SIR JAMES HUGH MARTEL WAS NOWHERE TO BE FOUND!

Byron walked up and down the street, but his search was futile. Swearing, he gave up, and hating the crowd of people, he decided to take a walk on the empty white beach. He stopped to watch a fisherman mending his nets. The man's black hair was turning grey; his beard knotted and tangled. A threadbare tunic that had once been black hung from his shoulders.

The man did not look up. "Either help or go away," the man said in French. "I dislike people who stare."

"I meant no offense. You're not Greek."

"No, but you're a Norman. I hear it in your speech. From Britton?"

"Sir Byron Fitzwalter of Gowen Ireland."

"Humph, a knight marked with the cross," the fisherman said as he tied broken cord into a knot. He held up the repaired section of net and looked at his work. "So, how goes the war?"

Byron crossed his arms. "Not well."

The fisherman looked up at Byron with one eye closed. "Humph, an inevitable end. So, Sir Byron Fitzwalter of Ireland, what brings you to Crete?"

"I am on my way to Rome."

The fisherman opened his eye to give Byron a piercing stare. "The war is not going well. A disaster from what I hear, and you are going to Rome. Do you think the Holy Father will aid you?"

"How do you hear such things?" Byron snapped. "As far as my business in Rome, that is my affair."

THE SECRET OF ETEMENANKI

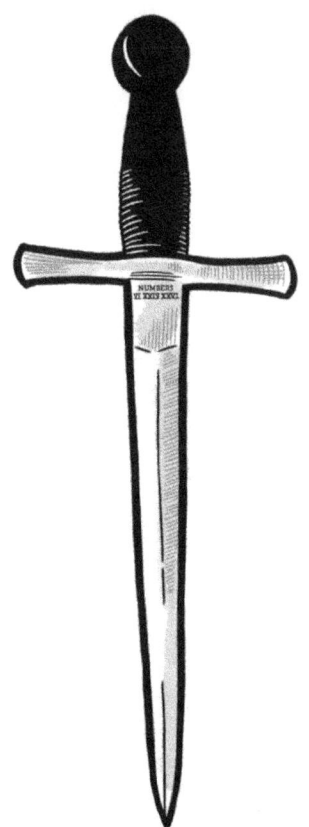

By James Ragon

Bay Horse Publishing
Salem, Oregon

The characters in this work, with the exception of some well-known historical figures, are products of the author's imagination. While some historical characters and settings are inspired by actual people and events, the dialogue and incidents described are fictional and are not to be construed as accurate portrayals of historical events. In all other respects, any resemblance to actual persons, living or dead, or actual events is purely coincidental.

The Secret of Etemenanki
ISBN 978-1-7362424-0-7
Copyright © 2020 by James Ragon

Published by Bay Horse Publishing
Salem, Oregon
All rights reserved

No part of this publication may be reproduced, stored in a retrieval system, stored in a database and / or published in any form or by any means, electronic, mechanical, photocopying, recording or otherwise, without the prior written permission of the publisher.

Cover illustration and book design by Casandra Johns/House of Hands

Printed in the United States of America

This book is dedicated to the memory of my niece,
Kate Christofferson.
A lover of books.

CONTENTS

Prologue: The Roman Empire 10
1: In the Shadow of the Hills 24
2: The Priest and the Monk 32
3: Salah al-Din Youssef-ibn Ayyub "Saladin" 40
4: The Saracen Knight and the Sultan's Son 52
5: The Caverns of the Apostles 58
6: Grim Tidings 66
7: Of Papaver Somniferum 70
8: The Dream of the Banshee 78
9: The Road to Tyre 94
10: The Merchant and the Assassin 104
11: The House of the Archbishop 116
12: The Lord of Tyre 126
13: The Failure of Husam al-Din 146
14: Sir James Hugh Martel 156
15: The Gift of the Cross 172
16: Crime in the Streets 182
17: The Worries of Jabbar 190
18: The Storm 196
19: Paying for Damages 202
20: The Cretan Adventure 208
21: Byron Visits Rome 220
22: The Lateran Palace 228
23: The Cardinal and the Priest 234
24: Mene, Mene, Tekel and Parsin 240
25: Silk Merchants 256
26: The Confession of James 262
27: The Shadow of Empire 272
28: The Don and the Count 282
29: The Little Cardinal and the Pope 294
30: Good Cardinals and Bad Cardinals 302
31: The Mercy of Husam al-Din 322
32: What Shall We Do With the German 330

33: The Graf Opens His Mouth 338
34: The Devil Comes to the Lateran 352
35: The Journey Begins 364
36: The Loss of a Good Servant 378
37: Alexandretta 384
38: James at the Gates of Aleppo 404
39: The Lord of Aleppo 410
40: Byron's Prayer 426
41: Husam al-Din and the Prince 440
42: Saracen and Christian Ghosts 446
43: Muhtadi Loses the Christians 456
44: Qala' at ar-Rahba 464
45: Noddaba 478
46: Quest par Excellence 490
47: Zahirah 496
48: The Staff of Al-Tusi 504
49: The Tale of the Emerald Necklace 510
50: Ali ibn Ubaydullah al-Aziz 516
51: The Secret of Ali and Zahirah 526
52: The Centurion's Men 534
53: The Ishtar Gate 542
54: The Palace of Nebuchadnezzar 548
55: The Adventures of Isma'il and Muhtadi 564
56: Etemenanki 574
57: Silken Bowstrings 588
58: The Army of the Tower of Babel 596
59: Short Swords, Long Swords, and Shamshirs 624

ACKNOWLEDGEMENTS

I would like to thank the following for their assistance in creating my book.

To my wife Laura who spent hours editing the story.

To my editor Tina Roese for helping me improve this tale.

To Steph Flora for editing my first draft.

To Al Bathke who assisted in writing Byron's prayer.

To William McGill for his support.

To my draft readers: Whitney Padilla, Mariah Stephens, Kim McGill, Rita Wyatt

To Tim Rogers for his advice and assistance in publishing this story.

PROLOGUE
THE ROMAN EMPIRE
408 AD

The day was ending and the shadows were lengthening beneath the trees lining the Via Ostiensis. The centurion, marching at the head of his centuria, ignored the beauty of the countryside. He could feel the sweat beneath his armor trickling down his back. He glanced up and muttered a curse. The sun would be gone soon and he was late. He needed to be at the gates of Ostia by sunset. He looked behind him at his soldiers and wagons stretching into the distance.

The centurion set a brutal pace. Two more miles passed as the sun came to rest on the horizon. He looked back at the fatigued faces of the men who followed. He raised his hand and called a halt. From the back of the column, his optio[1] jogged up to stand next to him and leaned on his hastile, the long staff he used to keep his troops in line.

"Achatius," he said softly, "do you think the barbarians still follow?"

The centurion looked back down the road. Nearing thirty, he was still trim and muscular, although grey was starting to creep

---

1 *optio centuria*, was the second in command of the century and were generally chosen by the centurion. They marched at the rear of the century to keep the troops in line and enforce the centurion's orders.

into the edges of his dark hair. His face assumed its habitual frown, made more severe by the deep scar on his cheek, a reminder of the battle of Pollentia. "Yes. The Visigoths travel light. We have four, maybe five hours before they catch us."

"Do you think we can afford to rest?"

Achatius looked into the worried face of his optio and shook his head, the white horsehair crest of his helmet swished with the motion. "No, Sulla, but I can push the men no farther. Order them to stand fast in the ranks and give them five minuta prima."

Sulla nodded. He was shorter than Achatius. The red cloak draped over the chain mail armor made him look broad. Sulla's arm crossed his chest as his fist rapped the lorica hamata and then extended in a salute. "Yes, centurion." Sulla turned to carry out Achatius' orders. "Stand fast! Five Minuta!"

Achatius watched his shadow grow as he calculated the passage of time. It seemed that only three-minuta prima had passed when he heard Sulla bark, "Centuriae to your arms! Centuriae Inten- Te!" With a crisp snap, the men came to attention. "Shoulder arms. Spearward face!"

Achatius smiled. It was a short rest. His optio was worried and he had a right to be. Achatius had fought the barbarians on the frontier, he knew that their deaths would be cruel and merciless if the Visigoths caught up to them.

The soldiers shouted three cries of ready as Achatius took his place at the head of the column next to his signifier. The signum standard with its silver hand of loyalty to the emperor was held aloft. Achatius raised his arm.

From the back of the column, Sulla shouted, "Forward march! Follow the standard."

With a swift wave of his hand, Achatius motioned his column forward.

With each step, the miles passed. Achatius could feel the wind shift as a cold wind blew from the east. The sun disappeared below the horizon, but the centurion did not slacken his pace. At last, the shadows of Ostia came into view. As he neared the arch of the Porta Romana, the statue of Salus Augusti looked imperiously down at him from the top of the gate. In her hand, she grasped the head of a snake coiled around a staff. Achatius raised his hand, and his men came to a halt beneath the gate.

Achatius looked back. The spears of his men rose towards the sky like a black thicket of thorns. A few faint stars showed along the edges of the clouds. In the failing light, he could see the towering spires of a thunderstorm brewing in the east. There was no sign of the Visigoths, but that did not mean he had shaken their pursuit. He passed through the archway and peered down the deserted streets. All was silent and still. Achatius motioned his column to follow. The centurion led his men and wagons through the empty streets to the docks.

He rounded the corner of a building. A feeling of elation filled him. In the dark waters of the Tiber, sat a merchant ship tied to the wharf. She was a large grain ship of Roman design. Twin masts rose to the sky. The foremast was set just behind the bow that curved gracefully up to the beakhead that jutted out over the water. In the center of the deck, a large mast with a single yardarm furled with a canvas sail. The head of a swan carved from the ship's stern post looked out over the deck.

The column picked up the pace. As Achatius drew closer to the ship, he could faintly make out the ship's name painted on the weathered, grey planks of her hull. A harsh voice broke the stillness. "Prepare to cast off." The feeling of relief turned to alarm as Achatius watched sailors running across the deck. The sailors lifted the gangplank to toss it off the ship. With more speed than he thought possible, Achatius dashed to the ship and jumped on the plank causing the sailors to drop it to the deck. Running the length of the board, Achatius sprang on to the deck. The surprised sailors backed away. A thump behind him caused Achatius to glance over his shoulder. Sulla had followed him.

"Get off my ship!"

A large chested man charged out from beneath the wooden swan. "Damn you and may Pluto take you to the underworld below," the man cried, his mouth hidden beneath a black beard, braided into a long point. "Get off my ship!"

Achatius placed his hand on the hilt of his sword. "Tarquinius Syrus?"

The man stopped. His eyes rested on the centurion. "I know him not! Get off my ship! I have a schedule to keep." Turning to the sailors, the man shouted, "Get these boarders off my ship."

The sailor next to Achatius reached out to grab his arm. Achatius jerked his arm away and struck the man across the face with his vitis.[2] The man staggered back.

"This ship is the *Septimia Zenobia* and you are Tarquinius Syrus," Achatius cried. "You were hired by the magistar officium Olympius to transport my men and my crates. Caesar commands it."

"And you were supposed to be here yesterday!" Tarquinius shot back.

"I was delayed by the mob in Rome."

"I don't care. You're late! Get off my ship." Tarquinius motioned to more of his sailors to help evict the centurion and his optio.

Achatius drew his spatha.[3] "Are you refusing to fulfill the desires of Caesar?"

Tarquinius opened his mouth to reply and then looked up. Achatius' centuria was now lining the dock looking at him. Unfazed, Tarquinius leaned forward and pointed his finger at the centurion's chest. "Don't threaten me! Ravenna is a long way from here. I don't care what Caesar wants."

Achatius scowled. "You will transport my men and my crates or everyone here will die." Achatius' men drew their swords.

Tarquinius sighed, glanced at Achatius, and raised his hands as he appealed to the soldiers. "Look boys, no one needs to die. Come with me before it is too late."

"No one move!" Achatius shouted as he faced Tarquinius. "These men are under my command. How dare you try to incite a revolt?"

"Revolt?" Tarquinius looked mystified. "Revolt from what? Rome is dead. Only you and the fools in Ravenna have not figured that fact out yet."

---

2 Vitis, the grape vine staff carried by a centurion as a symbol of rank. It was used as a disciplinary tool. *"The centurion's vine staff is an excellent medicine for sluggish troops who don't want to advance..."* Pliny.

3 The spatha was a long sword issued to cavalry. By the late Roman empire, as the legions fought a defensive war against Germanic invasions the spatha was issued to the infantrymen.

"Rome is not dead!" shouted Achatius.

Tarquinius shook his head. "If you say so." He eyed the soldiers. They were all young men, most of them in their late teens. As he looked into their eyes, he saw fear. Fear of the centurion. There would be no dissuading them from following the centurion to their doom. Tarquinius shook his head and shrugged. "Do what you will, but I will spare no one to load your cargo."

Achatius shoved his sword in Tarquinius' face. "You will load my crates!"

Tarquinius scoffed as he stared down the blade of the spatha to the centurion. "My crew have their own tasks. If you want your crates on board, you do it!" He brushed the sword away with his hand and looked up at the approaching thunderstorm in the east. "I would have sailed yesterday but for Favonius. The god of the west wind kept us here. I feel the god of the unlucky east wind upon my face and now you show up." Tarquinius looked down at the deck muttering to himself. He looked up again, his eyes bored into Achatius. "Twenty of your men below decks, and I will supervise their work."

Achatius sighed, his threat had failed; he needed Tarquinius and Tarquinius knew it. "I'll send twenty men."

Tarquinius smiled. "Good!" Before Achatius could reply, Tarquinius stalked off back to the stern of the ship shouting orders. Achatius watched Tarquinius walk away.

Sulla frowned. "I guess we load the crates."

The centurion looked at his wagons. "Get the men moving. I will pick who will work below."

The centurion walked across the gangplank to the dock tapping twenty of his men with his vitis sending them to the ship. Achatius pulled his red cloak around him to ward off the night chill. He glanced at the warehouses lining the dock. Not a sound came from the city. The only sounds came from his men laboring to unload their wagons. An oppressive pall hung in the air as Achatius' men worked to move the heavy wooden crates to the edge of the dock. More than one soldier apprehensively glanced over his shoulder for fear the Visigoths might suddenly appear and attack.

Fear increased as the work dragged on. Every minute brought the Visigoths closer. The men were tired. Achatius began to pace the dock to relieve the tension. Time was slipping away. His soldiers were not working fast enough. The soldiers carrying the crates from the wagons had stopped working. He glanced at the ship. Crates were scattered about the deck. His soldiers were leaning on them as they waited for their turn to deliver their crate to the hatchway. Minutes slipped by.

Achatius could stand it no longer. "What is going on down there?" Pointing to a soldier standing near him he shouted, "Go! Find out what is taking so long!"

The soldier stiffened to attention. "Yes, centurion!"

The soldier hurried to the ship and disappeared below the deck. Time passed, and finally the soldier reappeared and clambered onto the dock. He jogged over to Achatius and saluted.

"Well?" the centurion demanded

"It's not the men, it is the captain. He is worried about the cargo. He fears that if the weight is not properly balanced, it will capsize the ship. He is making the men move them over and over again."

The centurion tipped his head back. "Christ! I knew it. The entire Visigoth will be here at any moment, and his only concern is the weight in the hull of his ship! He pointed at the soldier with his vine-stick. "If Alaric catches us here on the docks, the first man to die will be Tarquinius. I will make sure of it."

The centurion's eyes swept the ship's deck and then the dock. Crates were everywhere. He was counting the remaining crates on the dock when he glanced up at the sky. The somber clouds glowed a dull red. The Visigoths were putting the countryside to the torch.

Achatius stopped his count, he was out of time. The Visigoths were near. "Optio come here!" Sulla came running over. Achatius grabbed Sulla by his Lorica hamata[4] and pulled him close. "Look!" Achatius pointed his vitis at the warning in the sky. "Time is short. Get down there," he rasped in Sulla's ear as he pointed to the ship. "Get the men to work faster. Beat them if you have to. If Tarquinius Syrus gets in your way, do what you have to. Do you understand?"

---

4 Lorica Hamata - chain mail worn by the Roman legions in the late empire.

Sulla nodded. "Go!" Achatius pushed his optio away. "Do whatever it takes."

Sulla raised his eyebrows. "Kill him?"

"For God's sake no... restrain him. I will deal with him when I have time."

"Yes, centurion." Sulla saluted and then jogged to the gangplank and onto the deck of the ship.

Achatius turned his wrath to the soldiers on the dock. "Move your asses, damn it!"

The soldiers stopped what they were doing and looked at Achatius pointing at the sky. They saw the danger. Furiously, they began shoving the cargo onto the ship. Achatius looked back at the somber omens in the night sky warning of the approaching Visigoths.

He heard a crash. Men were yelling curses. Achatius turned to see a crate split open on the deck spilling its contents of golden coins minted in the reign of Constantine.

Men were scrambling towards the crate. Sulla jumped in front of the ruptured wooden box yelling, "Leave it!" Several sailors were already grabbing up the coins stuffing them into their pockets.

"Damn it," Achatius swore to himself. The last thing he needed was for the ship's crew to know the contents of the crates. Achatius ran across the plank and leaped onto the deck. Standing beside his optio he drew his sword. "Put those back. Get back to work."

The sailors weighed the consequences of ignoring them. Achatius saw their look of hesitation. The empire's days were ending and they knew it. A barbarian army near Rome, a centurion fleeing the country with treasure, the signs were clear. Achatius felt the menace of their hardened stares as they faced him.

"Get back to work." A hint of desperation crept into his voice. He did not have time to put down an insurrection. Out of the corner of his eye, he could see Sulla back up as the sailors pressed forward. Achatius prepared to be rushed. He scanned the sailor's faces looking for the leader and he saw him. He was taller than the rest. Tangled grey hair hung down to his shoulders. Confidence emanated in his face. The face of a man who hated authority. This man would die first. Achatius prepared to attack the sailor, several of his soldiers came running up with their swords drawn. The sailors realizing the odds had changed, stopped their advance and began to back away. Those pocketing the gold began to drop the coins onto the deck.

The centurion seeing the tide turn shouted, "This gold belongs to the Senate and People of Rome. The next man who doesn't do what he is told is a traitor to the empire and will be executed!"

An angry murmur swelled up from the sailors. One of the sailors whispered to his mates, "Not yet. We'll get it later."

Achatius sheathed his sword. "Sulla, I swear the gods are against me."

Sulla nodded. "The gods do enjoy their mischief."

The centurion scoffed. "Well we are not done for yet. Take care of Tarquinius. I will take care of this."

Sulla nodded. "Yes, centurion."

Achatius turned to the soldiers who were milling around talking excitedly about the contents of the crates. He pointed his vitis at two of the nearest soldiers. "You two stay here. The rest of you, back to work!" The soldiers stopped talking and reluctantly turned away.

"I did not say tomorrow," Achatius roared as he smacked the nearest soldier with his vitis. "Now! Move your lazy asses!" Scrambling to avoid Achatius' blows, the soldiers hurried off to resume loading the ship with crates of gold.

Achatius turned to the two soldiers standing near the broken crate. "Don't stand there. Clean this up!" The soldiers kneeled down on the deck and started scooping up the coins pouring them back into the crate. Achatius bent close, his face inches from the two men. "If either of you pinch a coin, I will bind you to the dock and leave you as a gift for the Visigoth king. Do you understand?"

The men nodded. "Yes, centurion."

Achatius stood up and walked a short distance away so he could watch. The gods were definitely against him. He swore bitterly as he thought about the events that had led him here. Olympius, chief minister to the Emperor Honorius, had given him the order to remove the treasure and take it to Syracuse, far beyond the Visigoth's reach. Olympius had promised to be waiting there to receive the treasure, to keep it safe for the emperor until the current crisis had passed. Achatius did not trust the minister, nor was he certain that the emperor knew it had been moved, but he was in no position to question his orders. To do so would be fatal.

The wind came up and ruffled Achatius' cloak, bringing with it the sounds of distant cries. The Visigoths had reached the city. They were here. It was time to go. Now! Achatius looked at the dock. Only a few more crates remained to be loaded.

"Get on the ship!" Achatius shouted to his men. "Leave the rest. Maybe fortune will favor us, and Alaric's men will fight over it." The soldiers, hearing Achatius' command, dropped what they were doing and ran to the ship. Two of his men continued lugging one of the heavy crates across the dock. "Drop that damned thing," Achatius cried, "or I will leave you."

Startled, the soldiers let go of the wooden crate. It crashed to the dock, its sides splintering into several shards of wood. Coins flowed through the cracks like water pouring onto the dock. This time no one went to retrieve the gold. Every man saw the danger and did all he could to get the ship underway.

Crates cluttered the deck of the Septimia Zenobia. Achatius ran to the hatch that led to the lower deck. In the dim light, he could see Sulla with his sword drawn. Two soldiers grasped the captain's arms as they held him firmly against the side of the ship. The tip of Sulla's spatha pressed against Tarquinius' throat.

"Let him go, the Visigoths are here."

Sulla lowered his sword and stepped aside as the soldiers released the captain's arms.

Tarquinius glared at the optio and then rounded on Achatius. "If this ship founders..."

Achatius cut him off. "If this ship founders, we drown. Right now, our severed heads will decorate the ship's railing if you don't get us underway."

"Get out of my way," Tarquinius snarled as he shoved past Achatius. Achatius followed Tarquinius onto the deck. Figures with torches were running towards the dock. Tarquinius was shouting to the sailors to get his ship into the channel. The sailors were getting into each other's way as they tried to free the ship. At the bow, Achatius could see two sailors with axes hacking at the rope that held the ship to the dock.

"Loose the sail and brace up fore and aft!" Tarquinius shouted. The old sailor who Achatius almost killed, ran to the main mast and began untying the ropes that held the main sail up. The ropes slid through the metal rings, and the sail dropped. The cold east wind blew into the sail, moving the ship backward. Tarquinius, standing on the roof of the stern cabin, cried to the helmsmen at the steering oars. "Bring her around."

The steering oars were turned to port as the ship swung out stern first into the current. The old sailor was now singing an old Roman song, setting the cadence as the men hauled on the ropes to set the braces. The wind drove the sail against the mast as the ship was driven backwards, laboring towards the main channel.

Achatius looked back at the wave of Visigoths closing on the edge of the dock. A flash of lightning split the sky. In the searing light, he could see hundreds of barbarian soldiers. In the midst of the barbarians, rode a man on horseback, his silver armor flashed in the light and then faded as the thunder boomed, shaking the ship.

"Alaric is here!" Achatius shouted. "Sulla! I want a fighting formation. Two ranks."

"Orbem Formate!" Sulla cried. "Contendite Vesrta Sponte!"

The soldiers scrambled to fulfill Sulla's commands. Falling into place, they circled the edge of the deck, facing out with their shields in front of them.

Achatius' eyes swept the formation. "Soldiers, to the left. Shieldward, about face." The soldiers on the left spun to face the approaching mass of barbarians.

An arrow flew past Achatius' head and he ducked. More arrows struck the ship. He could see the faces of the Visigoths; their iron caps shone red in the firelight of their torches. Like a flood, the numbers increased, filling the dock. Kneeling to draw their bows, the Visigoth soldiers sent their arrows to stop his flight. A German war cry filled the air.

The masts creaked as the wind drove the ship back. The dock

was slowly receding. Achatius needed to buy time.

"First rank, javelins ready!" Achatius barked. The soldiers hoisted their javelins to throw.

"First rank, throw."

"Enecate," the soldiers shouted as they hurled their javelins at the line of Visigoths on the dock. The barbarians scattered as the Roman pilums rained down on them. Achatius saw a German sink to his knees, a javelin in his chest.

"Testudinem Facite," Achatius cried.

The first rank of soldiers knelt behind their shields as the second rank of soldiers lifted their shields overhead. Stumbling across the cluttered deck filled with crates, the second rank of soldiers moved forward in a desperate race to form the turtle. The ship was nearing the main channel as the men at the steering oars strained to turn the ship so her bow faced down river. The wind began to fill the sail, they were almost free.

Achatius watched as the second wave of Visigoths dropped to one knee. The Visigoth king rode behind his archers, his golden helmet glowed in the torchlight. Rising in his stirrups, Alaric drew his sword. His harsh voice rose above the din. The Visigoth soldiers bent their bows.

"Move, you sons of whores!" Achatius cried as he as he ran behind his men lashing them with his vitis. The second rank of soldiers was about to bring their shields over the heads of their comrades when the Visigoths unleashed their volley of arrows.

"Down!" Achatius cried as he pulled one of his soldiers to his knees and ducked beneath his shield.

A shower of arrows rained down on the ship. Achatius saw a sailor crumple to the deck. Through the thump and clatter of arrows, a sickening, high-pitched wheezing sound filled the air. A soldier, with an arrow in his throat, toppled over and fell onto the sailors who were hauling on the braces to set the sail. Curses rang out as the soldier's body, encumbered with sixty pounds of armor, smashed down on the men. The sailors let go of the rope as the yardarm spun, letting all of the wind spill from the sail. As the sailors struggled to shove the dying soldier out of their way, the ship lost headway and turned sideways in the river.

A cry of triumph erupted in German as the Visigoths, encouraged by the sight, loosed another volley. Achatius was on the edge of a catastrophe. He sprinted through the shower of arrows and grabbed the dying soldier by his armor. It was the boy he had sent below decks. The boy's body was twitching in his death throes. His face was white, the arrow's fletching protruded from the side of his neck. Achatius dragged the body out of the way and turned back to the brace line. He grabbed the rope. The sailors joined him. Hauling the line down the deck, they dragged the yardarm around. The sail luffed as it filled with wind. The ship had steerage again, as the men at the helm slewed her back into the channel. As the sailors secured the brace line, Achatius looked back over the ship's stern. In the distance, Achatius could see Alaric sitting on his horse watching his escape. Harsh German voices filled the air with taunts and insults. The ship gained speed, shooting down the river.

A heavy rain began to fall. Achatius watched the Visigoths disappear, hidden by the curtain of falling rain. He turned away and walked back to the dead soldier. The boy's face was upturned, his lifeless eyes staring at the sky. Achatius bent down and closed the boy's eyes and with a sigh stood up and motioned to two of his men. The soldiers picked up their dead comrade and carried him to the ship's rail. Lifting the body over the rail, they heaved it into the Tiber.

Achatius turned away, walked up to the bow of the ship, and stood there looking at the dark water of the Tiber. It gurgled and slapped at the bow of the ship. He glanced around the ship. How many more were certain to die. He debated what to do. Syracuse would be his grave. Olympius would take the treasure, execute him as a traitor, and transfer his men to different posts to die at the hands of the Visigoths. Looking back in the darkness, Ostia had disappeared from sight.

He mulled over his situation and laughed bitterly. Several of his soldiers, huddling under their shields to ward off the rain, looked over at Achatius, but Achatius ignored them. An idea had come to him as if Minerva herself had whispered it into his ear. An old tale from the Christian book echoed in his memory. The idea grew and took shape.

The ship reached the mouth of the river and passed into the open sea. The ship rolled in the heavy seas, hindering the tired soldiers as they struggled to move the rest of the crates below deck. The last crate was safely lowered into the hull as the sky began to brighten. The storm had passed, and the somber grey turned yellow and then to a brilliant blue. The seabirds flew around the ship, calling to the crew in the early morning air. It was time. Achatius walked beneath the swan's outstretched neck and climbed up onto the roof of the stern cabin. Tarquinius was standing next to the sailors at the helm.

Achatius walked over and stood beside Tarquinius. Without looking at the captain he asked, "Do you know our destination?"

"No," Tarquinius snapped.

Achatius smiled. Olympius had made a mistake. Maybe fortune had favored him after all. He turned and whispered in the captain's ear the destination. His destination - one Olympius would not like.

CHAPTER 1
IN THE SHADOW OF THE HILLS
July 1187

Byron's eyes opened to darkness. The smell of rotting flesh filled his nose. Something was holding him down. Panic swelled within him, he was suffocating. He started pushing frantically. The object rolled off, revealing the bright, blue sky. Breathing hard, he tried to twist onto his side, but his left leg was pinned by a heavy weight. He pushed himself up on one arm. His bay horse, with a spear sticking from its side, was lying on his leg.

He needed to get free. Now. Byron placed his right foot on the cantle of the saddle and pushed. He did not move. Byron pushed harder. He could feel the stirrups digging into his ankle. Slowly, the dirt and sand began to give way. Ignoring the pain, he pulled his leg free from under the dead horse.

He jerked the skirt of his chain mail out from under the horse, rolled over, and grasped his sword that lay in the sand near him. He struggled to his feet. Pain shot through his body as he forced his knees to straighten. Swaying from the sudden rush of blood, he fought to keep his balance.

He brought his sword to a position of on guard and looked around in the eerie stillness. No dull beat of sword on shield, no ringing of swords, no shouts or screams of men. All was quiet except for the soft hiss of the wind in the grass. His eyes slowly focused. Dead horses, their legs stiffened and straight. Dead men, in the places where they fell, bloated and turning black in the desert sun. Grotesque faces, contorted by the heat, stared up at him. Flies disturbed from their feast, rose in a black cloud from the rotting corpses. He glanced down at the headless body at his feet. Ragged dark red flesh, curled and turning black at the edges, surrounded the white vertebrae that stuck out from the neck. The blue surcoat was torn, but Byron could still see the embroidered yellow shield with a broad red stripe running down the center. He knew the surcoats device. "Rodger Beauvallet," he sighed.

Trembling, his strength gave way and he sank to his knees. Kneeling on the windswept plains of Galilee, he gazed at the bodies of twenty thousand men. "Mon Dieu, Mon Dieu," he whispered. Byron shoved his sword into the sand, and grasping the hilt, he struggled to his feet. Sighing, he took off his Norman helmet and wiped his brow as he pushed the mail coif from his head. The wind felt good in his hair. He could feel his knee swelling. He looked down at his blood-soaked gauntlet. Hands shaking, he carefully pealed back the top of the leather glove. He winced as it tugged at his skin. A long, deep cut ran from beneath the mail sleeve to his wrist. Curiosity satisfied, he gently let go of the edge, and the glove sagged back into place.

This was not his first battle. Sir Byron Stephen Fitzwalter was a descendant of Normans who had crossed the channel and fought for William on the field of Hastings. Twenty winters had come and gone, and the long white scars on his body testified to years of fighting. He had trained for war his entire life. Years of combat with Celts of Ireland had removed any of the shades of the doubt that troubled other men. He was confident, for he knew what he could do, and he was self-reliant, for there was no one else to rely upon.

Byron pushed his dark hair out of his face. Brown eyes set beneath thick eyebrows gave a sternness to his countenance. The slight crook to his nose, the result of a shattered lance, was only noticeable if one looked closely at his face. He took a deep breath as he pulled his black surcoat straight so that the white Maltese cross of the Knights of Saint John was centered on his chest.

Byron staggered over and sat down on a large rock. He glanced up at the vultures circling above him in the blue sky and then to the hill. The red pavilion was gone.

Beneath the red shelter, Guy Lusignan, the King of Jerusalem, Gerard di Ridefort, the Grand Master of the Temple, and Raynald De Chatillon had commanded the fight against Saladin's Army. He closed his eyes as he put the pieces of his memory back into place.

News had reached King Guy that the Sultan Saladin had surrounded the city of Tiberias, on the Sea of Galilee. Gathering his army at the springs of ar-Saffuriyah, the King of Jerusalem had marched to relieve the siege of the beleaguered town.

Byron opened his eyes and looked out over the foolishness of that decision. There had been no water on the road to Tiberias. The dust rose as the sun blazed down on the Christian soldiers marching in their heavy armor, striking men down as efficiently as if they had been killed by Saracens. Saracen horsemen with wild cries, swept within range, shooting arrows into the ranks as the Christians tried to force their way to the safety of the Sea of Galilee. As the day wore on, the Saracens numbers grew until it became clear to the Christian commanders that they would not make their destination. Surrounded, the Christians made camp near two hills known as the Horns of Hattin.

At sunrise, Saladin's soldiers lit the grass in the valley on fire, choking the thirsty and suffering Christians with smoke and ash. Saladin led the first charge, and in the swirling smoke, the Christian lines collapsed. King Guy, seeing a disaster unfolding, commanded Count Raymond of Tripoli to make a cavalry charge, in hopes of relieving the beleaguered army's desperate position.

Byron, sent to rally the infantry, had watched the Crusader cavalry as they formed their horses into a line and went from a trot to a run. The sun shone through the smoke. Mail shirts flashed crimson and silver as Christian knights rode at a gallop towards the ranks of Saladin's horsemen. Like a silver crested wave, Christian Chevaliers crashed upon the Saracens who broke and fled. A great shout went up from the Christian Army. They might yet fight their way out of Saladin's trap.

The Saracens were not fleeing. Taqi-al-Din commanded the

portion of the sultan's army that was under the crusaders assault. Having fought the crusaders many times before, he had instructed his men to part and let the enemy pass unfought. As the crusader cavalry thundered ineffectively through the enemy's lines, the Saracens reformed and turned to face the Christian knights. Through the swirling smoke that rose into the sky, Byron had watched as Raymond's horsemen wheeled to face the Saracens. A moment passed, and in the distance, Byron saw the Count of Tripoli ride out in front of his men. The count rose in his stirrups, his light blue cloak billowing in the breeze. Byron watched intently, waiting for the count to raise his sword and charge. Each drop of sweat down Byron's neck marked the seconds that passed, and then to Byron's horror, Raymond bowed his head. Turning his horse away from the Saracen Army, the Count of Tripoli led his men away from the battle.

That moment changed everything. He remembered now. In that awful moment, he knew all was lost. He had looked to the red pavilion to see what the king would do, and he saw Rodger Beauvallet motioning for him to join him. From the midst of the battlefield, the remaining mounted knights were being summoned to make one last charge.

With Beauvallet riding beside him, he had galloped down the hill towards the Saracens. With a crash, he fell upon his enemy. His spear had driven deep into the chest of a Saracen, forcing the man backwards off his horse. Byron remembered letting go of the entangled spear and sweeping out his sword. A Saracen on a black horse rushed him from the left. Byron raised his shield as the Saracen's shamshir struck with a crash. With their horses side by side, the two knights fought until the Saracen foolishly exposed his head and neck. Byron had raised his sword for the kill. As he prepared to strike, a Saracen foot soldier ran up and plunged a spear into his horse's heart.

All he could remember was that as he had leaned forward to make a stabbing thrust, his horse's legs buckled and began to fall. His sword went down, the tip driving into the pommel of the Saracens saddle. He was off balance as the horse fell to its knees. Pulling on the reins to keep the horse standing, Byron tried to get his feet out of the stirrups. He was almost free of the saddle when the horse toppled onto its side smashing his left leg. Byron's head slammed into a rock, and everything went black.

That was the last memory he had. Byron looked up at the desert sun. It was past midday. He looked at his dead horse. He needed to make a decision. He stood up. Moving stiffly, he found his water-skin still hanging from his saddle. He tugged at the skin, but it was tangled beneath the horse. "God's bones!" he swore, and reaching for his dagger, he cut the water skin free. He sat down on the dead horse and uncapped the skin. He held it up to his cracked and bleeding lips. It was empty. Byron sighed as he held the water skin to his eye. In disgust, he tossed it away. With a groan, he stood up and shuffled off to start searching the dead for water.

Through the swarms of blowflies, Byron made his way around the rotting corpses until he came upon a row of a hundred or more headless Templars. He paused to stare at them. Knights Templar would not ransom their captured men. Their hands still bound, Byron could see evidence of repeated cuts, where an unskilled swordsman had taken several attempts to sever the head.

Despite the heat, a shiver went down his spine. The wind whispered the ghostly voices of the dead. "Saladin did this," it whispered in his ear. Byron sighed. He did not care for Templars, they were rich and arrogant. But the sight of the headless bodies mollified his feeling, and he felt pity for these men. They had been marked with the cross and had fought tenaciously. They were Christendom's most dangerous warriors. Their unbending faith had left Saladin no choice but to execute every last one of them.

He stood transfixed in this awful place. The birds pecked and tore at the flesh of the dead. The horror overwhelmed him, and he could stand the sounds of the macabre feast no longer. He turned away and limped off; continuing his task of finding what little water remained. The fate of these young Templars haunted Byron as he continued the grisly search, but at least he had been fortunate enough not to watch their cruel demise.

His search was not fruitless. Here and there, he found several skins, where men believing that they would see tomorrow had saved some of the precious fluid. Byron stopped and took stock.

He had collected as much water as he could find. He did not have all day to wander the fields of death looking for the life-giving fluid. The Saracens would return. He looked up at the sky, considering the time of day and the journey that lay ahead, the little water he had collected would have to do.

Trudging back to his horse, he wondered how many of the Christian soldiers the sultan had captured. Saladin would soon send demands of ransom. Each man had a value and Aleppo, the great Saracen fortress, would be the captured men's prison. Some would wait in vain and die there.

He reached his dead horse. His knee ached, and he sat down on a rock to rest while he considered his choices. It was fifteen miles to the springs of ar-Saffuriyah. The ride from Jerusalem to Hattin on horseback had been punishing. To walk back to ar-Saffuriyah in the heat, wounded, he doubted he could do it.

After resting a moment, he stood up again gathering his resolve. Standing up straight, he unsheathed his sword. Holding his sword in the sign of the cross, he bowed his head, and in a hoarse whisper, said a prayer for the dead.

"Our Father who art in heaven hallowed be thy name. Thy Kingdom come, thy will be done on earth as it is in heaven. Give us this day our daily bread and forgive us our trespasses, as we forgive those who trespass against us. Lead us not into temptation but deliver us from evil, for thine is the Kingdom and the power and the glory, for now and forever."

He paused and looked up. It was the only prayer he knew. From birth, he had trained for war. Byron had had some training in letters, but that had been long ago. He did not feel any loss for his lack of literacy, which was the function of priests and clerics. His rank in feudal society placed no value on education or learning. Warfare and personal bravery in combat were the lofty pursuits of his class. Writing brought no glory. No cleric had ever been crowned a tournament champion. Books had a tendency to fill men's minds with dangerous ideas that often resulted in an unpleasant demise in the tower of London.

He weighed his chances to survive the long walk to Jerusalem. He looked at the Sea of Galilee shimmering in the distance. The fresh water lake was inviting, but he knew that the road would be dangerous. Saladin would have gone that way on his return march to Tiberias. It would not do to blunder into a Saracen rearguard. He made his decision. Without water, he would die. No matter how dangerous, he would have to try to make it to the lake. Maybe he could hide there and rest, wait for his wounds to heal. Maybe by that time the Saracens would have moved on. The night would conceal him from any unfriendly eyes watching the road.

He turned and began trudging stiffly along. The horns of the hill frowned down upon him as he made his way from the battlefield. The shadows were already beginning to lengthen on the roadway, fading to blue as the sun began to set in the west.

Out of the corner of his eye, he saw something move. He spun to meet the threat. Standing fifty yards to the left of him was a chestnut horse. Even at that distance, he could make out a large bloody gash on its neck. A saddle was turned onto the horse's side. Byron walked towards it slowly. "Mon ami," he repeated just loud enough for the horse to hear. He needed to catch this horse. His chances of living would improve considerably. He watched it, gauging his approach to see if the animal showed any sign of running off. The horse stood still. He reached out to stroke the horse's white blaze.

"Hello, friend," he said quietly. "I am glad to see you."

The horse pushed his hand as if acknowledging the greeting. With his other hand, Byron grabbed the reins, which hung to the ground. He again spoke reassuringly to the horse while undoing the straps of the breast collar and loosening the cinch. The saddle fell to the ground with a thump, and the horse spun away. The pull on Byron's arm caused him to gasp. Gritting his teeth, he shrugged off the pain. His hands were shaking.

"I need your help," he told the horse softly. "We must leave here, you and I, but first I have something for you."

He took his Norman helmet from his belt and poured all of the precious liquid he had just collected into it. He carefully held it up to the horse's muzzle, letting the horse drink. The horse was a gift from God. He would surely be a dead man without this beast. He had to make sure this horse would live to carry him home.

After the horse drank all the water in the helmet, he led the horse around and positioned him so the saddle was on the left side. Byron lifted the saddle blanket out of the sand and shook it clean. He put the blanket on the horse's neck and pulled it into place, smoothing the horse's hair. Pain shot down his back as he lifted the saddle up. His arms were trembling as he set the saddle onto the horse's back. He leaned against the horse to rest. After a moment, he put his hand on the pommel, rocking the saddle until it fit well behind the horse's shoulders, and then cinched the girth. Byron led the horse around in a small circle and tightened the girth. He took a moment to admire the saddle. The cantle was covered in silver. In the center of the cantle were two gold chevrons. The saddle skirts were embossed with the fleur de lies. Whoever owned the saddle had prized it. He also had shorter legs. Byron took a moment to adjust the stirrup leathers. With his stiff, swollen knees, he would need every advantage to mount.

His first attempt was a failure. No matter how much he tried, his left knee would not bend, and he could not get his foot in the stirrup. He moved the horse to several nearby corpses that had fallen on each other. Using the dead bodies as a mounting block, he clawed his way into the saddle, and started down the road.

From his new vantage point, he could see the trampled ground. Thousands of hooves and boots of men in heavy mail had ground the earth to dust; clear evidence the Saracens had headed to Tiberias to finish off the city. Byron had no illusions of what was happening at Tiberias. With any luck, the Saracens were so busy looting, or worse, they would not notice a lone horseman on the road. It was just a matter of time before Saladin's Army moved on. No place in the Christian Kingdom was safe now. With a little good luck and the blessing of Saint Patrick, maybe he could stay ahead of the enemy and reach safety.

CHAPTER 2
THE PRIEST AND THE MONK

Byron cautiously made his way down the road. His sword was drawn, resting across the pommel of the saddle, ready to ward off a surprise attack. He was alert, listening to any telltale sound that might warn him of a Saracen rearguard watching the road. He kept an eye on the horse's head. If there were Saracens lurking nearby, the horse would know it long before he was aware of the danger, but the horse kept walking, relaxed, its ears forward. His new mount had an easy gait and gave him confidence that the horse had some good sense. Whoever had owned this horse must have prized the animal.

The road was empty. Byron grew uneasy. As he got further from Hattin, a sixth sense warned him that danger was lurking somewhere ahead, and he knew he should soon leave the road. He hated the thought, because the road was easy to travel, and going cross-country was rough riding and time consuming. Nevertheless, the chances that he would run into the enemy increased the closer he got to Tiberias. The defeat of Jerusalem's Army left Saladin unopposed, but the sultan was no fool. He would leave a rearguard on the road just as a precaution.

Years before, King Baldwin the leper had caught Saladin's Army marching unaware in the ravines below the fortress of Montgisard. The sultan had been careless, believing he was safe from attack. Baldwin had attacked with five hundred knights, and in the ensuing battle, the king of Jerusalem completely routed Saladin's soldiers. The defeat at Montgisard had almost cost the sultan his life. Byron had heard the story told many times while drinking wine with his friends. Even though the Christian Army was dead, Saladin would still exercise great care. He would not make the same mistake twice.

Byron rode along keeping an eye out for any trail that led away from the road towards the lake. In the twilight, he could see what appeared to be a small trail leading down off the road in the direction of the water. The knight stopped for a brief moment to examine the path. It went in the right direction, but he had never been here before. Unknown trails could be deceitful. Just because a trail looked like it went the way you wanted to go, did not always mean that it did. After some indecision, he committed himself to taking the trail. He guided the horse off the roadway and down the steep bank, hoping it would lead to the lakeshore.

The horse slowly worked his way down the steep and winding path. In pain, Byron did his best to lean back in the saddle to take his weight off the horse's shoulders. He sat up again when he reached the bottom of the hill. He stopped to listen and looked the countryside over for any sign of the sultan's soldiers. He saw nothing. The only noise he heard was the sound of crickets and the distant croaking of frogs.

He rode on. The lake was getting near. His thirst was beginning to burn. Even the horse was picking up the pace. He could see the water's edge in the fading light. A few more yards and he would reach the water. Suddenly, the horse jumped and snorted with fear, its ears forward as a dark object hurled up at him. Without thinking, Byron swept his sword off the saddle and aimed a blow at the figure as it slammed into him. A powerful hand seized Byron's arm and wrenched the sword from his grasp. Another hand grabbed him by his hauberk and pulled him from the saddle. Byron slammed onto the ground. His horse bolted. Byron struggled, but the pain of his most recent body blow was unbearable, and he passed out.

"Got him," the man said in a strained whisper in Italian.

"I see that, Brother Carl," another voice replied in Italian from the darkness. "The plan was to pull him from the horse unharmed so I could question him."

"Father Villhardain, I did not strike a heavy blow." Carl paused and looked down at Byron. "It looks like he has passed out."

Father Villhardain stepped out of the shadows. A tall, gaunt man, caused from living by the example of Saint Augustine. His priest's cowl was thrown back revealing his silver hair, cut short. He was educated to the highest standards of the time, fluent in several languages. He knew scripture. He had dipped his fingers into Becket's blood. Learned in the teachings of Christ he had shunned ecclesiastic rank, adhering to his devotion to the savior. Despite his desire for piety, he had attracted the attention of the Holy Father. Notwithstanding his low position, he now served the highest circles of the Church. Because of this service, Father Villhardain had traveled many countries on assignments for the Church, but his passion was Roman history.

It had been an evil day, and Father Villhardain was in a hurry. This unexpected encounter would delay him. He assumed that the sultan had sent the rider to track him down. If one had found him, there would be more. The priest was unsure how much Saladin knew about his mission for the Church, but when the rider appeared to be following the same trail they were traveling, he feared the worse.

He bent down to look at what he thought was a Saracen Knight but saw a ghastly-looking young man with terrible wounds. The priest could see the tattered and bloodstained surcoat of black that bore a dirty white Maltese cross of a Knight of Saint John. Undoubtedly, the young man's armor hid other grievous wounds. "Carl, help me get him up."

Brother Carl and Father Villhardain got on each side of Byron and slowly raised him into a sitting position.

"Give him some water," Father Villhardain suggested.

Carl lifted a water skin to Byron's mouth and poured water into his parched, cracked lips. Byron coughed.

Byron started to stand up but two powerful hands on his

shoulders held him down. For the second time that day, he tried to focus his sight. Facing him, stood a tall older man. The priest's black dalmatic was plain and unadorned, covered in dust. A dark cloak thrown over his shoulders.

The priest bent close in the fading light and looked carefully at Byron's face. After a moment's examination, said to his companion, "Carl, release him." Carl released his grip. Byron tried to stand, but it was beyond his strength anymore. Father Villhardain's blue eyes stared directly at the knight, making him uncomfortable.

"Tell me who you are, my son," the priest said in a kind voice. Byron stared blankly at the priest. "Do you speak Italian, my son?"

Byron shook his head. He could speak Italian, but not well, and he did not want to look like a fool.

"I see," the priest said, changing to French. "Tell me who you are, my son? What brings you here to the shore of Galilee? I assume you know how dangerous it is for a Christian to walk the lakeshore tonight."

Byron sat for a moment, looking at the priest in front of him, considering how much he should tell the man. "I know it's dangerous. I had no other choice. Pray what gives you the right to attack a Christian soldier traveling the road? I have no money if that is what you desire."

The priest laughed softly. "We are not thieves, my son. Who are you, and what brings you here?"

"I am Sir Byron Fitzwalter, and I came to the lake to get some water ere starting my journey south to Jerusalem." Byron decided not to mention the destruction of the Army of Jerusalem until he knew more about the man.

A knowing smile flashed across the old priest's face but faded to a grim worried look. "Well, Sir Fitzwalter, I apologize for Brother Carl's greeting." Father Villhardain stood up and cautiously looked around. "I thought you were a servant of the sultan. I see now, that is not so." Byron started to protest, but the old priest cut him off. "You need not say more. Time is pressing, and I can guess what has happened." Father Villhardain paused and looked around, scanning the hillsides. "We must go. You will come with us, or by morning you will be a prisoner of the sultan."

"Father Villhardain," Carl interrupted, "a word of counsel?"

For the first time, Byron saw the man named Carl. He was tall with broad shoulders. His hands and arms knotted with muscles. He wore a brown dalmatic with frayed sleeves; his cowl was pulled up covering his head, the hood overshadowing his face. In the dim light, he could make out the edges of a red beard and a misshaped nose, protruding beyond the edge of the hood. The monk's nose was flat, slightly bent to one side, apparently the result of having been broken several times. The nose, nor the size of the man, seemed consistent with the soft men of the Church. Byron stared at the shadowed face. In the twilight, he could see the glimmer of the monk's eyes, and it gave him an unfriendly impression.

Father Villhardain stood up and walked over to where Carl was standing. "Father," the monk whispered, "are you sure we should take him with us? We are in haste, and already he has slowed us down. He is not worth the risk. He is almost dead now." Carl paused. "If we leave him, he may slow the Saracen's pursuit."

"Brother Carl, I cannot, in good conscience, leave this soldier of Christ here. Now find his horse."

"What about Brother Aaron?"

Father Villhardain shook his head and looked sadly in the direction of Tiberias. "I fear the worst. He should have been here by now. We can wait no longer. If by some miracle he escaped, he knows how to find Youssef."

Byron watched the two churchmen. Their conversation ended, and Carl walked away from the priest and returned with Byron's horse. Byron, relieved, knew his chances of surviving were getting better. Father Villhardain picked up Byron's sword and handed it back to the knight who put it back into its sheath. After a struggle, and some help from the priest, Byron was back in the saddle and riding away from the lake. They stopped after a short distance. Carl walked off into the dark and returned leading a donkey loaded down with several boxes and tools.

It was a dark, moonless night. For Byron, each mile was more miserable than the last. Father Villhardain led the way. Brother Carl, leading the donkey, walked behind him. Byron watched the priest confidently make his way through the dark, apparently having walked this trail many times. After toiling through the rolling hills for several hours, they stopped. Father Villhardain walked back to Byron, put his hand on his leg, and looked up at him.

"My son, I am going to ask you to put this hood over your head. I am taking you to a secret place that the early Christians have used over the years to hide from persecution. No harm will come to you, but I must have your word as a knight that you will not try to look."

"I am at your mercy, Father. You have my word."

Father Villhardain nodded. "I wouldn't ask, my son, if it was not necessary." Father Villhardain handed Byron a dark hood that he put over his head.

With each mile, the ache in his shoulders and back increased. His right foot had gone numb from riding in the saddle with his knee bent in the same position for too long. From the start of the journey, he had kept his left foot out of the stirrup to avoid having his knee take the shock of each step of the horse, which meant Byron had taken every jolt of the journey in his groin. To make matters worse, it was difficult to breathe with the hood over his face. He had to remind himself that he was not suffocating.

Just when he felt he could take no more, he heard Father Villhardain whisper to him, "Just a little further, my son, we are almost there."

The encouragement helped, but a little further seemed like forever. Suddenly the air temperature changed. Byron felt cool, damp air on his face. The horse balked, and Byron could hear the priest and the monk softly encouraging the animal to go on. The horse lurched forward, its hooves echoing. He sensed he was riding in a confined space, no longer outdoors. They went on for several minutes, and then he tilted forward as the horse started down a gentle slope. Suddenly they stopped. He sat in the saddle wondering what was going to happen next. He could hear a conversation in Arabic, but whoever was speaking was talking softly, and he could not make out what they were saying. The conversation stopped. Byron was starting to worry when Father Villhardain said, "My son, our night's journey has come to an end. We are safe." He felt hands gently help him from his horse.

"It's all right, my son," Father Villhardain said, "we are among our friends."

Byron relaxed as they removed the hood from his head. He was in a cavern. Torches lit the rock walls. Father Villhardain was standing near him. In the red glare of the flickering light, he saw that two Arab men were holding him up. A third Arab was standing next to Father Villhardain. The Arab was shorter than the priest, a beard covered his face. He was wearing a green tunic, the edge embroidered in silver. The sleeves of his light blue shirt extended beneath the sleeves of the tunic. A leather jerkin, polished smooth from years of wear, covered the tunic. A shamshir[5] hung at his side. The Arab's dark eyes stared at Byron.

"This is Youssef," the priest said. "You are his guest. He has agreed to give us a place to stay." Byron nodded. "You are fortunate Youssef feels pity for you. He has agreed to let his daughter tend your wounds. So be comforted, for the daughter of Youssef is a great healer. Go in peace. You are under the protection of Youssef, no harm will come to you. The coming days will bring more ill tidings I fear, and you will need to regain your strength."

Byron was too exhausted to care. All he could do was hope for the best. The next thing he knew he was lying on a comfortable mattress made of straw as he drifted off to sleep.

---

5 Shamshir is a curved sword of Persian origin. The sword has a curved slender blade with long quillons forming the hilt guard. The Saber is descendant of the Shamshir.

CHAPTER 3
SALAH AL-DIN YOUSSEF-IBN AYYUB "SALADIN"

It was a glorious day. The sun shone through the palm trees, and the Sea of Galilee shimmered silver in the distance. A man in a yellow silk surcoat smiled to himself. It had been a most satisfying week. He had attacked Tiberias and drawn the Christian Army from its stronghold in Jerusalem. He had forced the Christians to take the most difficult, waterless route, trapped them, and destroyed them. He had fulfilled his vow to kill Raynald Chatillon, the deceitful truce breaker. Salah al-Din Youssef, or as the Christians knew him, Saladin, smiled inwardly with satisfaction as he stood on the ramparts of the newly captured Christian fortress.

Salah al-Din's rise to sultan had not been an easy path. He was a Kurd, a self-made man. Through diplomacy and war, he had advanced himself through the ranks of the Arab nobility. His deadly cunning earned grudging respect from his enemies. His victories on the battlefield had made him a legend in his own time. Even in the far away kingdoms of Europe, mothers admonished their children to be good least the Sultan Saladin come and punish them for their misdeeds. He had great courage in the face of enemies, but his legendary wrath struck fear into friend and foe alike.

For years, Salah al-Din's war against the Christians had ebbed and flowed, though none of his victories had been as spectacular as the defeat he delivered to the Christians at Hattin. Years before, Salah al-Din had suffered a humiliating defeat at Montgisard. He had revenged himself upon the Christians with a bloody victory over the Templar castle at Jacobs Ford. The campaign against the Latin kingdom had been hard fought, and the Templars in particular had been a dangerous foe. The victory at Jacobs Ford had been costly to Salah al-Din and the Christians. For a time after these horrific battles, the war smoldered as each side rested their battered armies.

A two-year truce with Baldwin, the leper, had lasted until the Lord of Krak des Chevaliers, Raynald de Chatillon, broke the peace. Chatillon had made him look weak and put his position as sultan at grave risk. Salah al-Din had forged a weapon by uniting the Arab princes in jihad against the Christian invaders, but it was not a strong coalition. At any moment, any trifling disagreement could flare up and destroy all of his efforts. For the moment, his victory at Hattin had removed all doubt in his leadership. He had good reason to feel satisfied, if not relieved.

On the ground, below the rampart wall where the sultan stood basking in the sun, were lines of demoralized Christian soldiers, chained and fettered. The faithful were already flocking to Tiberias to purchase new slaves. The revenue raised from the sale of the Christian prisoners would greatly offset the cost of this campaign against the Crusader Kingdom.

A smaller group of Christians sat apart, their heads bowed down, talking amongst themselves, the leaders of the recent battle. Salah al-Din could only guess what they were discussing, but whatever their conversation, it mattered not. The sultan smiled to himself, they were powerless. He was the master of their fates. Let them talk. Their defeat would fester like a cancer, eating at them until they began to chew on one another like rats in a basket. Salah al-Din stood watching the small pathetic group of Christian nobility. He could make out King Guy and Grandmaster Ridefort sitting next to each other. Good. Their families would pay large ransoms for their freedom. Salah al-Din would soon consider what their lives were worth.

He had already ransomed several minor Christian lords, knowing his goodwill gesture would weaken the enemy's resolve to oppose him. The released Christians would explain away their defeat by embellishing his army's strength, and unwittingly spread rumors of his invincibility. The leaders of the defeated Christian Army were a different matter. They were dangerous. He needed to hold them captive until the time was ripe for furthering his political purpose.

Salah al-Din turned away from the walls and headed into the citadel, making his way to the great hall that was now his temporary throne room. Only one thought troubled him on this perfect day. He had taken Tiberias by storm, yet his soldiers had failed to capture a certain Christian priest. Even as he looked out at the captured Christian Army, his followers were searching the city for the priest and his assistants. The sultan had little doubt that his soldiers would find him. Tiberias was his, and there were only so many places a man could hide within the city's walls.

Salah al-Din walked into his newly acquired throne room. At the far end of the darkened hall, his servants had built a makeshift dais. On the dais sat a large chair.

Salah al-Din reached the dais, sat down on the chair, and made himself comfortable. Once settled, he took a moment to admire the walls of the room. His servants had hastily covered the decadent western art with woven tapestries embroidered with the shahada in gold thread. The room would be cleansed later, but for now, the new appearance met the sultan's approval. Satisfied with the room's decor, he rested his feet on a piece of worn wood, oddly out of place with the rest of the comfortable furniture. The relic was a trophy recently acquired at the battle of Hattin, the true cross, if indeed it was.

Salah al-Din was skeptical. Not that it mattered. The Christians believed the wood was from the cross of Christ's crucifixion. It was the battle flag of the Crusader Army. They believed it made them invincible. He scoffed at the thought of such idol worship and wondered if their recent defeat had disabused them of the cross' invincibility. No matter. It was in his hands now, and he enjoyed its new use as a footrest. Such an item would be dangerous if it fell back into Christian hands. It would revitalize them to fight on. He needed to keep the cross from falling back into the possession of the Crusader Kingdom. On his orders, it would be taken to Damascus and buried under the threshold of a mosque. The faithful could tread on it on their way to prayer. Salah al-Din would make sure it stayed out of Christian hands forever.

He looked up from his musings about the relic as his seventeen-year-old son, al-Afdal, entered the room.

"Have you found the priest?" the sultan demanded.

Al-Afdal bowed to his father. "No, we have not. I followed your direction father, and we have questioned the monk we captured in the city."

"And what have you learned?"

"I have learned he was a member of the priest's order. But it has taken considerable effort to convince him to talk."

"That is not unexpected. What did he tell you?"

Al-Afdal frowned. "The monk's name is Brother Aaron. He is an assistant to Father Michael Jean Villhardain. The monk revealed he traveled from Rome to Outremer with the priest and another monk by the name of Carl. We have learned that Father Villhardain is in the highest circles of the Roman Catholic Church. He is close to the infidel Pope Urban."

"Hmm, what else did the man tell you?"

"Brother Aaron told us that the priest was outside the city on a search for artifacts when we surrounded it."

Salah al-Din sat for a moment in thought. "Have the infidels found the Roman treasure?"

"Yes, but he professes he doesn't know where it is hidden."

"Do you believe he is being truthful?"

"Yes, father. The monk was in great pain." Al-Afdal, glanced away from the sultan to look at one of the tapestries. "I don't think there is anything more we can extract from this man."

"Perhaps a new interrogator would be more successful. Send a new man to talk to this monk, perhaps a new approach might get better results."

Al-Afdal looked back to his father and then down at his feet. "That is no longer possible."

"And why not?"

"The man is dead."

Salah al-Din's eyebrows lowered as a scarlet hue filled his face. The sultan leaned forward in his chair. "I told you to keep him alive!"

Al-Afdal took a step back. "Father, it is not my fault. We had just finished the first series of questions, and I had ordered the man be returned to his cell when he turned pale and stopped breathing."

"When I send men to be interrogated, I don't send them to be killed! If I wanted him dead, I would say so! Who was the interrogator?"

Al-Afdal hesitated, uncomfortable in the silence, then he mumbled, "Fayyad".

"Fayyad. That clumsy fool! He needs to be taught a lesson." The sultan paused, his fingers tapping out cadence on the armrest of his throne. The drumming stopped. "Fayyad must pay for this. Have Fayyad scourged. Perhaps then, he will have a deeper understanding of how far he can torture a man."

"Yes, father, I will see that your punishment is carried out."

The death of the monk had been an accident, but al-Afdal knew his father. He had been in such a mood just before he killed Raynald de Chatillon. Al-Afdal knew better than to argue with his father once the sultan pronounced judgment.

Salah al-Din massaged his forehead. "This is a most unfortunate development. I had hoped we might learn the location of the treasure. Now things are much more difficult." Salah al-Din paused. "The other monk and the priest were outside the city when we besieged it?"

"Yes, father. Nevertheless, just to be sure, I have had the men turning this city upside down, but no one has found them."

Salah al-Din sighed. "Circumstances are now what they are, it cannot be helped. We must find the priest. We must thwart the Christian's efforts to recover this treasure, or all our efforts will come to naught." The room became quiet. Salah al-Din tugged at his beard, thinking. He considered which leader in his army would be trustworthy and capable of finding the priest and possibly the treasure.

Al-Afdal shifted uncomfortably in the silence. He wanted to accompany the army, to be there for the conquest of Jerusalem. He now feared his father would choose him to lead this fruitless chase to find a priest that probably had already fled.

At last, Salah al-Din spoke, "Go find Husam al-Din and bring him here."

Al-Afdal bowed and hurried from the room to go search for Husam al-Din before his father changed his mind and chose him.

†

Husam al-Din was resting in the shade. It had been a hard fight, and he was enjoying a well-earned respite. He had led the attack on the crusader column as the Christians had marched from ar-Saffuriyah. His men had swept down upon the enemy ranks, shooting stragglers with arrows, delaying the Christians advance. The unrelenting assault had forced the Christians to halt and fight at the Horns of Hattin. Hattin was the place where his master, the sultan, had chosen to destroy them.

The fight at Hattin had been hard fought. The Christians were trapped, but they knew how to fight. He lost several of his best men as he charged the Christian infantry, breaking their line of spearmen. Once through the lines, he had gathered his remaining knights and charged uphill to the red pavilion. Shamshir in hand, Husam al-Din had cut down the defenders as he recklessly rode his horse towards the red tent. A Templar bolted from beneath the red awning. Husam al-Din rode after him. The Templar glanced behind him as he ran. It proved to be a fateful mistake as he tripped over a rock and fell to the ground. As the templar rolled in the dust, the red cross of his white surcoat twisted about him as if binding him with a cord. The Templar was struggling to get to his feet. Husam al-Din sprang from his horse and leveled his shamshir at the Templars face. As he stared down his sword, he realized his good fortune, for he recognized the face of Grandmaster

Ridefort. Husam al-Din looked into the agonized grandmaster's eyes. The realization of the immense ransom for Ridefort's freedom entered his mind, and he mocked Ridefort with the Templar battle cry, "Christ may be your life, infidel, but death will not be your reward. You are worth more alive!"

The pleasant memory faded as Husam al-Din saw al-Afdal approaching. The sight of al-Afdal did not fill him with joy. The sultan wanted something. His rest would have to wait.

"Peace be to you."

"And to you," Husam al-Din responded.

"The sultan requests your presence."

Husam al-Din rose. He was tall with broad shoulders. A steal cap covered his black hair. Between large, dark eyes, his roman nose was the most prominent feature of his face. He bowed to al-Afdal. "I am at the sultan's service." Husam al-Din turned to his men, who were now on their feet in the presence of the sultan's son. "Wait here," he growled to Isma'il, his second in command, and then turned and fell in behind al-Afdal.

Both men walked through the streets, making their way past a large number of Saracen soldiers who were too busy looting to notice the sultan's son. After being jostled several times by pillagers, they came to the entrance of the citadel. The guards in yellow silk surcoats bowed to al-Afdal and swiftly admitted them into the castle.

The posted guards, with shamshirs drawn, saluted the two Saracen Knights as they entered through the doorway of the great hall. Salah al-Din was sitting in his chair at the far end of the hall, deep in discussion with a group of his commanders. Al-Afdal and Husam al-Din approached the throne and bowed low to Salah al-Din. The sultan finished the meeting by giving orders to the leaders of his army, and then motioned for his son and Husam al-Din to approach the throne.

"Bring seats and some refreshments for this hero of Islam."

The sultan's recognition pleased Husam al-Din. The servants hurried off, and within moments, returned with two carpets. They rolled them out for them to sit on. The two men sat down before the sultan, and the servants reappeared with qahwa and sweet cakes. When the trays of sweet cakes and qahwa had been placed before them, the servants bowed to the sultan as they backed out the door. When the last servant had crossed the threshold, the guards saluted and shut the doors.

The sultan looked down from his throne at Husam al-Din and held him in his gaze. After what seemed like an interminable length of time, Salah al-Din spoke, "It was you and your valiant men who kept the Christians from reaching the safety of the Sea of Galilee. Your valor is to be commended. I cannot think of anyone who did more to bring about our victory."

Husam al-Din bowed his head to the sultan. "You honor me, Great Sultan. The Christians fought hard and asked for no quarter, and none was given. It was one of the hardest fights I have had in some time, and I lost several of my best men."

"The loss of good men is always hard. Especially considering that this campaign to destroy the Christian Kingdom has only just begun. I assume you have acquired adequate compensation for your trouble."

"My soldiers worked hard to relieve the infidels of their earthly cares and burdens."

The sultan nodded and then cleared his voice. "I will get to the point. A pressing matter has arisen, and after careful consideration, I have chosen you to carry out an important undertaking." Husam al-Din looked up at the sultan in surprise. "This will not be an easy task, and that is why I chose you."

Husam al-Din mustered his enthusiasm before he answered He had really hoped to spend some time resting in Tiberias before the army's next move. No matter, he knew that Salah al-Din had made his choice, and he would have to do his best to carry out the task. "Thank you, Great Sultan. How can I be of service to you?"

Salah al-Din could guess the thoughts of the man in front of him. One did not become a successful leader without such skill. A tyrant could compel men with fear but only for a short time before they began working covertly to undermine you. Salah al-Din was too great of a leader to resort to unnecessary force. He had many tools to motivate men.

"Husam al-Din, this task I am appointing to you will test all of your ability. Your effort will be rewarded if you are successful. What I am going to tell you must be kept to yourself. Do not fail to heed my warning."

Husam al-Din nodded. The sight of the infidel Chatillon's head on a stake was cautionary enough not to become the subject of Salah al-Din's wrath.

The sultan cleared his voice and began his story. "Several years ago, a group of Christian pilgrims traveling by ship to the Holy Lands were blown off course by a storm and forced into one of our harbors. Unfortunately, for the pilgrims, the now dead truce breaker, Chatillon, raided our seaports at the same time.

"When I demanded compensation for our losses, the Christians in Jerusalem refused. In retribution for the wanton loss and destruction by Chatillon and his miscreants, I sold every one of the Christian pilgrims into slavery. One of the pilgrims attempted to bargain for his freedom. He was brought to me, and he told me he was a bishop in the Christian Church and a close friend of the pope. He seemed to have the mistaken belief that such friendship was important to me. The man considered himself to be important, but to be candid I have forgotten his name."

Salah al-Din took a sip of qahwa. "He said he would share valuable information in exchange for his freedom. I told the bishop I would grant his freedom if I found his information of value. I also told him that if he failed to impress me, or told me a tale full of fabrications, I would have his eyes blinded and tongue cut off for wasting my time."

The sultan paused. "After I told the fool my conditions, the man became highly motivated to be truthful. The bishop told me that in the closing days of the Western Roman Empire a treasure ship loaded with gold left Rome just before the Visigoths stormed the old capital. The ship sailed for the Levant with a centurion of the emperor's guard in command of the expedition. When the centurion reached the Levant, he and his men hid the treasure in the desert where it was forgotten."

Salah al-Din set his cup down on the arm of his throne and leaned forward. "But that is not where the story ends. At first, the bishop felt the story that you have just heard was sufficient, but

I felt that there might be more. I had one of my guards help the bishop's memory, and I was correct, there was more to the bishop's tale. The bishop, with some encouragement, found he could remember more details. It turned out that the Roman Catholic Church had recently found evidence of the treasure's existence. The bishop also remembered that the Church had sent a priest, learned in Roman history, to the Kingdom of Jerusalem with instructions to find the treasure, and return it to Rome."

Salah al-Din sat back in his chair and looked Husam al-Din in the eyes. "This must not happen!" He then paused for a moment to let his words sink in before he continued. "I was inclined to blind the bishop and have his tongue cut from his mouth for trying to withhold information from me, but then," Salah al-Din made a dismissive wave of his hand, "I reconsidered and decided that this treacherous fool would learn a better lesson in humility through hard labor, so I sent him back unharmed. I still remember the look on the man's face when I told him that he was going to be sold."

Salah al-Din picked up his cup and took another sip of qahwa. "Not long after that, a wealthy merchant of Mecca told me that he had been trading with the Crusader Kingdom, and that he had sold an old Roman clay vessel to a Catholic priest for an enormous sum of money. The merchant, eager to continue to exploit the Roman Church, inquired of relatives and other business associates and found they had also had similar experiences with a priest matching the same description. The merchant told the story as a jest of the foolishness of Christians and their obsession with useless artifacts and scrolls."

A sly smile crossed Salah al-Din's face. "As you can guess, I reached a different conclusion of what the priest was doing, and I sent spies to find him and watch him. The reports I received from my spies only served to confirm my guess. The last information I had regarding the priest, before my war to capture Jerusalem, was that he was here in Tiberias working on collecting more information and artifacts. I am disappointed that he was not captured when we took the city." Salah al-Din stopped and looked down from his throne directly at Husam al-Din.

"This is the task I have for you. Find the priest. Find out all that he knows, and then find the treasure. Husam al-Din, you must not fail. If the Christians are able to recover the treasure, it will prolong our struggle for the city of Jerusalem and will hinder our efforts to rid our country of these invaders."

In shock at the enormity of what had just been thrust upon him, Husam al-Din stammered, "All will be done as you desire, Great Sultan."

Salah al-Din smiled. "Indeed, it will. You must succeed. I will provide every resource I can, directing my servants great and small to aid you." Husam al-Din nodded. Salah al-Din set his cup down and rose. "You do not have much time to prepare. The priest will know that Tiberias is no longer safe. I cannot guess if he is in hiding, or fleeing the country. All is as Allah wills it to be. My hope is that he will bless you and guide you. Go, and may Allah be merciful to you."

Husam al-Din bowed to Salah al-Din and then backed from the room, never turning his back on the sultan. Salah al-Din whispered to his son, "Stay for a moment. I want to have a word with you."

Husam al-Din walked from the throne room like a man in a trance. When he reached the outside walls of the citadel, he stopped and leaned against the wall. His mind reeled with the enormity of the sultan's request.

The impossibility of finding one man, who could be anywhere, was a huge undertaking. If the priest had fled the region, how would he know?

The only thing his mind kept coming back to was what would happen to him when he failed, because he was sure failure would be the likely outcome. What would happen to his family, his wife, his children? What would his father say of him? It was unthinkable. If he failed, he would have to die in the attempt.

These thoughts passed through his mind as he leaned against the wall. He was not the kind of man to dwell on failure, Salah al-Din had chosen well. He shook his mind free of these destructive thoughts and began to consider how he was going to make this work. He started making his plans as he walked from the citadel. His confidence began to return. It was a long shot, but who knows, he might even find this priest and maybe even recover the treasure.

CHAPTER 4
THE SARACEN KNIGHT AND THE SULTAN'S SON

Salah al-Din motioned for his servants to return to the room. "Bring more qahwa." The servants bowed, and within moments, one of the servants returned with a steaming kettle.

"May I ask a question?" al-Afdal asked as the servant filled his cup.

"Of course, my son."

"Why did you pick this man? There are other brave men in your service who have done greater deeds of valor."

Salah al-Din smiled. "I chose this man for several reasons, none of which has to do with valor. Husam al-Din has already proved his worth on the battlefield. No, in this instance, I need someone who has qualities beyond bravery.

"Husam al-Din is the son of Sheikh Abdul al-Subayil," continued Salah al-Din. "The sheikh, as you may know, is a wealthy merchant with an extensive network of trading partners in the Levant, the Far East, and Christendom. His caravans import exotic goods from the Far East, which he then sells to the Christians at exorbitant prices."

"Ah, I see the wisdom of your choice."

"Indeed, my son. When I renewed my effort to take Jerusalem, the sheikh presented to me a gift of one-hundred knights, lavishly equipped, and his only son to lead them. I chose Husam al-Din for many reasons. He is brave, he is resourceful, and he has his father's connections. He will not only have access to information at the ports in our kingdom but those in Christendom as well."

"That will prove useful if this priest flees Outremer."

"As he is certain to do. The Christians will sell their souls if the price is right. All Husam al-Din must do is strike the right bargain, and we shall know everything necessary about this priest."

"Their greed is insatiable."

"And it will be their undoing. I have forced the priest out into the open. My war has disrupted his plans. It has made it difficult for him to retrieve the treasure, but the priest will not give up. I have chosen the huntsman. He will find his trail. With Allah's blessing, this priest will soon be captured, and this threat will evaporate like a mist in the wind."

Al-Afdal smiled. "Before long, the priest will be a prisoner in Aleppo, and we will once again be masters of our own country."

Salah al-Din looked towards the windows. "Husam al-Din said he suffered losses. Do you know how many men?"

Al-Afdal shook his head. "No, father."

"The army will march soon. When you meet with Husam al-Din, tell him he can have his choice in men to replace his losses. Soon, I will take the city of Acre and then Ascalon. Jerusalem will be isolated and weak. I will offer generous terms to the Christians to surrender. If they do not give up the city, then I will destroy it."

Salah al-Din turned and motioned to one of his servants. "Summon my scribe. I want to draft a letter."

The servant hurried out of the room and returned, accompanied by a corpulent, elderly man. "I want a letter drafted," the sultan said, "directing the faithful to assist my servant, Husam al-Din, with anything he might request. Further, I want it to be clear that Husam al-Din speaks for me. If they fail to aid him, they will feel my wrath, which will be swift and terrible. I want this letter before me for my seal as soon as possible."

The scribe bowed low. "All will be done as you wish, Great Sultan. I will have it ready for your exaltedness within the hour."

"Then make it so." The man bowed and backed out of the room and hurried off.

Salah al-Din and al-Afdal spent the time waiting by rehashing the recent battle at Hattin. The scribe returned within the hour with several drafts of the letter for the sultan's seal. Salah al-Din read them carefully and appeared satisfied with one of the copies.

He placed his seal to the letter and turned to his son. "Take this to Husam al-Din. Give it to him and see how he is progressing." Al-Afdal took the letter and bowed. "And I want you to take care of Fayyad after you finish delivering the letter." Al-Afdal frowned. "Do you think I am being too harsh my son?"

"Yes, father, I do."

"My son, when I give a man a task to do, I expect his best efforts. Fayyad has killed a man I wanted questioned. Fayyad has been trained by the best to do this kind of work, and he has gotten careless. Now, I have to send Husam al-Din and his men to repair his mistake at a time when I would much rather have them with the army. Do you understand?" Al-Afdal nodded. "Someday, my son, you will have to act on such matters. Men must see consequences for their failures. It will be your job to enforce the standards, no matter how unpleasant. You must do an even more difficult task at the same time…enforce those standards upon yourself. If men perceive that you have rules for everyone but yourself, then my son your days as sultan are numbered and Allah will be the one to enforce his judgment upon you."

Al-Afdal bowed again.

"Now go give Husam al-Din my letter and then take care of Fayyad." Saladin was pleased that even though events had not worked out the way he had hoped, he was still able to use them to prepare his son to be a sultan.

Al-Afdal turned and walked out, his mind contemplating his father's lessons.

He found Husam al-Din at the edge of town in his tent. He was sitting at a wooden box that he was using for a table. Several maps lay scattered on its weather-beaten surface. Two of his knights stood at the entrance of the tent. The knights bowed as al-Afdal entered the tent.

Husam-al-Din looked up from his work and started to rise to his feet.

"Don't get up, I won't be here long. I have a letter for you." He handed the letter to Husam al-Din. "This letter commands all who reads it to assist you with whatever you require."

Husam al-Din nodded distractedly as he looked at the sultan's seal on the letter and then carefully opened it.

"How are your plans coming?" al-Afdal asked as Husam al-Din read the sultan's letter.

Husam al-Din looked up. "After giving the problem some thought, I believe that the priest will try to escape the Holy Lands," Husam al-Din said as he pulled a map out from under several other maps and spread it across his makeshift desk. Al-Afdal bent down to get a closer look.

Husam al-Din pointed to the map. "I think he will try to leave the country at either Acre or Tyre. There are other ports he could try to use, but they are farther away." Husam al-Din paused and rubbed his forehead with his hand. "I believe he will go to Tyre. Jerusalem is the sultan's prize making Acre a dangerous destination. The priest will know this. That is why I think he will go to Tyre."

"Very good," muttered al-Afdal.

"I have decided to send my best men to watch the roads to Tyre. I will send a few to Acre, Ascalon, and other possible places of escape, but I intend to focus most of my efforts on all the routes that lead to Tyre."

Al-Afdal nodded. "You have done well in such a short time."

"You are very gracious, my prince. One thing I have not been told is the description of the priest. Does he have servants?"

Al-Afdal's lips twisted into a faint smile. In all of his father's instructions to Husam al-Din, the sultan had neglected to tell his servant what the man he was seeking looked like. Al-Afdal found the oversite amusing, but as he inwardly chuckled, he decided he would keep his father's mistake to himself. "A good question. The information I am going to tell you came from a monk we captured. The priest, Father Michael Jean Villhardain, is about fifty years old. He has short-cropped, silver-grey hair. He is tall and thin, almost gaunt looking. He has blue eyes. He travels with an assistant, a monk whose name is Carl. He is stout and strong. He wears the monastic robes of the infidel faith."

"Anything else?"

"The monk told me, as Fayyad was breaking his fingers, that Carl had been an Anglo-Saxon warrior before he became a religious man. Beyond that, I have nothing more to tell you."

Husam al-Din nodded. "Well that should make things interesting. I am going to draft a letter to my father and ask him to help me make contact with his most trusted trading partners."

"That would be wise. What else do you have in mind?"

"I am sending men out in groups of two with instructions to capture this man alive."

Al-Afdal nodded. "Speaking of men, you told my father you suffered losses. How many men did you lose?"

"I lost twenty-four...fifteen dead, nine will never fight again."

"That is a pity, especially for the widows and orphans." Al-Afdal looked down for a moment. "My father has given orders that you will have your pick of men from the army. I suggest you do so before the commanders start hiding their best men."

Husam al-Din smiled. "No one ever gives up his best fighters willingly."

"No, they don't." Al-Afdal turned to leave. "You have done well. I will let my father know your plans. I am certain that he will be pleased. Now, I will take my leave. I have another task that demands my attention."

Husam al-Din went back to studying the maps on his makeshift desk. He looked over at the sultan's letter. He would put it to use. He picked up a quill and wrote a list of names on a piece of parchment.

"Isma'il!" he cried. He waited a moment, but his second in command did not appear. Husam al-Din went to the entrance of his tent and shouted again. "Isma'il!"

From the doorway of another tent, Isma'il's head appeared. "What do you want? I have a visitor."

"I have something for you to do... now."

"Right now? Can't it wait?"

"No, it can't wait."

Isma'il shook his head and muttered something as he disappeared into his tent. Husam al-Din went back to his desk.

After some time, Isma'il entered Husam al-Din's tent. "What do you need? I have a servant girl I am entertaining."

"I have been given an important assignment by the sultan. The sultan has given me first pick to replace my losses. I don't have time to hunt down replacements, therefore you are going to do it."

"That could take hours."

"Indeed. I suggest you start now. The sultan has sent word to his commanders to give me whoever I want. Knowing my fellow commanders, I am certain they are already trying to find a way to ignore the command. Take this letter with the sultan's seal. If anyone refuses your requests, show them the letter. It will help remind them of the severity of refusing the sultan's commands." Isma'il sighed and nodded. "Here is a list of the men I want."

Isma'il took the list and glanced at it. "Is this all?"

"Unless you can think of anyone else?"

Isma'il looked at the list again. "Kasim. He is a fearless man."

"Then take him and get the rest. The sultan has given us first choice. A few extra men might prove useful."

Isma'il nodded. "Once I am done, is this all? Or do you need something else?"

"This is all for now. Your servant girl will wait."

Isma'il scowled at Husam al-Din as he turned and left the tent. Husam al-Din frowned. Servant girls indeed. He had bigger issues to worry about. The priest would not escape. Husam al-Din would turn loose one-hundred battle hardened men to chase a priest and a monk. He smiled at the thought. The outcome was not in doubt.

CHAPTER 5
THE CAVERNS OF THE APOSTLES

Byron awoke in a strange room lit by candles. He stared at the sandstone wall decorated with a fresco of Christ on the cross. He scanned the other walls of the room and saw there were more frescos of Christ, dulled by years of soot and dirt. He wondered who had made them. He looked up at the ceiling. Jesus, his arms outspread, stared down at him with a reproachful stare. He lay on his back thinking of Hattin, the men he had slain. The Celts he had slaughtered in Ireland. He rolled over and tried to go back to sleep. He closed his eyes, but after several minutes, he sat up. His muscles ached. Carefully, he moved his legs to the edge of the bed and put his feet on the floor. He sat there for a moment in the quiet room. A feeling came over him that he was not alone. He glanced around, but the room was empty.

Byron looked down to find he was dressed in a floor length dressing gown of white cotton. The wound on his arm was bandaged. He thought about getting up and going outside. The sun would feel good, but it seemed like a lot of effort. His head hurt, and he sat weighing whether or not he should move. A crutch had been placed at the head of the bed. He leaned over to grab it. Groaning, he stiffly pulled himself into a standing position.

He hobbled across the room to look at his reflection in the copper mirror that hung on the wall. Someone had washed the blood from his face, but savage cuts remained. He reached up to touch his face. None of the wounds were deep, they would soon heal. His face would be as good as new. He smiled at his reflection and then looked away. He wondered how long he had been asleep. He slowly shuffled to the doorway of the cavern and made his way down a dimly lit rock passageway to an arch.

Byron passed through the rock archway into the brilliant sunlight. He blinked several times as his eyes adjusted to the light. He was standing at the edge of a courtyard surrounded by tall sandstone walls. At the center of the courtyard, a garden of white and purple flowers encircled a small pool, fed by a spring. Byron stood admiring the garden. The sun felt good, and he took a deep breath of fresh air. He was still alive. He wanted to see the flowers, so he hobbled along the path to get a closer view. A gutter filled with running water sparkled in the sunlight as it rushed past him, flowing to a dark opening cut into the sandstone wall.

Byron stopped at the edge of the garden. The flowers, on tall grey-green stems, swayed in the gentle breeze. The knight reached out and cupped one of the purple flowers in his hand. Several flowers had lost their petals, leaving only a large pod behind. He heard a voice, and he looked up to see the priest standing near the pool talking to Yousef and another Arab dressed in black.

"Your plan is fraught with risk, Father," Yousef whispered in Arabic. "Salah al-Din's army is on the march. The sultan has left Tiberias; his army marches towards Jerusalem. It is immense. It stretches for miles. If you must travel to Tyre, you should go by night, and hide during the day. I warn you, Father, stay away from the roads. They are being watched. My brother has seen several riders traveling the roads, asking all they meet for information concerning a priest and his assistant."

Father Villhardain sighed. "I have been fearful of this," he replied fluently in Arabic. "Have you found any sign of my missing assistant Brother Aaron?"

"I have heard nothing. We cannot get into Tiberias. I know not what has happened to him." The priest shook his head. "I wish I could tell you his fate for certain," continued Youssef, "but his disappearance... it speaks for itself."

Father Villhardain nodded and then looked at the ground. "You have my thanks for any inconvenience you suffered to search for him. I will heed your warning about the road to Tyre. For your trouble," the priest said, taking several coins out of his robe and handing them to Youssef.

Youssef bowed and turned to the man with him. "We must go." Then, to Byron's surprise, the Arab made a sign of the cross. "Have faith, my friend, our Lord Jesus Christ will hear your prayer. Brother Aaron may be lost, but the Good Shepherd has not forgotten him, and he will find him wherever he may wander." Youssef turned and walked with the other Arab to the dark opening at the far end of the garden and disappeared.

Leaning on his crutch, Byron shuffled over to where Father Villhardain stood looking down, deep in thought. The priest glanced up at the approaching knight. "I see that you are up and moving about, my son," Father Villhardain said in French.

"I am," Byron replied.

Father Villhardain motioned to a nearby bench. Byron hobbled over to it, and with a groan sat down. Father Villhardain sat down next to him. Byron looked at the old priest who appeared worn and tired.

"Tell me your name again, my son."

Byron smiled. "Sir Byron Stephen Fitzwalter of Gowran Ireland."

"Hmm, Sir Byron Fitzwalter," repeated the priest thoughtfully. "A Hospitaller, or so I remember from the livery you wore. I am glad to make your acquaintance. Tell me, my son, I have heard an evil rumor: the Army of Jerusalem has been destroyed. Is this true?"

An awkward silence followed. "Yes," Byron replied, not wanting to discuss the subject.

"Hmm," the priest said thoughtfully, looking at the battered young man sitting next to him. "You were there, were you not?" Byron nodded. "And yet, death passed you over, taking others and leaving you. How did you escape when so many others perished or were captured?"

"I don't know, Father," the knight said, looking at his hands. "I was fighting a Saracen and my horse started to fall. I awoke and found myself alone, surrounded by the dead. By some miracle I was overlooked among the corpses."

"Tell me what happened at Hattin? What has become of the king?"

Byron looked down at the bandage on his arm. "Father, the rumors you have heard are true. The army has been destroyed. The king? I know not what has happened to him." Byron looked up. "I shall tell you the tale of our march from the springs of ar-Saffuriyah to the defeat at Hattin, but beyond that I do not know."

Byron coughed, and then began his tale. The sun shone down on the priest and it grew warm as Bryon told his story. Father Villhardain looked at the young knight when he had finished. The truth of his account was evident in the fading marks of battle still marring his face. The two men sat quietly. The water gurgling from the spring was the only sound in the garden.

At last, Father Villhardain spoke, "The rumors of Saladin's victory are true. Dark tidings indeed, and I fear they are a harbinger of worse days to come." The priest sagged back against the bench and looked down at his hands.

"Forgive me, Father, for overhearing your conversation, but it sounds like the roads have become very dangerous. What did Youssef mean by riders are asking questions about a priest?"

Father Villhardain looked up, his eyebrows raised. "You speak the Saracen tongue?"

"Yes, Father. I have been told I could pass for a Saracen, though it was not kindly meant."

"So, my son, you can speak the language of the Saracens," the priest replied in Arabic. "That must be a great benefit to you here in the Holy Lands."

"It has been helpful."

Father Villhardain smiled and lifted his chin as he examined Byron's face with his piercing blue eyes. "Indeed. It may come in very useful."

"Father, I appreciate your care and hospitality, but I should return to my order in Jerusalem."

The smile on the priest's face faded to a frown. "My son, I fear you will have to stay here for a while. Saladin's army are on the road to Jerusalem. It would be unwise and dangerous for you to travel that way." Father Villhardain pointed to the knight's bandaged arm. "You have fulfilled your obligation to the Church. Let your wounds heal."

"You are very kind, Father," Byron replied as he struggled to pull himself up with his crutch. "Saladin is not resting, therefore neither should I."

The priest watched as the knight struggled to stand. Byron's face grew pale from the strain and collapsed back down on the bench. "My son, give yourself time to heal. You will only hinder your comrades in this condition."

Byron nodded in defeat. "Yes, Father."

"My son, I have a question. Who commands your order?"

"The Grand Master, but ultimately we serve the Holy Father in Rome."

Father Villhardain nodded. "If the Holy Father, Christ's representative on earth, gave you a command, would you follow it?"

"Of course."

Father Villhardain smiled. "You asked me earlier about Saracen Knights searching for a priest. What if I told you the Holy Father in Rome has given me an assignment and I will soon be returning to that city?"

"I would find that interesting," Byron replied politely, unsure where the conversation was leading.

"And what if I told you my task here in the Holy Lands is of vital importance to the Church, Christendom, and the crusade?"

"What is your task?"

"I cannot say... at least not here, but would you consider traveling with me to Rome." The priest paused, seeing Byron's eyes narrow.

"I have sworn an oath to my order. To leave would break my vow of faith."

"Your vow as a knight to your order and your church will be fulfilled if you assist me. I am returning to the Lateran Palace to meet with the Holy Father. If your vow troubles you, you can ask his Holiness for intercession."

Byron started to cross his arms across his chest, and he grimaced as the pressure on his arm reminded him of his injury. He dropped his arms to his sides.

"My son, at least travel with us to Tyre. It would be a great comfort to me and Brother Carl if we had your protection on the road." Father Villhardain let these words sink in. "What do you think of my proposal?"

Byron was uneasy. He had assumed as soon as he was healed, he and the kindly priest would part ways. It troubled him to think he would be abandoning the men of his order. Still, he had taken the cross to defend his faith and the Holy Lands against the infidels no matter the cost to himself or others.

At last, Byron spoke, "If all you say is true, then it is my duty to defend you and to make sure you arrive safely at Tyre. I owe you that much for the kindness that you have shown me, but I owe fealty to the Order of Saint John. Once you have reached Tyre safely, I must ride for Jerusalem."

"An oath cannot be lightly set aside," Father Villhardain said. "It speaks to your character. I would welcome your company to Rome, but your protection on the road to Tyre will suffice. We shall wait here until Youssef deems the roads are less watched, and then we shall travel to Tyre. That will give you more time to mend."

"Father, who is Youssef?"

"Youssef? He is a Christian. A descendant of Christ's first followers when Our Lord walked this land preaching the gospel. They are still here, after his crucifixion, preserving the secret places where his disciples prepared to go out into the world to spread the good news. The cavern you are sleeping in was one of the early places where they met. Very few of them remain, and they rarely admit outsiders into these special places. When the first crusade seized Jerusalem, they greeted us as deliverers. Unfortunately, they were treated with contempt, tortured, and murdered. They despise the Templars, who they hold the most responsible for the atrocities inflicted upon them. It is fortunate that you are not a Templar."

Byron's face stiffened. "No, I am not."

"I see you hold some animosity against them."

"I don't care for them. The Knights of the Temple are arrogant."

"Yes, my son. Their pride has grown, and it is their pride that hurts them. Even in something as simple as finding refuge. During my travels, I befriended these Christian Arabs. They have been of great help to me in my work. They have opened their doors to us, and it has proven to be a great boon. We can now hide and wait for Saladin to tire of his search for us. If we were Knights of the Temple, we would not be welcome."

"When do you expect Youssef's return?"

"He has gone to scout the roads, to see which ones Saladin's soldiers watch and which ones may be safer to travel. Youssef and his men will return soon. When they do, I will listen to their counsel and then decide when it is best to travel. My hope is that they will escort us part of the way to Tyre." The priest shook his head. "It is in God's hands, though in my heart, I could stay here forever. Alas that is not my fate."

"It is a pleasant place," the knight said, admiring his surroundings.

The old priest looked up at the sky for a moment and then slapped his knees with his hands. "Well I have many tasks, and sitting here is not accomplishing any of God's work. Do you need help to stand?"

"I can manage, Father. I did it once. I can do it again."

Father Villhardain nodded. "Indeed, but I will still send someone to check on you. Enjoy the day, and I will see you for the evening meal." The priest stood up and walked away, disappearing into one of the many passages leading away from the garden.

CHAPTER 6
GRIM TIDINGS

Father Villhardain walked through the sandstone hallway. Shafts cut in the rock revealed islands of light that aided him as he traveled through the darkness of the hall. The old priest was distracted, Brother Aaron was missing, and now Saladin's soldiers were searching the roads for him. He could only assume that the sultan had captured Aaron and tortured him until he talked. Even more concerning, ever since he had reached the caverns, he had heard rumors of the Christian Army's crushing defeat. Fitzwalter had just confirmed his fear. He just hoped he could make it to Tyre. The archbishop would help him.

He walked along, head down, his hands behind his back, until he came to doorway. He knocked and opened the door without waiting for an answer.

Brother Carl sat at a small wooden table, his head bowed in meditation. Without looking up, the big monk asked, "What news did Youssef bring?"

"Nothing but bad tidings," the priest replied as he pulled a chair close to the table and sat down.

Brother Carl looked up from his prayers. "Is the Norman still resting?"

"He has risen, but he is still pale and very weak."

"Humph!" The monk was unimpressed. "So, what did Youssef tell you? Did he find Brother Aaron?"

"No, and they can't get into Tiberias to search for him. More concerning, is that Youssef told me that Saladin's men are searching the road for a priest and a large monk."

Brother Carl leaned back into his chair thoughtfully. "Saladin has Brother Aaron. I can't imagine the agony he must be enduring. Brother Aaron would die before he told them too much."

"Things have become very dangerous."

"Do you still wish to see if the treasure remains where the centurion left it?"

"No, my plans have changed. I think it is now too perilous."

"What do you want to do?"

"I don't know. What do you think?"

The monk crossed his arms across his chest. "We need to leave the Levant. My suggestion is to wait here until Saladin's men tire of their search, and when they become careless, we make our way back to Tyre."

"I agree. I have been thinking about our current difficulties. Saladin's war was unexpected, but I never thought the Army of Jerusalem would be annihilated. Youssef told me only ten knights are left in the city of Jerusalem. We will not be able to recruit the men we need to travel to Babylon. No one is going to release his retainers to aid us. Looters are taking anything of value. Food will be scarce as the cities brace themselves to withstand a possible siege by Saladin. We will be fortunate to escape the levant alive."

The monk nodded. "Events have turned grim. It is ill tidings."

"We need to return to Tyre. I have sent messages to the archbishop regarding our progress. I expect a response from Rome."

"What is the Norman's tale?"

"He was left for dead on the battlefield after the Army of Jerusalem was destroyed."

"Did the Norman tell you what happened?"

"Yes," Father Villhardain said as he sat back in his chair and related to Brother Carl the army's march to Hattin and the disaster that befell the Christians.

"Fools!" the big monk snorted. "The housecarls of Harold the Saxon would have fought better."

"Like at Hastings," the priest replied.

"Harold Godwinson would have won Hastings if we had not had to first fight Harold Hadrada at Stamford Bridge. It was just bad luck."

"Hmm, perhaps... war's outcomes are never certain. It was ordained in heaven that Harold the Saxon would die at Hastings, and you know as well as I, nothing on earth can change that."

"So, what do you want to do with the Norman now?"

"Take him to Rome."

"Surely, you jest!" the monk cried. "The man's wounds make him a burden. You can't even be sure he is trustworthy. What if he gets drunk with some harlot and tells her everything?"

"First, you have not talked to him. I have. He is not the kind to spend time with harlots. Second, I do not intend to tell him what we are doing. I will appeal to his oath and his code of chivalry. That will keep his silence."

The monk pushed his chair back from the table. "Chivalry? Oaths? I think you are over trusting of Normans. Their empty codes of chivalry and their damnable castles! Leave him behind. It will be weeks before he is able to travel. He is useless to us."

"Nonsense! We will have to assemble enough fighting men to bring the treasure back." The priest tilted back in his chair, his eyes narrowed into an icy stare. "He speaks Arabic."

Brother Carl sat back with his arms crossed, glaring. "He is a Norman."

"I don't care if he is a Norman," the priest continued forcefully. "He is a Knight of Saint John, he serves the Holy Father, and right now I need him. We will wait until he is healed, and then we will travel to Tyre."

"Then, Father, you will have to wait until the Norman is fit to travel."

"Then it will be God's will. In the meantime, I will send a message to His Grace, Archbishop Joscius, to expect us." Father Villhardain stood up. "I have letters to write. It will be time for the evening meal by the time I am done. I expect you to dine with me and our Norman guest, and I expect you to be cordial." Father Villhardain turned and left the room, leaving Brother Carl to brood over having to be kind to a man whose kindred he despised.

CHAPTER 7
OF PAPAVER SOMNIFERUM

Byron sat in the sunshine the rest of the day, enjoying the garden and the cool air from water evaporating from the pool of water. Several women came to tend the garden. He watched them at their work as they watered the plants. To his surprise, the women drew knives and began to slice the seedpods. From the wounds, a sticky substance seeped as the women collected the sap. Once the pod was drained, the women moved on, selecting other victims for their blades. A young girl looked over and smiled at him, her dark hair covered by a scarlet silk scarf. Byron nodded his head and smiled back. She sheathed her knife and approached the knight, her slim figure covered by a brown dress.

"You look better," she said, her dark eyes looking him over. "How is your arm?"

"My lady, it is better. Do I have you to thank for my care?"

The woman smiled, her teeth flashed white against her tan face. "I applied the bandage, but you should give your thanks to Al-Zahrawi and his books, the Kitab al-Tasrif. He is the great Arabic physician whose writings directed my care of you."

Byron nodded. "Then, my lady, thank him for me."

The girl laughed as she held out a spoon filled with a milky substance. "That will not be possible. He has been dead for a long time. Take this, it will ease your pain."

"What is this?" Byron pointed to the spoon.

The girl smiled. "The Romans called it Papaver somniferum?"

"My lady, speak plainly."

"It is called the sleep-bringing poppy. Take it." She pushed the spoon towards him. "You will feel better. Just don't take too much."

Byron took the sap and put it in his mouth. He screwed up his face at the bitter taste and the woman started to laugh. "I will send someone to check on you." She smiled at him and then turned to go back to her work.

Byron watched her walk away, skeptical that the sap would do anything. His body still ached. Then, as if by magic, he felt the pain slipping away. He felt relaxed, sleepy. A stupor came over him and he felt his cares melt away. The day passed, but Byron cared not. He sat on the bench until he fell asleep. When he awoke, the sun was setting in the west. He could see Brother Carl approaching. The big monk had his cowl over his head as he lumbered along the path.

"Come, Norman, Father Villhardain wants you to join us for the evening meal."

Byron looked up at the big monk and then fumbled with his crutch as he struggled to rise. The monk reached out his hand and pulled the knight up to stand. Byron shuffled along the path, following the monk until he came to a stone table set beneath the canopy of a flowering vine tree. Father Villhardain was sitting at the table in front of several platters of cheese, sliced meat, bread, dates, and olives. Byron was famished. He hadn't eaten since the night before the battle of Hattin, and he had not had much of an appetite on that night. Father Villhardain poured some water into a wooden bowl and passed it to Byron.

"You must be hungry," the priest said. "Don't wait for us, Carl and I have business to discuss."

Byron ate as he listened to Father Villhardain and Carl talk about the events of the outside world. All the news was bad. Yousef's servants had returned to report that Saladin's army had besieged the citadel of the Knights of Saint John Belvoir. To Byron's dismay, he learned that several surrounding forts had surrendered without a fight. Soon, Jerusalem would be under siege. It was inevitable. There was no Christian force left to slow Saladin's advance. Byron listened quietly, knowing he was powerless to aid his order and his comrades.

After sharing the last of the news, Father Villhardain glanced at Brother Carl and then turned to Byron. "Would you care for a glass of wine?"

"Yes," Byron said as he held up a metal goblet placed near him on the table.

Father Villhardain asked, "You have heard our discussion. What do you think? Can Jerusalem hold out against Saladin?"

Byron shook his head. "Every knight in the city marched to Hattin. The city will fall."

"The walls of Jerusalem are stout," Brother Carl retorted. "The infidel will not pass through them easily."

"Walls will do nothing if there are not stout men to defend them," replied Byron. "Saladin will terrorize the city. He will bombard the city with Greek fire and the corpses of the dead. He will beat down all resistance. When all have fled in fear, he will breach the gate and take the place by storm. The only real hope is that a new army is raised in Europe to relieve the siege."

"The chances of that happening is unlikely," Father Villhardain replied.

"Saladin has planned well," Byron said. "The war ended at Hattin."

Brother Carl nodded. "The Norman is right. Saladin will not make a mistake. He has struck down the only force that could have prevented his takeover. Jerusalem is beyond aid."

"Let's not give up all hope," the priest replied. "Europe will not come to our aid, but from what I hear from Youssef, Saladin's hold on the Saracen princes is fragile. Anything could happen. Fighting could break out among the Saracens and their army could disintegrate."

"And that would be our good fortune," Byron said, glancing at the priest and the monk. "But that would be a miracle."

"Well, it is in the hands of God," the priest said. "There is nothing I can do to prevent Saladin from retaking the city. The only thing that can be done is to return to Rome and see if what I have found will help."

Byron almost asked what Father Villhardain had found but then thought better of it. He decided to wait and see if the priest would share what he had found, but the priest did not say another word. Father Villhardain poured another round of wine for Byron and Carl. The three men sat in silence contemplating the unpleasant future.

The sunlight disappeared beneath the horizon and the sky turned red. Blue shadows slowly crept across the garden. The light faded and the sweet scent of the flowers became stronger in the evening air. Sleep began to creep up on Byron, and he knew he should make his way to his chamber to rest. He leaned against the table and groaning, pushed himself up. Tottering, he thanked Father Villhardain and Carl for the food and their kindness, and then using his crutch, he made his way back to his bed.

He lay down. It felt as if someone was with him in the room. It filled him with an enveloping feeling of peace. The scars of living had covered the deep wounds to his soul, but nothing ever truly eased his pain. In this room, the peace he felt lifted his burden. Soon, he knew he would have to shoulder the burden again and carry it to its distant and unforeseen end. For the moment, he enjoyed the respite. Slowly, his eyes grew heavy and he was slipping away. The strange room was taking away the cares that filled his mind. He drifted off into a dreamless sleep.

He spent the next few days resting in the sun by the pool of spring water. He was starting to feel better. The sap from the seedpods eased his pain and his headaches were starting to lessen. His wounds were healing, his scars fading. The swelling had gone down in his knee, but the bruise on his ankle remained as black and purple as ever. By the end of the week, he felt well enough to ask Carl to help him with his sword skills.

He was feeling restless, though the monk was not his first choice. Churchmen were soft, but he needed someone, even if his only ability was to hold the sword upright in front of him. At least he would get some practice and rebuild his strength. If Brother Carl had any skill with a weapon, it was probably with the Anglo Saxon, two-handled, battle-ax. Perhaps he could enlighten Brother Carl on the use of a refined weapon, such as the sword. Perhaps he could even teach the arrogant monk a lesson or two in humility.

At first the monk refused, but Byron persisted and the monk grumpily agreed, on the condition that if he did so, Byron would leave him alone. To his astonishment, Brother Carl proved to have great skill with a sword. The knight was surprised at the big man's grace as he found himself fighting a master swordsman. The fact that this churchman was better than he, damaged his pride. It hurt to admit that the Anglo Saxon Monk was superior. Yet, each day he practiced with the monk, his deadly skills improved, even if it was under the tutelage of someone he never would have expected to be a master.

One afternoon, Byron was sitting on a bench by the pool, resting from his sword practice when Father Villhardain sat down next to him. "Brother Carl tells me that your sword skills are improving."

"Yes. Brother Carl is a difficult opponent to defeat."

The priest laughed. "Indeed, fortunately for you, he has been taking it easy on you, but he did say that perhaps there is hope and that when he is done, your sword skills might become passable."

Byron frowned. "That sounds like something he would say."

Byron and Father Villhardain talked about the places they had seen and people they had met. After they had talked for some time, Father Villhardain asked, "My son, why did you take up the cross?"

Byron frowned at the question as his mind thought of his family's fief in Gowran Ireland and the rude castle built on a mound of dirt. It was very different from the mighty fortresses in the Holy Lands such as Krak des Chevaliers or the city of Jerusalem. "It was my father who suggested I take the cross."

"I see, so, why did your father make the suggestion?"

"That is a long tale. I was in love with Lady Isabella de-Clare, the daughter of Strongbow, and she loved me. But Strongbow died, and the king gave her, with all her lands, to another man, William Marshal."

"I am sorry to hear that," the priest replied sympathetically.

Byron smiled sadly. "I loved her and then she was gone." Byron paused. "Can we speak of something else?"

"Surely, my son. How did you choose the order of Saint John?"

"The king summoned my father, along with the other barons, to London to give counsel. He took me with him because he was worried that I might do something rash and left my brothers to watch over our lands. King Henry had been offered the crown of the Kingdom of Jerusalem after the death of Baldwin the fourth and his young nephew, Baldwin the fifth. Henry summoned his advisors to give counsel on whether he should accept the crown and the council of Barons met at the House of the Knights of Saint John of Jerusalem.

"I was there when Herclius, the Patriarch of Jerusalem, laid before Henry the keys to Jerusalem, the keys to the Tower of David and the keys to the Church of the Holy Sepulcher. Henry consulted with his barons on accepting the crown. After considerable deliberation, the barons advised the king that it would be better for him to manage his existing kingdom than to become embroiled in the politics of Outremer."

Byron sighed. "I remember watching the king reject the offer. At the end of the council, the patriarch was taking oaths to take the cross. My father, seeing an opportunity to move past my loss, encouraged me to go on the crusades. So, I joined the Order of Saint John of Jerusalem, becoming a Hospitaller."

"Interesting," the priest said.

"It was the hardest thing I had ever done. I always admired William the Conqueror. William started with little, but through audacity and courage, he defeated the oath breaker, Harold the Saxon, to become the King of England. Nothing but heartache waited for me at home. I thought, perhaps something good would come of all of this if I went on the crusade and followed William's example."

Father Villhardain looked at the young knight for a moment. The knight obviously idolized William Duke of Normandy, and knew nothing about the cruel and ruthless man known as the conqueror.

"Well, my son, I think you have made something of yourself," the old priest said smiling. "The journey is not complete, but you have made a good start. I have enjoyed our visit, but I must take my leave. Enjoy your afternoon." The old priest stood up and left, leaving Byron alone in the garden.

Byron picked up his sword and leaned back against the stone bench. It was a good sword. The blade was flexible, it would bend and not break; the fuller the sword smith had hammered down the center of the blade, gave it strength. He turned the sword over, the sun flashing on the silver blade. He raised the blade until it was level with his eye. Straight and true. Lately, the events in his life had not been so. He had not had been the master of his destiny at all. Clearly, a path had been chosen but not by him. He sighed at the thought. He had seen inferior swords shatter in battle because they were strong but brittle.

He would have to give the priest's request some thought. Byron stood up and sheathed his sword. He was tired and decided to pass on the evening meal. He returned to his chamber to lie down, paying no attention to his surroundings until he reached his room. Pushing aside the heavy curtain, he shuffled to his bed and lay down. After tossing and turning, he found a comfortable position on his side and fell asleep.

CHAPTER 8
THE DREAM OF THE BANSHEE

Fog shrouded the simple huts of the Celts. Byron's father was sitting on his grey horse. His mail coif tossed back revealed his silver hair matted with dew. Baron Robert Fitzwalter leaned forward in the saddle and demanded the return of several stolen cattle. The Celtic chief standing in front of the baron's horse crossed his arms across his bare chest and denied any knowledge of the theft. The baron's retainers surrounded the village and the air was thick with tension and fear as the villagers banded together to resist the onslaught that was coming.

The baron exploded in rage. Spurring his horse forward, he swept out his sword, and with a swift stroke, felled the chief with a mighty blow. The Celtic warriors drew their swords and rushed to the aid of their dying chieftain. A Celt, stripped to the waist with blue stripes painted down his chest, lunged at Byron with a spear. Byron instinctively batted the spear away with his shield. He drove his spurs into the sides of his horse to run the man down. Drawing his sword, Byron stood up in the stirrups and stabbed the Celt in the neck. The Celt fell, his blood spilling on the green grass. Byron wheeled his horse away and rode towards his older brother, who was shouting to his father's men to burn the village. They began firing the thatched roofs of the houses. Yellow and red flames rose against the grey sky.

Wails filled the air. The women scurried to grab their children and whatever meager belongings they could salvage. A Celtic warrior darted among the burning huts, and Byron turned his horse to pursue the man. The Celt was running in front of him, the blue stripes painted down the Celts back contorted with every stride. Byron's horse was closing the gap. Byron rose in his stirrups and leaned forward, his sword raised to strike. A small girl with a green cloak darted in front of his horse and froze. She stared up at him, her blue eyes wide as Byron's horse bore down on her. Before he could stop or change course, the girl went under the hooves, thrown down into the dirt like a twisted rag doll.

Byron watched the Celt dart between two huts and disappear. He brought his horse to a stop and turned in his saddle to look back at the dead girl lying on the torn sod. He could not remove his gaze. A mist formed as her body started to wither. Her blond hair turned into yellow flame. The flesh on her face shriveled. He watched in horror as her eyes snapped open revealing empty sockets. With a snarl the girl rose. He could not move.

"Go away foul banshee!" he cried.

The door to one of the burning huts flew open. The banshee gave a loud wail as she grabbed the reins of his horse. Struggling to move, he tried to strike her with his sword, but his body refused to obey his commands. The dark entrance of the door drew close. Red and yellow flames curled from the entrance. He winced at the heat and made a desperate attempt to turn the horse. It was to no avail. The banshee led the horse through the flames. All went black.

He found himself sitting on the horse in the Holy Lands. The earth was no longer green but was dry and burnt in the desert sun. The banshee looked up at him, the flesh on her mouth was gone and her teeth now showed through.

"Remember?" she rasped.

He nodded. From a mist, a group of Saracen women, with their children, was kneeled before him. In the distance, he could see the Knights of Saint of John looting a caravan. Two knights pushed past him. He heard the sinister metallic rasp as they drew their swords.

The children were screaming. The woman directly in front of him defiantly lifted her chin and held Byron in her baleful gaze. The knight closest to him swept off her head. The other women screamed as they held out their hands begging him to help.

"Help them," the banshee hissed.

Byron glanced at the banshee but did not move. He stood and watched as one by one each woman and child were slain. The bodies lay twitching on the blood-stained sand. The banshee looked up, the empty black sockets boring into him. Slowly, she raised her emaciated arm and pointed at him. "You stood by. You did nothing! Fail again and it will be your life and your blood."

With a wild scream, he started upright in bed. Sweat poured from his body. His heart pounded in his chest. He had killed many men in combat, and on occasion, the memories haunted him, but he had never had such a dream. He had not thought about the Celtic girl in years. The Saracens he had all but forgotten. Now, their memory was back. The banshee had opened the door and let them out. In the room of the apostles, his forgotten past filled him with deep shame.

In the gloom, he could see Christ looking down at him from the ceiling. Remorse welled up and overtook him. He flung himself onto the floor. On his knees, he looked up at the ceiling and prayed for forgiveness. He stopped and waited in the dark, but no answer came. He had never been troubled like this. His head was throbbing in pain. He was dizzy. Slowly, he got up and carefully laid back down in his bed. "Do not fail again" he pondered the wraith's words. His mind drifted back to the first time he had ever heard of banshees.

He was a boy, and he had been riding his pony down a muddy lane when he stopped to explore a large green mound. He had heard tales of Viking mounds and the treasure some contained. The large green mound looked the right size to contain a Viking lord's treasure and so he dismounted and tied his pony to a nearby tree. Picking up a stick, he started to explore the mound. His head was down as he jabbed the stick into the earth, hoping to find a secret door. He looked up and jumped back in surprise. An old peasant was watching him. The man's grey locks hung beneath a black felt cap that framed his thin, sallow face. Thick black eyebrows furled over the peasant's dark eyes that were sunken deep into his eye sockets. A dagger was thrust into the weathered belt that bound the peasant's reddish-brown tunic at the waist.

"What are you doing, boy?"

Byron thrust the stick into the ground and put his hand on his hips in indignation. "Boy? My father is a baron! You would do well, serf, to address me as lord."

The peasant's lip curled into a contemptuous sneer as he doffed his black cap and gave a halfhearted bow. "My apologies, little Norman lord."

Byron pulled his stick from the earth and leaned on it as if it was a sword. "That is better. Well, serf, as you can see this is my treasure mound. I claim it, so be off! I will not yield my lawful prize."

The peasant's dark eyes bore into Byron as his jaw stiffened. "Lawful prize? Nothing in Ireland is the Norman's lawful prize... including this mound. There is no treasure to be found here, young fool. No, these mounds are home to fairies, they are. Old women, old hags, with fiery hair, back from the dead. Banshee's they are called, boy! They bring news of death. Disturb them not."

Byron's face twisted into disbelief as he scoffed. "Banshee's don't exist."

The old peasant raised his withered arm and pointed his finger at Byron. "Little lord, they do exist, and if you know what is good for you, you will leave well enough alone!" The peasant took a menacing step forward. Byron dropped his stick and ran to his pony. Scrambling into the saddle, he turned his pony towards the castle and took off at a fast trot. "Someday, Norman!" He heard the old man cry. "Someday you will hear the banshee cry. Then you will know. Then you will know!"

He had never believed such tales ...that was until now. Now that a banshee, or whatever dark spirit from hell, troubled his dream. It made the superstition hard to ignore. "Do not fail again." He sighed. He should have done something to save the Saracen women and their children. He had been unwilling to pay the price for such an act. It would have been unthinkable to turn against the knights of his order. He had just stood there watching. What new horror waited in the future for him to witness? He pondered this for a while. Tired of thinking of all sorts of unpleasant things, he rolled onto his side, closed his eyes, and fell back to sleep.

Two weeks passed, and the time to leave drew closer. Byron felt a tug of regret to leave this place. He had grown accustomed to resting near the fountain, smelling the sweet fragrance of the flowers while the cool air from the evaporating water filled the courtyard. He was sitting near the fountain one afternoon, after suffering another defeat at the hands of Brother Carl, when the old priest came and sat down beside him.

The dream of the Gaelic girl was weighing on his mind. The banshee had not returned, but he had no desire to have her visit him again. He glanced at the priest. What would the priest think if he told him of the dream? He was a knight. He had trained his whole life for war. The death of one Celtic girl was a trifling. When the first Christians captured Jerusalem, the entire population of the city had been put to the sword. Knights had waded through the blood of the dead and dying as they made their way to the altar to offer their prayers of thanks to God. He was a fool to be troubled by the death of a small child.

After wrestling with indecision, he turned to the priest. "Father, I have sinned, and that sin now troubles me deeply."

Father Villhardain turned to the face the knight. "Tell me of this sin, my son."

Byron looked down and frowned. "You will think I jest when I tell you what troubles me."

"Humph, my son, I will decide what weight to give this matter. Tell me of this sin." Byron told the old priest about the burning of the village and the death of the Celtic girl.

"Why do you think I would find the death of one of God's children insignificant?"

Byron chuckled mirthlessly. "Father, I have watched hundreds of men slain in a matter of minutes. I myself have killed an untold number of men. Heretics, infidels, Saracens." Byron shook his head. "But this child's death troubles me. She haunts my dreams.

I see her blue eyes staring at me just before she goes under the hooves of my horse... and then she changes."

"She changes?"

"Yes...she changes into a foul banshee ... she is back and she has foretold my doom."

The priest raised his eyebrows. "A banshee or a daemon?"

"Her flesh shrivels away. Her eyes are gone. Her golden hair turns to fire."

Father Villhardain frowned. "Banshees are nothing more than pagan lore, and I doubt a daemon would dare come here."

"Well she has. I saw her. If she is not a banshee then she is a foul hateful creature from hell."

"Are you certain? "

"Yes, Father."

"What did this spirit say?"

"It told me not to fail, or it would be my death."

"My son, it sounds as if she is a messenger from your past."

"What past? I slay men in combat! Death is my past... and apparently my future."

The priest nodded. "Yet, she is back and the guilt is gnawing at you. What happened after the Celtic village was burned?"

Byron looked away to the fountain. "The cows were found. They had wandered off."

"So, the Celts did not steal them."

"No, the herdsmen were beaten for their carelessness."

"I see. You say you are a slayer of men. Yet, the girl was not a man; she was not a warrior at all. In fact, had your father exercised more patience, she would not be dead."

Byron's eyebrows knitted quizzically as he crossed his arms across his chest.

The old priest smiled. "You are a soldier of the crusades, engaged in a war with the enemies of our faith. You, of all people, should know nothing in life is certain. It is not for you to decide who lives or dies. Yes, you have been the agent of death, but you have suffered the same peril." Father Villhardain looked at him. "The fact that you survived Hattin is proof that God has a purpose for you."

"Humph," replied Byron skeptically. "I hadn't given it any thought; I considered myself fortunate, nothing more."

"You are not responsible for events you did not set in motion. We live in a time when perceived weakness can result in the deaths of thousands. However, there is a price with every act, and the price you will pay is to remember her for the rest of your life. You ignored the lesson, and it has come back with vengeance." The old priest's face became stern, and his voice turned harsh. "Learn from it! Perhaps when you are in the same position, you will gather the facts ere you act on your perceptions. And perhaps another little girl will get the chance to live because you did not act rashly."

Byron considered what the priest had just told him.

Father Villhardain paused for a moment and looked Byron in the eyes. "The seeds you sow will take root and grow, and unfortunately you can never predict when harvest time will come. The Gaelic Celts have not forgotten what you have done. Even as we speak here, they chafe with the desire for revenge. Keep that in mind. Perhaps you should ask them for forgiveness."

"Forgiveness?" the knight replied incredulously. "The villains would have set upon me even if we hadn't burned the village. They do not respect the law of the king, nor my father who the king has enfeoffed with lands in Ireland." He searched for the right words. "They live like beasts. No! I caused the death of the girl, an innocent. She is the life I must atone for."

Father Villhardain sighed. The knight was missing the point. "Yes, but sometimes you must ask for forgiveness of others even if you don't feel you owe it. Forgive us our trespass as we forgive those who trespass against us. I don't remember the Gaelic Celts being excluded. By your acts, did you deprive them of the chance for salvation? Can you read what is in man's heart?"

"Celts find grace?" Byron laughed. "I suppose you are next going to tell me that Saracens can find salvation."

Father Villhardain frowned. A look of anger crossed the priest's face. "Yes, my son, they can! Do you need to be a Jew before you can become a Christian?" Before Byron could answer, the priest answered his own question. "Of course not! If that were true, no gentile would have been saved! Christ did not exclude anyone from salvation! Even the common thief that was crucified next to our Lord was saved. All that is required from you is good works for the Church and a belief in Christ!"

"You make your point, Father." This new thought that a non-believer could find grace was troubling.

Father Villhardain jutted out his chin. "Of course, I do. Because it is God's will to save his children. He sacrificed his only son for that purpose." The priest paused. "This ghost has returned. Well, I will give you a penance so you may make amends with God. You must be sincere in your repentance; otherwise it will be for naught."

Byron nodded. "I am sincere, Father. I never wish to see her again."

"I can see you are deeply troubled, my son."

"Thank you, Father."

Father Villhardain smiled and stood up. "I will send Brother Carl to find you." The old priest departed, leaving Byron deep in thought about his past deeds of valor that maybe were not as glorious as he once thought. The water springs bubbled in the late afternoon sun. Brother Carl found him still sitting next to the pool of water.

"Come. Father Villhardain is waiting." Brother Carl tossed him a bundle of rough, ragged clothes. "Put these on proud Norman. It will help humble you in the sight of God, if such an act is possible."

When Byron was dressed in the hot, itchy rags, Brother Carl led him through a twisting corridor lit by the sputtering light of several torches driven into the rock walls. The corridor gave way to a large cavern that Byron had not seen before. He glanced at his surroundings as he crossed the rough stone floor. At the far end of the room, an altar glowed from the light of a multitude of candles. Flickering in the darkness, they cast their glow on the face of several images painted on the wall. A cross of polished wood, with the image of the Savior carved upon it, was on the wall behind the altar.

Byron drew closer. The image of Mother Mary stared solemnly at him. He prepared his soul to make amends for his actions. Father Villhardain stood next to the altar, waiting quietly. Byron knelt in front of it.

"Sir Byron Fitzwalter," the priest said, his voice echoing in the stillness of the room, "do you come here as a sincere act of contrition to repent your sins?"

"I do."

"Then prostrate yourself in front of the altar." Byron lay face down on the ground. "Byron Fitzwalter, say the prayer of the act of contrition," commanded the priest.

Byron recited the prayer, his voice a whisper in the stillness of the church. Byron finished his prayer of the act of contrition.

Father Villhardain stood solemnly as the echoes died away and the room became quiet. At last he spoke, "The act of penance I want you to perform..."

"I want the penance Henry preformed for the murder of Becket," Byron interrupted.

Father Villhardain looked down at the knight. "Are you sure, my son?"

Byron nodded. "Penance good enough for Henry is good enough for his knight."

"I will not have you beaten all night, we must travel soon."

"I must pay for what I have done!"

Father Villhardain shook his head. Fitzwalter was almost well enough to travel. The priest offered a compromise. "My son, if that is what you wish, then I will have Brother Carl lay ten lashes upon you."

"Father, that is not enough to absolve me for what I have done."

"My son, you have asked for my intercession and I say it does. If God demands more, you will soon know it." Father Villhardain turned and whispered to Brother Carl, "Fetch a lash, and go easy on the Norman, we need him."

"Tempt me and then take it away," growled Carl as he left to search for a lash.

✝

Byron thought of Ireland. He missed the land, the green grass. He then thought of Isabella de Clare, the daughter of Strongbow. He could see her face, her long dark hair, the mischievous look in her eye. He then thought about the time he had been caught killing the Bishop of Ossary's chickens. He had not thought about it in years. Isabella was adventurous. Most of the time, he, his brothers and Isabella had roamed the village near the castle tormenting the serfs with their pranks. The serfs endured the children's mischief without complaint. The nobility could do whatever it wanted and so could their children.

It had all been amusing, until Isabella de Clare decided it would be great fun to kill the chickens belonging to the Bishop of Ossary. She had encouraged Byron and his brothers to throw rocks at the stupid birds and shouted with glee at each kill. Seven chickens lay dead, yet that was not enough. It was exciting to watch the witless birds run as they tried in vain to escape the boys' deadly aim. Then one of the bishop's servants had caught them. Isabella disavowed any involvement in the murder of the chickens, and the servant dragged each of the boys by the scruff of the neck before the bishop.

The old bishop was angry at the senseless waste of his prized chickens and marched the boys into the St. Canices where each of them had to prostrate himself before the altar and pray for forgiveness. The ordeal was not nearly as terrible as the punishment of their mother when they returned home. To exorcise the demon of poor judgment, she had applied the rod in the form of their father's belt.

†

The past slipped away, and Byron forced his mind to focus on the present. He heard Brother Carl return and prepared to strip off his shirt.

"Leave the shirt," the priest commanded. Byron turned to

protest, but the old priest cut him off. "Sir Byron Fitzwalter, in warfare and chivalry I will heed your advice, but in the matters of the Church, my word is final."

Brother Carl drew back. The first blow fell with a thump that echoed in the empty chamber. Byron groaned as each blow fell. He could see the girl standing next to the Savior, and he hoped that she would understand that he was truly sorry for what he had done to her.

After Brother Carl counted the tenth lash, Father Villhardain spoke, "Byron Fitzwalter, do you repent your sins, are you sorry for what you have done?"

"I am sorry for each and every one."

"Then I absolve you from your sins. Arise, my son, and be comforted. Thy sins that thou hast committed are forgiven, because as it is written, a contrite humble heart God does not despise. Go, and sin no more."

Byron rose up slowly and looked at the old priest, who held up his hand. "Go in peace."

Byron bowed and turned to walk away, taking one last glance at the cavern painted with the images of the apostles. When he returned to his room, he lay down on his bed, quickly shifting to lie on his side: his back was on fire. He stared at the image of Christ on the cross. The adrenaline was wearing off. His pain was nothing compared to the pain Christ had endured. The need to rest came over him, and as he slowly drifted off to sleep, he heard the voice of the old priest say "I forgive you".

The next morning Byron awoke with a sore back. He glanced over his shoulder in the mirror and saw that his back was red but nothing more. He was certain that Brother Carl had not whipped him with all his might. The priest had interceded on his behalf. Perhaps God was satisfied. Even if Brother Carl had not used all his might, his back still hurt, and he decided to forgo sword practice. He spent the day resting in the shade, placing wet rags on his back. He got bored and started wandering. He climbed a set of steps onto the edge of the natural rock cliff that formed the walls of the garden and looked out at the world. He was looking towards Jerusalem.

"What do you seek, Hospitaller?" a voice asked in Arabic.

Byron turned to see that Youssef had climbed up next to him. "A miracle."

Youssef moved next to Byron and shaded his eyes with his hands as he looked into the distance. "Do not give up hope, Hospitaller. Miracles do happen. Maybe even to you, if you are observant enough to see them. But if you desire the miraculous defeat of Salah al-Din, then I fear your wish is unlikely. Heaven has it is own purpose."

"Perhaps that purpose is for me to lead men in the defense of Jerusalem. Yet, I am here, idle."

Youssef smiled, showing his yellow teeth. "Be not impatient. It is not your time. If God wanted you to defend Jerusalem, do you think you would be here?"

"No," Byron grumbled.

Youssef turned away from the wall and started to walk down the steps. "I have news for Father Villhardain. I suggest you adopt a more modest request to God. I think you should pray for your safe arrival in Tyre. I think if you arrive at the walls of that city unharmed, that will be your miracle."

Byron's eyes narrowed and he frowned as he watched the Arab walk away. He looked back in the direction of Jerusalem and then sighed as he turned to follow Youssef down the stairs.

Over dinner, Father Villhardain told Carl and Byron of his plan to leave, asking for their counsel. "Youssef has ridden close to the gates of Tyre," the priest said, his face full of concern. "He was accosted several times by Saracen horsemen asking if he had seen a Christian priest accompanied by a large monk. Saladin's men have not tired of their search."

"I find it hard to believe that Saladin would take an interest in capturing a priest?" Byron scoffed. "I should think by now he has larger concerns requiring his attention."

"Norman, do not question Youssef," Brother Carl said. "He has taken great risks to spy on Saladin. If Youssef brings news and advice, then it would be wise for you to heed what he says."

"Yes, Brother Carl," the priest said calmly, "but Sir Fitzwalter has made a reasonable observation."

Father Villhardain smiled at Byron. "My son, normally your observation would be correct, but in this instance, the Sultan Saladin, even with all of his concerns, would make the effort to capture a single priest."

"Well, I can't imagine what the sultan would want with a priest when his prize is Jerusalem."

"My son, it is what I know. That is why I have attracted the interest of Saladin."

Byron looked into the priest's blue eyes. What could the priest possibly know? Byron had never seen Father Villhardain before. The priest had not been a confidant in the inner circle of the Kingdom. Byron knew who sat in council. To Byron's knowledge, Father Villhardain had not been involved in any of the strategy discussions with the Marquis Montferrat, King Guy Lusignan, nor the Grand Master of the Temple. So, why would the sultan want to try to capture him?

At last, he asked. "Father, what do you know that makes you so important?"

"Ah... to learn the answer to that question you will have to come to Rome."

Byron shook his head. "Father, I will go as far as Tyre. Then I must ride for Jerusalem. It is there that my services are needed most."

Father Villhardain smiled. "I would not expect anything more. Now, I have thought about traveling cross-country to Tyre, but it will take us longer to reach our destination. If we run into a forage party for Saladin's Army, well, we will most likely be robbed and murdered. The road will be quicker and easier. I plan to travel at night. The light of the half moon will aid us." Father Villhardain looked around the table. "This will be our best and only chance. Youssef and his men can ride ahead of us, as well as serve as a rear guard. If we run into trouble, he and his men will eliminate the danger by killing or disabling our pursuers. I was hopeful that as time passed, Saladin's horsemen would tire and would watch the roads less closely, but now I know that is not the case. What are your thoughts?"

"You know my thoughts," Carl replied.

The priest looked at Byron. "I do not know why you are here in the Holy Lands or what the Church has asked you to do," Byron said. "You know the risk if you are discovered. The decision is yours. All I can do is fight to defend you and hope that will suffice."

"That is true. I know the peril, and I know that time now presses me," Father Villhardain replied. "Every choice is filled with danger. Tomorrow we will get ready to leave, and in the next few days, we will find out if God has further purpose for us here on earth." Byron nodded as he stood and then turned and headed for his room. When the knight was gone, Brother Carl rose from his chair.

"Father Villhardain, you might have doubts about God's purpose, but I feel that we will be blessed and will reach the end of the journey unharmed. You should have more faith." With that, the monk turned and walked away, leaving Father Villhardain alone at the table.

They spent the next day preparing for their departure. Byron was surprised when Father Villhardain came into his room late in the day with a bundle in his arms. It was a new surcoat and gambeson, the quilted garment that he wore beneath his hauberk of chain mail.

"Your old ones were beyond repair," the priest said. "So, I asked Youssef's wife to make you a new one."

Byron took the gift. "Thank you, Father. You are very kind. My old raiment was worn."

"Yes, I had it burned. Carl is bringing your hauberk. Your sword, shield, and spurs you already have. Carl had the rents in the chain mail repaired. You will be ready for battle."

Byron began putting on his gambeson. Brother Carl came into the room lugging the rest of Byron's gear. Byron sighed as he looked at his armor. "I miss my squire. He was with me at Hattin, but I have no idea what happened to the boy. Captured most likely."

"Then I will help you, Norman," said Carl gruffly, dropping the armor on the floor. He arranged the armor neatly, and skillfully began helping Byron. Carl surprised Byron by kneeling down to buckle the golden spurs to his boots. The spurs were one of Byron's most prized possessions. Once he had put his black surcoat, with its white cross, over his armor and buckled on his sword, Byron felt good again, in control of his destiny.

Father Villhardain draped Byron's black cloak over his shoulder and tied it in place. "My lord, we are traveling to Tyre and ask for your protection on the road."

"Last time he needed ours," Carl muttered.

"True," the knight replied. "But that is the vow of my order, to protect pilgrims on the road to Jerusalem. I owe you a great debt, and I will do all I can to protect you. Even if that means my death."

"Brother Knight," Carl said with a rare smile, "despite the fact that you're a Norman, let us hope it does not come to that. We have too much time and trouble invested in you."

Byron nodded. The seriousness of journeying through the war-torn land of the collapsing Kingdom was upon him. The trip would be dangerous and the likelihood of reaching Tyre safely was unsure at best.

CHAPTER 9
THE ROAD TO TYRE

The men walked to the courtyard of the garden where three horses stood saddled and waiting. Arab grooms held the animals and assisted the riders in mounting.

"I thought men of the Church rode on asses," Byron said.

Father Villhardain frowned. "They do when humility is required. When Saracens pursue them, they use horses."

"Swift ones," the monk added.

Father Villhardain tossed Byron a black hood. Byron pulled the dark cloth over his face. He could see nothing but felt his horse begin to move and heard hooves clicking on the stones as they led him out of the cavern. The horse began to climb and then the clicking stopped. He could feel the wind on his face as it passed through the fabric of the hood and the heat of the sun on the right side of his face as it set in the west. Byron's horse stopped. The sun slowly sank and the black hood grew darker. He felt his horse shift. It took a small step forward then another step. He gave the reins a sharp jerk, to make the horse stand still.

"You can take the hood off now," said the priest.

Byron removed the hood and saw that they were alone. The sun had set. The dark outlines of the sycamore trees showed against the twilight sky. Blue-grey shadows stretched across the clumps of grass among the rocks. The moon was rising and its pale light flooded the land. Byron pulled his black cloak close to ward off the cold breeze that was blowing from the north.

"The road is an hour's ride," Father Villhardain whispered. "Youssef and his men are already on it. They will ride ahead of us to make sure the road is clear of Saladin's men. I have been waiting to make sure that I time our arrival with their protection."

The three men began the long winding ride to the edge of the ancient road. The road had been built before the Romans, but the Roman engineers had improved the thoroughfare. A Roman sign marked the spot where the trail entered the roadway. Byron could still make out the faint outline of the name Tyre. Countless sandstorms had rendered the other Latin words unreadable on the weathered stone.

The crickets chirped in the night air, but other than the wind in the scrub brush, no other sound reached their ears.

"Father Villhardain, how long are you going to wait?" Carl whispered. "We have given Youssef enough of a head start. The longer we sit here, the more likely someone will come along. I don't want traveling companions."

The priest nodded. They turned north and moved out at a trot to conserve their horses' strength. The road was empty at first, but as the miles passed, evidence that the peasants were in flight from Saladin's host began to appear; a broken cart wheel, discarded clothes, household items thrown out in an effort to lighten the burden.

They slowed their horses to a jog as they picked their way through the discarded possessions. A cast-off spear lay in the roadway. Byron felt his heart sink. More weapons appeared. Christian soldiers had fled this way in disorder. Resistance to Saladin was crumbling. The soldiers had cast aside spears, armor, and other gear, now encumbrances, as they tried to gain more speed and endurance as they fled.

Each man was alert, watching and listening intently for any sign of danger as the rolling hills slowly passed by. The sky turned grey. The yellow glow of the rising sun expanded over the eastern hills revealing the empty road. They cautiously left the road and made camp in the shelter of an overhanging rock. Each man took a turn keeping watch as the others slept.

Byron felt a hand on his shoulder shake him. "Wake up," Father Villhardain said with a weary smile. "It will be time to go soon. We'll eat and then make our way back to the road." Byron groaned. The sun was setting in the west. He sat up and watched the priest walk away.

The three men sat in silence eating their dinner of salted meat, bread, and olives. When their meal was finished, they packed up their few belongings and saddled their horses, preparing for their last night's ride to Tyre. The moon had risen above the horizon and was shining in the night sky by the time they returned to the road. They rode again for hours, the silver-grey hillsides slowly passing by. No sounds disturbed the night other than the beat of the hooves on the roadway, the squeak of leather from the saddles, and the muffled sound of metal from Byron's mail.

The night dragged on and seemed to pass slower than the night before. After several miles, something new appeared in the distance. Byron could see the red light of campfires dotting the landscape. A few at first, but as each mile passed, they grew in number. As far as the eye could see, little red dots lit the hillsides in the dark. All of Christendom was in flight, fleeing to the city of Tyre, where safety and passage to Europe was still possible.

Father Villhardain halted. A new dawn reddened the sky. A stone marker stood at the side of the road. It was broken in half, and the top of the stone was missing.

"We are five miles from the city," Father Villhardain said. "We will stop and rest here ere we finish the last leg of our journey."

The men left the roadway and rested under a twisted olive tree, out of sight, off the road. They were sitting in the shade, drinking water from their skins, when two horsemen dressed in black appeared. Bryon rose to his feet and rested his hand on the hilt of his sword.

Father Villhardain reached up and stayed his arm. "Fear not. I'm expecting them."

The horsemen, on fine boned Arab horses, drew near. Byron recognized Youssef. Father Villhardain stood up and greeted him. "Peace be with you," he said.

"And to you, and all who travel with you," Youssef said as he dismounted. "We have ridden to within sight of the city gate and found no evidence that anyone waits on the road for you. My people also have told me similar reports. There are still many places to hide. I would be most careful now, for I fear the danger has not passed. The land is in disarray. Word of Salah al-Din's victory has spread fear among the Christians. They are fleeing from their villages to find a place of refuge. They are stacked deep at the gates of Tyre as they clamber to gain the safety of the city's walls."

Father Villhardain nodded. "I feared as much."

"The defeat at Hattin has crushed the Christians' will to resist."

Father Villhardain sighed. "Thank you, my friend, for everything."

"I will miss your company," Youssef said sadly.

Father Villhardain smiled. "Perhaps someday we will meet again, but until then farewell, my friend."

The men stood looking at each other. At last, Youssef bowed, then turned, and mounted his horse. Turning his horse to face the priest, he raised his hand and said, "Farewell."

Father Villhardain raised his hand in return. The two Arabs wheeled their horses around and rode out of sight. Father Villhardain watched them.

The three men mounted and returned to the roadway, only five more miles remained before they reached the safety of the city gate of old Tyre. They had gone less than a quarter of a mile when two figures, dressed in black, appeared and stopped on the edge of the road. Byron felt a stab of adrenalin. One of the riders stood in his stirrups and pointed in the direction of Byron and his companions. The rider wheeled his horse, and like an arrow shot from a bow, began thundering towards Byron. A flash of silver glinted in the sun. The Saracen had unsheathed his shamshir. The second Saracen put his spurs to his horse and was now running towards them.

Byron turned to Carl. "Defend the priest!" the knight cried as he urged his horse into a gallop.

Carl yelled something back, but with the air rushing past his ears, Byron could not understand him and could only assume that it was not a compliment. His horse was running hard. Byron flew down the road. He swung his shield into his left hand, and unsheathed his own sword. With each stride, he could feel the power of the horse, its hooves digging into the ground, driving him forward. His war-horse had done this before, his ears pinned back and his neck stretched out, rushing to meet the enemy.

The Saracens were now riding side by side, trying to press Byron between them. They drew closer. Byron drove his spur into the side of the horse at the last moment, and at a full gallop, the horse shifted his direction sideways. The Saracen, unprepared for this unexpected move, grabbed desperately to shorten the rein to keep Byron from passing him on the outside. The Saracen's hand reached down to pull on the rein. His shield dipped, leaving his body exposed. With a skilled stroke, Byron aimed his sword between the Saracen's steel collar and his helmet, striking him in the throat. Blood sprayed into the air as Byron swept by, covering his surcoat with a fine red mist.

The dying Saracen flashed by and was now behind him. Byron pulled on the reins. His horse slid to a stop; dust filled the air. Byron turned the horse back to face his second opponent. Spurring furiously, the horse leaped forward and slammed into the side of the second Arabian horse, almost knocking it down. The Saracen showed his skill as he stayed in the saddle. Turning his horse, the Saracen pushed beside Byron, striking the knight's shield with his shamshir.

The two warriors circled their horses, side by side, head to tail. Locked together in a duel, the dust swirled from the horse's hooves as master and horse tried to overpower the other. Byron's sword hewed through the Saracen's wooden shield, sending slivers of wood flying. The Saracen knew he was losing, and in desperation, he struck Byron with all his might, hoping to stun him long enough to escape. The Saracen turned his horse to flee.

Byron stood in his stirrups and raised his sword. The sword flashed in the sun as Byron delivered the blow to the back of the man's helmet. The Saracen's helmet split. The black turban that bound the steel cap unraveled. The dark ribbon drifted to the ground upon the dust and the sand. The man's head sagged forward, his chin against his chest as he swayed in the saddle. The Saracen rolled off his horse onto the ground.

It was over. Byron sat on his horse breathing hard. He dismounted and looked around. The road was empty, except for the dead men's horses standing near the bodies of their fallen masters. They were fine horses, a handsome prize. They would fetch a substantial price in Tyre. He thought of the adulation he would receive when he rode through the gates of Tyre leading his battle trophies. A new thought entered his mind and he frowned. The priest was trying to escape to Rome unnoticed. The horses would attract attention. A sure sign to any spy that he had killed Saladin's knights. If he were alone, who would care, but he was in the company of the priest that Saladin was seeking.

"Damn it!" Byron walked over to the horses of his fallen foes. He grabbed their reins and led them to the side of the road where he loosened the cinches of their saddles and dumped them into the brush. Stripping off the horse's bridles, he slapped each horse on the rump with the flat of his sword, yelling, "Laissez aller! Go home." The horses, unsure of their freedom, paused for a moment, but then realizing they were free, took off at a run and disappeared from sight.

Byron went back to the road, grabbed the ankles of one of the dead Saracens. Grunting and cursing, he drug the body across the dirt road and into the scrub brush. He was making good progress when the dead man's arm snagged on a thorn bush, bringing him to an abrupt halt. Cursing, he kicked the dead man's arm free from the bush and went back to dragging the body. Satisfied the dead Saracen was out of sight, Byron grabbed the other body and dragged it to the opposite side of the road. He paused to catch his breath. "That should keep you until the birds find you."

He led his horse back onto the road. He put his foot into the stirrup, preparing to mount, when he saw an object glittering in the sun. He stopped and walked over to look at it. It was a golden coin, half buried in the sand. He reached down and picked it up. At least he had some compensation for his efforts. He put the gold dinar into the pocket of his cloak and swung back into the saddle, starting on a dead run to Tyre. His horse was lathered with foam, but the animal's strength did not fail. The walls of Tyre came into view. Refugees, as far as the eyes could see, pressed against the gates. Byron broke to a trot, forcing his way up to the gate. The peasants gave way, staring at the blood staining his armor and surcoat.

He could hear the whispers among the crowd. "My God, Saladin has taken Acre! He brings news of the downfall."

The peasants fell back, bowing their heads, not daring to look at the knight. The gate was open, but soldiers in mail, armed with pikes, barred the way. Surcoats, bearing the livery of the city, covered their armor, giving the men a look of authority and power. But as Byron drew near, he could see the worry etched on their faces. A knight in armor stood in the center, flanked by the guards, his mail hood thrown back revealing his long dark hair. He stood with his hand on the hilt of his sword blocking Byron's way.

"Hail, Christian Knight," the knight said, saluting Byron. "Sir Geoffrey D'Auvay, captain of the guard. What news do you bring from afar?"

Byron returned the salute. "I bring none. I seek a priest and a monk. Have they passed through the gates?"

"Apologies, my lord. I have been expecting news from Acre." D'Auvay looked in the direction of the endless lines of peasants seeking refuge. "I know not about a priest and a monk. It has been an endless deluge of serfs." D'Auvay tilted his head and sniffed the air. "And the unwashed. Are they friends of yours?"

"No, traveling companions."

D'Auvay raised his eyebrows. "I see. What is your tale, my lord? I see the fresh signs of battle upon you."

Byron nodded. "Indeed, I have today fought two servants of Saladin, but I will not tell my tale here ..." Byron glanced at the serfs standing near him trying to overhear their conversation. "I would prefer to do so in private."

"Come," D'Auvay motioned, and he moved further into the archway of the gate.

Byron leaned close so only D'Auvay could hear him. "On the road to Tyre, I came upon two servants of Saladin."

"And do the sands run red with the blood of our enemies?" D'Auvay interrupted.

Byron nodded. "Saladin has two less men to trouble the kingdom."

The French Knight smiled. "Ha! Then all is well. If it is your desire, my lord, I can send a few of my men to collect your trophies."

Byron shook his head. "No, my lord, time presses me. If you wish to retrieve it, you can ransom it; but if you do, make sure the bodies stay hidden."

D'Auvay raised his eyebrows. "A strange request, my lord." D'Auvay stepped closer. "Only those who commit murder wish their crimes to be hidden."

Byron sighed. "It was not murder, though their deaths were untimely."

"I mean no offense, my lord, nor do I lament the death of a Saracen no matter the manner. It is just an unusual request."

"Yes, it is. I have sworn an oath to protect this priest, and to fulfill my oath, my own personal triumph must suffer. Let me pass so I can find my traveling companions. I need to know that they have gained the safety of the walls."

D'Auvay bowed. "You are very generous, my lord. You may pass, but before you go, would you do me the honor of telling me your name?"

"Sir Byron Fitzwalter of the Knights of Saint John."

"Sir Byron Fitzwalter, welcome to Tyre. I will have the heralds shout your victory from the walls."

"No, my lord, I would rather my victory remain silent."

The French Knight bowed again, a look of disappointment crossed his face. "As you wish, my lord, though the city could use some good news."

"And any other time I would enjoy such an honor, but not this time." Byron saluted. "Thank you for your courtesy, my lord."

He rode through the great gate of the city into a small courtyard. Serfs and peasants filled the courtyard, milling around, searching for companions or family before they moved on into the city. Byron sat on his horse searching the crowd. At last, he saw Father Villhardain and Carl standing near the wall holding their horses. Carl saw him first and tugged on Father Villhardain's sleeve. Father Villhardain looked over at Byron and surreptitiously motioned him to join them. Byron rode his horse through the crowd, the peasants jostling each other to get out of his way. When he reached Father Villhardain, he dismounted.

"Are they dead?" The priest asked quietly.

"Yes, and their bodies are hidden."

"Good." The priest looked around to see if anyone was watching them. "We should go."

"Father Villhardain, it is time I take my leave. I have fulfilled my oath, though it does not fully repay your kindness. You are safe in Tyre, and I must now turn towards Jerusalem. Already, I fear I have tarried too long."

"My son, even if you left right now, you would not get far. Your horse is spent. You have ridden all night and fought a hard battle. Come with us. In the morning, you will be refreshed and so will your horse. A few hours will not change the fate of Jerusalem. If anything, a fresh mount will carry you further and faster than one that is worn and tired."

Byron looked up at the sky. It was midday. He looked at the dried sweat that covered his horse's hair. The priest was right; his horse was in no shape for another hard ride. It was wiser to water and feed his horse than to ride a few miles from the city to camp in the dirt with no water and no food.

"Father, you are right. If it is not too much trouble."

"Norman, that is a surprisingly good decision," said the monk.

A continual stream of refugees passed through the city gates and into the courtyard, which slowly but steadily filled with new arrivals, grateful to be within the safety of the walls. It was becoming crowded in the confined space designed to force invaders who breached the gate to crowd together in the defenders killing field.

The noise from the crowd and the smell of unwashed bodies was making it uncomfortable. Father Villhardain led the way out of the courtyard, down the crowded and winding streets of the ancient city, built by the Phoenicians, to the residence of the archbishop.

CHAPTER 10
THE MERCHANT AND THE ASSASSIN

Jabbar ibn-Yasir al-Harthi was a successful merchant of Tyre. He traded extensively in silk, cotton, entertainment, and other exotic luxuries of the Far East. He was a Muslim, although he thought religion was a burden suffered by those who had been too long in the desert sun. He had never been troubled with what other men considered a conscience. After the first crusaders bloody purge of Jerusalem in 1099, their descendants had remained, adopting the Eastern lifestyle. They had made him rich. His wealth was as immense as his person was, and he denied himself nothing.

His business connections spread to Italy, France, Spain, and China. Because of his relationships with the Christians, his caravans traveled their territory unmolested. Even the Templars, through a monetary arrangement, left him alone. He liked Christians; they were like him.

His recent business venture to import three hundred beautiful Frankish women into Acre for the purpose of pleasurable entertainment had been a smashing success. He was still reveling in the amount of income this had generated, but the rumors of this new war troubled him now. War was bad for business. Salah al-Din and his followers would be far less understanding of his lifestyle.

On this day, he was sitting in his lavish apartment, which doubled as his business headquarters, enjoying the ocean view. He sat in his favorite chair, in his silk pajamas, musing over the future. He was not pleased with the prospect of Salah al-Din's takeover of the Christian Kingdom. The war was already disrupting his business. The Christians were fleeing as Salah al-Din's Army reduced his customer base, and he could do nothing about it.

At least he still had his Arab business connections. He had recently received a letter from Sheikh Abdul al-Subayil, one of his business associates. While he was not fond of the sheikh, the man was powerful in the Islamic trading community, so it was important to maintain the relationship. The letter had been a curious request for information concerning a priest and a traveling companion. He had dismissed the letter as a trifling request and shuffled it among his papers to be forgotten.

He was drinking qahwa and musing over news of the war. The Christians had been crushed at Hattin, and Saladin's host was on the march. He was trying to divine the murky future when one of his servants entered the room accompanied by a dirty street urchin, dressed in rags.

The servant bowed low. "Master," the servant said hurriedly, seeing the look of annoyance on Jabbar's face, "this boy has information that I thought you might find interesting."

Jabbar felt it was important to know everything that went on in the city, and he had a network of informants on his payroll. It had paid off from time to time, either by keeping him one-step ahead of his competitors or enabling him to blackmail those who wanted to maintain the illusion that their infidelities were a secret.

"What do you have for me?"

The boy bowed before the fat merchant. The boy was slight, his dark hair unkempt. He was wearing a brown sack that reached his knees. The hole cut for his head had split with wear and was now too wide. The boy's thin boney arms thrust through the slits cut into the sack's sides. A frayed rope gathered the excess folds around his waist.

"Master," he stammered, "I was at the city gate when I saw a knight ride up. He was covered with blood and his horse was lathered white with foam."

"What of it, boy," Jabbar interrupted.

"Yes, master... well the Frankish captain at the gate demanded the knight tell his tale. The infidel knight told the captain he would only speak to him privately, so they moved into the shadows of the arch." The boy smiled slyly. "I heard them talk. The knight told the captain that he fought two of Salah al-Din's soldiers on the road to Tyre and killed them. He said he hid their bodies near the road."

Patience was not one of Jabbar's virtues, and he erupted in anger. "You interrupted me for this? What possible interest would I have in the battle between a Christian and a Saracen? They fight all the time." He muttered to himself, "I just wish they were more successful in killing each other so I could get back to business."

He yelled at the servant, "Get out! And pray I do not have you beaten for your stupidity!"

The servant grabbed the boy and stumbled backwards, attempting to escape when the boy cried, "Master, wait! There's more."

Jabbar looked down at the boy and sighed in exasperation. He gave a casual wave of his hand. "Finish your tale, boy, but this better be worth it."

The boy could feel the servant's arm on his shoulder shaking with fear, and now he was worried. He needed to be very careful in what he said. The boy licked his lips and then swallowed. "The captain asked the knight if he wanted his men to go collect the dead men's armor. The knight said he didn't want it. He said he did not have time to ransom it. He said he was sworn to protect a priest. He told the captain that he could have the armor and keep the ransom. The knight then asked the captain to keep the bodies hidden. When the Frank captain asked the knight if he wanted his victory shouted by the heralds throughout the city, the knight said no. He said he wanted to keep his victory quiet."

Jabbar sat for a minute staring at the boy. "Is that all?"

"No, master. I followed the knight into the courtyard. An infidel priest and the largest man I have ever seen were waiting for the knight. The knight rode over to them. I tried to get close, but I could not push my way through the mob of infidels. When I did get through, they were gone."

"Hmm, come here, boy." The boy approached Jabbar. "Hold out your hand." The boy complied. Jabbar placed three silver pennies in his hand. "I want you to go back, find this knight and his companions, and keep watch on them."

The boy smiled. "Yes, master." He bowed and took the money from Jabbar's hand. The boy gripped the pennies tightly in his hand as he turned and hurried out.

Jabbar looked at his servant. "Get out." The man bowed and backed out of the room. Jabbar sat for a moment pondering what he had just heard. The boy was right. It was very strange that a Christian Knight would not have his triumph shouted across the city. Men of that type always relished their victories. To Jabbar, the thought of not ransoming the armor, weapons, and horses was almost a crime. There was something very odd about the whole affair.

He sat rehashing the boy's story. The memory of Sheikh Abdul al-Subayil's letter came back to him. He smiled. He had information to sell. Allah be praised. He got up from his seat and waddled to his desk. He frantically shuffled through the stacks of parchment until he found the sheikh's letter. He held up the letter in triumph and sat down at his desk to write. Jabbar pulled out a quill and some paper.

What to say. The boy's story just would not do, so he began to write.

> *Brother,*
>
> *As your humble and obedient servant, I am honored by your confidence. I was surprised by your request for information concerning an infidel priest and his servant. Your confidence was not misplaced. As soon as I received your letter, I began a diligent search of the city.*

He stopped and sat pondering the value of what he knew. Information had value, and he did not want to sell what he had just learned at too low of a price. It was obviously important. Then again, perhaps with the way things were going, it would be good to ingratiate himself with the sheikh and make sure he was on the winning side.

It was against his nature, but prudence dictated it might be wise to let the sheikh set the reward and hope it would serve as a future investment. After all, you could never tell when little investments paid big dividends. He made his decision and started to write again.

> My efforts to employ my vast network of informants was not in vain, and it pleases me to inform you that the priest you seek is in Tyre. The infidel priest is in the company of a barbarian knight who has recently murdered two of our faithful brothers. To my great dismay, I was informed that the murdered men were in the service of the great sultan, Salah-al-Din. Such a barbarous act has grieved my heart, and I have been in mourning ever since learning of such lawlessness.
>
> I pray for the moment of our revenge. I have sent my spies to watch the priest and his companions. I will send word if I learn anything more. It would be helpful if you would share why you have an interest in this priest. Such a boon would please me greatly and would aid me in providing the information you desire.
>
> It has been a long time since the banner of the crescent moon flew over Tyre. As a true believer in Allah and his prophet, I long for that day. My servants will wait and watch, as I shall await your instructions.

He ended the letter with the usual insincerities about being your humble servant, along with a few quotes from the Qur'an for good measure, signed the letter, and sealed it with his seal.

He leaned back in his comfortable chair. He had no doubt that the boy would bring more information. He usually paid one shaved silver penny. Three full sized pennies would ensure the boy's best efforts.

A thought came to him. He could capture the Christian priest himself. Information was one thing, but the priest was obviously important, and if he had the priest, then maybe the sheikh would richly reward him. He had never heard of a priest being worth anything, and that is what made this whole thing very fascinating. It was all he could think about now that he was curious.

He sat down at his desk and carefully reread the sheikh's letter. The sheikh not only asked for information about the location of the priest but also described the man and his associate. For the first time, he really paid attention as he read the most intriguing part of the letter. The sheikh wanted Jabbar to inform him of the priest's destination if the priest left Tyre. Now that was interesting, interesting indeed.

The priest must have something valuable to Salah al-Din. The timing of the letter after the sultan's victory at Hattin raised Jabbar's suspicions. A priest did not command armies, have personal wealth, or anything else Jabbar would consider useful. No! Whatever made this priest the subject of the sheikh's interest had to be knowledge of something. He couldn't have stolen anything of value from Salah al-Din, he would not have access to the sultan. What else could it be? Of course, it could be the sheikh, and not Salah al-Din, who wanted the priest. The sheikh was a good friend of the sultan. There were rumors that he had given the sultan a lavish gift of several hundred men at arms with his only son as their commander.

Jabbar put his head in his hands as he worked this complicated theory out. The fact the letter arrived shortly after the sultan's victory over the Christian's at the Horns of Hattin pointed more to Salah al-Din than to the sheikh. It made it a real good possibility that whatever the priest knows affects the sultan's latest effort to take Jerusalem. When Jabbar arrived at this conclusion, he shouted aloud "Ha!" as he slammed his hand on his desk. Salah al-Din needed the priest. It was the only logical answer, and if he was wrong, so what. But if he was right and the priest was his prisoner, well now, that would be really good for him.

Jabbar began seriously weighing the possibilities of pulling off a successful abduction. He knew a man who could do the job, but he usually employed him to kill off rivals, not take them hostage. It would be more difficult, but it could be done. He was already thinking that this could be successful, but where and how should he do it.

If the priest fled the country by ship, which his presence here would indicate, he could have his men capture him at sea. He liked this plan at first, but after giving this option more thought, he dismissed the idea. Captains and sailors were an independent lot. He would have to pay an exorbitant amount of money to get their cooperation, and then he ran the risk of being double-crossed. That just wouldn't do. Besides, ship crews were superstitious, and since the majority of the sailors were Italian, they would consider harming a Catholic priest very bad luck.

No. The ship idea would not work. He would have to capture the priest before he left port. He could have his men overpower the priest and his companions on the street, hold them in a safe place, and after certain payments made, hustle him out of the city to one of his many estates.

He smiled to himself and laughed, this was going to be easy. He could contact the sheikh once they were at his estate, negotiate a nice ransom, and that would be that. It was a double win. He would not only get rich, with any luck, he might even become a hero of Islam, and that would be a nice touch. Pleased with the thought, he decided to put his plan in motion. He picked up a small bell and rang. One of his servants whisked into the room and prostrated himself on the floor.

"Most gracious and wonderful master, it is my undying joy to serve you. What do you desire?"

Jabbar looked at the man with disdain. He leaned back in his chair and watched the man as his muscles gradually began to spasm in the uncomfortable position. Sweat was now running down the servant's face. At last, Jabbar spoke, "Go find Ishaq. Tell him to drop whatever he is doing and come here immediately."

The man stood up and bowed. "Most gracious master, I will not disappoint you."

Jabbar stuck out his chin and peered down at the man. "Humph, see that you do not." The servant turned and hurried out of the room as fast as he could.

✝

Ishaq was lounging at his favorite khan enjoying the afternoon. He was an average looking Arab. His clean-shaven face made him exceptionally good at his profession. Nothing distinguished him. His large, dark eyes gave him a look of kindness, but his looks were deceiving. He was anything but kind. He was a ruthless, cold–blooded killer. It did not matter who he killed: men, women, children, he could slay them all as long as the price was right. This unassuming man took his victims by surprise when he stuck a poisoned knife in the side of their neck and cut their throat, which was his preferred method of dispatching his victims.

What made him especially sought after by those in need of his vocation was his versatility. He used other methods of murder, such as poisons, darts, or arrows, with expertise. He was well known for his use of silken bowstrings to strangle victims of Islamic royalty. Some of his best customers had been princes or sultans who appreciated his discretion in removing troublesome royals who had become an embarrassment to the family, or proved to be a complicating factor in determining succession. To the delight of his customers, he ensured that once he was hired, their particular problem disappeared quietly.

He was stirring his cup of qahwa when Jabbar's servant brusquely bulled his way to the table, babbling that Jabbar needed to see him immediatly. Ishaq leaned back in his chair and tilted his head to look at the servant.

"What does Jabbar want?"

"I do not know. My master does not tell me. He just wants to see you now."

"Tell Jabbar I am busy."

"No!" the servant wailed. "No, you cannot be busy." The servant flung himself to the ground and hugged Ishaq's leg. "Please come, please, please, please. You must come. Jabbar will have me beaten. You must come."

Ishaq looked down as the servant began to weep. Ishaq shook his head. He wanted to cut the man's throat to stop the pitiful wailing, but the setting was too public and the man was so pathetic that killing him would provide Ishaq with as much enjoyment as swatting a fly. "Enough!" Ishaq cried. "I will come. Get up and go tell your master."

"You are most merciful. Thank you, Thank you."

"Enough. Be gone before I change my mind."

The servant got up, bowed, and hurried off.

†

It seemed like an eternity before Ishaq presented himself in Jabbar's apartment office. Jabbar was pacing, his hands behind his back, and muttering to himself when Ishaq entered his apartment.

Ishaq gave a bow out of courtesy. He had worked for Jabbar long enough to know his moods, and whatever put him in this mood was going to be profitable for Ishaq. "I came as soon as I was told you wanted to see me," Ishaq said in an amused voice. Ishaq did not fear Jabbar. They needed each other. Jabbar made him rich doing what he loved to do. Ishaq took care of the dirty, messy work and Jabbar made sure that the dirty, messy work paid well.

Jabbar cleared his throat. "I need you to arrange an abduction," he exclaimed with more excitement in his voice than he intended. "Can you do it?"

Ishaq raised his eyebrows. "You want an abduction?"

"Yes. Can you do it, or should I find someone else?"

"Find someone else. Abductions are troublesome. I am an assassin. I don't stoop to collecting ransom." Ishaq turned to leave.

"Wait!" Jabbar cried. "Ishaq, my friend, I was only jesting. No one can do what you do. I will pay double your rate."

Ishaq turned back to face Jabbar and frowned. "I can, but it will cost triple."

The demand for extra money didn't even faze Jabbar. "I don't care what it costs! I need it done, and I want it done as soon as possible."

If Ishaq was surprised, his face betrayed no emotion. Usually, the painful process of price negotiation accompanied any offer of employment. Ishaq had suffered through these many times. Several offers usually went back and forth before they agreed upon a price. Once they settled on a price, Ishaq would have to listen to Jabbar's whimpering about Ishaq's exorbitant rates. Jabbar was a pain in the ass, and if he were not such a good customer, Ishaq would have stopped doing business with him a long time ago.

"Who is the mark?" the assassin asked, expecting the name of some well-known person.

"A Christian priest."

Ishaq started to laugh. "A priest. Jabbar, you surely jest."

"He is being protected by a brutish monk and a knight who slew two of Salah al-Din's men today," Jabbar said, not amused.

"I heard this story about the knight, but then I heard a rumor from someone else that he killed four. You know how rumors are." Ishaq shrugged. "It was probably an old beggar with one arm and one leg who had the misfortune of asking the knight for money. Christians are such braggarts."

Jabbar shot Ishaq a look of irritation. "I had a spy at the gate when the knight rode in. The man killed two of Salah al-Din's men in fair combat."

"So, what is your plan?" Ishaq replied, no longer laughing.

Jabbar was glad to see that Ishaq was now taking this seriously. "I am waiting for more information from my spy, but my plan is for you and your men to surprise and overpower the knight and the monk while they are in the street. Capture the priest unharmed and take him out of the city to my estate near Damascus."

Ishaq shook his head. "That's your plan? I think this is going to be a little more difficult than that."

"Ishaq, my friend, I am hiring you for your expertise, and I will pay triple your rate if you are successful."

"Whatever you desire," the assassin said, a little irritated by Jabbar's oversimplification of what was required. "As soon as your spy returns with new information, send him to me. I make no guarantees about success. Killing is simple. Abductions take time to plan and requires several men. This is a rushed job. I usually need time to follow the targets and learn their habits." Ishaq looked Jabbar right in the eye. "If this works," he said, emphasizing each word, "and this is a big IF, then I demand that you pay my men my regular rate as well."

Jabbar didn't even hesitate. "Done. Just make it happen!"

"It will be done," Ishaq muttered. He turned and started to walk out of the room, then paused and turned to look at Jabbar. "Whatever did this priest do?"

"That is my business, and I will pay you very well to keep it my business."

"And so, it will be," Ishaq said with a shrug of his shoulders. "Unless this goes bad, and then, my friend, you will wish you had told me everything." Ishaq turned his back on Jabbar and walked out of the apartment.

Jabbar frowned as he watched Ishaq leave. "You will wish you told me everything," Jabbar said to himself in a mocking voice, tilting his head back and forth, as he said each word. Jabbar stopped and looked at the empty doorway. "I will tell you nothing!" Jabbar scoffed, "Nothing, nothing…and nothing."

All of the scheming was making his head hurt. He decided to visit his harem. Such visits always put him in a better mood to plan. He lifted his bulk out of his chair and headed to their apartment. He returned refreshed after several hours. The women might have had different thoughts, but the welfare of his harem girls was not even a flicker of concern to Jabbar.

He sat down with a smile on his face as he basked in his good fortune. Ishaq would capture the priest. The sheikh would be pleased. Salah al-Din would be overjoyed. He would reap the benefits with lucrative trade agreements, and the money would start pouring in. He could almost see himself wallowing in a mound of gold coins.

CHAPTER 11
THE HOUSE OF THE ARCHBISHOP

Father Villhardain, Byron, and Carl rode through the streets of Tyre. Refugees crowded the streets, bringing everything they possessed with them. The inns were full, and camps were set up in the open spaces in the city.

Byron rode in front, using his horse to clear a path through the human mass. To the knight's annoyance, the peasants would not yield the street. Using the unrelenting weight of the horse, he forced the ragged mass to move. As the horse pushed the peasants closer, a shoving match broke out. Curses filled the air as men came to blows. Household treasures were dropped and scattered, but the scuffle ended as the peasants caught sight of the knight in his blood splattered armor. Grumbling and with dark glances, the peasants gave way, allowing the three men to ride through. It took time to work their way through the twisting narrow streets, but finally they arrived at an imposing building that served as residence of the archbishop.

The house had survived the fall of the empire. It was still standing long after Pluto had taken the houses' last Roman master to the grave. A Roman equestrian, sent to govern the conquered provinces, had built the house. It had served as a symbol of Roman wealth and power. A fashionable building in the backwater of Judea, to be envied by the Romans and the conquered alike. Tall, white Doric columns held up the triangular portico. Inside the attic of the portico, the graven images of Roman horsemen in martial splendor had been carved to remind the subjected of the power of Rome. Roman cavalrymen, with crested helmets, were riding at a full charge. The horse's muscles bulged, their eyes wide, and nostrils flared as they thundered across the stone-carved grass.

Yet, the moment for the riders to strike a blow for Jupiter and the emperor had come and gone. A stirring image of Roman authority that faded long ago. Decay and vandalism had shorn the stone image of its grandeur. The riders' swords were broken at the hilt; the head of one of the equestrians shattered. Only the horses remained unmarred.

Behind this massive porch stood the yellow sandstone walls of the two story domus. The first-floor windows, decorated with fluted columns carved from the stone, filled the building with light. Graceful arched windows lined the second floor, which was crowned by a red tile roof. The archbishop, in need for larger accommodations for guests and servants, had added two wings built in the Romanesque style. The wings stretched from each side of the original building, each ending with a turreted tower. At the back of the house, a great hall and scullery had been constructed for the purpose of entertaining. The groin vault of the great hall loomed over the original domus; its narrow windows added the illusion of height while its back wall was pierced with a magnificent stained glass rose window.

No other residence was as grand as the house of the archbishop of Tyre. The German architecture would outlast the domus, but for the moment, the Roman architecture remained the heart of the building.

Father Villhardain dismounted at the steps of the portico. "Stay here," he said. "I will speak to Archbishop Joscius alone."

The priest turned, went up the steps, and into the building. A young man was waiting for him by the bronze door. He was dressed in a black dalmatic of a seminarian. His dark hair, neatly combed, framed his tanned face, and he wore an expression of self-assured superiority that only the son of a noble could emanate.

"Father Villhardain," he said in a clear voice, "the archbishop sends his greetings and welcomes your return. His eminence is anxious to speak with you."

"Excellent," the priest said. "I take it then my messages arrived."

"Indeed, they have," the young man replied. "I was sent to escort you." The seminarian opened the large bronze door, adorned with the lightning bolts of Jupiter, into the spacious hallway of the Vestibulum. The hallway opened into a large atrium lined with white marble walls. A statue of Plutus still stood in the corner of the atrium holding his cornucopia of grain, while hiding in the opposite corner, a statue of Bacchus frolicking in revelry. Father Villhardain frowned as he passed by the images of the god of wealth and the god of wine. He thought their presence was in poor taste, but he kept his thoughts to himself. Perhaps the archbishop enjoyed their artistic value, and it was not the priest's place to correct his superior. The seminarian walked through the atrium without giving either statue a second glance.

He led the way through the mosaic courtyard between the two wings of the domus. In the center of the courtyard was the compluvium, the marble basin filled with rainwater. As the seminarian passed beside the water, he glanced down to admire his reflection.

"How was your journey, Father?"

"Tiresome."

The seminarian looked up. "I would say that it was more than tiresome by the looks of the knight that is with you."

Father Villhardain's eyes narrowed. "It was tiresome, and that is all you need to know."

"I offer no offense, Father. I was merely observing."

"Observing or prying," the priest reproached.

The seminarian frowned.

"Young man, when you are old and grey perhaps you will be wise enough to be entrusted with the business of the Church. Until then, mind the tasks given to you. If you excel, then perhaps greater assignments will follow."

"Yes, Father Villhardain."

The seminarian opened the door. Father Villhardain shook his head as he entered the room. "Youth," he muttered to himself.

The walls of the room were painted in alternating shades of red and black and decorated at the top with a boarder of laurel. A mosaic of Hector and Apollo filled the back wall of the room. The Trojan hero was armed with spear and shield, his intense dark eyes glared from beneath his lofty helmet. Behind Hector, stood Apollo dressed in white, but the son of Zeus had turned his face, as if something else had caught his interest. Father Villhardain glanced at the image. Would Hector have fought Achilles had he known the gods had abandoned him? What of his own journey? He prayed every night for guidance and wisdom. He believed God had blessed his endeavor, but how would he really know? He looked away from the image of Troy's ill-starred hero and walked across the mosaic floor.

Archbishop Joscius, standing, framed by the window with his hands behind his back, looked out at the refugees filling the city. Hearing the priest's approach, he turned to greet his guest. "Michael, I have been praying earnestly for your safe arrival."

Father Villhardain bowed. "Your Grace, I thank you for your prayers. I was deeply concerned about the danger of traveling on the road to Tyre. God heard your prayer, and he delivered to me a young knight who heroically fought off Saladin's pursuers today. Had he not been with me, things would not have turned out well."

"God does not forget us in our times of need," the archbishop said with a smile.

"It is a good thing. Saladin's war came as a surprise. And it is only by the grace of our blessed lady that I was outside Tiberias when the sultan surrounded it."

"I can only imagine the anxiety of such a narrow escape and with the enemy so close. Even here, with the enemy miles away, fear is rampant. The city is in disarray. We have had our own divine intervention with the timely arrival of Lord Conrad de Montferrat from Constantinople."

"Yes, Yousef delivered your letter. How is the son of the Marquis de Montferrat? Does he know his father is a prisoner of the sultan?"

The archbishop nodded. "I delivered the ill news to Conrad. He took it better than I expected."

"Hmm, I was discouraged when I read in your correspondence that Reginald of Sidon was negotiating the surrender of Tyre to Saladin. The loss of Tyre would be a devastating blow."

"Indeed. Since the capture of the king and the elder Montferrat, not one lord has the vision to see the larger strategy." The archbishop sighed. "Not that Guy Lusignan was a great strategist. Hattin is proof of that."

"Well, it appears we have been saved for the moment by Conrad Montferrat."

"Yes. Conrad has put an end to such cowardice. He has rallied the city."

The archbishop motioned Father Villhardain to take a seat. The archbishop sat down across from him, his hands pressed together in front of his face. The archbishop looked over the tips of his fingers, his grey eyes bored into the priest. At last the archbishop spoke, "I have received an answer from Rome. Cardinal Morra has sent word that he wants your immediate return to the Lateran. He is impressed with your find, and he has asked me to congratulate you."

Father Villhardain bowed. "Thank you, Your Grace."

"Father Villhardain you have done well. You have found the resting place of Honorius's lost treasury."

"Indeed, but I had hoped to examine the site... but things have changed. Brother Arron has been captured, and now Saladin is searching for me. I fear we now have one chance to go and bring it back; otherwise, all my work will be for naught."

The archbishop leaned back in his chair and brought his hands down in front of his chest. Father Villhardain stared at the archbishop's hands as he waited for his superior to speak.

"This is a problem," the archbishop said as he tapped the ends of his fingers together. "Where does the treasure lie?"

Father Villhardain glanced around the room and then leaned close to the archbishop. "It lies in Babylon, deep in Saracen lands."

Joscius took a deep breath. "Babylon...I was afraid of something like this."

"When Rome held sway over these lands, the journey was

difficult. Now it is dangerous."

"How do you propose to retrieve it?"

"I am not sure, Your Grace. I have some thoughts. They started to take shape when I took the knight into my company."

"Does this knight know your purpose?"

"He does not."

"It is going to take more men than one knight."

"Indeed," the priest said. "The lords of this land are greedy and treacherous. They will gleefully stab each other in the back if they believe it will gain them an advantage. I cannot imagine what would happen if they were enlisted to retrieve a large treasure of gold."

"Father Villhardain, never were truer words spoken. Even if you found a lord willing to aid the Church, no one is in a position to spare you the men. Even here in Tyre, Lord Montferrat lacks the soldiers to man the walls. He has forbidden anyone of fighting age to leave the city."

Father Villhardain frowned. "Your Grace, I need my assistant, and if my plans come to pass, I need this young knight. Only Rome can raise the resources I need."

"Cardinal Morra has foreseen this, and that is why you are to return to the Lateran as soon as possible. Nothing further can be accomplished here."

"What do you have in mind?"

The archbishop frowned. "I will have to ponder this. Lord Montferrat is here. I invited him here as a guest to discuss the Saracen onslaught that is coming. He will be staying for dinner." The archbishop paused. "I will have places set at my table for you and your traveling companions."

"You are very gracious, Your Grace."

"Father Villhardain, Lord Montferrat is a skilled politician. He is not easily manipulated or deceived. I will have to gauge his mood. Whatever course I choose tonight, you must be prepared to follow."

"Yes, Your Grace."

"Excellent." The archbishop smiled as he stood up. "I must take my leave and return to my guest. Now that you have arrived, I will do what I can to aid you. Go back to your men. I have asked my servants to prepare rooms for you."

"Thank you, Your Grace." Father Villhardain bowed and left the room.

Father Villhardain entered the courtyard. The seminarian was gone. A priest stood next to the compluvium. He looked up as Father Villhardain closed the door. "Father Villhardain, God be praised for your safe return."

"Father Dominic, it is good to see you again."

Father Dominic began walking beside Father Villhardain. "His Grace, the archbishop, requested me to assist you with your horses and to set a place for you at the table."

"Father Dominic, that is very kind of you."

The two priests walked through the doorway and down the stairs to where Byron and Carl were waiting. Byron, still covered in gore, was relieved to see Father Villhardain return. The stench was starting to grow, and he was looking forward to cleaning up.

"Father Dominic, these are my companions, Brother Carl and Sir Byron Fitzwalter."

Father Dominic smiled. "Father Villhardain has arranged your lodging with the archbishop, and I am here to welcome you on his behalf. Take your horses to the stable," Father Dominic said, turning and pointing to the back of the residence. "I will have trenchers set for your evening meal." Father Dominic paused for a moment, looking at Byron. "I will also arrange for a place to clean up, as well as a change of attire."

Bryon nodded. "Father, that would be most welcome."

"I will see if I can find raiment suitable for a Knight of Saint John."

Byron bowed and turned leading his horse to the stable. Father Villhardain joined him and after a few steps, Byron stopped. "Father, I can unsaddle your horse."

Father Villhardain handed the reins to Byron. "If it is not too much trouble, my son."

"It is not," the knight replied.

"Father Dominic! Wait!" Father Dominic stopped and turned to wait. Father Villhardain was out of breath when he reached the place where Father Dominic stood.

Father Villhardain took a moment to catch his breath. "In my youth, I would have thought nothing of such a short jog."

"But now you feel as if you ran a mile," Father Dominic replied. The two priests turned and walked into the house.

†

Byron and Carl led the horses to the stone stable used by Archdiocese. Compared to the villa, it was relatively new and plain. It was feeding time when they passed through the doorway into the darkened building. Several monks were pitching hay into the mangers. The barn was alive with nickers of horses calling to their keepers. Byron paused to admire a well-built black charger standing in one of the stalls. A monk stuck his pitchfork into a mound of hay as he stopped to watch Byron.

"I see you like Lord Montferrat's horse," the monk said as he leaned against his pitchfork.

Byron nodded. "Indeed, this is a handsome horse."

"He brought it with him from Constantinople."

"Does Montferrat keep his horse here?"

"No, my lord, he is a dinner guest of the archbishop."

"I see." Byron motioned to the monk to come over. "Be of service and hold this horse."

"Yes, my lord." The monk set down his wooden pitchfork and took the reins of Father Villhardain's horse.

"My lord, what misfortune has befallen you?"

"Misfortune?" Byron looked down at his armor. "The blood is not mine. No, the misfortune belongs to the Saracens today." Byron led his horse into the tie stall and tied his horse up.

"Tell your tale, my lord."

"There is not much to tell... I killed two Saracens in combat today."

"The roads have grown dangerous."

Byron nodded as he started to unsaddle his horse. "Who is Lord Montferrat?"

The monk's eyes widened as he leaned forward. "You have

never heard of Lord Montferrat?"

"Should I?"

"My lord, he is a great captain in Constantinople. The emperor gave him the title of Caesar."

"Humph, I was unaware there were any great captains in Constantinople," Byron answered dryly as he pulled the saddle from his horse and placed it on a nearby railing.

The monk shook his head. "He defeated the army of the Holy Roman Emperor Barbarossa."

"When he defeats the army of Henry of England, I will be impressed," Byron replied as he started brushing his horse.

"You scoff, my lord, but I have heard that Saladin fears the Holy Roman Emperor."

"The Norman's right," interjected Brother Carl. "No German army, or Greek for that matter, is superior to the English." Byron looked up from brushing his horse. "The yeomen of England are the backbone of Henry's army," continued Brother Carl. "No finer infantry exists in all of Europe."

"Led by a Norman king," Byron interjected as he started to unsaddle Father Villhardain's horse.

"My lord, I beg your pardon," the stable monk said, "I am a holy brother, and I am only repeating what I have heard. I have seen Lord Montferrat, and he impressed me as a masterful man. Perhaps looks are deceiving."

Byron started brushing the priest's horse. "Looks are deceiving, and reports from afar can be faithless. We will meet Conrad Montferrat tonight and make our own judgment."

"Are you spending the night, my lord," the monk asked, "or are you here for the evening meal?"

"I am staying the night. In the morning, I ride for Jerusalem."

"I hate to interrupt your conversation," Carl groused as he stepped out of the stall where he had tied his horse, "but I am famished, and I am leaving without you if you don't get moving."

"Yes, Brother Carl."

"Young lord, be careful," the monk whispered as he grabbed Byron's arm. "Conrad Montferrat is a powerful lord. He has taken over the defense of the city, and he is in fell mood. His father is a prisoner of the sultan and he is displeased with the city's preparedness."

Byron cocked his head to the side and stuck out his chin. "Why is Montferrat displeased? There were knights at the gate, soldiers on the rampart."

The monk drew close as if he feared someone might overhear him. "After the defeat at Hattin, and much to the archbishop's dismay, the lords of the city were negotiating the surrender of Tyre to Saladin. Montferrat went into a rage when he found out. He demanded that the city resist Saladin to the bitter end."

"I might have to rethink my judgement of Lord Montferrat," Byron muttered. "Perhaps he is a worthy lord after all." Byron tied up the priest's horse and stepped out of the stall. "I am ready."

"It is about time, my Norman friend. It has been a long ride. I am ready to eat, and then to rest in a comfortable bed. Unless, of course you insult the lord of the city and we are turned out into the cold, cruel wilderness outside the city's walls."

"I will do no such thing. I am as tired as you are. I do not wish to sleep on the dirt among the rocks." The two men left the barn and made their way to the house.

"What do you expect will come of our dining with Lord Montferrat?"

Brother Carl stopped and turned to face the knight. "Father Villhardain did not say. The only council I can give you is to listen and watch."

CHAPTER 12
THE LORD OF TYRE

Brother Carl turned and started to walk to the back entrance of the archbishop's house. Byron hurried to catch up. "What could possibly happen?" The knight asked.

The monk looked at Byron out of the corner of his eye as he continued to walk. "Norman, Father Villhardain has been given a special assignment by the Church. Montferrat does not know why we are here. No one knows. A wrong word or misunderstanding with Montferrat might delay our departure and place all of Father Villhardain's efforts in jeopardy."

"You talk of this task, but you give no hint as to what it is."

The monk smiled. "Norman, when Father Villhardain feels it is necessary for you to know, then he will tell you. Until then, have faith."

Byron stopped at the door and folded his arms across his chest. "I think my deeds today earned that right."

Brother Carl leaned forward, his brow furled over his misshapen nose. "Norman, did you ever consider that by not knowing our secret, Father Villhardain has done you a great service. You are still free to leave our company, and in the morning ride to Jerusalem."

Byron laughed as he looked around at the churchmen going to and fro on their daily tasks. "Even if I knew the priest's task, who here could stop me from leaving?"

Brother Carl's eyes hardened as if he were looking through the knight. "I could, and I would not hesitate. I was not always a monk. Even today my past and the present sometimes cross in my service to the Church."

Byron looked at the monk as he thought back to their sword practice. He had been a fool. The monastic robes had blinded him. Not for one moment had he considered that monk had actually used his skill to slay other men.

Brother Carl saw the realization in Byron's face. "I was chosen to protect Father Michael and Brother Aaron at all costs and by all means. I have been granted an indulgence by the Holy Father to do whatever is necessary to keep our purpose in the Holy Lands safe from the enemy. Even if that means shedding blood."

"But Saladin knows, does he not?"

"Yes, and that is what troubles me most. I have failed. If I had known Saladin was going to surround Tiberias, I would have brought Brother Aaron with us. But alas, he wanted to stay and work on an old text that he was translating, and I saw no harm in leaving him behind. By the time I saw the error in my judgment, it was too late."

"Well, it appears Saladin does not know everything; otherwise, why would he trouble himself to capture Father Villhardain?"

"Indeed, the sultan's desire to capture Father Villhardain is perplexing."

"Perhaps he does not want the priest to report his information to Rome?"

Brother Carl sighed. "Ah Norman, you are much too clever, but that is not the reason, and I will tell you no more."

Byron paused and looked at the monk for a moment, but he could think of nothing to say and turned and opened the door. Two pages were waiting for them. The older boy had a slight build and dirty blond hair. He was leaning on a crutch to take the weight off his clubbed foot. Despite his deformity, he was doing his best to stand straight. A younger boy, with red hair, was hiding behind his companion.

"Welcome, lord and Holy Brother," the older boy said as he bowed. "Father Dominic has sent us to guide you to your rooms where you can refresh yourselves and change your attire before dinner with the archbishop and the Lord Montferrat."

"I don't need to change or be refreshed for that matter," grumbled Carl. "I want to eat and then rest. I am tired and I don't care."

"Holy brother," the older boy replied earnestly, "you must, the archbishop insists."

Carl looked down at the boy. "I must?"

A worried look crossed the boy's face as he looked at the towering monk in front of him.

"Holy brother, Lord Montferrat is here, and the archbishop would want you to make a good impression." The boy lowered his voice. "He has been among the Greeks, and the archbishop would not want the true Church to suffer in comparison."

"Boy, do you really think that my appearance is the one thing that will tip the scales and cause Montferrat to disfavor the Church?"

"It could. The Greeks are misguided heretics. Who knows what evil they have whispered in Lord Montferrat's ear."

"I see you are going to insist," Brother Carl grumbled. "Well, lead on and don't tarry. It will take some time to make my appearance suitable for our evening meal, if such a thing is possible. I would not want to disappoint Lord Montferrat."

The timid boy with red hair did not move. "Take the holy brother to his room," the older boy whispered, giving the younger boy a shove with his crutch. The boy stared up at the big monk.

"Come now, lad," Brother Carl said with a twinkle in his eye. "I won't bite, unless you make me late for dinner with his Eminence." The boy hesitated, and then began to hurry down the hallway.

"That's more like it," Brother Carl grumbled as he followed him to his room.

The older boy turned to Byron and said, "My lord, I will take you to your room." Byron walked slowly as the boy hobbled down the hallway. The boy, doing his best to hide his infirmary, looked up at the knight, his eyes wide in awe. "Are you the one who killed Saladin's men?"

Byron glanced down at his bloodstained surcoat. "How do you know that?"

"My lord, the news has gone all through the city."

"But I just arrived. How did you learn of this?"

"I don't know, my lord. All I can say is news reached the house that one who is marked by the cross was beset by two Saracens on the road. In fierce and righteous combat, the fell Christian knight dispatched the wicked non-believers to hell." The boy ended his statement by crossing himself.

Byron shook his head in disbelief. "Yes, I slew Saladin's knights."

The boy beamed. "I knew the moment I saw you that you were a true crusader, a true champion of our holy cause. Someday, I hope to be a great warrior like you."

Byron smiled at the boy. "Then work hard." Byron paused as the boy looked up at him despite the difficulty of walking with his crutch. "Remember your oath, for it gives you purpose, and perhaps your valor will not be in vain nor forgotten."

The boy nodded. "I will, my lord." The boy paused at a door and opened it. "I will remember what you said, my lord. I hope your room is satisfactory." Byron looked in and nodded. "My lord, do you need help removing your armor?"

"That would be helpful."

The boy smiled broadly. "It would be my honor, my lord."

Byron moved to a nearby chair. "Then come here boy and stand on the chair."

The page hobbled over and with the assistance of the knight, he scrambled up on to the chair. From the moment that he had killed the two Saracens, his surcoat had smelled of blood and flesh. As the day wore on, the smell had gotten stronger as the fermented gore began to dry and rot. He hated the sickly stench.

"Help me get this cloak off," instructed the knight, "and then we will start from the top and work down." The page untied the black cloak and carefully draped it over the chair. Next, he undid the laces that tied the hood to the hauberk and pulled it free. Byron pulled his gauntlets from his hands and tossed them carelessly onto a small table. The knight unbuckled his sword and handed it to the page, who carefully leaned it against the chair.

Byron pulled up the surcoat as the boy gingerly pulled the

garment off. "Toss it on the floor." The boy complied. "Now help me with the hauberk."

The page leaned forward to remove the hauberk. As the boy struggled to pull the heavy chain mail up, his face turned red from the strain. Byron, seeing the boy struggle, began to help gather up the mail. When the mail came free, it was too heavy for the page, who let it fall to the floor with a crash.

"I am sorry, my lord," the boy cried.

Byron laughed. "Do not fear, boy, it has suffered worse." Byron stretched, enjoying the feeling of freedom. He glanced down at his surcoat. The white cross of the Hospitaller was facing him.

"I can do the rest myself," the knight said as he reached up to help the page down from the chair.

"Are you sure, my lord?"

"Yes," he said tiredly as he sagged into the chair. He leaned back for a moment and enjoyed the comfort of the chair before beginning the task of removing the rest of his armor.

"Do you require anything else, my lord."

Byron looked around the room. Laying on the bed was a clean black tunic and a black cloak of the Knights of Saint John. "How does the archbishop come to have the livery of the Knights of Saint John?"

"The archbishop has livery for Templars, and other military orders kept here. You are not the first knight to stay here and need a change of raiment. It is a gift from the archbishop. You serve his Holiness in Rome, and the archbishop feels that such service should always be recognized. He also wants you to make a good impression on the Lord of Tyre."

"I see. Come here, boy. I have something for you."

The page approached as Byron fumbled in the pocket of his cloak and pulled out the gold dinar he had found on the road. The boy's eyes widened as he saw the flash of gold.

"For you. A souvenir," the knight said as he placed the coin in the pages in hand. "It came from one of the dead Saracens. Spend it wisely." Byron sat forward on the edge of the chair and looked down to remove the chausses. He glanced up and saw the page still standing in front of him.

"My lord, you said you lost your squire. I would be willing to be your squire if you accept my service." The boy looked down. "If you need one?"

Byron looked at the page. "Boy, I doubt not your courage, nor do I question your sincerity, but my road leads to Jerusalem. In the morning, I intend to ride swiftly, and I do not look to return."

The page looked up at Byron. "My lord, I do not fear the Saracens. I am willing to die for Christ."

"You do not fear the Saracens because you have not met them in battle. As far as dying, do not be in such a hurry. Dying is easy, living an honest Christian life is far harder."

"But, my lord, you are going to sacrifice yourself are you not?"

Byron sighed. "I swore an oath to the Knights of Saint John. How can I abandon them in such a dark hour? The only reason I am here is that I owed a debt to the priest, and now, that debt has been repaid. Now, I need to serve my order." Byron leaned forward and tussled the boy's hair. "Serve your master. If Christ demands your life, you will know, and your sacrifice will be rewarded with eternal life."

The page bowed. "Then I shall leave you, my lord." The page hobbled to the door and then paused. "If you return and you still need a squire, remember me."

Byron looked at the page. "I will indeed."

The page bowed. "I will ask His Grace, the archbishop, to keep you in his prayers." The page left the room and Byron was alone. He bent down and began to remove his chausses and the cloth wrappings around his knee and leg. He stood up and began to wash.

A monk stopped by his room and collected his bloody garments for cleaning. As he dressed in his new clothes, he wondered how many people in Tyre knew about his melee with Saladin's knights. He shook his head. His efforts to be discreet had failed.

A servant of the archbishop arrived and escorted him down the marble hallway to the dining room of the cardinal. Byron stopped at the hallway mirror to admire his new black tunic with its white Maltese cross. A black cloak with a crusader's cross was draped over his shoulders. He stared at himself thoughtfully as his reflection looked back at him. He looked the same. A little thinner, but still to his mind, handsome or at least good enough to attract a young maiden's attention.

He walked away after a moment and was about to enter the dining room when he saw Father Villhardain and Brother Carl standing near the doorway. Father Villhardain was dressed in a new black robe, and Brother Carl wore his usual monastic attire, except these robes were clean.

A long highly polished table with a green runner in the center of it stretched across the room. Candles lit the marble columns that lined the walls, and the smell of incense filled the air. The archbishop waited at the far end of the room to greet his dinner guests. Father Villhardain walked to the archbishop, knelt down on one knee, took his hand, and kissed his ring. Byron and Carl followed suit.

"Father Villhardain, my old friend," Archbishop Joscius said, "it has been a long time since you have sat at my table, please take your seats."

"Thank you, Your Grace,," the priest replied.

The archbishop turned to the dark-haired man seated at the table. "This is my guest Conrad de Montferrat, Lord of Tyre." Father Villhardain bowed. "Father Villhardain, would you be so kind to introduce your companions."

"Indeed, Your Eminence. Lord Montferrat, this is my assistant, Brother Carl, and this young Knight of the Order of Saint John is Sir Byron Fitzwalter of Ireland."

Montferrat looked at the two churchmen and then Byron. Byron gazed back at the lord of the city. Montferrat was thin. He was dressed in a silk tunic of light blue that fit loosely on his muscular body. A purple cloak, lined with ermine, draped over his shoulders. Conrad looked into Byron's eyes as if he were reading him, weighing the worth of his life's story. At last, the lord of the city spoke, "Welcome to Tyre, my lords. I hope your journey was not too arduous."

"My lord, our journey was not without its difficulties," Father Villhardain replied. "but by the grace of God, we reached the safety of your walls and we are grateful to be here."

Montferrat lifted his chin. "Father Villhardain, it is my honor to offer you sanctuary. You and your companions are my guests." Montferrat then turned to speak to Joscius.

Byron sat quietly in boredom listening to the mundane politics of keeping the Genoese traders' interests in Tyre. He perked up as Montferrat spoke of destroying the mole built by Alexander the Great. The mole was the bridge that linked Tyre to the island fortress in the bay. He had seen the island fortress from the old city, its formidable walls built along the water. The destruction of the wood and stone mole, would no doubt inconvenience Saladin, but he had no doubt that Saladin's engineers would have no problems in repairing the breach. Alexander had conquered Tyre by building the mole. Saladin would conquer the city by repairing it.

He sat staring at the table, turning over a dinner fork, a useless utensil of Byzantine and Italian decadence. He had never seen a fork until he arrived in the Holy Lands, and he still questioned its usefulness when fingers and a knife worked just as well. He glanced up at Carl who had his head down deep in thought.

Several pages arrived with fingerbowls and towels. A new set of servants arrived and placed several loaves of white manchet on the table. The appearance of the loaves of bread made Brother Carl sit up. Picking up his knife, the big monk eagerly started slicing the bread. More platters arrived with sliced apples and pomegranates.

Byron, who had pushed the fork out of his way, was placing as much as he could on the trencher of bread that had been set before him. He was hungry and to his delight, a new set of platters filled with fresh meat appeared. The knight was carving off a slab of boiled beef when he leaned over and spoke to Brother Carl, "Will the archbishop have a minstrel play?"

"No, Norman," whispered the monk. "This meal is to discuss strategy. Perhaps when the meal is ended, we might be entertained, but I do not expect it."

Byron sighed. "It has been a long time since I have heard a minstrel play. I was hoping the archbishop would have a good musician."

"Norman," the monk said, with his mouth full of food, "what did you expect. This is the church, not a castle. There are no fools and no minstrels. Be grateful for the fine fare placed before you. It will be a long time before you eat like this again."

Byron nodded as he stabbed a piece of mutton with his knife and began to eat. When Byron had eaten his fill, the servants began to clear the table. Byron gave his trencher to a page, who added it to the rest of the bread plates to be given to the poor. Byron saw Conrad de Montferrat looking at him from across the table.

"You must be the knight who killed two Saracen's on the road to this city?"

Byron nodded. "Aye, my lord."

"Well done. Too bad you couldn't have killed a few more of the bastards; although, Saladin will hardly be troubled by the death of a few of his soldiers. But tell me, how is it you end up in the company of this priest when all of your order marched with the army to Hattin?"

Before he could say a word, Father Villhardain interjected. "That is where we found him, my lord. He was on the doorstep of death when we took him into our care." Father Villhardain shook his head. "He is quite fortunate to be here at all."

Montferrat tilted his head to one side and looked at Byron. "I beg your pardon, Fitzwalter. I thought you were one of those skulkers who always fashions an excuse to hide while other men do the fighting." Montferrat took a sip of wine. "This worthy priest has corrected my misunderstanding. Tell me your story. How did you escape from Hattin?"

Byron recounted how his horse fell on him and how he woke up alone.

Montferrat listened with a grim look on his face. "Damn the stupidity of Lusignan. He should have heeded the counsel of Raymond, Prince of Galilee, and not Gerard and Chatillon. Lusignan should have known that Saladin could never hold Tiberias. Not that it matters now, this is the circumstances we have inherited. Either we fight to victory, or we die an honorable death."

"Well said, my lord," Byron replied. "Better to die a man with your sword in your hand, than an old dotard lying in your own filth."

"It will be a hard fight," Montferrat replied, "but I will not lose this city. Will you be with me, Sir Fitzwalter?"

"My lord, my duty is to return to Jerusalem. I swore an oath to the Knights of Saint John to defend that city against the enemies of Christ. How can I not return to her in her hour of need?"

Montferrat washed his hands in his finger bowl and then wiped them with a cloth. "An oath cannot be lightly set aside, but in this matter, I can give you advice. The roads to Jerusalem are impassible. Saladin has cut off all access to the city. Yesterday the sun was only an hour old when a knight from the marshal of Jerusalem arrived requesting our aid. I had none to offer, but alas, the marshal will never know. The knight had scarcely left the city when he was forced to return. Sir Fitzwalter, you are on one of the last Christian islands in the Saracen sea.

"Yet, all is not lost," replied the archbishop. "You have prevented the unnecessary surrender of this city. A Christian island, you say my lord, but it is a strong place and the Italians still control the sea. As long as we have the sea to our backs and the Italian's to bring supplies, we can hold this place indefinitely."

The room became quiet and Byron changed the subject. "My lord, what has happened since Hattin?"

"Nothing good," Montferrat growled. "Ever since I arrived, the survivors from the battle have been straggling in. I would never have imagined such a disgrace would befall Christian arms. Most of the men are weaponless; their lords are either dead or captured. The few lords that did escape have proved useless. Balian of Ibelin's only concern has been to negotiate a deal with Saladin so he can pass through Saracen lines and return to Jerusalem to retrieve his family."

"I am not surprised, my lord," replied Byron. "The road to Tyre was littered with weapons."

Montferrat shook his head. "The King of Jerusalem is a prisoner of the sultan, so is my father. Raynald de Chatillon is dead. News arrived that the sultan relieved Chatillon's shoulders of a burden by cutting off his head."

The archbishop bowed his head as he crossed himself. "I have heard the same."

"My lord, what do you intend to do next?" Father Villhardain asked.

"Nothing. Saladin has taken every outlying fort in the area and has lain siege to the city of Acre. I do not have the men at arms to go on the offensive. The best I can manage is to improve the cities strength and defend it to the last man. We must advise the Holy Father of our desperate situation and request a relief force ere all is lost."

Out of the corner of his eye, Byron saw the archbishop give a slight nod to Father Villhardain. In that moment, Byron understood the meaning of Brother Carl's admonition: Father Villhardain and the archbishop were planning something. Montferrat's presence here was no accident. He shot a look at Father Villhardain who smiled back at him. With the knowledge that a plan was about to be launched, he sat back to watch the churchmen's stratagem.

Conrad leaned forward. "Father Villhardain, I have been told that Rome sent you here to find religious relics. Have you found anything of interest?"

Father Villhardain smiled. "Depends on your interest, my son. I found a treasure trove of scrolls written at the time of Diocletian's persecution of Christian martyrs. I think I might have even found an original letter written by Saint Paul."

"Your work must be enthralling," Montferrat replied dryly. "War is upon us and the Church sends a priest to devote his time to such a useless pursuit."

"God wills it," Father Villhardain said. "Is that not the battle cry of those marked with the cross? And if God wills it, then looking for those things that guide us in doing God's will would not be a waste of time."

"Humph," Conrad snorted. "I have never been convinced that God's will is all that clear. Especially in light of our recent defeat. Which brings me to my request. You are close to the Holy Father. Is this so, Father Villhardain?"

Joscius glanced at Father Villhardain and then spoke, "It was the Holy Father who sent Father Villhardain here, if that is what you wish to know."

Montferrat leaned back in his chair and crossed his arms across his chest. "It is indeed. Father Villhardain, I know the relics of the past is your passion, but would you be willing to stop your work and undertake a journey to Rome. I need someone to deliver a message to his Holiness. The Holy Father needs to know how desperate our situation is, and I need someone who has the confidence of the Holy Father. I fear that if Rome does not come to our aid, Jerusalem will be lost by Christmas."

Father Villhardain nodded. "I hate the thought of stopping my research and traveling, but our situation is desperate." Father Villhardain paused. "I will go and do what I can. I will deliver your request and ask the Holy Father to call for another crusade."

"Father Villhardain," Joscius said, "your selflessness will be remembered and rewarded. The archbishop then paused. "Yet, I have concerns...Such a plan has merit... but there will be others who must be convinced. I am certain the Holy Father will seek advice from the cardinals. I am certain that the princes of the Church will want evidence."

"What evidence could the priest present?" Montferrat asked. "Do you intend for Father Villhardain to take Christian corpses with him and lay them at the Holy Father's feet?"

"Heavens no," Joscius replied. "No... we need a witness, someone who was there." The archbishop looked at Byron. "Sir Fitzwalter, you were there. You saw the battle. You know of the King's defeat."

Byron, tired and on his third glass of wine, was not paying attention. He had slumped in his chair and was quietly humming a tune, hoping that a minstrel would soon show up to play a ballad or two. He sat up and stammered. "Ah... yes, Your Grace, I was there."

"Then there! There is your witness, Father Villhardain," Joscius cried.

"You... Your... Your Grace," Byron stuttered, "my intention is to return to Jerusalem to fight Saladin. I can't go to Rome."

"Sir Fitzwalter, did you not swear an oath to fight the enemies of Christ. Are you not a soldier marked with the cross?"

"Yes, Your Grace...but."

"Sir Fitzwalter, I am an archbishop of the Church. Times are desperate; your service is needed in Rome, not in Jerusalem. The Lord of Tyre has reported that the roads are impassable. I am releasing you of your service to the Knights of Saint John of Jerusalem and commanding you to accompany Father Villhardain to

Rome. Do you not think that if your testimony raises an army that you have not done a great service?"

"Sir Fitzwalter," Montferrat added, "I am short of knights, but I am willing to release you as well."

Byron looked at the men seated at the table. His face was turning red as he felt his anger rising. He had sat back to watch the churchmen's stratagem, not realizing that he would also be a victim of their scheme. Doing his best to mask his anger, he said in a clipped voice, "I will go, but it weighs on my heart that I am not fulfilling my oath. I am abandoning my comrades in their hour of need." Byron took a sharp breath as he looked at the wall beside him. "But if you feel my service is needed in Rome, then I will go."

"A knight never turns away from a challenge," Montferrat replied, "but in this matter you will have done so with honor. The heralds may not shout your deed, but if an army rises from your bearing witness, then a mighty deed you have done."

Byron shifted uncomfortably in his chair. He and Father Villhardain had talked about Rome, but now he felt trapped. There was a war going on, and the fate of Jerusalem was uncertain. He had trained his whole life for this moment. He could make the difference in leading the defense of the city, and now he was being told to go a different direction, far away from the battle for God's holy city.

Montferrat turned to Father Villhardain. "How soon can you travel?"

"I will start making arrangements tomorrow." The priest glanced at the archbishop who nodded.

"God bless you, Father." Montferrat said. "We are on the edge of a catastrophe. I hope the Holy Father can do something ere it is too late." Montferrat stood up. "I must leave. I have too many pressing matters demanding my attention." He turned to the priest. "Father Villhardain, God's speed. May the wind be in your favor and the waves part before you as you sail in swift passage to the city of the Caesars." Montferrat turned to face Byron. "Sir Fitzwalter, I understand the restless desire for combat. Do not despair. You may not strike your enemies down one by one, but in

Rome, your testimony, in one swift stroke, might kill thousands." Montferrat turned and bowed to the archbishop. "Your Grace, you are a gracious host. I shall soon return the favor." Montferrat bowed to the archbishop and left the room.

Byron sat drumming his fingers on the table in irritation as he watched Montferrat leave. Rome. He did not want to go to Rome. He looked over at Father Villhardain who was deep in discussion with the archbishop about which ships would soon sail to Rome. He glanced at Brother Carl who was still eating. He rose to his feet. "Your Grace, thank you for the new attire and the excellent meal, but alas, it is time for me to take my leave."

Joscius looked up. "Sir Fitzwalter, I am sorry to see you leave so soon."

"Your Grace, it has been a long ride, and I find I am in need of rest."

"Then take your leave, and may your night be filled with dreamless slumber."

Byron bowed and left the great hall. A page jogged to catch up to him. "My lord, I will take you to your room."

"I can find my own way," Byron snapped.

Byron walked down the hall, flung open the door, and found himself standing in the courtyard. He glanced around angrily; he had taken a wrong turn. Night had fallen and the shadows of the columns stretched across the tile. In the center of the courtyard, he saw a marble basin, now grey in the evening light.

All was quiet, not even a whisper of wind disturbed the air. He walked over to the compluvium and glanced down into the water. His dark faceless shape stretched across the water. The silver beams of starlight encircled his shadow. He stood transfixed in thought. He was his own master. He could still ride to Jerusalem. He mulled it over. What to do? The archbishop could have him excommunicated. He looked again at the black shadow, and then with his hand, he slapped the water. As the ripples destroyed the image, he turned and went back to the hall.

"Damn it! Damn them all!" If he rode for Jerusalem, the Church would punish him. His journey had now changed towards Rome. After a few wrong turns he found his room. He threw the door open with a bang and stalked into the room. Ripping off his cloak, he flung it on the floor and then slumped into a chair muttering curses to himself.

He hated sailing. He hated the ocean. The journey to the Holy Lands had almost killed him. He had been so severely afflicted with seasickness he had almost died. Now, he would have to suffer the same miserable trip once again.

Byron sighed and rubbed his forehead. He felt a headache coming on. "Damn it," he swore as he stood up. He was tired and there was nothing he could do. He started to get ready for bed when he heard a knock at the door. Byron opened his door. "Father Villhardain."

"My son, may I enter?"

Byron motioned to a chair, and the priest came in and sat down. Byron pulled a chair from the corner of the room and sat down across from the priest.

"My son, I know that you are angered."

"You should have asked if I wished to go. You do not realize what you are asking."

"My son, it was not my desire to force you into going. The Lord of Tyre has forbidden any man of fighting age from leaving, and I need you in Rome. You were nothing more than a victim of circumstances."

"A victim of circumstance? How did fate come into this? You and the archbishop planned this, and you did not even ask if it was my desire to go. At least, do me the courtesy of telling me why!"

"My son, the Lord of Tyre brought up the idea of a delegation to Rome. In that moment, he was amenable to any request I might have." Father Villhardain shrugged. "In that moment, I had to ask for your release; otherwise, he might not have been so agreeable to losing a knight."

"And now I am fated to travel to Rome. The last sea journey almost cost me my life."

"My son, I understand you are angry, but listen to my tale before you decide that this journey is a waste of time. For the present, I will tell you enough to answer your questions as to why I need you. In the presence of the Holy Father you will learn more, but only when we are safely in the Lateran Palace."

Byron nodded. "I am listening, Father."

"Brother Carl and I belong to an order which takes its direction directly from the Holy Father. Most of our work involves investigating allegations of Church corruption, correcting heretical beliefs or practices. Anything that threatens the integrity of the Church. I had a second assistant, but he was in Tiberias when the city was surrounded. Since I have not heard from him, I fear the worst. Brother Aaron was a true and pious monk." Father Villhardain stood up and began to pace. "I have traveled to many places working for the Church. It might surprise you that I have been to England and the court of King Henry Plantagenet. It was many years ago when the Holy Father sent me to assist my mentor, Cardinal Morra, with the investigation of the murder of Thomas Becket, the Archbishop of Canterbury."

"I remember my father talking about that."

"Indeed, it was, and still is, a very troubling matter. The archbishop and the king had quarreled over who had authority to punish the clergy. The debate between the archbishop and Henry became heated, and in a fit of rage, Henry demanded 'who will rid me of this troublesome priest'. Much to Henry's regret, this statement set in motion the murder of the archbishop. Four of Henry's knights hearing their master's demand rode to the Cathedral of Canterbury where they slew the archbishop, dipping their brands in Saint Becket's holy blood. When His Holiness received the news that his archbishop had been murdered in his cathedral, he demanded an investigation."

"Yes, Father, I know."

"Indeed, you do. Henry wisely submitted to the judgment of the Church, and was scourged by the clergy of Canterbury. All night he suffered for the sin of his impetuous statement, and he further atoned by giving a large ransom to the church. That ransom has been used to pay for the current war against Saladin."

"Father, I have heard the story of the murder of Thomas Becket. That still does not explain why my presence is needed in Rome."

Father Villhardain smiled. "My son, do not be so impatient, I am getting to that point. Several years ago, I was given a new assignment. Before the Western half of the Roman Empire collapsed, part of the imperial treasury was sent out of the empire to keep it from falling into the hands of the Visigoths."

"Treasure. Like a treasure of gold?"

"Yes. All the gold the Emperor Honorius had on hand at the time of the Visigoth invasion."

"Where did it go?"

The priest leaned in close and whispered. "It is here, in the Levant."

"Why here? Why would anyone send such a treasure here? The Levant would be the last place I would have sent it."

Father Villhardain's blue eyes locked onto Byron with a piercing stare. "It was not sent here by the emperor. No. It was brought here without the emperor's consent."

Byron raised his eyebrows. "Who brought it?"

Father Villhardain, seeing the knight's interest, smiled. "It was brought here by the centurion who had been given the task of guarding the treasure."

"And what prey tell is a centurion?"

"A centurion was the rank of a Roman officer who commanded a century of men, which usually had eighty soldiers."

"I see," replied Byron. "So, where is this treasure's resting place?"

"My son, if you wish to know the answer, you must come to Rome with me. That is, if you wish to go with me to find it."

Byron sat back and looked at the priest with narrowed eyes. "Father, if the treasure is here, why go to Rome? Why not go and retrieve it now?"

"My son, it is not that easy. The treasure lies deep in Saracen lands. It will be a dangerous journey, and Saladin's war has complicated matters. I need men. Our recent defeat has made fighting men scarce. Only the Holy Father has the men and the supplies I need to bring the treasure back to Rome."

"What of the lords here? Would they not suffice to help you?"

"Would you trust them with an immense treasure of gold?"

Byron sighed. "No, Father... I would not."

"Indeed, neither would I. I need your help, Sir Fitzwalter. I want you to help me find Honorius' lost treasure and bring it back to Rome." Byron folded his arms across his chest and looked at the priest. "My son, this journey will be difficult and dangerous. But if we are successful, it could change the strategic situation here in Levant. I am even hopeful it could strengthen the Church's position to reestablish order in Europe. The west is mired in poverty, ignorance, and brutality. The Church could restore stability in Europe Think of what the treasure could do. It could bring about a new empire born from the darkness. A place where Christian values of love and charity are practiced; where enlightened thought is esteemed and respected."

"Father, I am not sure Europe is ready to embrace such ideals, nor will the kings willingly submit their authority to the Church." Byron sighed and glanced around as if looking for someone to give him an answer. "As a Knight of Saint John, I will do everything within my power to aid the Church." Byron sighed again. "My path is now clear. I will go with you to find the treasure."

"Fitzwalter, you have my thanks. In Rome, you can ask the Holy Father to intercede if breaking your vow troubles you."

"Father, it does, and if the Holy Father will hear me, I will ask for intercession."

"I am certain the Holy Father will hear you, especially if Cardinal Morra asks in your behalf. Tomorrow, I will begin working on securing passage to Rome. I will set up a meeting with His Holiness. Once we arrive, we will start arranging an expedition to go and retrieve the treasure. Montferrat is right. We are on the edge of a disaster. All I can do is pray to God that the gold is still there."

"Is there a chance it won't be there?"

"I don't know. Thieves could have found it long ago, but I think not. I don't think many would dare to touch it."

"And why is that, Father?"

"Because the place where the treasure lies is cursed."

"Cursed... cursed by God. Then Father why are we going? I will not risk eternal damnation."

"My son, that is another reason why we are going to see the Holy Father. If the Holy Father, Christ's representative on earth, blesses our expedition, then you need not fear. All will happen according to God's will. In Rome, such a treasure would confound our enemies by raising and equipping an army. Such an army marching beneath the papal banner would drive the Saracens from Jerusalem and the Holy Lands would have peace for all time." Father Villhardain stood up to leave. "I don't need to tell you how delicate this information is. I have placed great trust in you. Do not betray me."

"Father, you have my word. I will not breathe a word about this."

The old priest replied as he opened the bedroom door, "Good night. With God's blessing, and a little good luck, we will soon be in Rome."

Byron sat on the edge of the bed. After a while, he was just too tired to think any more, and he lay down and fell asleep.

CHAPTER 13
THE FAILURE OF HUSAM AL-DIN

Husam al-Din was camped on the outskirts of Nef. Nothing about the location elated him. Nef had nothing to offer other than dust and sand. He had chosen the place because of its central location between Acre and Tyre. He was convinced that the priest would flee to Tyre so he had focused his efforts on watching the roads leading to the city. At the same time, his master had surrounded Acre. He wanted to stay close to the army just in case Salah al-Din requested his presence.

A week earlier, Nef had been in the possession of the Christians. The crusader garrison had vowed to defend the city to the death, but as the Christians saw the dust rising from thousands of marching feet, they had chosen to abandon the city instead. It had taken days for the Saracen infantry and cavalry to pass through the town. Husam al-Din had been tempted to continue on to Acre. Acre would have been a pleasant oasis compared to Nef. He had his task, and he was hopeful Allah would favor him and that his men would quickly find the priest. Should that happen he was within a day's ride of Acre and if he hurried, he just might arrive in time to be part of the assault.

At the moment, he was sitting in the shade of his tent looking at the surrounding reddish-grey hills dotted with trees, wishing he was with his master preparing for the assault. He glanced at the deserted crusader castle that guarded the road. The walls were distorted by the waves of heat rising from the land. The castles battlements were empty and the open gate revealed a vacant courtyard littered with trash. He had thought about setting up his headquarters in the castle, but the heat was stifling and at least his tent allowed the cooling breeze to pass through.

He had sent his men to scour the lands in search of the priest, but his carefully crafted plans were going awry. It was proving difficult to find one man in the mass of humanity that was now traveling the roads, seeking the safety of the walls of Tyre. Husam al-Din had heard rumors that Tyre was on the verge of surrender, and he had been disappointed when news reached him that Conrad Montferrat had taken over the city's defense. Now that the great Byzantine general was in charge, all hope of an easy victory disappeared. Husam al-Din had no illusions of the number of Saracen lives it would cost before the city was once again in the sultan's control.

His men were straggling in from their search for the priest. Over the last several days, they had returned tired from the long miles of a fruitless search, but still Husam al-Din held out hope. He had sent two of his best men to watch the Tyre road. They had not returned, and Husam al-Din was optimistic that his men's absence was a good sign.

"I see you have ridden hard to find the priest."

Husam al-Din looked away from the crusader castle to see Isma'il standing in the shade of his tent. His second in command's face was streaked with dust and sweat. "What news do you bring?" replied Husam al-Din, ignoring the sarcasm of his second in command.

"None. No one has found your priest. We have ridden every road, every camel trail, searched every dung pile, and found nothing."

Husam al-Din closed his eyes and rubbed his forehead. "Then you need to go back and look again!"

"We have looked! He is nowhere to be found."

Husam al-Din opened his eyes and stared at Isma'il. "I must report to Salah al-Din. If you feel that your efforts are beyond reproach, then stay and rest in the comfort of your servant girl. Otherwise, you and your men get back on your horses and search again!"

Isma'il glared at Husam al-Din and then took a drink from his water skin. "Has Kamal and Fadil returned?"

"No, and I consider that a hopeful sign. The Tyre road is the priest's most likely route to take."

"Then you should have sent more men to watch that road."

Husam al-Din was about to reply when a dusty rider on horseback rode up to the tent and dismounted. Without ceremony, he handed Husam al-Din a letter. "From your father, Sheikh Abdul al-Subayil."

Husam al-Din took the letter. "Something for your trouble," Husam al-Din replied, handing the man two coins. The man bowed.

"You are very gracious, my lord. Do you have a letter for me to take back?"

"Not yet. I will read this and then decide." Husam al-Din turned to Isma'il. "Take our guest and offer him some refreshment after his long ride."

"Is that before or after I leave to search for your missing priest," Isma'il snapped.

"Before," replied Husam al-Din as he ripped open the letter.

"Come," growled Isma'il. "Be thankful you only have to make a ride back to the sheikh." Isma'il turned and stalked out of Husam al-Din's tent.

Husam al-Din ignored Isma'il's departure and sat down at the wooden box which served as his desk to read his father's letter:

Beloved son,

News has reached me that you have won glory on the battlefield and have upheld our family name. I am pleased that the sultan has found your service satisfactory, and it was with great joy that I learned of your triumph over the wicked infidels at Hattin. It is therefore unfortunate that I must be the bearer of bad news.

I received your letter requesting assistance in finding a Christian priest. I found your request surprising, but the sultan must have his purpose. I have sent letters to all of my trusted business associates. I also sent a letter to Jabbar ibn-Yasir al-Harthi who resides in the city of Tyre. He recently responded by sending a pigeon with a letter declaring that your priest is safely within the walls of Tyre and that a Christian knight slew two of your men on the Tyre road.

Husam al-Din gasped and then slammed the letter down on the box.

"Damn it!" The priest was in Tyre. He leaned forward with his head in his hands, anguishing over the loss of his men and his failure to capture the priest. After several minutes of mourning his loss, he picked up the letter and continued reading.

Jabbar ibn-Yasir al-Harthi of Tyre is a wealthy and a very untrustworthy brother of our faith. It would be wise, should you have to deal with him in person, that you take those you can rely on, and that you make sure you never impart to him the honorable duty that the sultan has bestowed upon you.

Jabbar assures me that he is working diligently to find out more information about the infidel priest of the nonbeliever. He professes to me that he is a good servant of Allah and his prophet, and he is doing all within his power to assist the effort to expel these foreign invaders from our lands.

My beloved and faithful son, I warn you that I do not trust Jabbar's intentions. He has never been a faithful servant of Allah, and I fear that only the promise of an earthly reward will produce the information you seek.

As a man seeking to be a true servant of Allah and his prophet, I am making a sacrifice by sending Jabbar a large sum of money to ensure his best efforts in providing you the necessary assistance you will need. I pray that we can soon cleanse our lands and our holy places of the infidel invaders.

My son, be vigilant in following the teachings of the Prophet. Be faithful in your duty to the Great Sultan that Allah has raised up to lead our people, and rejoice in the great honor that he selected you above all others to be of service.

Above all, take care so you can return a hero to your aged father who has always esteemed you, and so he may look upon you once more with great joy.

Your Father

The grave misgivings that had first occurred to him when the sultan bestowed the so-called "honor" were now starting to reveal themselves. Husam al-Din had received a summons yesterday from the sultan to come to Acre and report on his progress. Well, he now had something to report. Failure.

He walked to the entrance of his tent. "Isma'il," he shouted, "our plans have changed. Have my horse readied and prepare yourself. We are going to see the sultan. Tell the courier I have a message to take back to my father."

He might as well get this over. He decided it would be wise to take Isma'il with him, just in case his company abruptly needed a new commander. He drafted a letter thanking his father and closed it by asking his father to remember him kindly in his prayers. He walked out of his tent. A servant was holding his dapple-grey horse. The horse nudged Husam al-Din with his nose as the knight patted the horse's neck, smoothing down the black mane.

"El-Marees has missed you, my lord," the servant said as he bowed.

"I have missed him as well. It has been several days since our last ride."

When the horses were ready, he gave the letter to the courier.

"Why are we going to see the sultan?" Isma'il asked.

Husam al-Din sighed. "Kamal and Fadil are dead. The priest has made it to the safety of Tyre. He is most likely at this moment sailing away."

Isma'il's mouth sagged open. "Kamal is dead?"

Husam al-Din paused. "Yes. I am sorry Isma'il. He was killed by a Christian on the Tyre road."

Isma'il's face turned white as he turned and pointed a finger at Husam al-Din's chest. "I told you. You should have sent more men!"

"Yes, so it appears," Husam al-Din said as he stepped into the stirrup and swung into the saddle. "Come, I have to deliver these ill tidings to the sultan." Isma'il stood holding his horse, staring at Husam al-Din. Husam al-Din rode near to Isma'il and looked down at his lieutenant. "Nothing will change what has happened. It was Allah's will. Come, I must report to the sultan."

Isma'il sighed and then nodded. Mounting his horse, he turned and followed Husam al-Din to Acre. They rode in silence. Husam al-Din brooding on what he was going to tell the sultan. Isma'il said nothing.

As they approached Acre, a pall of black smoke hung over the city. In the distance, thousands of Saracen soldiers moved in formation, the sun flashing on their armor as they marched into position to surround the city. Husam al-Din sat on his horse and scanned the battlefield. Behind the lines of the main army, the engineers worked to erect the trebuchets, to hurl massive stones against the city walls. In front of the trebuchets, ranks of archers stood ready with their bows as they prepared to shower the city with arrows to keep the Christians from defending the walls. There was no doubt that the Christian commander was also watching the spectacle.

After a moment of watching, Husam al-Din and Isma'il turned and rode to the golden tent of Salah al-Din. Husam al-Din dismounted and handed the reins to Isma'il. "Hold my horse until I return. If I do not return, may Allah be more merciful to you than he was to me."

Isma'il started to speak, but Husam al-Din held up his gauntleted hand, turned, and strode to the entrance of Salah al-Din's tent where he waited for a few moments before being admitted into the sultan's presence. Salah al-Din was standing in the shade of the tent, which had its side rolled up so he could watch his army's preparation for the assault on the city.

He turned and greeted the knight. "Husam al-Din, do you bring good news?"

Husam al-Din blanched. "No, Great Sultan, I only bear news of failure."

Salah al-Din gave the knight an icy stare. "Tell me of this failure."

"Great Sultan, the priest has made it safely to Tyre..... I apologize. I sent two of my best men to guard the Tyre road, but the priest was in the protection of a knight who slew both of my men, Kamal and Fadil."

"And, where were you?" asked the sultan.

"Great Sultan, I was in Nef."

"You were in Nef?" The sultan scowled.

"Great Sultan, I was directing the search."

Salah al-Din sighed. "If you thought the main road to Tyre was that important, then you should have been there!"

Husam al-Din looked down. "Yes, Great Sultan."

"Tell me about Tyre."

"Conrad de Montferrat defends the city. None of my men can get in."

"So, I have heard," the sultan replied. "I expected Tyre to fall, but Montferrat has thwarted my negotiations. His father is my prisoner. Perhaps that will give me some leverage."

"Yes, Great Sultan," Husam al-Din answered. "The only good news I have is my father's contact in Tyre is in the process of gathering more information about the priest and what he is doing."

Saladin thoughtfully stroked his beard. "The priest is in the city?"

"Yes, Great Sultan."

"Hmm, and he is accompanied by a knight who bested two of your men?"

Husam al-Din nodded. "He must be a skilled crusader. My men were experienced fighters."

"Too bad," the sultan grumbled as he looked away and stared out at his army as it moved into position. "How do you intend to repair your failure?"

Husam al-Din took a deep breath. "I can only wait for my father's associate to report the priest's departure and destination." Salah al-Din was about to speak when a servant entered the tent and bowed.

Salah al-Din motioned to the servant to speak. "Great Sultan," the servant said, "al-Afdal sends his greetings. He wishes to know if you want to continue assembling the siege towers."

"No. Tell him to wait. I sent the Christians an offer to surrender. If they agree, I don't want to spend time disassembling them before the next march."

"Yes, Great Sultan, I will inform the prince of your desire." The servant bowed and backed out of the tent.

Salah al-Din turned back to Husam al-Din. "Where were we? Oh yes, your plan. What is your alternative?"

"We could assassinate him. That would keep the treasure out of Christian hands."

"No!" Salah al-Din snapped. "I want this treasure in my possession. Wait for your father's spy to make his report. Once we know what the priest is doing, we will act accordingly. The treasure is here in the Levant. He will return."

"Yes, Great Sultan, but he could return at any location. How would we know when and where?"

"Husam al-Din, with the victory at Hattin I now control this war. Think. Why does the priest need to leave?"

Husam al-Din paused. "The priest will have difficulty finding the men necessary to help him. The Christian lords will not release their retainers."

"Yes."

"He needs to return to Rome. Only the infidel Pope has the power to raise resources to aid the Church."

The sultan smiled. "Very good."

"But that does not help us find him."

"What if I leave one Christian port unmolested? What If I left, say... Alexandretta alone? Do you not think that would be an inviting place for the priest to return?"

"Yes, Great Sultan."

"And the only road that leads to our land passes through?"

"Aleppo."

Salah al-Din smiled. "Ah, yes. Aleppo. I will send messages to my other son to be on guard for anything unusual. We shall set a trap and we will wait."

"Yes, Great Sultan, but what if the priest returns to Tyre? Would he not return there to seek Montferrat's aid? That port still remains in Christian hands?"

Salah al-Din dipped his chin as he fixed his dark eyes on Husam al-Din. "Then pick a central place to wait. You have a spy in Tyre, do you not?"

Husam al-Din bowed. "Yes, Great Sultan." Salah al-Din waved his hand to dismiss him.

As Husam al-Din started to back out of the tent, Salah al-Din spoke, "Husam al-Din I suspect you were afraid to come and give me what you consider bad news." Husam al-Din stopped and nodded. "I gave you a difficult task, but I did not expect miracles. All things in war are uncertain, and I know this. Someday, perhaps when you are in a position like mine, you will remember this. You must accept bad news with the good. Your servants must be able to bring you the unvarnished news of failure, as well as news of success."

"Yes, Great Sultan."

"It is a fine line between fear and respect. Your servants must respect you while they fear your wise and just decisions. If they are slothful, derelict, or deceitful, you must act to correct their misbehavior. But if you give a task to a man that is beyond his capabilities, then whose fault is it when the task fails?"

"The task giver, Great Sultan."

"Indeed. If my servants misrepresent the true state of affairs, then a disastrous decision could be the result. Always be wary of men who only bring good news and are too cowardly to tell you when things have gone badly."

The sultan smiled. "Now that you understand, go do my bidding." Husam al-Din bowed and backed out of the tent.

Isma'il was looking down, pacing as Husam al-Din approached. Isma'il looked up. "What did the sultan say?"

"We have more work to do. We shall find this priest, and we will avenge Kamal and Fadil."

"The priest and all those with him will die a painful death," Isma'il growled.

"Indeed, they shall," Husam al-Din said as he mounted El-Marees and began the ride back to their camp.

CHAPTER 14
SIR JAMES HUGH MARTEL

Byron awoke to the sun pouring through the dust-streaked windows of his room. He was tired. He lay in bed for a moment debating if he should get up. At last, he rose. He washed his face, then dressed and walked out into the hallway in search of the smoke kitchen.

A grey haired monk, withered and bent, approached him. The monk bowed. "My lord, are you Sir Byron Fitzwalter?"

"Yes, friar," Byron said as he nodded.

"My lord, the archbishop sends his greetings. He and Father Villhardain have gone to the port in search of a ship to take you to Rome. They will be gone all day. His Eminence asked me to make sure you got breakfast."

"You are gracious," replied Byron with a smile.

The monk screwed up his face in a scowl. "Humph, it was not my choice, and after you see the smoke kitchen... you will question the favor."

Byron tilted his head and looked at the monk. "I have seen kitchens before."

The monk chuckled. "Well, I leave you to judge the favor then, follow me." Byron walked slowly, trying to keep pace with the old monk's shuffling gait. He knew he was drawing near the kitchen as the smell of smoke from the cooking fires grew stronger. The monk opened the door. "See for yourself, my lord."

The whitewashed walls of the kitchen were stained with soot from the large open hearth that stretched across the back of the room. In the hearth, a fire burned beneath two black iron kettles. A serving wench in a dirty brown dress was stirring the pot. In the center of the room was a large wooden table. At the far end of the table, a cook in a stained black robe with wide sleeves was wielding a cleaver, beheading chickens. Four other cooks, stripped to the waist, were plucking feathers from a pile of dead birds.

Byron stepped into the sweltering room, avoiding the feathers that covered the floor. Thunk! The cleaver fell as the cook severed a chicken's head from its body. The head fell to the floor. The cook wiped his brow and tossed the bird on the pile of dead chickens. The headless chicken, as did Lazarus hearing his master's call, rose from its deathbed and ran down the table. Reaching the end, it fell to the floor, tottered in a circle and took off again across the blood-soaked tiles. The cook dropped his cleaver and gave chase. Blood sprayed the walls as the headless bird ran towards the serving wench who was stirring the boiling pots. She lunged at it and with a shriek, fell sprawling across the floor. The cook, in close pursuit, could not stop. Tripping over the woman, he crashed into the wall.

The old monk started to laugh. The chicken was now running towards the door. Byron grabbed a nearby copper pot and slapped it down over the headless bird.

"Wonderful work, my lord," the old monk cried. "You have caught your breakfast!"

Byron put his boot on the pot, holding it firmly to the floor. A dull thumping came from the pot. As the thumps subsided, Byron surveyed the carnage and then looked at the pot. "I think I have lost my appetite for fowl. I think a loaf of bread and some cheese will do, and a different place to eat."

The monk, still chuckling, carefully crossed the kitchen floor. Taking a loaf of stale bread and a large piece of cheese from the larder, he retraced his steps. The cook rubbed his head and groaned as he got up. Reaching out his hand, he helped the wench from the floor.

The monk handed Byron the loaf of bread and the cheese. "Brother Knight, take these and go with this blessing.

"*Benedic, Domine, nos et haec tua dona quae de tua largitate sumus sumpturi. Per Christum Dominum nostrum. Amen.*"

Byron raised his head. "Thank you, friar, for your hospitality."

The monk smiled as he made the sign of the cross. "My lord, you have earned this. If it were not for you, the bird would have escaped and who knows what further misadventure it would have caused."

†

Byron ate his morning breakfast alone in the large hall. When he had finished, he went back to his room and buckled on his sword. He picked up his double-bladed dagger and drawing it from its sheath, he checked the blade. The dagger had been a gift. The black hilt was polished and wrapped with wire. Long steel quillons formed the hilt guard protected the wielders hand. Near the hilt, the blade was engraved with the word, Numbers, followed by the Roman numerals six, twenty-four, and twenty-six. He had always wondered at the significance, but he had never asked anyone, least he show his ignorance.

He sheathed the knife and thrust the dagger into his belt. He never walked the streets without the weapon. He stopped to check on Brother Carl, who let him know that he was looking forward to spending time alone. After ensuring he was free to spend his time as he saw fit, he made his way to the front door and out into the street.

He walked the narrow stone street, keeping a wary eye for thieves. Beggar children crowded around him and he tossed a few coins to clear his path. It grew hot, and Byron was starting to regret bringing his cloak. As he neared the center of Tyre, the street became more crowded. He stopped at the corner of an old sandstone building, not wanting to be subjected to the press of the peasants.

The city was alive. Frightened refugees set upon the marketplace to buy food. Local merchants, who normally crowded into the street to attract customers, were fighting to keep looters out of their shops. Byron watched from a distance, his hand resting on the hilt of his sword. Those who saw him, feared to accost him, but this was only temporary. It was dangerous to be here. A cry went up as Montferrat's soldiers came marching into the market to restore order. This was not his fight, and he turned to go. He had no desire to watch the heavy hand of authority as it put the serfs back into their place.

Byron thought he heard someone calling his name. He turned back to see the soldiers rushing the crowd.

"Fitzwalter!"

From the midst of the crowd, he saw a knight in the blue surcoat of the Marshal of Jerusalem. He looked closer and saw that it was his friend, James Martel. James started shoving to clear a path, but the peasants, with no place to go, pushed back. James, cursing, drew his sword and grasping the blade with his other hand, began to wield the weapon as a baton to force his way through the human mass. The peasants gave way, except one recalcitrant knave who James delivered a blow to his head that sent the man staggering out of his path. Clear of the mob, James sheathed his sword and came jogging up.

"Well, I'll be damned, it is you! I thought you were dead."

Byron smiled. "No, not dead.... surprisingly."

James looked at his friend. "No, you look remarkably well... at least for you."

Byron glared at James. "It is good to see you too."

James laughed. "When the news arrived in Jerusalem of the disaster at Hattin, it was said no one escaped alive. I feared that I had lost my friend, but I am glad to see that has turned out to be false." James paused, as he shook his head in disbelief. "I can't believe you are here in Tyre."

"Humph, I can't believe that either. My intent was to ride to Jerusalem, but alas, my plans have changed."

The right corner of James' mouth turned up in a sarcastic smile. "That is well. Your ride to Jerusalem would have been short and fatal. The Saracens have cut roads to the city. No one gets in and no one gets out." James looked at Byron's face and then paused. "I see that is not what changed your plans. There is some strange story here. Do you have time to tell your tale?"

"At the moment," Byron looked over at the serfs running from the market place as Montferrat's soldiers chased them, "I do."

James stopped. "Is Lord Beauvallet with you?"

Byron shook his head. "He lives no more."

James glanced down. "I see. He was a worthy man." Byron nodded. James changed the subject. "Let's sit on the wall by the sea, and you can tell me your story."

The two knights made their way to the old rock wall to sit and talk. In the distance, the forbidding walls of the island fortress of new Tyre cast its shadow over the water. Byron could see men working on the causeway, the mole of Alexander, as they worked to destroy the bridge that connected the Island to the old city of Tyre.

James sat quietly listening to Byron tell the story of the battle of Hattin. Byron had grown. James thought back to the first time they met, on the streets of Jerusalem.

†

James had been busy with his own affairs and had no time for new comers from Europe, let alone a poor Norman knight from a place such as Ireland. As James had approached him on the narrow street, he had sized him up as a country knight, whose questionable lineage was probably slightly better than a commoner.

In comparison, James Hugh Martel was a relative of the Duke of Loraine, a descendant of Charlemagne. He could trace his lineage all the way back to Charles the Hammer. Inwardly, he had scoffed at Byron, dressed in an outlandish blue wool cloak, the white crusaders cross poorly stitched onto the garment. James had been on his way to meet the Constable of Jerusalem, and as he approached the country knight, he had given him a dismissive nod. The Constable, Aimery of Lusignan, was not a patient man and James knew he should not be late. But as he walked past the country knight, he could tell that the man was lost and the look of distress on Byron's face filled James with pity, and he had stopped.

The impulsive, gregarious side of his character had won out; the constable could wait. Despite James' high lineage, he was not unkind. He reached out his hand to the lowly newcomer and welcomed him to the Holy Lands. From that moment, James became the teacher and Byron his protégé. James, born in the Holy Lands, had been a crusader all of his life. Skilled in the art of fighting in the Levant, James had passed on to Byron the necessary expertise that made the crusaders of Outremer a first-rate fighting force. It was not long after that first meeting that James had been rewarded for his kindness.

Riding in the vanguard to a skirmish with Saracen raiders, James had been cut off from the rest of the crusader cavalry. The dust swirled in the air as six Saracen knights circled him, drawing their noose ever tighter, their black robes, like spectral wings, fluttered behind them. In the distance, behind his circling attackers, the two opposing bodies of horsemen crashed into each other with the shattering of lances. No one could see him, nor could his comrades come to his aid.

Turning his horse, he had set his lance. Not that it mattered, the nimble Arab horses were faster and the chances of bringing down the Saracens closing in upon him was remote. All seemed forlorn as James prepared for the inevitable. It was at this grim moment that Byron had recklessly rammed his horse into the side of one of Saracen's mounts, knocking the Arab horse to the ground. The Saracens, confused by the sudden attack, had scattered, opening up an avenue of escape. James smiled at the memory as he listened to his friend recount his deeds on the battlefield of Hattin.

†

When Byron's tale had reached the fight on the road to Tyre, James interrupted. "Was that you, Fitzwalter? That story has gone all through the city. The tale is, you killed five Saracens in a wild mêlée after you were ambushed."

Byron shook his head. "People will believe anything. No, I defeated two, and it could have easily gone the other way."

"No, people don't believe everything. They just want to hope things aren't as bad as they really are."

"Well, unfortunately the dreadful truth is now upon them. There is no escape." Byron looked at his friend. "Why are you here? And why are you in the company of Montferrat's men? Should you not be in Jerusalem?"

A grim look came over James' handsome face. "Indeed, I should. There are only thirteen knights left in Jerusalem to defend the city. When the master of the city finally learned the truth that stragglers were retreating to Tyre, it was hoped that the bulk of the army might have escaped to the safety of this city. The city master sent me to Tyre with a message for Montferrat, requesting aid, believing the rumor that the army might still be intact. It was a dangerous ride, and I rode as swiftly as my horse could run. I arrived here, two days ago and met with Lord Montferrat." James looked around. "I am sad to say that rumor proved false. Montferrat was sympathetic to our plight, but in the end, he has no one to spare."

"I feasted with him last night. Things are grim indeed. Especially if a knight with your lineage and reputation is now chasing serfs out of the market place."

James tilted his head back and laughed. "My friend, that was an accident. I happened to be in the company of Lord Montferrat when a messenger arrived with the news that the peasants were rioting. Montferrat asked me to accompany D'Auvay to crush...the insurrection," James said with a hint of sarcasm, "and so, here I am."

"Indeed, and here we are chasing rioting peasants while Jerusalem fights alone and unaided. So, what do you think Saladin will do next?"

"Ah! Saladin," James said with a smile, "that devilishly clever infidel. I don't know. What I do know is, when I tried to return to Jerusalem with Montferrat's answer, the roads were full of Saracen soldiers. My friend, I had a real opportunity to achieve martyrdom. You slew two on the Tyre road? I could have slain a hundred Saracens and what a glorious battle that would have been... but alas, there were thousands. Despite my prowess with a blade, a thousand is just too many for me alone, and what good is being a martyr? When I go down fighting, I want a witness so that the minstrels will someday be able to sing the song of James Martel."

Byron laughed. "The song of James Martel. I wonder if there is anyone good enough to sing such a melody."

"Probably not," James snorted. "So, I passed on the opportunity for my head to grace the top of a Saracen's lance and rode as fast as I could back to Tyre!"

"Do you think Saladin will take Acre?"

"I fear so. Saladin is fiendishly clever. He has been using a powerful weapon."

"And what is this new weapon?" Byron asked, knowing the Saracens fondness for engineering.

James gave a disgusted look. "Generosity. That devil of a Saracen is being generous."

"Generous?"

"Generous," James repeated. "Yes, he shows up with his army, surrounds the fort or town, and sends one of his men to parley. The lord of the city comes out, and the nice Saracen lad tells the lord, 'the Sultan Saladin will grant you safe passage to Christian lands if you surrender. You can take all of your men at arms, your people, and your possessions. Refuse the sultan's generous terms and he will kill every man, woman, and child and burn this place to the ground.' The lord of the fort or city ponders this request for a moment, looks at the vast army of bloodthirsty infidels surrounding him, and replies, 'I surrender under those terms'. And that, my friend, is how, without much fuss or fighting, Saladin is taking over the Kingdom."

Byron sat pondering the implication. No wonder Saladin was making such incredible progress. Saladin was preserving his army for the important battles, while causing the Christians to give up valuable fortresses through a show of overwhelming force. With the main Christian Army destroyed, the forts were worthless.

James smiled as the look of realization crossed his friend's face. "Saladin's no fool. Jerusalem's days are numbered and so are the Kingdom's. Which brings me back to my question, what made you change your plans to ride to Jerusalem?"

Byron sighed. "I was ensnared by the archbishop and Lord Montferrat. Last night, and much against my desire, I was chosen to accompany a priest to Rome."

James tilted his head back as he gave Byron a quizzical look. "Why Rome?"

"Montferrat has asked the priest to deliver an appeal to the Holy Father requesting a new crusade. I am going to Rome to give an account of the defeat at Hattin." Byron paused, seeing the doubtful look on James' face. He drew close to James and pressed on in a low voice. "But that is not the only reason. This priest is laboring on an important endeavor for the Church and our Christian cause. He told me last night of his work. It could win the war. You should come with me. Another sword would be welcome."

James laughed. "Aid the Church? You surely jest. Fitzwalter, this priest has beguiled you. The Church has beguiled us all. Christ on a stick! Fitzwalter, the Church has betrayed us all. Do you really believe all the bloodshed, murder, and rape will be forgiven because the Church has granted indulgences?" James laughed bitterly. "I think not. Not that it matters now. Your priest says he can win the war. What good will it do these people? Those who are delaying the inevitable by fleeing to Tyre." James chuckled mirthlessly. "Whatever mysticism this priest is conjuring, it will not be instantaneous, or for that matter, bloodless. No indeed. A lot of men will yet die before war tires of this land." James shook his head. "There is no turning back. We are now fighting for our survival. There will be no surrender, and there will be no mercy."

"James this is not magic. This is real, and it will work... I swear it! It will save Jerusalem."

"Save it, how?"

"I cannot say," Byron stuttered. "Would you at least be willing to meet the priest and see if he would be willing to take another knight with him?"

James looked at Byron for a moment and thought about the

first meeting. The man across from him was now a battle tested knight wearing the black cloak of the Hospitaller, its white cross neatly sewn upon the shoulder. Beneath this mantle, was the black tunic emblazoned with the Maltese cross. Symbols of service and valor.

James laughed. "Fitzwalter, I don't know. I was thinking of returning to France."

"If you are leaving, then come with me. You will have the opportunity for some adventure."

"Adventure," James repeated as if he hated the word. "Adventure is for fools and the soon to be dead. I have had enough of adventure. The adventure that brought me to Tyre almost got me killed."

"Yes, but if you come with me, you will have something to show for your valor. Here, there is just death and a forgotten grave. Byron motioned to the peasants near them. "These people are not fleeing to this place because they want to. Can't you feel the fear in the air?"

"I feel it. That is why I think it is time to return to the land of my ancestors," replied James. His handsome face frowned as he looked around at the few peasants who had taken refuge near the waterfront. "Priests are too serious, too dull, and usually disapprove of my pursuits. As I see it, the chances of my life being short... well... it is highly likely, so I intend to have the best time I can as long as the women are willing, the wine is good, and my money lasts. Priests, on the other hand, disapprove of anything resembling the pleasures of life."

"James, come with me," Byron said shaking his head. "I would welcome your company, and this journey will be worth your time."

James paused again, taking his time to survey the wretched refugees. The peasants were dirty. Their garments reflected the miles traveled to reach the refuge of Tyre. James could see the lines of worry and stress in their faces as they huddled in groups discussing the uncertain future of slavery or death should Saladin take the city. James felt pity for them, but it was beyond his means to aid them. He had already taken a great risk to ride to Tyre, on the vain hope reinforcements would be sent to break the army of Saladin at the walls of Jerusalem. There was nothing left to do but wait for the end to come.

"Byron, I will talk to your priest, but I make no promises without hearing more." He scanned the beach and shook his head. "There is no reason to stay. There is not one pretty maiden in sight."

Byron looked up at the sky. The afternoon was getting late, perhaps Father Villhardain had returned. "Let us go then and have you meet Father Villhardain."

The two men got up from their seat on the rock wall and began walking back to the residence of the archbishop. Byron had a strange sensation of power as the common people scrambled to get out of the way of the two knights at the height of their skill and strength. It was an intoxicating feeling and the knight had to remind himself that such feelings were in actuality a sin.

When they arrived at the house of the archbishop, Byron told his friend to wait in the Vestibulum of the Domus while he went to find Father Villhardain. He searched the hallways, but everywhere he looked the priest was nowhere to be found. At last, Byron stopped. He was about to give up when he heard a voice speaking in French coming from the great hall.

"Behold, the days come, saith the Lord, that I will make a new covenant with the house of Israel, and with the house of Judah:" Byron tilted his head listening. "Not according to the covenant that I made with their fathers in the day that I took them by the hand to bring them out of the land of Egypt; which my covenant they break, although I was a husband unto them, saith the Lord:"

Byron recognized the voice of Father Villhardain.

"But this shall be the covenant that I will make with the house of Israel; after those days, saith the Lord, I will put my law in their inward parts, and write it in their hearts; and I will be their God, and they shall be my people."

He reached the doorway and paused in the shadow of the door to listen. His head bowed, a secret listener, eavesdropping on the priest's private musings. "And they shall teach no more every man his neighbor, and every man his brother, saying, Know the Lord: for they shall all know me, from the least of them unto the greatest of them, saith the Lord: for I will forgive their iniquity, and I will remember their sin no more."

Father Villhardain grew silent, and at last, Byron knocked on the doorjamb. "May I enter, Father?"

"Indeed, come in, my son," the priest said pleasantly. Father Villhardain was sitting at the table. His bible rested on the table next to him, closed.

"Father, I heard you speaking aloud. Who were you talking to?"

Father Villhardain smiled. "Ah...I was speaking to no one. No, I was reciting Jeremiah. I love to hear it in French. I like to do that sometimes when I am tired, or discouraged. But enough of that. You have returned, what do you think of Tyre?"

"Father, the town is in chaos and the serfs are frightened and unruly."

Father Villhardain nodded. "A sign of the times I am afraid."

"Yes, well I dare say it is. I met an old friend, Sir James Martel, a knight in the service of the Marshal of Jerusalem. He is the messenger from Jerusalem that Montferrat spoke of last night. He is caught here with nothing to do. He is a good friend and a brave man. I thought perhaps you might have need for another knight for your quest."

The old priest sat back in his chair and examined Byron's face. "Do you trust him?" asked the priest.

"Yes, I trust him. When I first arrived in the Holy Lands, I was alone and friendless. James befriended me, when it was not in his interest to do so. He gave me good counsel on the art of war. I have fought in many battles with him. He is an honorable and chivalrous knight, although that does not do justice to praising his martial prowess."

The priest's blue eyes bored into Byron. "Would he be tempted by gold to betray his friends?"

"No... James?.... No," Byron shook his head. "Gold has no hold on James. If the question was about women...well they seem to enjoy his attentions. No, he would fight to the bitter end to protect his word, his honor, and his friends."

Father Villhardain paused for a moment. "I will meet him," the priest said thoughtfully.

"Where do you want me to bring him?"

"Bring him here." Byron nodded, turned, and left the room. He returned to the main entrance and found James waiting for him.

Father Villhardain was reading when both men entered the hall. He looked up at the knights as he slowly closed his bible. James was taller than Byron. He was clean-shaven, although a dark shadow of a beard was starting to appear, making his square jaw more prominent. His dark hair, cut short, curled in wisps, cascading like waves on a dark sea. James smiled graciously; his perfect teeth, unusual for the time, flashed white in contrast with his deeply tanned face, but as James smiled, Father Villhardain also saw the twinkle of mischief in those deep dark eyes, and he understood why Byron spoke of women desiring James' attention.

"Father Villhardain, this is my friend, Sir James Hugh Martel."

"My lord, please sit. Are you a relation to Charles Martel, the Hammer, Grandfather of Charlemagne?"

James nodded as he sat down in a chair and leaned casually back. He was dressed in a light blue tunic, embroidered in gold with the cross of the Kingdom of Jerusalem. Over this tunic was a light blue cloak clasped at the throat, with a broach shaped like a silver eagle. He wore grey tights, stuffed into a pair of tan boots that were turned down at the top.

"I am a distant relative of Charles Martel, the man who saved France, but my glorious lineage is somewhat diminished by my present circumstances."

"I see," Father Villhardain replied. "So, how long have you crusaded in the Holy Lands?"

"I was born here. My great, great, great, grandfather took the cross and came with the first crusade along with his kin, Godfrey of Bouillon, the Duke of Lower Lorraine. I have lived here all my life."

"So, you are familiar with the customs of the Saracens and the politics of the Kingdom?"

James nodded. "My father was a member of the king's council. As far as the customs of Saracens, one cannot live here without being aware of what is considered good manners."

"I had to spend a good deal of time learning the manners and customs myself, but it is time well spent if you wish to accomplish anything in these lands. Fitzwalter tells me you might wish to aid me in my work," Father Villhardain said in Arabic. "Do you have a desire to serve the Church?"

James smiled and then replied in Arabic. "Fitzwalter told me some vague story about a task given to you by the Church. I was considering returning to France, but if your work interests me, I could change my plans." Byron shifted on his feet uncomfortably.

"My son, I cannot tell what my task is. At least not here. I will say, that the road I intend to travel will be filled with hardship and it will lead deep into Saracen lands. If you come with me, I have nothing to offer you, other than your service will be a great work that will be remembered in heaven."

James frowned. "Hmm, we shall see what heaven remembers. Father, I lived here all my life, and I know the hardships of the desert. I have crusaded against the enemies of Christ in the land of thirst. There is nothing you can say about these lands or the Saracens that will cause me to shrink away or abandon my friend, but for me to give you a commitment, I must know if your quest is worthy of my time."

"As I told Byron, when we are safe in Rome, I will reveal the purpose of our quest."

"Father, it is my experience that when such secrecy is required, so is great valor. You have my interest." James looked around the room and then fixed his gaze upon Byron. "I will at least travel to Rome. If I find that your quest is worthy of my aid, then I will join your company."

"My son, I must warn you, if there are any earthly rewards, it will be up to the Holy Father. I myself am poor, and so I can give you nothing."

James frowned. "Rewards don't interest me."

"That is well. It is likely your death will be your reward."

James smiled. "Then, Father, nothing has changed has it?"

"No, my son. Is there anyone who will miss you if you leave with us?"

James shifted uncomfortably in his chair. "My family died of the plague many years ago. No one remains but me."

"I am sorry to hear that."

"Nothing to be sorry for, Father. There is nothing that can be done. When they died, I was left with nothing. I was not of age, and my family's lands were enfeoffed to my uncles, including my father's titles. My only inheritance is what I have achieved by the sword, and I must confess that is a precarious way to live."

"It is the times we live in," the priest said.

James nodded. "Father, Byron has also told me you are traveling to Rome to deliver a request to the Holy Father."

"Yes, my son. I intend to leave as soon as the arrangements can be made. I assume Sir Martel, you can be spared from your previous commitments."

James sat back in his chair and an odd smile crossed his face. "Father, my commitments ended when I could not return to Jerusalem."

"Good. Do you have any equipment you need to retrieve?"

"My armor and other gear remain at the inn," James replied. "I also have my horse and saddle."

Father Villhardain frowned. "You must sell your horse or give him to the archbishop to keep, should you return."

"I will see what can be done. Selling a horse might be difficult."

Father Villhardain nodded. "You will need to sell him by tomorrow. We are leaving the day after."

"So be it. Can you release Fitzwalter? I need to get my accoutrements, armor, and weapons."

Father Villhardain nodded. "If you need more help, you can ask Brother Carl."

"That will not be necessary. Fitzwalter's aid will be sufficient."

†

Byron was pleased with himself as he and James passed through the gate and into the street. Events were going his way. He glanced down at a small Arab boy wearing a brown sack tied at the waist with a rope. Reaching into the pocket of his cloak, he pulled out a silver penny and tossed it to the boy. Fate had been generous to him and he decided it would be best to pass the generosity along.

"There you go lad," he said as he walked by.

"What was your impression of Father Villhardain?" Byron asked once he was past the boy.

"Frankly, he impressed me." James stopped walking and turned to face Byron. "I liked the man. I will wait to see what he has to say when we are in Rome. If I am going to go on some dangerous quest, I would like to make sure that it is worth the sacrifice. Otherwise, I will go on to France." James turned and began walking again. "Fitzwalter, you are much too trusting. If I go to France, will you travel with me?"

"No, I gave my word to the archbishop."

James frowned. "A knight's word is binding. Well, we shall see."

It was dark when the two men returned to the residence with James' horse, armor, and other tools of his trade. Byron had no illusions that he was embarking on an arduous journey. At least James would hear the details of the priest's quest in Rome. He had no doubt that once James heard Father Villhardain's tale, he would agree to go. He hoped.

CHAPTER 15
THE GIFT OF THE CROSS

The word had spread through Tyre that Ishaq's men had work to do, and they gathered at the usual khan to meet with their boss. It had taken his men longer to arrive than Ishaq expected and his impatience mounted. As his men slowly filled around Ishaq's table, the other patrons began to leave, not liking the rough group of men who were congregating around the baby faced Arab.

"I hear you have work for us," growled a tall, dark man who was missing his left ear.

"You hear right, Sahl," Ishaq replied, stirring his qahwa, the corners of his mouth turned up in a slight smile at the irony of Sahl's statement.

"Who's it for?" Sahl demanded.

"Jabbar. He has hired us to kidnap a Christian priest." The men sitting at the table started to laugh all at once.

"You called all of us together to capture a priest," Sahl roared.

"There is more to this," Ishaq said mildly. "Jabbar is paying good money. Unless you have something better to do."

"If Jabbar wants to waste his money, let him," Sahl said.

"That's the spirit I am looking for," Ishaq exclaimed, looking around the table as the rest of the men nodded.

A loud crash and then a thump interrupted Ishaq, and he

turned to look for the source of the commotion. A small boy wearing a brown sack had knocked over a small table and had fallen to the ground. Getting up, the boy brushed the dust from his bare knees. Ignoring the stares of the seated men, the boy tipped the table upright, and then as if nothing happened, walked to where Ishaq was sitting.

The boy looked up, his unblinking eyes fixed on Ishaq. After a moment, he stammered, "I, uh, I am looking for Ishaq of Tyre."

Ishaq's men stared at the boy. The boy, ignoring the motley collection of thieves and killers, shot a glance to the side of the room, looking for an exit should he have to run. He then looked back up at Ishaq. Ishaq stared at the boy. The boy looked like him at that age, and it reminded him of his life as an orphan on the street, begging for scraps and fighting to keep his meager handouts from the older boys. That was until the day the Hashshashin took him in.

†

Everyone feared the assassins of "The old Man of the Mountain". The Hashshashin could be anywhere, lurking in plain sight, waiting to strike anyone deemed an enemy. Even Salah-al-Din feared the Nizari Ismaili after an assassin had infiltrated the sultan's bedchamber and placed a poisoned cake with a threat on the sleeping sultan's chest.

Ishaq had been taken to the Nizari Ismaili fortress of Alamut where he learned the art of killing. There he was educated. Reading the Koran, learning writing and mathematics. He had studied the ways of the Nizari's enemies. He had grown from a poor street urchin to a man who could blend in with the people of culture, and kill them.

Ishaq's skill grew and he rose to the rank of a Lasiq, the most feared assassin, an adherent, ready to sacrifice himself for the order. He had been a loyal Hashshashin, but all that changed when he failed to kill an emir of Salah-al-Din. He had skillfully blended in as a soldier, drawing close to his victim. He had drawn his knife when one of the emir's soldiers saw him and cried, "Assassin!" In the fight that followed, he had been stabbed in the chest and had been left in the street for dead. Bashshar had found him and had nursed him back to health.

He had recovered from his wounds, changed his name to Ishaq, and moved to Christian lands. He now killed for money. He was successful and rich and he had never looked back. That is until this moment, when he found he was face to face with a ghost from the past. The boy and the memories of his cruel past stirred in his heart, and he felt pity for the boy.

†

"I am looking for Ishaq," the boy repeated, almost in a whisper.
"What do you want, boy?"
"Jabbar sent me."
Ishaq sat back and nodded. "What do you have for me?"
The boy took a deep breath. "The priest is staying at the big Christian house. You know, the one where the important Christian lives. They were down on the docks today. They are sailing in a big ship to a place called....Rome?"
"Yes, boy," Ishaq said, "it is called Rome. Continue."
"They are leaving the day after tomorrow. I overheard the captain tell the priest to have his men on the dock by morning."
"Is there anything else, boy?"
"The ship is Christian. It is the Lady Mary Grace. The priest said he liked the name Mary."
"Hmm. Come here, boy." The boy approached tepidly. Ishaq leaned forward, held out a gold dinar, and gave it to him.
The boy took the coin, holding it carefully with both hands. He looked at it, turning it over, taking his time to examine it. At last the boy looked up, his eyes shining, a smile on his face. "Thank

you, master."

Ishaq smiled and rubbed the boy on the head. "I like you boy. Go and keep watch. If something changes, come back here and tell me."

"I will, master," the boy cried and he ran off.

A large man with bushy eyebrows and dark beard leaned forward. "Boss, why did you give that boy a dinar?"

"We are getting older, Bashshar. Someday, that boy will grow up and I don't want him working for someone else, or cutting into our business. I consider that a small investment in the future. Besides, he reminds me of myself at that age." Bashshar shook his head.

"Very nice," Sahl sneered, irritated at the interruption and Ishaq's sentimentality. "Can we get back to business? What is your plan?"

"I have not decided yet. As soon as I have a plan, I will let you know," Ishaq snapped. "I would have turned this job down if it were not for the amount of money Jabbar is willing to pay."

"What's in it for us?" Sahl pressed, hoping Ishaq would be generous.

"Your usual cut, plus a ten percent bonus," Ishaq replied curtly.

"Fifteen percent!" one of his men shouted.

"Ten percent," Ishaq snapped. "Unless you are questioning my generosity." No one said a word. "I didn't think so," Ishaq continued softly, pausing thoughtfully for a moment. "I have made my offer, if you think you are owed more you can leave now." No one left the table. "I see," Ishaq continued. "That is all I have for now. I need time to consider the boy's information. Come back tonight and meet me near the docks at the usual place. I will have something by then."

All of the men except Bashshar got up and began to leave. When they were alone, Ishaq turned to Bashshar. "Bashshar, what do you think?"

"I think Jabbar is a fool."

"So do I, but the money is good. In fact, it is too good and I am puzzled. Jabbar is not a generous man. There is more to this, I can feel it."

"Who cares? This is an easy job. Jabbar is an idiot. For all you know, the priest stepped on Jabbar's toes in a crowd, and Jabbar now wants him captured so he can force the priest to apologize."

Ishaq got up from the table. "Yes, Jabbar is conceited and it could be as simple as that. The reasons are not important... just the money."

Bashshar got up. "It has always been about the money; otherwise, I will never understand why you work for Jabbar. The man is an arrogant swine."

"Yes, he is, but he pays well," Ishaq replied as he walked next to his lieutenant. Ishaq grew silent. The feeling that he was missing something important nagged at him. He shrugged. He had never cared before. Jabbar could keep his secretes. He pushed the matter from his mind.

†

The next day, James had been unable to sell his horse. He gave the animal to the archbishop, grumbling about the greed of the Church. Byron had to make the same choice, and it saddened him to part with the horse that had saved his life. The monk in charge of the stables promised the horse would be well cared for, and Byron hoped that would be the case, the horse deserved it.

When Carl learned there was another knight in the company, his only comment had been to growl, "So, now there is a Norman and a Frank. Lord, what did I do to offend you?" James almost answered Carl's rhetorical question but thought better of it.

They spent the day packing to leave. They oiled the armor and other equipment and packed them for the journey at sea. Byron was not looking forward to the trip. While the idea of seeing Rome excited him, he hated traveling by ship. Every sea voyage he had ever taken had caused him to spend the first several days horribly seasick. The trip to the Holy Lands had almost killed him. He had spent every day retching until there was nothing left. Even the water would not stay down. He had gotten so weak his comrades had given up hope, leaving him in peace to die. It was on the third day that he was strong enough to sit up. After that, he had gotten better to the point where the trip was just miserable, but at least he could eat. He had learned that if he stayed at the back of the ship watching the horizon, he was able to manage. If he looked down at the deck or went below, his stomach began to roll and the terrible watery feeling in his mouth returned. The only good thing about sea travel is it always made him grateful to set foot on land.

They had their final meal that night with the archbishop. The food was excellent as usual; although Byron enjoyed his meal exceedingly, he was already wondering how much grief it would cause him the next day when they got under way.

When the meal was finished, Archbishop Joscius stood up at the head of the table. "The time has come for us to part ways. Once you leave here, you will be on your own and beyond my aid. Therefore, I wish to pray for each of you."

Byron looked up at the archbishop, who smiled.

"I have gifts for each of you. I hope it brings you comfort when times are dark and reminds you each day that anything worthwhile comes with sacrifice." He then made a sign, and one of his servants walked over to the table with a silver tray covered with a white cloth. On the cloth were four gold crosses. Each cross, bound with silver and gold, hung from a finely woven gold chain. "I hope when you wear these, you remember me and the people of the kingdom who depend so much on your success."

The archbishop took a cross from the tray and motioned for each man to approach. When Byron received his gift, he bowed. "Thank you, Your Grace. I shall always wear it and remember your kindness and hospitality."

"My son, I know you do not wish to go to Rome. Your heart yearns to defend the walls of Jerusalem, and that is a worthy deed, but so is this. This journey will not be heralded throughout Christian lands, but it is no less noble. So be comforted, for you are chosen for this task and therefore you are blessed."

Byron was unable to speak. He bowed again and returned to his chair in silence.

"Go now and rest. Tomorrow will be the beginning of a long journey." The archbishop turned to Father Villhardain. "Could I have a word with you before you retire?"

"Of course, Your Grace."

Once the room was empty, Joscius spoke, "In the morning, my servants will hitch up the mules to the wagon and deliver your belongings to the ship. Do you wish to ride with them?"

"No, Your Grace. The wagon will be crowded, and it is a short walk."

Joscius nodded. "I would not pass on the opportunity for one last walk on dry land."

"Is there anything else, Your Grace?"

"Yes." The archbishop lowered his voice. "There is discord in the Lateran. The vice chancellor's influence over the Holy Father has grown. In his letter, Cardinal Morra writes that Cardinal Fulcher is advising Urban and the papal consistory to excommunicate the Holy Roman Emperor Frederick Barbarossa. This does not bode well. Only the Holy Roman Emperor can defeat Saladin. We do not need a house divided. I have suspicions that Fulcher has designs on becoming the next Pope, and I fear that the excommunication of Barbarossa is the first step in that plan."

"Did Cardinal Morra give any guidance?"

"No. Perhaps when you meet with Cardinal Morra you will learn more." Father Villhardain nodded. "We have tribulations enough without creating more. God's speed, Father Villhardain, I will pray for you."

"You are very gracious, Your Eminence," Father Villhardain said as he bowed.

Father Villhardain was about to leave when the archbishop grabbed his arm. "Be careful, Michael. Be wary of Vice Chancellor Fulcher."

Byron and James walked down the hall that led to their room. James paused to admire a tapestry celebrating the first crusades capture of Jerusalem that hung on the wall. Knights in armor knelt before the walls of the city, while those standing looked to heaven with outstretched hands singing their praises to God. James reached out his hand and brushed the dust from the wall hanging.

"Amazing how time and a few stitches of thread can hide all the blood that flowed in the streets of God's city," James said.

Byron stepped closer, inspecting the colored threads and knots. Each thread by itself was insignificant. The knots made the thread stronger. Woven together with each stitch of the needle, the threads were bound together to form the full image. Byron ran his fingers along the tapestry to the edge that was starting to fray. He pulled the fabric closer to inspect the damage, but as he pulled the tapestry away from the wall, Byron realized it had been hung there to cover a large dark hole punched into the plaster.

"Humph. This tapestry has more than one purpose."

James came over to look. "I wondered why they would hang this here," James replied as he glanced at a nearby image of Mercury casting his net to ensnare a nude Venus. "It seemed out of place."

"Everything here seems out of place." Byron let go of the tapestry, which hit the wall with a dull thump, causing a small cloud of dust. He turned and started to walk down the hall. "I would have expected the house of the archbishop to be more somber." Byron glanced up at the image of Venus. The nude goddess, half turned towards Mercury revealing her large breasts, was running, her golden hair flowing behind her. Her flirtatious eyes wide as she laughed. The messenger of the gods, dressed in a white tunic, laced with gold, had his eyes fixed upon his prey as he leaned to throw his steel net to ensnare the goddess of love.

"These," Byron gestured at the image of Venus and Mercury, "seem a bit too worldly for a man of the Church."

James smiled. "I don't know, Fitzwalter... I like her. A beautiful woman should always be admired."

Byron scoffed, "Of course, you would say that."

James laughed. "Fitzwalter, you have no appreciation of women do you."

"I don't think a lady should ever be displayed in such a manner. Especially in the house of a man of God."

James cocked his head and eyed his friend. "Fitzwalter, as a man who appreciates beautiful women, I can assure you this painting is a fine representation of womanhood. I hope someday,"

James pointed to Venus, "you get to enjoy the company of a beautiful woman such as her. Perhaps then you will be able to appreciate this image."

Byron scowled at James. "I hope someday to marry a lady who will worship me as her husband and represent my house in a dignified manner."

James laughed. "Then I wish you well, my friend. Which reminds me, do you really believe this priest's mystery journey will alter the kingdom's fate?"

"I do. When Father Villhardain reveals his purpose, I think you will agree."

Byron expected James to ask more questions and was surprised when James said, "Hmm. Well, whatever Father Villhardain is up to, Saladin thought it important enough to send his knights to try and intercept him."

"And it would have succeeded had I not been there."

"Yes, and we must use care. Saladin has many spies. He will soon learn of your victory and will try again."

Byron shook his head. "I had hoped that my victory would have gone unnoticed."

James laughed. "If you thought that, it was truly wishful thinking. You were still covered with blood when you passed by hundreds of refugees at the gates. Not all of them are loyal. Even the nobility cannot be trusted if they believe that the sultan has something to offer them. Christ! The treacherous bastards were trying to surrender Tyre without a fight."

"I suppose it was foolish to think my entry into Tyre would escape notice." Byron threw up his hands. "Even the news of my triumph arrived here before I did."

The two men reached the room they were sharing. Once they entered the room and the door closed, James spoke, "Do not worry. The fastest rider in the land could only have arrived in Acre today. It will take time for the sultan to react, and by that time, we will be safely on our way to Rome."

Byron smiled. "I wonder what the sultan thought when he found out his plan to capture Father Villhardain had failed."

"I am glad I was not that messenger," James smirked. "Just

think, Fitzwalter, without any effort on your part, you have probably killed a third Saracen."

Byron pulled off his cloak and draped it on a chair. "Hmm, a pleasant thought. Well, at the very least, I caused Saladin some difficulty."

James was checking the bed to see if it was stretched tight. "Well, Fitzwalter, this is it. Rest well. This will be your last night on dry land."

Byron blew out the candle and lay down on his bed. He closed his eyes as the memory of his last sea voyage filled his mind. Cold, wet, and sick. He could almost feel the bed rocking. He was not looking forward to tomorrow. He rolled onto his side and pushed the thought out of his mind. He was not going to let his anxiety ruin his sleep. Moon light shown through the window, its soft white light cutting a path across the darkened floor. Byron reached up and gripped his new gold cross that hung around his neck. The feeling of the cross in his hand filled him with comfort, and before long, he fell asleep.

CHAPTER 16
CRIME IN THE STREETS

The morning sun was shining in the window when both men woke to the sound of someone banging on the door. James groggily got up and walked to the door. "I am coming you knave," he shouted. Opening the door, he saw Brother Carl scowling at him.

"Father Villhardain is in the kitchen waiting for you," the monk grumbled.

James yawned and replied, "Good Morning to you to." Carl started to leave. "Brother Carl, are you ready?"

"Yes and no," Carl said with a frown. "I am ready to return to Rome, but the sea is fraught with danger. When I was a young man, I traveled in the longboats of my ancestors. I have seen the oceans might. I have been praying for a swift and safe journey, one without storms." With that comment, he turned and walked down the hallway.

Byron turned to James and said, "I couldn't agree more."

"Well, I love sailing," James replied. "To be free upon the water. The ship sailing swift upon the sea, wind filling the sails." James gave a mischievous smile. "I love sitting on the ships rails singing. I always hope that the sound of my voice will attract a beautiful sea nymph, and we will be bound together making love upon the rolling waves."

"I too will spend my time at the rail, but it will not attract a sea nymph," Byron grumbled as he headed out the doorway.

Father Villhardain sat at a small table eating his breakfast when the two men entered. The priest looked up. "Are you ready for the journey?" Byron nodded. "Good," the priest said. "I went for a walk on the grounds this morning. The winds are fair, and I think it will be a great day for sailing."

Byron forced a smile as he picked up a piece of bread. When their morning meal was finished, the men picked up their belongings and headed for the door. The archbishop greeted them when they reached the main exit. "My servants have left to deliver your armor and other baggage to the ship. Perhaps we will meet again, but until that time, farewell and God bless you."

Father Villhardain bowed. "Thank you for everything, Your Grace."

"You are welcome, Father Villhardain. May God grant you safe passage and keep you in his care."

Father Villhardain, Carl, and Byron were about to exit the main gate when James stopped and patted his tunic with his hands. "I left my gift in our room."

"What gift?" Byron asked.

"My cross. Go! I will catch up."

"Don't be late," Carl said. "We will leave without you." James turned and dashed back to the house of the archbishop.

Byron shrugged. "At least he remembered."

"He will have to run to catch up," the monk replied. "Perhaps he will learn to be less forgetful."

"I am not sure running is the cure for that malady," Father Villhardain said.

The priest, the knight, and the monk walked in the early morning light. Most of the inhabitants of the city were not out of their houses yet, and the streets were not crowded. The street vendors were busy setting up their shops. The few people who were out and about walking the streets were too busy with their own affairs even to say good morning. A pall of despair hung over the city, affecting everyone who lived behind the walls. Simple courtesy vanished as the realization slowly consumed the citizens that eventually

Saladin and his Saracen horde would descend upon them. The constant fear of being overwhelmed was grinding the citizens of Tyre down. People felt isolated and alone, with their backs against the sea, trapped with no means of escape in sight.

Byron felt pity for the poor and dispossessed, knowing they would never have the means to pay for their escape. However, he did not dwell on the thought of the fate that awaited them. He glanced over his shoulder, but he could not see James. He smiled, he had no doubt his friend was hurrying to catch up to them. He rounded the corner to the next street that would take them to the ship. The street was empty.

Bang! A door flew open, and with a rush, several men dressed in black ran out of the doorway. Byron, drawing his dagger, spun to face the attack when the first man hit him, knocking him down. The second man, who was missing an ear, jumped on top of Byron and raised his arm to stab him with a knife. Out of nowhere, a sword flashed over the top of Byron, and the man's headless corpse toppled off. The second man was scrambling off to engage the unseen attacker when Byron drove his dagger into the man's heart.

Byron got to his feet and drew his sword. James was in front of him, running to Carl who was bashing one of his attacker's head on the ground.

"I have got these bastards," Carl roared, "help Father Villhardain!"

Byron rushed past Carl, James was still ahead of him. He could see three men on top of Father Villhardain holding him down. A bag was over the priest's head, and his assailants were in the process of tying him up. James' sword flashed in the sun as he struck a downward blow to the man who had been sitting on Father Villhardain's legs. With a dull smack, James' sword cleaved the man's skull, splitting his face in two.

The man tying Father Villhardain's legs together was struggling to his feet as Byron ran up. The Saracen turned his head, and his mouth gaped open. The man screamed as Byron drove his sword through the man's body up to the hilt. Dark blood gushed out of the grooves in the blade of the sword. The man fell forward to the ground, his face twisted to one side. Byron put his boot on the man's back to pull the weapon free from the twitching body.

The third Saracen was now on his feet with a shamshir in his hand. James waded in, striking at the baby faced Saracen who was skillfully deflecting each blow. The ring of steel echoed in the empty streets. James towered over the smaller Saracen. His sword strokes fell like hammer blows as he advanced. The Saracen, retreating from the onslaught, stumbled and fell backwards.

"Run master!" a small Arab boy screamed as he jumped between the Saracen and James. James, who was starting to deliver a sweeping stroke with his sword, was unable to stop, and the small boy caught the entire force of the blow meant for the man. It cut him completely in two. The Saracen, seeing the boy's body split in half, rolled to his feet and began running down the street away from the fight.

"You bastard! James shouted as he started to run after the Saracen. He was starting to pick up speed, when he felt a hand on his shoulder.

"Let him go!" Byron cried.

James stopped and bowed his head, breathing hard. "I just killed that boy!" he gasped between breaths.

"I saw," Byron said. "There was nothing you could do. We need to go before they come back." James hesitated as he looked down the road at the fleeing Saracen. "That man is not our errand today," Byron shouted.

James nodded, stooped down and wiped the blood from his sword on the body of one of the dead Saracens. Byron was untying Father Villhardain as James bent down to help.

"Father, are you okay?" Byron asked.

"Yes," replied Father Villhardain, gasping for air. "I'm unharmed."

Brother Carl came running up, puffing hard, and with surprising gentleness, he lifted Father Villhardain off the ground. "Come, lads, follow me."

Carl started walking as fast as he could while holding Father Villhardain up. Byron and James followed behind as a rear guard, watching for any sign of another attack as they hurried down the deserted street to the city harbor.

Byron saw the bay come into view, and he could see the Genoese ship tied up at the wharf. The forecastle of the large, two-masted ship hung over the walkway, the sailors were working on the deck. They reached the docks and several men dressed in mail, with swords drawn, challenged them. The first guard approached Byron. "Halt!" the man called out in a commanding voice. "The Lord Montferrat has forbidden any fighting men to leave Tyre without permission. State your names and your business."

"I am Sir Byron Fitzwalter, with me are Father Villhardain, his assistant Brother Carl of the Roman Catholic Church, and Sir James Hugh Martel of Jerusalem. We have permission from the lord of the city to leave. We are traveling to Rome."

"We have been expecting you," the guard said in a softer tone. As the man drew closer to Byron, he noticed the blood and saw Carl holding Father Villhardain up. "My god, what has happened?"

"We were attacked by Saracens. Their bodies still lie in the street. One of them got away."

"Saracens? Are you sure, my lord? Are you sure they were not Christians?"

"I am sure."

The captain turned to his men. "Go! See if you can identify the villains who attacked these lords!" The captain turned to Byron. "With so many refugees within the walls, crime is out of control." The captain then pointed to Father Villhardain. "Is he unharmed?"

The priest smiled weakly. "I'm fine. Just got the wind knocked out of me."

"The villain who got away, what did he look like?"

"Like a Saracen," Byron replied. "No beard, with the face of a boy."

One of the guards returned as they were talking. "Captain, my lords are right, they were Saracens. There are six bodies in the road and a dead boy."

The leader nodded as he turned to Byron. "My lord, do you want to stay and have us search for the man so justice can be done upon him?"

"My lord, our journey is our concern," Byron replied.

The captain nodded and bowed. "Yes, my lord. May God grant you safe passage. Hopefully, Rome has not forsaken us."

Byron walked onto the deck of the ship. James and Carl helped Father Villhardain up the gangway. Father Villhardain, getting his wind back said, "Just let me sit down on the deck." James and Carl eased Father Villhardain down onto the deck and propped him against a bulkhead.

"God bless both of you, I will be all right." at the sound of approaching footsteps. "Captain Antonius Vercelis," the priest cried in Italian.

"Father Villhardain." Captain Vercelis reached out his calloused hand, hardened from years of hard work with canvas and rope, and helped the priest stand up. A smile crossed Captain Vercelis' tanned face.

"Father, welcome on board the Lady Mary Grace. I hear from my men you have already had quite an adventure today."

"More than I would have wanted."

"Your baggage is aboard. Are your traveling companions here?"

"Yes, we are all here."

Captain Vercelis glanced up at the sky. "Excellent. Then we shall get underway. Everything is stowed, and we are ready. The wind is fair and the sky is clear. God is with thee, Father Villhardain."

The captain began shouting orders to the sailors. The ship was untied from the dock and two small boats, rowed by Arabs who worked in the harbor, began towing the ship away from the dock. When the ship was clear, the tow hawsers were tossed free. Standing in their small boats, the Arabs waved as the wooden hull of the ship slid by. The captain, standing near the sailor with the steering oars, shouted commands for the sails to be set. The white sails emblazoned with black crosses filled with wind, the ship picked up speed. A bow wave began to form as the ship cut through the water.

James stood by the ship's rail watching the waves slide by. Carl walked up and stood beside him looking at the sea. "If it were not for you, Father Villhardain would be in the hands of Saladin, and Byron and I would be dead. What happened was not your fault."

James shook his head. He slapped his hands on top of the ship's rail. "Had I not forgotten my crucifix, things would have turned out ill. Fate is such a strange creature. It is not the first time I have killed someone unjustly, but each time it has happened, I feel as if a little piece of my soul is torn away."

"Your cause was righteous. Your combat was honorable and manly. It is unfortunate the boy took the blow that was meant for the man," the monk answered, "but his death is not your fault."

"It is unfortunate." James sighed. "I doubt now that any nymph will come to hear the song of a child murder."

The Lady Mary Grace was clear of the harbor. The captain ordered more canvas spread, and in no time, she was running before the wind. Tyre faded into the distance. The ship was now alone on the open windswept sea.

CHAPTER 17
THE WORRIES OF JABBAR

Ishaq ran down a deserted alley. He had used this alley many times, but today it was crucial to his escape. His black robes were splattered with the boy's blood. His men were dead. With each step, his anger grew. This was Jabbar's fault. Jabbar had rushed him. He needed more time to stalk his prey, to learn their habits. There were two knights, not one. What would the old man of the mountain have said? That greed had blinded him? That he had not planned the attack properly? He hissed through his teeth. He may have made a few errors in judgement, but Jabbar had not told him everything, and now Jabbar would pay.

Jabbar would pay, and he was going to make it slow and painful. Revenge! The Christians would have to wait. Jabbar, on the other hand, was about to get a surprise. Jabbar's house was now in view. He took a deep breath as he mastered his rage and cleared his mind. The time was not right. He stopped at a side street café to watch and drink qahwa. His hands shook with anger, causing his qahwa to slosh out of his cup. He needed to calm down. He would wait until the sun had set, and then he would make sure Jabbar understood the magnitude of his error.

†

It had been a bad day for Jabbar. News had arrived that Acre had fallen. His warehouses had been looted. Jabbar, exhausted from his day of trying to keep his business empire afloat, wearily got up from his desk to go to bed. Even his harem did not interest him. His women, that he had spent a fortune on, would have to pass on his attentions. He lit a candle and walked down the hall to his bedchamber in a depressed mood. Perhaps tomorrow would be a better day. He lit an oil lamp as he entered his luxurious bedroom. He turned and gave a start. Ishaq was sitting on his bed looking at him. His back against the wall and his legs stretched out in front of him. He had been so distracted by his losses that he had forgotten all about the plan to capture the priest, and with a jolt, he remembered. A feeling of fear crept over him, and he stuttered, "H-h-how did things go today? Did you capture the priest?"

Ishaq sat quiet for a moment before he answered. "We made our move," the assassin said coldly.

Relief spread across Jabbar's face. "So, you have them?" he asked excitedly.

"No," Ishaq replied in a measured tone. "I warned you that it would be bad for you if you did not tell me everything." Ishaq paused, letting his words hang in the air.

Jabbar became thoroughly frightened. "I t-t-told you everything. I told you everything I know."

Ishaq's face hardened, the corner of his mouth twitched as his eyelids narrowed. "No, you did not. I lost six good men today," Ishaq continued, cold and menacing. "Do you know why?" Jabbar shook his head as he stood paralyzed with fear.

"They died because there was another knight with the priest. My men are dead because of you!"

Jabbar was visibly trembling, tears were streaming down his fat face. "I am sorry Ishaq, I am so sorry!" Ishaq stood up and began to walk towards Jabbar. Jabbar collapsed on his knees. "Please! Please! Don't kill me!"

"Jabbar, we have been business partners for a long time. You know the arrangements. I take care of your problems, and you pay me."

Jabbar started to beg. "Please! Please! I will pay! I will pay you six times our original agreement!"

Ishaq reached out and grabbed Jabbar by the beard as he drew his dagger. "Jabbar, you will pay. You will pay ten times the amount, to cover the cost of what you have done. I have widows to compensate, but that is only the start. I need to send a message. Do you understand?" Jabbar's head bobbed. Ishaq bent close and whispered in Jabbar's ear. "Good. We are now going to renegotiate our business arrangement. You are going to tell me everything about this priest. If you don't, I will butcher you, slowly, and feed your body to the pigs, making sure you live long enough to watch."

A puddle of urine appeared on the floor beneath Jabbar. Ishaq looked down for a moment. He smiled inwardly, he was getting his message across and that was good. "Who is this priest?" shouted the assassin as he shook Jabbar by his beard. "Why is he protected by two knights? Why do you want him?"

"Sheikh Abdul al-Subayil. He wants information concerning a Christian priest, Father Michael Villhardain. I think the Sultan Salah al-Din wants him. I don't know why?"

Ishaq's face turned red. His dark eyes lit as if a fire raged inside him. "You think!" he screamed as he shook the fat merchant. "You risked my men on a hunch? " Ishaq drew back his knife. The curved blade, suspended in air, flickered in the candle light.

Ishaq's knife jerked towards Jabbar's neck, and in an effort to save himself, the fat merchant squealed, "Salah al-Din has already tried to capture the priest. The Sultan has sent Sheikh Abdul al-Subayil's only son to search for him. He is important to Salah al-Din. The Christians are coming back!"

Ishaq stopped. "The Christians are coming back? How do you know this, you fat swine?"

"Because the sheikh asked for me to send information if the priest returns."

"That means nothing!" Ishaq drew back his arm again to stab Jabbar.

"I will give you anything. I will pay you a hundred times what you demand. I will give you women, camels, anything! Just let me live."

Ishaq looked down at the fat merchant who was now weeping. His face softened and he frowned. He felt disgust. Not with

Jabbar but with himself. He never let his emotions control him, especially during a kill. He had never let his victims plead for their lives. He was violating all of his rules, and the thought cooled his anger. Salah al-Din wanted this priest. The sultan had his men searching the desert for him. Why? He needed to sift through this before he acted rashly. Jabbar might prove useful yet.

The room was silent, except for the soft sobbing of Jabbar. Ishaq finally broke the silence. "I need time to think."

Jabbar's revelations had put a new twist on things. There was more to this after all, and Ishaq decided that perhaps a different approach might be more rewarding than the instant gratification of killing the fat merchant. Jabbar was not going anywhere. There was no place he could flee. With some regret, he let go of the fat merchant's beard.

"Jabbar, I will be back. You will have my money ready and waiting for me." Ishaq shoved the fat merchant down into the pool of urine. "I will see you tomorrow." Ishaq turned, walked out of the bedroom, and left the apartment.

The street was dark. Not a gleam of light from the nearby houses lit the thoroughfare save for the stars above. Ishaq stealthily walked among shadows, making little noise. He was irritated with himself for his lack of self-control. He was also perplexed at what he had just learned. The sultan wants the priest. He knew an opportunity when he saw one; the problem was how to make the most of it. Jabbar had better be ready with the money, or he would butcher him alive.

Jabbar lay on the floor for a long time, unable to move. Finally, he got up. He was still shaking. His first thought was to have his servants killed for letting Ishaq get into his house, but then he thought better of it since Ishaq was the one he would hire to do it. What a mess. Why did he ever start this? All he had to do was send a letter with information to the sheikh, but because of his greed, he now had a real problem on his hands. He made his way to a bureau where he took out a change of clothes.

Tomorrow he would need to get his funds together and pay Ishaq. Maybe that would placate him. Perhaps time would cool his wrath and things would get back to normal. He knew better.

Things would never be the same until Ishaq had killed all he held responsible; hopefully, that would not be him. Maybe he could buy his way out of the tight spot he was in.

    He cleaned himself up, put on a new night shirt, and crawled into bed. He pulled the covers over his head and tried to sleep as his mind turned over and over all sorts of unpleasant thoughts of what perhaps was waiting in his future.

CHAPTER 18
THE STORM

The weather was pleasant and Byron was not seasick. The first day at sea the dreaded feeling had plagued him, but by the second day it had disappeared. He was now able to move around the ship without clutching to the railing, waiting for another round of retching.

James had remained detached and spent his time leaning on the ships rail as he watched the sea birds fly. The death of the boy had brought back memories. He listened to the splash of the water as the bow of the ship drove through the sea, reflecting on his life. He had grown up in Outremer, and he was leaving the only life he had known. His grandfather had died in the Levant, so had his mother and father. He was the only living child of that union. Three brothers and one sister had died as infants, a curse that his mother had stoically born despite his father's constant reminders of her failure as a woman.

He had spent years fighting, never taking any time to establish a house, or take a wife. He had relationships with numerous women, but the encounters had been, in the eyes of the Church, a sin. When he died, there would be no one to remember him, to lament his passing. Father Villhardain walked to the rail and stood next to the knight.

"Father, I have heard told that sailors believe seabirds are the souls of dead men."

"You know that is not true."

James turned away from the water to look at the priest. "Too bad. I think I would like to be a bird, to be free of it all." His dark eyes softened. "Father, I have killed many men in battle. Most of the slain were killed in close combat, one after the other, to the point I cannot recall them. I remember one hard fight, years ago, when I had won my spurs. I had ridden with Marshal Lusignan to punish a Saracen incursion into the kingdom. We found them and attacked. I rode straight at a Saracen mounted on a horse and drove my lance deep into his chest. What I did not realize is there were two of them. The Saracen must have picked up another man whose horse had fallen. My lance had pierced them both."

James stopped and looked straight into Father Villhardain's eyes. "I can still see the look on the rider's face. He was crying, praying to Allah as I smote him and his companion to the ground. Two friends died together." James sighed. "The extra weight slowed his horse, making him easy prey. If the Saracen had not pulled his friend onto his horse, he probably would have escaped. His act of kindness ended with his death. The Saracen boy jumps in front of his master, and I reward his loyalty with death." James became silent as he watched the waves in the distance.

"I suppose you are looking for an answer as to why God, who sent his only son with the message to love one another, allows such violence to go on."

"It is a fair question, Father."

"I have a question for you. Did you choose to be a knight?"

James frowned. "My destiny was never a question. I have trained for years to earn my spurs."

Father Villhardain smiled. "Yet, you could have renounced it all, left your life of privilege, returned to France, and been a peasant farmer."

"A scion of Charles Martel and Charlemagne, a peasant farmer?"

"I do not jest. You have chosen to retain your privileges and your rank, and you chose to stay in the Levant," the priest said gently.

"Of course, I did."

"Then do not blame God if the circumstances you placed

yourself in are not working the way you planned. You have killed many men. You have fought in wars. You have grown older and are now starting to question the righteousness of your acts."

"Father, I don't question what I have done. It is done and there is no going back."

"Then what do you want?"

"I do not know what I want anymore," James said as he walked away.

The day passed as the ship tacked, keeping the wind in its sails. As the sun began its descent below the horizon, the wind increased. Dark ragged clouds raced across the sky, covering the stars with ominous blackness. The waters became troubled, and the ship pitched and rocked in the rising sea. The cry went out to shorten the sail. Large waves crashed against the ship, sending the spray over the decks.

Byron, below decks swaying in his hammock, could not sleep as he listened to the waves smashing into the sides of the ship. The ship pitched violently, tossing him from his hammock onto the deck. In the dark, he stood up. The hull creaked and groaned. He felt the ship closing in on him. The fear of being trapped began to fill him with dread. He could not breathe. He decided he would rather drown beneath the sky than be entombed in a sinking vessel. He got up and struggled to the deck. "If it is not seasickness, then it is something else," he grumbled to himself.

Keeping out of the way of the sailors, he watched them struggle to reef the sails in the blowing winds. The ship crested a mountainous white capped wave and then plunged straight down into the trough. The ship began to rise again on a new swell towards the darkened sky. A flash of lightning split the night, its stark searing light revealing the face of every man on the deck. In that moment, time stood still. The light faded and all went dark. The wind howled while the rain lashed down. In the darkness, the pale crest of a rogue wave glimmered in the darkness, rolling towards the ship's starboard side. A cry went out, and all hands turned to look in fear at the approaching menace.

"For God's sake turn into it!" Captain Vercelis cried, but the men at the steering oars were powerless to change the ship's fate.

With a crash, the wave slammed into the ship's side. The timbers of the hull groaned and creaked. The ship heeled over, rolling on to its side. The yardarm of the mast dipped into the water, the sail gathering water, threatening to drag the ship over.

Byron was thrown across the deck. The ship refused to right itself. He grabbed onto a rope and held tight as the waters reached up to take him. He could hear a sailor, his voice filled with fear, praying to God to keep the cargo in place. Clutching to the rope, he looked down at the dark abyss waiting to take him. He hung there suspended in air, and with a groan, the ship slowly righted. The mast rose skyward, and the water from the sail poured down on him. Byron felt his boots hit the deck as he let go of the rope.

Another streak of lightning shot across the sky as another black wave rolled towards the ship. Byron stood transfixed, watching the dark water rising higher and higher. He had just escaped death, but the sea had not given up. The bow of the ship rose violently with the swell. Tons of water crashed down onto the deck. Byron, knocked from his feet, slammed to the deck. Ropes and tackle washed past him. Salt water burned his eyes, and his mouth filled with its foul taste. The water hissed in his ears. He felt himself being pulled along the deck. The water was dragging him from the ship. As he was flailed about to save himself, someone grabbed his leg.

"You cannot have him!" a voice bellowed. Byron looked back to see Brother Carl holding onto his leg. "Norman, where are you going?" The monk said, pulling him back as the water rushed past him. Grabbing him by his shoulders, the monk helped him to his feet.

"The sea is going to take me willing or no," Byron sputtered.

"Not if I can thwart it," the monk growled.

Byron's teeth were chattering from the cold. Brother Carl pulled his cloak from his shoulders and wrapped it around Byron. "Fear not, Norman, I have survived worse nights than this. Stand with me, and we will face the beast together." Moving to the mast, Brother Carl and Byron stood together looking forward into the face of the storm. The spray from the waves soaked them to the bone. Byron was starting to think the night would never end when Brother Carl spoke, "Norman, I shall lift your spirits and sing the Lament of Doer. It is an Anglo Saxon song that recounts the sufferings of men who overcame their own tribulations." Above the shriek of the wind, the monk began to sing in the sonorous Anglo Saxon tongue.

Weland, tasted misery among snakes. The stouthearted hero endured troubles,
He had sorrow and longing for companions, cruelty as cold as winter- he often found woe. Once Niðhad had put fetters of so many supple-sinew bonds upon the better man.

That went by, so can this.

In Beadohild's mind, her brothers' death was not as painful to her heart as her own trouble, when she realized that she was pregnant; nor could she ever foresee without fear how things would turn out.

That went by, so can this.

We have heard that the Geat's love for his lady Maethild passed all bounds,
that his sorrowful love deprived him of his restless sleep.

That went by, so can this.

For thirty winters, Theodric ruled the stronghold of the Maerings with an iron hand;
Many acknowledged this and they groaned.

That went by, so can this.

We have heard of Eormanric's wolfish thoughts; how he cruelly held dominion over the kingdom of the Goths. A grim king. Many warriors sat, bound with woes and sorrow, wishing that his kingdom be overthrown.

That went by, so can this.

If a man sits in despair, deprived of joy, with darkness in his thoughts; it seems to him that there is no end to his troubles. Then he should consider that the wise Lord follows different courses throughout the earth; to many men he shows honor, certainty, yet, misery to some. I myself will say I was the bard of the Heodeningas, my Lord's favorite. My name was Deor. For many winters, I had a good position and a gracious Lord, until Heorrenda, a man of skillful songs, has inherited the land once given to me by the protector of warriors.

That went by, so can this.

The wind began to slacken and stars appeared through holes in the clouds. The ship sailed on, smashing its way through the swells, but the waves were growing smaller. Captain Vercelis ordered the sail lengthened, and the ship picked up speed.

"Norman, you have a stout heart. The storm has given its last. It is time for a well-earned rest for those who stood before the mast to witness the wonders of the deep." Brother Carl turned and disappeared below deck.

Byron followed the monk into the gloom. He reached his hammock and felt it with his hand. It was damp with salt water. He lifted up his wet blanket and held it out. Water dripped from it, and he tossed it down into a pile. Shivering, he was about to lay down when he looked over in disbelief at James who was on his side still asleep. James had slept through it all. Byron looked at his friend, wishing he could have stayed asleep, and with a sigh, he lay down. Rocking with the swaying of the ship, he fell into a deep sleep.

CHAPTER 19
PAYING FOR DAMAGES

Jabbar used every connection he had to collect the money Ishaq demanded. After the money had been gathered, counted and recounted, he sat in his office, waiting, the money piled on the table in front of him. He was chewing on his fingernails until Ishaq finally arrived.

"Do you have the money?" Ishaq demanded. Jabbar's head bobbed. Ishaq smiled as his eyes bored into Jabbar. "I am going to Rome."

Jabbar stopped chewing on his fingernails and sat up. "Rome? Do you think it is safe for one of the faithful to tread the streets of the capital of the infidel religion?"

"I have a friend who has an import business in Rome. I feel it would be beneficial for me to go there in person."

"I always find that things work more efficiently when I am there to supervise in person." Jabbar laughed nervously.

"I am not going to supervise anything, you fool. I am going to find out what the priest was doing here." Jabbar resumed chewing his fingernails. "Jabbar, you will send one last letter to the sheikh. Tell him that the priest has left for Rome. Send him nothing else. Do you understand?" Jabbar nodded. "That should satisfy the sheikh. Perhaps when he learns the priest has fled, he will drop his interest in this matter." Ishaq opened one of the bags of money to make sure Jabbar had not cheated him.

"I am not sure that will suffice," Jabbar replied. "The sheikh wanted me to keep him informed. Something he needed for his son. He promised me that I would be rewarded for my efforts."

Ishaq closed the bag of money and rolled his eyes up at the ceiling as he shook his head. "Do I care? Send the sheikh a letter and then drop the matter. If he sends you anymore requests, ignore them!" Jabbar nodded. Ishaq moved over to the rest of the bags of gold coins sitting on the table and picked them up, opened them, and looked at the coins.

"Jabbar, you have made a mess. You had better be on your best behavior while I am gone. If not, I swear I will feed you piece by piece to the pigs."

Jabbar turned pale. "I would never cheat you."

"Yes, you would," Ishaq said as he held up a misshaped coin, its edges clearly shaved. "You are trying to cheat me now with coins that are not their full value." Jabbar whimpered. "Enough! I know you, and I am a man of my word." Ishaq glared down at Jabbar. "I assume the rest of the bags of gold are in the same condition." Jabbar nodded his head sheepishly. "Be thankful that I have too much to do, and that I am in a merciful mood. Otherwise…" Jabbar looked down.

"I will be back. Do not forget that," Ishaq said as he turned and walked out of Jabbar's apartment and wandered out into the street. He could see the women sweeping their doorsteps, and he saw the ragged urchins playing in the gutter. His mind whirled with thoughts of how best to leave the city. Montferrat's men had tamped down on anyone leaving Tyre. Not that it would stop his departure, it was just an inconvenience. He could have had Jabbar use his connections to get him passage to Rome, but he did not trust Jabbar, who would undoubtedly do something stupid, like trying to kill him. He laughed to himself. Jabbar might have a great business sense, but he was inept when it came to getting rid of rivals. Besides, his Italian friend would probably have a ship departing for Rome. It was just a matter of finding out when.

He made his way to the café and sat down at a table. He waited patiently. After some time had passed, Bashshar appeared and sat down with him. At least his trusted lieutenant had not been with him when his attack failed.

"News of our losses is starting to circulate," Bashshar said.

"I knew it wouldn't take long," Ishaq replied. He tossed the bags of money on the table. "Take this money to the widows. Tell them this is their husband's share, plus extra to compensate them for their loss. Tell them Ishaq will not forget them. Be generous. I want it known Ishaq takes care of his people."

"Your reputation does not seem to be damaged by this setback. In fact, it appears most of the men who are interested in our kind of work look at your setback as an opportunity."

"Good. Bashshar, I am going to Rome to see to some business. Continue to find replacements and train them while I am gone. Shake down a few merchants, and then I want you to kill a few of our small-time rivals." Ishaq pushed a list of names across the table. "I want to send a message that I am still running the show."

Bashshar nodded. "What are you going to do in Rome?"

"I am going to visit a friend. Do you remember Count Marcellus Theophylact?" Bashshar shook his head.

"His family is powerful and they have had considerable influence in Rome. Once upon a time, the Theophylact family controlled the infidel Church. Marcellus has a large shipping empire that brings him considerable income, and a mercenary army that he uses to fight turf battles with rival lords. He controls large sections of the city as well as the land surrounding Rome."

"Does this have something to do with the infidel priest?"

Ishaq scowled. "Yes."

"Do you think the count will be able to help you?"

"Of course." Ishaq stood up to go. "I expect to be back in Tyre by the end of the month."

"I will look for your return."

Ishaq smiled. "Good, I will see you then."

Ishaq walked down the crowded streets of Christian peasants, ignoring their hostile stares. A peasant with dull blue eyes, breathing through his mouth, looked at Ishaq and then stepped in front of the assassin's way. Ishaq stopped and looked up at the peasant. The man was tall; he had stooped shoulders and a fat gut hanging over his belt.

"Where do you think you're going, rag head?"

Ishaq lowered his eyes and bowed. "I mean no offense, good Christian sir. I am running my master's errands."

Another peasant, wearing a dirty black cap that covered his head and ears, came over. "Richard. Do you think this dirty little Saracen has any money?"

"I don't know Phillip. Perhaps we should find out."

Phillip chuckled. "He looks small. Maybe we should kill this dirty little Saracen and send him on his way to infidel hell."

"Masters," Ishaq said, still looking down at the ground, "I am poor, and I am doing my master's bidding. Let me pass, I have no money."

"You Arabs are such liars," Richard said as he reached out to grab Ishaq. "I think I am going to ring your dirty little neck."

All the years of training of the Nizari Ismaili flowed through Ishaq. Without any thought to what he was doing, he spun sideways. Drawing his knife, Ishaq slashed Richard's throat. The dimwitted peasant's eyes widened in shock. His blood poured out down the front of his leather jerkin. Richard sank to his knees, Phillip turned to run. In two steps, Ishaq caught Phillip and jumped up onto his back. Grabbing him by the hair, Ishaq savagely slashed his throat. The rest of the peasants watching the death of two of their comrades scattered, leaving Ishaq alone in the street. Ishaq started to chuckle. He bent over, yanked Phillip's hat off his head, and wiped his hands and his blade clean. Smiling, he threw the hat down and turned to walk away. This was turning out to be a pleasant day after all.

He ducked down an alleyway and headed down another street. After a considerable walk, he found himself at a line of row houses near the waterfront. He walked up to a decrepit old building that was the shipping office of Count Theophylact. The building was Greek, built in distyle in antis. Two weathered and chipped Corinthian columns supported the doorway. Above the columns was the attic, but the frieze that had once decorated the building was demolished. All that remained was two disembodied outstretched arms that reached skyward. At the corners of the building stood two gorgons that reminded Ishaq of vultures crouched upon their prey. Ishaq shoved open the bronze door and entered the building. A table, littered with papers, was in the middle of the room.

A small man with thinning grey hair sat behind the desk. His face was pale, and he had dark circles under his eyes. He was furiously scribbling out a bill of lading. "What do you want?" he said without looking up.

Ishaq smiled. "I am an old friend of Count Marcellus Theophylact, and I need to pay him a visit."

The man laughed. "Lord Theophylact has no friends."

Ishaq changed tact and walked up to the desk. Instinctively, the clerk looked up from his papers. For some reason, the hair on the back of his neck had stood up as Ishaq loomed over him.

"My name is Ishaq of Tyre, and I would like to arrange passage to Rome to visit my friend Marcellus."

The clerk's demeanor changed when he heard Ishaq's name. He pushed back from the desk. "I wish you had told me your name in the beginning. I am in such a hurry. Montferrat is demanding a list of everything leaving the city. His soldiers are searching all of our cargos."

He sprang up from the desk. "Can I get you anything? Would you like some qahwa?"

"No, all I need is a ship to take me to Rome."

The clerk smiled. "God favors you. A ship leaves tomorrow. I can inform the captain that an old friend of Marcellus Theophylact seeks passage, and I will list you as a member of the crew to get around Montferrat's men."

"That will do just fine."

"I will make the arrangements. Be here in the morning, and I will get your baggage brought on board. I will also have the captain send a couple of sailors to help escort you past the guards on the dock."

Ishaq smiled broadly, pulling a stack of coins out of his pocket. "Excellent."

The clerk beamed and bowed. "Thank you, thank you."

Ishaq smiled again. He liked the power money always brought to the table, and he enjoyed using it to make people do his bidding. He had no doubt that he would now receive royal treatment on this voyage. "I will be here in the morning," Ishaq said as he turned and walked out of the office.

Tomorrow would be his last day in Tyre for a while, which was good, he needed a change of landscape. Marcellus would roll out the red carpet for him. He had no doubt. He had eliminated some troublesome competitors for the count, and he was sure Marcellus had not forgotten. He headed back to one of the many places he stayed. The Nizari Ismaili had trained him to avoid a permanent residence; therefore, he was always on the move.

His life's goal was to someday disappear and establish himself in a faraway town. Far away from his past. Far away from people. He would build a home, settle down, and enjoy the good life with all the luxury that the money he had been saving could buy. He needed to pack for his journey. He was going to find this priest, he had no doubt, and he was going to find the answer to why Salah al-Din was interested in this man.

CHAPTER 20
THE CRETAN ADVENTURE

Byron was on deck when he heard the cry high up from the mast. "Land off the windward bow!" Byron moved to the front of the ship. He was dressed in a loose fitting, white cotton shirt. Leaning against the rail, he could feel the wind in his hair, and he could see the rugged landscape of the island of Crete far off in the distance.

Father Villhardain at the stern of the ship turned to Vercelis. "I thought we were sailing straight to Civitavecchia?"

"Father, I wish it were so, but for this trip to be profitable, I must transport cargo. Otherwise I cannot pay the crew."

Father Villhardain frowned. "I see. How long will we be here?'

"Depends on how long it takes to unload the cargo of olive oil. As long as the wind holds, we will leave in the morning. Do not fear; I intend to leave as soon as I can. The longer I stay, the crew will start disappearing from the ship. The dark-haired sirens of Crete will start calling the sailors away, and finding replacements," Captain Antonius Vercelis shrugged, "is difficult."

The rugged hills of the island drew closer.

"Why not leave today?" asked the priest.

Vercelis raised his eyebrows. "And risk a mutiny? These sailors look forward to these stops. I shudder to think what would happen if I did not give them time ashore...just not too much time."

Father Villhardain looked at the weathered, muscle bound sailors on the deck. "I understand, my son."

"Have you ever been to Crete, Father?"

"Yes…but I was younger. I tramped the hills of the Minoans, admiring the ruins of the palace, but that was long ago. I don't wish to see them again."

The ship entered the harbor of Chandax, and a small boat came alongside the ship. "Pardon me, Father, I need to negotiate with the harbor pilot."

A man with a red fez stood up in the back of the small boat. "Twenty nomismata to pilot your ship to the dock," he cried.

"You are drunk," Vercelis shouted back. "Five nomismata, or I will lower my own boat to sound the channel!"

The Greek's face turned red. "Lower your boat, and when you ground your ship, I will buy the salvage rights." The Greek paused. "Ten nomismata, and that is only because your ship is not worth salvaging."

Vercelis leaned over the rail and laughed. "Ten nomismata, but only because my men are tired."

"Agreed!" the Greek cried as he clambered on board the *Lady Mary Grace*. The Greek's skin was burnt from day after day in the sun. He took off his fez and ran his hand over his bald head to wipe away the sweat. Replacing the fez, he shouted up to the sailors standing on the yardarms, "Shorten the main sail and slow the ship."

Captain Vercelis tossed a small bag of coins to the pilot. The Greek opened the bag and then shook it. Satisfied that the coins were all there, he stuffed them in his pocket. The ship slowly came about. From the bow of the ship, a sailor threw a line into the water and called the depth as the Greek skillfully maneuvered the ship. In the distance, Byron saw the fortress that guarded the harbor. A red flag emblazoned with the gold tetragramic cross of the Byzantine Empire floated lazily above the battlements.

A white sandy beach spread out next to an ocean of blue. Byron was ready to leave the ship even if it was only for a few hours. A few hours ashore were better than being stuck in this wooden hell of wet misery. Working the sails, the Greek guided the *Lady Mary*

Grace to the dock were the ship was made fast.

On the dock, a man in a blue silk tunic was lounging on the chair of his litter. He held a black cane. A servant behind the man was holding a parasol over his head to shade him from the sun while the rest of the servants stood next to the litter sweating. "Captain Vercelis," the man in the blue tunic shouted, "I trust your journey was uneventful."

"Master Domninus. It is kind of you to ask. The ship almost capsized, but other than that it, was no worse than usual."

"Ah, well... I hope there was no breakage. You know I will not pay for damaged amphora."

"Master Domninus, your cargo fared well. It was packed tightly in the hull, and it was the only thing that kept the ship from rolling over."

"Excellent." Master Domninus thumped his cane on the dock. "Well, my good captain, unload my cargo of olive oil here. My servants are on their way to retrieve the amphora."

"As you wish, Master Domninus. You heard the lord," Captain Vercelis cried to his crew, "on your feet! I want all of the amphora unloaded." The sailors grumbled. "The faster it is done, the more time you can spend ashore. We weigh anchor in the morning for Civitavecchia." The sailors cheered.

"Do you wish to go ashore?" Byron asked James.

James frowned as he looked at the unimpressive village of stone buildings. "I don't know." Just then, two dark haired women walked down onto the dock. James saw them and smiled. "Perhaps a few hours ashore will do no harm."

A plank was tossed onto the dock. Byron hurried below deck to buckle on his sword and then stuffed his dagger into his belt. He returned to the deck and looked for James, but he was not there. Going to the ships rail, he could see James on the dock talking to the women.

"How does he do that?" Byron asked aloud.

"It appears to be a misspent gift or a curse," Brother Carl replied as he leaned against the rail watching James walk away. "I have never seen a man woo a lass so quickly in my life."

Byron hurried to the plank, but James was already strolling

down the dock with a woman in each arm. The sailors, lugging the amphora of olive oil down the deck, blocked the plank that led to the dock. Byron stood impatiently waiting for his turn to leave the ship. At last, the plank cleared, and Byron was able to go down to the dock.

He looked up but James was gone. "Damn it!" He hurried to catch his friend. He reached the end of the quay and looked down the crowded street, but James was nowhere in sight.

Byron walked up and down the street, but his search was futile. Swearing, he gave up, and hating the crowd of people, he decided to take a walk on the empty white beach. He stopped to watch a fisherman mending his nets. The man's black hair was turning grey; his beard knotted and tangled. A threadbare tunic that had once been black hung from his shoulders.

The man did not look up. "Either help or go away," the man said in French. "I dislike people who stare."

"I meant no offense. You're not Greek."

"No, but you're a Norman. I hear it in your speech. From Britton?"

"Sir Byron Fitzwalter of Gowen Ireland."

"Humph, a knight marked with the cross," the fisherman said as he tied broken cord into a knot. He held up the repaired section of net and looked at his work. "So, how goes the war?"

Byron crossed his arms. "Not well."

The fisherman looked up at Byron with one eye closed. "Humph, an inevitable end. So, Sir Byron Fitzwalter of Ireland, what brings you to Crete?"

"I am on my way to Rome."

The fisherman opened his eye to give Byron a piercing stare. "The war is not going well. A disaster from what I hear, and you are going to Rome. Do you think the Holy Father will aid you?"

"How do you hear such things?" Byron snapped. "As far as my business in Rome, that is my affair."

The fisherman laughed. "Is it your affair? Or does your business affect others. There are no secrets, Sir Byron Fitzwalter. Ships stop here from all over. I know more about what goes on in the world than you do. As for Jerusalem, I know every inch of the city, its history. I was there long before you ever set foot in the Levant."

"You were a crusader?"

"You could say that, but alas, now I am here and I cast my nets upon the sea. Some days I catch fish… other days not."

"My lord, tell me your name."

"My name is not important. I am what you see. Either you accept my story or you do not. If you knew my name, would it improve my credence?"

"No, it would not." Byron looked out at the sea. "Well, tell me fisherman, if you know so much about the world, will the Holy Father aid us?"

"Yes…and no."

The corner of Byron's mouth turned down into a slight frown. "Your skill as a seer is lacking."

The fisherman smiled. "You want more then."

"Indeed."

The fisherman gathered his nets. "The Holy Father will aid you. You will find something of great value, but it will come at a terrible cost."

"I don't like your future."

The fisherman stood up and draped his nets over his shoulder. "It is not my future. It is yours. God be with thee, Sir Byron Fitzwalter." The fisherman started to walk away, his bare feet leaving impressions in the sand.

"Fitzwalter!" Byron turned to see James walking towards him.

"I have been looking all over for you." James motioned to him. "Come. I have found an inn. There is good wine, and the women are waiting for us. You have to see the women of Crete. Mon Dieu they are such beautiful creatures. I should have come here years ago."

Byron turned back to say farewell to the fisherman, but he was gone. James furled his brow. "What are you looking for?"

Byron turned back to James. "I was talking to a fisherman."

James tilted his head and looked at Byron. "If you say so, my friend. When I saw you, you were alone, looking out at the sea."

Byron looked at the sand where the fisherman had walked, but no footprints remained. Byron stared at the sand. The man was just here. He glanced up at James and decided to drop the matter.

Maybe he was crazy. The banshee, now this. He was losing his mind. He could feel another headache starting.

James could see the confusion in Byron's face. "Come, my friend. You need a rest. Drink some wine, a kiss from a serving wench perhaps, and you will feel better."

With a glance over his shoulder in the direction of the fisherman, Byron followed James back to the streets of Chandax. His head hurt, and the fetid smell of sewage and trash made it worse. James shoved two slumbering drunks out of his way as he entered a plain white washed stone building. Byron entered the courtyard and could hear lutes playing accompanied by a lyra. Two girls were dancing to the music. He stopped to watch their graceful bodies swaying to the music.

James grabbed Byron by the shoulder. "Come, Cyra and Megoris are waiting."

"And who are they?"

"The girls that I told you about!"

James led him to a table where two women sat at a table drinking wine from wooden bowls. James sat down on the bench next to the women. "This is Cyra. Megoris is for you."

The woman named Megoris wore a low-cut, black dress that clung to her slender body. She smiled as she tilted her head back to run her hand through her long, dark hair. Uncomfortable, Byron sat down next to her.

"James has told me about you," she said in halting French. "I ... glad you...join us." She handed Byron a bowl of wine and cuddled up next to him, laying her head on his shoulder. James was already kissing Cyra. Byron took a big gulp of wine from the bowl. "You...crusader?" Megoris asked, her broken French slurred from the wine.

"Yes," Byron said as he felt Megoris' arm slip around his neck.

James stood up, taking Cyra by the hand. "I see you and Megoris are getting along. I think I will take this charming lady for a walk." Before Byron could say wait, James turned leading Cyra from the room. He was about to call to James when he felt Megoris' hand on his jaw. She pulled his face towards hers and began to kiss him. Their lips parted and Megoris lifted a wine bowl to

Byron's lips.

"Drink. Wine. Nectar of gods. You wish to be a god."

"There is only one God," Byron replied.

"Serious," Megoris said as she pulled at Byron's cheek. "James right, you...need... rest."

Megoris started to kiss him again. Byron wanted to resist, but he found his will power slipping as the wine and the music took effect. His headache was going away, and he was starting to relax. Who cared? Megoris was now breathing heavily. Her hand was on his neck giving him a massage. "Ooh, tight muscles."

Byron took another drink of wine. The Greek musicians were now playing a slow song and Byron felt sleepy. He felt a tug. At first, he ignored it, and then he felt another tug. He looked at Megoris and saw a glint of gold shine in her hand. Instantly, he reached to his neck. His gold cross was gone. He sat up and grabbed her hand.

"Let me go!" Megoris cried out in Greek. Two large Greek men stood up in the corner. Byron grabbed Megoris' hand and slammed it repeatedly against the table until it opened revealing his cross.

"You filthy wench. How dare you steal from me!" Byron cried as he grabbed up his cross and put it back around his neck.

"Help me!" Megoris cried to the two Greek men now lumbering across the courtyard, shoving tables and chairs out of their way. Byron drew his sword and backed up to a wall. The Greeks drew their knives and spread out to flank him. With a nod, they rushed him. Byron moved sideways. He struck the Greek in the sleeveless leather tunic with his sword, opening a gash in the man's arm. The man screamed. Dropping his knife, he instinctively grabbed his arm. Byron kicked the man in the stomach with his boot and shoved him out of the way. Turning, he faced the other Greek who was wearing a heavy leather jerkin. The Greek crouched in front him, his arms stretched out ready to strike.

"Your blade is a little short for a sword fight," Byron cried.

The Greek smiled and then charged. In a swift and fluid move, the Greek wrapped his arm around the sword, pulling it close to his body so Byron could not strike. The man slashed at him with his knife. Byron leaned back, the blade just missing his throat. Byron tried to pull the sword free, but the Greek had it bound so tightly it was no use. The Greek slashed at Byron again, and Byron let go of the sword hilt as he drew his own dagger.

The Greek laughed. "Now we are equal." He let go of the sword, and it clattered to the stone floor. Both men circled. The music stopped, and the crowd gathered to watch. Out of the corner of his eye, Byron could see money changing hands as wagers were being placed.

The Greek charged again, and Byron stepped sideways as he moved past the attack. Both men spun to face each other. Byron backed up next to a table. The Greek pressed forward. The Greek charged and Byron kicked the table over. The table flipped and the Greek tripped over it, falling forward. Byron stabbed him repeatedly in the back. With a gasp, the Greek fell to the ground. Byron swiftly stepped past the dying man and grabbed up his sword. Holding the weapon in front of him, he backed down the hall.

"James!" Byron shouted. "James!"

James stumbled out of a side room, holding his sword in one hand while tucking his shirt into his tights with the other. "I leave you in the company of a beautiful woman, and you still manage to get into a fight?"

"It's time to go!" Byron cried. The crowd of angry Greeks began to push close. Backing to the exit, both James and Byron held their swords out to fend off the coming attack.

A serving wench came out of a side door. James snatched a wine skin from her hand. "Thank you my dear," he cried as he pushed through the doorway. Once they reached the street, they turned and ran. The crowd of Greeks poured out into the street behind them.

James laughed. "Is this a retreat? Or, are we just running?"

"Call it what you like," Byron snapped. "That worthless wench tried to steal my gold crucifix."

They ran down the street and ducked into an alley, running beneath hanging laundry strung between the two buildings. They came out onto a deserted street. Byron paused to look around. In the dim light, he could make out the darkened shapes of two derelicts passed out on a doorstep. Byron started to run. He could hear the sound of James' boots slapping on the ground behind him. They ran down two more streets until James glanced behind him. No one was following. He stopped and leaned against a wall. Uncapping the wine skin, James took a drink and then handed it to Byron.

"Ah well, I was done with that girl anyway. My God, Byron, you know how to have a good time. Did you at least steal a kiss?"

Byron finished drinking, capped the skin, and handed it back to James. "I was assaulted with kisses."

"And to think I wasted her beauty on you." James started to laugh, and then throwing his arm over Byron's shoulder he started walking. "Do you remember how to find our ship?"

"Keep walking, we are headed in the right direction."

James took another big gulp of wine from the skin and passed it back to Byron who did the same. James started to hum a tune and after a few more steps, he started to sing.

> *"In Calais, lives lonely maiden*
> *her beauty is known far and wide.*
> *And every time I see her, I want to make her mine.*
> *Her eyes are blue and her face is fair,*
> *though a serving wench she be,*
> *but....,"* James slurred, *"but....* Byron how's it go?"
> Byron began to sing,
> *"But forever in my heart*
> *she will always reign a queen."*
> "That's it," James cried.
> *"But forever in my heart*
> *she will always reign a queen."*

"Fitzwalter help me sing the chorus. Don't be a churlish knave." Byron looked at James and reluctantly began to sing with James out of key.

> *"Girl fetch a round and hurry.*
> *And sit with us and sing*
> *Sing with us beneath the moon.*

For tonight we will be merry.
For once the morning sun, tops the golden hills.
To our deep regret we bid adieu and swiftly ride away."

James stopped singing. "Byron, you're my friend. You know that...You know that."

"Yes, James, I know that." James started to sing again.

"In empty streets of Calais,
  my maiden walks alone.
Beneath the stars she awaits,
For me return to home.
Jerusalem's need has called me away,
  and though leagues lay between us.
In my heart the maiden of Calais still remains my queen."

James nudged Byron and together they began to sing.

"Girl fetch a round and hurry.
And sit with us and sing
Sing with us beneath the moon.
For tonight we will be merry.
For once the morning sun, tops the golden hills.
To our deep regret we bid adieu and swiftly ride away."

A shuttered window above them flew open, and a hoarse voice shouted at them in Greek. Before James could answer, the window banged shut. James and Byron started to laugh as they staggered down the cobblestone road. At last, they reached the dock and stumbled aboard the *Lady Mary Rose*. Captain Vercelis was on deck, leaning against the ship's rail.

"My lords, I see that you had a good time in town."

"Indeedy," James sniggered. "Well I did. I rode a lass and Byron....despite my best efforts to find him a suitable maiden.... got into fight."

Captain Vercelis stopped leaning against the rail and stood up. "Did they follow you?"

"They did not follow," replied Byron.

"No, we retreated faster than they could run," James laughed.

"My lords, perhaps it would be best if you went below and stayed out of sight."

"How dare you suggest we hide," James snapped.

"My lords, if it comes to a fight, then I will call upon you, but I would rather avoid a fight. The last thing I need is to be detained here by the Byzantine authorities."

"A sound strategy," James said. "Lay in wait and then strike the knaves. Don't you think so, Byron?"

"Yes, and we shall slay them all."

"Good night, my lords, in the morning we shall be underway."

"Good night, captain," Byron replied. Byron nodded as he helped James down the stairs to the lower deck. Stumbling around in the dark, Byron found their hammocks.

"What a great night," James sighed as he lay down." Without another word, he was fast asleep.

CHAPTER 21
BYRON VISITS ROME

Byron awoke to the swish and slap of the waves hitting the hull of the ship. His head hurt. Groaning, he got up and made his way to the main deck. He stood for a moment watching the ships bow rise and dip with each swell. With a sigh, Byron turned and stumbled to the ship's rail, leaned over and retched.

"Too much merriment?" Brother Carl asked. Byron did not answer as he clutched the rail and looked down at the sea. Brother Carl laughed and walked away as Byron vomited again.

The days at sea slipped by. The captain may have known where they were, but it came as a surprise to Byron when land appeared and the ship stood off the Italian port of Civitavecchia. The *Lady Mary Grace* slowly made its way through the press of vessels, each crew competing to force their ship's way to the docks to unload their cargo and get paid.

"We cannot get any nearer to the dock," Captain Vercelis complained. "The other bastard captains have taken every available space of the dock. We must wait our turn, for I see no way to dock this ship, so I am lowering the ship's boat. The first mate and a few volunteers from the crew will take you into the harbor." In a lower voice he continued, "I know why you are going to Rome, my lords, I only hope you can persuade the Holy Father to intervene ere it is too late."

"The Holy Father has many concerns," the priest replied, "but the safety of Jerusalem will be priority."

"I hope so. Many of us depend on the trade that comes from Outremer. I hope the Holy Father understands that."

"The welfare of all Christians is his concern."

"Father, I know you will do what you can," Captain Vercelis replied, stalking away shouting orders.

They lowered the ship's small boat over the side and tossed the men's baggage aboard as the waves tossed the small craft about. A large swell almost slammed the boat into the side of the ship, making Byron less than enthusiastic about getting into it. At last, everyone was in the boat and the sailors began to row away. The first mate raised a mast and small sail. The boat picked up speed as they sailed into the harbor of Civitavecchia.

Father Villhardain breathed in deeply. It was good to be home, no matter how short the stay. A great fortress guarded the harbor, and the boat glided past in the darkened waters from the shadow of its walls. Father Villhardain looked up at the towering wall with pride, knowing Pope John X had marched at the head of the Papal Army to liberate the city from the oppression of the Saracens. The boat moved beyond the wall's shadow as it tacked to an empty space at a small dock. A sailor jumped from the boat's bow and tied it to the dock.

Byron could not wait a moment longer, and to the amusement of the sailors, he clumsily scrambled his way out of the boat. Father Villhardain stepped off the boat behind him. "You already look better."

"My favorite thing about traveling by ship," Byron said with relief, "is the moment I leave it."

"It is always a blessing to reach one's destination safely," Father Villhardain replied.

The sailors tossed their baggage onto the dock, and after a second trip, their armor and other gear was brought ashore. Once the last of their belongings were deposited on the dock, Father Villhardain took Brother Carl in search of transportation.

The dock was busy with barges bringing the wealth of the

Far East to the Italian merchants of the Papal States. James paid no heed to the commercial bustle of the dock. He spent his time admiring the few women who happened to be at the waterfront. Byron noticed his friend's distraction. "Do you not think of anything else?" Byron asked.

James glanced at Byron and frowned. "Of course, I do."

An hour passed, and Father Villhardain returned with a wagon driven by a young man dressed in a black tunic. Brother Carl, riding a donkey, was leading two black Spanish jennets. The baggage was loaded on the wagon and they started off for Rome. They passed through the gates of Civitavecchia. The wagon bumped along on the uneven stones of the Via Aurelia. Byron and James rode ahead in silence, watchful for brigands.

The sun was shining, but there was a coolness in the north wind. Lines of green vines stretched across the hills of brown grass, burnt dry from the summer sun. Groves of olive trees shaded the road, which wound along the Italian coastline, passing through the small Italian towns. After two days, they entered the outskirts of Rome. In the distance, he saw the imposing brown walls of a large fortress. In the center of the battlements, rose a large round stone keep. A white flag with the golden keys of Saint Peter snapped in the wind.

They approached the city gates. Peasants with their wagons were jammed chaotically at the arches of the gates waiting to pay duty on their imports. The chatter of their Italian voices filled the air with cacophony of sound. Pale faced merchants in brown tunics had come out of the city to inspect their shipments of silks or rare spices. Byron sat on his horse waiting for their turn to pass.

"Ah, the Castle of Saint Angelo is a welcome sight," the priest sighed.

James eyed the fortress. "A strong castle indeed."

The priest smiled. "Yes, it serves its new purpose well, but it was not built to be a fortress. It was built as a tomb for the emperor Hadrian."

Byron turned in his saddle to face the priest. "They built that as a tomb?"

"Indeed, but when the Visigoths sacked Rome. They entered the mausoleum and desecrated the emperors remains. After that it sat derelict and empty, but the Holy Father has now put it to good use."

Byron looked at the castle. He could see the sun glinting on the armor of the men manning the ramparts. He pushed his horse forward a few steps, stopping next to a large wagon to get a better look. A woman with fair skin and high cheekbones glanced up at Byron. She was sitting in a wagon surrounded by bolts of silk and bundles of fur. Her dark hair was covered with white lace. A green cloak draped over her shoulders concealed most of her yellow dress. Their eyes met and Byron tilted forward in his saddle and gave a slight bow. A faint smile blushed across the woman's lips, and then faded away as she looked to the grey-haired man in a black tunic standing next to her. The man engrossed with making notations into his black book paid her no heed. Byron looked at the woman, but she did not look back.

The man closed his book with a dull snap and motioned for his servants to move the wagon forward. The woman pulled the hood of her cloak over her head. The wagon lumbered forward through the arch of the gate and disappeared amidst the other merchants entering Rome.

James rode up next to Byron and winked. "There goes a fine catch, Fitzwalter. You should have got her name."

"I think she was already caught."

"She was not caught. That man was her father. I doubt if he even remembers how to pleasure such a young woman." Byron frowned at James and said nothing. James shrugged. "Well, I doubt if he does."

Byron and James pushed their way to the gateway. Father Villhardain followed behind. Knights in red surcoats emblazoned with a white cross leveled their spears and blocked the way. To Byron's surprise, a knight with blond hair that hung to his shoulders stepped forward. He bowed to the priest as he motioned to his men to let them pass.

"Father Villhardain, it is good to see your return," he said with a German accent. "His Holiness sent instructions for us to watch for your return. He extends his blessings and his greetings."

"Thank you, my son. It is good to be home, however brief. Peace be with you." The guards bowed again and let them pass. Byron's black cloak with its white crusader cross flowed behind him as he crossed the Tiber. His black horse pranced as it clattered across the bridge. James rode beside him. The handsome image of a chevalier in his blue cloak with the emblems of the marshal of Jerusalem. The Italian peasants stepped aside as they passed. Byron caught snippets of their conversations as they payed homage to them as soldiers of the crusades. They rode down the street between the old and dour buildings of Rome. Columns, chipped and worn, lined the way. Here and there stood stone statues of the grand monuments to the faded power of Rome. Byron glanced at each of the life-like carvings as he rode by, but he noticed that the Italians paid them no heed.

They entered a square where a large fountain bubbled and splashed water upon the stone street. It was growing hot, and a cool breeze wafted across the plaza. They halted to enjoy the feeling. Byron sat on his horse watching the Italians lounging in the cool air. The image of a soldier carved into a marble panel caught his eye. The panel was not as grand as the statues of Rome's ruling elite. The soldier's helmet was adorned with a crest that ran from the front of the helmet to the back, his armor decorated with medallions. In one hand, he was wielding a short sword, his arm bulged, the sinews of his forearm taught. In his other hand, he held by the hair a bearded head that he had just severed. The soldier, bent forward, was pressing his attack; his greaves pressed against the body of a fallen man. Byron stared down from his horse into the soldier's face. The man's brow furrowed over empty eyes, his jaw clenched.

Byron wondered at the image. "What was this man?" he asked the priest as he pointed at the marble frieze. The priest, sitting next to the page on the wagon seat, leaned forward to get a better look.

Father Villhardain smiled. "My son, that is a centurion, a Roman soldier. The panel represents Rome's wars against the barbarians."

Byron nodded, as he remembered Father Villhardain's tale of the centurion and the treasure. Now he had an image to put with the title. He knew little of Rome and nothing about the history of the empire. Byron had heard of Rome, the city of the Holy Father of the Catholic Church, but that was all he knew. He had never given much thought to politics or history, the dominion of kings and their advisors. It was not necessary to know such things. It was not his to question a decision of the king, nor was it safe to do so.

The only history he did know, as every good Norman Knight should, was that William the Conqueror had defeated the usurper Harold the Saxon at the Battle of Hastings to become the King of England. It was God's righteous judgment for Harold's oath breaking to William, and Harold had paid with his life, dying on the field of Hastings. It was all the history he had needed to know. Now, walking through the city of Caesars, it brought home to Byron the magnitude of his ignorance.

The wagon slowly lumbered through the countryside of olive trees and up a hill to a sprawling house. The Lateran Palace, the home of the Bishop of Rome, stood amidst a lawn of brown grass. It was a haphazard collection of structures, as if the architects could not agree on course or direction. The buildings of limestone pillars had walls of light tan plaster. Arches adorned the windows, while red tiles covered the roof. Largest of all was the basilica of Saint John Lateran. It had a great bronze door centered beneath a white marble arch. Above the arch, a stained-glass window depicting a red rose glistened in the afternoon sun. Against the blue sky, two square bell towers, each topped with a golden cross, crowned the basilica's roof.

Byron stopped his horse in the shadow of the cross. "Is this our destination?" he asked Father Villhardain.

"Yes. The house of the Holy Father. It is very old. The palace once belonged to the Plautii Laterani family. During the reign of Emperor Nero, Plautius Laterani was accused of conspiring against the emperor. The palace was confiscated along with all of the family's property. Long years passed until the Emperor Constantine gave the house to the Bishop of Rome to be his residence." Father Villhardain leaned back and stretched. "I am looking forward to this journey's end. It will be good to see my old friend and mentor, Cardinal Morra." The priest looked at Byron. "How is your Italian?"

"My Italian is fair."

"James?"

"Father, I speak it like a native tongue."

"Good, then there will be no problems."

The wagon rolled past a large bronze statue of a man on horseback and came to a stop in front of the palace. The courtyard was empty. Byron glanced around. He had expected a large reception of churchmen anxious to learn the condition of the Kingdom of Jerusalem. Yet, he could only see one man waiting for them near the doorway of the palace.

CHAPTER 22
THE LATERAN PALACE

Cardinal Morra stood in the shade of the doorway with his hands behind his back waiting to greet Father Villhardain. A red, broad brimmed hat shaded his face. A white cloak was draped over his red cassock. Father Villhardain got up stiffly and stepped off the wagon. He approached the cardinal and started to kneel when the cardinal surprised the priest by embracing him.

"Father Villhardain," the cardinal exclaimed with a smile, "my prayers for your safe arrival have been answered. I have been worried for your safety. Ill news, brought by the Genoese traders of Outremer, speak of a terrible Christian defeat. They say that Saladin is moving unopposed to take Jerusalem. I feared the worst for you."

"Your Eminence, once I tell my tale, it will only confirm that the news you have heard from afar is true."

"I thought you might say that," responded Cardinal Morra with a frown. "I see we have much to discuss. Come, my servants will take you to your rooms, and once you are unpacked and refreshed from your long journey, we will talk."

"You are very gracious, Your Eminence. It has been a tiring journey, more so than I expected."

Byron watched the two churchmen talk. Only one cardinal

was here, and it appeared as if the priest expected nothing more. Servants appeared to unload the baggage from the wagon. Byron dismounted his horse as a page took the animal and led it away.

"I see you have also lost your horse," James said as he came over and stood next to Byron. "The knave was in such haste to take my horse I did not think he was going to give me the courtesy of dismounting... I wonder if they were afraid we might not give their horses back."

A young man wearing the livery of the keys of Saint Peter walked over and gave a crisp bow. "My lords, welcome, I will show you to your room."

"Room?" James replied. "Does this mean I must spend more nights listening to Fitzwalter snore?"

"I don't know why you are worried," Byron replied. "I am sure you will make arrangements to stay with some maiden who desperately needs your attention."

"Aye, and normally that would be true," said James with a chuckle, "but I am afraid Father Villhardain would disapprove. After all, we are guests of the Holy Father."

The servant looked at both men, his lips pressed together tightly as if he disapproved of their conversation. "My lords, follow me." The page led them though a bronze doorway and into a hall lined with mosaics.

James whispered to Byron as they walked. "I am starting to think that I will go on to France. You should come with me. These church people don't know their business."

"Of course, they don't," Byron replied. "That is why we are here."

"And what makes you think they will listen?"

Byron looked at James and frowned. "I made a promise to the priest, one that I intend to keep."

James held Byron in his gaze. "Fitzwalter, Jerusalem is on the verge of collapse, and the Church sends one cardinal to meet Father Villhardain? I would have thought the loss of Jerusalem would have earned an immediate meeting with the Holy Father. We may be here for weeks before the Pope grants the priest an audience, and by that time, the issue may be moot." James glanced at the page to see if he was listening. "This journey is most likely a waste of time."

"Saladin's victory is assured if we stand idle," Byron snapped. "This journey is far more worthy of my efforts than dying in the service of a minor lord, in some muddy field, fighting over land."

"I thought you would say something like that," James sighed.

They came to a stop and the servant opened the door. "Your room, my lords." James walked into the room. Their belongings were piled neatly in the middle of the floor. Byron collapsed in a chair near a window.

James looked at the room. "Well, at least they got us two beds." The servant closed the door.

"I was also surprised by the lack of reception," Byron said. "Perhaps the Church is better informed than I thought."

"Or they don't care." James replied.

"I am certain they care. After all they sent Father Villhardain to the Holy Lands to find..." Byron stopped. He had almost let Father Villhardain's secret out.

"To find what? Fitzwalter we are in Rome. In the Lateran. You could at least now give me some idea of why we are here?"

Byron took a deep breath. "I suppose I owe you that. There is no harm in telling you what I know." Byron paused and looked around as if he suspected there was a spy hiding in the corner. "Father Villhardain has found the treasure of a Roman Emperor, and we are going to go and bring the treasure back to Rome."

James sat down in a chair and tilted his head holding Byron in a skeptical gaze. "A treasure hunt? For what purpose?"

"To finance a new crusade to defeat Saladin."

James laughed. "France is looking more inviting. Fitzwalter, do you really believe that these churchmen, once they have a treasure, will use the money wisely?" James lowered his voice. "Despite the fact these churchmen hide behind the façade of doing good works. The truth is, they are all about enriching themselves and increasing their power."

"I don't believe that! Look at the crusades! If it were not for the Church, Jerusalem would still be in the possession of the Saracens. It was the Church that reopened the Holy Lands for Christian pilgrims."

"The crusades had nothing to do with the capture of Jerusalem,"

James interrupted bitterly. "The crusades were nothing more than a means to send the violent and the lawless somewhere else to fight."

Byron shook his head. "I don't believe that the Church has a higher purpose, nor do I believe Father Villhardain would go to all this trouble just to have his efforts wasted."

"Father Villhardain is not making the decisions. Others, who have risked nothing, will have the final say. And because they have not worked for it, how it is wasted will not trouble them."

A knock at the door ended their discussion. "Careful, my friend," Byron whispered. "You never know who will take offense, especially when we are guests."

James turned and walked over to the door and opened it. Father Villhardain was waiting at the door with a servant of the cardinal.

"Byron, would you come with me?" the priest asked. "I am going to a meet with his Eminence Cardinal Morra, and I would like for you to give your account of the Battle of Hattin. James, I assume you wish to see Rome, so I have brought you a guide."

James looked at the young man who fidgeted under the knights stare. "Well," James said jauntily, "it is my plan to go and stretch my legs. I welcome the company." James smiled and looked down at the servant. "Do keep up." James glanced at Byron with a grin. "Enjoy. I am off to see Rome. Laissez Aller! Sally forth."

The servant looked at Father Villhardain and whispered, "Father, this knight lusts for the harlots of Rome."

"Do what you can," Father Villhardain replied. "I do not expect a miracle, nor do I expect you to follow him into a lion's den." The servant nodded, and with the look of a lamb being led to slaughter, he left running to catch up with the self-assured knight.

Byron shook his head. "I hope he doesn't get into too much trouble."

Father Villhardain frowned. "God looks after children and fools. We should go. The cardinal is waiting." Byron and Father Villhardain walked down the hallway to the cardinal's chamber. "Urban is frail," the priest whispered. "Certain cardinals are positioning themselves to be chosen as the next Pope. You and I will meet with His Holiness in a few days. Our meeting today is to prepare our presentation to His Holiness. Cardinal Morra will have many questions, and he will give you advice on what to say or not say." Byron nodded. "My son, the Holy Father wields more power than any king, but he is growing old and becomes distracted easily. Pay attention to Cardinal Morra and follow his advice."

Byron looked at the priest. He did not like Father Villhardain's insinuation, and he was beginning to suspect that James' cynical view of the Church might have been more accurate than his own view.

Father Villhardain stopped beneath the image of an eagle with two heads and turned to face Byron. "What do you know of the history of Rome, or for that matter, the crusades?"

"What is there to know father? We are fighting the enemies of Christ; there is nothing else to know."

Father Villhardain frowned. "In this instance, it would be helpful if you had some understanding of the events you are a part of. I don't have the time to teach the history of the world. This short lesson will have to do."

The priest glanced down the empty corridor and then looked back at Byron. "In its final years, the Roman Empire was split in two with two co-emperors. One ruled from Constantinople, the other from Ravenna. The Western half of the Empire did not survive, as a series of invasions by Vandals, Goths, and Lombards destroyed it. The Eastern half lasted long after the destruction of the West but became more Greek than Latin."

Father Villhardain paused. "The Byzantine empire is in grave danger. Many years ago, before you were born, a new threat arose in the east. The Seljauk Turks invaded the Holy Lands and overran the lands of the Eastern Roman Empire. The Emperor of Constantinople, Romanus Diogenes, led a massive army to turn back the invasion, but at Manzikert the Byzantines were defeated and the Emperor captured. More defeats followed, and the Eastern Roman Empire was opened for invasion.

"In an effort to save his empire from the Saracens, the new Emperor Alexis Comnenus appealed to his Holiness, Urban the second, for assistance to push back the Saracens, and reopen the Holy city of Jerusalem to Christian pilgrims. Urban called upon the kings of the West for a crusade, and the call was answered as

Christian armies marched to the city of Jerusalem, waging war to bring it back under Christian control.

"God favored us. Against tremendous odds, Jerusalem was captured and a new Christian Kingdom was established. Unfortunately, none of this goodwill healed the breach between the East and the West. The Emperors in Constantinople consider themselves the heirs of Rome and all others usurpers of their authority, including the Holy Father. That double-headed eagle," Father Villhardain pointed at the image on the wall, "is the symbol of the emperors in Constantinople. It represents the Eastern and Western Roman Empire. If you know nothing else, that symbol embodies the mindset of the emperors in Constantine's city."

"And now we are losing," Byron replied.

Father Villhardain glanced down the hallway to make sure it was still empty. "If the situation in the Levant is going to be stabilized to our advantage, the cost will be tremendous in resources and treasure. That is why finding the treasure of Honorius is so important. It is also why the Holy Roman Emperor, Frederick Barbarossa of the House of Hohenstaufen, must not be excommunicated."

"Excommunicated?"

Father Villhardain sighed. "I should not have told you that. We must go, Cardinal Morra is waiting."

Byron and Father Villhardain walked the rest of the marble hallway in silence. Byron looked up at a painting of Jesus Christ hung on the wall. It reminded him of the rustic frescos in the caverns of the apostles. It was the work of a great master, but Byron could not help feel that they were superficial in comparison with the simple frescos in a far-away cave in the Holy Lands. After climbing a flight of stairs, they reached the chambers of Cardinal Morra. Two servants opened the door, and Byron and Father Villhardain entered the room.

CHAPTER 23
THE CARDINAL AND THE PRIEST

Cardinal Alberto di Morra sat behind a richly carved table near a window. Light streaming through the window cast its light on his careworn face. "Welcome," said the cardinal, smiling. "Come sit down." He gestured to two chairs near the table. "I have been looking forward to this conversation for some time."

"Your Eminence," the priest said, "I am looking forward to receiving your wisdom and guidance on this difficult matter that affects the Church."

Father Villhardain turned to Byron. "Your Eminence, Sir Byron Fitzwalter of the Order of the Knights of Saint John of Jerusalem. He has returned with me from the Levant."

"Your Eminence," Byron said as he bowed.

Cardinal Morra leaned back in his chair. "I have heard from the Genoese that the Army of Jerusalem has been destroyed by the Sultan Saladin who is now unchecked and running rampant throughout the Kingdom. Is this true?"

"It is true," Father Villhardain sighed. He then motioned to Byron. "Sir Fitzwalter rode with the Army of Jerusalem. I think he can best tell you what befell the Christian host."

Cardinal Morra turned to Byron. "Tell me your story, my son. How did Christendom's best soldiers come to be defeated?"

Byron told his story of the Christian Army's march to defeat at the Horns of Hattin. When he finished Cardinal Morra sighed. "It is worse than I thought, much worse." Cardinal Morra turned to Father Villhardain. "Do you think your efforts will bear fruit? Will it aid in reversing our misfortune?"

"I don't know, Your Eminence. Saladin's war came at a most unfortunate time. By the miracle of God, I had just found the scrolls of Achatius Licinius Gaeta. I know where the treasure was, but I was unable to journey there to see if it still remains." Father Villhardain paused. "I fear I will have to present to his holiness my incomplete work, and hope the Holy Father will send an expedition to retrieve the treasure based on faith."

"But it was there at one time, was it not, Father Villhardain?

"Yes. The centurion left the treasure in Babylon."

"Babylon!" the cardinal exclaimed. "Nebuchadnezzar's city?" Cardinal Morra tilted back in his chair and scoffed, "How appropriate."

"Yes. Finding the treasure will be hard. Getting it back to Rome will be difficult, especially with the recent developments in the Levant."

Cardinal Morra nodded. "It would be much easier to convince the Holy Father to risk sending an expedition deep into the lands of the Saracens if we had proof. Lack thereof will make our plans more difficult."

"Yes, but that is not the worst. Saladin is aware of our plans."

Cardinal Morra sat up. "The sultan knows our designs?"

"Brother Aaron disappeared when Tiberias fell."

"Dead or captured?" Cardinal Morra interrupted.

"I don't know."

"Dead might be wishful thinking."

"Well, since then Saladin has made two attempts to capture me. I suspect Brother Aaron is dead."

"Two attempts? Your journey has been more dangerous than I thought."

"The second try was almost successful. Had it not been for my young friend sitting here it probably would have been."

Byron nodded, uncomfortable with the praise. "Actually, it was

Lord James Martel who defeated the Saracens second attempt."

Father Villhardain smiled. "Yes, my son, it was James."

"Who is James?" the cardinal asked.

"Lord James Martel," Father Villhardain replied. "I accepted his service in the name of the Church. He is a relation of Godfrey of Bouillon."

"Hmm, Saladin knows," Morra grumbled. "This is most unfortunate news. If Brother Aaron is in the clutches of Saladin, it is only a matter of time before he tells them everything. Does Brother Aaron know the location of the treasure?"

Father Villhardain paused. "Yes, Your Eminence, he does. But I fear Brother Aaron is dead. If he were still alive, the sultan would not waste his time trying to capture me."

"Hmm, I don't know," the cardinal replied slowly.

Father Villhardain leaned forward and put his hands on the cardinal's desk. "If Saladin knew the location, he would quietly go and retrieve the treasure, and we would never be the wiser."

"Perhaps he already has," the cardinal said, shaking his head. "This is all terrible news. Brother Aaron is a tremendous loss. He was a gifted and dedicated man, a pious Catholic monk. He had a brilliant future. I will pray for him, and hope that God grants him release from his suffering. Are there any other revelations I should know about?"

"No," Father Villhardain sighed. Cardinal Morra rubbed the stress from his forehead. "Do you intend to tell the Holy Father that Saladin might know our plans?" the priest asked.

"Heavens no!" the cardinal cried. "That would just confuse the issue. We are in a difficult position. We need the treasure to reverse the tide that flows against us, but we have no way of knowing if it is there, or worse if Saladin has it." Cardinal Morra stared down at his desk as if he were searching for an answer written on its polished surface. "We must go to Babylon. If it is there, we will be blessed. If it is not there, then perhaps the Saracens will leave evidence that they took it."

"I agree, Your Eminence. When do we meet with the Holy Father?"

"The Holy Father is busy in meetings on Church business all day tomorrow. The first available time I could arrange is the day after tomorrow. The Vice Chancellor Cardinal Fulcher is setting the schedule for the consistory, and the subject of tomorrow's meeting is Barbarossa and his son's inheritance of Sicily and Southern Italy."

"Do you think the Holy Father still intends to excommunicate Barbarossa?" the priest asked.

"I have argued against it," Morra replied. "But alas, Fulcher's influence over his Holiness has grown. I cannot say which path the Holy Father will choose."

"Why is any of this important?" Byron interrupted.

Father Villhardain tilted his head to eye Byron. "The Hohenstaufen inheritance has grave consequences for the Church. It was not very long ago that Italian princes controlled the Church. The family of the Theophylacts were the worst, murdering popes when they would not do their bidding. The Church is now free from secular influence. Should Barbarossa's son inherit Sicily and Southern Italy by marriage, that independence could change. That is why Holy Father is resisting Barbarossa's designs with the only weapon he has, excommunication."

Byron looked perplexed, "I thought excommunication was for a grave sin."

"My son," the Cardinal said, "none of this is relevant to you. It is an ongoing matter for the Church. What is relevant is that when you address the Holy Father, you speak loudly and you keep your story short. Under no circumstance should you discuss anything else. You are here to talk about the defeat at Hattin. If anything else is required, I will address it." Byron nodded. Cardinal Morra smiled. "You have had a long journey. Do you think you can find your way back to your quarters? I have several issues I would like to discuss with Father Villhardain."

"I think I can find my way back."

"I will stop by your room when it is time for the evening meal," the priest said.

Byron stood up, bowed, and left the room. He wandered the hall looking at the artwork, the mosaics framed with marble. At last, he reached his room.

Byron opened the door, entered the room, and took off his

cloak and tunic. With a sigh, he flopped down on the bed. He had closed his eyes when he heard a noise that made him jump up and grab his sword. To his great surprise, he found himself looking at a beautiful nude woman with long black hair. She had popped up from behind the couch on the other side of the room. She smiled at him, and then giggled as she grabbed up a cloak to cover herself. From the other end of the couch, another nude woman stood up and winked suggestively at him. She placed her hand on her hip and leaned against the couch. Byron stood there with his mouth open in shock looking at her.

James, without the slightest hint of embarrassment, sat up between the two girls. "My friend, you came back!"

"You Fool, damn it!" Byron hissed. "You are in the Lateran Palace, for the sake of Christ!"

James laughed. "What does it matter? My friend, these two lovely girls wanted to see my weapons, and I did not wish to disappoint them. Did you know that if you put monastic robes on a person and pull up the cowl, no one can tell who she is?" Byron was speechless. James was kissing his way up the arm of one of the girls who was giggling. "I am sure one of these girls would like to get to know you."

"The last girl you introduced me to tried to steal from me," Byron said as he put on his tunic. He grabbed his cloak and hastily tossed it around his shoulders. Buckling on his sword, he headed to the door. Turning to James as he was leaving, he said, "Father Villhardain will stop by at dinner time. I would have these wenches out of here by then if I were you."

"As you wish."

Byron stalked out of the room and slammed the door wondering what to do next as he stood on the other side of the door. He walked towards the palace entrance and made his way to the open grounds of the residence. Only James would be so bold as to bring two girls into the residence of the Holy Father.

A pang of regret entered his mind, and he had to admit that the desire to enjoy the touch of a woman clung to him. Isabella de-Clair. He could see her face and he missed her. He still had not come to grips with his broken heart, and the thought of another heartbreak filled him with sadness. He at last found a shade tree that looked inviting. Leaning against the tree, he sat tossing pebbles as he watched the finely dressed Italians pass by. He wondered if Isabella de-Clair even thought of him anymore.

He pushed the thought away and tried to think of something else. Babylon. He had heard the name, but he had never paid much attention to religious matters. In church, he had gone through the motions as he attempted to stay awake, but he never expected that anything said would be relevant. It was clear Father Villhardain and Cardinal Morra had concerns about the place.

It was warm and the wind whispered in the leaves of the trees. He felt drowsy and before he knew it, he was asleep. Only a few passersby noticed him, and those that did, had too many worries of their own to spend any time wondering what he was doing there sleeping in the shade of the tree. Drunk perhaps, or out of money and evicted from wherever he was staying. No one cared. They hurried on errands of their own. In the end, Byron spent his first afternoon in Rome asleep and undisturbed.

CHAPTER 24
MENE, MENE, TEKEL AND PARSIN

It was late afternoon when Byron awoke. He got up, dusted the twigs and dust from his clothes, and set off for the Lateran palace. The guards at the door eyed him suspiciously. He made his way down the hallway to his room. He slowly opened the door and looked in. James was gone. Hopefully James' escapade would not embarrass him. He had vouched for James' character, and he did not want James' misconduct to tarnish his reputation. He picked up the water ewer and poured some water into the bowl. He was washing up when he heard a knock on the door. He opened it and saw Father Villhardain standing there.

"Where is Martel?"

"Ah-I don't know, Father."

Father Villhardain crossed his arms across his chest. "The page came back and told me James lost him in a crowd. Then I learned from the guards that he returned in the company of two women disguised as monks. The only reason they let them enter was they knew James was my guest." Father Villhardain shot Byron an accusing stare. "Do you know anything about this?"

"No, Father," Byron said, bending the truth. "I have been out. I decided to look around the palace grounds."

"I see," Father Villhardain said as he shook his head. "Hmm, something troubles him deeply. Do you know what that might be?"

Father Villhardain's blue eyes bored into Byron. "No, Father."

Father Villhardain closed his eyes for a moment. "I see. Well, it must be dealt with. You realize that James could undo all my work if the Holy Father found out about this... this scandalous behavior?"

"I suspect all chances of persuading him to aid our cause would be futile."

"Indeed. I want to see Martel when he returns. This will not happen again."

Father Villhardain had just finished saying this when the door swung open and James walked in with a smile on his face. "Father, so gracious of you to stop by. Byron, how was your rest?" James winked at Byron.

"How was your afternoon, James?" the priest said.

"It was most excellent."

"I am glad to hear that. Your first day in Rome must have been pleasant by the look on your face."

"I enjoyed it fully," James replied truthfully.

"My Lord Martel, are you aware the guards at the palace door report everything to me? They report who comes, who goes, and who is with them."

The smile on James' face vanished. "Ah no, Father, I was unaware you took such an interest."

"So, did you enjoy your religious experience with the two holy brothers who were with you when you returned?"

"I did as a matter of fact."

Father Villhardain turned to Byron. "Lord Fitzwalter, give us a moment. I must speak to Lord Martel alone."

Byron nodded and stepped out into the hallway. He expected a shouting match, and was relieved he would not have to witness what was coming next. Yet, as he stood in the empty hallway, he did not hear the exchange of raised voices. He could barely hear Father Villhardain speaking. The priest continued for several minutes and then everything became quiet. After several more minutes, the door opened, and Father Villhardain motioned to Byron to come back into the room. James' face was red.

Father Villhardain spoke softly, "There will be no more of this insolent behavior. You are guests of the Holy Father." James nodded. "James, I have much to do. I will speak to Brother Carl regarding this. I will see what his thoughts are regarding your penance." James frowned. "That will be dealt with tomorrow," Father Villhardain said. "It is time for the evening meal. We will dine with the cardinal." Father Villhardain turned and walked into the hallway. Byron followed, but James remained standing in the room. The priest stopped. "Are you coming?"

"Perhaps it would be best if I dined alone," James replied.

"Nonsense!" Father Villhardain snorted. "You said you wanted to hear my story. At least hear my tale before you decide to go to France." James' eyes widened at the priest's mention of France. "Despite your poor judgement," the priest continued, "I need a man of your experience. Tomorrow, you will atone for your misdeeds. Don't think you are the first to do such a thing. Tonight we are going to discuss our upcoming expedition and I would like you to be there so we can benefit from your expert knowledge." James' face brightened. Father Villhardain smiled. "Now let's go. I do not wish to keep the cardinal waiting."

Servants had placed a small table in Cardinal Morra's apartment suite. As Byron entered the room, he could see the first course of the meal had been set and Brother Carl seated at the table. Cardinal Morra greeted his guests as they took their chairs at the table.

The dinner conversation centered on the dire peril of the Crusader Kingdom. Rumors that Saladin was moving to besiege Jerusalem had continued to pour in from the Genoese merchants who traded with the kingdom. The Christian defenders had refused an offer to surrender.

The walls of the apartment slowly turned crimson as the light of the setting sun filled the room. As the shadows from the objects of the table lengthened, the servants reappeared and began lighting the candles and clearing the plates from the table.

"Let us now discuss the task that our Lord has appointed to us," Cardinal Morra said. "I will now ask his divine guidance." The men around the table bowed their heads. Byron listened as

Cardinal Morra prayed in Latin.

"*Michael Archangele, defende nos in proelio; contra nequitiam et insidias diaboli esto praesidium. Imperat illi Deus;*" Byron felt his interest drift as he found himself admiring a silver ladle resting next to him on the table.

"*Supplices deprecamur: tuque,*" the cardinal droned on as Byron admired the ladle's handle which had been fashioned to represent intertwining vines of ivy. He wondered how long it had taken the craftsman to fashion such a work of art.

"*Princeps militiae coelestis, Satanam aliosque spiritus malignos, qui ad perditionem animarum pervagantur in mundo, divina virtute in infernum detrude.* In the name of the Father and of the son and of the Holy Ghost, Amen"

Byron looked up from the ladle and muttered, "Amen."

Father Villhardain rose from his chair. "We are here tonight to develop a plan to recover a treasure that in the last years of the Roman Empire was sent from this city and lost. I have spent years trying to find it," Father Villhardain paused. "I have finally found it. Tonight I will tell you the tale of the centurion's treasure. May it aid us in turning back the tide that now flows against us."

Cardinal Morra nodded. "The news has not been good, but let's not give up hope. *Dues Volt!* God wills it! If God wills it, Saladin will fail!"

James looked down at the table and then spoke, "This is not about hope. This is about the means to resist Saladin. When I rode from Jerusalem to seek the aid of Lord Montferrat, there were only thirteen knights left to defend the entire city. When I delivered the plea, not one Christian soldier marched to our aid. God will not help our cause if we are too cowardly to leave the safety of the walls of Tyre. Saladin is strengthening his hold. God wills it. I swear the only thing that is going to save Jerusalem is men in armor, horses, and crossbows." James turned to the cardinal. "In Rome, God may will it. In Jerusalem, God has turned his back on us because we do not have the will to fight."

"You are cynical," the cardinal scoffed. "God's will is not always clear, yet you fear that my optimism is not based on true circumstances." The cardinal fixed James with a cold stare. "My optimism is based on faith in God. This meeting is not about wishful thinking, nor is cynicism warranted. When we have made our plans, and they come to naught - then you can be cynical. Do not make the mistake of thinking you are the only one who cares about the fate of Jerusalem. I will not sit idle while we lose this war. Money creates armies, it keeps them in the field, it supplies them, and it feeds them. That is why we meet tonight, to plan, so when we strike, the blow is well aimed and effective. We will recover the Imperial Roman treasure to finance a new crusade." Cardinal Morra leaned forward. "In our moment of great need, God has placed the evidence in front of us. Now, it is up to us to find it and bring it back to Rome."

James leaned forward as he looked back at the cardinal. "Your Eminence, I fought in many battles. I understand the need for plans. It is the will to carry them out that I question. If you are willing to put your prestige behind this, then I am willing to make the journey."

"My son, I put my prestige behind this when I sent Father Villhardain to the Holy Lands," Cardinal Morra said as he turned to the priest. "Father Villhardain, please continue, and tell us what you have learned."

Father Villhardain looked at James and frowned. "Your Eminence, as you have just pointed out you were the one who sent me to the Holy Lands to find this. It has taken many years to piece together the story of the fate of the treasure of Rome. It is by the grace of God that I found what I sought."

Father Villhardain stood up, pulled out a leather case from under his black dalmatic, and placed it down on the table. He carefully opened it, took out several pieces of parchment discolored with dark stains and very old, and placed them on the table. Unrolling the document, the old priest reached across the table. He picked up a candlestick and several other table items, and placed them on the corners to weigh the parchment down. The men stood up and leaned over the table to look at it. The handwritten script was chaotic, which appeared as line after line of random pen strokes.

Father Villhardain glanced up and smiled. "Writing has

changed a great deal since this document was written. You are looking at old Roman cursive. This is the handwriting of everyday business. It was used by emperors to issue orders, and by the common man to conduct business."

Byron felt a rush of excitement as he stared at the ancient writing. There was no doubt that he was one of very few people to have ever seen it, and he wished he could read it. He knew he would have to wait for Father Villhardain to decipher the meaning. He was in awe of the priest, who was wise and learned. Like a great wizard, the priest had the magical power to take random symbols and translate them into meaning, to discern the thoughts of a man who had been dead for years.

The candles flickered on the table. Each man turned to Father Villhardain in anticipation, wanting to know what had happened to the treasure of Imperial Rome lost so long ago.

"Several years ago, Brother Aaron found the first evidence while translating several of Saint Augustine's writings into French. He was copying an original document when he found a curious letter stuck between the pages. The letter was an order written by a Roman bureaucrat in Ravenna to officials in Ostia. The letter directed that a ship be made available to transport an important cargo of gold out of the reach of the Visigoths should they reach Rome. The order went on to say, the cargo would be in the custody of a centurion of the emperor's guard, Achatius Licinius Geta. Brother Aaron, in his excitement, brought the letter to me, and I met with Cardinal Morra to seek his guidance."

"I knew Brother Aaron had made an important find when I saw the letter," the cardinal interrupted. "It had been rumored that before Alaric's sack of Rome, the Imperial treasure had been sent beyond his reach, but no one ever seemed to know what happened to it. I knew the rumor was true when I saw the letter. While that was a starting place, it was obvious it was going to take a lot more research, so I asked Father Villhardain to look into it."

"Fortunately for us," Father Villhardain said, "the ship's name, Septimia Zenobia, was in the letter, and with the blessing of our lady, and after looking through various records, I was able to find it listed in the records of Ephesus. While that was a good start, I still had many doubts. I searched the great library of Constantinople, but as I searched, my doubts increased. I grew to despair that I would ever find the resting place of the treasure... that is until I found this scroll written in Achatius' own hand."

Curiosity got the better of James. "Forgive me, Father, but why did the Romans ship the gold out of the empire?"

Father Villhardain smiled. "Good question, My Lord Martel. I beg your pardon, my son. I will start my tale a little further in the past. At the death of the Emperor Theodosius the Great, the Roman Empire was split in half. The sons of Theodosius ruled as co-emperors, Honorius in Ravenna and Arcadias from Constantinople. Arcadius died and the Emperor Honorius, fearful the Roman General Stilicho was attempting to overthrow him, had the general executed for treason.

"Honorius believed Stilicho was attempting to reunite the empire under one emperor and was suspicious that he was building a barbarian army to seize power. After executing the general, the emperor commenced a pogrom to cleanse the Roman army of barbarian influences. Honorius, playing to popular sentiment of Roman citizens, ordered the deaths of the families of the Visigoths serving in the legions. Madness reigned in the cities of the empire as Visigoth women and children were cruelly put to death. The Visigoths who escaped with their lives brought tales of horror to their king, Alaric.

"Alaric was already seething with rage. Years before, Honorius had reneged on paying Alaric and his barbarian army for their service to Rome. With tales of the emperor's new atrocity, and his army now swelled with angry Roman-trained Visigoth soldiers, Alaric seized on the opportunity to recover the money his men were owed. In the year 409, the Visigoths invaded the west. Following the tall figure of the Visigoth king mounted on his horse, the Visigoth army marched unopposed across the empire."

Father Villhardain paused as he chuckled grimly. "Sadly for Honorius, the execution of Stilicho removed the only competent general in the Roman army. With no capable leadership left to lead the legions, no one could stop the invasion."

"Amazing," James said in shock. "This is true?"

"More or less," replied the priest.

"Only a fool would kill the man capable of leading his armies and then provoke his enemy to attack," Byron muttered.

"Worse," replied Father Villhardain sadly, "Stilicho had been Honorius' regent since he was a child. Stilicho was Honorius' father-in-law. The general had already defeated several invasions of the empire, preserving his son-in-law's rule."

"So, why kill him?" Byron asked perplexed.

Father Villhardain took a deep breath. "My son, Honorius fell under the influence of an unscrupulous minister named Olympius, who removed the general as means to advance himself at the expense of the empire. This brings me to the part in the story of the treasure. As the Visigoths advanced, Olympius conceived a plan to move part of the treasure to Rome as a way to entice Alaric to bypass Ravenna. I doubt if Olympius told the emperor that the treasure was being moved. If he did, I suspect he did not tell the emperor all of the details. I think that Olympius thought Rome's days were numbered, and he saw an opportunity to steal the Imperial Treasure so he could live in luxurious exile."

"So, the centurion was a conspirator and a traitor," James muttered.

"No, I think not," Father Villhardain replied. "Don't judge the centurion too harshly. Olympius, in control of Ravenna, had already executed Stilicho's family, as well as hundreds of his supporters. I believe the centurion found himself caught in a predicament with no way out."

"Father Villhardain," Cardinal Morra interrupted, "how do you know this? Men don't leave evidence of plans like this?"

"Ah, Your Eminence, no they don't, but the centurion did in the scrolls that lie on this table. Apparently, the Septimia Zenobia was supposed to sail for Syracuse."

"Still, that does not mean Olympius was going to steal the treasure," Cardinal Morra argued. "Records that the Church possess do not mention the loss of the Imperial Treasury. Such a tremendous loss of revenue would warrant some investigation. If this had occurred in Old Rome, the Tiber would have run red from the mass executions for corruption."

The priest frowned. "I disagree. I think the loss was so egregious and so embarrassing the emperor made the whole incident disappear. Honorius would have had to admit to the Senate that Olympius was the true traitor, which would call into question the execution of Stilicho." The priest paused. "I think Honorius chose the lesser of the evils and ignored the catastrophic loss."

"Sending the treasure to Syracuse does seem suspicious," the cardinal muttered.

James was incredulous. "Only a foolish knave would have put a treasure on a ship and send it to sea. Storms, shipwrecks, and not to mention the risk of the crew finding out what was on board."

Father Villhardain picked up a goblet from the table and looked down into it as he swirled the wine in the glass. Frowning, he lifted the goblet to his lips and took a sip of wine. "You are absolutely right, My Lord Martel. And I think Olympius was counting on all of those possibilities as a plausible way of explaining why the treasure disappeared."

Byron, who had been intently listening, spoke, "Obviously Olympius' plans failed. He did not end up with the treasure; otherwise, we would not be here."

"No," the priest replied. "His plans failed thanks to Achatius."

The room became quiet as Father Villhardain took another sip of wine. "The centurion knew Olympius would execute him to hide the theft so, in self-preservation, he took the ship to Ephesus. At some point in the voyage, the crew must have learned what was in the crates. For once the ship was in the harbor, the ship's crew tried to kill the soldiers. Achatius brutally put down the attack by killing the entire crew. With the ship now useless to him, he organized a caravan and moved the treasure inland."

Father Villhardain paused. "It appears that Achatius was a Christian, or at least the faith influenced his decisions. The treasure belonged to the people of Rome, it also represented hoarded greed and evil. He needed an out of the way place to hide it." The old priest paused as he looked at each man seated at the table. "He chose Babylon." Father Villhardain stopped for a moment to let his words take effect.

Byron could see the look of apprehension on the churchmen's

faces, and he wondered at it. He straightened up from leaning on the table.

"Babylon," the priest muttered, a troubled look on his face, "sits astride the Euphrates River. Babylon was the first great empire of man. The city was the pride of the great king Nebuchadnezzar. It was the first city to have all of the excesses of this world: vanity, pride, the sinfulness of man. It as a place of evil, a warning against earthly indulgences. The book of Daniel is important to our quest. The centurion was very clever in hiding the treasure. He knew Daniel had lived in the city of Babylon and he used the Bible as a guide to the treasure's location."

"So, who is Daniel?" James asked. "And what does he have to do with Babylon?"

"My son, Daniel was a Jew who was known as Belteshaz'zar to the Babylonians. He was a seer who rose to great fame in the court of Nebuchadnezzar, but it is the fall of Babylon that is relevant to our quest. King Belshaz-zar, the son of Nebuchadnezzar, held a great feast and invited many guests. During the feast, the guests proceeded to drink from the silver and golden vessels taken from the temple in Jerusalem. As the party went on, a ghostly hand appeared and began writing on the wall. As you might imagine, this unnerved the guests and filled the king with fear. Daniel was summoned to interpret the words, which I will read to you."

Father Villhardain placed a well-used bible onto the table and opened it. The paper crackled in the quiet room as Father Villhardain turned the pages searching for the right place. After a moments search, he began to read.

> *"Then from his presence the hand was sent, and the writing was inscribed. And this is the writing that was inscribed: Mene, Mene, Tekel and Parsin. This is the interpretation of the matter: Mene, God has numbered the days of your Kingdom and brought it to an end; Tekel, you have been weighed in the balances and found wanting; Peres, your Kingdom is divided and given to the Medes and Persians."*

"These are the words written on the wall the very night Belshaz-zar was slain and Darius of Mede took Babylon." Father

Villhardain looked up. "The centurion developed a method of landmarks using the book of Daniel to mark the treasure's location."

"How did you find all this information?" James asked in astonishment.

"It was divine intervention," the priest said. "An old Saracen, who had lived in Tiberias all of his life, heard I was buying old Roman artifacts. The man sought us out and offered to sell to us a plain old Roman clay vessel, along with whatever it contained, for a modest price. At first, I was not very interested in the object. However, Brother Aaron was fascinated by it. So reluctantly, I purchased the vessel and took it back to the church in Tiberias.

"At the time, I was busy working on deciphering several other artifacts, and the vessel sat in the corner of my room forgotten. After a week had past, Aaron began cleaning the dirt from the old clay jar and discovered the lid was still intact. When we opened the vessel, we found several scrolls of sheepskin darkened with age but still readable. With great care, we slowly unrolled them. At first, I was uncertain about their origin. The writing had faded and difficult to read, but as I examined them closely, I found that it was Latin. To my great shock, I found that I was reading the journal of Achatius Licinius Geta's travel from Ostia to Babylon. Apparently, he must have used the jar as a hiding place for his important papers. Along with the journal, I found a rudimentary map of the city."

"Did the man who sold you the jar tell you how he came to possess it?" the cardinal asked.

"No. Fortunately, Latin is a dead language used only by the Church. Even if the man knew about the scrolls, it is unlikely that he could have read them. Only someone who could read Roman cursive writing could understand them."

"It looks like scribbling," Byron said.

Father Villhardain nodded his head. "You are quite right, and that is why I am certain that no one has ever read this."

James picked up the centurion's map. "What happened to the Roman Soldiers? I can't imagine all of them just walked away and didn't try to help themselves to a reward for their efforts."

"The centurion states that only he survived. Once he hid the treasure, he paid his men, and began marching back to Ephesus. He writes that on the road, bandits attacked as they were going through a narrow pass and that only he escaped. I assume he died of old age in the Roman town of Tiberias," the priest shrugged. "Whatever the case, it appears his jar of papers was forgotten." Father Villhardain sighed. "I don't believe Achatius' story about bandits on the road. Something else happened to his men, but what, I don't know."

"What makes you believe that?" Cardinal Morra asked.

"When he describes the flight from Ostia to Babylon, his writing is filled with lots of information about the journey. However, when he describes the death of his men, he provides no details other than a brief statement that they were killed by bandits in an ambush, while he alone survived. I find that odd. One would think that if your men, with whom you had faced dangers and hardships, were killed you would display some emotion or document their memory. I think their deaths lack description because he was unable to fabricate a good explanation of what happened."

"I can tell you what happened," James said smugly. "He killed them to keep the treasure hidden. He was probably afraid that if his men returned to Rome, Olympius would learn where he was hiding it."

"It would seem likely the centurion did murder his men in an effort to keep the hiding place secret and safe," the priest replied. "His soldiers would not have been the most trustworthy guardians of a secret of that magnitude, but I don't think that is what happened either. He quotes Jeremiah when he writes about the death of his men.

> "Flee from her midst of Babylon, let every man save his life, be not cut off in her punishment for this is the time of the Lords vengeance."

James leaned back in his chair and folded his arms across his chest. "What does that mean?"

"Something evil happened to them in the midst of Babylon," the priest said, "and I think Achatius is afraid to tell us what it was."

"So, how do we find the treasure?" Byron interrupted.

"First, we need to find the city of Babylon," the priest said. "The city has been abandoned for some time. The desert has been at work reclaiming the land, which might make it difficult to find. Once we find the city, we need to locate the royal palace where the ghostly hand wrote Mene, Mene, Tekel, and Parsin on the wall."

Father Villhardain paused. "There are other signs to the treasure's whereabouts, but first we need to find the palace of Nebuchadnezzar. Once that is accomplished, we will worry about mastering the other obstacles."

James leaned forward. "Obstacles? What do you mean by obstacles?"

Father Villhardain tilted his head back and looked down his nose at James. "The centurion writes that whoever seeks the treasure will be tested and judged, just like Belshaz-zar was tested and judged by God."

James smiled. "Or like Belshaz-zar, you will be found wanting and then dead."

"My son, that appears to be the point of the centurion's message."

"What are these obstacles?" Byron asked.

"Traps, my son. Devices designed to kill or maim, to keep out robbers or anyone else who might try to steal the treasure. The centurion states it was his desire to return the treasure to the Roman people, but only God knows what was truly in his heart."

Byron sat down and leaned back in his chair, his hand on his chin. "Did the centurion say what these traps are?"

"No," the priest said, "other than they have something to do with numbered and ended, weighed and found wanting, and divided."

"What are these obstacles, or traps, and how do we get around them?" James asked.

"Until we are there, I am not sure," Father Villhardain said. "Unfortunately, he appears to have only written down enough information to serve as a general reminder to himself. The actual details of the mechanics of the traps he kept to himself, or wrote them on a separate parchment that remains lost. Whatever the case, we must exercise great care when we think we are in the vicinity of one of these infernal devices Achatius has left behind."

Cardinal Morra read the Latin inscription as they stood looking at the map. "Here, drawn by the hand of Achatius, is a map of mighty Babylon built for the glory of Nebuchadnezzar." Cardinal Morra picked up the first two pages of the scroll and started looking through them. "Is there anything else the centurion warns us about?"

"He does. He writes the following,

"I am growing old and the judgment for my sins draws near. I am writing this not as justification but as an explanation. It was not my desire to take the treasure in the first place. During the Visigoth invasion, I found myself receiving orders from men who only looked to their own welfare and not to the welfare of the empire. I have known many good men who have died defending Rome, and yet when I found myself in the distinguished post protecting the center of power, I came to realize it was nothing more than an empty honor. Honor flows from great men, and it is a great honor to be of service to men larger than themselves. The men I served were small, self-serving men, nothing compared to the great emperors who occupied the throne of Caesar. There was little honor in the acts I preformed and I look back with bitterness at the idea of Rome knowing what Rome should have been instead of what it had become.

"What happened in Babylon cannot be undone. Now all I can do is ask Christ for forgiveness. The treasure was removed from Ravenna for a selfish purpose. It will now rest forever, forgotten in Babylon until this wicked world passes away. A fitting resting place among the heap of ruins, the haunt of jackals, a land without inhabitants, and where no son of man passes by."

Father Villhardain looked up. "He then quotes Revelations,

"I saw another angel coming down from Heaven, having great authority: and the earth was made bright with his splendor. And he called out with a mighty voice "Fallen, fallen is Babylon the great! It has become a dwelling place of demons, a haunt of every

foul spirit, a haunt of every foul and hateful bird; for all nations have drunk the wine of her impure passion, and the kings of the earth have committed fornication with her, and the merchants of the earth have grown rich with the wealth of her wantonness.

"*Then I heard another voice from heaven saying, 'Come out of her, my people, lest you take part in her sins, least you share in her plagues, for her sins are heaped high as heaven and God has remembered her iniquities.*"

CHAPTER 25
SILK MERCHANTS

Father Villhardain looked around the room at the faces around the table. James broke the silence. "Traveling through enemy territory is dangerous enough, but if everyone is going to start worrying about hobgoblins and ghosts, maybe we should not go."

"This is not about hobgoblins or ghosts," replied the cardinal. "This is the word of God. Evil can be subtle and not easy to recognize."

"If entering Babylon is that grave of a concern," James said forcefully, "then we should leave the treasure were it lies. I have no desire to risk my immortal soul."

"And I would agree," the cardinal replied, "but the holiest city on earth hangs in the balance. We must do everything we can to keep the infidels from recapturing the city of our Lord's sufferings."

"What is the Church prepared to do to protect us?" James demanded.

"If the Holy Father decides this trip to Babylon is in the interest of the Church, then you shall have the protection of the Church from whatever evil lurks in Babylon," Cardinal Morra answered.

"But even if we recover the treasure," Byron said as he was looking at the map, "it will take some time to bring it back to Rome.

Saladin will most assuredly have Jerusalem under his control by that time."

"Perhaps," the cardinal replied, "but nothing is certain in war. We must at least dare to act, and maybe God will reward us with a miracle. If we do nothing, then defeat is certain."

"How do you plan to get there?" James interrupted.

"That is why we are here," Cardinal Morra said. "To discuss the best options to successfully bring the treasure home."

Father Villhardain reached into his leather case, pulled out a stained and tattered paper, and began unfolding it on the table. "I have brought a map of the Levant to aid us with our plans."

"We could ask the Holy Father for a papal bull to raise a force of fighting men to go into the city and bring it out through force," Carl interjected.

Byron shook his head. "Babylon is near Baghdad, the heart of the infidel religion. We would need an army as large as the one Louis of France led from Ephesus. And even he with all the men he had under arms, had difficulty in keeping the Saracens at bay."

"Fitzwalter's right," James agreed. "We don't have the time to assemble the number of men necessary to overcome the kind of resistance the Saracens will mount to protect the heart of their empire. No, I am afraid that in the short amount of time we have, the best we could muster is a small company of mounted knights who would only succeed in arousing the wrath of the Saracens."

"You are correct," Father Villhardain replied. "Do you have an alternative?"

James sat quietly in thought for a moment. "We could travel in disguise. Travel to Babylon as Saracen merchants returning to Baghdad. No one would question an Arab caravan on the road. Silk traders perhaps."

"You mean dress as infidels?" Carl asked, looking at James with disdain. "I will not have any part in masquerading as the accursed race."

"I am not telling you what I want to do," James replied. "I am suggesting what I think would possibly work to bring the treasure back to Rome, if that is what this group wishes to accomplish."

"James is right," Father Villhardain interjected. "I have had the same thoughts for some time. In fact, when I recruited Byron, I was already thinking we would have to travel in disguise."

Byron spoke, "So once we get there, how do we move the treasure? I assume we are talking about a large number of crates, which will be heavy since they are loaded with gold."

Father Villhardain nodded. "I have given that some thought. I wrote Cardinal Morra and asked him about the possibility of arranging for a large ship that could travel to Levant, sail up the Euphrates, and bring the treasure back."

"Does such a ship exist?" Byron asked.

James, looking at the map, shook his head. "That won't work."

"What won't work?" Father Villhardain said, looking at James in surprise.

James looked up from the map. "It won't work. You can't sail a ship up the Euphrates. It is too shallow. The only kind of craft that can navigate the river is a small boat or shallow barge."

"We could barge it down the river to the sea and then load it on the ship," the cardinal suggested.

"I would not take that risk," James said. "The river is full of reeds, with lots of twists and turns, and it branches off in several different directions once you get to the Persian Gulf. It will take a lot of manpower to manage the boats, and they will be difficult to handle. I suggest we look at another alternative."

"I agree with James," Byron said. "We should move the treasure over land like the Romans did."

"I fear you're right," Father Villhardain said, nodding, "but the quickest route over land is filled with danger."

"Why is that?" the cardinal asked.

"Because the best port still in crusader hands is Alexandretta. It is close to the Euphrates. But the road takes us through Saladin's Fortress of Aleppo... I don't need to tell you how dangerous that part of the journey would be."

"Surely there is a safer way," James snapped. "Aleppo is the prison for captured Christians. It has an evil reputation."

"There is no alternative," Byron replied. "It is the only road open to us."

"Fitzwalter is right," Father Villhardain said. "That is why we must travel as Arab silk merchants taking their caravan and their Christian slaves to Baghdad."

The room became quiet. James finally broke the silence. "We could tell them we are trading with Sheikh Abdul al-Subayil," James suggested tentatively.

"Who is that?" Cardinal Morra asked.

"The richest and most powerful Saracen merchant in the region," James answered. "Rumor has it, he is a favorite of Saladin and stands to make great gains if the Christians are run out of the Levant." James turned to Byron. "What are your intentions, Fitzwalter? Clearly you have some thoughts?"

"We travel to the Levant as silk merchants with their Christians slaves. You would be a prince," he paused, grasping for a name, "Prince...Prince Hashim. Prince Hashim, the second son of... of... Emir Azahar al-Umari."

James eyed Byron skeptically. "I'm not convinced."

"No," Byron replied, "it can succeed. You are being punished by your father for your indiscretions, by having to accompany one of your father's caravans on its trek to the Far East."

"And your role in this charade?" James asked.

"The overseer," Byron replied.

"I see, Fitzwalter," James said, "but I have not said that I would go on this quest."

Father Villhardain looked at James. "What is your decision?"

"I will give you my decision tomorrow. The thought of riding to Aleppo does not appeal to me. I will have to consider this," James said as he frowned.

"So, once you get past Aleppo, where will you go next?" the cardinal asked.

"We follow the Euphrates River to Babylon," the priest said. "Once there, we find the treasure, turn around, bring it back to Alexandretta, and then to Rome."

"Well, I have heard enough for now," the cardinal said tiredly. "I think we have the beginnings of a plan. I will start working on preparing the way for our meeting with the Holy Father."

"What about the caravan?" Byron asked. "How are we going to arrange getting enough camels together to move the treasure?"

"I will seek out some of the Italian merchants I know and see what I can learn," the cardinal replied. "Now, if you please, I am old, tired, and I need my rest."

Each man told the cardinal good night and left his chamber. The hallways of the Lateran were dark, and the men followed Father Villhardain who was carrying a single candle to light their way. The darkness gave way as the candle pushed away the emptiness. In the light, they could see the elaborate marble carvings and the great paintings of art that brought the illusion of life to the cold stone walls. But once the priest had passed, the darkness closed in behind them, resuming its gloom. The light from the candle faded away as the shadows crept across the painted faces that soon disappeared into the darkness.

The priest stopped. They had reached their rooms.

When they were inside and the door was shut, Byron asked, "What is your decision? Are you going on to France?"

"I will tell you in the morning," James replied curtly.

"So, do you still think bringing those serving wenches into the Lateran was worth the trouble?"

"Of course not," James snapped. Byron shook his head. "Fitzwalter, I will sleep on this tonight. If I am still here by the morning, it is likely that I will go."

Byron was tired, and without any more discussion, he crawled into bed. He lay on his back thinking about Babylon. Babylon, he had never heard of the place. Clearly, the name bothered the churchmen. He rolled onto his side listening to James softly breathing as he drifted off into an uneasy sleep.

He dreamt that he was standing in the desert. The silver moon had not yet risen. He watched the stars as they flickered in the night sky. All was silent and still. Suddenly, a huge fire lit the eastern sky, and as he watched the fire burn, he saw a dark shape slowly form into a stair-stepped pyramid. Within the red and yellow flames, a great lion with the outspread wings of an eagle leaped out of the fire, and with a roar ran towards him.

Fear overcame him and he turned to run, but his legs would not move. He looked back; the beast was closing in on him; its shaggy mane shook with every stride. It was almost upon him. He cried out, but despite all of his effort, his feet remained firmly planted. Then the great beast came to a sudden stop. He stared at the lion face to face. Its hot breath on him, and with a low growl it said, "I am waiting." The lion turned to dust the moment it said this and blew away with a sudden gust of wind. The stars began falling from the sky, arcing in crisscrossing patterns as they fell to the earth. The world turned black. He was spinning, and the wind roared in his ears as if he were being pulled into an invisible vortex.

He awoke and sat straight up in bed. Breathing hard, he looked around the room. He could see the chair, the other bed. He could see James lying on his side, and he heard the rhythmic breathing as his friend slept. He lay back, took a deep breath, and then let it out again. The terror gone, he relaxed and fell back to sleep. If he had any other dreams, he could not remember them.

CHAPTER 26
THE CONFESSION OF JAMES

Byron woke to the early morning light flooding into the room. He was tired, and the memory of the lion made him uneasy. James was standing near the window covered with dew.

"You are still here?" James nodded. Byron got up and stretched. He walked over and stood next to his friend who was staring out the window.

"You seem troubled?" James asked.

"I had a strange dream," Byron replied, not wanting to discuss the matter. "Are you going to Babylon?" James sighed and then nodded.

Byron was about to say more when Brother Carl opened the door and entered the room. The monk's cowl was over his head, shadowing his face. "James Martel, come with me. Father Villhardain and I have discussed your sin. Since I have been ordained, he thought that I should hear your confession. It is not something I normally do, but Father Villhardain was insistent."

"I don't need to confess anything," James said. "You know what I have done."

Brother Carl's voice softened. "Come. We shall see."

James held up his hand as if to defend himself. "Brother Carl, you and I are men of the world. We have done things and we have said things. Some turned to evil. Some deeds were evil on purpose. How can a man walk away from his past?"

"Brother knight, if God can forgive you, perhaps then you should forgive yourself." Brother Carl looked at Byron. "Norman, Father Villhardain will be here soon. Do not keep him waiting." Brother Carl opened the door. James looked at Byron who nodded to him, and James followed Brother Carl out of the room.

The monk walked through the Lateran's marble halls. James was starting to question if he had made the right choice, or if he should have saddled a horse and ridden away before the dawn. They passed two cardinals deep in talk. One of them looked up and then went back to the conversation about Barbarossa's possible excommunication. Brother Carl opened the door to a small chapel in the Lateran and entered.

The room was small. Several benches lined the center of the room. At the far end of the room, was an altar where candles burned in the gloom. Brother Carl threw back his cowl and motioned James to sit across from a mural on the wall. As James sat down, he realized it was of Christ. The Savior dressed in white was on one knee, his finger touching the ground. A woman kneeled before him. Her brown dress was torn and her head bowed. Surrounding them, a group of angry men held rocks in their hands. With a screech, Brother Carl pulled a bench next to James and sat down.

James cocked his head to one side and looked at the painting. "Brother Carl, I assume you have some reason for me to see this image. At least tell me the story of the painting."

The monk glanced over his shoulder and then back to James. "It is called the *Test of the Scribes and Pharisees*." The monk leaned back, his grey eyes fixed on the knight as he stroked his beard. "The Scribes and Pharisees brought a harlot before our Lord. The Law of Moses commanded that a woman condemned of adultery should be stoned to death. Knowing this, the Scribes and Pharisees demanded our Lord's judgement in the matter, hoping he would defy the law. Ignoring their demands to kill her, our Lord knelt down and began drawing in the sand. At last, he looked up and said, 'Let he who is without sin cast the first stone.' One by one, the Pharisees and Scribes dropped their stones and left. When the last had departed, Jesus asked the woman, 'Where are your accusers? Has no one condemned you?' The woman replied, 'No one Lord.' Our Lord then told the woman, 'Then I don't condemn you. Go and sin no more.'"

James leaned back and crossed his arms across his chest. "Is this the reason you brought me to this room? To show me this? Get me to confess?"

Brother Carl's face twisted into a faint smile. "Yes and no. This room is a quiet place to pray, and it was not being used. And yes, I brought you here to see this image. Many wonder what our Lord wrote in the sand. Some say it was the names of the Pharisees and the Scribes; others believe it was their sins; the Bible does not say. But there is more to this tale than just the forgiveness of the harlot." Brother Carl paused. "The Lord ignores our false accusations and judgments just as he ignored the Pharisees and Scribes demands to kill the woman. When the Lord told them to cast their stones, in that instant he had convicted them of their own sins. But instead of staying in the presence of Christ, the one who could forgive them, they ran away." The monk leaned back. "Martel, what are you running from?"

James looked at Brother Carl. "I have nothing to confess."

The monk's face softened. "I disagree. A man does not bring two women into the Lateran for carnal pleasures, unless he wishes to insult God."

"Brother Carl, I did not wish to insult God. It was a long trip, and they...were willing. It was a mistake."

Brother Carl frowned. "Indeed, it was. Fornication is a sin, but even if you were going to engage in sin, you could have found someplace else. I suspect they suggested someplace else. Yet you chose this place. Why? Are you angry with God?"

James scowled and shook his head. "I enjoyed the company of the two women. There is nothing more."

"Except you chose the Lateran Palace. Why are you so angry with God?" James looked back at the painting. "I know how hard this journey of confession is. Pride, fear of disgrace. Therefore, I will briefly tell you my own tale of sin." Brother Carl paused and looked at the knight. "I have slain men. I have taken women as war trophies. I did what I wanted and no one could stop me. My ancestors were the housecarls to Harold Godwin and died defending the king at Hastings. Alas, in Norman England my Anglo-Saxon lineage brought me no favors, so I left England. My mother was a descendant of the Earl Guthrum, or Æthelstan as he became known after his conversion to Christianity. I went to live among my mother's kin, the Norsemen. There I achieved fame. I have led men in many raids and fought in many battles."

Brother Carl sighed. "I loved it. The smell of blood, the terror in my victim's face. It made me feel powerful. It all ended when I accidentally killed the son of a powerful Jarel. I was instructing the lad in the art of swordsmanship." Brother Carl looked down and shook his head. "The boy was clumsy. He tripped and fell upon his own sword. I could not believe the fool had impaled himself... not that it mattered. In that moment, I became a villain, an outlaw. I took a few followers and a longboat and fled to the coast of France. At first, I enjoyed my new life as a brigand, robbing and killing."

Brother Carl smiled. "I captured a priest. Churchmen were always worth robbing. But to my surprise, I found him penniless. I was going to kill the priest, and as I drew my sword to cut off his head, the man thanked me. He even forgave me. The priest was Father Villhardain, and I found that I could not do it. In that moment, I was saved, and I stopped running from the Lord. I asked for forgiveness, and from that day, my burdens were gone. I still owe a great debt, and I have worked hard to repair what I have done."

James slouched against the bench. The monk leaned in, his grey eyes cold. The crooked and flattened nose inches from James' face. "What is your tale?"

James' face hardened and his jaw was set. "That is my business!"

"Do you wish to take it to the grave like the Pharisees and the Scribes? I will not force you to confess, James, that is up to you. I have walked the road that you walk, and I have carried the burden you now carry. As one man to another who has walked that dark road, stop. Let me help you lay down your burden."

James weighed telling the monk his sins. He was thirteen when his mother had died. At last, James scoffed, "You wish to know my sin? My father killed my mother in a fit of rage. I watched her die."

†

James could still see the mosaic floor and the marble walls lined with tapestry. The Star of David carved into the wall was the only evidence that the house had once belonged to a rich Jewish family. His mother and father were standing in the great hall. He had heard shouting, and he had come to investigate. Near the entrance, he could see his mother in a dark blue dress; her dark hair was loose, falling about her shoulders. Standing in front of her was his father, his dark hair matted and unkempt. A dark wine stain, splashed across his white shirt.

"You come home drunk from your night with whores, and then you lie to me!" His mother cried.

Count Martel's face was scarlet, the veins in his neck bulged. "How dare you woman! What I do is not your concern!" His father stepped closer. "Your place is to be silent and to bear my children. You speak to me of honor and duty? How many of our children live! Four to the grave and only one still lives! If anyone has neglected their duty, it is you! My dogs are more obedient. Now my line relies on one unmanly disgrace of a boy!"

His mother's face turned white. "James is not a disgrace! How dare you speak of our son in such a manner? As for the others, I cannot help that God chose to take them away. If anyone is a disgrace, it is the drunken fool in front of me. Raynald de Chatillon was with you! Tell the truth. You and that foul, evil man!"

James watched his father lean forward menacingly. "Do not speak ill of His Grace!" He struck her across her face. His mother reeled, and then raising her fist, she struck back, hitting the count in the jaw. With a cry of rage, the count grabbed her by the hair, drew his knife, and stabbed her in the chest. James' mother staggered back and looked down, her eyes were wide. Gasping, she sank to her knees and fell forward.

"Bitch!" James' father said as he looked down at her and then stepped over her, leaving the hall.

James stood for a moment in shock as the monstrousness of what had happened sank in. He ran across the room and knelt beside her. Tears filled his eyes as he gently turned her over. His mother looked up at him, her dark eye's wide. She smiled weakly. "James," she whispered. "James, my son, avenge me."

James cradled her head, running his hands through her soft hair. "I will," he whispered. "I most surely will." Her lips moved, but no sound came as her eyes slowly became fixed and dull. James began to sob. Footsteps echoed, and James looked up to see his father approaching. The count had changed into a clean shirt and was pulling on his tunic. The steward of the house was following the count, carrying his father's sword and cloak.

"I found her on the floor," the count said. "Died by her own hand." The count shook his head. He looked at the steward. "I want this cleaned up," he said as he took his sword and buckled it on.

"She did not kill herself!" James shouted.

James' father grabbed him and struck him, knocking him to the floor. Bending close, he looked James in the eye. "Yes, she did, and that is the story you will tell boy!"

The count stood up. "I have been summoned to the king's council. This mess had better be gone by the time I return." James' father looked at the steward who had placed the cloak around the count's shoulders and was fastening it with a broach shaped like a falcon. "Summon the bishop. Tell him what has happened." The count tossed the steward a bag of coins. Give this to the Church with the understanding that the Lady Martel's death was caused by the plague." He looked down at the body of his wife. "Make sure she gets a Christian burial."

The count then turned back to James. He reached down dragging him to his feet. "No son of mine cries!" He shook James. "Only unmanly cowards cry, whimpering before they die." The count waited a moment for his son to wipe away his tears. "Now, I am leaving you to instruct the servants to clean this up! It is time to become a man." James nodded. "Understand!" the count roared as he shoved James away.

"Yes, my lord, father," James replied.

The steward's face betrayed no emotion as he stared at the tapestries. The count reached down grabbing the dagger still buried in his wife's chest and pulled it free. "I will need this," he grumbled as he strode out of the room.

†

James looked away from Brother Carl as a fly buzzed nosily in the corner of the room, disturbing the stillness of the chapel.

The monk leaned back and crossed his arms across his chest. "And does your father still live?"

James looked back at the monk, his face a mask that betrayed no emotion. What did it matter, he had already started down the path, why not tell the monk the truth?

James' dark eyes flashed in anger. "No, I avenged her. I shot a bolt into his cold black heart with a crossbow, and I left him in the wastelands for the jackals."

James stared at the candles that burned on the altar. "There," James said, "I have confessed my mortal sin. What absolution do you have for me? None?"

The monk held James in a steady gaze. At last he spoke, "Father Villhardain asked me to hear your confession because he knew I could understand your pain better than anyone. Therefore, that is for me to decide."

James nodded, still looking at the candles. The great cross above the altar glowed in their light. "She was a descendant of Robert, Count of Flanders," James said softly. "She deserved better. Their marriage was arranged of course, but she still deserved respect. She asked me to avenge her." James looked at the monk. "Knights fight for their lady's honor, in a quest par excellence. What greater woman was there than my mother? I have avenged her, and the man who took her life lies dead."

"Perhaps, but was your combat honorable?" the monk asked.

"My mother was a devout Catholic. She prayed every night on her knees to God. Yet in the end, where was God when she needed him most?" James ran his hand through his hair and then down his face. "You ask if I am angry with God. Yes, I am angry. He did nothing! I had to avenge her death. God did not aid me! He watched as a terrible burden was thrust upon me. And when I acted to give my mother justice... it was sin." James bowed his head and was silent. After a moment, he softly spoke, "His death was trifling. I have paved my way to heaven and back to earth again with the bodies of Saracens."

"How did your father die?"

"Ah...It was not long after her death that my father and I rode beyond the walls of Jerusalem to hunt gazelles. It was a large hunting party, and I accompanied my father as his squire. We had stopped to water the horses, and as my father prepared to dismount, he handed me his crossbow. I touched the trigger and the bolt was loosed. The shaft buried itself deep in his chest. He fell from his horse, dead." James looked at his hands and sighed. "I am not sorry. I wanted it to happen and it did."

Brother Carl leaned back and fixed his gaze upon James. "So, your revenge to God was to bring harlots into his house and commit sin. Are you sorry now for your sin?"

James sighed. "I am sorry for my mother." James looked up at the monk. "I should never have brought the wenches to this house. I regret that."

The monk fixed his gaze upon the knight. "Is this why you find commitment so difficult? That you fear if you commit to someone that they will be taken from you?"

"How dare you monk. You forget yourself. I have no problems in honoring my word."

The monk smiled. "I do dare, and I ask if you are certain? You will not commit to one woman, that is obvious. You will not even commit to this journey to Babylon."

"That is not true," James snapped.

"Humph. When you first arrived in the Lateran you were

overheard by a page telling Fitzwalter that you were thinking of going to France." James looked at the monk but said nothing.

"The normal acts of contrition are not sufficient," the monk continued. "To say you are sorry is not enough. You must prove your desire to be forgiven. You ask if your mortal sin can be forgiven, and I say yes. Christ died on the cross. He shed his blood so that you are forgiven. Consider Henry, King of England, who was guilty of murder. The archbishop of Canterbury was killed on the king's command. Yet, the king has atoned for his sin, and he was forgiven. I was there, and I was one of the monks who lashed the king. It was a strange fate because my deeds were far worse than the king's casual comment of wishing his enemy dead. I tell you James that I did not lash the king because I was righteous, or because I was without sin. I lashed the king because he was my brother, and as a brother, I wished to give him the means for atonement." The monk paused. The chapel became quiet.

At last the monk spoke, "You are my brother as well, James, and I will now give your penance, but only you can decide the sincerity of your contrition. You will recite the Lord's Prayer every day, and you will wear a chalice. It will remind you of the cost of your sin. And you will do a good work for the Church."

James' eyes narrowed. "And what is this good work?"

"You will go to Babylon with Father Villhardain and bring back the treasure. You will go, no matter the cost, even if it means your death."

James shook his head. "I knew you were going to leave me no choice but to go."

Brother Carl ignored this as he continued. "I will decide how long you will wear the chalice that will be a shirt of goat hair. Your service to the Church will end when you are either dead or standing in the Lateran with the Treasure of Honorius."

Brother Carl rose and placed his large calloused hands on James' head. "I will pray for you.

"Confiteor Deo omnipotenti, beatae Mariae semper Virgini, beato Michaeli Archangelo, beato Joanni Baptistae, sanctis Apostolis Petro et Paulo, omnibus Sanctis, et vobis, fratres (et tibi pater),

quia peccavi nimis cogitatione, verbo et opere: mea culpa, mea culpa, mea maxima culpa. Ideo precor beatam Mariam semper Virginem, beatum Michaelem Archangelum, beatum Joannem Baptistam, sanctos Apostolos Petrum et Paulum, omnes Sanctos, et vos, fratres (et te, pater), orare pro me ad Dominum Deum nostrum. Amen."

Brother Carl removed his hands. "James Martel kneel before me and repeat what I say.

"Deus meus, ex toto corde poenitet me omnium meorum peccatorum, eaque detestor, quia peccando, non solum poenas a Te iuste statutas promeritus sum, sed praesertim quia offendi Te, summum bonum, ac dignum qui super omnia diligaris. Ideo firmiter propono, adiuvante gratia Tua, de cetero me non peccaturum peccandique occasiones proximas fugiturum. Amen."

When James finished repeating the prayer, Brother Carl looked at him and smiled. "James Martel, I absolve you from your sins in the name of the Father, and of the son, and of the Holy Ghost. Come, I will find a chalice for you to wear. The journey to Babylon has yet to begin."

James stood up. He looked at Christ and the woman and then followed the monk out of the room.

CHAPTER 27
THE SHADOW OF EMPIRE

Byron watched his friend leave. He pulled his black cloak over his tunic and buckled on his sword. He stood in the empty room, his arms folded across his chest. After several minutes, Father Villhardain entered. "Did Brother Carl come for James?"

"Yes, they are gone."

"Hmm. Well, we shall see what comes of that. In the meantime, are you ready?"

"Yes, where are we going?"

"To the Campo Vaccino."

"A cow pasture?"

"Yes, you will see."

The two men stopped by the kitchen to eat and then headed for the door and out into the outskirts of Rome. It had rained during the night, and Byron could see there was more rain on the way. The weather was changing as summer fled and fall slowly began to grip the land.

They came upon a group of peasants from the country dressed in browns and reds. Their carts were loaded with vegetables bound for the city markets. They were festive; a young man juggled apples as he walked. A girl in a green dress with a garland of white flowers in her dark hair smiled at Byron. Her mother handed Father Villhardain a flower and asked the priest to pray for them. They journeyed with the peasants until a fork appeared in the road, and they parted company.

Father Villhardain stopped and waved goodbye to the peasants. Once they were out of sight, he turned to walk the lane less traveled, overgrown with grass.

"My son, do you know anything of Rome?"

"No, Father? Should I?"

"Yes, my son, you should. Rome is the foundation of all kingdoms. All kings wish to emulate the power and traditions of the Roman Emperor."

"So, what was Rome?"

"We spoke of Rome last night. Rome's empire stretched from Britton to Germania to Egypt and across the Levant. It was ruled by a Senate and an Emperor. The Roman legions policed the empire, defending its borders, while imperial bureaucrats collected taxes and paid for public projects. For two thousand years, there was peace and prosperity until darkness fell. Some believe the barbarians destroyed the empire. Others argue that Rome disintegrated because the Romans became self-indulgent and no longer cared to defend their lands."

"Is that what we are going to see?"

"Yes, the remnants of the heart of Imperial Rome."

They reached a broad pasture beneath the Lateran. The white orbs of dandelions waved among the stalks of brown grass. New shoots of green brought to life by the autumn rains were starting to grow from the dead turf. Byron walked through the damp grass following a trail of dirt packed hard by the cows traveling the same route over and over again. Hanging in the few remaining taller stalks of grass, he could see the silver lines of cobwebs wet with dew. In the distance, cows lumbered along unconcernedly grazing, ignoring the threat of rain. It might have been like any other rural setting, except for the marble columns rising from the grass.

Father Villhardain stopped and turned to smile at the questioning look from the knight beside him. "This is Imperial Rome."

"This is it?" the knight asked.

"Yes, there is not much left now."

The priest began walking towards a colossal elliptical building that dominated the field. Graceful arches rose three levels high. At the base of the colossus, a number of peasants were building a wall. The first few stones of the wall had been set, and several peasants were applying mortar. Other peasants, stripped to the waste, were working in the cut of the earth to push another foundation stone into place. The cut of stripped turf stretched like a brown ribbon to a large marble structure in the distance.

A man with a black velvet hat adorned with a red feather was sitting on a horse watching the peasants work. He had a long face, made longer by his neatly trimmed beard that ended in a point. Over his mail, he wore a garish purple cloak. He looked at Byron and the priest and then shouted. "What is your business here?" Before either the priest or the knight could answer, the Italian lord put his spurs to the horse, and with a great leap, the horse broke into a gallop.

Two soldiers with pikes, lounging against a low wall, stood up and began running after the lord. Byron, seeing the threat bearing down on them, threw his cloak aside and grabbed the hilt of his sword.

Father Villhardain smiled as the Italian noble approached. "Lord Frangipani, I see that you are well and in good health."

Frangipani stopped his horse in front of Father Villhardain and looked down at the priest. "Father Villhardain, I heard a rumor of your return."

Villhardain looked up and nodded. "Indeed, I have, although the business of the Church has many requirements, and I fear my stay will be brief."

"Hmm, if the Lateran spent less time meddling in the affairs of this world, you would not be so busy."

"It is the conduct of the souls of this world that concern me."

Frangipani smiled. "That is your reputation. I beg your pardon Father. I thought you were spies of Theophylact." He spit on the ground.. "Did you come to see the start of my new fortress?"

"No, I brought my young friend, Sir Fitzwalter, to see Rome."

"A knight marked with the cross, I see. Going or returning?"

"A brief return," Byron replied.

"Well, my crusader friend, there is nothing of interest here, just crumbling buildings." Frangipani stood in his stirrups and pointed. "Except for that damned arch. It is as solid as the day it was built, and it is right in the middle of my new wall. It will take great effort to tear it down. So, my architect is trying to decide what to do with it. A gate perhaps."

"The past shapes the future," the priest replied.

Frangipani scoffed, "Ha! No one affects my future. You are looking at the building of the present. I may be stuck with the past, but the future is mine to shape. Once this fortress is complete, I intend to govern from the security of its walls as I move Roma forward." Frangipani looked around and then leaned forward. "If you see that ass, Theophylact, in your travels, you can tell him for me that if he sets foot near here, I will send his soul to hell. But then again," he said as an afterthought as he sat up straight on his horse, "maybe, out of courtesy, I should display his head from the ramparts." Frangipani again spit on the ground.

"I should remind you that vengeance belongs to God."

Frangipani laughed. "Father, I intend to be the instrument of God's vengeance should Theophylact decide to trespass on my lands."

"With your permission," Father Villhardain changed the subject, "I would like to spend a few moments looking around."

"Look as long as you wish, Father. Now if you will excuse me, I must keep an eye on the serfs, or nothing will get done." Frangipani turned his horse and trotted back to supervise the work on the walls of his future castle.

"Come," the priest said, "let's see what we can before it disappears forever."

The priest in his black robes and the knight with his black cloak walked the dirt path torn into the green earth. The dead turf lay here and there tossed on top of the mounds of dirt. At the end of this gash, stood a forlorn structure silhouetted against the sky. Weeds grew among the broken slabs that surrounded the base. The walls, once white, were brown and stained. As Byron drew closer, he could see large capital letters inscribed at the top of the arch. Seeds brought by the birds had sprouted and now festooned the arch's top with grass and shrubs. In contrast with the wild appearance of the arch's top, the builder's martial intent still remained as the images of men and horses, carved in relief, remained visible upon the walls.

The priest stopped and looked up. "I brought you here because this arch records a dark day in the history of Jerusalem, as dark as the troubles that surround her now."

Byron walked through the arch and stopped to face a marble carving of a chariot drawn by four horses. A man stood in the chariot, robes cascaded down in folds over his armor. In his one hand, he held a baton. The other arm, outstretched, ended with a severed hand. Behind the man was a goddess placing a crown on his head. Her dress clung to her body, barely concealing her breasts as it displayed her upper chest and bare arms. Her feathered wings stretched protectively around the man. On the other side of the structure, soldiers crowned with laurel were bearing a table, trumpets, and a large candelabrum.

The priest walked into the arch to stand next to the knight. "This is the Triumphal Arch of the Emperor Titus."

The knight turned to the priest. "Who was Titus?"

"Well, my son, that depends. To the Jews, Titus is a monster. In the seventieth year of our Lord, the Jews revolted against Rome. The Romans demanded as a sign of loyalty that the Jews worship the Spirit of Rome and the genius of the emperor. The Jews of course refused, insisting on worshiping the God of Abraham. As a result, the Jews revolted and it was a bloody war. In the end, Titus sacked Jerusalem and burned the Jewish Temple. When there were no more Jews left to kill or crucify, he returned to Rome with the Temple Treasure." The priest pointed to the large building in the distance. "The Flavian amphitheater, or Coliseum, was built with the spoils from that war."

"The Jews," Byron muttered. "Usury is their God, and the ungodly rates they charge. My Father is still paying off his debts for my horse and armor. It is outrageous that they should charge a man interest on a loan just so he can send his son to fight the infidels."

"My son, there is more to the Jews than money lending. They

are God's chosen people. Never forget that Jesus was a Jew."

"Yes, but the Jews rejected Christ and demanded his death," the knight said. "What does this have to do with the crusades?'

The priest smiled. "Everything, my son. The decisions of the Emperor Titus and the Emperor Hadrian affect us to this day. It was sixty years later that the Jews revolted against Rome once again, and the Emperor Hadrian in his anger cast the Jews out of Israel, and Jerusalem ceased to exist. Hadrian rebuilt the city and proclaimed it Aelia Capitolina. That is why to this very day the Jews live separately among us as the wandering people. You find their usury unchristian, but if you have been dispossessed of all you own, would you not do whatever you could to survive?"

"Yes, not that it matters. If Saladin is victorious, the Christians will be the next to be expelled, but at least I can return to my home." Byron walked out of the arch and looked up at the imposing words carved into the marble at the top. "Father what does this say?"

The priest looked up at the Latin words carved in stone and read, *"The senate and people of Rome dedicated this Arch to the divine Titus Vespasianus Augustus son of the divine Vespasian."*

Father Villhardain sighed. "If Saladin is victorious, it will be many years before another Christian sets foot on her sacred streets."

"Then we shall not fail. Jerusalem arose once again, did it not?"

A faint smile appeared on Father Villhardain face. "Yes, and that reminds me, I want to show you something else."

The two men turned their back on the Arch of Titus. It took some time to walk to the massive walls of the Coliseum. The wind picked up as the blue sky disappeared, turning to a grey slate of clouds. Near the Coliseum stood another triumphal arch. Standing at the top of the three archways, stone men with bearded faces looked down at them.

The priest stood in the center arch. "This is the Arch of Constantine the Great." The priest looked up at the attic and began to read, *"To the Emperor Caesar Flavius Constantinus Maximus Pius Felix Augustus the senate and the people of Rome dedicated an arch with scenes of triumph, since by divine inspiration and great wisdom with his army and righteous weapons he liberated the state from tyranny and all faction.*

"We should take hope from Constantine," the priest smiled. "Jerusalem's fate is not sealed. The tyrant Maxentius' army was twice as large. Yet, as Constantine approached Rome to fight Maxentius at the Milvian Bridge, he saw the cross in the midday sky surrounded by the words *In Hoe Signo Vinces* - In this sign thou shall conquer. Christ visited him that night in a dream and told him to remove the Roman eagle of Jupiter from his standards and replace it with the sign of the cross. On the day of the battle, Constantine's standard was the cross, and he ordered that his soldiers shields be emblazoned with the Chi Rho." The old priest paused at the knight's questioning look. "The Chi Rho is the letter P crossed by the letter X, the first two letters in Greek spelling of the name Christos. My son, Christ was with Constantine, and he was victorious. We should take hope from that story. All is not finished."

Byron looked at the priest shaking his head. "How do you know this?"

"Reading my son. I have read a great deal. Reading gives great power."

Byron looked up at the letters. To him the words were meaningless, but the priest could recite them just as they were spoken long ago. It was a skill worthy of great respect. "So, how did Jerusalem arise again from utter destruction?"

"It was Constantine's mother, Saint Helena, who influenced her son to restore Jerusalem. It was Helena who found the location of the crucifixion and the Tomb of our Lord. She destroyed the temple of Venus that Hadrian had built on the place of Christ's crucifixion and sponsored the building, the Church of the Holy Sepulcher. In fact, you have seen one of the holy relics that she found."

"Which was?" Byron asked.

"The true cross."

Byron's brow furled as he looked down. "We marched from Jerusalem with the holy relic before the army. I never thought...we could be defeated as long as we possessed it. I wonder what she would say of our valor since we lost it. Saladin has it now. God knows what that cursed infidel has done to it."

Byron glanced up at the Coliseum and to his surprise, found people looking down at him from the arches. They were dressed in rags. Some were barely dressed at all; their wretched bodies burnt brown from the sun. Unlike the peasants on the way to the market, there was no gaiety. They looked down at him with hollowed eyes. Curtains draped the arches in an attempt to give privacy to the dwellings of the poor. As he scanned the arches, his eyes fell upon one with black curtains filled with rents. It was different from the rest of the dirty white cloths erected by the poor. A small girl with a pallid face stepped out to look down at him.

Byron's face turned ashen as a sudden pain filled his head. It was almost as if he could hear screaming. He closed his eyes in agony as a voice hissed, "Change your path."

Father Villhardain reached out and put his hand on Byron's shoulder. "Are you ill, my son."

"Do you see her, Father?"

Father Villhardain looked up. "See who?"

"The Celtic wraith. The banshee. She is standing in the arch with black curtains."

The priest looked up. "My son, I see nothing." Father Villhardain's face tightened as he looked at the knight. "Perhaps you hear the voices of those who died here." Byron was holding his head; his eyes were watering from the pain. "Come, my son, the peasants are watching. This is an evil place. They will not try to rob us because they fear you, but if they see you are weak, then events might turn ill."

Byron, his head bowed, followed the priest. He was in great pain as if a lightning storm was raging in his head. His vision was blurred, and he could only make out the vague outline of the priest. They started up Palatine Hill when Byron asked the priest to stop.

"Are you feeling better, my son?"

"Yes," Byron said as he wiped the tears from his eyes. "Father, you said I was hearing the voices of the dead. What did you mean?"

"My son, the Romans used the arena to entertain the masses. Gladiators fought each other to the death. Christians were coated in pitch and lit on fire to burn as candles. For years, men, women and children perished there. Perhaps you heard the echoes of their agony." Father Villhardain took a long look at Byron. "My son, are you sure you are well enough to journey to Babylon?"

Byron's jaw tightened. "Father, if it were not for the Archbishop Joscius, I would be in Jerusalem defending the walls. I can journey to Babylon. It is now my duty to go." Byron wiped the sweat from his brow. "The affliction has passed."

"Do you wish to go on?"

"We are half way up the hill now... I want to see the ruins."

The priest smiled. "Then we shall."

They walked up the hill towards the remains of the palace of the emperors. Byron stood on Palatine Hill and stared at the heart of Rome and the remnants of the empire. His head ached, and he turned to face the cool wind that came from the west. The wind ruffled his black cloak. He looked up at the sky and watched the clouds, black with rain, as they scurried beneath the grey canopy above. No rain fell, but as the cold wind came up, he knew it was not far away.

It occurred to him as he looked out over Rome that the descendants of the people who had built the city were now living in poverty of its ruins. How could such an empire disappear so completely? He wondered if the men who had lived here, would have ever conceived that all of their efforts would come to this. That their immense and powerful city, the symbol of their empire, their myths, their culture, would be erased. That their mighty capitol would become a pile of rocks, with a few columns here and there to mark the spot where marble temples and other important civic buildings had once stood. The great men of Rome, imprisoned in marble relief, lurked here and there in the remains of their city, ignored and forgotten.

Byron turned away from the view as he pondered the words of the banshee. "Change your path." Was it something he had imagined? What did that mean? He had almost died at Hattin. Maybe it was time to become something more than a cold-blooded killer. Perhaps it was time to start looking for a way to become something more.

"Father, I would like to learn to read."

The abrupt request surprised Father Villhardain and it showed on his face. "Absolutely, my son. It would be a privilege to bring you into a broader world, but it will take some dedication and practice on your part."

"I am aware of what it will take."

"Do you wish to start today?"

"Yes, I have seen enough." Turning his back on the ruins of power and prestige, Byron walked with the priest down Palatine Hill towards the Lateran palace.

CHAPTER 28
THE DON AND THE COUNT

Ishaq stepped off the ship and on to the dock. He was carrying a silver cane. A dark grey traveling cloak was draped over his black tunic embroidered with elaborate designs of silver thread. His new moustache and beard was starting to fill in, and it gave him a distinguished look of a Catalan Don. In his other hand, he carried a sealed letter that he had written to Marcellus Theophylact.

Ishaq looked around and sighed, it was late in the day. He needed a place to stay. He was in the land of the infidel, and he despised the sight of the serfs. Several were working on the docks. He tilted his head to look down his nose at their unwashed faces and their ragged dirty clothes, but it was the smell of them that he hated most.

"My lord, do you need your baggage carried?" Ishaq turned to find a peasant standing next to him. A brown cap was pulled over the peasant's ears. A brown leather jerkin with patches of hair covered his torso. A smile revealed the few yellow teeth that remained in the man's mouth. The peasant pointed at Ishaq's bag.

"Yes," Ishaq replied as he put Marcellus' letter into his cloak pocket and fished out a coin. He tossed it to the peasant who deftly caught it. "If you find me a suitable place to stay, there will be another coin for you."

"Thank you, m' lord," the man said as he doffed his cap and bowed.

Ishaq followed the peasant to a two-story building with a red tile roof. A painted sign in Italian proclaimed the place as "The Red Rooster Inn." Ishaq looked at the modest building.

"It don't look like much, m' lord, but the fare's good and the keeper honest."

Ishaq looked at the failing light. It would have to do, and he handed the peasant another coin. Ishaq walked through the small courtyard and entered a hall with a long table in the center of the room. Several guests, already seated, looked at Ishaq with unfriendly stares. A thin man with wisps of grey hair was ladling soup. He looked up. "My lord, do you need a room."

"Indeed, at least for this night, and I need to send a message to Rome."

"May I ask the lord his name?"

"Don Hernandez de Fuego of Catalonia."

"My lord, you honor me with your visit to my humble inn."

Ishaq looked around at the surly lot of commoners as he took his place at the table. "It was recommended to me as a respectable place with boon company and good food."

The innkeeper bowed. "Is there anything else you require?"

"Yes, I need a message sent to Count Marcellus Theophylact." Several guests gasped. "And I will pay well."

The muscles in the innkeeper's face tightened. He dropped the ladle, and it fell into the pot of soup with a splash. "Count Theophylact is known. Well known. Are, are, you a friend?"

Ishaq smiled. "Indeed, the count and I have done business together."

"I, ah see," the innkeeper stuttered. "I will find a rider at once."

Ishaq looked around the room. The mention of Count Theophylact had a welcome effect. Most of the guests were moving as far away from Ishaq as the room would allow. Ishaq smiled as the innkeeper placed a bowl of stew in front of him and then left the room. He looked around at the men seated at the table. Most avoided his gaze. He had dreaded having to engage this lot in conversation, but with the mention of the count's name, he was able to eat in peace.

When the meal ended, the innkeeper came up to Ishaq and whispered in his ear. "My lord, the courier is here."

Ishaq nodded and got up from the table. In the darkened courtyard, a young man wearing a black cloak and tall riding boots was waiting. Ishaq handed the man the letter and a gold coin. "Deliver this swiftly to Count Marcellus Theophylact in Rome and no one else."

The rider bowed. "Yes, my lord. I will ride as fast as my horse can carry me. Hopefully, God willing, there are no bandits on the road tonight."

"Humph, should you be waylaid, tell them what you carry and who it is for. Ask them if they intend to commit suicide by interfering with my letter."

"I will do what you ask, lord." The rider bowed and left the courtyard.

"Come, my lord, I will take you to your room," the innkeeper muttered. "Since you are a friend of Count Theophylact, I will give you a room to yourself."

"That is kind. I will make sure to let the count know of your graciousness."

The innkeeper bowed. "That would indeed be kind." He led Ishaq up the stairs and opened the door to small room with a single bed. "May our Lord and Savior keep you from harm this night, my lord, and see you safely to dawn's light."

Ishaq smiled. "I am certain he will." Ishaq closed the door and set his bag down. He rummaged through it for his prayer rug. He rolled the rug out on the floor and then paused. He had no idea which way to face. He stared at the wall and then turned to look at the door. With a sigh, he gave up and knelt down to pray. After his prayer to Allah, he turned in for the night. The bed was uncomfortable, and he tossed and turned, laying on his back, then laying on his side. After an hour, he got up and sat on the edge of his bed. He had been a poor street urchin, and now here he was in the land of the infidel conversing with them, masquerading as a Catalan Don. He was using all the training the Nizari Ismaili had given him when he was a boy learning to become an assassin. As he thought about it, he thought of the fortress of Alamut.

†

It had been long ago since he had seen the great fortress. He thought of his old master the old man of the mountain. He remembered the candles stuck into iron candelabrums that cast their dim light on the floor. His shadow flickered on the stone walls, growing larger and then smaller as he passed from one candle to the next. The floor was smooth, and his feet made a soft padding sound. It had been five years since the Nizari Ismaili took him in. He had grown. He could speak Frankish, and he was learning Italian, soon he would learn Spanish. He was becoming fluent in the languages of the enemies. He was gaining skill as a killer. He had mastered the bow; he was learning the chemistry of poisons. He was growing into a dangerous man. Ishaq was pleased and his pride was growing. He had just won praise from master Saqr for his skill with the knife.

He was reflecting on his lesson with master Saqr when he felt the presence of someone. He turned to find the old man of the Nizari Ismaili behind him. The old man's hood shadowed his visage. Ishaq felt the hair on his neck stand on edge as a jolt of fear went through him.

"Habib, how goes your studies."

Ishaq bowed. "Very well, master. I have become skilled at the art of using the knife. Master Saqr is pleased with my control and my position of attack."

"Hmm, so I have heard. Master Saqr is impressed, but that is not why I am here. Can you guess why I am here?"

Ishaq looked wide-eyed at the shadowy figure of the Master of Nizari Ismaili. "No, master."

Beneath the hood's shadow, Ishaq saw the corners of the master's mouth harden into a frown. "Humph, I thought you might have some idea. It has come to my attention that you have been less than kind to the new boys inducted into our order. You have been bullying and stealing from them." Ishaq looked down. "Is this true, Habib?"

"Yes, master."

"Do you know the penalties for being a thief according to Sharia law?" Ishaq nodded. "Fortunately for you, none of the boys will bear witness against you, but that is not a reprieve." The old master grabbed Ishaq and jerked him close. "These boys are your brothers. They are our future. They will be the only ones who will aid you in the tasks I give you. Do you understand?" Ishaq sucked in air as he nodded. "Habib, you are gifted and Allah has blessed you, but this behavior will cease." Ishaq looked at the master, his eyes wide with fear.

"I will give you your first task." The old man's eyes glistened in the darkness of his hood. "You will defend our youngest recruits. You will guide them and you will look after them. Do you understand?"

"Yes, master."

"Good." The old man let go of Ishaq. "Do not fail me, Habib." With a swish of the master's cloak, the old man disappeared into the darkness of the corridor and was gone.

†

Ishaq sat in the darkness of the inn's room thinking of that moment. It had not been easy, but the master was not one to disappoint. He had been diligent in becoming a leader, and he had learned from it, but after his near death in the streets of Tyre, he had found himself alone. Taking the lessons he had learned at Alamut, he had remade himself, changed his name to Ishaq, and assembled men to do his bidding.

The street urchin from Tyre would have been a new addition to his group. A spy, an errand boy, and if he did well, then other things would have followed. The boy had died to save him. He had failed to protect his protégé. The tall handsome knight would pay for that. He lay back down on his bed and stared at the ceiling. The handsome knight would pay. He would not fail to reap vengeance.

In the morning, Ishaq was roused by the sound of rain on the tile roof. With an effort, he got up. The scar from the old wound in his chest ached, and he gingerly rubbed the mark to make the pain go away. "Damn this cold weather," he muttered. He dressed and made his way downstairs. He sat apart from the other guests and ate his breakfast of cold bread and butter.

The innkeeper came up to him as he finished eating his simple meal. "My lord, a coach has arrived to take you to Rome."

"Very good, tell the driver to wait." Ishaq went up to his room and gathered his few belongings.

The carriage was parked in the courtyard. Chickens wandered next to the black wheels with golden hubs shaped like lion heads. The top of the carriage was made of black leather with golden finials at each corner. Red and black canvas curtains hung down from the top, protecting the passenger from the weather and prying eyes. The driver in a black tunic with a purple cloak was standing holding the reins of the two white horses.

The driver bowed. "My lord, the Count Marcellus Theophylact sends his greetings."

Ishaq nodded. "I trust our journey will be swift."

"Those are the count's instructions. He desires to see you as soon as possible."

The driver took Ishaq's bag and placed it in the coach as Ishaq took his seat. The driver mounted one of the white horses, and with a lurch, the wagon started moving.

In the early morning light, the rain beat steadily on the roof of the coach. The rolling countryside of vineyards and olive orchards passed by as the coach rocked and bumped along the old Roman road. The driver hunched forward, his head bowed enduring the rain that poured down on him. Ishaq could see the few peasants working in the fields staring at him. He ignored the peasants, enjoying the splendor of the coach that was considerably more comfortable than traveling in the rain by horseback.

Hours passed and the morning rain lifted. Ishaq passed the time by rehearsing his role as a Spanish Don from Catalonia whose mother was of Moorish decent. He had used this disguise before, and it had worked well. It was convenient that the Moors had invaded Spain, a valuable historical event that he used to explain away his obvious Arabic features. The Nizari Ismaili had trained him to speak Spanish. He was grateful for the training at times like this. Just in case someone should doubt his authenticity, he wore a large gold cross prominently displayed on a heavy gold chain. If that didn't work, he had an extra supply of gold coins on hand to help solve any problems should someone suspect his true identity.

The coach rumbled to a stop at a pleasant wayside. The driver, wiping the rain from his face, approached the door. "My lord, I need to rest the horses."

"I think I shall take a walk and stretch my limbs," Ishaq said, looking at the sky to see if the rain would start again.

His foot touched the ground, and he heard several small voices calling out. "Lord, lord, have pity on us we are poor. Please lord. Do you have any spare pennies?" Ishaq turned and found that several small children, their hands outstretched, had set upon him.

"Go away you gutter rats!" the driver cried irritably as he shooed the wretched children away. "This lord has nothing for you."

"Not true," Ishaq said sharply. "Come here." The children meekly gathered around as Ishaq handed each boy two silver pennies. When he finished, Ishaq smiled. "That is all I have for you, now go home."

He smiled inwardly as the children ran off. He remembered the days before the Nizari Ismaili, when the gift of a penny was a treasure. He hoped the pennies would ease the boys' misery for a day. At least the little wretches would not be throwing dirt clods, or something worse, at his carriage.

The carriage reached the outskirts of Rome and steadily began to climb a small hill. The drive lined with cedar trees led to impressive battlements of a large fortress of the House of Count Marcellus Theophylact. At the gate, the coach came to a stop as two mercenaries with long pikes blocked the road. Ishaq could hear one of the guards questioning the driver. The other guard, who had an evil looking scar stretching from the corner of his eye to his neck, looked in the coach at Ishaq, verifying the driver's story. Satisfied with the driver's explanation, the gate opened.

The coach passed through the wall, stopping in front of the white walls of the villa.

The driver opened the door, and Ishaq pushed his silver cane through the doorway and stepped out of the coach. Count Theophylact stood at the portico. He was tall, his dark hair was combed back, his beard neatly trimmed. The count was smiling, but his dark eyes were a window to an empty soul. He was wearing a fur-lined cloak draped over a red tunic embroidered with threads of gold. Ishaq tensed as Marcellus greeted him with a hug. "My old friend, it is so good to see you." He then kissed Ishaq on both cheeks. Ishaq frowned as Marcellus stepped back. "What brings you to Rome? Business?"

"Ah, you could say that."

"Who is the poor soul who will not be with us long?" Marcellus asked with a sly grin.

"I am afraid it is more complicated. I have come to ask for your assistance. I need some information about Rome."

Marcellus raised his eyebrows. "I see. Come, my friend. I expect you to stay as my guest as long as you are in Rome."

"I am honored to be your guest."

Ishaq walked between the two marble columns of the portico looted from a Roman temple. They gave the house an aura of stability and wealth. Several female servants dressed in white togas greeted them as they entered through the open bronze door.

"This is my guest, Ishaq of Tyre. I want him treated well. Take his belongings to the guest room." He turned to Ishaq with a smile. "Come, my friend. Follow me to where we can sit in comfort and talk."

Ishaq set down his meager belongings. A tall dark-haired woman with sensuous brown eyes approached. She smiled at Ishaq as she collected his bags. She turned slowly making sure that he could see her shapely body and then walked away. Ishaq stared after her.

"Do you like her?" Marcellus asked.

Ishaq looked again at the Italian woman as she disappeared from sight. Everything here had a price, including the girls. What that price was, Ishaq did not know, and he never made a deal until he knew the full cost.

"My business does not allow for that."

"Too bad," Marcellus replied slightly disappointed.

Marcellus led Ishaq beside a pool lined with marble statues. The intricate mosaic floor of a sea was filled with nymphs and mermaids. To make the illusion real several nude girls were swimming in the pool.

Marcellus looked at them and smiled. "These are my mermaids. But don't linger, their siren song will have you swimming in the pool." Ishaq glanced at the girls and then ignored them.

Marcellus walked up to the half-dressed sculpture of a woman. Her toga draped around her body in folds that cascaded to the floor. Her face with its delicate features was turned sideways "Venus," Marcellus said as he patted her breasts. "Exquisite. I like the sculptor's attention to detail." Before Ishaq could answer, Marcellus moved to the next statue of a man crowned in laurel holding a cup and a vine of grapes. "Bacchus came from a temple near the forum, but the next one is my favorite."

Marcellus stopped beside a sculpture of a man wearing a helmet that covered his cheeks. A crest of faded and chipped red paint topped the helmet. The narrowed eyes of the god stared out into the distance; stylized muscles bulged as he grasped a spear in his right hand. Marcellus put his arm around the statues neck. "Mars. What do you think Ishaq? Do you see the likeness?"

Ishaq had studied Roman mythology. The Arabs had preserved many of the great works of the Greeks and the Romans. His old reading master had made sure he learned the lore.

Ishaq smiled. "I see a resemblance." Inwardly, he thought that Marcellus was more the Greek version of the god of war; a double-faced liar bent on ruin and destruction.

"Yes indeed," Marcellus beamed. "They are all early empire, not the later crude works before the fall of Rome. Come, Ishaq, I have more to show you." Ishaq sighed as Marcellus chatted away about his collection of treasures. Ishaq had no interest in Marcellus' possessions, but he feigned his attention out of politeness.

They arrived in the sitting room, the walls painted with life size frescos of Italian rural scenes of women harvesting grapes and olives. The floor was a mosaic depicting a Roman gladiator garbed as Murmillo cutting the throat of a defeated opponent. Dark red tiles imitated a pool of blood in the center of the floor. Ishaq frowned as he stepped over it.

"Sit, my friend," Marcellus said. "Wine?"

"Do you have qahwa?"

"I do." Marcellus turned to his servants in the room. "Coffee for my guest, and a flagon of wine for me." After several minutes, the servants returned with coffee and wine.

"What can I do for you?" Marcellus asked.

Ishaq, sitting in a comfortable chair, was enjoying the heat from a bronze brazier of burning charcoal. The warmth drove the autumn chill from the room, and it made him sleepy. He took a sip of qahwa, or coffee as Marcellus called it, to ward off the effects.

"I am looking for a priest. He has recently returned to Rome from the Levant. I have a client interested in learning what the priest was doing in the Holy Lands. He is, or was, in the protection of two knights."

"That sounds odd," Marcellus said, raising his eyebrows. "I have never heard of a priest meriting that kind of protection. I wonder why."

"So, does my client. My client also wishes to know why Salah al-Din has an interest in capturing the priest."

Marcellus sat up in his chair. "Did my ears just deceive me, did you just say the Sultan Saladin attempted to capture a Catholic priest?"

"I did."

"Do you have a name?"

"Villhardain."

"I have heard of him. He is well known in Rome, a favorite of Cardinal Morra, an extremely powerful cardinal of the Roman Catholic Church. Why Villhardain? I have never heard anything bad about the man, and I make it my business to know those sorts of things." Marcellus paused in thought. "I am surprised; he is not your usual target."

"That is true, but the Roman Church is engaged in some sort of plot. A plot that has caught the interest of Salah al-Din, and

Villhardain is at the center of the Church's designs. My employer is extremely curious. Do you have any contacts with the Church that might tell you what Villhardain was doing in the Levant?"

"I might be able to aid you," Marcellus replied, "for a fee. Do you think whatever Villhardain is doing in the Levant might be profitable... say for us?"

"That is why I am here."

"Do you need a business partner?"

"Perhaps," Ishaq said, weighing the decision to cut Jabbar out of the picture. The fat merchant was too much of a coward. Marcellus, on the other hand, was ruthless, and if things went wrong, too far away to exact revenge.

Marcellus nodded. "My friend, you are fortunate. I have recently made the acquaintance of Cardinal Fulcher. He is the vice chancellor of Urban, and I think he would be amenable to helping us. He is campaigning hard to ensure he succeeds Urban as the next Holy Father. He has asked for my support. I control Rome, so my support is necessary for Fulcher. I must add, for a churchman, he has the soul of Lucifer."

"I knew you would have a source."

"I am fairly certain he will see things our way. He has a fondness for young men. It would not do if something like that became public information, now would it?"

"No, indeed not. Something like that could be very damaging." Ishaq shook his head. "So, what does the fool think; that he can keep his perversions secret?"

"He has so far," Marcellus chuckled. "Actually, he has done far worse."

"Are you concerned that Fulcher will try and destroy you first?"

"No, the man's a coward. Besides, we have an understanding. Within the next few days, we shall know what the Church finds so interesting in the Levant."

Ishaq nodded. "Enough business for now," Marcellus continued. "You have had a long trip. Why don't you go to your room and I will send a girl to entertain you. I will make arrangements to meet with Fulcher."

"Thank you, my friend, but the girl will not be necessary."

"Are you sure?" Marcellus asked in surprise.

"Yes."

Marcellus shook his head. "Well, if you change your mind, all you have to do is ask."

Ishaq sat drinking his qahwa as Marcellus got up and left. He found it irritating that Marcellus kept pushing him to spend time with his girls. He had no desire to become trapped and manipulated like Fulcher, and he was sure that Marcellus had some impure motive behind his generosity. He poured himself another cup of qahwa, stood up, and walked outside to admire the grounds of the estate. He would now sit back and wait. He had come a long way to solve the mystery of Villhardain. Hopefully, this corrupt cardinal would have the answer.

CHAPTER 29
THE LITTLE CARDINAL AND THE POPE

A small man walked hurriedly down the hallway of the Lateran, his red silk robes billowing behind him. Although he looked like a boy, as vice chancellor he was the most powerful cardinal in the Church. A red biretta covered his blond hair. About his shoulders, he wore a red cape lined with ermine. Cardinal Fulcher was angry. His schemes to become the next Holy Father had so far come to naught. Yesterday, he had tried with all of his powers of persuasion to get the old fool Urban to excommunicate Frederick Barbarossa, but no matter how much pressure he put on the doddering old man, the Holy Father would not take the next step to excommunicate the emperor. He wanted to spend today putting pressure on the consistory and the Holy Father to carry out the excommunication. Instead, he was summoned to a meeting requested by Cardinal Morra. He was irritated by the distraction, but he was even more irritated at Morra who kept thwarting his plans.

He stopped and entered a side room. As the door opened, a blond, middle-aged German with a pockmarked face turned to look at him. "Is everything ready?" the man asked.

"No! Urban still threatens excommunication, though he lacks the courage to go through with it."

"You promised you would be done today," the German said in

anger. "You told me Urban was under your control."

"Graf VonDurenberg, this process requires delicacy. I will have Frederick excommunicated, and I promise you will succeed him as Holy Roman Emperor. It is going to take more time, but I will back Urban into a corner where he has no other choice but to excommunicate Frederick."

The German tilted his head back and looked down his nose at the cardinal. "Good, I traveled all this way to receive the title of Holy Roman Emperor; another day or two will not hurt."

Fulcher shook his head in exasperation. "I remind you, Helmuth, that you must first be elected by the German princes to become emperor. Our purpose here is to prepare Urban to recognize you. Once you are emperor, you will support me to become the next Holy Father once Urban is dead."

"Don't patronize me. I know how the process works," VonDurenberg snapped. "All it will take is for Frederick to be excommunicated, and the German princes will rise up against him."

Fulcher sighed. "I cannot make the Holy Father move any faster. Be patient. Frederick will be excommunicated. Now come with me."

"Why? I have my own commitments to attend to. The emperor has seized the lands of my lord and kinsman Henry, the Lion of Saxony. Saxony is rife with resentment against Barbarossa, but now I must send messengers to Henry that you have failed."

Fulcher looked up and rolled his eyes. "I have not failed! You can send a messenger later. Right now, I must attend an audience between Urban and that fool Morra who will prattle on about a worthless treasure hunt. Once Morra is done wasting time on whatever rash project he and his assistant have been working on, we can start working again, playing on Urban's fears that Frederick is threatening to seize the papal states."

"Treasure? What kind of treasure?"

Fulcher tilted his head slightly to the side and frowned. "A fool's tale."

"Indulge me."

"After the fall of Rome, a rumor circulated that the Imperial Treasure of the Roman Empire was taken out of Italy ahead of the

Visigoth Army. I have heard this story over the years and I believe it is nonsense."

"I see," the graf said, unconvinced. "I cannot believe Morra would waste the Holy Father's time with nonsense."

"Yes, he would. He is trying to put on a show so the Church will have a favorable opinion of him when the time comes to name a new Pope. Now come, I must speak to the old fool."

Both men made their way through the Papal Palace. Fulcher led the way to a curious set of stairs leading to the Sancta Sanctorum, the private chapel of Urban III. At the bottom of the stairs Fulcher stopped.

"I will speak to His Holiness about the approaching meeting of the sacred college of cardinals. I need you to go to the Basilica and wait for me near the papal altar."

"I should accompany you," the graf said as he placed his hand on the hilt of his sword. "Perhaps I could impress upon him the need to act."

Fulcher scoffed, "I think not! Such crude methods might work in the world of chevaliers but not here!" The diminutive cardinal turned and marched up the twenty-eight steps to the private chapel of the Holy Father. At the top of the stairs, he glanced at the image of Christ on the cross and then walked past. The last thing he needed right now was for VonDurenberg to open his mouth and for Urban to learn the true extent of VonDurenberg's stupidity.

Urban was on his knees deep in prayer when Fulcher entered the chapel. Fulcher stopped and listened to the Pontiff's prayer. He could see the old man shaking as he struggled to maintain his balance. What a fool, Fulcher thought, no one would ever know if the Holy Father prayed on his knees. He would never put himself in such a position. After several moments, the old man stopped his devotions and then struggled to his feet.

"May God's blessing find Your Holiness," Fulcher said as he kissed Urban's hands, "and grant you the discernment to guide your flock through the tribulations of this unhappy world."

Urban reached out with a faltering and shaking hand and patted Fulcher on the shoulder. "My...my... young friend, I don't know what I would do without you. It is a beautiful day, and I have been in prayer all morning, but I must say I have not been able to enjoy it as I should. It has been such terrible business dealing with Frederick's treachery."

"It is a terrible burden you carry, Your Holiness. It is always distressing to discover those closest to you have betrayed your trust. What is worse, Frederick should have the best interest of the Church in his heart, but he has chosen to pursue his own earthly interest of sin instead of preparing his soul for the afterlife. Charlemagne protected the Church from its enemies. Frederick should follow that example. It is clear he has fallen from grace. His soul has been corrupted by the devil.

"His disobedience has been troubling. I am incensed at Frederick's insistence on his son's marriage, which has not been blessed by the Church, and is nothing more than a thinly disguised land grab by the emperor. He knows his son's inheritance of the Kingdom of Sicily and southern Italy will bring him in conflict with the Church. I am concerned that Frederick's next move will be to threaten the independence of the Papal States, and then it is only a matter of time before he will be the master of Italy. He will control Rome and the Church if he succeeds.

"Disobedience to the authority of the Holy Father is a sign that he has turned his back on the Church. I fear the only recourse you have, Your Holiness, is to remove the corrupt through excommunication."

"Cardinal Morra," Urban said, his voice quivering from old age, "does not think Frederick's soul is lost. Yesterday, he offered to mediate once again; to bring the lost lamb back to the flock and return Frederick to the path of righteousness."

"I believe Cardinal Morra is deceived. Frederick is lost. He wants to rule as Charlemagne did; yet, he does not have Charlemagne's greatness, nor would he respect the Church or papal authority. You must act. We are at war with the forces of evil. You are the heir of Saint Peter. Christ will hold your immortal soul accountable if you fail to protect his Church. As your loyal friend and advisor, I warn you, you must act before it is too late."

"Yes, I know. I am torn with anger at Frederick's disobedience, but I will indulge Cardinal Morra's request. Excommunication is not to be taken lightly; therefore, I will wait before I begin the rite that condemns Frederick's soul: bell, book, and light."

Fulcher sighed. "I will bow to your wise judgment in this matter, but if I learn of any further evidence of Frederick's sins against the Church, do you want me to bring that evidence to you?"

"As much as it breaks my heart, I must know if he still transgresses against my authority. He has done this before to other Popes, but I always had hoped he would have had more consideration for me."

"Then, if anything else is learned, with deep regret, I will bring the sins of my brother to you."

"What other matters are on my schedule for today?" Urban asked with a sigh, changing the subject.

"Cardinal Morra has requested an audience with Your Holiness," Fulcher replied in a businesslike tone. "His assistant, Father Villhardain, has returned from Jerusalem with news on the condition of the Kingdom. He also wants to present information on his investigation into the lost Imperial Treasure of Honorius."

"What is the condition of Jerusalem?"

"Rumors have circulated that the Saracens have launched a new war of conquest, but my reliable contacts have informed me that King Guy Lusignan and the gallant Knights of the Temple have defeated the Saracen Sorcerer Saladin, and his army has retreated back to Damascus in disgrace."

"God be praised. Wonderful news, tell me more."

Fulcher was caught and he struggled to create a story. "Ah..., your Holiness, well..., ah... I have been told that, ah..., Saladin was engaged in communication with the devil when his army was attacked by our soldiers marching with the true cross before them. Our valiant army routed the Saracens in a short, decisive battle. I was also told that many of the enemy soldiers were struck down by lightning bolts which emanated from the cross itself, a true miracle witnessed by several Knights of the Temple."

"Oh, that is wonderful," Urban exclaimed. "A true verdict that God wills it and favors our crusade to punish the infidel." Urban paused, his brow furled in thought. "But if that is true, why are members of this Church whispering in the hallways that the

Christian Army has been defeated and that Jerusalem is in grave danger?"

"It is a lie! A lie spread by the devil-worshiper Saladin that our misguided brethren have embraced."

"Men always see the worst," Urban said, shaking his head. "Do you know what Father Villhardain has found out about Honorius' lost treasure?"

"I have not been told. Cardinal Morra is very protective of his assistant. I can only assume he is here to report nothing has been found. I anticipate this meeting will not take very long. If, though by some unlikely chance, the treasure has been located," Fulcher said, keeping his options open, "I would like to offer my service as an advisor to the recovery effort. I would also take it upon myself to take charge of the gold and ensure that it is used wisely to promote the Church."

"My faithful friend, I thank you for your selfless offer. I know how burdened you are already, but it would ease my cares if you were involved in this matter."

"I will do my best," Fulcher said dolefully. "And while it is an additional burden, I think it would be best if some oversight was provided to Cardinal Morra. His continued support of Frederick Barbarossa makes me question his judgment."

"I disagree. Cardinal Morra has always been a staunch and pious member of the Church. I have spoken to him about this, and I know he believes he can redirect Frederick's energies. I am willing to let him try. I don't think you need to question his devotion to the Church, or his judgment for that matter."

"You are right, Your Holiness," Fulcher said, doing his best to smoothly retract his comment. "I must confess that Frederick's transgressions have caused me so much anxiety and anger at his obstinacy that I have been a little quick to judge the motives of others who only wish to help."

"I can understand your frustration," Urban said, giving the cardinal a look of warning. "But you must guard against speaking rashly about a fellow cardinal of the Church."

Fulcher's face assumed the look of complete repentance. "You are right, Your Holiness. I appreciate your just chastisement for my impertinent comments." He had practiced this facial expression many times for a moment such as this. In truth, he wanted to make more disparaging comments regarding Morra, whom he considered a threat to his plans to become the next Pope.

"Are you ready to go Your Holiness? I expect Cardinal Morra and Father Villhardain will be arriving soon."

"I am ready to go. I must say, I am still marveling at the miracle about lightning from the cross. Amazing!"

"Indeed," Fulcher said, smiling at his clever deception. Hopefully, the old man would be dead before he learned the truth, or more likely, forget about it in his senility.

"Take my arm," Fulcher said gently.

"You are much too kind," Urban said as he walked with halting steps through the Basilica. "I will remember your generosity when the time comes." The two men walked across the mosaic floor between the marble archways of the Basilica.

"I have asked a member of the German delegation to be present at this meeting," Fulcher said, broaching the subject of VonDurenberg's presence. "I have known his family for a long time, good Catholics, staunch defenders of the faith. Graf VonDurenberg is a brave, generous knight and an experienced warrior. While he has not had an opportunity to take the cross to go to the Holy Lands, he has spent his time campaigning in the Holy Roman Empire, helping to keep the peace despite the emperor's neglect."

"Whatever you desire," Urban muttered distractedly. "I assume you have advised him that whatever Church business is discussed is not to be repeated."

"Absolutely. Graf VonDurenberg has complete integrity and is completely trustworthy."

"Good. Anything discussed must remain in the Church. If I hear our internal business is the general knowledge of Rome, it will not bode well for the person who sponsored the layman to attend this meeting."

"Yes, Your Holiness," Fulcher muttered, already preparing to look for a scapegoat if and when VonDurenberg opened his mouth, which despite his earlier statements, was likely to happen.

"I assure you nothing will be said."

They reached the end of the hall and Urban took his seat on his throne, a white chair near the apse of the Church. VonDurenberg, standing near the dais, started to open his mouth to speak, but after a withering glance from Fulcher, he shut his mouth and stood silently. Fulcher took his place near Urban, turned towards the entrance of the Basilica, and waited for the arrival of Cardinal Morra.

CHAPTER 30
GOOD CARDINALS AND BAD CARDINALS

Rain was falling as they reached the grounds of the old palace, and Byron was thankful to get inside out of the weather. He stopped at the entrance to shake the rain from his cloak. Father Villhardain looked out the doorway and watched the rain beat down on the stones in the courtyard.

"I don't think this is going to let up," the priest said as he watched the puddles grow. "Come with me. Bad weather makes this a good a time to begin your lessons."

Byron followed Father Villhardain through the Lateran to his room. The priest opened the door. "I don't stay here often. The Holy Father has many tasks for me. Most of the time, Brother Carl and I are traveling the roads on our labors for the Church."

Byron entered the room, long disused. Two worn chairs sat next to a worn table devoid of any varnish. A large wooden cross adorned with the Savior dominated the wall. The room was a stark contrast to the lavish palace. Perhaps the priest's long absences from the Lateran had made it unnecessary to furnish the room more comfortably, but deep down, Byron knew that was not the reason. The room reflected the man, everything in it was necessary, and that was all that was required.

"My son, what do you know of letters?"

"I know some. Long ago, when I was a boy my mother asked the Bishop of Ossary to teach me to read."

"Well, that should make this task easier."

Father Villhardain strode purposefully to a shelf lined neatly with books. The priest sorted carefully through the books, his most prized possessions. Every man had a weakness; books were expensive, and most of these had been gifts. Owning books was the one worldly indulgences Father Villhardain allowed himself. Byron watched the priest shuffling through his books, he found himself thinking about Kilkenny castle and his last reading lessons.

†

He remembered the cold November drizzle as he stood on Kilkenny castles palisades and watched his father's retainers gather for their westward march towards the river Shannon, where the lawless Gaelic remained unconquered. The wooden baily of newly hewn timbers was still light brown, and the smell of fresh sap still clung to the wood. In the gloomy mist, Byron watched the ghostly forms of the knights assemble; their spears rising like thorns in damp air. The Lord Strongbow standing beside Byron leaned on his crutch, his foot a mass of bloody bandages was still too painful to walk on.

Byron's father, on his grey horse, rode to the front of the column. He could see his eldest brother beside him. Envy filled Byron's heart as he watched his brother, and he wished that he were riding with his father to meet the Celts in battle. The flat dull sound of a horn echoed, and with the rattle of metal, the army of knights moved forward at a trot.

Strongbow looked down at Byron, his long grey hair hung to his shoulders. The old warrior's eyes twinkled as he winked at the despondent boy beside him. Clapping Byron on the shoulder, Strongbow exclaimed, "All knights wish for battle, but fear not lad, your day might come sooner than you think." Strongbow bent down and looked Byron in the eyes. "Now come and gird yourself, for the Celts may yet come. They have destroyed this castle once, but should they come again, you and I will ride forth to defend this motte and give the pagans a taste of cold steel." Byron did his best to smile as he glanced back at his father's men disappearing in the grey curtain of fog.

Richard de-Clair, or Strongbow, was the most famous and most powerful lord in Ireland. So much so, that King Henry of England had come to Waterford with an army not only to bring Ireland under Norman control, but more importantly to keep an eye on his wayward vassal, least Richard de-Clair entertain the idea of becoming an Irish king. Despite Henry's concern, Richard de-Clare realized that he was not strong enough to fight the Plantagenet king. In a display of fealty, Strongbow bowed to his master's desire and led the conquest that swept across Irish land.

The Gaelic kings did not submit easily to a Norman overlord, and as they fought back, Norman strength faltered. In a change of fortune, Donal O'Brian, the intrepid Irish lord, defeated Strongbow. As Richard de-Clair's castle at Kilkenny burned, Strongbow, with the remains of his army, fled. All seemed lost for the Norman cause, until Lord FitzGerald landed at Wexford and turned defeat into victory. In revenge, the Normans laid waste to the city of Athlone on the River Shannon, and from Athlone tower they hanged the Irish King of Meath, lest the Irish rise again. From the ashes, Kilkenny Castle was rebuilt, but Strongbow would not lead another charge. A wound to the foot had hobbled the doughty Norman lord. As Henry's armies rode to battle, he remained behind.

Baron Fitzwalter, answering his Kings call, had gathered his retainers for war, but to ensure his families safety he had sent them to live at Kilkenny Castle under the protection of Strongbow. Despite Byron's disappointment at not getting to accompany his father, it was still a great adventure to live at Kilkenny Castle. He enjoyed every moment, sitting in the great hall surrounded by trophies of war, listening to Richard de-Clare tell rousing tales of the great battles he had fought in and the valor of their Norman ancestors. His mother had different ideas how he should spend his time and arranged with the Bishop of Ossary to teach him to read.

In a dim room of Saint Canices Church, lit by the filtered light of the stained glass windows, he had started his reading lessons. In the gloom, the candles flickered in the air as the wind seeped through the window frames. The pale face of the old bishop, watched him as he slowly turned the pages of the book. His small halting voice sounding out the words echoed in the empty room.

His mother had dreamed her favorite son might someday make the Church his life, becoming a man of learning and letters. It was not his dream, and he did not put forth the effort. His dream was to follow in the footsteps of his heroes, Richard de Clare and William the Conqueror. He had wanted more than anything to learn the family trade of war, to win his spurs, and find immortal glory in combat.

He did make some progress in his education for the sake of pleasing his mother, but he never really put his heart into learning the unmanly art. Each day, as he rode to the church to toil in the tedious drudgery of reading, he found himself daydreaming of assaulting the ancient round tower that stood next to the church.

In his imagination, the white tower, built hundreds of years before the church, became a great fortress filled with treacherous Anglo-Saxon traitors defiant against the crown. He saw himself a great captain leading his army to assault the dreaded fortress of Harold the Saxon. Through a hail of arrows, he led his knights, storming the citadel and cutting down the villains with his sword and battle-axe. When the battle came to an inevitable and glorious conclusion, he could almost hear the adulation of the multitudes as they cheered for his heroic bravery. No one ever cheered a cleric. No one ever remembered the cold pasty-faced men who spent their days writing about the deeds of what great men had done. Violence, audacity, and bloodshed were the hallmarks of great men, not the tepid, mousy creatures that scurried about in the dark damp hallways of the church. No, he would never be like them.

The reading lessons ended when his older brothers found out about his academic pursuit and began to tease him. From that moment, he resisted any attempt to read. It was only after his mother saw she could not overcome his obstinacy that she gave up. He could still see the hurt and disappointment in the old bishop's eyes when he rudely told him he would never read another word as long as he lived. Now, he was paying for his shortsightedness. The decisions he had made as a boy held him back, and he deeply regretted the stupidity of limiting who he could become.

†

"No, I don't think this one will be interesting," Father Villhardain muttered as he continued his search. "No, too advanced." He shuffled through his collection, picking up several books and judging them unfit for a variety of reasons. At last, he found what he was searching for. "Ah," he said with a smile, "I think you will enjoy this one. A very old tale, but it is a favorite of mine." Byron felt his curiosity rise as the priest carried the book over and placed it on the table. "Homers Odyssey," the priest said. "A tale of adventure and bravery. It is the story of the Greek hero Odysseus and his journey home from the Trojan war."

"I have never heard of a heroic Greek."

Father Villhardain smiled. "I think once you begin to read it, you will understand why I chose it, but I think we will first start with letters and their sounds."

As Byron started sounding out the letters, he remembered why he thought reading was dull, but this time he was determined to succeed. The priest had written out the alphabet and had the knight repeat each letter sound. He found to his surprise that his lessons from long ago came back to him.

Father Villhardain smiled. "Ah! You remember the sounds. Very good. How about the words?" Father Villhardain opened the book to a random page. "Start here."

Byron stared at the page for a moment and then slowly sounding out the letters he started to read, "A,a,and n,n,now as... D..awn r,r,r,rose from h,h,er c,couch b,b,beside..." the knight looked up at the priest, "I cannot say this."

"Tithonis," the priest said.

"Tithonis," Byron repeated. Byron took a deep breath and continued his laborious reading. Daylight turned to night. It was frustrating.

Father Villhardain pulled his chair close to Byron. "I shall now read and you can follow along.

"Odysseus followed," the priest read, *"in her steps; so the pair, goddess and man, went on and on till they came to Calypso's cave, where Odysseus took the seat Hermes had just left."*

"When you read, the story makes more sense," Byron said interrupting the priest.

Father Villhardain nodded. "It will come with practice. You are impatient, but you have already made great strides. Whoever taught you years ago did you a great service."

"The Bishop of Ossary, although at the time I thought it was torture."

Father Villhardain laughed and then started reading again. At last Father Villhardain stopped. "I think that is enough. We will start again tomorrow."

Byron closed the book and bid farewell to Calypso and Odysseus. He headed back to his room with the precious book tucked under his arm.

He found James sitting on the edge of his bed wearing a shirt of black goat hair. Byron looked at his friend for a moment. "Does this mean you are going?"

James nodded. "Yes, Fitzwalter, it means I am going? Deny yourself and take up your cross if you wish to follow in the footsteps of Christ. At least that is what Brother Carl told me."

Byron smiled. "Well, I am pleased you're going."

James shrugged. "It will be a long journey. I have my doubts, but I cannot say that part of me is not curious."

"How long must you wear that?" Byron said, pointing to the hair shirt.

"That is not your concern."

"It looks uncomfortable."

"That is the point Fitzwalter. Now, if you please, I do not want to discuss this any further."

Byron, finding the sight of his friend's discomfort somewhat amusing, inwardly chuckled as he lay down on his bed.

The autumn sun was shining through the window of his room when Byron woke the next morning. The rain clouds had blown away, and the pale, blue sky shone in the window as early morning light streamed into the room. He put on his tunic decorated with the symbols of the Knights of Saint John and his cloak with a crusader cross visible on the shoulder. Lastly, he buckled on his sword. He was not looking forward to meeting the Pope.

James got out of bed and stiffly began to put on his blue tunic embroidered with its silver shield and its gold Jerusalem cross surrounded by four smaller crosses; the device of the Marshal of Jerusalem. There was a knock at the door, and without waiting for an answer, Father Villhardain entered the room while Cardinal Morra waited in the doorway.

"Are we ready?" the priest asked, brimming with confidence.

"Yes, Father," Byron replied without much enthusiasm.

Father Villhardain smiled again. "We must not make the Holy Father wait. We need to be going." Father Villhardain stopped in the doorway, turned to James and said, "Sir Martel, you should come as well."

James picked up his light blue cloak and threw it about his shoulders. The four men headed to the entrance of the Lateran and into the courtyard past the bronze statue of Marcus Aurelius on horseback. The warm fall sun shone down on them as they walked the short distance to Saint John's basilica in silence. They approached the marble stairs leading to the massive bronze door that had once been the door to the Roman senate. Byron stopped to look at the line of marble figures on the roofline depicting Christ and the apostles. He stood gazing at Christ and the heroes of the Christian faith and pondered the strange twist of fate that had brought him here. He shook his head and walked across the threshold into the church.

The marble walls with their arches and gilded columns rose above him. In the middle of the great basilica, stood a large golden pinnacle of the papal altar. The statues of the saints, immortalized in stone, stood in the alcoves along the marble walls. Byron felt out of place. He started to walk towards the apse of the church with its massive arch. At the far end of the hall, there was another altar beneath a half-dome ceiling painted with images of Christ and the saints. He noticed an old man sitting on a white throne. The Pontiff, dressed in white, wore a red camauro trimmed with white ermine. Next to him, sat a small blond man, boyish in appearance, dressed in the robes of a cardinal.

On each side of the aisle, the cardinals were starting to arrive taking their chairs in front of the Pope. Behind the line of chairs, Byron noticed a man who was not a member of the clergy. The man's blond hair hung to his shoulders. His pockmarked face had a ruddy complexion made worse by the light of the candles in the room. He was wearing a white cloak emblazoned with a black German cross. As Byron approached the papal throne, the German knight looked at him, and Byron nodded to him. The knight looked at Byron for a moment and then turned away without acknowledging the courtesy. Byron knew he had been snubbed, and it did not make a favorable impression of the man.

The diminutive cardinal stepped forward and stood beside the Holy Father's Cathedra and cleared his throat. "Pope Urban, the third by that name, calls to order the consistory of the Sacred College of Cardinals." The room became quiet as all the assembled cardinals turned to face the small cardinal. "Primum ordinem is the condition of the Kingdom of Jerusalem. His Eminence Cardinal Morra and Father Villhardain, who has returned from the Levant, wishes to address the consistory."

"Wait here," Father Villhardain whispered. James and Byron stopped short of entering the presence of the Holy Father. Both Cardinal Morra and Father Villhardain continued forward until they reached the foot of the cathedra. Both men genuflected, and the Holy Father nodded in return to the obeisance. The old Pontiff held out his hand, his arm shaking with age. Both men gently took his hand in turn and kissed the Pope's ring.

"Cardinal Morra, rise," Urban said.

"Most Holy Father," Cardinal Morra said, "I have come here with my assistant, Father Michael Villhardain, to give to you a first-hand report of the Kingdom of Jerusalem. Father Villhardain also wishes to report on his project that I believe will bring a great benefit to the Church."

Fulcher leaned over and whispered something to Urban. "Ah yes," the Pontiff muttered aloud, "quite right." He paused for a moment and then addressed Morra. "I understand your desire to share the good news, but Cardinal Fulcher has told me of the glorious victory of King Guy Lusignan over the infidel sultan." The Pope turned his gaze to the priest. "Father Villhardain, it is good to see you in the Lateran safe and well. I have had you in my prayers since you left on your long journey. I cannot think of any priest who has selflessly done more than you." Urban looked back to Cardinal Morra and raised his hands. "Since I have already received news of our crushing victory in the Levant, why don't you address your project. I am curious to hear what you have found." The old Pontiff smiled kindly.

A cardinal with short iron-grey hair, stooped by age, rose from his chair. Cardinal Fulcher frowned and nodded to the old man. "Cardinal Cattaneo."

Cardinal Cattaneo turned to face Urban. "Holy Father, I have not heard of a great victory? Instead, I have heard from abroad that the Kingdom of Jerusalem is in grave danger. Surely, my esteemed colleagues of the consistory have heard the same rumors?"

"All falsehoods spread by defeatists," Fulcher snapped. "We have won a great victory!"

The corners of Cattaneo's mouth twitched into a faint smile. "Defeatists or the truth? Cardinal Morra, I see Father Villhardain. I see a Knight of Saint John. What do they say on this matter?"

Cardinal Morra nodded to Cardinal Cattaneo and then turned to face Urban. "They have much to say. Holy Father, I fear you have been told a false tale. There has not been a glorious victory. Instead, Father Villhardain and Sir Byron Fitzwalter are here at the urging of Lord Montferrat of Tyre to deliver the news of great defeat."

Urban leaned forward with a scowl. "And what information are you here to report."

Cardinal Morra turned to face the consistory. "Your Holiness, the entire Christian Army was destroyed. Jerusalem is in danger of falling to the Saracen forces." Morra turned back to face Urban. "Holy Father, already Tiberias is lost, and Acre is surrounded."

"Do you know this defeat first hand," Urban asked as his chin dipped to give Morra a skeptical glare from beneath his long white eyebrows.

Cardinal Morra glanced at Fulcher and then Urban. "Father Villhardain has been a witness, and I have brought Sir Byron Fitzwalter of the Knights of Saint John of Jerusalem, a witness to the destruction of the Army of Jerusalem." Cardinal Morra motioned back towards Byron who bowed to the Pope.

Urban nodded and motioned to Byron. "Come closer, my son. Tell me what you saw."

Byron approached the cathedra. Bowing on one knee, he took the old man's hand and kissed the ring of the Pope. As the statues of Saint Peter and Saint Paul looked down at him, Byron took a deep breath, rose to his feet and began his tale. As he spoke, he saw several of the cardinals watching him, intently engrossed in every word as he told about his horse's death and of being trapped beneath the animal.

Urban sat back and looked at the audience of assembled churchmen when Byron finished. "Do any of you have any questions for this Knight of Saint John?"

"I do," Cardinal Fulcher said with a malicious smile. Fulcher had not expected Morra to produce a witness from Jerusalem. He knew the danger and he needed to destroy this witness. His plan to excommunicate Frederick Barbarossa was stalled, but if the old fool learned that Jerusalem was in jeopardy, then the Holy Roman Emperor would suddenly be in favor. Only Frederick had the means to defeat Saladin. He needed more time to put VonDurenberg on the throne. He looked at Byron. He needed to discredit this young knight, and he decided to attack him by sowing confusion in his story. With any luck, this uneducated young rube would become frustrated and destroy his credibility in front of the consistory himself.

"Sir Fitzwalter, I want to first thank you for your valiant service to the Church. I want you to know that you will not be forgotten, nor will your sacrifices go unrewarded. I know it must be difficult for someone of your rustic background to address His Holiness. Your valiant attempt at Italian with a Norman accent is commendable, and given your limited ability, I just want to clarify several things I heard in your story."

Byron was not oblivious to the subtle jabs at his deficiencies. He felt his blood rising at the insults. Nevertheless, he made an effort to check his anger as Fulcher continued.

"First," the cardinal asked in a polished voice, "I wonder. Did I hear you correctly that once your horse was killed, you fell beneath the animal?"

"Yes, Your Eminence, that is true."

Cardinal Fulcher frowned as he shook his head. "That must have been a terrible blow to have a horse fall on you with so much weight. I could see how you would be left insensible. Once your horse was down, did you see the rest of the battle?"

"Of course not."

"That is a pity. So... you have no knowledge of what transpired. You did not see what really happened to King Guy or the army because by that time you were unconscious."

"No, I was in a swoon for a day at least."

"Then it is possible, Sir Fitzwaller, the Christian Army was victorious and Saladin's forces were defeated?"

"Fitzwalter," Byron corrected.

Cardinal Fulcher paused. "My apologies, Sir Fitzwalter. But is it not conceivable, the army was victorious, and after its glorious victory, it moved on and you were unfortunately left behind? That could have happened, could it not?"

"No, Your Eminence! You were not there! I saw the bodies. I saw the executed Templars."

Fulcher smiled. He had expected Byron to say something like this, and he skillfully renewed his attack, cutting him off before he could finish. "All casualties of war." Fulcher shook his head as he looked down at the floor. "Most unfortunate, but you have no proof other than the bodies you saw. I am sure that in the desert heat it would be hard to distinguish the blackened corpse of a Saracen from the corpse of one of our brave soldiers who is in paradise with our Lord and savior."

"Except for the devices on their shields and surcoats."

"But you did not go and look at each individual corpse, now did you?" Cardinal Fulcher said in an accusatory tone. "After all, you were gravely wounded and disoriented, by your account."

"I walked the battlefield! I know what I saw!" Byron could feel the frustration rising. He was just about to tell the short, smug cardinal what he thought of him when he felt Cardinal Morra's hand on his shoulder.

"Thank you, My Lord Fitzwalter," Cardinal Morra said gently. "I agree with Cardinal Fulcher's comments about your true and loyal service. I think His Holiness has enough information."

Byron was livid but saw the warning look in Morra's eyes. He rejoined James who was fidgeting uncomfortably from the hair shirt. Urban on his cathedra looked confused.

A tall cardinal rose to his feet and jabbed his finger at Fulcher. "Come now, Fulcher, this young knight has told us the truth and yet you belittle him?"

"I am only trying to get to the truth, Cardinal Paltinieri," Fulcher snapped.

"The truth is, Fulcher, your version of events is not sooth. You are trying to beguile us."

Cardinal Fulcher's face turned scarlet. A cardinal with a dark tanned face and narrow eyes rose from his chair. He brushed the dark bangs that hung beneath his berretta aside. With a dark glance at Byron, he turned to Cardinal Paltinieri. "Come now, Paltinieri, why are you so willing to believe this nonsense. His Eminence Fulcher was only trying to get the facts and so he did. We learned that this so-called witness was unconscious for the last parts of the battle. He knows nothing of what happened. Are you willing to base the policy of the Holy Mother Church on this man's word?"

Every cardinal jumped to their feet and began to argue. Byron turned to James who shrugged and shook his head. As the arguments became more heated, Urban sat on his cathedra looking at his hands ignoring his cardinals as if this was a normal behavior. Cardinal Fulcher was yelling for everyone to sit down, but none of the members of the Sacred College paid him any heed.

Cardinal Morra raised his hands and shouted, "Princes of the Church! Cardinal Paltinieri! Cardinal Fulcher! Enough! Please sit down. We have much to discuss." The arguing slowly stopped as the Cardinals resumed their seats.

"Sir Fitzwalter is not the only source." Cardinal Morra turned and gestured towards James. "When news reached Jerusalem of the defeat, the Master of Jerusalem sent Sir James Martel to ride to Tyre to request reinforcements from Lord Montferrat. Further, The Genoese traders have brought news of Jerusalem's woes! I agree with his Eminence Cardinal Cattaneo. Jerusalem is in danger. While others might debate the extent, perhaps it would be prudent to make a call for a new crusade."

Morra paused to look around at the cardinals seated beside the aisle. Cardinal Morra looked at Byron and smiled. "For the sake of this discussion, let us say that Vice Chancellor Fulcher is correct. Let us say that Guy has been victorious. If that is true, then now is the time to capitalize on this victory by going on the offensive. The opportunity to strike is before us! Now is the time to send reinforcements to the Kingdom. If Saladin has been defeated, he is vulnerable, and the arrival of more crusaders would allow us to take the initiative. We could call on Frederick, the Holy Roman Emperor, to march on Mecca, crush the infidel religion, and end this war once and for all."

Cardinal Morra smiled at Fulcher. Fulcher looked uncomfortable at this unexpected turn, but before Fulcher could speak, a heavyset cardinal with large jowls and bulging eyes rose to his feet. Fulcher rolled his eyes in annoyance. "Yes, Cardinal Melior le Maitre." The heavyset cardinal folded his hands together and looked at Fulcher with calculating shrewdness.

"His Eminence, Cardinal Morra is right. Perhaps now is a good time to make another call to the soldiers of Christendom. If Saladin has been weakened, then maybe one good push should be considered. However, as Camerario of the Holy Roman Church, I suggest that we look to Frederick Hohenstaufen for aid. At this time, we do not have the finances to fund a new assault on Saladin."

"And I agree with Cardinal Morra as well," Fulcher said as he looked for a new avenue to forestall anyone from requesting

Barbarossa's aid. "This is something I had not considered. We should discuss this further. Perhaps Your Holiness could choose a small committee from the princes of the Church to explore the feasibility of sending additional forces. I would urge caution before calling upon Frederick, in light of his transgressions against the Church."

"And I would agree," Morra replied, "but if Saladin has been weakened, time is critical. This opportunity will disappear if we don't act quickly. Only Frederick has the means to defeat Saladin in the time allotted by heaven."

Urban raised his palsied hands bringing the discussion to a close. "Cardinal Fulcher is right. I need more time to consider this matter carefully. After all, this is an important decision and merits further discussion as a private Church matter."

Urban glanced at Morra. "I will keep in mind that we need to act quickly, but I don't think a day or two of careful consideration will change the outcome should we decide to intervene."

"Thank you, Your Holiness," Cardinal Morra said as he bowed. "I look forward to this continued discussion of Church strategy, and now I have another matter for you and the consistory to consider." Cardinal Morra motioned to Father Villhardain who stepped forward and once again genuflected before Urban.

Cardinal Morra turned to face the Cardinals of the Consistory. "As some of you may remember, one of our Holy Brothers found evidence that during the Visigoth's invasion of the Roman Empire, the advisors to the Emperor Honorius sent the Imperial Treasure out of Rome where it was lost. Father Villhardain has spent the last several years working, at my direction, to find… and if possible, recover the treasure and return it to its rightful city, Rome. He has just returned from the Levant." Morra turned to the seated cardinals. "The treasure exists. Father Villhardain has found its resting place." The group of assembled cardinals gasped. Several clapped in their enthusiasm at this revelation.

"So, Father Villhardain, where is it hidden?" Urban cried.

Father Villhardain cleared his throat. "Your Holiness, after several years of searching, I have found that Honorius' treasure, or to be precise, the treasure of the people and the Senate of Rome is hidden in the ruins of Babylon."

The cardinals began talking excitedly. Urban looked surprised. Cardinal Melior le Maitre clapped his hands, and the excited voices became quiet. "Babylon? Father Villhardain, are you certain?"

"Yes. I intended to go myself to find the truth, but with Saladin's incursion into the region, I was unable to travel to Babylon and had to flee. The Levant is no longer safe."

Fulcher shifted his weight from one foot to the other uncomfortably at the priest's statement of the region's instability, but said nothing.

"What do you propose?" Urban asked.

"I propose to lead a small party of men disguised as Saracens to Babylon and recover the treasure for the Church. It belonged to Rome then, and it belongs to Rome now! We have nothing to lose other than time and some traveling expense."

Fulcher started to open his mouth, but before he could interfere, Urban asked, "Father Villhardain, what do you require?"

"Your Holiness, I need twenty men at arms, several servants, and a caravan of camels. I will also need an experienced captain and a seaworthy ship to return the treasure to Rome."

Fulcher was about to speak when Urban cut him off again. "Done! All will be provided as you request."

"Thank you, Your Holiness," Father Villhardain said with a bow.

Urban turned to Cardinal Fulcher. "Vice Chancellor, see that Father Villhardain receives everything he needs."

The color drained from Father Villhardain's face. He had hoped Cardinal Morra or another cardinal in the assembled audience would be assigned to assist him. He did not expect the Holy Father to give Cardinal Fulcher the mundane task of outfitting his expedition.

"As you wish, Your Holiness," Fulcher replied. "Might I suggest that Graf Wilhelm Helmuth VonDurenberg, who is here before you, be sent on this quest? I think a representative of the German knights would be a welcome addition to Father Villhardain's expedition. It would be an excellent goodwill gesture considering the recent relationship between the Church and the Empire."

VonDurenberg's eyebrows raised as his eyes widened in

surprise. He opened his mouth to speak, but after seeing Fulcher's face, he shut his mouth and nodded his head in agreement.

"I think that is an excellent proposal," Urban said thoughtfully. "I don't see a problem with the request. Do you have concerns, Father Villhardain?"

Father Villhardain, already forming a poor opinion of the German knight, wanted to protest, but he knew there was nothing he could do to refuse. "I accept Your Holiness' judgment on the matter," the priest muttered without much enthusiasm.

"Good! Good!" Urban cried. "A united effort by members of this Church will set a positive example to all our brethren."

Fulcher was not finished causing mischief. His mind was already calculating how to covet the gold for his own purpose. "You mentioned the need for camels," Fulcher said helpfully. "I know a man in Rome who can help us, Count Marcellus Theophylact. He is a good Catholic and has contacts with the Levant. I think he would be a great resource to us. I believe he may own several caravans that he uses to transport his imports across the desert from the Far East."

"Well, ah, Your Eminence, I appreciate your offer of assistance," Father Villhardain said as he glanced at Cardinal Morra, "but how can we trust Count Marcellus Theophylact?"

"He absolutely can be trusted," Fulcher retorted. "After all, you're the one who suggested that you needed assistance in procuring a caravan, and now I am offering you one. Do you not trust my judgment?"

Father Villhardain looked at Cardinal Fulcher. Before he could answer, Urban spoke putting an end to the debate. "Cardinal Fulcher has offered a solution, and I suggest you accept his judgment in this matter." Father Villhardain bowed in acquiescence without saying a word. The issue was settled, much to his misgivings.

Urban rose from the cathedra. "Are there any other pressing matters to discuss?"

"Yes, Your Holiness," Cardinal Morra said. "Babylon is a place of evil. Will your Holiness give his blessing to keep our men safe from whatever evil lurks in the shadows of the city."

"I will give my blessings, and I will pray for their protection from evil as they do the work of his Holy Church. Is there anything else?"

Cardinal Morra bowed. "No, Your Holiness. Thank you for your wisdom with these difficult issues."

"Cardinal Morra," the old Pontiff said in a quivering voice, "it is my responsibility to help where I can. I will send a servant with an invitation to you tomorrow so you may come and discuss Jerusalem." All the members stood up and bowed as Urban rose from the cathedra and left the room.

Cardinal Morra whispered to Father Villhardain, "Let us go. We have many new issues to discus in private."

Cardinal Fulcher walked up to Morra as they prepared to leave. "Cardinal Morra. I must say I enjoyed your presentation. I was very much surprised at the revelation that you and Father Villhardain have located Honorius' treasure. I wish you had taken me into your confidence sooner so I could have been of more assistance."

Morra smiled. "Cardinal Fulcher, I assure you, had I been more certain of my information I would have brought you into my confidence. But as you know Father Villhardain has only just returned, and I have only recently learned of its final resting place. You can appreciate such information is sensitive, and since there are so many untrustworthy and unscrupulous people, I had to keep the knowledge of such riches a closely guarded secret."

Fulcher's face discolored in anger. "I do not question that it is important to keep such information close, but I assure you, when a new Pope is named, he may not be so forgiving of those who do not share information with other members of the Church. After all, you must agree that such an act, no matter the reason, shows a lack of faith and could be interpreted as self-serving."

Morra frowned. "I disagree. It is not selfishness or a lack of faith in the members of the Church to withhold information. Timing is an important consideration when determining to release information. It is important to weigh carefully who needs to know and what the consequences of sharing that information will be. I have not withheld information from the Church regarding the treasure. I have just been careful to reveal what I know to those who have the power and the intellect to use that knowledge properly."

Cardinal Morra paused and glared down at the diminutive cardinal in front of him. "However, if it's the desire of the next Holy Father to make everything public, then I would also think information on the personal habits of all church members should also be shared in the same manner."

This statement stopped Fulcher in his tracks. While he had exercised the utmost care in his personal transgressions, he could not be sure Morra did not know about his immoral habits. He quickly decided to drop the subject completely. "I look forward to tomorrow's continued private discussion on the situation in the Outremer," he said nervously. "I am sure our discussion will lead to a well-balanced policy to bring stability to the region."

"I agree," Cardinal Morra said as the corner of his mouth twitched into a slight sarcastic smile. "King Guy Lusignan and his victorious army will be pleased to see new forces at his disposal. I am quite certain these additional troops will be just what he needs to march on Mecca."

Byron and James quietly gathered around the churchmen as Cardinal Morra made this statement. The diminutive cardinal was starting to feel uncomfortable under the unfriendly stares of the two crusaders.

"I am quite sure," Fulcher muttered as he made furtive glances at Byron and James, "King Guy will be pleased indeed. I must go," Fulcher said as he looked at the opening between Father Villhardain and Cardinal Morra. "His Holiness requires my aid." The little cardinal forced his way between Cardinal Morra and Father Villhardain and hurried off.

Cardinal Morra turned to Byron and James. "Not a word until we meet in private. Father Villhardain, I must speak to Cardinal Scolari and Cardinal Melior le Maitre. Take Martel and Fitzwalter to your room... I will meet you there shortly. We have much to discuss."

"Yes, Your Eminence," Father Villhardain replied.

Byron and James followed the priest out of the basilica and into the Lateran Palace. Byron leaned close to James and whispered, "If I could, I would have split that little bastard from his nuts to his head."

James laughed. "And then you would have had two bastards to

deal with instead of one."

"Do not jest. That man is a liar. He needs to be taught a lesson."

"Indeed, he does, my friend," James replied, "but let it go. Your day of vengeance will come, but not yet."

"Yes, well woe unto him when that day does come, because I will not forget this."

CHAPTER 31
THE MERCY OF HUSAM AL-DIN

The sun was relentless. Under the shade of his tent, Isma'il looked out at the hill. Vultures were circling, riding the thermal drafts as they ascended into the blue sky. Isma'il was bored. Nef was a dung heap. There was nothing to do. Dispatch riders bearing the sultan's messages had brought news of Salah al-Din's crushing victory at Acre. Soldiers were getting rich on captured Christian loot. Isma'il turned his gaze away from the hill. He was bitter. Kamal was dead, and Husam al-Din had done nothing to avenge his death. Husam al-Din should be fighting the enemies of Allah. Instead, in his shame for losing the priest, he was hiding here.

He got up and stepped out into the sun. He was twenty. A neatly trimmed beard covered his face. A white ghutra covered by a steal helmet protected his head. He was wearing a light green tunic trimmed with blue and silver embroidery. His white trousers were stuffed into a pair of worn brown boots. He looked at the empty Crusader castle and muttered a curse under his breath. Not one thing of value had been found within its cursed walls. To his surprise, he saw a figure on the castle's ramparts. His eyes narrowed, and he recognized Husam al-Din pacing, looking down at something in his hand. It appeared that Husam al-Din was holding a bird. A feeling of anger coursed through Isma'il at the sight of his commander. The man was a coward.

Out of the corner of his eye, he saw someone approaching. He turned to face the man; a tall knight with a black turban wrapped around his steel helmet. The man stopped. The knight's thin face was made even longer by his black beard which had been trimmed to a point.

The knight smiled, showing his yellow teeth. "Enjoying the view?" the knight asked.

"No. What do you want, Kasim?"

"You know what I want. The request is the same as yesterdays. When are we going to kill Husam al-Din? The men are close to revolt and you have done nothing. I am only here as your friend. Isma'il, you must act. Husam al-Din has been disgraced. He is being punished by Salah al-Din for losing the priest. Let's be rid of him and then ride to Jerusalem and the war. Every man will follow you."

Ismail looked at Kasim and scowled. "Killing Husam al-Din will not be easy."

"Come now, Isma'il. Allah does not favor Husam al-Din. You will strike him down with ease. Surely, you see this. Was it not Husam al-Din who sent Kamal and Fadil to their doom? Was not Kamal your friend? Does his death not demand revenge?"

Isma'il's eyes narrowed as the muscles in his jaw tightened. He rubbed his face with his hands. "Yes..."

"Well, you need to avenge him, and you need to do it soon or the problem will be taken out of your hands." Kasim turned and walked away.

Isma'il looked back at the castle walls. Husam al-Din had stopped pacing and was now leaning against the rampart as he looked out over Nef. If Husam al-Din was dead, then the sultan's task would fall to another commander and his men. He drew his dagger and looked at it. Kamal was dead. Husam al-Din should have sent more men to watch the Tyre road. The blade glittered in the sun. Sheathing it, he looked at the half-opened gates of the crusader castle. Isma'il weighed what to do and then made up his mind. He turned and strode to the open gate.

The tall wooden doors, barbed with iron, were ajar. He

stopped in the doorway, his right hand near the hilt of his knife. Husam al-Din was approaching. He was holding a pigeon in his left hand while his right hand stroked the bird's feathers. Isma'il's muscles grew tense, and he cleared his throat. "Did you find anything of interest?"

Husam al-Din stopped. "No."

Isma'il scuffed the sand with the toe of his boot as his hand went to the hilt and gripped his knife. "Why are we still here? There is nothing here."

"We wait because the sultan has given me this task." Husam al-Din frowned. "Why do you ask such questions?"

"I ask such questions because the men are questioning your leadership. They say you are a coward and hiding here. Are you being punished for failure? Does your ego demand that everyone shares in your despair?"

Husam al-Din's eyes flashed in anger as his face turned scarlet. "None of this is your concern."

"You promised that we would avenge Kamal and Fadil, yet you have done nothing. You sent Kamal to his death. You knew the priest would go that way, and you only sent two men!"

Husam al-Din tilted his head back to look at Isma'il. "I had no way of knowing which road the priest would take. Kamal and Fadil were brave men. It was Allah's will."

"Allah's will! Do not hide in your shame and stupidity behind the name of Allah! If you will not avenge Kamal then I will! I will lead the men to Jerusalem, and I will avenge Kamal. All of Islam is at war. If you are to craven to fight the Christians, then I will!"

"No, you will not." Husam al-Din let go of the pigeon to grab the hilt of his sword. Isma'il drew his knife and sprang upon Husam al-Din knocking him down. The dust swirled as the two men rolled on the ground. Husam al-Din grabbed Isma'il's wrist. The knife hovered over Husam al-Din's face as each man struggled to overpower the other.

"Stay this madness!" Husam al-Din grunted. "At least hear me."

"And what is there to hear from a liar!" Isma'il cried as he used both hands to try and push the dagger into Husam-al Din's face. Grunting, Husam al-Din held on to Isma'ils wrists as the dagger hovered over his nose.

"Read the sultan's letter," Husam al-Din gasped.

Isma'il did not reply but pushed down harder. Both men's arms were shaking with strain. Husam al-Din kicked his leg out and thrusting his hip, he rolled over pinning Isma'il on his back. Husam al-Din jerked his head forward and sunk his teeth into Isma'il's wrist. Isma'il screamed as he let go of the dagger.

"Truce!" Isma'il cried.

Husam al-Din grunted. "Why should I show you mercy, traitor." Husam al- Din reared back breaking free. Raising his fist, he struck Isma'il in the face. Blood began to flow from Isma'il's nose. Husam al-Din jumped to his feet and drew his shamshir. "Get on your feet, traitor!" Isma'il, gasping with pain, rose to his feet. "You have betrayed me. Is there any reason why I should not slay thee?"

Isma'il, looking down, shook his head. "You killed my friend," he muttered.

"A Christian knight killed your friend. I told you we shall avenge him and we will. You must learn to be patient Isma'il," Husam al-Din replied. Holding his shamshir by one hand, Husam al-Din used his other hand to pull out a small roll of parchment tucked in his sword belt. He thrust the small scroll towards Isma'il. "This is from the sultan. Read it for yourself."

Isma'il, holding his injured wrist, took the letter. The sultan's mark was on the parchment. Isma'il opened the note.

Husam al-Din.

I am disappointed by your request. I have many soldiers capable of storming Jerusalem. I do not need more.

Finding the priest is your priority. You will wait and you will capture him. The next message I expect from you is that the priest is your prisoner.

I hope this clarifies your priorities.

Isma'il looked up at Husam al-Din. He felt like a fool. The men had used him by sowing words of doubt into his mind. He had made a fatal error. He hung his head. "My life is yours to take."

Husam al-Din lowered his sword. "And what good would that

do. Until this moment, you have served me well." Husam al-Din sheathed his sword. "Isma'il, I am disappointed. Do you not think I know the men are unhappy? Do you think that I would not at any moment call for my horse to ride to war?" Husam al-Din's dark eyes bored into Isma'il. "You have betrayed my trust, but I will spare you. However, I will not forget this incident. You will have to work doubly hard to regain my trust."

Isma'il, still looking down, nodded as he handed the note back to Husam al-Din. "The sultan has made his orders clear," Husam al-Din continued. "We will not join the army."

"The men will not understand."

"Then what do you suggest?"

"Perhaps it would be more palatable if we at least waited somewhere else...such as Homs?"

Husam al-Din looked at Isma'il. "Homs..." Husam al-Din looked around as he surveyed Nef and then shrugged. "Perhaps you are right. Homs would be better than this."

Husam al-Din nodded as he moved closer and put his hand on his lieutenant's shoulder. "Isma'il, next time come and talk to me. I need your loyalty. Now, go clean your face and bandage your wrist."

"Yes, my lord."

"When you have tended your wounds, you can tell the men the good news that we are moving our camp."

Ismail bowed again. "Yes, my lord. I suppose you will want to know the names of the men who have conspired against you?"

"I know who they are. I will deal with them in my own time."

Isma'il nodded and walked away. Kasim and several of the men were waiting for him in camp. "Is he dead?" Kasim asked.

"No."

"You swore to take care of the problem." Kasim hissed.

"And you lied to me. Husam al-Din is not in disfavor. I have read the sultan's note."

Kasim leaned forward. "He has deceived you. Does not Kamal's death trouble you? Husam al-Din lied to you, and yet you let him live? What kind of man are you?"

"Kamal was my friend, and I will see him avenged when the time is right. Husam al-Din has not deceived me. It is you who has deceived me. Kamal was killed by the Christians, and yet you used his death for your own wicked end." Isma'il shook his head. "Husam al-Din has shown me mercy. He bested me and let me live."

Kasim looked at Isma'il in disgust. "Perhaps I was mistaken. Perhaps you were never worthy to lead."

"Kasim, I have read the sultan's note. He has ordered that we are not to march for Jerusalem. Revolting against Husam al-Din will bring the wrath of Salah al-Din upon you."

"That is irrelevant."

Isma'il pointed his finger at Kasim's chest. "You raise arms against Husam al-Din and you will suffer the same fate as the Templars at Hattin. I stand by Husam al-Din. I am indebted to him, and I am certain that most of the men will follow me."

"Isma'il, this is not finished. We will have this discussion again." Kasim turned and walked away. Isma'il watched him go. Turning, he raised his arms and called out to the men to gather round.

Husam al-Din stood in the empty courtyard. He tilted his head back to look at the blue sky and exhaled. He looked down, straightened his tunic, and brushed the dust from his clothes. Young men are always impatient. He had almost lost the fight. He hoped his decision to spare his lieutenant would bring a greater reward. His men on the other hand, disappointed him. Salah al-Din had given him a great responsibility, and all his men could think about was their own selfish interest. He heard a shout from the camp and looked in that direction. Isma'il must have told the men they were moving to Homs. Already tents were being dismantled.

Husam al-Din walked to the camp. Smiles greeted him as he made his way to his tent. He stepped inside his pavilion and stopped by the box that served as his desk. His father's letter was on it. Next to his father's letter, was a letter from Jabbar bearing the news that the priest had left for Rome. He picked up the letters and folded them carefully.

"Bring me a bird," Husam al-Din cried to a passing soldier. "I must inform the sultan of our move." The soldier bowed. Husam al-Din sat down at his desk and scribbled out a short message to the sultan advising that he was moving his men to Homs.

The soldier returned holding a pigeon. Husam al-Din took the note and placed it in the wooden tube on the bird's back. Once the note was secure, the soldier released the bird. Husam al-Din smiled. The Christians were always amazed at how swiftly messages traveled in the lands of Islam. It was not with the wings of eagles, but on the wings of pigeons that the armies of the sultan received their orders.

The camp was dismantled quickly. The horses were saddled and the men were forming two columns. Husam al-Din's horse, El-Marees, was brought to him.

Husam al-Din stood up in his stirrups and surveyed his men. There were traitors among them. He could see Kasim whispering to the man next to him. All things in their own time, he thought to himself.

Husam al-Din turned back to face the road and started off at trot. It would take a few days to reach Homs. He looked back at the crusader castle. Shorn of its martial banners it looked forlorn in the afternoon shadows. He was glad to be leaving this place. Perhaps a new location would bring him better fortune. His master's trap was set. He hoped the priest would take the bait and return to the Levant at Alexandretta, but Husam al-Din could not be sure. The priest had eluded him so far, and Homs would ensure that if the priest did return to Tyre, he could ride in either direction to intercept the Christians.

CHAPTER 32
WHAT SHALL WE DO WITH THE GERMAN

The priest opened the door to his room. Byron, still seething with anger, strode across the floor and sat down next to the worn table. James spun a wooden chair backwards to the table and sat down, resting his arms on the back of the chair. Father Villhardain looked at the two men and then stepped out of the room to summon a page to fetch some wine and mead. After a few moments, the page entered the room with two pints of mead and a flagon of white wine.

Brother Carl came into the room carrying a chair. The monk was obviously acquainted with its sparse furnishings. He placed the chair on the floor and sat down, surveying the grim and angry faces.

Brother Carl looked at Byron who was staring at the table, then James and then Father Villhardain. When he could no longer suppress his curiosity, the monk asked, "How was your audience with the Holy Father?"

James smirked and Byron frowned. Father Villhardain smiled. "It went surprisingly well."

"I have other thoughts," Byron growled. "That little cardinal would be dead had we been anywhere else. The man is a liar!" He picked up the tankard of mead in front of him and took a long drink.

Father Villhardain smiled. "You are allowing your anger to

cloud your perception. Cardinal Fulcher did not get what he desired. Yes, he managed to confuse the issue on the condition of the Kingdom of Jerusalem, but if you were observant, Cardinal Morra turned his lies against him. It will be very hard now for Fulcher not to send new forces to the Holy Lands."

Byron scoffed, "Yes, well he was able to get his German spy into our company."

Father Villhardain nodded. "Yes, but the Holy Father has made his decision. We need to wait and see what the future brings before we pass judgment."

"My heart tells me the German is not a good choice," Byron grumbled.

Cardinal Morra entered the room as Byron said this. "The German is not a good choice? Did I hear you correctly?" The cardinal answered his own question before anyone could respond. "Indeed, he is not, but I have every confidence the people in this room are smarter than he is. I suspect the person who sent him on this journey will come to regret his impulsive decision."

Byron turned to face Morra. "Your Eminence, why would a cardinal lie about Jerusalem's danger? What does he stand to gain if the city falls into Saladin's hands?"

Cardinal Morra sighed. "I will not attempt to beguile you by portraying Fulcher as something he is not. All I will say is, he does not want to see Jerusalem fall to Saladin, and he is gambling that will not come to pass. What he does not want to see is Urban, in his need for troops, request Frederick Barbarossa to gather an army. If that happens, Frederick will once again be in the favor of the Church, and that will undo Fulcher's current enterprise to have the emperor excommunicated."

"Why does Fulcher want Barbarossa excommunicated?"

"Because it aids Fulcher to become the next Holy Father."

Byron emptied his tankard and slammed it down on the table. "Well I hope that does not happen."

"Indeed," replied the cardinal. "There are many in the Church who fear that."

Byron stood up. "I think I have heard enough today. Father Villhardain, the mead was excellent. With your leave, I am going back to my room."

James stood up. "I think I will take my leave as well."

Cardinal Morra sat down in a chair. Father Villhardain moved the chair James had been sitting in closer to Morra. Cardinal Morra rested his elbows on the arms of the chair as he folded his hands in front of him.

"We did well this morning even though we have new problems to contend with. Fitzwalter did not do too badly, and that turned out to be a blessing in our favor. I have spoken to several cardinals who were in the audience. They are convinced the knight's tale is true and that Jerusalem is in grave danger. Cardinal Fulcher will have a harder time stalling after this. I am quite certain he will do all he can to make sure a decision to send a relief force will be bogged down in a Church council, which is good, because it will make his plans even more transparent to those who are watching."

"Do you think they will want to see what Cardinal Fulcher is doing, or will they ignore the obvious?" the priest asked, suspecting his fellow churchmen to take the path of least resistance.

"They will pay attention. I have spoken to the members who will most likely sit on that council. They share the same concern I do, Jerusalem must be saved, and we must do all we can to make sure the Holy Father will not become confused and succumb to indecision. I think we can work around this, with a little time and effort, but the Holy Father will do what is right."

"I have every confidence you will succeed. In the meantime, what do I do with VonDurenberg? I do not like the idea of Von-Durenberg being part of this expedition."

"Your instincts are correct, Father Villhardain," the cardinal said with a sigh. "Rumor has it, he is Fulcher's choice to depose Fredrick. Fulcher has been grooming him for some time."

"What do you recommend?"

Cardinal Morra laughed. "Nothing. Fulcher has made a foolish mistake sending him on this expedition. It takes his protégé out of Rome. VonDurenberg has never gone on a crusade, so he has no experience with the Levant. He is a fish out of water, powerless and dependent on you. I hope Fulcher will have destroyed his credibility by the time you return, and this whole affair will be a closed chapter."

"Your Eminence, I will do what you ask. But I don't like the thought of taking such a dangerous assignment with a house divided. I hoped to have knights that could blend in with the Saracen population. VonDurenberg will stand out."

"I don't disagree. But these are the circumstances we are in, and while it's not ideal, you need to do your best. As far as VonDurenberg is concerned, I suggest you pass him off as a Christian slave." Cardinal Morra laughed. "That will be a blow to his immense ego."

"That is what I fear most," the priest retorted, shaking his head. "It's not his looks. He is too arrogant. No slave has such an air of superiority."

"If the fool can't do what is required, then let the infidels take care of him. Or if necessary, our two knights are capable of coming up with a solution to your problem."

"I hope it does not come to that," the priest exclaimed.

"That will be VonDurenberg's choice. Remember how many lives hang in the balance. Not only those you lead through the lands of the enemy, but those living in peril in Jerusalem, knowing nothing of your labors to aid them."

Father Villhardain nodded his head. "I have one other concern. This caravan Fulcher is procuring, can we look elsewhere? I know the reputation of the House of Theophylact, and I don't like the thought that, once again, they may resume their involvement in the Church."

"The House of Theophylact?" Brother Carl asked. "What is your concern, Father Villhardain?"

"The House of Theophylact was an influential family in the early Church," the priest replied. "They were a powerful family who placed several popes in the chair of Saint Peter. Pope John X was thrown into prison when he opposed their wishes, and the family had him smothered. It was only after Otto the Great crossed the Alps and rescued the Church from the influence of the Theophylacts, that the dignity of the Church was restored. I have never heard anything good about Count Marcellus Theophylact. I know he is maneuvering to reestablish his family's prominence in

Church affairs. Do you think the Holy Father was aware of what he was doing when he blessed Fulcher's suggestion to reestablish ties with Count Theophylact?"

"No," Morra replied. "I doubt he was even paying attention, but the caravan does not concern me as much as the internal politics once the treasure is returned. Marcellus will want the treasure back in Rome as much as we do. While we may have to pay an exorbitant rate for the use of his animals, my guess is Marcellus will expect Fulcher to reward him."

"What kind of reward?" the priest asked.

"I am not sure what the reward will be. But Marcellus will want something in exchange for his support of Fulcher's candidacy to become the next Vicar of Christ."

Father Villhardain shook his head. "I don't like this at all."

"I agree, but this is the result of your own error I am afraid. You should have kept your request to a minimum and then let me make further arrangements as time went on. Unfortunately, Cardinal Fulcher is now procuring your caravan, and there is nothing you or I can do to change that."

"There must be something you can do," the priest replied.

"I fear not. The Holy Father has made his decision, and now we need to follow his direction. To do otherwise will cause a long delay. Besides, we know what Marcellus is. Are you willing to risk everything on someone you don't know, or who might be worse?" Father Villhardain shook his head. "See, as this expedition grows in manpower, the risk of betrayal becomes greater. It cannot be helped. Only God can help us, so trust in his will. Now, do either of you have anything further you wish to discuss?"

"No," the priest replied.

"Anything you want to add, Brother Carl?" Morra asked.

"He who troubles his own house shall inherit the wind," the monk said as he stood up and picked up his chair. "Already, I feel a light wind on my face." The monk frowned as he turned and carried his chair out of the room.

✟

Byron had gone back to his room, but his anger remained. He decided to go for a walk on the grounds of the palace. The pale sun light shone, but there was a chill in the air. He stopped by a tree and leaned against it. He looked up at the leaves and watched them as they moved with the breeze. He listened to the rustle as he watched them sway, and the noise reminded him of the thunder of horse hooves. He bowed his head and thought of his bay horse in Ireland. It had been a good horse. Smooth to ride, a gentle disposition. The horse had been his companion, taking him faithfully wherever he wished to go. The horse had never betrayed him. As he thought of his horse, his mind drifted to his brother Guillaume.

†

Guillaume dressed in chain mail was looking at him. His nose covered by the long guard of his Norman war helmet. He was riding next to him shouting excitedly as he waved his sword.

"We got him! We got the Celtic swine! Run you bastard!"

Byron smiled as he urged his horse on. He could see the Celt painted with blue stripes running just ahead of him for the tree line. The Celt passed under the dark bows of the fir trees and disappeared into the shadows. In two strides, Byron's horse reached the edge of the forest. Byron slowed to a trot and then stopped. He looked around. The Celt was gone. The dark pillars of the tree trunks rose in front of him. Everything was quiet, except the water dripping from the fir bows.

"Come on, Byron! The Celt porker is hiding."

Byron frowned. "No." His eyes swept the trees in front of him. "Strongbow warned us not to chase the Celts into the forest."

"Don't be a coward!" Guillaume cried as he spurred his horse forward.

"Let him go," Byron shouted, but Guillaume ignored him and rode deeper into the woods. Cursing, Byron followed his brother. Byron ducked under a branch. Byron felt his breathing quicken, the trees were getting closer together. Dead branches crackled under his horse's hooves, breaking the oppressive stillness of the forest.

"Guillaume come back," Byron cried as his horse snorted and bolted backwards. Several Celtic warriors armed with spears, appeared from behind the trees.

"Christ!" Turning his horse, Byron spurred the animal furiously to escape. The big bay leaped forward at a run. A spear went by him. Dodging the trees, he saw his brother's horse running beside him. A tree was in his path, and Byron leaned to the right, his blue cloak snagging on a branch and tearing. His brother was now running ahead of him, his black horse disappearing out of the trees. Byron was nearing the edge of the forest where the tree boughs hung low, and he leaned forward hugging the withers of his horse. With a swoosh, the branches slid over his back as he shot out into the open field. He looked up to see his brother drop over the other side of the hill. Byron's horse crested the hill. A blood-chilling cry went up as more Celts rose from their hiding place among the rocks.

Guillaume's horse swerved sideways as the mass of blue painted warriors rushed him. Byron watched in horror as Celts dragged his brother from his horse. A scream filled the air as the Celts began stabbing and beating his brother to death. With a cry of rage, Byron charged them. As his horse closed with the nearest warrior, Byron stood up in his stirrups to strike him with his sword. The nimble Celt dodged to the side and drove his spear into the ground, tripping the horse. Byron's horse fell to its knees and rolled onto its side. With a crash, he was thrown, and he rolled across the turf, his chain mail twisting around him. Byron came to rest face down, his sword still in his hand.

He jumped to his feet and pulled his armor straight. His helmet was gone and his mail hood pulled back. He turned to face his enemies who were gathering around him in a ring. He raised his sword, his arm shaking. "Come on you bastards!" he cried. A Celtic warrior with a silver helmet pushed through the circle to face him. The warrior slammed his blue shield emblazoned with two running dogs into the ground and leaned on it.

"Take your dead Norman and go home! This is our land!"

Byron hesitated, but before he could move, he was knocked to the ground. Two Celts wrenched his sword out of his hand and using the nearby rocks, broke it in half. Massive hands grabbed him. He looked up into the merciless blue eyes of the Celtic warrior. The man's braided blond hair hung down from his iron helmet Another Celt grabbed his arm, and they started dragging him to his horse.

"Get on your horse, Norman." Byron looked over as his brother's lifeless body was thrown over the back of the black horse and tied in place. "Get on your horse."

Byron stepped into the stirrup and swung into the saddle.

The Celt with the silver helmet walked over and handed him the reins. "Tell your king to never come here, or we will slay him and all his men."

†

Byron sighed as he rubbed the wetness from his eyes. He turned away from the tree. They had foolishly chased the Celt, and the lesson had cost him his brother's life. He had grown wiser. He was still angry, but he would not chase Cardinal Fulcher, especially in a place where the cardinal had the advantage.

CHAPTER 33
THE GRAF OPENS HIS MOUTH

Cardinal Fulcher lounged in the back seat of the coach. The morning fog was thick; wisps of grey hid the surrounding countryside. The cardinal was wearing a red fur-lined cloak to ward off the cool damp air. A cap trimmed with ermine was pulled down over his ears. Fulcher was in a hurry to reach his destination, and the coach ride from the city seemed longer than usual. VonDurenberg sat across from the cardinal, his white cloak drawn tightly around his black tunic. The graf was looking down, his face was drawn and his lips pressed together.

"I don't see why it is necessary for me to go to Babylon," VonDurenberg said. "I have retainers loyal to me. I can find someone else to go. I have many important tasks that require my attention and prestige."

Fulcher raised one eyebrow as he looked at VonDurenberg. "More prestigious than being chosen by his Holiness? Whether you like it or not, the Holy Father has chosen you."

VonDurenberg's brow furled and he scowled at Fulcher. "After you suggested I go."

"I gave you the great honor to serve the Church. There are many who would leap at the opportunity to be chosen personally by the Holy Father."

"I understand, but the timing is inconvenient."

"Well, you are going. I want someone I can trust to bring this treasure back to Rome. It must be kept out of Morra's hands. Morra will push for a new crusade. If that happens, the Church will need Barbarossa, and all hope of deposing him will fade. We must maintain control of the gold. A large sum of money will buy the support of the German princes, smoothing the way to remove Frederick from the throne. With a large treasury behind your rule, you will become as powerful as Otto the Great."

VonDurenberg could not suppress the slight smile at the suggestion. "Be patient. Everything will fall into place," Cardinal Fulcher said.

VonDurenberg sat back and stared out at the variations of grey in the fog. Perhaps the cardinal was right. A large treasure would give him immense power, besides the trip would not be so terrible. If he had to go, his retainers and the right number of servants might make the journey comfortable.

The coach started up a long drive lined with somber cedar trees, their bows laden with silver drops of dew. It rounded the corner, and the wall of the fortress of Count Marcellus Theophylact came into view. Cardinal Fulcher leaned forward. "I will do the talking."

VonDurenberg frowned. "Then why did you bring me?"

"Because I want you to meet this man. Count Theophylact can be very generous with his gifts. You will find that when you depose Barbarossa, the count is a very useful friend to have."

The coach came to a stop near the portico of the villa. Cardinal Fulcher and VonDurenberg got out, and one of Count Theophylact's female servants came out of the house to greet them. "Cardinal Fulcher," the woman said sweetly, "it is good to see you again. My master is entertaining a guest from Catalonia. I will let him know you are here."

"You are very gracious, my child," Fulcher replied, ignoring the woman's flirtatious smile.

VonDurenberg walked over to the woman and stared at her, admiring her beauty. The woman, feeling uncomfortable under his unblinking gaze, drew away and walked as fast as she could back to the house.

VonDurenberg stared as if in a trance as he watched her walk. "Such a beautiful woman. I should like to have such a woman as a servant to..."

"I don't want to hear another word," Fulcher interrupted the graf.

The graf looked down at the cardinal. "It is my right to take my servants wherever I please."

"What you do with your servants is your business. You are in another man's house. Do not covet his possessions. At least not out loud."

They waited for only a few moments before Marcellus walked out the doorway of the house and embraced Fulcher. "Cardinal Fulcher, what an unexpected surprise."

"Count Theophylact, I apologize for this sudden and unannounced visit. An urgent matter has arisen, and I have come to seek your assistance on a Church matter."

Marcellus smiled broadly. "Your Eminence, you honor me. A Church matter, how interesting." Marcellus' smile faded. "Nonetheless, your visit could have been better timed....I am entertaining a merchant from Barcelona....but no matter, follow me."

Fulcher followed the count, trailed by VonDurenberg who was looking around at the house. Marcellus escorted his guests to the garden where he and Ishaq had been sitting down to coffee. The fog was lifting, and the warm sun was starting to shine though the tendrils of grey that curled in the morning breeze. Ishaq, seeing a Roman Catholic Cardinal, immediately assumed it was Fulcher and rose to greet Marcellus' guest.

"Your Eminence, such an honor." The assassin knelt swiftly and kissed the cardinal's ring. "Allow me to introduce myself, I am Don Hernandez de Fuego. I cannot believe my good fortune in meeting an esteemed member of the Church," he gushed. "The blessed Mother Mary must be smiling upon me." Fulcher pulled back his hand as if he had been violated.

"Don Fuego," Marcellus said slowly, looking at Ishaq to see if he got the name right, "may I introduce my esteemed friend, Cardinal Fulcher."

"Cardinal Fulcher," the assassin said, "I have heard so much about you. And who is your worthy escort?"

"This is Graf Wilhelm Helmuth VonDurenberg."

Ishaq eyed the proud German, standing erect, looking down his nose at him. "Ah, giraffe that is an unusual title. I have seen a giraffe once. Long necks, strange creatures. Why do you use such a sobriquet? Was it bestowed upon you, because as a warrior you have qualities of a giraffe? Or was it given to you because you have a long neck?"

VonDurenberg's mouth dropped. He could not believe this fool. "That is graf, you imbecile! It is the honorable German title for a count, and I don't have a long neck."

Ishaq's smile faded. "Ah my sincere apologies, my lord. I am not familiar with Germania. I did not mean to offend."

Marcellus chuckled as he sat down in his chair and looked at Fulcher with the glint of amusement in his eye. "What do I owe the honor of a visit from such an esteemed member of the Church?"

"I would like to discuss business with you," Fulcher said.

"A proposition?" Marcellus said as he stroked his beard. "Is this a business proposition or a personal request?"

"Church business," Fulcher said.

"Church business," Marcellus repeated as he looked at Ishaq with raised eyebrows. "What kind of business?"

"Can he be trusted?" Fulcher asked as he pointed his finger at Ishaq.

"Of course," Marcellus replied. "Why, Don Hernandez may even be able to assist you if you will confide in us your needs."

Ishaq frowned at Marcellus' use of the wrong name. "Your Eminence, tell Don Fuego what you desire, and I assure you that I, Don Fuego, will do everything with my considerable financial power to make it come true."

Fulcher had a confused look on his face as he glanced at Marcellus and then back to Ishaq. At last he said, "What is said here must stay here."

Marcellus leaned back in his chair with his fingertips pressed together in front of him. "As you wish."

Fulcher eyed the men in front of him. Marcellus was wearing a red silk shirt. The Spanish Don was dressed in a black tunic embroidered with fanciful designs that reminded Fulcher of a spider web. "The Church is sending an expedition to the Levant, and I need someone who can supply a caravan of camels."

"Camels?" Ishaq asked in surprise.

"And what is your destination?" Marcellus asked.

"I am not in a position to discuss that," Fulcher replied.

"Hmm...well if you want my help, then I need some information," Marcellus said. "Where are you starting from?"

"Those details have not been decided," Fulcher replied.

"Then I am afraid we will not be able to help you," Marcellus replied, standing up. "I am sorry, Your Eminence. You have journeyed here in the fog for nothing. I will not put anything at risk until I have the details. Our caravans are already committed to existing trips to the East. It will be a considerable financial hardship if we use them for something else. Perhaps when the Church has finalized its plans, you can make your request."

"All you need to know is the Church will pay your costs," Fulcher said in exasperation. "I assure you if you assist me, you will be well rewarded."

"I wish it was that simple," Marcellus said, "but I like to know the risks before I say yes."

"Hmm," Fulcher grumbled with disgust. "I came to you hoping you could assist me, but now I will have to look elsewhere."

"I am sorry, Your Eminence," Marcellus said, "but I think I can speak for myself and Don Fuego that until you can provide me with more information, I am not willing to take the risk."

Marcellus stood up to conclude the discussion. Ishaq added, "I wish I could help, Your Eminence, but Count Theophylact is right. There are too many unknowns."

Fulcher turned to leave. "I had hoped as good Catholics you would aid the Church on faith."

VonDurenberg was incredulous. They had wasted the entire morning to get here, and Cardinal Fulcher was about to leave. He could see more trips to the villa and more time wasted. "Enough of this foolishness!" VonDurenberg cried in frustration. "For the love of God, I have other things to do that are more important." The graf spun to face Marcellus. "We are going to Babylon to retrieve a lost treasure. Is that enough information for you?"

The garden became quiet. Only the chirping of the birds in the trees broke the silence. Marcellus spoke after several moments, "It is indeed," he said as he smiled, thinking to himself, 'ah-ha so that is what the Lateran had been up to, you fools should have kept that to yourselves'. He felt a pang of disappointment that VonDurenberg had ended the game so quickly.

"Now that I know what we are attempting to do," Marcellus said in as relaxed manner, "I think Don Fuego can help you."

Ishaq did not answer at first. He was still in shock that Jabbar had been right. At least partially right. The fat merchant would have happily sold the priest to Salah-al-Din not realizing the magnitude of the knowledge the priest possessed. A treasure! No wonder the priest was being protected.

"Don Fuego, you can help them, can't you?" Marcellus repeated.

"Oh yes, indeed, indeed, indeed," Ishaq repeated distractedly. "Oh my, yes. God has smiled upon you and rewarded you for your trust. At this moment, I have a caravan returning from the Far East. All I need to know is when and where to meet you." Ishaq leaned forward. "Your Eminence?"

Cardinal Fulcher, still in shock of VonDurenberg's foolish outburst, stood with his mouth slightly open. He blinked and then let out a deep sigh. "Ah... if you bring the treasure back unharmed and intact, I assure you, your reward will be substantial."

"Agreed," Ishaq exclaimed, clapping his hands and rubbing them together. "Let me know when you have the details: where you intend to embark, when you and your entourage are going to arrive in the Holy Lands, and I will have my caravan there."

"As I said," Fulcher replied, "I am not privy to that information yet. Other members of the Church are making those plans, but I think I could arrange a meeting with Cardinal Morra."

"Send a messenger when you know," Marcellus said. "This must happen soon. Don Fuego must have enough time to make the necessary arrangements." Marcellus smiled as he directed the conversation away from the graf's foolish outburst. "Enough business, stay for the noon meal ere you return to the Lateran?"

"Count Theophylact, you are gracious," Fulcher said as he eyed VonDurenberg angrily, "but no, we must be going. I have much to do today. I will send a messenger to let you know when and where the meeting will be."

"Such a disappointment," Marcellus said, not at all disappointed to be rid of the cardinal and the graf. There was so much to talk about, he could hardly contain himself. "Until we meet again, Your Eminence. Farewell."

Fulcher turned and stalked out of the garden and down the hallway without saying a word. VonDurenberg followed behind him. Once the coach had pulled out of the driveway, Fulcher exploded in a rage. "You fool! You should never have revealed to Marcellus our quest. I just hope that by the time you leave Rome, the entire world does not know about this. I certainly hope Morra does not learn you told Theophylact what we are doing and where we are going. If Morra finds out, he will use this against me. What possessed you?"

VonDurenberg glared back at the cardinal. "You were wasting my time. They are going to find out. No man agrees to go on a journey without knowing his destination. Even men on the road to hell know where they are going."

Cardinal Fulcher looked at the graf, opened his mouth to speak, then shut his mouth, and slumped back into his seat. Even if he explained all the subtleties, VonDurenberg would still not understand. With a sigh, the cardinal resigned himself to the fact that VonDurenberg was a fool. Nothing he could do or say would change that simple fact.

"What is done is done," Fulcher said softly. "I just hope not to pay too dearly for your stupidity."

The rest of the journey back to Rome was in complete silence. Cardinal Fulcher brooded over what had happened, contemplating how he was going to repair the damage. When the coach reached the Lateran, Cardinal Fulcher stepped out and then turned to face the German. "Tomorrow," he snapped, "I want you to meet with Father Villhardain. He is starting to select men for the journey."

VonDurenberg frowned. "I told you I have my own men."

"That is why I want you there. I am placing you in charge of this expedition. Tell Father Villhardain his choices are unnecessary. It is a simple task. Do you think you can manage this?" Before the graf could answer, Fulcher turned and walked off leaving VonDurenberg standing by the coach.

†

Byron sat quietly next to Father Villhardain, maintaining a look of interest as he listened to a knight in the service of the Papal States regale the priest with his boastful exploits of his deeds in a small war between two Italian Princes of the Lombard league. At last, the old priest cut him off politely and told him he would give him some consideration.

When the man had left, Byron turned to Father Villhardain in exasperation. "I never thought finding experienced soldiers would be so difficult."

"Why do you think I asked you to join me?" the priest replied sleepily.

"How much more time are we going to spend looking for knights marked with the cross who have spent time in the Levant?"

"The weather will soon change, and the sailing season in the Mediterranean will end. We must be under sail in the next few weeks. It will not do to find the treasure if we cannot safely transport it back to Rome. We will make our choices in the time given us and then live with our decision."

The door to the room opened with a bang, and VonDurenberg marched in. "I was told by Cardinal Fulcher to seek you out. I understand you are looking for knights. That is not necessary. I will be leading this expedition, and I will be bringing my own retainers."

Byron and Father Villhardain sat looking at VonDurenberg in complete surprise. "I don't think you will be leading anything," Byron replied with irritation.

"Yes, Cardinal Fulcher has chosen me. I am a graf of the prestigious house of Durenberg. Do you think I will answer to a priest or," VonDurenberg sniffed, "Norman riffraff?"

Father Villhardain's blue eyes hardened. "My son, you were chosen by the Holy Father to be part of this journey, but there was no discussion of you leading the expedition."

Graf VonDurenberg threw back his shoulders and scoffed, "I do not take commands from priests."

Byron rose to his feet. "You have not taken up the cross. You know nothing of the lands we are going to travel. You have never been to war with the Saracens. Being a graf does not give you knowledge to command!"

"War is war," VonDurenberg replied. "Who it is against is irrelevant. My men are dependable knights and my servants do my bidding."

"My son, Cardinal Morra will have to be consulted on this. We are not going to fight. We are going disguised as traders. We are going to slip though the lands of the Saracens and then return to Rome."

VonDurenberg laughed without mirth. "I am a German graf. I will not go as a thief or a peasant."

Byron scowled. "My lord, are you certain?"

VonDurenberg turned red in the face and rested his hand on his sword. "I will not be spoken to in such an insolent manner."

Byron's face flushed. "Are you challenging me to combat?"

"Yes, or are you a coward?"

Byron swept out his sword and leapt across the table despite the protest of Father Villhardain. "I will teach you the same lesson the porker Saxons received from William's Normans, you arrogant German ass!" he cried as he raised his sword.

VonDurenberg, surprised by the sudden attack, was backing away fumbling to draw his sword. He pulled his sword free just in time to block Byron's first blow. The ring of steel echoed in the room. Byron shoved his blade to pin the German's sword against his chest. With his free hand, Byron repeatedly struck the German in the face. VonDurenberg's nose was bleeding. Byron stepped back and raised his sword for the kill when he heard a voice say, "No!"

James had entered the room to deliver a message to Father Villhardain when he saw Fitzwalter standing in front of the German, whose face was covered with blood. "No! Fitzwalter not here," James yelled.

Father Villhardain shouted, "Listen to him. Not here. Turn the other cheek and let this pass, you must let this pass."

Byron relaxed and sheathed his sword. He walked a few paces, turned, and pointed a finger at the graf. "You are unworthy. You will lead nothing."

The doorway was now crowded with several churchmen who had heard the commotion and come to see what was happening. Byron shoved passed them and left the room.

"Father Villhardain," a cardinal asked, "what is the meaning of this?"

Father Villhardain bowed. "Nothing, Your Eminence. Just a swordsmanship demonstration, nothing more."

The cardinal looked skeptical. "This is not the place for such acts of war. See that it does not happen again."

Father Villhardain bowed. "Yes, Your Eminence." The crowd of churchmen muttering among themselves left the doorway.

VonDurenberg, shaking and breathing hard with fear, wiped the blood from his face. "Fitzwalter is fortunate that I at least have respect for the Church. Otherwise, I would have slain him."

James tilted back his head and laughed. "You are fortunate to not be dead."

"I will not tolerate this impudent behavior," VonDurenberg snarled belligerently as he stooped down to pick up his sword. "I will talk to Cardinal Fulcher. I am leading this expedition, and Fitzwalter will not be going."

James looked at VonDurenberg with surprise. "I have not heard this." James turned to the priest. "Is this so? Is VonDurenberg leading us to Babylon?"

"That is the recent issue of contention," Father Villhardain said. "Nothing has been decided. I have yet to discuss this issue with Cardinal Morra."

"I see," James said, turning to VonDurenberg. "You wish to be the leader?"

"I am a German graf, of course I am the leader," VonDurenberg said as he was feeling his nose to see if it was broken.

"Where are you taking us?" James asked.

"Babylon," VonDurenberg snapped. "You know that as well as I."

"I do," James said with a smile. He loved this. He was the cat that had caught a small mouse and was now going to torment it until it could play no more. "How do you get to Babylon?"

VonDurenberg stopped feeling his face. "That is not your concern, My Lord Martel."

"It is my concern. I want to hear your plans for traveling the lands of the Saracens."

"I don't see the need to share my plans, especially after being unjustly assailed in the house of God by your friend Fitzwalter."

"My lord graf, I can see why you would feel that way. Fitzwalter should not have done that; although, combat is an acceptable form for settling a dispute among fighting men, wouldn't you agree?"

VonDurenberg sensed he was being trapped, but he could not think of a way out. "I do agree, among equals, but..."

"I see we have the same opinion," James said abruptly. "You are certainly not Fitzwalter's equal."

VonDurenberg became flustered, uncertain if James was paying him a compliment. "Yes, Fitzwalter is not my equal."

James laughed. "Now that the issue is settled, what is your plan?"

"I don't have one yet," the German said, starting to suspect James was making fun of him.

"I see. It is a good thing you are fluent in the Saracen tongue. Plans can change quickly, and the one thing I have learned, it is important to speak the language of the lands you travel. I cannot begin to tell you how useful it is to get information from the people who live in the Levant. But you know that already."

"I don't speak the language of the damned," VonDurenberg exploded in frustration. "I have no desire, whatsoever, to converse with devil worshipers. I am done! I promise you, you and Fitzwalter will both live to regret this."

"That is my fear," James quipped, doing his best to suppress a smile. "I am curious though, once you reach the ruined city, what do you expect to find, a sign stating Roman treasure buried here?"

"I do expect to find something of that sort," VonDurenberg

yelled. "I am certain such a marker exists. No one would bury a treasure without making some mark as to its location."

"My lord, I almost wish I had the time to watch you look," James laughed. VonDurenberg glared at James and then left the room.

"My son, you should not have antagonized him," Father Villhardain said.

"No Father, what I shouldn't have done was stop Fitzwalter from killing him. The only reason I did was for fear of what would happen to Fitzwalter if he had given the German what he deserved."

"This will complicate things you know."

"Father, the man needs to be put in his place. Our demise will be cruel and slow if his stupidity exposes who we are." Father Villhardain shook his head. "All will turn out well, Father," James said with a smile. "Byron and I will deal with him, just not here."

"That may prove unlikely my son. VonDurenberg is threatening to bring his own retainers. The last thing that I need, is a man with his own private army and a treasure. It is one of the reasons that I returned to Rome. I need men loyal to the Church."

"That is a problem." James paused as he looked at the priest's pale face. "You look tired. Are you well?"

"No, my son. I have not been feeling well, but it is nothing more than the worries and concerns that have been placed upon me. Once things are organized, I will feel better."

"How many knights have you found?" James asked.

"Not as many as I would like. I am afraid with our limited time they will have to do. I found one converted Moor from Castile, Sir Narvez, he speaks Arabic and has crusaded in Spain. He has been involved in the heavy fighting on the Iberian Peninsula to remove the infidel threat. The rest have no experience at all, but are willing and seem eager to aid the Church."

"As long as they can keep their tongues still. That is all I care about. Which reminds me, Cardinal Morra wanted to see you."

"No harm, my son. I am sure the cardinal is just seeking a report on our progress." Father Villhardain walked out, leaving James by himself in the room.

James took a moment to reflect on a large mosaic of Adam and

Eve driven from Eden. Adam was looking over his shoulder. Behind him, robed in white, was an angel holding a flaming sword as if pointing where to go. Eve walked beside Adam, her head bowed and her face obscured by her hands. Adam had wrapped his arm around Eve's shoulder as if to console her, but the anguish on Adam's face suggested that he himself was consumed by the same grief.

James looked at the mosaic for a moment longer and sighed. Women and war had consumed his life. He had not once considered his future. Life was precarious at best. Without warning, it could suddenly and violently end. The concept of paradise had never entered his mind. He had no time for foolish daydreams. He had just started his journey to atone for his sins, but as he looked at paradise lost, he wondered if this journey was sufficient, or would God demand more.

After taking a moment to examine the emptiness of his life, he turned his back on the mosaic. Like Adam and Eve, God's judgment had been rendered. The angel standing guard to the forbidden garden had denied him entrance. Not that it mattered. The signs were gathering all around him, like storm clouds, and he knew this journey to Babylon would be ruled by the sword.

CHAPTER 34
THE DEVIL COMES TO THE LATERAN

Father Villhardain was waiting in Cardinal Morra's apartment when the cardinal returned. The cardinal poured himself a glass of wine and sat down at his table, taking a moment to look at his friend sitting across from him. The priest was pale, the lines of stress etched in his face.

"You look tired, my friend."

The priest sighed. "I am tired, but I have lots to do."

"I wish I could offer you relief from your responsibilities, but I am afraid we have come too far for that."

"To him who much has been given, much is required."

Cardinal Morra nodded. "Indeed. How much progress have you made in selecting men?"

"It is as we feared. There are no fighting men left who have any experience with the Levant. Even if the Holy Father calls for a new crusade, it will be as if we are starting all over again."

"Let's hope the few experienced warriors we do have can impart their wisdom to the new recruits who take the cross. How many of the men you recruited have crusader experience?"

"Aside from Fitzwalter and Martel I found one knight who has been to war. The rest will provide the labor we need, and God willing, we will not have to discover what their fighting skills really are."

"I was afraid it would come to that."

"I am already having problems with VonDurenberg."

Cardinal Morra nodded. "Yes, I have heard all about it. I just left a meeting with His Holiness. Fulcher demanded that VonDurenberg not only lead the expedition, but also be allowed to bring his retainers and his servants."

Father Villhardain frowned. "And the Holy Father's judgement in the matter?"

"Fulcher made the claim that one of your knights assailed the graf." The cardinal raised his eyebrows as he looked at the priest in front of him. "Fortunately, the Holy Father did not hear him or did not believe him. Despite this claim, I was able to convince his Holiness that it would be wiser to use our own knights in the service of the Papal States, but I did have to make some concessions."

"Which are?" Villhardain asked, not daring to breathe.

"I had to concede that VonDurenberg will assist you in any military matters that might arise."

Father Villhardain sighed with relief. "I expected worse. VonDurenberg has demonstrated his martial incompetence. Without his retainers, he will be much easier to ignore."

"Indeed. There is one more pressing matter," the cardinal continued. "Count Theophylact is coming to the Lateran tomorrow, and he is bringing a Catalan with him. We will be meeting with them and Fulcher in the late morning."

"As you wish, Your Eminence," Father Villhardain replied, looking as if he would rather do anything else than have a meeting with the largest rogue in Rome. "What is the purpose of this meeting?"

"Fulcher did not say." The Cardinal glanced down at his desk. "I have one last problem. Your assistant, Brother Carl Honeywell. If you intend to slip through Saracen lands unnoticed then I suggest he remain behind. Brother Carl has been valuable to you, but in this instance, his size will draw attention. The kind of attention people remember. The men you choose should not leave any lasting impression."

"Yes, Your Eminence, I know. I have struggled with this decision."

"If it will make it easier, I will give him a task within the Church as a reward for his loyal service. That should help take the sting out of being left behind."

"If you would, Your Eminence. It will help, although he will not be fooled."

"True, but it must be done. When you leave here, tell him I want to see him. We might as well do this soon, rather than let him make preparations for a journey he will not take."

"I will do as you ask."

"Good."

Father Villhardain stood up. "Your Eminence, do you have anything else?"

"No, Michael. This expedition must be ready to sail in the next few days. The longer you stay, the more time Fulcher has to meddle. Do you think you can manage it?"

"Yes, Your Eminence, I will be ready."

Father Villhardain walked down the hall with his head bowed in thought. When he reached Brother Carl's room, he knocked and entered. The monk was not there. Father Villhardain looked at the few meager possessions of his friend: a cowl draped over a chair, an extra robe hung on the bedpost to dry, a small canvas bag lying on the floor. Brother Carl took his vow of poverty seriously, and when he was gone, nothing would remain to mark he had ever lived. The priest left the room and headed to the small chapel where Brother Carl had heard James' confession. He found the monk kneeling in front of the altar praying, his deep voice whispering in Latin.

The monk stopped and glanced behind him. "Father Villhardain, I have been expecting you."

"You have?" the priest said.

"Hmm, yes. I have heard the rumors that I will not be going."

The priest looked at the monk for a moment before he spoke, "Brother Carl, you have been my friend. You have been my assistant."

"Yet you are leaving me behind," the monk interrupted. "All my years of toil and service meant nothing."

Father Villhardain sighed. He knew this would be difficult, but he had hoped Brother Carl would understand. "You know that is not true."

The monk stood up and crossed his arms across his chest. "Was it your decision?"

The priest nodded. "Yes. Cardinal Morra will find a place for you while I am gone."

The monk shook his head. "I have protected you on the roads we have traveled. Yet on the most dangerous road of all you leave me behind."

"Yes, and you know why."

"I have heard the whispering. The man is too big. He will stand out. People will remember him." Brother Carl scoffed. "Foolishness. The Saracens capture all manner of men and enslave them."

"I understand, but the decision has been made. As difficult as it was, I did it in the best interest of the Church."

Brother Carl looked at the priest for a moment. "I fear for you, Father Villhardain. I fear for your safety. I will pray for you every day when you are gone, but my heart tells me it will be to no avail."

"Brother Carl, I will return. When we meet again, we will resume our work and our travels as if nothing has happened."

The monk pulled the priest close, embraced him, and then stepped back. "I hope it is so. You have more faith in the Frank and the Norman than I do. I have improved the Norman's sword skills, but I fear for the Frank's commitment. I have done my best to set Martel on the path of redemption. This journey will be his test. I hope these labors to improve these men will serve you well, otherwise you are in God's hands."

"And in God's hands I will be safe no matter the outcome." The priest smiled. "It will turn out as God will's it. In the meantime, Cardinal Morra wishes to speak to you."

Brother Carl nodded. "Will the cardinal change his mind about my going?"

Father Villhardain looked at the monk. "No."

"I thought not." The monk turned and left the room.

✝

That night, Byron sat down with the priest to read. After an hour, he found the reading tedious and his mind distracted as thoughts about the future trip to Babylon kept intruding. "I wonder what Odysseus felt before he left for Troy," the knight said. "It is a shame that my lessons will end tonight."

"Odysseus was wise. He knew that the Trojans would exact a terrible toll upon the Greeks," Father Villhardain replied. "But why do you fear your lessons will end tonight?"

Byron pointed to the tome sitting on the priest's table. "Surely, Father, you do not plan to take that book with us."

Father Villhardain smiled. "Of course not. May I see your dagger?" Byron drew his dagger from his belt and handed it to the priest. Father Villhardain looked at the dagger. "Is your weapon sharp?"

"Of course, Father."

"This is curious," the priest said as he eyed the blade. "Numbers 6, 24, 25, 26. Did you inscribe the blade?"

Byron lowered his eyes. "No, it was a gift from the Lady Isabella de Clare."

"My Son, do you know what it means." Byron shook his head. The priest smiled. "It is a quote from the book of Numbers. *The Lord bless thee, and keep thee: The Lord make his face shine upon thee, and be gracious unto thee: The Lord lift up his countenance upon thee, and give thee peace.* The Lady Isabella must have cared deeply for you to give you such a gift."

Byron looked away and stared at the wall. "That was a long time ago, Father."

"Hmm, yes, well let me see if it is truly sharp."

Byron gasped as the priest opened the book and began to cut out the pages. "Father! You're destroying the book."

"Indeed! Pages are easier to carry. Learning to read is more important than this book. Besides I never liked its cover."

When the priest had finished dissecting the last chapters from the book, he rolled them up and tied them with a red cord. "Now you shall learn the fate of Odysseus." The priest tossed the book to Byron. "I expect you to complete this task. I would like to think that I did not destroy this book for no purpose."

Byron bowed. "I will finish this task."

"Excellent. Now I think it is time to part for the night. We will start again. In the meantime, I expect you to read on your own."

Byron bowed again and then turned to go. Byron walked the halls of the Lateran, gripping the pages in his hand. He was still amazed at the priest's desecration of one of his prized possessions, but even more, he understood the magnitude of the gift.

†

It was nearing midday when Marcellus' coach reached the Lateran. Ishaq made an amusing observation as the coach pulled into the drive. "I don't think anyone that I know would ever believe that I received an invitation to be a guest at the center of the infidel religion."

"I assure you, there are those who would rather receive you as a guest at the Lateran before they would even consider extending an invitation to me," Marcellus said as he opened the door and stepped out onto the grounds.

Ishaq and Marcellus stood in the grounds looking at the door of the palace. A page approached and bowed low. "My lords, Cardinal Fulcher extends his greetings. Follow me and I will guide you to the meeting."

"The Church has welcomed me home," Marcellus said with a hint of sarcasm in his voice. "Come, Don Fuego, a good Catholic such as yourself should enjoy this."

Ishaq chuckled as he followed Marcellus who had his head up and a smile on his face. The page led them through several marble hallways until he reached a bronze doorway. The page opened the door revealing a room with a vaulted blue ceiling. The edge of the ceiling was painted with white clouds, tinged with pink and gold. Angels peering from the edges of the clouds looked down at the men below. A dark wooden table was in the center of the room. At the far end of the room, sat Cardinal Morra. Standing beside him was Father Villhardain.

"Cardinal Morra," Marcellus beamed, "good to see you."

"Count Theophylact," Morra replied, "it has been a long time."

"It has indeed. I don't often get invitations to visit the Lateran."

Cardinal Morra frowned. "Considering history, should you be surprised?

"I am surprised," Marcellus said. "The past is the past. It is time to move forward." Marcellus turned to face Father Villhardain. "Father Villhardain, I did not know you were back in Rome."

"Count Theophylact," Father Villhardain said as he nodded. "Yes, I have recently returned from the Levant."

Marcellus smiled. "Ah yes. Find anything of interest there?"

Father Villhardain frowned. "No, my lord. Nothing you would find interesting. Most of my time was spent translating old texts from the early Church. Dull tedious work, but to me rewarding."

"I'm sure it was rewarding."

Cardinal Fulcher entered the room. Marcellus turned to greet Fulcher. "Cardinal Fulcher, I must thank you for this invitation. I must say I admire your visionary style. I am glad to see a member of the Church has a progressive vision. Wouldn't you agree Alberto?"

"Count Theophylact," Cardinal Morra replied, "I really never have given it much consideration. Personal agendas were never a concern of our Lord."

"I understand and that is regretful." Marcellus looked down at the table. After a moment, he glanced up and smiled. "Down to business."

Marcellus threw back his cloak and pulled out a chair. The count sat down so that he faced Cardinal Morra. Ishaq pulled a chair back from the table and sat down resting his black and silver cane in front of him.

"I understand the Church is need of a caravan of camels," Marcellus said.

"Yes," Cardinal Morra replied. "Cardinal Fulcher was given the task by the Holy Father to procure a caravan."

The corners of Marcellus' mouth twitched into a brief smile as he nodded to Fulcher. "So, His Eminence has told me. My associate, Don Fuego of the Kingdom of Catalonia, has a caravan you can use. When do you intend to leave Rome?"

"We intend to leave within the next week," Morra replied. "A ship is being prepared to sail, and we leave as soon as the winds are favorable. The destination is one of the few ports still in Christian hands. Alexandretta."

Ishaq leaned forward, his hand on the top of his cane. "Your Eminence, thank you for this invitation and this opportunity to serve the Church. I, Don Fuego, am a humble man, and it is a great honor for me to be here. I have but two questions. Who will lead this quest and what is your purpose?"

"Father Villhardain will lead this quest," Cardinal Morra replied as he looked at Cardinal Fulcher. "We intend to recover some lost artifacts that once belonged to the Roman Empire. The artifacts are of a religious nature dating to the reign of Constantine the Great. The Church greatly desires to have them back in our possession."

Marcellus smiled. "They must be of great value indeed, to venture into a war-torn region."

"To the Church, they are important; although, I am not sure you would consider them of value."

"Well, it is hard to know what I value, but I do value my relationship with Don Fuego. I expect that he will be well compensated for the risk he is taking."

"I am sure you and Cardinal Fulcher have already discussed terms for your time and trouble. I assure you, whatever monetary arrangement has been made, the Church will honor that agreement."

"Good! Because considering the importance of this journey, Don Fuego has agreed to go in person."

Cardinal Morra had not expected this. The last thing he wanted was this Spaniard going along. "That won't be necessary. I assure you that your caravan will be quite safe. If anything should happen to the animals, the Church will compensate you for your loss."

Ishaq gave a low bow. "Your Eminence, do any of you have experience with camels or the drivers? Someone must supervise, and since your destination is a bit vague, I think it is best that I am there to make sure that everything is done satisfactorily. Besides, I was traveling to Outremer anyway, so it is not an inconvenience."

"Father Villhardain intends to cover as much distance as possible every day, and when the work is completed, depart the Levant as soon as he can."

"I understand," Ishaq replied. "This is not the first time I have traveled in the Levant. I know the hardships."

"Is there anything else you would like to discuss?" Marcellus said as he looked around the room. "Excellent!" he exclaimed. "We will look for Father Villhardain in Alexandretta. Now, I think it is time for us to go before my welcome expires. I hope someday soon my visits here will be less infrequent." He glanced at Fulcher with a smile.

Cardinal Fulcher beamed with delight at the sign of the count's support. "Before you depart, Count Theophylact, I would be honored if you and Don Fuego would break bread with me."

"Ah, yes. I would welcome your hospitality."

Marcellus bowed, turned his back on Cardinal Morra, and followed Cardinal Fulcher out of the room. Ishaq stood up, and taking his cane in one hand, he did a sweeping bow to Cardinal Morra. "I look forward to this adventure. I am very certain it will prove rewarding." Ishaq followed Marcellus out of the room.

"This keeps getting worse and worse," the priest groaned.

"I agree," Morra grumbled. "But this has not run its course. Be patient, perhaps things will work out better than you expect."

It was late afternoon before Marcellus and Ishaq returned to the Fortress of Theophylact. Ishaq could see one of Marcellus' men standing in the drive waiting for his master as the coach turned the corner. The servant bowed as Marcellus stepped from the coach.

"My lord," the man said with his head still bowed, "Frangipani has seized our shipment of spices and is demanding a tax."

"What?" Marcellus shouted, his eyes alight with rage. "What is this outrage? You tell that son-of-a-bitch I am not paying anything."

"I have, my lord. I threatened that if he does not turn over what belongs to you, my lord, we will come and take it from him."

"And what did the drunken fool on Frangipani's payroll say?"

"All Frangipani's servant did was laugh."

"Insolent cur," Marcellus yelled. "Call the men. This cannot and will not stand! I will not be robbed of my hard-earned goods. I run Rome, not this upstart."

Marcellus turned to Ishaq. "My plans have changed. I will not have time to see you leave. I trust you will manage our affairs to our advantage."

Ishaq smiled. "Of course, I will make sure we are amply rewarded for our work."

"My coach will take you to *Gaeta*. My ship, *Esperia*, will be there waiting for you. She sails with a shipment for Tyre. I anticipated time would be short, but I did not expect the Church to be so efficient."

"Why *Gaeta*?" Ishaq asked in surprise.

"That worthless cur Frangipani controls Terracina," Marcellus snapped. "I can't get my ships into harbor without paying enormous taxes to that thief."

"That is unfortunate."

"Yes," Marcellus fumed. "How do you think he can afford to build his new fortress? Next, Frangipani will control *Gaeta*, and sending my ships to Genoa is out of the question."

"My friend, Frangipani is slowly squeezing the life out of your business."

"It is true. When I heard Frangipani was building his new fortress, I knew there would be trouble."

Ishaq nodded. "One does not start such a project without a purpose behind it."

A servant leading a horse walked up. Marcellus took the reins and mounted. "Ishaq of Tyre, I look forward to your return. I trust your generosity for my help."

"Ishaq always rewards his friends."

Marcellus mounted and turned his horse to face Ishaq. Standing in the stirrups, he doffed his cap and bowed. Marcellus rode to the head of his mounted retainers and led them through the gate. Ishaq watched them go and then hurried into the house to pack. He had a lot to accomplish before the Christians returned to the Levant. He hoped Bashshar had done what he had asked and trained his men well because he was going to need them.

CHAPTER 35
THE JOURNEY BEGINS

VonDurenberg paced the hallway outside Cardinal Fulcher's door. At last, a servant opened the door and admitted the graf. Fulcher dressed in a red silk robe was at his desk writing. The cardinal set down his quill and looked up. "I have finished meeting with Cardinal Morra regarding your demands."

"And?" VonDurenberg demanded.

"Father Villhardain will lead the expedition, but he is to consult with you if any military matters arise."

"That is not acceptable!" VonDurenberg shouted as he threw his hands in the air. "I will not be led by a priest! And what of my retainers? Am I at least allowed to take my men?"

Cardinal Fulcher looked at VonDurenberg. "No, your men will not be going, but Martel and Fitzwalter are."

VonDurenberg's mouth twitched as he glared down at Fulcher. "Damn it. Whose side are you on?"

The cardinal leaned back in his chair and folded his arms. "I suggest you calm yourself, Graf VonDurenberg. Cardinal Morra is in charge of this expedition, and I remind you that only Father Villhardain knows the precise location of the treasure." Cardinal Fulcher looked up at the graf. "Morra has chosen Fitzwalter and Martel because they have crusaded in the Levant and they speak the Saracen tongue."

"Irrelevant," VonDurenberg snapped. "If I had my men, we could drive right through the Saracen lands. After all, one Christian Knight is worth twenty Saracens."

"Well, you do not. You are not there to wage war. You are to pass through the lands unnoticed, and speaking the language may prove invaluable."

"Hmm and what if it is not? What if it comes down to a fight?"

"If it comes down to a fight, then you will have failed and your return will be unlikely."

"Martel and Fitzwalter will thwart our plans."

The cardinal sighed and waved his hand in front of his face as if to dismiss the concern. "Do you think I have not thought of this? There is nothing more I can do. You will have to win over the men who are traveling with you. Get possession of the treasure. That is your task."

"And Fitzwalter and Martel."

Cardinal Fulcher looked down at the letter on his desk. "That is up to you."

VonDurenberg smiled. "Yes, Your Eminence."

Cardinal Fulcher leaned forward again and picked up his quill. "Is there anything else?"

"No, Your Eminence."

"Good, then I will look for your triumphal return." VonDurenberg bowed, then turned and left the room.

†

The ride to Civitavecchia was pleasant. Byron and James took full advantage of the last few days of freedom from responsibility. The fall air was crisp and invigorating as the horses clopped along the polished stones of the roadbed. Father Villhardain, not trusting that the ship was ready, had sent them ahead to find out if it was true.

They were several miles into the journey when James asked, "I have been working on a song. Do you want to hear it?"

"No," Byron replied, fearing his friend was going to sing anyway.

"Fitzwalter, you have no appreciation for power of song sung by a great troubadour such as I."

Oh God he is going to sing, Byron thought, and before he could say a word, James stated his song.

> *The breeze of summer drifts across the golden fields*
> *Together we lie beneath the deep blue sky,*
> *You and I, in loves embrace,*
> *A gentle wind caresses us,*
> *As we pass the day away*
> *I kiss your lips as I hold you close*
> *And tell you Sweet lady,*
> *Tomorrow I must sail.*
>
> *Sweet lady wait for me.*
> *Sweet lady remember me.*
> *Sweet lady if I fail,*
> *Lay me on my bier in a hauberk of golden mail.*

James stopped and looked at Byron for approval.

Byron frowned. "Your song needs work."

James' eyes narrowed. "And what is wrong with it?"

"It is depressing. You sing of failing, of death, and golden mail?"

"It is a love song, Fitzwalter, full of romanticism. Something which you have no experience." Before Byron could answer, James began to sing again.

> *Before the walls of Jerusalem, as I face Muhammad's hordes*
> *I think of you, as you walk alone,*
> *on France's sandy shores,*
> *I long to see your smiling face,*
> *to spend the idle time of day,*
> *But as I set my spear to the enemy's face,*
> *I whisper and I pray,*
> *As I remember you to my sorrow,*
> *Sweet Lady*

in a land so far away.

Sweet lady wait for me
Sweet lady remember me
Sweet lady should I fail
Hide your tears with a long black veil.

"Why are you in such fine spirits today?" Byron said, hoping to avoid having to give another critique of James' song.

"Who can't help being in fine spirits on such a day. We have left Rome. VonDurenberg is not with us. What could be better?"

Byron had to agree. It was nice to be away from Rome.

After two days of riding, they arrived at Civitavecchia. Riding through the gates of the city, they headed for the docks. A forest of masts rose near the wharf as a number of ships were unloading their cargos. Byron stood with his hand shading his eyes looking at the weather stained hulls of the vessels. "Do you remember the name of the ship?"

"*La Seynte Grace*," James replied. Byron dismounted and tied his horse to a post. He walked down the length of the dock looking for the ship. At last, he stopped before the black hull of the *La Seynte Grace*. The ship's forecastle loomed over the dock. Her bow was broad and rolled back from the water line to the forecastle. The ships trim, once white, was chipped and worn so the grey wood now shown through. Several sailors mending the rigging took no notice of the two knights. Byron walked the length of the hull. Satisfied that the ship appeared seaworthy, he went onboard and began looking around the deck. He was standing next to James looking at a rigging block when an Italian with a short beard and salt and pepper hair confronted them.

"What is your business on the *La Seynte Grace*?"

James turned. "I believe the proper address is, 'my lords, welcome. How may I be of service?'"

The man crossed his arms across his chest and leaned back fixing his gaze on James. "I am Captain Borgesse. This is my ship. Who are you and what is your business?" He scoffed, "my lords."

James smiled. "I beg your pardon, captain. I thought you were a common sailor." Borgesse scowled at the suggestion. "We are your passengers. Do you still sail in two days?"

"No," the captain growled. "The wind does not favor us. I will be surprised if it is any better in two days. With luck, it will change, but until then we must wait." Borgesse gave an evil smile. "Enjoy the last few days while you are here, my lords. The season is getting on, and the sea will be rougher as it nears winter."

Byron frowned. "What do you mean by rougher?"

"Nothing a common sailor can't handle," the captain replied with a harsh laugh. He turned and walked off, giving orders to his crew regarding the stowage of the cargo in the hull of the ship.

Byron sighed and walked off the ship. He was dreading the thought of sailing. He would not spend a minute more on this future wooden prison of misery, not until it was necessary.

Byron and James left the dock, and leading their horses, found an inn to spend the night.

James scrawled a message to Cardinal Morra advising the ship was ready, but the weather was not. Paying a messenger, James watched him ride away. The next day, a large number of men on horseback approached the city from the east. The knights in chain mail were wearing white cloaks with the red cross of Jerusalem on the shoulder. Behind the riders was a large number of servants and retainers, along with a number of pack animals and wagons. News quickly spread through the city of the approaching knights, and Byron and James went to the city's gate to wait.

VonDurenberg, at the head of the riders, raised his hand and the column stopped. Byron turned to James. "VonDurenberg has brought his entire household. Surely, he is not foolish enough to think he can bring that mob on the quest."

VonDurenberg motioned to his squire. The squire was a lanky young man wearing a black tunic with a white German cross emblazoned across his chest. He wore a black velvet cap that covered his dark hair. VonDurenberg leaned over and spoke to him. The squire turned his pale face towards Byron and James and nodded. Spurring his horse forward, the squire rode to James and stopped. He dismounted and gazed at the knights in front of him with his unblinking blue eyes.

"Graf...you dine," the young man said haltingly, and he turned to point beyond the city walls. "You dine....Night."

"Where are your manners?" Byron said. "When you address a lord you bow and address the lord with his title."

The squire ignored Byron as he continued to stare at James. "You dine. Night." The young man repeated as a grin spread across his face.

James stepped forward. "We accept the graf's invitation." The young man leered at James and then turned and led his horse back towards the cavalcade.

Byron watched him walk away. "What insolence."

James shrugged. "Can't you see the boy is disturbed? It does speak to VonDurenberg's lack of respect in choosing such an emissary."

That afternoon a pavilion was set up outside the city's wall. A number of tents ringed the pavilion as servants went to and fro on their master's errands. Evening approached as Byron and James stopped at the camps edge and watched the spectacle.

"Fools," Byron grumbled as he motioned towards the tents. "Where do they think they are going? Surely they do not intend to bring all of this?"

James put his hand on Byron's shoulder. "My friend, let them enjoy a little comfort. They will know hardship soon enough." James smiled at Byron. "Come. Graf VonDurenberg is being gracious. Perhaps he wishes to make amends."

"Humph!" Byron scoffed as he followed behind James.

The tables were filled with platters of meat and cheese. A minstrel sat in the corner strumming a mandolin while he sang the ballad of Count Roland. A page escorted Byron and James to the table. A trencher was placed in front of Byron as he carved a piece of beef from the platter in front of him. He sat eating, listening to the boastful comments of the men around him. VonDurenberg sat at the end of the table, his squire stood behind him waiting on his master. A round faced English knight with a shaved head, was chatting loudly to another knight. Sir Parker of England was regaling Sir Stephen Maurice de Vale of his desire to slay his first

Saracen and carry his head on the end of his lance. De Vale smiled faintly at the young knight's enthusiasm, but a sideways glance at the knight that was sitting beside him suggested he would rather discuss something else.

Next to Byron, sat the Italian knight Giodonni. The Italian's chiseled face was tanned. He had a frown on his face, which was made more severe by his thick moustache. "Parker should be silent," the Italian grumbled. "It is bad luck to boast, and he is making a fool of himself."

"Aye," replied Byron.

Giodonni leaned closer. "I have been told you have returned from Jerusalem. That you were at Hattin?"

Byron stabbed the piece of meat he had just cut and held it up in front of him. "I was at Hattin."

"What happened? I still cannot believe we were defeated?"

"What happened?" Byron said as he twisted the knife, looking at the rare meat as blood ran down the blade. "We were foolish, and we were slaughtered because of it." Byron placed the meat in his mouth and began to chew, ending the conversation.

"We were betrayed," muttered a knight next to Giodonni. "I hear that Count Raymond fled the field." Byron looked over at the knight named Simon De Courcy. De Courcy had been muttering to himself, chewing his fingernails. Up till now, Byron had ignored him. Now that he had spoken, Byron regarded him. De Courcy's grey shaggy hair hung down over his blue watery eyes lined with red as if he suffered from a lack of sleep. De Courcy's lips curled into an unpleasant smile. "Isn't that right, My Lord Fitzwalter."

Byron scoffed. "It is. The Count of Tripoli fled. He abandoned the army to its fate. I watched the coward ride away while braver men stood and fought to the death."

De Courcy nodded. "That is what I heard when I was a prisoner in Aleppo. The Saracens bragged about the defeat. God favored me," De Courcy sighed. "I escaped that wicked cruel place." He looked down and resumed chewing on his fingers.

Byron frowned as he watched De Courcy resume muttering to himself. He looked up and caught sight of the Spanish Knight Sir Narvez across the table. The Spaniard shrugged. Narvez had fought against Almohad Empire. A savage white scar ran along his jaw as a testament to his combat. Narvez held Byron in his gaze for a moment and then nodded. Byron returned the informal salute and went back to eating.

"My Lord Martel," VonDurenberg cried from the head of the table as he waved a chicken leg in James direction, "we have heard My Lord Fitzwalter's tale. Why did you leave Jerusalem?"

James turned to face the graf. "My lord, it is a simple tale...I left because I left."

VonDurenberg leaned forward in his chair. "Hmm, my lord, you mean you fled." VonDurenberg set the chicken leg on the table down and dipped his fingers in a bowl of water held by his page.

"The water is cold!" VonDurenberg shouted as he knocked the bowl form the page's hands and slapped him across the face. The boy started to cry and VonDurenberg slapped him again. "Get me another bowl!" The page turned and bolted out of the tent.

VonDurenberg turned back to James as if nothing had happened. "Where were we? O' yes, Sir Martel why did you leave the Levant?"

"Because I left. A knight does not need a reason. I decided to pursue another noble quest."

"My lord, what noble quest?"

"To protect children from abusive lords. Does it make you feel powerful when you strike a boy? Does beating children fill you with satisfaction?"

VonDurenberg rose to his feet. His face turning scarlet. "I will not be spoken to in that manner by a man who fled the Levant. If I beat my servants, that is my affair."

James lifted his chin, his lips pressed tightly as he glared at VonDurenberg. "Indeed, my lord, you may beat them, but you look like an ass when you do. As far as the Holy Lands, if you must know, I rode to Tyre at the request of Jerusalem's master. I was sent to ask Montferrat to send reinforcements. Down that perilous road, filled with Saracens, my gallant horse ran, for I was in great haste to beat the army of Saladin, but when I reached Tyre, I found that Montferrat had no help to send. My return to Jerusalem was not to be, for I found that the Saracens cut off the roads." James rose to his feet. "It was God's will, not mine, that I was unable to return."

Narvez leaned forward. "Well spoken, my lord. Only God knows true valor." Narvez turned towards VonDurenberg. "Graf VonDurenberg, Sir Martel has spoken. Are you questioning this lord's bravery? If you so...then challenge him! It will be my great joy to be the marshal of the field of combat, and we will let God decide the matter."

VonDurenberg looked at Narvez. "My lord, I am not questioning Sir Martel's bravery. I was just asking the circumstances of his leaving Jerusalem."

Narvez' dark eyes flashed. "It sounded to my ears as if you were questioning My Lord Martel's honor."

"Ah... My Lord Narvez. That was not my intent to impugn Lord Martel's honor. My French is not as polished as it should be."

"Perhaps, my lord," Byron said as he cut another piece of meat, "but it sounded to me as if you were insulting Sir Martel. I suggest you improve your French." Byron looked up at the graf. "Misunderstandings in the Levant can be fatal." Byron looked around the tent. "I assume, my lord, that you have no intentions of taking any of these comforts with you." Byron motioned to the tables and the servants.

VonDurenberg sat down. "No, your priest has already made that clear."

"Good," Byron said as he looked over at a tray of beef and cut off another slab of meat. James turned away from the graf and sat back down. Byron chuckled, "A quest for abused children?"

"It was all I could think of at the time," James whispered.

"It was well done. The look of anger on VonDurenberg's face was worth coming here tonight. I thought he was going to split with rage."

That night at the inn, Byron sat alone reading the pages Father Villhardain had torn from his book. In the darkened room, the light of the candle flickered, illuminating the letters. Sounding out each syllable, he slowly read until he could read no more. Tiring of his work, he placed the pages back into order and carefully tied the string around them. He was still stunned by the priest's gift, and he vowed to care for the pages. At last, he lay down. Soon the trip would begin.

The next morning, the men were on the dock preparing their belongings to be taken aboard the *La Seynte Grace*. Fishing boats were tied nearby unloading their mornings catch. Gulls circled the boats as the fishermen cleaned the fish, throwing scraps to the birds. As Byron watched, the sound of the birds sent a shiver down his spine at the memory of the birds feasting on the bodies at Hattin. He stood up and walked a short distance to sit on a pier. The morning sun felt good as it warmed the air. A coach appeared, rumbling along the road. A pennant bearing the symbols of the keys of Saint Peter was next to the driver. Following the coach, was a monk riding on a mule. The coach drew near and stopped, and Father Villhardain stepped out of the coach.

The priest reached out his hand and helped Cardinal Morra step down. The cardinal stretched, and then followed by the priest, walked down to the dock to the assembled men. Brother Carl dismounted his mule and stood at a distance as Father Villhardain and the cardinal said goodbye to the men. Byron got up from his seat on the pier and walked over to stand next to the monk. James, wearing his light blue cloak, joined them.

"Brother Carl, are you ready for another voyage?" Byron asked.

Brother Carl looked down. "Norman, I am not going."

"Not going?" James said.

Brother Carl shot a glance at James. "No, His Eminence has given me a new assignment within the Church."

"Brother Carl, you will be missed," Byron replied.

"Indeed. It will now fall upon you to protect Father Villhardain." Brother Carl looked again at James. "I want to speak to Lord Martel alone." James followed the monk to a small grove of olive trees near the waterfront. When they were out of earshot, the monk stopped walking. He leaned close, the nostrils of his flattened nose flared, and his grey eyes became narrow slits as he held James in his cold gaze. "I am not going, and I expect you to take my place. I release you from wearing the chalice. It will be nothing more than an encumbrance. The journey itself will be uncomfortable enough. Now, more than ever, you must fulfil your vow." James nodded. The monk did not blink as his eyes bored into the knight. "God will hold you to your word."

"I know," James replied.

Brother Carl turned to see Father Villhardain approaching. The priest stopped and called out, "Come join us! Cardinal Morra would like to bless us all before he returns to Rome."

"Do not fail me, James." Brother Carl turned and followed Father Villhardain.

The knights gathered around Cardinal Morra. "This journey," the cardinal said, "is of great importance to the Church. His Holiness has bestowed upon you the title of Knights of the Holy Sepulcher, and he has granted you indulgences. It is now time for you to show you are worthy of that honor. I will now bless each of you." The men bowed their heads as Cardinal Morra prayed.

> *"Credo in Deum Patrem omnipotentem, Creatorem caeli et terrae. Et in Iesum Christum, Filium eius unicum, Dominum nostrum, qui conceptus est de Spiritu Sancto, natus ex Maria Virgine, passus sub Pontio Pilato, crucifixus, mortuus, et sepultus, descendit ad inferos, tertia die resurrexit a mortuis, ascendit ad caelos, sedet ad dexteram Dei Patris omnipotentis, inde venturus est iudicare vivos et mortuos. Credo in Spiritum Sanctum, sanctam Ecclesiam catholicam, sanctorum communionem, remissionem peccatorum, carnis resurrectionem, vitam aeternam. Amen."*

Bryon looked up as Cardinal Morra touched each one of them on the head with his hands.

"Go in peace, my sons, May God grant you success." He turned and walked back to his coach.

Brother Carl moved closer to Father Villhardain and spoke in a low voice, "God be with thee, Father."

"Brother Carl, you have been a faithful friend. God bless you."

Carl stood for a moment with a strange look of sadness on his face. Without a word, he walked back to his mule and deliberately gathered his reins, paused, and then mounted. Turning his face from the priest, the big monk pulled the hood of his cloak over his head so it hung over his face, shadowing his features. With a gentle nudge of his heels, he started the long ride back to Rome.

Byron, James, and Father Villhardain stood silently watching the coach and rider pass down the road and out of sight. When they were gone, Father Villhardain asked, "When do we sail?"

"It is undecided," James said. "The captain said the winds are not favorable."

"We are now at the mercy of God," the priest said.

"No," James grumbled, "we are at the mercy of the weather, but it would be nice if God would step in and help out."

The wind changed on the seventh day. Byron stepped on the deck and took a long look at the land. Father Villhardain was at the gangplank making sure that all of the men were accounted for. Byron was standing next to James at the bow as the sails filled with wind. He was looking forward at the murky future. What awaited them he could not tell. He glanced around at the men standing on the deck. Did any of them have a feeling of presentiment, or was this just another passing day with no special significance? He looked down and watched the foaming water pass by as the ship knifed through the waves, cutting its path through the deep blue sea. He wondered if a man felt a tug on his soul when the Fates cut the string, ending his life, or did death reach down with no warning, taking a man unawares.

VonDurenberg disturbed this moment of reflection. Out of the corner of his eye, Byron could see the graf approaching. VonDurenberg's head was up and his shoulders were back. He was almost strutting. Next to VonDurenberg, walked the lanky squire with black hair.

"This is my squire, Peter Speer. He is my nephew. I will send him on errands from time to time, and I expect you to extend to him courtesy."

"My lord graf, I assure you we will treat him with the same courtesy and respect that we extend to you," James said.

"See that you do," VonDurenberg growled as he turned and walked off. Speer did not move or say a word, but just stared with an odd grin on his face as he scanned the handsome knight in front of him. Speer gave a knowing smirk and then turned to follow his uncle to the stern of the ship.

James cocked his head to one side as he watched the squire

walk away. "That was odd?"

"Indeed, but what did you expect? That he had somehow grown in intelligence since our last meeting."

James shrugged and turned away.

Captain Borgesse was right. The sea was rough. After several miserable weeks of sailing in rough weather, there was a shout from the mast. Alexandretta had been sighted. Byron was overjoyed. The wretched voyage had finally ended. A certain amount of excitement crept into his mind, only to be dashed by the thought of the work that was about to begin. He knew the hardships. Days spent in the saddle, riding in the heat and the dust, in the land of thirst.

All hardships paled though when he thought of Aleppo. He could envision the great gaping gates of steel waiting like teeth to shut behind him, trapping him forever in the belly of the beast. Aleppo, the Saracen prison, the place of dread where all Christians feared internment should they fall into enemy hands. A Temple Grandmaster had died a prisoner of Aleppo when he vainly refused to be exchanged for a Saracen prisoner, boasting that no Saracen was his equivalent. Other young men, of less fame, whose adventures had reached an unfortunate end, had found themselves imprisoned in the great Saracen fortress waiting in vain for a ransom that would never be paid. Most of these unfortunates, sold as slaves to Saracens, would be worked to death. Their masters not caring to spend the money to keep them alive.

It was a future he did not like to dwell on, because it was unpleasant and it was a very possible real ending. A better ending to his story, one that he liked, was to be rewarded by the Church for his role in saving Jerusalem, settling down with a beautiful young woman, raising children, and growing old in his own manor house.

Aleppo: living in a dark cell, fighting for food, overworked and dying in the hot sun from exposure. He refused to accept the fact that his current course made the nightmare very possible. Each time he cracked the door open to the future and peeked in at the very real possibility that this disaster could happen, he recoiled from the thought and slammed the door shut, not liking what he saw. It just could not happen. He would not let it happen. He would die fighting in front of the gates before he would ever succumb to being a captive of Aleppo.

CHAPTER 36
THE LOSS OF A GOOD SERVANT

Jabbar sat working at his desk, desperately trying to keep his business empire intact. It had been a week since his servants had brought news that Salah-al-Din had taken Acre. As the days passed, bad news became worse news. His warehouse had been sacked. The loss of his warehouses at Acre had been a blow, but Salah-al-Din's war had driven his Christian customers away. No Christians. No income. The only Christians left, were refugees who possessed only the clothes on their backs.

In desperation, he had stopped all imports of silk and spice and was now working feverishly to supply the armies with the materiel of war. He was composing instructions to his buyers to purchase food, spears, arrows and other expendable weapons of war now in demand by the soldiers engaged in the struggle for the Kingdom of Jerusalem.

He heard someone enter the room. Watching his life's work disappear was taking its toll, and he was in no mood to be interrupted by one of his servants. Without looking up, he said irritably, "I am busy! Get out! Whatever it is, it can wait!"

Footsteps came closer and with a thud, something dropped on his desk. Blood seeped over his letter. Jabbar looked up at the severed head of his steward.

"Jabbar," Ishaq said coldly.

"Ishaq," Jabbar stuttered and pushed away from his desk. "I had not heard that you had returned to Tyre."

"Hmm. So, it seems. Your servant told me I was no longer welcome in your house. He seemed to believe you had instructed him not to let me in."

"I would never do such a thing," squeaked Jabbar.

Ishaq smiled as he leaned forward. "I know. And I know you would not want such a disobedient servant."

Jabbar looked at the face of his trusted steward. The man's eyes were rolled back in his head and the bloody stump of the neck continued to ooze blood over his expensive teak desk. Jabbar opened his mouth to reply, but Ishaq continued, "Do not worry, my friend. There will be no demand for compensation for ridding you of a disloyal servant." Ishaq motioned to the head. "Consider this a gift."

"Th...th...thank you, my friend," Jabbar said, shaking. "I...I...I don't know w...w...where he would have gotten such an idea to keep my old friend out of my house. I h...h...humbly apologize for his behavior."

Ishaq's eyes glittered as he smirked. "No need to thank me. Now down to business. I would like to introduce my lieutenant, Bashshar."

Jabbar had not noticed the burly man with a sour look standing behind Ishaq. Bashshar gave a short bow but said nothing.

"I need a favor Jabbar," Ishaq continued. "I need a caravan of camels for the next several weeks."

"I can't do that," Jabbar stammered. "Salah-al-Din has seized most of my caravans. He is using them to supply his army. I only have one caravan that is still mine, but it is in Alexandretta. I am in the process," he said, looking down at the letter now covered with blood, "of putting a shipment together."

"Excellent," Ishaq said enthusiastically. "I will take it. I am sure you don't have any objections to me using your animals do you."

Damn! Jabbar thought and not meaning to, he pushed himself even further away from his desk. He had hoped Ishaq would be disappointed to learn his only caravan was too far away and would drop the request.

"I...I... I don't care," Jabbar said in resignation.

"That is good. Don't you think so Bashshar?"

Bashshar stepped forward. "It is good, considering the recent misunderstanding."

Ishaq nodded. "That is true. I knew my old friend would not treat me in such a manner. It is clear the servant was disloyal to his master, and now Jabbar has made amends by allowing us the use of one of his caravans." Jabbar could see it was in his interest to go along with the charade in hope that Ishaq would not take anything else. "Draft a letter to your overseer, and tell him to expect me. Tell him that he is working for me."

Jabbar sat stunned. He was so thoroughly frightened he could not hear Ishaq's instructions. "Do it now!" Ishaq shouted.

Jabbar fumbled for his papers and ink. He stood up, moved to another table, and wiping the blood from his hands, began writing. When he was done, Jabbar sealed it with his mark.

Ishaq picked up the letter. "I will deliver this myself. I would not want it to be lost or misplaced." Jabbar looked down at his desk. Ishaq smiled. "You shall see me one last time when this is over, and then we will be done for good." He turned and left the room.

Ishaq meandered through Jabbar's house, taking his time. Spying several small knick-knacks he knew Jabbar prized as having great value. Each time he found an item he knew Jabbar would miss greatly, he picked it up. Satisfied with his choices, he walked out of the house, past the headless corpse, and down into the street where he came across several urchins playing in the street.

"Why are you not home where you belong?" the assassin demanded.

"What does it matter to you?" the oldest boy snarled.

Ishaq laughed. "I like that. But come now, I asked you a question."

The boy stuck out his chin in defiance. "This is our home."

"Come here and take these," Ishaq said, as he held out the looted treasures from Jabbar's house. "This is not a gift, it's a test. Get as much as you can for them."

The boy's eyes were wide and shining as he took the gift. The other boys quickly gathered around as each took one of the looted treasures from Jabbar's house and quickly stuffed them under their ragged clothes.

"I am Ishaq of Tyre. I am going to be gone, but when I return, I will find you. When we meet again, tell me what you did with my gift. If you were wise, I might have a job for you."

The small boy with a runny nose looked up at Ishaq. "You would give us a job?"

Ishaq smiled. "I only give jobs to those who are tough, smart, and loyal. I have no use for fools. Pass this test, and I will find a place for you."

"I will pass your test," the small boy said, and he hurried off with his comrades to find a place where he could sit and examine his gift.

"Boss," Bashshar said, shaking his head, "I will never understand you."

Ishaq scoffed, "That's because I am always thinking of the future."

They walked down the shadowed streets of the city. Windows were shut and doors closed as the inhabitants went indoors from another day's toil, eking out an existence that provided sustenance, but nothing more. As the blue shadows lengthened, Bashshar and Ishaq swiftly made their way down the empty street. At last, they came to a side gate in the city's wall, guarded by two Christian soldiers. Bashshar took the lead as they approached. He walked up to one of the men and handed him a bag of gold.

"Damn your eyes, infidel, and be quick," the soldier growled in a harsh whisper as he opened the gate partway and motioned for Ishaq and Bashshar to pass through.

Once they were outside the walls of the city, Bashshar led the way while Ishaq followed behind. They walked quickly to a bend in the wall where the shadows were darkest. Bashshar slipped into the concealing gloom and motioned to a man holding two horses next to the city wall. The man led the horses to Bashshar who handed the man a small leather sack of gold coins. The man nodded, then turned and slipped away into the shadows.

Bashshar waited for the man to disappear from sight and then mounted his new horse.

Ishaq put his foot into the stirrup and swung into the saddle. "To Alexandretta then." Bashshar nodded. Both men rode casually from the city. Ishaq anxiously listened for a cry of alarm that horsemen were near the city. The only sound he heard was the music of the crickets as they played their ancient song in the cool night air.

Once Ishaq was sure they were beyond the sight of the city's guard, he kicked the horse into a gallop. Riding swiftly, the lights of Tyre disappeared from sight. Time was short, and Alexandretta was a long way from Tyre. Ishaq needed to get to Alexandretta before Father Villhardain's ship arrived. Bashshar had fresh horses waiting ahead. His men would begin following him on the next day.

Worry filled his mind. He had lost his most experienced men. He hoped his replacements would do as well. He hoped Bashshar had chosen well. It was too bad he had to start such an important enterprise with men new to the business, but that was the way it was, and nothing was going to change it.

Ishaq pushed the thought from his mind and leaned forward, urging the horse to keep up the pace. He had a long way to go and already he was tired.

CHAPTER 37
ALEXANDRETTA

The sails on the *La Seynte Grace* were shortened as the ship entered the bay of Alexandretta. Father Villhardain called all the knights below deck.

"It is time," the priest said. "Rid yourself of anything that identifies you as a Christian Knight. Captain Borgesse has assured me that all your things will be safe."

Each man slowly began to change clothes, exchanging the garments of the cold north to the light cotton clothing fashionable in the Levant. Byron slipped on a cotton shirt and a light tan tunic. On his head, he bound, with two black rings, a blue and white checkered ghutra that hung down to his shoulders. Byron took out his dagger and then unbuckled his sword belt. He grasped the hilt of his sword and looked at it. The black sheath, worn from miles on horseback, was polished brown in places. He admired the hilt, its broad straight hand guards of steel nicked and gouged from battle. The sword made of Spanish steel had been an expensive gift from his father. It was the only tangible thing that reminded him of home. He thought of the day that his father had given it to him.

†

The sky had been grey, and he was standing on the dock waiting to board the ship that would take him to France. Water lapped against the shore, and a heavy mist blurred the nearby group of knights marked with the cross. He was alone, looking out at the water when out of the corner of his eye, he saw his father and his older brothers. To his surprise, he saw that Isabella de Clare, wearing a somber black dress, was with them. About her neck, she wore a yellow silk scarf that added a splash of color in the dreariness of the grey fog. Isabella came up and embraced him, giving him a kiss on the cheek. His older brothers stood back solemnly as he and Isabella said goodbye. Byron looked into her eyes to see if any feelings of love remained, but to his sadness, he saw only pity. Isabella stepped back as his brother placed into her hands a wooden box. She held the box out in front of her. "A gift for you to remember the lady Isabella by, and to keep you safe."

Byron leaned forward and whispered in her ear. "Come with me. We can sail to the Levant where we can live together, far away from the authority of the king."

Isabella shook her head as her eyes softened, glistening with tears. "You know I cannot. The king has betrothed me to William Marshal. He is a good man." She pushed the box forward, and he reached out and took it. Isabella brushed a lock of his dark hair from his face. "I wish you well, Byron. May God keep you in his care." She then took the yellow silk scarf from around her neck and draped it over his shoulders. Before Byron could say anything, Isabella bowed her head and walked away.

Byron watched her go. He wanted to rush forward and ask her to reconsider, but he knew it would be in vain. He opened the box and looked down. Inside was a double-edged dagger with a black sheath. He took the dagger from the box and held it up in front of him. After a moment of looking at it, he shoved it into his belt. He would have time later to examine the dagger. Each of his brothers stepped forward and took his hand, wishing him Godspeed. It was the last time he would ever see any of them. At last, his father stood before him. The baron embraced his son and then motioned to his squire, carrying an odd shaped bundle, to approach.

A strained smile crossed Baron Fitzwalter's face and in a husky voice, he spoke, "My son, we fought the oath breaker at Hastings. We conquered Ireland for Henry's son, John. We endured the reign of King Stephen, and we have prospered under the rule of Matilda's son, Henry, but we have always faithfully served our king. You now journey far beyond my aid, beyond the aid of your brothers, only God can protect you. I can do nothing, except give you this." The baron motioned again, and the servant unwrapped a sword.

"The Gaelic Irish speak of luck, but I know no such thing. A man stands on his own, makes his decisions, and lives with consequences. I have had this sword made for you." The Baron drew the sword. "Wield this brand with honor, and when the enemies of our Lord are no more, return home, and sit next to me at my table and tell me how you bore yourself in battle."

✝

In the fetid heat of the dim hold of the ship, Byron looked at the sword for a long moment. He wrapped the weapon with reverence in rags and placed it in the wooden box along with his clothes. He was about to take off the gold cross Archbishop Joscius had given him, and then impulsively decided to keep the crucifix. No one would ever know he had it, so he buried the golden symbol deep under the layers of cotton clothing. Only when he was dead, would they find out he had kept it. And under those circumstances, what would he care.

Two sailors brought a crate up from the hold and pried the lid open. Father Villhardain walked over to the crate and lifted up a gold hilted shamshir. "Sir Martel, here is a weapon worthy of a prince."

James walked over and took the shamshir from the priest. He was wearing a steal helmet bound with a white turban that fell down over his neck. A long black silk tunic laced with intertwining gold thread hung down to his knees. James nodded to the priest. "I will bear the sword with honor."

Father Villhardain lifted another shamshir from the crate. It was plain with a steel hilt guard. "Sir Fitzwalter, a sword worthy of an overseer." Byron nodded, took the sword, and buckled it to his belt.

When the shamshir's were passed out, Father Villhardain turned to the rest of the men. "Your weapons will be with the camels. You are Christian slaves. Should it come to a fight, then you will be armed, but these swords will only delay your death. We are in the land of the enemy, beyond aid. Your best protection will be to convince those who see us that we are silk merchants." De Montgris muttered a curse under his breath.

"For God's sake," De Courcy cried. "You are not going to have us walk among the Saracen devils unarmed?"

Father Villhardain looked at De Courcy. "Have courage, my lord. God will not forget us. Did he not deliver Daniel from a den of lions?"

"Christ! This is not a den of lions! You have never been to that hell hole, Aleppo!" De Courcy shouted back.

James leaned over to Father Villhardain and whispered in his ear, "Father, give the poor man a dagger. He was just ransomed from the Saracens."

Father Villhardain nodded. "Perhaps you are right."

James stepped over to De Courcy and handed him a dagger. "Keep this out of sight."

De Courcy reached out his trembling hand and took the dagger. "You are very kind, my lord." De Courcy took the dagger and held it in his hand, gripping the weapon tight.

Once the transformation was complete, Father Villhardain spoke again, "His Holiness has granted absolution to each of you for your sins, or any sins that may occur in the service of the Church. The same conditions granted to the crusaders who now fight to save Jerusalem." There was a murmur of approval from the men. "Once we've docked, I will go ashore with Fitzwalter and Martel," the priest said. "Saladin has many spies, so use care if you go up on deck."

VonDurenberg stood up. "What if you do not return? Do you

think it wise for you to leave with so little protection? If something happens to you, all is lost."

Father Villhardain paused. "I trust in God. If it is God's will that I die today, then none of you can change that. Be comforted. If I do not return, then you only need to sail for home."

"You make light of your safety, Father Villhardain," VonDurenberg replied as De Vale and Montgris rose up to stand next to the graf. "I am in charge of military matters. This is not about you or your relationship with God. There are lives at stake."

"Father Villhardain's life is safe with us," James replied.

"That brings me no comfort, My Lord Martel," VonDurenberg snapped.

"We are in Christian lands. Three men will draw less attention than a large group of knights surrounding a priest as he walks the streets of Alexandretta," Byron said.

VonDurenberg eyed Byron for a moment. "And if we all leave at once, then there is no doubt in the priest's safety."

Byron rested his hand on his shamshir as he squared off with the graf. "And if we all go together, we attract attention."

"Fitzwalter is right," Father Villhardain said, waving his hands to end the discussion. "Martel and Fitzwalter have been in the Holy Lands. None of the rest of you have ever been here, and I do not want to attract the attention of the sultan's spies. You will wait here for my return."

"I am a graf and I insist on going," VonDurenberg snarled.

Father Villhardain sighed. "My son, you will wait here. I promise, I shall return." Without waiting for an answer, Father Villhardain went up the stairs to the upper deck. VonDurenberg glared at Byron who brushed passed the graf and jogged up the steps after the priest.

James followed Byron up the stairs; he felt something grab his boot. He glanced down to see Speer hiding in the shadows of the stairway. The boards of the steps cast dark lines across the squire's face. "Get out from there," James said as he kicked Speer's hand free from his boot. "Fool of a squire," James grumbled. Speer continued to sit in the shadow of the stairs: not saying a word, watching every step James took, his face twisted in an odd evil grin.

Father Villhardain and Byron waited for James on the dock in the hot afternoon sun. The only relief was the cool breeze that occasionally blew across the waters. James missed the heat of the desert, he was home and it felt good to be back.

✝

Ishaq had spent the last few days at the same shoreline funduq, waiting for the Christians to arrive. Crusader castles glowered down at him, watchful for any approach of the armies of Salah-al-Din. He did not feel particularly comfortable, and he kept a watchful eye on anyone he perceived might approach him and ask what he was doing. No one did, no one heeded him at all.

Ishaq sat drinking his usual qahwa while Bashshar sat across from him, slowly gazing around the streets. A ship with a weathered hull of grey planks was entering the harbor and caught Ishaq's eye. He set down his cup as he looked intently at the brown stained sails. He could hear the captain of the ship shouting orders in Italian.

Ishaq leaned forward. "Bashshar, I believe it is time to go." Standing up, Ishaq began walking towards the harbor, pushing his way through the crowd.

"What does this priest look like?" Bashshar asked.

"The man is tall, has grey hair. I met him at the Lateran, but I never spoke to him."

Swarms of men were unloading cargos of amphora, filled with oils, or moving heavy crates. Ishaq threaded his way through the crowd. He caught sight of the ship tied to the dock. Ishaq picked up the pace. A tall man with short grey hair was walking away from him. Unsure if it was the priest, he decided to shout, "Padre... Padre!"

Father Villhardain heard someone shouting "Padre". He

stopped and turned. He was about to turn away when he heard a voice shout again "Padre!"

This time he saw Don Fuego, in a white tunic with a white ghutra on his head.

"Don Fuego," Father Villhardain cried. "I pray you have not been waiting long."

"Two days," Ishaq said.

"I trust that all is ready?" asked the priest.

Ishaq nodded. "Yes, we have been waiting for you to arrive." Ishaq paused as he eyed the priest, whose face was a sickly grey hue. "Are you sure you do not want to rest after such a long journey? Perhaps you should stay a day or two in this jewel of the Mediterranean?"

"No," the priest muttered. "I want to get underway as soon as possible. I plan to move my men out of the city in two groups today."

"I understand Padre," Ishaq said, looking at James and Byron. "Moving your men in small groups is very wise. Padre who are these worthy men that are with you," Ishaq said, pointing to James and Byron.

"Don Fuego, this is Sir Byron Fitzwalter and Sir James Martel."

"Knights!" Ishaq exclaimed, smiling as he bowed. "How fortunate we are to have fighting men. Sir Byron, is this your first time in the Holy Lands?"

"No," Byron replied, "I am returning."

"Oh, Sir Byron, it must be wonderful to be home then. And you, Sir James, is this your first visit? Are you planning to go on a pilgrimage?"

"No," James replied, "I was born here."

"Then let me welcome you home. I have procured several fine horses for you to ride. Pride of the Saracens. Their pedigrees are long and distinguished."

"Excellent," James said. "Have you any news of the war?"

Ishaq frowned. "Rumors mostly. I have heard Ascalon and Acre have fallen. It is said the Christians are desperately short of men to defend the walls of Jerusalem."

"Has any Christian Lord formed an army to march to the city's defense?" Byron asked.

"I have not heard anything of that sort, Sir Byron," Ishaq replied.

Father Villhardain spoke abruptly. "We should go. We can talk of rumors on the way. Where is your caravan?"

Ishaq smiled. "Not far, Padre."

Father Villhardain sighed as he looked around at the pleasant city, the sun and the sand. He wanted to rest, but a feeling clung to him that he needed to hurry.

Ishaq led them through the crowded streets, pushing his way through the press of men buying and selling until he reached the outskirts of town where a large caravan of camels were bedded down. Several men were tending the animals which had yet to be loaded with the provisions they would need for the journey. As Ishaq approached, Bashshar clapped his hands and began shouting orders to the men. The drivers stopped what they were doing and began scurrying around, packing their gear.

Father Villhardain turned to Byron and James as they stood watching the men pack. "Can you find your way back to the ship?" James nodded. "Then return to the ship. Bring the men and their equipment, and meet me here. I plan to leave as soon as everyone is assembled and the animals are ready to go."

James and Byron walked back through the streets of Alexandretta, dodging the gauntlet of merchants trying to entice them into their shops. Here and there, crusaders moved among the crowds, eyeing the Arabs with suspicion.

"What do think of the Don?" Byron asked James.

"I am unsure," James replied as he looked around. "I would like to stay here for a few days, but alas it is not to be."

Byron and James reached the ship. The deck was crowded with sailors unloading cargo from the *La Seynte Grace*. Below deck, they found VonDurenberg waiting. "Where is the priest?" the graf demanded.

"He is with the Spanish Don," James said.

VonDurenberg's face turned red. "You left him unguarded?"

"The priest is safe," James snapped. "If I thought he was in danger, I would not have left him."

"I knew I should have gone. This quest will come to naught if something happens to the priest."

"Yes!" James said. "But someone has to guide you back." James looked around. "I want ten men who are ready to go."

Giodonni stepped forward, several other knights gathered around. "Bring your possessions," James said, "and follow me."

"I will go as well," VonDurenberg said. "Peter come." VonDurenberg's squire appeared, lugging his uncle's possessions.

James started to ascend the stairs. "If any man gets lost, you are on your own. I will not look for you."

Once James was gone, Byron waited for half an hour. As his men assembled on deck with their baggage, Captain Borgesse came up to him and put his hand on his shoulder. "May the wind be at your back, my lord. I will look for your return in a month."

"And you will be a welcome sight. The voyage home will not look so bad after a month in the desert living with camels."

Captain Borgesse smiled. "Most assuredly."

Byron took one last look at the ship then walked down the gangplank and onto the dock. Before he left, he gathered his men together. "Stay with me," he said in a low voice. Memories of the attack in Tyre came back, and he kept a sharp eye out for anything or anyone out of place. After some time, he found himself outside the city walls.

James and Father Villhardain were waiting for him. Several men were already starting to grumble when they found out they would not be on horseback.

The Arab drivers stood watching, talking among themselves. Byron watched them out of the corner of his eye. This was going to be a hard journey, and it would be harder still with a group of men who had no loyalty to each other. Byron hoped that once they started on the road, some semblance of a bond would form. Byron's men dropped their gear. The Arab drivers gathered to collect it. De Courcy stood, his red eyes fixed on the Arabs as he gripped the dagger in his belt. Byron was watching the drivers pack the camels when he saw Bashshar walking towards him, leading a bay Arab horse with white socks.

"For you," he said in an unfriendly voice as he handed Byron the reins. Bashshar turned and walked away before Byron could give his thanks.

Byron stood looking at the horse. He had never cared for Arab horses, but they were as tough as the land that bred them and it was better than walking. If he could have his wish, he would rather ride the big chestnut he had left in Tyre. In his business, where the horse made up fifty percent of the partnership, it could mean the difference between life and death.

He looked into the horse's large brown eyes. The horse looked back at him. It pleased him that his new horse had a kind eye, and it gave the knight a favorable impression. He would have to gain his new mount's trust. He reached out his hand and stroked the horse's white blaze. "I shall call you Enam, or... if you prefer Frankish, the Gift." The horse put its ears forward. "I knew you would like the name," Byron said as he pet the horse. He hoped his new partner would serve him well, and that whoever had trained this horse had done a good job. He did not want to spend his journey trying to retrain the horse to unlearn bad habits.

He checked the saddles cinch. It was tight. Putting the reins over the horse's neck, he stood next to the shoulder as he turned the stirrup towards him. Grasping a tuft of mane near the withers, he put his foot in the stirrup and swung into the saddle. He sat still for a moment waiting to see what the horse would do. The horse stood waiting. Satisfied that the horse would not buck, he gently nudged the horse forward with his leg. The horse started to walk and Byron smiled. His new friend might work out after all.

"Where are we going?" Ishaq asked.

"We journey to Aleppo," the priest muttered. "Then south to the Euphrates. I think that should be enough information for now. I will tell you the rest once we get a little further from Alexandretta and spies."

"Aleppo?" Ishaq exclaimed. "Are you sure you want to go there? I have heard Aleppo is a dangerous place for Christians."

"That path has been chosen. With God's blessing, we will make it past. If we do not, then I shudder to think of our fate."

"You know best, Padre," Ishaq said, shaking his head. He had to give credit to the Christians for their courage. When the first crusaders took Jerusalem, it had been against impossible odds. Wiser men would not have attempted it, and yet, almost on faith alone they had conquered the city. This attempt to ride straight to the fortress of Salah-al-Din was foolhardy. Yet, he wondered if the Christians, in their audacity, might not pull it off. He had been to Aleppo when he had been with Nizari Ismaili. He had killed an enemy of the old man in the streets. It had been difficult to escape, but he had done it. As he looked at the priest and the Christian knights, he doubted if they would be as fortunate. If the Christians failed, he could plead ignorance to their identity. Perhaps the authorities would only think that he was nothing more than a fool and let him go.

Ishaq pushed the thought out of his mind as he stood up in his stirrups, raised his hand, and cried, "Up." The camels rose and began to move down the dusty road. Ishaq rode in the lead with Father Villhardain, followed by Byron and James as the rest slowly found a place in the dusty line.

The landscape slowly passed by. The road rose steadily up from sea level into the rugged hills that formed a border to the city. It was rough and slow going as they paused frequently to let the animals rest. Byron enjoyed the beauty of the land, the mountains crowned with trees that rose up to touch the sky. Slowly, they made their way south. The heat was punishing as they moved across the land. Byron could feel the heat as it radiated upwards from the dry earth, covered with grass and scrub brush.

Byron's knees were beginning to ache, and he found himself taking his left foot out of the stirrup. He had not fully recovered from his injuries. His left ankle still had an evil dark bruise from being crushed by his horse at Hattin.

"I have been watching this Spanish Don," James whispered to Byron as they rode together.

"And?"

"It is almost as if I have seen him before."

"Hmm, it is just your imagination."

James shrugged. "Agreed, but for some reason I have this feeling."

It was late in the day when they came to a halt and moved off the road to a small clearing. The camels were unpacked, and the horses were unsaddled and tied to a high line. Byron wiped the dust from his face and strolled off to stretch his legs. He looked at the few trees that surrounded him as the dust rose with each step. Byron leaned against a tree, watching the setting sun sink out of sight. When he returned, he found the men gathered around in small groups eating dried meat and dried fruit. Byron sat down next to James who tossed him a haversack. Byron was rummaging in the haversack for something to eat when he heard Narvez ask to join them. He looked up as the Spanish knight sat down and crossed his legs.

"I hear that you crusaded in Spain," James said.

"True," Narvez answered. "The reconqista against the Almohad Empire has been an ongoing war. My Order of Alcantara has been heavily involved in the bloody fight to rid Spain of the Moors."

"It has been a long struggle," James replied. "My ancestor, Charles the Hammer, defeated the Saracens at Tours. It was through his bravery that France was kept free from the Saracen scourge."

Narvez tilted his head to look at James. "Charles Martel was a great man. You must be honored to have such a great ancestor."

James frowned. "It is an honor and a curse."

Narvez nodded. "The expectations of others can be a burden. As far as Spain, we are winning, and we are pushing them back but at a cost." The Spaniard pointed to the savage scar on his face. Narvez looked up as Simon De Courcy came and sat down next him. De Courcy did not speak, but sat staring at the fire, his grey locks hanging down hiding his face.

Byron watched De Courcy for a moment. "What of your story, my lord?"

De Courcy looked up from the flames and shook his mangy hair. "My story? Hmm. My story. Six years I was a captive of the Saracens."

"And how did you come to be captured," Narvez asked.

De Courcy scoffed, "I went on a raid with Chatillon. Deep into Saladin's lands we rode, riding the road to Damascus as far as Tabuk, but alas my horse grew lame and I was left behind. My Christian friends left me." De Courcy looked back into the red flames. "On the road, I wandered lost in the desert, left to die. God how I wished I had died. The Saracens found me and stripped me of my armor. They took my horse, my honor. They took everything and then threw me in Aleppo." De Courcy's jaw hardened as he clenched his fists. "Aleppo is hell on earth." De Courcy sighed. "Six years I waited, sending letters to my family. I had given up hope, and then one day, my ransom was paid and I was released. I left the Levant. I vowed never to return, and I sailed for Rome. I was going to return to France when I met De Montgris who told me of this quest. It was as if God had given me a chance to strike back." De Courcy laughed. "I seized it, and now I shall have my revenge on the Saracen swine."

De Courcy finished speaking as Father Villhardain came to the edge of the firelight. The priest paused and placed his hand on De Courcy's shoulder. "My son, you have suffered. We spoke of this." De Courcy nodded. "I brought you so that you could find redemption on this journey. That you could see your efforts help our cause. Do not hinder the greater good that you could do with small acts of revenge."

De Courcy stared into the flames but did not say a word. The priest patted De Courcy on the shoulder. "Aleppo is in the future. Tomorrow will bring its own troubles."

"Is there a concern?" James asked.

"Yes. In the next day or so, we will pass through the Syrian Gate. It is the only pass through the Nur Mountains. The pass is narrow, and I fear an attack by bandits, or worse."

"And what do you consider to be worse?" Byron demanded.

"Templars," the priest said. "Bakras Kalesi, the Castle of Gaston, guards the mountain passes from Antioch to Alexandretta. No one can use the mountain road without passing the fortress."

James frowned. "The caravan will draw their attention."

"Yes," the priest said. "But God willing, the war has drawn the Templars away."

"Or made them more watchful," Byron added.

The next day the expedition slowly labored on the mountain road, the Syrian Gate drawing closer. Byron was watchful as they neared the narrow choke point, listening intently for any warning of a sudden attack. Quietly, he drew his shamshir and rested it on the pommel of the saddle, ready and alert as the rock walls closed in. He half expected to see Templars, their white surcoats emblazoned with a red cross, blocking the way, but the pass was empty. Nothing appeared to oppose them as the men guided the column of camels and horses between the narrow pass. The Templars were away, busy with cares far larger than a caravan of silk traders and their camels. Saladin had struck fear into the region, and all Christian efforts were now bent on self-preservation.

Byron breathed a sigh of relief as the Syrian Gate receded behind him. In the distance, he could make out the great castle built upon the hillside, looking down from its commanding height. Beau seant, the black and white banner of the Templars, floated above the top-most tower. No challenge came as they passed by the great fortress, and he could envision the Templars scurrying about, doubling and tripling their efforts to make their fortress ready for the coming storm.

The men settled into a steady routine as the week and the miles passed. The land changed as they descended from the mountains down into the plains. The trees gave way to grassland. The sparse grass was brown and dried. It had been a long time since water had touched the land, and as they went south, the earth became more barren and desolate.

The road was empty. It was evident the war was taking its toll on trade. The normal caravan traffic that brought silk from the Far East was nonexistent. No dust from the long lines of camels disturbed the horizon. It was evident from the roadway that it had been some time since anyone had traveled this route. The hot winds swept the empty lands, making Byron apprehensive as it whispered to him that things were wrong. Inwardly, while he heeded the warning, he was powerless to do anything about it.

That evening, as James and Byron sat eating their meal, Father Villhardain sat down to join them. When they had finished eating, Byron stood up and retrieved the pages of the book from his saddlebags. Sitting next to the priest, he untied the red leather thong and unrolled the pages. In the failing light, he started to read aloud quietly. Montgris gave Byron a dark look as he walked by, but Byron ignored him as he concentrated on sounding out each word. He was getting better, and the story started to flow. Byron could see that James, sitting across from him, was even listening to the tale of Odysseus. At last, it grew too dark to see the letters on the pages and he stopped.

"Your reading has improved." Father Villhardain smiled as he motioned to James to move closer. James came over and sat down across from the priest.

"We are near Aleppo," Father Villhardain said. "By tomorrow, we will be at the city gates and by the time the sun sets, Aleppo will be nothing more than a memory. Do you still want to carry out your plan?"

James picked up a stick and began to draw in the sand. After a moment of doodling, he answered. "I think the plan is good. It will catch the Saracens off guard. If we try to slip by, it will raise suspicions. What do you think Fitzwalter?"

"I would rather pass on the whole venture," Byron grumbled. "But since it was my idea, I guess I should see it through."

"I will gather the men together," the priest said as he stood up. "I want to go over the plan so everyone understands what is at stake."

James and Byron stood up as Father Villhardain gathered the Christians together. Byron saw Don Fuego join the assembly and watched him take a seat next to the priest to listen. The priest sat on a rock in the middle of the group as he told the men of the plan to pass Aleppo.

"As the military leader of the group, I demand to go with Fitzwalter and Martel," VonDurenberg said.

A look of surprise crossed Father Villhardain's face.

"Absolutely not!" Byron cried.

VonDurenberg frowned. "I will go. I do not trust either of you. You left the priest unguarded in Alexandretta." VonDurenberg pointed at Father Villhardain. "If anything happens to this man, this journey is over."

"Father Villhardain was in the protection of Don Fuego," Byron replied.

The German threw back his head and started to laugh. "The protection of Don Fuego! Surely you jest."

Ishaq looked at the German. His eyes glinted with malice, but the assassin did not speak.

"I am going," VonDurenberg said with finality. "My feudal rank says so."

"If you go," James interjected, "you go as a slave."

"How dare you make such a suggestion," VonDurenberg yelled. "I will go as a prince and remain silent."

The priest frowned. "If you go, you must go as a slave. It is too great a risk. Someone might ask you a question."

"I refuse to be a slave," VonDurenberg said. "I am a graf and I will be treated as such."

"No," James cried furiously placing his hand on the hilt of his sword. "This trip is not your personal pilgrimage to the Holy Lands. Either you go as a slave, or you do not go at all!"

VonDurenberg snapped, "Then it must be. I will make this sacrifice for the good of our men who have bravely and selflessly volunteered to serve the Church. I have no trust in either of you. I will go just to make sure you don't betray us."

Byron took instant offense and was about to reply angrily when James exclaimed, "Be ready then! We leave ere the sun rises."

"Do not go to Aleppo," De Courcy whispered. "Do not go to Aleppo. Only death waits for you there. Cold, hunger. Even the rats fear Aleppo, for they are a great prize, if you are fortunate enough to catch one and eat it." De Courcy started to weep.

Speer began walking around the circle of men, throwing dust in the air. He stopped in front of James and gave him a leering grin.

"Enough!" James thundered. "Our road takes us to Aleppo. We either go or we turn back now."

Speer began to cackle insanely. "Peter!" VonDurenberg shouted. "Come. Leave the Frankish lord in peace." Speer looked at VonDurenberg as if he was weighing the consequences of disobedience, but then shuffled over to his master.

"I will see you in the morning!" VonDurenberg snapped as he left the circle of men with his squire in tow.

Father Villhardain, a little unnerved by what had just happened, turned to Ishaq. "Don Fuego, what of the caravan? How do you intend to pass the city?"

"Bashshar has been to Aleppo," Ishaq replied distractedly as he watched VonDurenberg and Speer disappear into the darkness. Ishaq paused and then turned to face the priest. "The road bypasses the city and there are basins to water the animals. As you can imagine, the Saracens have no desire to have hundreds of camels passing through their city.

"That is well," the priest said. "Go and rest. Tomorrow we will test our fate. If it goes well, we will continue our journey to the great river. If not, we perish and it will not matter." The group slowly got to their feet and walked off.

De Courcy did not move. "Forgive me, Father, but I will not be taken again."

Father Villhardain put his hand on De Courcy's shoulder. "My son, it will not come to that."

"Father, I will not be taken again!" De Courcy snapped as he rose to his feet and walked off.

Byron was still fuming as he and James went back to where they were going to sleep for the night.

"Are you ready to test your fate?" James asked.

"No!" Byron snarled throwing out his bedroll. "It was bad enough when it was just you and me making the attempt. Now we have that idiot German going with us, and we have a knight who is almost unmanned at the mere mention of Aleppo's name. We will be lucky if we are not prisoners of the Saracens by tomorrow."

"Have faith. All will be well," James reassured him. "If VonDurenberg opens his mouth, no one will understand him and De Courcy will bypass the city with the camels." James chuckled. "If anything, De Courcy's demeanor fits perfectly for a slave. He is terrified of his Saracen masters."

Byron furled his brow as he scowled at James, "All will be well."

Byron lay in his bedroll, tossing and turning. He rolled onto his back and looked up at the stars flickering brightly in the night sky. The stars glittered in the sky as the crescent moon rose above the hills to shine down upon him. He looked at the moon and then turned onto his side. The moon must rise he thought. It was nothing more than the normal cycle of the moon. It meant nothing, or did it? Byron finally drifted off to sleep.

He dreamed he was at Hattin, alone in an empty land, walking slowly in the field below the twin hills. He was searching for something, but he could not remember what he was looking for. He saw Rodger Beauvallet ride up, dressed in mail, carrying a spear. He called to his friend, but Rodger did not hear him. Instead, Rodger pulled back on the reins, and the horse came to a stop. Rodger sat still, intently watching something Byron could not see. His horse's ears forward and alert. The horse snorted as it slightly reared and started to back away from an invisible threat. Byron began to shout at the top of his lungs, but Rodger still ignored him as he spurred his shying mount forward.

Putting his spear in rest, Rodger brought his shield up. The horse reared and then turned to flee as an unseen hand threw a spear, hitting Rodger in the back, killing him instantly. Byron watched in horror as his friend rolled from his horse and fell to the ground. Byron tried to run to Rodger's aid, but he could not move his legs. As he struggled, the ground gave way, slowly pulling him into the earth. As the earth slowly swallowed him, the vision was gone, faded to black, and his mind wandered elsewhere.

James woke him early the next morning. It was still dark and there was a chill in the air. Half asleep, he saddled his horse and made his preparations to ride to Aleppo. VonDurenberg had already saddled. Byron mounted his horse stiffly and stretched as he worked out the aches and pains from sleeping on the ground.

Father Villhardain had risen and was standing watching them prepare to ride. He went over to James who was sitting on his horse. "I will take the caravan past the city and we will wait for you on the south side of the city in the olive groves."

James nodded. "Do not fear. God will be with you, my son. All will be well and by the time the sun sets, we will be far from Aleppo."

James smiled. "Father, it will be, but if we fail, would you have the minstrels write a song of the brave crusader knight, James Martel, who fought the Saracen hordes at the gates of Aleppo."

The corner of Father Villhardain's mouth twitched upwards into a slight smile. "My son, if you fail, we all fail. I will most likely not be able to fulfill your request, but maybe God's angels will sing your praise instead."

Byron sat on his horse and thought about the dream from last night. It troubled him to see his deceased friend, whose headless body had concealed Byron from the victorious Saracen soldiers. If the dream had a meaning, he did not understand it. He could only hope that if the dream were a warning, its message would become clear before it was too late.

CHAPTER 38
JAMES AT THE GATES OF ALEPPO

The sun rose above the horizon, its light revealing three horses and their riders traveling on the road to Aleppo. The early morning darkness had concealed the roadway, slowing their progress. As the shades of night retreated to the shadows beneath the rocks and shrubs, the men picked up the pace. The horses moved faster, and the dust from their hooves rose in swirling clouds, irritating the nose and throat of horse and rider, before it returned to the earth from where it came.

On a distant hill, Byron saw the fourteen towers of the Saracen fortress. The heat was beginning to grip the earth, distorting the view. As they neared the stronghold of Saladin, they faintly heard the clear call of a man singing in the Saracen tongue.

"They have seen us," VonDurenberg cried, turning his horse to flee.

"Fool," James said, grabbing VonDurenberg's reins. "It's the call to prayer. Keep going."

The land was flat, burnt, and dry. A few groves of olive trees stood here and there to break the monotonous landscape. The horses slowly closed the distance. Every second dragged by, each man deep in his own thoughts about what awaited them. The great gate of the Saracen fortress drew closer. The road ran along the massive city wall to the archway of the city gate. Recessed into the wall of white stone, the gates to the city were open. Guards in silver mail, with green and black tunics, stood in the shade of the recess blocking the roadway. Byron continued riding alongside the towering battlements where the only Christians who had ever passed had been in chains. Only the lucky few, whose relatives were wealthy enough to pay ransom, had ever returned from Aleppo. The stories passed down solidified its reputation as a place of evil. Byron rode to the gates with the knowledge that if this ruse failed, he would never leave. He glanced at James, who looked back at him with a confident smile and winked.

The Saracen guard called out in challenge as they drew near the gate, demanding they halt and state their business. James rode up to the commander of the Saracen guard and pulled himself to his full height. "I am Prince Hashim," he said arrogantly. "The son of Emir Azahar al Umari. I am bringing my beloved father's caravan back from the infidel city of Antioch, having concluded a sale of silk to the infidel dogs. I am here to pay any road tax the Sultan Salah al-Din may require for the use of his road before we turn south to Baghdad."

The guard eyed James for a moment and then bowed. "My lord, welcome to Aleppo. Once you pass through the gate, continue into the city, go to the citadel, and there you will find the tax collector. He will gladly receive your gift to the Great Sultan."

VonDurenberg, who was just behind James, felt his fear rising. The sense of danger was almost tangible, and as he listened to a language he could not understand, his imagination was racing with dreadful thoughts. Any moment they would all be prisoners. He glanced at the Saracen guard, imagining they were starting to converge on them, hemming them in and preparing to attack.

James was starting to relax. This was almost too easy. He was about to thank the guard for his directions when VonDurenberg, no longer able to suppress his fear, blurted out in a high-pitched voice, "Martel! Run you fool! They're gathering to take us!"

Byron was aghast. Their disguise was blown. He stared in shock at VonDurenberg, who was pulling his horse around in an attempt to flee. The Saracens would know they were spies. Byron reached for his shamshir. James stood in his stirrups and grabbed the headstall of VonDurenberg's horse. Drawing his whip with his free hand James began thrashing the graf unmercifully. "You insolent, infidel dog," he shouted. "You're not going anywhere, nor did I give you permission to speak!"

James leaped from his horse and dragged VonDurenberg from his horse, throwing him to the ground. "Crawl on your belly like the worm you are!" James screamed as he kicked VonDurenberg in his buttocks. "Kiss the feet of these worthy men! Beg them for your undeserved forgiveness! Kiss them!" he yelled in a towering rage.

VonDurenberg groveled in front of the Saracen guard as James continued to whip and kick him. VonDurenberg, realizing his only escape was to comply, kissed the guard's feet. A look of disdain at the infidel groveling in front of him crossed the face of the Saracen soldier, while other soldiers gathered around and began striking VonDurenberg with the butts of their spears as they yelled encouragement to James in his discipline of the insolent and unruly slave. When the beating ended, James grabbed VonDurenberg by the collar of his tunic and pulled him upright. "Back on your horse!" he yelled, looking VonDurenberg in the eye. "One more outburst and I will leave you here!"

"My lord," a Saracen of authority cried, "if you wish to sell this troublesome Christian, I will buy him."

Byron looked at James. The proposition was tempting. Byron could see by the flicker in James' eyes that he also thought the prospect was alluring. VonDurenberg, not understanding a word of the conversation, guessed the meaning. Color drained from the graf's face, his eyes now wide with fear.

Byron looked at VonDurenberg for a moment and sighed. "Your father would be most upset if you sold this infidel," he said, shaking his head.

James stared at Byron for a moment and then turned to the Saracen. "I must confess, while I find your proposal pleasing, my father enjoys this particular slave. For my part," he continued as he eyed VonDurenberg in disgust, "I would sell him, but alas I cannot. I am afraid it would be unwise to return home without this dog of a Christian."

"I understand," the Saracen said with a smile.

James turned to VonDurenberg. "Get back on your horse."

The Saracen raised his eyebrows as VonDurenberg got back on his horse. "You are very generous to let your slave ride."

James scoffed. "No, I am not. I am in haste, and I have no desire to prod along in the heat of the day while the slave walks. I have business in Aleppo, and I need the slave to mind the horses while I tend to my business."

The Saracen bowed. "Yes, lord, I did not mean to offend. It just is unusual for a slave to ride a horse or a prince to accompany a caravan. Does your father not have servants?"

James looked down at the man. "Indeed. No, you are witnessing my father's punishment."

"My lord, your offense must have been very grave to have been given such a punishment."

"Indeed," James said. "Let us pass into the courtyard, and I will tell you my tale."

"The lord wishes to tell us a tale," the Saracen shouted. "I for one want to hear it."

With a look of satisfaction, James rode through the gate of Aleppo and into the courtyard of Saladin. The group of eager listeners crowded around him, and he began regaling them with a story. Byron stood on the outside of the gate, still reeling in shock from all that had just happened. VonDurenberg bowed his head and fell in behind Byron.

One of the guards approached him as he was about to cross through the gate. "Tell me your story," he said, in the manner that servants do when their master is not listening.

"The prince," Byron replied softly, "disobeyed his father. My master finally had enough and so he banned his son to go on this trek to the Far East, and he has been a pain in the ass the entire way."

Byron shot a glance at James, like a servant fearful his master might overhear the criticism. "It has been a long trip, and I am ready to go home and be rid of the prince."

The Saracen guard smiled. "Just remember, my friend, that in paradise your suffering will be rewarded."

"I pray every day that Allah remembers me kindly." Satisfied, the

Saracen returned to his post and Byron turned to VonDurenberg.

"Move, you worthless dog," Byron commanded in broken French, using the tone and style of the Arabs of Jerusalem as they attempted to converse with the Frankish crusaders. "Move or I will accept the offer to sell you." To Byron's satisfaction, VonDurenberg lowered his head and fell in behind him.

Byron entered the courtyard and saw James sitting on his horse surrounded by Saracen soldiers. To Byron's astonishment, James was telling the story of how he had snuck into the bower of a Frankish princess and had his way with her. Unfortunately, her father had been awakened by their lovemaking, had chased James out of his house, almost catching him. In this current version, the daughter was a Saracen beauty and the aggrieved father, an emir of caliph of Persia.

Byron could not believe what he was witnessing. They had just narrowly escaped discovery, and now James, emboldened by his success, was telling the Saracen soldiers this outlandish story. To Byron's amazement, James held the group of Saracen soldiers captive with his tale. Had any of them guessed his identity, they would have dragged him from his horse and killed him on the spot.

At last, the story ended, and James, to the disappointment of his listeners, told them he must take care of his father's business and be on his way. The soldiers returned to their posts, leaving Byron, James, and VonDurenberg alone. James leaned over to VonDurenberg as they rode through the crowded streets filled with merchants. "I told you to stay, but you did not heed me. Now do you understand why speaking the Saracen tongue is important?"

VonDurenberg glared at James. "This is not over. How dare you humiliate me in such a manner?"

"Listen fool. I had to do something. I will not suffer your stupidity again. Next time, I will stab you to death and leave you for the crows." VonDurenberg, covered in blood from his beating, looked away and said nothing.

The streets were crowded with peasants. The smells of raw meat and unwashed bodies filled the air, mingling with the odor of raw sewage thrown in the streets. The smell was overpowering in the fetid heat, and Byron felt sick to his stomach. He could see banners and signs in the graceful Saracen script as he rode down the winding street. The massive citadel was visible. It rose above the rest of the city, its white square cut battlements were set on a massive sloping hill. It made the directions from the guards unnecessary as they made their way to the office of the tax collector.

CHAPTER 39
THE LORD OF ALEPPO

A sixteen-year old boy watched the sunrise from the ramparts. He thanked Allah for the blessings of another day. A white turban covered Malik az-Zahir Ghazi's dark hair; his white robes embroidered with gold. He was thin, a youth of average height, although this year, he had grown several inches. He heard the call to prayer, and turned away from the walls to return to his room to pray. When he finished his prayers, he walked to the great hall of the citadel to receive his morning reports of the condition of the fortress and the city from his Grand Vizier.

Malik az-Zahir Ghazi, the third son of Salah al-Din, governed Aleppo for his father, which was a responsibility he took seriously. Aleppo was an important conquest. The sultan had made several attempts to take Aleppo, and now that it was in his possession, he had no intentions of letting it slip away. This point he had impressed upon his son. The morning sun felt good as it streamed through the windows of the armory. Malik az-Zahir nodded to his Vizier as he sat down. The Grand Vizier stood up, bowed to the sultan's son, and started his report. The Grand Vizier was droning on about the number and the types of weapons cached in armory. Malik az-Zahir had heard this before.

Bored, he looked out the window at the orchard surrounding

the city. To his surprise, he saw a large caravan of camels making its way past the city. Malik az-Zahir held up his hand. "Grand Vizier. I thought the sultan commanded that all caravans of the faithful help support the war effort."

The Grand Vizier paused and raised his eyebrows. "Yes, my prince. The sultan's instructions went out far and wide. Why do you ask?"

"Because I see a caravan approaching the city from the north." The prince rose and walked to the window and stared out at the approaching caravan.

"My prince," a servant replied, "it is probably silk merchants, nothing more."

The prince turned to stare at the servant. "That does not matter. Silk merchants or not, they are returning from Christian lands," Malik az-Zahir snapped. "My father warned me to be on the lookout for something such as this! Find out who they are."

"Send a runner," the Grand Vizier commanded. "Get the name of the man leading the caravan and learn its destination."

"It will be done, as you command," the chief steward said, rising with a bow. He swiftly left the meeting.

As the meeting continued, the chief steward returned and whispered something into the ear of the Grand Vizier.

"What did you learn?" Malik az-Zahir asked.

"My prince, the caravan belongs to Emir Azahar al-Umari," the steward replied. "His son, Prince Hashim, is here in person. According to the commander of the guard, the caravan is returning to Baghdad after trading in Antioch."

Malik az-Zahir sat in silence for a moment. ""Hmm, have any of you ever heard of Emir Azahar al Umari?"

His servants shook their heads.

"I have not heard of him either," the Grand Vizier said.

"How dare the Emir not obey my father's commands? Does the Emir wish to profit while these Christian butchers are murdering our people? Or are they something else?" Malik az-Zahir crossed his arms across his chest. "I want an explanation. Find this Prince Hashim and bring him to the great room."

"It shall be done as you command," the chief steward said,

rising from the meeting. "I will go and send my knights to seek him out."

When the chief steward left, Prince Malik az-Zahir motioned for the Grand Vizier to approach. "I want you to find out the truth. Who are these people?"

The Grand Vizier nodded. "I will not fail you."

Prince Malik az-Zahir's mouth twitched at the corner. "See that you don't. You know what is at stake."

†

James had just finished paying the road tax when four Saracen Knights, in green and black, wearing fine hauberks of woven steel, appeared and surrounded them.

"Prince Malik az-Zahir, son of the Sultan Salah al-Din and ruler of Aleppo requests your presence."

James glanced at each of the Saracens surrounding them and then bowed. "I am at the prince's service."

"Come with us. Your slave can wait here with your horses."

Byron handed the reins to VonDurenberg.

The Saracen looked at James as he motioned to Byron. "Your servant need not come."

James drew himself up and glared at the Saracen. "You do me a discourtesy. My slave is one thing, but I demand the courtesy of bringing my servant."

The Saracen paused for a moment, then glanced at one of his comrades who nodded. "As you wish, bring your servant."

The Saracen turned and motioned for James and Byron to follow. They followed the Saracen to the hill, crowned with a great citadel. The sides of the hill sloped upward to the great battlements that towered above them. It would have been almost impossible for an army to scale the walls in an attempt to overpower the defenders of the citadel. They skirted the sloping walls and came to a stone keep with a great gate in the middle of it.

Broad steps led up to the gate, and a narrow bridge spanned the chasm that separated the fortress from the rest of the city.

The Saracen Knight stopped and turned swiftly. "Wait here!" he commanded sternly.

Byron glanced over his shoulder to see the three other Saracen knights standing behind him to make sure they obeyed. The Saracen strode proudly up the stairway and approached the guard hidden in the shadows of the arched opening. Byron watched the Saracen whisper something to the guards, which he guessed must have been the password. Byron could see the guard nod and reply. The Saracen straightened up, looked back, and motioned for Byron and James to approach the narrow bridge.

Byron crossed the bridge which rose steadily up to the castle on the other side. He did not pause to admire the crevasse to the moat below, instead focused on the guards at the other end of the bridge, who were eyeing them suspiciously. Byron could not help but admire the engineering that had gone into building the fortress. Whoever had designed this castle wanted to make sure anyone trying to take it by force would pay dearly.

Once they were on the other side, they entered a great stone hallway covered by an arch, leading to a flight of stairs. At the end of the stairs, they were admitted to a large plush room, carpeted with brightly colored Persian rugs covering the cold stone floor. The smell of incense filled the air. Light streamed through the windows, giving the room an open feeling and making the décor appear bright and cheerful. Couches with deep pillows faced a small dais where Prince Malik az-Zahir was sitting and drinking snow water, brought especially for him from the distant mountains. The youthful, smooth faced lord surprised Byron. Standing beside him was an old man with a snow-white beard.

Byron and James bowed low before the young prince. James stepped forward and bowed again. "Peace to you, great prince," he said solemnly. "It is a great honor to be invited to an audience with the son of the great Sultan Salah al-Din. We have journeyed far, and are honored by your request and your hospitality."

Not a flicker of emotion showed on Prince Malik az-Zahir's face.

"And peace be to you, Prince Hashim," the Grand Vizier said in a deep, pleasant voice. "When we learned that you were in the city, we had a great desire to meet you. We have been informed..."

"Why are you trading with the Christians?" the prince interrupted as he pointed a finger at James. "My father has commanded that all caravans of the faithful supply his armies!" The prince leaned forward. "How dare you defy the sultan!"

James licked his lips and nodded. "I have been in the East. I did not know that war had broken out between the faithful and the infidel Christians. We are now heading home."

The prince looked at James intently. "No rumor of war reached you?"

James was about to speak when the Grand Vizier interrupted him. "My prince, Prince Hashim is your guest."

Prince Malik az-Zahir looked at the Grand Vizier and leaned back in his chair. "Yes, Grand Vizier. Yes, indeed. Offer my guests refreshments."

The Grand Vizier clapped his hands. The servants in the room disappeared, and then returned bearing a tray of water and pastries which they placed before James and Byron. James took one of the pastries and began to eat it. Byron picked up a finely hand-blown glass from the tray and poured himself a glass of water. The water was cold and clear, and Byron was grateful to have a drink that did not taste like the leather of a water skin. The Grand Vizier stood quietly watching them as they ate their refreshments of light sweet cakes and drank the cold clear water. Byron had the uncomfortable feeling that the old man was suspicious, and that they were being evaluated. It was unnerving to know that the smallest detail could give them away. He was being exceedingly careful to do everything right, in an effort to conceal his identity.

James had the same uneasy feelings. His confidence left him for the first time as he looked up at the old man before him. He knew how thin the veil of secrecy was. As he looked into the face of this wise man, he saw someone who would take whatever fabrication he told him and pull it apart thread by thread. "My prince, we have had a long journey. It was at Alexandretta that we first learned of the war. We had silks to sell, and I decided to sell them to the Christians since silk has little war value."

"I am surprised that with the disruption in trade, no one in the lands you have traveled spoke of the latest conflict," the Grand Vizier replied. "Where did you go?"

"We were in the land of Mongols and then China. I confess," James said, not having the slightest idea of what to say since he knew nothing about the Far East, "I cannot answer your question, because I don't remember the names. The speech of the Far East is foreign to me. I had a slave from that region, but he died on the return trip." James shook his head. "A great loss."

"Indeed, how very sad. Yet, surely Prince Hashim," the Grand Vizier chided, "you must have some idea where you traveled?"

"No, my lord," James replied, "I don't know." Byron, without realizing he was doing it, shook his head.

"Hmm," the Grand Vizier replied, deciding to change the subject. "While you were trading, how did you find the Christians? Are they preparing for our onslaught? The sultan's threat to take Jerusalem must be demoralizing."

"They are preparing," James said, "but I don't think they are aware of the true nature of their peril."

"Well spoken," the Grand Vizier said. "How could they? Jerusalem is far away. Men always want to deceive themselves into believing things are better than they really are."

"The Christians believe they will prevail," James said. "They think that God favors their cause. That their Savior will come to their aid."

"So far he has not," the Grand Vizier replied. "Their sins are heaped high to the heavens, and I don't foresee a change in their shameless behavior. Allah favors our sultan. I have no doubt that before much longer, Jerusalem will once again be beneath the banner of the crescent moon."

"The Christians are resourceful," James countered, doing his best to suppress the pride in his voice. "It was against great odds that they took the city. The division in the Arab world has made that possible, even now our coalition could fall apart very easily."

"I disagree," Prince Malik az-Zahir snapped. "My father, the Sultan Salah al-Din, is a great leader who creates unity instead of division. His efforts have been rewarded by his carefully thought out decisions. He has a mighty weapon, the people, which makes him the most powerful sultan in all of Arabia."

James nodded. "Yes, prince, I am only reporting what I saw."

The Grand Vizier turned to Byron and said, "What do you say, servant. You have been with your master. How did you find the Christians?"

Byron bowed to the Grand Vizier. "My master has spoken and his observations are true. The Christians are resilient. They have suffered a great defeat, but they will not give up... not yet."

"Then we shall slay them," the prince interjected, "and their heads will decorate the ramparts of our citadels."

The Grand Vizier looked up at Prince Malik az-Zahir. "My prince, I think Prince Hashim should be forgiven. I think we should invite him to dine with us. If you give me leave, I will make preparations for our guests."

Prince Malik az-Zahir's eyes narrowed as he looked down at his Grand Vizier. The Vizier nodded and then the prince spoke, "Yes, I see the justice in what you say. Prince Hashim, I accept your excuse, and I insist you remain for dinner as my guests."

The Grand Vizier left the room. Byron and James waited in the awkward silence as the prince sat on his dais looking at them. After a moment, the Grand Vizier returned. "Why don't you enjoy a bath and put on some suitable clean attire before joining the prince at his table."

Byron's heart sank. He had half expected the interview to end with the prince sending them away, but instead, he now wanted to have the midday meal with them. Byron shot a side glance at James, who Byron could tell did not know what to do. Byron saw the old Grand Vizier watching them intently.

Before either of them could answer, the Grand Vizier clapped his hands together. "Shannon! Come here!"

Out of place with the setting, the woman's Christian name startled James and Byron. From a recess in the wall, a dark-haired woman of European descent appeared. She was dressed in the finest silk, clearly an important slave in the service of the prince. She approached the dais and bowed.

"Take these men to bathe, and find suitable clothes for them. They are my guests!"

"As you wish, my lord." She motioned for James and Byron to follow. She led them through the hallways of the palace. Not a word was spoken as James and Byron followed Shannon, but a glance between them showed the unspoken concern. Shannon threw open the doors to a room, revealing several large copper tubs and steaming kettles of water.

Byron glanced around the room. Two women dressed in silk were the only occupants. A slight smile crossed his face. It was a bath after all. At least the enjoyment of an eastern bath would help compensate him for his worries, it was one of the few guilty pleasures he enjoyed. He had all the superstitions of the northern race, fearing water carried diseases and other imagined malignant illnesses caused by the immersion of the body into water. He had only bathed when absolutely necessary. Since he had arrived in the Holy Lands, he had learned from the Orientals to enjoy bathing, along with the feeling of being clean. He now felt uncomfortable when he was unable to wash.

Two slave girls began filling the tubs with steaming hot water.

"Disrobe," Shannon said. James, without hesitation, took off his road stained garments, threw them on the floor, and climbed into one of the steaming tubs. A look of pure satisfaction filled his face as he leaned back in the tub and relaxed.

Byron stood for a moment, not wanting to shed his clothing in front of this woman. The cross of the Archbishop Joscius was still around his neck.

"Disrobe," she said softly, "you need not be ashamed. You don't have anything I haven't seen before."

"Well, lady," Byron said, "that is not true. I assure you, while all men are built the same, more or less, I am not less and I have no desire to offend you."

James, hearing Byron's comment, looked over at Shannon with a sly smile. "He does not jest. He just doesn't know what to do with it."

The woman started to laugh. "Take off your clothes, I don't have all day."

Byron felt foolish, but he needed her to turn away so he could get the cross off from around his neck. "Lady, would you please turn your back so I can undress?"

"I can hardly wait to hear tales from your wedding night," James taunted. "The poor girl will die of boredom before you get around to servicing her."

Byron was about to reply when Shannon sighed in exasperation. "I am turning around." She whirled her back to him.

Byron deftly undid the chain from around his neck and hid the cross in his ghutra. He was starting to slip out of his road stained robes when he heard a giggle. He whipped around to see Shannon's back to him while the two servant girls were standing in front of her looking at him admiring his body.

"Turn around!" he shouted embarrassed. "You did that on purpose!"

"You said I needed to turn around," Shannon replied with a smirk. "You said nothing about my girls."

Byron decided that arguing with Shannon would get him nowhere, so he finished undressing and disgustedly tossed his clothes on the floor, making sure to keep the head rag with the cross in his hand and out of sight.

Shannon turned around as he was walking over to the tub. She glanced at him, admiring the lean muscled body, strong and well proportioned. But, as she looked closer, she could see the savage scars that a lifetime of combat had left behind. Though they detracted from the masculine ideal of beauty, they testified that this was a man of worth. Only a man who had stood close and fought his enemies, sword to sword could earn such stripes, paying the price of hard lessons learned in victory as well as in defeat. She had seen those men who marked their bodies themselves with ink drawings designed to intimidate, but only a great warrior could earn the scars that covered the body of this young man.

"As I said, you have nothing I haven't seen before," she said with a mischievous smile. Byron turned red and sat down in the hot water. He relaxed after a moment or two and closed his eyes. The feeling of hands rubbing his shoulders made him sit up with a start and he turned to find one of the women rubbing down his aching muscles. His first instinct was to say something, but the protest died on his lips as he began to enjoy the massage.

Time passed, and like all pleasant experiences, it came to an end way too soon. Shannon told both men to rise, and she would towel them off. As she approached, Shannon knocked over a boiling kettle, spilling the water over the towels she was about to use.

"Fetch new towels!" she commanded to her two serving girls. "And make haste, we don't want these two lords to be late for their meal with the prince!" The two girls hurried out of the room in an effort to quickly do their mistress' bidding and avoid her wrath for being slow.

Shannon swiftly turned to James when they had left. "You are Christians are you not?" she demanded.

"No," James replied in surprise.

The question was unexpected. Byron squeezed the cross tightly in his hand. His mind raced, reviewing everything he had done.

"Don't lie," Shannon said. "I know you are Christians, and I don't have time to play foolish games. You are in grave danger. The Grand Vizier knows who you are, and he plans to take you prisoner!"

Byron was now in shock. How could she know who they were! He paused, uncertain whether to confirm her accusation. Several seconds of awkward silence passed as he debated what to do.

"I know who you are, you fools," she hissed. "Quit this foolish pretense or I will not help you!"

"Woman you know us not," Byron said in attempt to dissuade her. "How dare you insult my master with such an accusation?"

Shannon crossed her arms. "Only a Christian would be so foolish to think he could deceive the Grand Vizier. Either you let me help you, or you will die within the dungeons of this castle. Prince Malik az-Zahir may look young, but he has the heart of a lion. He will have you tortured without mercy."

Byron sighed. Somehow, they had given themselves away. She was a Christian and so were they. It was obvious she knew. Byron decided to trust her. He had no other choice. He wondered how she came to be here in the servitude of the Saracens.

"Why do you think we are Christians?" James demanded, testing her conviction. "You are mistaken! We are Saracen lords."

"I know what you are," Shannon hissed. "I suggest you listen to me, unless you want to die a prisoner!"

"And how should we escape?" Byron asked. "If the Grand Vizier and the prince know, they surely will not let us leave by the front gate."

"Get dressed," Shannon said, "and I will take you out the secret way that will lead you back into the city."

Byron was already starting to dress. "How did you end up here?" he asked.

Shannon, who was looking out the door to see if her servants were returning, glanced back at Byron. "I came with my father on a pilgrimage to Jerusalem. We were captured. My father was killed, and I was sold into bondage. Quit asking questions and make haste."

"Come with us," James said.

"No," Shannon said sadly. "You can't save me. You will be fortunate to save yourselves."

James and Byron finished dressing. Shannon led them to a door at the back of the chamber. She opened the door and peered out for a moment. No one was in the hallway. She motioned them to follow. She led them down the twisting hallways, pausing several times to see if the next hall was empty.

Byron felt his heart stop each time she paused, every muscle tense, waiting to strike, to fight his way to freedom. They reached the edge of a flight of stairs that twisted in a downward spiral. Torches on the walls flickered, lighting the way. The stairway seamed endless. As they went down, the air grew colder. At long last, they reached an empty rock hallway. Shannon, picking up a torch, lit it and stepped into the hallway. The hallway was straight and did not bend. She motioned them to follow.

Byron wondered what terrible fate she was leading them to. Finally, they reached another spiral staircase. This one climbed up. Byron's heart sank, for he knew that he was now going to have to climb the same number of steps that they had just done in their downward descent. It was a long, slow climb and when they reached the top of the stairway, all of them were sweating and breathing hard.

Byron was so absorbed in catching his breath, that he did not consider that their escape might have been too easy. When they had rested for a moment, Shannon led them down a short hallway to an unguarded secret entrance, leading to an empty street.

"Now go, and God bless you," Shannon said. "Follow this street, you will find your servant waiting for you with your horses."

Byron paused and looked at her. She looked so sad and forlorn. A woman lost, and abandoned from friends and family; serving at the whims of her cruel masters. He shuddered to think what those whims might be, and what fate waited her when her looks faded and they tired of her. It broke his heart to think he would have to abandon her here.

"Come with us!"

"No, I cannot leave."

Byron shook his head. "Then before we part, I want to give you this." Byron took out the gold cross Joscius had given him. "Keep this, and may it bring you comfort when the days are darkest and there is no hope in sight."

Shannon leaned forward and kissed both of them on the cheek. "Go!"

James and Byron walked swiftly down the street. Every once in a while, they looked behind them to see if anyone was pursuing them. To their relief, no one followed. Just as James was starting to worry that they might be on the wrong street, he saw the office of the tax collector and VonDurenberg slouched against the wall, his hood pulled low over his head.

"Get on your horse," James said as he took the reins and mounted his horse.

"What happened?" VonDurenberg demanded.

"We have been discovered. Get on your horse, we are leaving Aleppo."

VonDurenberg mounted his horse. "You have not answered my question. What have you done?" he hissed.

"Nothing!" James said as he led the way to the city gate, going as fast as he could without trying to look suspicious. Once clear of the city gate, James and Byron broke into a gallop and raced down the road to where Father Villhardain and the rest of the caravan were waiting.

†

Father Villhardain was pacing under the shade of an olive tree. As the day slowly passed, the priest became worried, and muttered under his breath as he walked back and forth. He was exhausted. The pain in his chest was getting worse, and he was starting to cough uncontrollably.

Ishaq approached the priest. "What is taking so long, Padre?"

"I don't know."

"And if they don't return? We can't wait here indefinitely." Ishaq took a furtive glance at the ramparts, as if he expected to see Saracen soldiers issuing from the gate to capture them. Instead he saw three horses racing towards them as he glanced up at the city. As they came closer, he recognized the horses and could see James and Byron riding at full speed into the camp.

"We need to make haste," James cried as he leapt from his horse. "I don't know how, but the lord of the city knows who we are!"

"Are you certain?" Father Villhardain said. "What happened?"

"No! I am not certain," James said hastily. "I will tell you the story when we are on the road." Byron began to shout orders and the men began scurrying around.

"Do you really believe with camels we can outrun horsemen?" Ishaq asked after he heard the Saracens might know their true identity.

"No!" James exclaimed. "What I hope to do is put enough distance between us and them before they can organize a pursuit. And maybe, if God favors us, we can hide our trail so they cannot find us."

Ishaq weighed the option to abandon the Christians, and then quickly dismissed the thought. He needed the Christians to find the treasure. It was still in his best interest to keep helping them. Bashshar looked at his boss, waiting for an answer on how to proceed.

"What are you waiting for, Bashshar?" Ishaq yelled. "You heard the man. We need to hurry!"

Bashshar nodded, and ran off, urging his men to do all they could to escape from the soldiers of Aleppo. The camels were hurriedly loaded, without regard for balancing the load, or consideration of the order of the animals. As they moved out, Byron was incensed to see Speer sitting in the middle of the road, looking back at the Saracen fortress.

"Get out of the way!" Byron shouted as he rode up to the dark-haired squire staring up at him, not moving.

"Dead," the squire said, "Dead!"

"Move!" Byron shouted, and he spurred his horse forward, causing Enam to jump at Speer. Speer did not even flinch.

"Dead," he said as he pointed down the road away from Aleppo.

James galloped past Speer. The squire stood up and pointing, "Dead!" James ignored the squire. He had enough to think about, such as evading pursuers that would likely ride out of the gates of the fortress to hunt them down.

†

The Grand Vizier stood next to Malik az-Zahir as the prince sipped snow water. The Grand Vizier watched the sunlight change patterns on the carpet before the dais. Several servants entered the room, waiting for their master's commands. The door to the room opened and Shannon meekly appeared.

"Do you have something for me?" The Grand Vizier asked.

"Yes, Grand Vizier," Shannon replied as she held up the gold cross. "They are Christians."

"I suspected this," the old man replied.

"Do you wish to seize them?" one of his knights asked.

"No. Assemble your best scouts. Follow and watch them. That is all you are to do. When the time is right, I will send new instructions."

"As you command," the knight said. Bowing, he backed out of

the room.

"You!" The Grand Vizier pointed to another servant. "Send a bird and your swiftest messenger to Homs. I will not have something this important left to fate! Husam al-Din is camped near the city. Tell him his Christians have returned to the Holy Lands. Tell him to make haste. I will have fresh mounts waiting for him." The Grand Vizier turned to Shannon as his men left to fulfill his commands. "We had an agreement and now I will honor that agreement." He turned to one of his knights. "Take this woman to within sight of Antioch and turn her loose unharmed." The knight bowed, grabbed the woman by the arm, and swiftly escorted her out of the room.

The Grand Vizier turned and motioned to one of his knights to approach. "Yes, Grand Vizier," the man said as he bowed.

"Send a pigeon to Qala' at ar-Rahba. Tell them to be on the lookout for a Christian caravan disguised as Saracens. Make it clear to Mohammad that he is only to watch and to let them pass unmolested on pain of death."

"All will be done as you say, Grand Vizier," the man replied. The knight turned and left the room, leaving the Grand Vizier alone with Prince Malik az-Zahir.

"Grand Vizier, how did you know they were Christians?" The prince asked.

"My prince", the Grand Vizier replied, "I didn't know. It was a guess, and I used the Christian woman to help me find the truth."

The prince smiled. "You are very wise, Grand Vizier."

"You are gracious, my prince, and now it is up to Husam al-Din to do the rest." The old man then lowered his voice. "Or risk the wrath of Salah al-Din."

CHAPTER 40
BYRON'S PRAYER

Homs was a jewel in Salah al-Din's Empire. Isma'il was right, the change had worked wonders on the attitude of his men. Husam al-Din was sitting in his tent reading a message from Jabbar. Since the priest's departure from Tyre, Jabbar's letters had become less and less. He had sent several messages to the merchant demanding that Jabbar keep him informed, but the only response he had received to his requests was the letter currently in his hand. Husam al-Din scowled as he read Jabbar's vague excuse that the war was hurting his business, and that he did not have the time nor resources to keep watch on the Tyre docks. He heard a voice calling his name. He stood up and walked out of his tent. One of his soldiers was running towards him.

"Husam al–Din! A bird has arrived from Aleppo bearing a message for you."

"What does it say?"

"It is from the Grand Vizier of Prince Malik az-Zahir. The Christians have returned. They are near Aleppo."

Husam al-Din's mouth sagged open, the sultan was right. "When did they arrive?"

"Two days ago," the soldier replied. "The prince has sent his scouts to follow them. The Grand Vizier urges you to make haste to Aleppo. Fresh mounts will be waiting for you."

"Summon the men. We leave today."

The soldier bowed. "Yes, lord."

Husam al-Din went in search for Isma'il. He walked through the camp and found his lieutenant sitting in front of his tent sharpening his sword. "We must strike camp."

Isma'il looked up. "Where are we going?"

"The Christians, they have returned. They are near Aleppo!"

"Aleppo?" Isma'il stood up. "That is foolish."

Husam al-Din frowned. "No, they are taking a great risk because that is the only route open to them. Strike the camp! I want every man ready to ride within the hour. Leave anything unnecessary!"

While his servant saddled his horse, *El-Marees*, Husam al-Din returned to his tent and packed a few necessary items he would need. Slowly, the men trickled in. The hour passed, then two, then three. Husam al-Din watched with impatience. His fears of Homs were coming true. He counted the number of men present. It was sufficient. To his satisfaction, he noted that several of the troublemakers were among the missing. His decision was made, he would wait no longer. He mounted his horse and rode to the center of camp. Several of his men were finishing packing; others were already mounted, waiting for their leader's appearance.

"Men!" Husam al-Din shouted. "It has been difficult to watch and wait while others, less worthy, have enjoyed the glory of great deeds, and the rewards such valor brings. Patience has its own rewards, and our time has come! I promise that all the rewards you have seen others enjoy will pale in comparison if we succeed. Now let's ride to success, with the blessing of Allah, and glory immortal!"

Standing in his stirrups, with his hand raised, he cried, "Allahu Akbar!"

His men repeated the cry. "Allahu Akbar!"

"Allahu Akbar," he repeated, and his men returned the cry.

With his men following, he rode down the road to Aleppo. Time was his enemy, and he needed all the speed he could muster if he was going to catch the Christians. He hoped in his heart that the men shadowing the Christians would not do something stupid and give themselves away, or worse, take them prisoner.

It was in the hands of Allah; maybe he had used up all of his bad luck. With his slate clean, events would now go his way.

†

James kept up a punishing pace all through the night. Resting once before the sunrise, he started out again at a trot. Byron's Arab horse was smooth to ride. Trotting was the most efficient way to cover distance without wearing the horse out. Byron kept scanning the horizon looking for any telltale sign of pursuit. If someone was following them, he could see no sign.

Miles passed, yet there was still no sign of pursuit. At noon, they stopped to rest. The men sat in groups talking in low voices. Byron took the opportunity to take a short nap. He sat in the shade of a rock and lay down on his back, shading his face against the sun. He lay there mulling over all that had happened. He was still amazed that they had escaped Aleppo. He thought of Shannon, and it filled his heart with pity thinking he had abandoned her to a life of misery. He looked up at the blue sky and sighed. He should have done something. He sighed again as he turned onto his side. His eyes grew heavy and he fell asleep.

He woke as he felt James nudge him with the toe of his boot. Byron rose and stretched. He looked at the sky. The sun was setting, and the subtle shades of approaching darkness were spreading across the land.

"What do you think? Shall we make another night's ride?"

Byron looked at James. His silver helmet, bound with a white turban, reflected the red light of the setting sun. Byron yawned. "If the Saracens are in pursuit, they will not rest. Therefore, neither should we."

James nodded. "Now begins the endurance test. Who is stronger? We are about to find out." James turned and shouted, "Make ready to ride. As soon as every mount is ready, we leave." An audible groan was heard as the men rose to make the animals ready.

James led the way, again trotting the endless miles. The land, covered in darkness, passed by in its shapeless form. They followed the trail like a ribbon in the darkness. As the horizon brightened with the promise of the morning sun, James stopped. He could go no further. Byron glanced behind him. In the morning light, he clearly saw the priest's face, and he twisted abruptly in his saddle. The priest was pale, he was breathing hard as he clutched at his chest with his right hand.

"Father," Byron cried, "you are ill?"

"It is nothing," the priest grunted as he dismounted stiffly. He began to cough. When he stopped, he wiped something from his face. Byron caught a glimpse of blood in the corner of Father Villhardain's mouth, though the priest did his best to hide it from him.

"Sit down, Father. I will unsaddle your horse."

"If you insist," Father Villhardain said. The priest bent down to sit, his knees buckled, and he fell over onto his face.

"Martel!" Byron shouted. James came running over, and both of them slowly rolled the priest on to his side.

"He's still breathing," James muttered, looking up at Byron with worry on his face. "Cover him with a blanket and put a cloak under his head for a pillow."

"What do you think ails the priest?" Byron asked.

"Old age. Too many miles."

Byron scanned the desert. The wind had picked up and was blowing in his face. "Fate is against us. We must pause, willing or no."

Byron and James moved the priest into a comfortable position as Giovanni placed a blanket over Father Villhardain. "What is wrong with the priest?" the Italian knight asked Byron in a low voice.

Byron shook his head. "I do not know, but whatever it is, it has come upon him suddenly."

Byron sat by the old priest watching. Clouds formed in the distance, but in the land of thirst, their presence came to naught. Byron passed the time drawing in the sand with a stick, but as the hours went by, exhaustion overtook him and he fell asleep. Byron woke with a start. The stick had fallen from his hand and lay beside him. The sun was setting again. He looked over where Father Villhardain had been, but the priest was gone. Byron jumped to his feet and saw the old priest sitting up.

"I see you finally decided to wake," the priest said.

Byron gave Father Villhardain a searching glance. The old man was smiling, but something was not quite right. His face was still lined and his eyes were red and watery.

They mounted again after they had eaten, and began the brutal bone-numbing ride through the broken landscape. James rode with Bashshar. Bashshar, in his youth, had traveled this country and had become the guide to the Euphrates River. The dark-haired Arab had taken a liking to James. The two of them spent the miles talking about philosophy, life, women. Byron rode behind them keeping an eye on Father Villhardain. Byron's concern grew as the hours passed. The same pallid hue returned, and even though the priest tried his best to hide it, he was coughing uncontrollably, clutching his chest, his body twisted in pain.

Ishaq rode up next to Byron. "Sir Byron, the Padre is not looking too good."

"I know."

"We should rest again. If he dies, your journey's destination dies with him."

Byron's eyes narrowed as he looked at Ishaq suspiciously. "What makes you think the priest is the only one who knows our purpose or destination."

Ishaq looked at Byron. His dark eyes glittered. "Do not try to deceive me, Sir Byron. I can see that only the priest knows our destination. If you wish to finish what you started, then it would be best if he lived."

Byron paused as he looked at Ishaq, and then putting his spurs to his horse, he galloped up to James. "I think we need to stop for the night."

"Already?" James grumbled in annoyance. "Bashshar told me if we keep this pace, we will reach the river by tomorrow."

"We may reach the river," Byron replied, "but Father Villhardain will not be with us." James looked back. In the gloom, he could barely make out the ghastly look on Father Villhardain's face, and he understood the gravity of Byron's concern.

"In another mile or more, there is an oasis," Bashshar said, overhearing the conversation.

"Is it safe?" James demanded. "I don't want to run into Saracen Cavalry."

"Safe enough."

Bashshar rode off ahead to see how much further they had to go before they reached the camp. Father Villhardain was doubled over in the saddle, gasping from the pain in his chest. Byron and Giodonni were now riding on either side, steadying the priest so he could stay in the saddle.

Byron was about to give up hope of making it when Bashshar reappeared and shouted, "The oasis is just over this hill." Byron felt the concern in his heart ease a little, as a group of palm trees rose from the desert near a small depression of muddy water. It would have been nothing more than a glorified mud puddle in any other place, but here, any water was a welcome sight.

Giodonni and Byron helped Father Villhardain dismount from his horse as James held the reins. Father Villhardain was now shaking uncontrollably. Byron sat beside the old priest all afternoon, giving him water. Father Villhardain was deathly pale; chills gripped his body, causing him to shake uncontrollably despite the heat of the day. Nothing worked, no matter what Byron did. A feeling of sadness slowly crept over him as he realized that the life of his friend and mentor was now in the hands of God. He was helpless to interfere. The day wore on, and the old priest began reciting mass in Latin, absolving unseen people of their sins.

James walked over to check on Father Villhardain's condition. He paused for a moment, listened to the priest recite mass, shook his head, and without a word to Byron, walked away. Byron sat patiently beside the old man, who even near death, labored on in his devotion to the Church.

De Vale and De Montgris sat with Parker at a distance watching to see what would happen. VonDurenberg showed no interest in Father Villhardain's struggle to live. De Courcy kept watch on the trail for Saracens, while Speer skulked around the oasis, an unpleasant grimace on his face. Speer never approached Byron or the priest, but clearly kept an interested eye on the state of the old man, almost as if he were expecting something to happen.

Byron's fears were realized as evening approached. Nothing stemmed the tide flowing inevitably towards the shores of death. Only one power could stop this, and he felt the need to urgently appeal to God. Byron had no illusions. The world was a violent place where life and death were summoned frequently to sort the souls subject to their dominion. If anyone deserved to live, it was the priest, yet the unmistakable signs were there, Father Villhardain would not live to see the new day.

He could not speak Latin. He searched his memory, but he could not remember the words to any prayer for a moment such as this. In desperation, he kneeled and silently began to pray.

"Lord help me, if the priest dies, the means to deliver Jerusalem from the armies of the Saracens dies with him." He paused. He knew this did not measure up. After a moment of vacillation, he decided to continue and not give up.

"Lord, I have traveled far, and I have tasted the bitterness of defeat. I have watched good men die, and I do not presume to question your reasons, but Lord, please spare your servant. Spare the priest so that those who stand guard at the city of Solomon are not left to wait in vain. I can't find Babylon without Father Villhardain's guidance, it is too great a loss."

He paused for a moment and sighed in defeat. His head was starting to ache. His eyes hurt from the glare of the mirage off the sand. He wiped the sweat from his face with his hand. In the afternoon heat, the mirage shimmered as the restless wind moved the silver sheen across the land.

In the shapeless bands of heat, a distorted small human image appeared. Byron watched as it grew and took form. The shape drew closer. The priest was dying and now the banshee chose to appear. He was too tired and too distraught. He closed his eyes to focus on the task at hand. He needed to do better. If he tried harder perhaps God in heaven would hear him. He sighed and sat for moment but his mind was blank. He could think of nothing. He was about to give up in despair when the words came to him, it was almost as if someone was whispering them to him.

"Lord, I am an unworthy sinner, lost in a desolate and empty land, journeying through life with other travelers facing the same or worse hardship. Do not think less of me if my troubles are not worthy in comparison to others seeking your intervention. I only ask now for your aid because my need is great. Your Holy Church gave Father Villhardain this undertaking. You sent him to find me when death was near. Your hand brought us together so that I might aid him to do your will. You have appointed me to this task although I would have rather ridden to the defense of Jerusalem. Instead I have labored to help Father Villhardain, to bring relief in defense of your holy city.

"Lord, help me finish what you sent me to do. Your will, will be done, but it would ease my burden if you would spare Father Villhardain. Do not leave me alone without a guide in this land of desolation. Time runs short and Jerusalem will fall. Saladin's bloodthirsty army surrounds the city like jackals at the door. Only this man, a righteous man, an educated man, a servant of your holy will, can find what was lost. A great treasure, the means to stop the enemies of Christ. Lord, do not abandon me in my time of need. In the name of the Father, and of the Son, and of the Holy Ghost, I offer this prayer, amen."

His eyes were closed as he waited for the headache to pass. The pain eased and he opened his eyes. The shadow was gone. He became quiet and waited, watching for a change, to see if God would answer him. A hot breeze gently blew in Byron's face as the cold feeling of isolation and loss settled in, dragging him down with the realization that the answer was no. He looked down sadly, defeated. Father Villhardain opened his eyes.

"Where are we?"

"In the desert, Father Villhardain."

"I have been in the desert. I have something for you." The old man struggled to retrieve from under his robes the leather binder containing the scroll of Achatius. "Open it." he said. Carefully, Byron opened the folder. Several papers written in French were on top of the scrolls. "I have translated all you will need to know into these papers."

"Father Villhardain," Byron said hopefully as he tried to push the folder back, "you still need this."

The old priest smiled and weakly pushed the folder back. "That is not true, and I am afraid that it is not our choice." He paused again for a moment and then, with a sigh, "I did want to see Nebuchadnezzar's city, to see my work to its end." Father Villhardain began to cough again and blood filled his mouth. "Before I leave, I want to bless you. Do what's right, no matter the cost, and even though the reward is not apparent, be assured that our Father in heaven will always smile upon you, even though you may not see it at first."

"Father, you will die without confession?" Byron asked, concerned the old man would die without last rights.

Father Villhardain smiled weakly. "There is nothing to confess. My sins are the sins of man. My savior shed blood for me, and I have labored to carry the message of his sacrifice. I hope he finds that I was worthy to speak his holy word." The old priest began to cough. Father Villhardain became silent. Just when Byron decided that Father Villhardain was gone, the priest spoke again, making Byron jump. "Do not camp in Babylon and do not stay within the walls after dark."

The old priest sighed and closed his eyes. His breathing was labored, and Byron knew death was only moments away. "Can you see the river?"

"No, Father, we are at least a day's ride from it."

"My son, that is too bad because I can see it. It looks peaceful, the sunlight sparkles on the water as it flows on its way to the deep blue sea." The priest sighed. "I think I am going to cross the water and rest in the shade of the tree on the other side. I see a man motioning for me to join him."

The old priest closed his eyes, took a rattling breath, and lay still. Byron kneeled beside the body of the old man, wiping the tears away from his eyes. The priest was gone. Byron sat staring at the body in disbelief. He felt empty.

The sun was starting to sink below the horizon, turning the evening sky a deep red, stretching out over the land in subtle variations of color. The colors gradually changed to azure and then faded to black. One by one, the stars appeared. Byron grew cold.

When he could no longer stand it, he got up and covered Father Villhardain's body with his cloak. Byron stiffly walked over to join James, who was waiting near a small fire with the rest of the men in subdued silence.

"Is he gone?" James asked.

"Yes," Byron said after a long pause.

Speer began a gurgling laugh. James swiftly stood up and backhanded the squire, who fell into a heap in the dust. The squire rolled over and then rose to his feet, a venomous look of hatred in his eyes as he backed away from James.

"My Lord VonDurenberg," James cried, "if your squire utters another word, I will slay him! Here and now!"

"You will do no such thing!" VonDurenberg yelled back as he leapt to his feet to defend his nephew. "He is my liege! How dare you strike my servant!" VonDurenberg spun to address the men. "The priest is dead. He was the only one who knew how to reach our destination! This is nothing more than a waste of time!" VonDurenberg turned back to Speer. "Peter come here! I have had enough of this foolishness." VonDurenberg walked off into the dark night, muttering. Speer followed behind him.

The rest of the men slowly got up. Giodonni stopped in front of Byron, his face shadowed by the night. "I know you were close to the priest. He was a good priest. You need not fear for his soul." Giodonni turned and walked away, leaving James and Byron alone.

"VonDurenberg is right," James said as he sat back down. "All we can do now is bury Father Villhardain's body and return to Rome."

"No," Byron whispered as he reached beneath his tunic and pulled out the leather binder. "Before he died, Father Villhardain gave me the parchment he had written for himself on how to find the treasure. He also gave me the scrolls of Achatius." Byron sighed as he pushed a stone on the ground with the toe of his boot. "I did not even want to make this journey. If it had been my will, I would be at Jerusalem defending the walls. I was chosen by the Archbishop Joscius, and I will be damned if I abandon this now."

"Do you think you can find it?"

"I know not, but I know I don't want to go back to Rome yet. Not until all of our attempts to find Babylon have failed."

"No, of course not," James said as he stood up. "I have had my doubts. I doubt if Babylon ever existed, or even if this treasure is there. Come, my friend, this has been a terrible day. Our choice will be clearer in the morning. Let us retrieve his body and bring it close so that no creature disturbs his rest tonight. We will bury him in the morning and then decide what to do next."

Byron stood up and walked with James to the place where the body of Father Villhardain lay. They carefully lifted him from the ground and carried him back to their fire. They laid the body of the priest on the ground.

Byron pulled his blanket over his shoulder and stared out into the night. James rolled up in his blanket and fell asleep. Byron could occasionally hear the horses and camels as they shifted around in the darkness. As the stars wheeled overhead, he dozed off with his back to a small hill. He awoke with a start. The grey sky was brightening in the east. The sun would soon rise.

James groaned and rolled out of his blankets. He walked over to sit next to Byron. "Anything happen last night?" he asked.

"No. Other than the jackals howling in the distance, it was quiet." Byron paused. "What is your decision? Are you going to continue the quest? If you abandon this journey, I will have no other choice than to give up as well."

James looked out, shading his eyes against the rising sun. "We are halfway there. I promised God I would see this to its end." Byron nodded. James stood up. "I asked you last night... are you confident you can find Babylon?"

Byron looked up. "You know this is filled with uncertainty. I have the priest's papers and the scroll of Achatius. It gives us a chance. That is all I can promise."

James scoffed and stretched. "Then we trust God. We will truly find out if he wills it. The first test will be to see if the men will follow us."

Byron nodded. "Yes, that will be the first of many mountains to climb. Let's bury the priest and then find out where the men stand."

Bashshar found a suitable place to dig a grave near the oasis. Using cups and the two shovels carried on one of the camels, the Christians slowly fashioned a shallow grave into the sandy earth.

A gloomy pall settled on Byron as he scooped up the sandy earth with his metal cup. Tragedy and death were not uncommon. Men lived and died in their short and violent span of life. In the cruel and violent times he lived in, it was hard to distinguish what was deserving of grief and what was nothing more than a mere incident in the cycle of life.

The shallow depression was finished. Giodonni and James lifted Father Villhardain's body up and carefully placed it into the grave. James looked down at the body of the priest for a moment, then took out the priest's Bible and carefully placed it in the dead man's hands.

Byron stood next to the grave. The priest's face was pale and waxy. On impulse, he pulled out his dagger and laid it on the priest's chest in the sign of the cross. "Father, farewell in heaven."

James and Byron helped gather rocks to cover the shallow mound of earth. As they did, James caught a glimpse of Speer watching him. The squire darted out of sight as soon as he made eye contact.

The Christians gathered around the shallow grave to recite the Lord's Prayer as the Arab drivers packed the camels for travel. The prayer ended, VonDurenberg folded his arms across his chest. "The priest is dead. With him, died the knowledge of our destination. I see no reason to continue this journey. Who is ready to follow me home?"

"We are not turning back," James said, interrupting VonDurenberg. "I am not ready to give up. We have never talked about our destination, but now is the time. I will not deceive you, for the journey will only get more dangerous. We are traveling to Babylon." Byron saw the look of astonishment flash across the faces of the assembled men.

"Babylon does not exist and you know it. You can do as you like," VonDurenberg exclaimed. "I see no reason to continue traveling in this God forsaken country. The priest is dead. God has made his will clear. I will waste no more time, nor will I follow fools who do not know when to quit. Let's go home! Let's go home to soft beds, good meals, and to the pleasures of a woman's company. This is a fool's quest, the delusions of a priest who played upon the weakness of the Church. Nothing awaits us, other than misery and maybe death."

James could see the appeal of going home on some of the men's faces. Brother Carl was not here to hold him to his word. He looked around at the camels and the drivers who were watching him. The treasure was probably long gone. If the men would not follow him, it was not his fault. With a shrug, he pushed the desire away. He knew he had better say something to change the men's minds before it was too late.

James laughed. "VonDurenberg, before we left, you were willing to travel to Babylon, believing the treasure would be easy to find!" James looked around at the bewildered look on the faces of the men. "Yes, I said treasure! Now that you have run into some difficulty, you are ready to give up and go home!"

"How can you be certain the treasure is there?" VonDurenberg demanded angrily. "Are you willing to risk the lives of these men on the hope of an old fool who is now dead?"

"Father Villhardain was no fool," Byron said. "He would never have risked anyone's life if he did not believe the treasure was there! It is there and we will find it!" Byron paused to scan the faces of the men. "All of you came because you wanted to serve the Church. If this is the best service you can give, then I release you."

"What kind of treasure are we talking about?" Narvez asked.

"A Roman treasure, lost when Rome fell. It was placed in the city of Babylon."

"Babylon?" Giodonni gasped.

"That is why we are here?" Narvez demanded. "We are risking our lives on a hunt for treasure?"

"You are risking your lives," James said, ignoring Narvez's disgusted expression, "so the gold from this treasure can be used to raise a new army. We are going to Babylon to save Jerusalem."

"Humph," Narvez grumbled. "What makes you think the Church will respect this noble purpose?"

"I had the same thoughts," James retorted. "But I am willing to take the risk. It is an act of faith. This journey is worthy of a song. If you are not worthy, then run back to your soft beds and women! Be forgotten! When I die, it will be with my face to the enemy and a sword in my hand!"

"Don Fuego will follow Sir James and Sir Byron," Ishaq said. "I have not come all this way just to turn around and go home." Several other knights shuffled around uncomfortably, looking at their comrades to see what they would do.

"I will also continue," Narvez cried. "I will not be shamed."

"My lords," De Courcy said as he scanned the hills with his hollow eyes, "whatever decision you make you should do it soon. The Saracens are following us. I can feel it."

"I am going to saddle my horse," Byron said, walking away. Narvez and James followed. Most of the men were saddling by the time Byron mounted his horse. He could hear them talking among themselves about the surprising revelations about the reason for their journey. He could already anticipate a flurry of questions, but not now, he would deal with them later.

Byron rode over to stand next to James. Bashshar rode up to join them. "We should make the river by nightfall," the Arab said.

When the last camel was loaded, James led off at a trot. Byron paused and watched as the caravan left the oasis. Camel after camel jogged along, dust rising as they passed by in a long line. He turned in his saddle. The palms of the trees swayed in the breeze. He took a long look at the mound marking the grave of Father Villhardain. It was the last memory he would ever have of the priest. Turning away, he looked forward. Putting his spurs to his horse, he galloped off to join James and Bashshar at the head of the caravan.

CHAPTER 41
HUSAM AL-DIN AND THE PRINCE

After a long punishing ride, with little rest, Husam al-Din was grateful to see the grim silhouette of the fortress of Aleppo. He had ridden hard to the summons of Prince Malik az-Zahir. Hopefully, the Christians were not too far ahead of him. The lights of the city flickered in the evening light. He rode to the gates without slacking his pace, hooves clattering on the stones.

"Who goes there?" cried the guards in challenge.

"Husam al-Din!"

"Allah be praised! We have been expecting you. The prince and his Grand Vizier awaits. He has news for you alone."

Husam al-Din dismounted and handed the reins to an orderly. A servant of the prince, waiting in the shadow of the gate, stepped forward and bowed. "I have been instructed to bring you into the presence of the prince. He has been most anxious to see you."

Husam-al Din followed the servant through the darkened city streets. The Saracen Knight was grateful for the guide who led him by the quickest way to the citadel. Husam al-Din was ushered into the same room, where only days before, Byron and James had been guests. The prince was dressed in a blue robe adorned with crescent moons, and seated on the dais. The Grand Vizier was standing next to him. Lamps lit the room, but in the dim light,

Husam al-Din could see two knights standing in the corners with drawn swords.

"Husam al-Din," the Grand Vizier said, "how was your journey?"

Husam al-Din bowed to the prince. "It was long and tiring. I rode swiftly, sparing neither man nor horse."

"You were right to do so," the prince said. "My father, the Great Sultan, would have expected nothing less."

"Yes, my lord. Where are the Christians now?"

"My chief scout is trailing them," the prince replied. "The Christians are heading towards the Euphrates."

"Interesting? The river was an artery of Roman invasion." Husam al-Din smiled. "Perhaps history is repeating itself. I shall capture the Christians just as our forefathers captured the Roman Emperor Valerian after his legions were annihilated in a glorious battle."

"Humph!" the Grand Vizier snorted. "And I remember that the Emperor Trajan at the zenith of Rome's power launched a war of conquest, looting the entire region and taking all the riches back to Rome. I consider this relevant, since it appears the Christians are attempting to do it again!"

"Enough. I have no patience for boasts or prognostications," the prince snapped. "History is ours to make. My father is making his own legend as we speak. The Christians are moving towards the Euphrates. They are traveling towards a region once known to the Romans. Perhaps the treasure has been hidden in one of the former subjugate cities. I have had horses gathered for you. How many men are still with you?"

"Eighty-six."

The prince looked at the Grand Vizier. "Grand Vizier, do you think that is sufficient, or should we send more men?"

"My prince, the chief scout Muhtadi estimates that the Christians and their servants are no more than thirty men. Even if Husam al-Din loses a few men along the way, he should have a sufficient force to overwhelm the Christians."

The prince raised his eyebrows. "I remind you, Grand Vizier, my father wants success."

"My prince, my men can overpower thirty Christians," Husam al-Din said.

Malik az-Zahir nodded. "Then let it be so. You know your men. What are your plans?"

"I intend to rest my men for a few hours and then continue the pursuit."

"That is well. The man who brought news from Muhtadi of the Christians path will guide you. My chief scout has been marking their trail."

Husam al-Din smiled. "Good. Then I shall make better time."

"Husam al-Din, ride hard. I have sent a message to Qala' at ar-Rahba. The commander of the garrison is expecting you, and I have advised him to have replacement horses should the need press you."

Husam al-Din bowed. "Thank you, my lord."

The prince nodded. "Go and rest. I have other matters that have come this night. The Christians have rejected my father's offer to surrender Jerusalem. The sultan has asked me to empty Aleppo of all remaining soldiers and send them to join the main army. Many will not return if we are forced to assault the walls of Jerusalem."

"They will come to rue that decision," replied Husam al-Din.

"Indeed, they shall."

Husam al-Din bowed again and backed out of the room.

†

When Husam al-Din departed to meet the prince, Isma'il led the men through the city gates to a wide place in the courtyard. On the command to dismount, each man began to look for a place to rest. Grooms appeared and began taking the horses away in small groups to exchange them with new mounts. Isma'il sat down and leaned his back against the cold stone wall.

"Isma'il, what are we doing here?" asked Kasim. "We are now riding in the opposite direction of Jerusalem. Has Husam al-Din lost his mind?"

"Kasim," snapped Isma'il, "I have heard enough. Stay here with the other women and children if you don't like the journey!"

"I think Husam al-Din has ridden to Aleppo for just that purpose," Kasim complained angry at the rebuke. "He is hiding from the war. I came to kill infidels, not chase phantoms across the desert."

"Kasim, if you wish to leave, do so now."

"You want that, don't you?"

Isma'il was about to reply when Husam al-Din returned and sat down next to him.

"Husam al-Din, how was your audience with the prince?" Kasim asked. "Do we ride again soon?"

"Yes. In a few hours we will continue in pursuit."

"Excellent," Kasim said. "It is an honor to ride in your service. I hope to bring these infidel dogs to bay, to punish them for their rash incursion into our lands."

"We shall," Husam al Din replied. "We have a long ride ahead of us."

Kasim rolled up in his blanket. Isma'il gave him a dark look of disgust as Kasim smiled maliciously back at him.

It seemed to Husam al-Din that he had just closed his eyes when he woke with a start. A servant of the prince was shaking him. "Lord, it is time."

Husam al-Din was disoriented for a moment and would have gladly given twenty gold pieces to be allowed to go back to sleep. He pushed himself up and sat for moment. With a groan and a sigh, he got up and started waking his men.

A groom from the prince brought him his new horse, saddled and ready. The black stallion was fresh and full of energy. "This is Antar. He is a gift from the prince. He is swift and he is strong. May he bear you to great fortune."

Husam al-Din nodded. "Tell the prince of my great gratitude." He could feel the horse tense as he mounted. The horse danced and jigged in anticipation of the journey as his men saddled their new mounts. Husam al-Din walked it in a circle, forcing it to wait until all his men were mounted.

The horse had great power, and it was a relief when the last man was on his horse and his column was ready to travel. Husam al-Din moved into the lead and started down the street, the horse jigging sideways in the early morning darkness. The few flickering lights that lit the dim streets guided him as he led his men to the city gate. He felt relief as he drew near the gate, knowing that at any moment he could pick up the speed and wear some energy out of his new horse.

A company of men in armor were waiting. Prince Malik az-Zahir was standing in their midst. Husam al-Din drew up his reins and stopped. The horse started to jig in place as the prince spoke, "I wish to impart to each of you a greeting from my father the great Sultan Salah al-Din. Many of you may feel cheated in your chance to prove your worth on the battlefield. Many of you desire to prove your valor to Allah and his Prophet Mohammad. That time has come! You are fortunate to have a great leader, Husam al-Din, and it would be wise to serve him well. At the end of this journey, you will understand why you were made to wait. With the blessing of Allah, go! Ride to great fortune!"

The men cheered the prince, who motioned to Husam al-Din to come near. "Husam al-Din, catch the Christians and crush them."

Husam al-Din bowed. "Fear not, my prince, they will come to rue the day they dared to enter our lands." Husam al-Din wheeled the black horse towards the open gate and releasing the tension on the reins, the horse surged forward breaking into a gallop. The black charger clattered down the cobblestone road, his column of knights followed him. He would slow the black horse soon, but for the moment, he would let the horse run to wear off some energy. He would catch the Christians, and then he would stalk them. They would lead him to the treasure. He smiled to himself. They would never know he was there until it was too late, and when it was too late, he would destroy them.

CHAPTER 42
SARACEN AND CHRISTIAN GHOSTS

Bashshar sat on his horse on a ridge and looked out over the Euphrates flowing south towards the Persian Gulf. The river stretched out before him like an artery in a wasted land. James rode up and stopped beside him.

"There is your river Christian."

James glanced up at the afternoon sun as it baked down upon them. "I think we have earned a rest."

"I don't know what you deserve Christian."

The rest of the men rode up and fanned out along the ridge. The green riverbank was inviting, the sound of the moving water called to the men to come and enjoy its cool, refreshing embrace. James looked at the water, and putting his spurs to his horse, he galloped down the ridge and rode his horse into the river with a giant splash. The rest of the men followed in a mad dash to the water's edge and jumped into the river.

The animals lined up along the banks, drinking their fill. It was several hours before the men tired of the river's water. After swimming in the river, several of the men gathered some wood for a fire to cook the first hot meal they had eaten in days.

Byron sat by the fire that night reading quietly from the pages that Father Villhardain had cut from the book. He felt relaxed as his mind drifted away with the story. His only annoyance was the fire, and he found himself moving every now and again to avoid the grey pungent smoke. James came over and sat down beside him.

"Should we rest another day ere we head south?" James asked.

Byron looked up from reading. "I see no harm. I have not seen any evidence we are being pursued."

"I agree. The animals could use the rest, and so could the men."

Byron frowned, thinking of Aleppo. "What do you think? Shannon seemed to think we were in danger, but now, nothing. De Courcy thinks we are being followed, but he is just overly fearful. If the Saracens were truly chasing us, they would have attacked by now."

"I don't know what to make of it, other than she was a captive servant. She could have been imagining things or overreacted to something she heard and did not understand. De Courcy is just mad."

"Well, it was strange that she would tell us we were in danger when clearly we are not."

"Why do you insist that everything make sense?" demanded James in exasperation at his friend's paranoia. "Accept the fact that sometimes things happen without a reason. Now, I insist you stop worrying about some slave girl's irrational fear or a madman's delusions and enjoy the moment."

Byron smiled ruefully. "You're right."

"Actually, I wish she were here. I could use some female company."

Byron shook his head, rolled up the pages, and tied them. He got up, put the pages into his saddlebags, and then wrapped his blanket around himself. He walked over to the most inviting spot he could find and lay down.

James, not ready to sleep, continued to talk. "I am still troubled by Don Fuego. I still can't seem to place where I know him."

"Your imagination is getting the better of you. Don Fuego is from Spain, and you have never been there," Byron mumbled sleepily.

"No. I have seen him before... somewhere." James stared into the coals of the dying fire. "There is something about him. He claims to be a merchant, but I am not convinced."

"Well, you won't solve anything tonight," Byron groaned,

wishing his friend would go to sleep.

"No. But it's stuck in my mind and I can't seem to stop thinking about it. Not that it matters I suppose. I wish the girl were here. I could relax in her arms and then everything would fall into place."

"A girl will not help you with this problem," Byron grumbled in annoyance, turning his back to his friend in an attempt to end the conversation.

James got up and threw more wood on the fire. He wrapped his blanket around himself, and lay back against the sandbank that served as a windbreak.

Byron said a silent prayer for Father Villhardain before he drifted off to sleep. He was used to James' womanizing comments, but tonight he was not in the mood to hear them. He could not see James smiling at him in the firelight, enjoying the thought of needling his friend about his shyness around women. He missed the priest. The loss of leadership and the loss of wisdom had yet to be felt.

Byron was right. The slave girl's warning bothered James a great deal. De Courcy might be overly fearful, or perhaps he was more sensitive to clues that James might be missing. James sat by the fire mulling over his worries. At last, he decided that he needed to act. He would slip out of camp in the morning and scout the surrounding hills. Maybe they were not as alone as they thought.

†

It was a moonless night with only the stars to light the edges of the desert road. Husam al-Din kept up his pursuit. The shadows of each horse and rider passed before the diamond studded backdrop. Above the land of dust and earth, the heroes of the ancients, immortalized in the stars, looked down at the exhausted men as they rode on.

Husam al-Din strained his eyes in the dark to keep his course on the roadway, a grey ribbon barely visible in the darkness. He could not afford to get lost. He rested his men only when necessary, and then rode as hard and fast as the stamina of the horses would allow.

After two days of riding, a cloud of dust appeared in the distance. As they drew nearer, a horse and rider became visible traveling at great speed. Husam al-Din's hand rose as he called a halt. The approaching rider's horse was covered with flecks of white foam. There was dust on the rider's black robes. When the rider saw the large body of Saracen cavalry, he checked his horse to a trot and then stopped.

Husam al-Din kicked his horse into a slow gallop to where the rider waited.

"Husam al-Din?" the rider asked.

"I am."

"The chief scout for the prince sent me to find you."

The black stallion towered over the scout's horse, and Husam al-Din tilted forward in the saddle to get a better look at the scout. Thin wisps of hair were starting to grow on the boy's face. His brown eyes were wide with excitement; no doubt, this was his first military expedition. He was slight, which was made worse by the oversized tan tunic that he wore. He wore a steel cap, bound along the edge with a white turban that draped over the boy's neck.

Husam al-Din smiled. "And you have. What is your name?"

The scout bowed his head. "My lord, my name is Nadim."

Husam al-Din nodded. "Nadim, what news do you have for me?"

"The Christians are a day's ride ahead."

Husam al-Din sighed with relief. "We are closing the gap."

"Yes, my lord, they are steadily riding towards the Euphrates."

"Do you have anything else?"

"We have also found the grave of a man."

"A Christian?"

"Yes, my lord."

"An older man?" Husam al-Din demanded. "What was he wearing?"

"The rags of a Bedouin. He was tall and thin with short, grey hair. Muhtadi told me to show you this." The boy reached into his saddlebags and pulled out a worn leather bound book. "This was found on the body. He also told me to show you this." The scout held up a dagger.

Husam al-Din took the book, opened it, and thumbed through the pages. He had seen the book before, and he knew what it was. The priest was dead. Husam al-Din sat quietly on his horse pondering this new development, weighing what to do next. He decided to keep what he had learned to himself. Perhaps a new leader had been chosen to guide the Christians to their destination. That they had not turned back with the death of their leader was a good sign.

Nadim watched Husam al-Din flip through the pages. "My lord, what is it?"

"The book?" Husam al-Din muttered distractedly. "The book is the Christian Bible. It is the Christian holy book. It's time we go!"

Nadim held up Byron's dagger. "Do you wish to examine the dagger?"

Husam al-Din looked at the dagger. "Keep it. A reward for your trouble."

Nadim bowed. "You are gracious, my lord."

Husam al-Din nodded. Time was precious, and though he was closer to his prey, he still did not have time to waste. Husam al-Din started to hand the Bible back to the boy.

"Keep it," Nadim said. "The dagger is reward enough. I don't want anything that belongs to the religion of the infidels."

Husam al-Din nodded and put the Bible in his saddlebags. The scout turned his horse and began the return ride back. Husam al-Din pondered this recent revelation. He lifted his spurs, nudging Anton forward. All he could do for now was follow the Christians and see which way they went.

†

Muhtadi lay quietly on a hilltop looking down at the river through his glass. A steady breeze was blowing into his face, keeping any scent that might give him away from reaching the animals below. It was hot and he was bored, he was tired of watching and waiting.

The Christians were not moving. They seemed to be content to stay in their camp today, perhaps resting their animals. It puzzled him that the prince had not sent a cavalry detachment to capture them. Instead, his orders had been to follow them and wait for Husam al-Din. It was not his place to question orders. He backed down from his vantage point and walked stiffly to the men he had left waiting with the horses. Muhtadi's faded blue tunic was dark with sweat stains, his white pants were stuffed into a pair of scuffed brown boots. He had served Salah al-Din for many years and now he served the sultan's son. The grey hairs of his beard testified to his years of service to the sultan and gave Muhtadi a look of wisdom but his hooked nose was the most distinguishing feature of his face.

"Are the infidel pigs going to move?" demanded a muscular young man with black hair and the dark eyes of a fanatic.

"No Ahmed, it looks as if they are going to stay camped today."

"I am tired of following them," Ahmed grumbled irritably. "We should slip in tonight and kill them in their sleep. I am ready to go home!"

"Those are not my instructions," Muhtadi growled testily as he took a drink of water. He had heard this, or similar rash comments, since the day they had begun to follow the Christians. He was tired of listening to them. Young men never had the sense to do what they were told. He had to listen to their boastful talk, which made him want to give them what they desired so they might learn a sharp lesson.

He had watched the Christians now for several days, and it was clear there were some experienced crusaders in this group. He had no doubt that if it came to a fight, it would not be as easy as these young hotheads thought. He would almost enjoy watching these youngsters get an education, but that was not going to happen.

Muhtadi lifted his water skin to his lips and was about to take another drink when he stopped abruptly, capping the skin. The sky brought news. Someone was approaching, a faint trickle of dust appeared on the horizon, and he thought he could hear the distant jingle of metal upon metal.

Quickly, Muhtadi picked up his bow and quiver of arrows. Grabbing the reins of his horse, he mounted. "Stay here! Keep an eye on the infidels, and don't do anything foolish! I will go see who is approaching."

He rode out swiftly, keeping the signs of whoever was drawing near in sight. Strangers were never welcome, and as he covered the rough terrain, he spied a group of horsemen approaching rapidly at a trot. Muhtadi stopped and pulled out his eyeglass. He needed to identify these men quickly, to do otherwise could be fatal. He scanned the riders. They were riding fine Arabian horses. The riders carried round shields with a boss in the center. A knight at the head of the column held a banner emblazoned with the graceful calligraphy of the Shahada. Riding next to the Saracen knight, he could see Nadim. It pleased Muhtadi that Nadim had been successful in his first real assignment. Muhtadi rode cautiously forward. His fear now was not to be mistaken for a foe.

Husam al-Din felt a jolt of surprise as a lone horseman appeared out of nowhere. He stabbed his hand into the air, commanding his men to halt as he studied the man intently to see if he was an enemy that would have to be swiftly slayed. Nadim put his spurs to his horse and rode out ahead of the column.

When Nadim was halfway between the stranger and the column, he halted. Standing in his stirrups, he turned back to Husam al-Din and shouted, "All's well! It is Muhtadi, the chief scout."

Husam al-Din put the spurs to his horse, Isma'il did the same, and they rode out to meet Muhtadi. He raised his hand. "Peace be to you."

"And to you," Muhtadi answered. "Are you Husam al-Din?"

"I am."

"My lord, I have been praying for your safe arrival. The Christians are just ahead."

Husam al-Din smiled. "Praise Allah! Take me to them. I want a look at the Christians to see how many foes we face."

"Yes, my lord." Muhtadi bowed.

Husam al-Din rode with Muhtadi and Nadim to the vantage

point overlooking the Christians. Ahmed, lying prone on the hilltop, was watching the enemy below. They carefully crawled up beside him.

"He is one of us," Muhtadi mumbled, seeing Ahmed's look of surprise at the sight of Husam al-Din. "What has happened since I have been away?"

"Nothing, other than one of them just returned on horseback."

"Did you see him leave?" Muhtadi demanded.

"No," Ahmed replied defensively as he eyed Nadim. "He returned to the camp just moments after you left." Muhtadi lay there mulling over the implication. A Christian had slipped out of their camp and he did not see him. How could he miss a horseman riding off?

"What have they done since the rider returned?" Husam al-Din asked.

"Everything has remained as it was," Ahmed replied. "They continue to graze their animals and the men seem to be resting."

"Good," Muhtadi replied in relief. "Maybe we have been fortunate, and they are still unaware of our presence."

Husam al-Din watched the Christians through his spy glass. He counted twenty-one men, although it was hard to tell the exact number as they moved about their camp. It was nothing his men could not handle if it came to a fight. They did not appear to be heavily armed, but that could be deceiving. Husam al-Din, satisfied he had at last found his prey, turned his back on the Christians and carefully slid down the hill. Muhtadi followed him down.

"I am going to find a place to camp my men," Husam al-Din said as he mounted his horse. "I will leave this in your capable hands, Muhtadi. Come get me if anything changes."

"It will be as you wish, my lord."

Ahmed turned to Nadim. "I see you did not get lost."

"No. I found Husam al-Din just as Muhtadi told me to."

"And you did well on your first assignment," replied Muhtadi.

"Yes," Ahmed replied as he gave Nadim a shove. "But one success does not make a tracker. Do not forget your place."

Muhtadi sighed. "Nor should you forget yours."

Ahmed glared at Muhtadi as he grabbed the dagger stuffed

in Nadim's belt. "Well, at least I follow instructions. You were supposed to give this to Husam al-Din, but it seems you coveted it for yourself!"

"Husam al-Din gave it to me!" the boy protested. "He said I earned it."

Muhtadi held out his hand and Ahmed handed him the dagger. "Is this true Nadim?"

"Yes. If you doubt my story, you can ask Husam al-Din yourself."

Muhtadi held Nadim in his gaze for a moment and then handed the dagger back to him. "Then it was well earned. Come, we have work to do. Nadim, take the horses downstream and water them. I will take the watch while Ahmed rests." Nadim took the horses as Ahmed glared at him.

Muhtadi ignored Ahmed and lay down on the dirt. He watched the Christians go about their chores as a hawk floated lazily in the air. The hawk's wings were outstretched as it soared circling the land. In an instant, it folded its wings and dived to the earth. Muhtadi followed its trajectory to the ground, where it pounced in a puff of dust on its prey. In an instant, it rose again, a snake dangling in its talons. Muhtadi smiled and went back to watching the Christians.

CHAPTER 43
MUHTADI LOSES THE CHRISTIANS

James woke before dawn. Quietly, he slipped over to where the horses were picketed and saddled one of the animals. James mounted the horse and rode towards the hills away from the river. His horse scrambled through the series of switchbacks to the top of the ridge as the rays of the sun broke the horizon. He paused to look out over the empty land. He rode in an arc around their camp looking for any evidence that would indicate they were not alone. The sun felt good on his face as it chased away the chill, and he enjoyed the stillness and solitude of being alone in the desert.

He rode aimlessly among the hills until midday when he paused near an ancient brick wall half buried in the sand; the remains of a great fortress built by a people time had forgotten. He dismounted. The fortress of mud bricks had slowly sunk into the sand. He rode along the wall until he came upon an arch. He paused. The arch had once been a gate, but the elements had filled it in until only the top of the archway remained. He decided to dismount. Hobbling his horse, he let it graze as he sat with his back against the wall of the arch. James rested in the shade, drinking from his water skin. The land appeared quiet, and yet the unease in James' mind steadily rose. An intangible sense warned him he was being watched, yet he could find no evidence to substantiate his suspicion.

He glanced at the odd weathered symbols and marks pressed into the bricks of the arch. What they meant, he could not tell, nor did he care. But as the desert breeze rustled past the ruins, it whispered to him that complacency only brought disaster. He would talk to Byron. They would leave tonight. He mounted his horse and with his mind made up, he rode swiftly back to camp.

James saw Byron sitting with his back to one of the few trees that grew near the river. Byron, reading the pages of the Odyssey, looked up as the shadow of James' horse darkened the pages. "Where have you been?"

"I went for a ride," James replied, dismounting.

"Find anything?"

"No," James said as he pulled the saddle off the horse. "You know the Saracen's as well as I. Just because you cannot see them, does not mean they are not there. They will hide in the hills and they watch and wait. When the time is right, they will strike."

Byron nodded as he rolled up the pages and bound them. "Agreed, we should leave tonight. If we are being watched, they will not expect that."

"It will buy us time, perhaps even throw them off our trail."

Byron stood up and scanned the hillside for any sign of the enemy. "The men will not be pleased."

"That is not my worry," James replied as he turned to lead the horse to the picket line. "My worry is an unexpected attack."

Byron gathered the men and told them of his plan to leave after dark. His plan was to build several fires with enough wood to keep them burning: giving the illusion they were still in camp, while in fact, they were leaving. If anyone was watching, they would not realize what was happening and the fires would cover their escape. Byron finished outlining his plan, and the men walked away to begin getting ready for their night ride. Von-Durenberg remained standing with his arms crossed. Byron and James started to leave.

"Did you find any evidence the enemy is near?" VonDurenberg demanded.

"No," James replied, "but that does not mean they are not here."

"And yet, you are willing to risk getting lost in the dark, or worse!"

"We are in the land of the Saracen," Byron replied. "They are cunning, and they are patient and will watch from afar, waiting for a moment of weakness. When they see a weakness, they will attack."

"Foolishness. The Saracens are miles away. I would rather get another night's rest than to go off and wander like a fool in the dark."

James stepped close to the graf. "My lord, you should heed Fitzwalter's warning. Do you not know the tale of the valley of DoryLaeum?"

VonDurenberg, face red and sunburned, looked down his nose at James. "My Lord Martel, should I?"

"Yes. It serves as a lesson. After its victory at Nicaea, the first crusader army had marched deeper into the Saracen lands. The Sultan Kilij Arslan followed the Christian host, watching, waiting for a moment of weakness. That moment came when Bohemond and three thousand men of the vanguard became separated from the main army. With twice the number of men, the sultan attacked. For hours, the battle was in doubt. Only through the grace of God and the courage of Bohemond were the Saracens held off. It was in the last grim hour, my great kinsman Godfrey of Bouillon arrived to drive the Saracens away."

"Interesting tale," VonDurenberg scoffed, "but the Saracens are not here. We are not an army. The Saracens will not care. The wench that told you that you were in danger was lying." VonDurenberg looked around, holding his hands in the air. "Clearly, they don't care."

"The Saracens will care," Byron replied. "Our very presence contaminates their land. Their reason for not attacking is a mystery, but do not discount that they are here and they are watching. When they decide to attack, they will do so when we least expect it, and they will kill us all. If you wish to stay the night, then you and your follows should stay. That is yours to command, but the rest of us will march tonight."

"I would not give you the pleasure of leaving me," VonDurenberg replied, "nor will I abandon the men, but I will demand satisfaction if you get us lost." VonDurenberg spit on the ground as he turned and stalked off.

The night gloom began to fall, and they lit several fires. In the twilight, as the men gathered for their evening meal, they grumbled about missing a night's rest. When dinner was finished, they quietly saddled their horses and packed their gear. When total darkness had descended, they threw more wood on the fires and quietly prepared to depart from their camp. One by one, the men gathered on the trail, careful not to be silhouetted by the firelight. When all the men and animals were accounted for, Byron led the way as they stealthily slipped into the darkness.

☦

The next morning before sunrise, Muhtadi relieved Nadim to begin his watch. As he lay flat on the hillside looking at the location of the Christian camp, the sun rose, spreading its light over the land. Muhtadi stood bolt upright. The enemy was gone! Nothing of their camp remained. Cursing, he ran down the hillside to his horse.

"Nadim, did you fall asleep!"

Nadim turned white. "No, Muhtadi. I watched them all night. They built several fires that burned brightly. When the fires went out, I assumed the Christians were asleep."

Muhtadi moved closer to the boy. "Did they keep one fire burning?"

Nadim took a step back his eyes wide. "No, they all burned low and went out one by one, until none remained."

"What is it?" Ahmed asked as he stood up with his blanket over his shoulders.

Muhtadi looked at Nadim and then slapped him across the face. "Damn it. The Christians left in the night."

"What?" Ahmed exclaimed.

"It is an old trick," Muhtadi snapped. "They left fires burning to make us think they were still in camp."

"I am sorry, Muhtadi," Nadim stammered as he rubbed his face. "I did not know."

"Well boy, now you have learned a lesson. Had one fire burned all night, you would know that someone still watched the camp."

"Do you intend to tell Husam al-Din?" Ahmed asked.

Muhtadi looked at Nadim. The boy's eyes were brimming with tears. "No. He might demand a more severe punishment for such a mistake. We will say nothing, but you had better pray I can find their trail!"

"You will find it, Muhtadi," Ahmed said. "There is no way they can conceal the trail of over a hundred camels."

"We will see how crafty these Christians are."

Muhtadi, Nadim, and Ahmed saddled their horses and quickly rode down to the Christian's camp. Muhtadi dismounted and walked around staring at the ground, looking at the hoof prints in the dirt. He knelt down examining the shape of the camels' pads, looking for the direction of travel. He walked back and mounted his horse, following the Christians trail. He pulled his horse to a stop when he was confident he was on the right path.

"Ahmed," Muhtadi ordered, "ride to Husam al-Din. Tell him the Christians are on the move and heading south."

"Anything else?" Ahmed looked at Nadim.

"No," Muhtadi snapped.

†

The night's ride had been long and uneventful. The sun rose and Byron called a halt to rest the animals. Sitting next to the river, he pulled out Father Villhardain's notes. Looking at the priest's map, he glanced at the river. He was following the right course. Rolling up the notes and the map, he stuffed them into his saddlebags. Byron guided the caravan through the small, dusty villages built near the river. The illiterate peasants paid no attention. They had seen caravans before, although several took the opportunity to shout insults at the Christian slaves laboring for their Saracen masters. Most, however, stayed away from James, the image of a great Saracen Lord, impatiently shouting orders, imperiously demanding his servants to care for his personal wants. Few of the peasants wished to arouse the ire of the Saracen prince who would not hesitate to punish anyone who annoyed him.

Byron halted by mid-morning, and the men sat beside the road and rested. Byron was stretched out on his back half-asleep when James came over to him. "My friend, why don't you take Bashshar and ride ahead and scout the road. Bashshar has told me that somewhere ahead lies a small Saracen outpost. Most likely, it is abandoned."

"Then why are you worried?" Byron asked tiredly.

"I do not know, but take Bashshar and look it over. See what we are facing. I will lead the men."

"Why don't you go?" Byron sighed "You like riding the countryside?"

"Does a prince scout the road?"

"No," Byron groaned as he stood up and stretched. "But they should." Walking to his horse, he stroked the horses face. "Sorry Enam, it is time for another ride."

It was a pleasant ride down the length of the river. Byron would have enjoyed this part of the journey if he were not in the company of Bashshar. No matter how hard he tried to befriend the dark-haired Arab, the man rebuffed him by keeping his distance. James seemed to get along with Bashshar, but James' infectious personality caused everyone to like him, except Von-Durenberg, and that was an understandable exception.

After several hours of riding in silence, Bashshar stopped abruptly. "Christian," the Arab growled, "we are almost within sight of Qala' at ar-Rahba. What do you intend to do?"

"What do you mean?"

"I mean how do you intend to get around the castle?"

"What castle? What are you talking about? James told me it was a small abandoned Saracen outpost."

Bashshar started to laugh. "You will wish it was abandoned. No, Qala' at ar-Rahba was built by Nur al-Din to keep the

Mongols at bay. Didn't any of you illiterates look at a map before you decided to venture into hostile territory?"

"I have never been here!" Byron snarled. "No Christian has ever been here."

Bashshar laughed. "I have to give you that. So, what are you going to do?"

Byron looked up at the sun, considering the time of day and sighed. "We will wait here for James and the rest of the caravan to discuss this."

"I tell you Christian, you can wait here, but it will not change your choice. You will have to make a decision. Either you go past the castle, or you return to your Christian lands. There is no way around."

"I will make a decision when I damn well feel like it!"

"You're the boss," Bashshar replied mockingly.

Both men sat on their horses in the heat of the day waiting for James and the caravan. Byron was getting bored. He shifted in his saddle and looked around restlessly. Sweat was dripping into his eyes and down his back. "It would do no harm to ride to within sight of the walls."

"That is your choice, Christian." Byron glared at the Arab as he nudged Enam forward towards Qala' at ar-Rahba.

The fortress, built on a steep hill, was made of brown stone and brick. Even from far away, Byron could see the massive walls of the citadel, each wall rising above the other. In the center, he could see the stone keep of the fortress rising above the desert floor. Towers rose to great heights against the blue desert sky. From the topmost tower, the banner of the crescent moon flapped in the breeze. The blur from the heat rising from the land made it difficult to see any details, but he did not need to see the exact layout of the fortress. Its immense size was enough to tell him it was a bastion of military power, built with the purpose of reminding everyone who saw it of the power of the Sultan Saladin. He scanned its looming walls for any sign of activity. The view was clear enough to see that it was going to be impossible to slip by the fortress unnoticed.

Byron sat on his horse watching. Nothing stirred along the

walls of the castle. He grew hopeful that maybe, like Gaston, perhaps the war had drawn the garrison away.

"Perhaps Saladin has left the castle unguarded?" Byron asked hopefully.

"Christian, the sultan has not consulted with me for weeks."

"I was hoping to hear your opinion."

"Let me ask you, Christian, if you were the sultan, would you abandon a military stronghold that guards your frontier?"

"No. Only in great need."

"Then, Christian, I think you have your answer."

Byron sat and watched the walls for a few moments more. It was hot. Anyone with any sense would be lounging in the shade, which was probably what the garrison was doing. He envied the men in the castle, who he suspected were enjoying a simple luxury that he was denied. He turned his horse and started riding back up the trail. Perhaps James or Narvez might have a better plan than riding past the front of the castle.

CHAPTER 44
QALA' AT AR-RAHBA

The castle was not abandoned, and the men who kept watch from its walls saw Byron and quickly relayed the report to the commander of the garrison. When the commander received the news of horsemen on the road he turned to his lieutenant. "What do you think, Mundhir? Do you think these horsemen are part of the caravan we were warned to watch for?"

"My lord, does it matter? Do you really wish to meddle in affairs you have been warned to stay away from?"

"No. It just makes me wonder," the commander said defensively. "It could also be the sultan's men, this Husam al-Din, whoever he might be."

"Some worthless favorite of the sultan who probably saw this as a chance to gather laurels and avoid the fighting. Those of us who dream of fighting for Islam and martyrdom rot out here, forgotten."

"Our time is coming, Mohammad. I have a feeling this war will last awhile. I don't think the Christians will give up so easily."

"Perhaps, but I tire of waiting while everyone else is fighting the infidels! I hear it has been a rout. The Christians are weak!"

"The war is not over. Things could change," Mundhir cautioned. "Let's go out on the ramparts and see if it is the caravan that we have been told is coming."

Mohammad walked across the courtyard and up the stairway that led to the rampart walls. Mundhir followed. When they reached the battlements, both men stood next to the wall and looked out at the desert. Several soldiers gathered around the castle commanders.

"Where were the horsemen?" Mohammad demanded.

"The horsemen were there, my lord," one of the soldiers answered as he pointed into the distance.

"I don't see them." Mohammad stepped back from the wall. "We shall wait and see if they return."

"Do you think I should alert the rest of the men in case it is Mongols on a raid?" Mundhir asked.

"I wish that were the case. I would welcome a glorious fight," Mohammad complained. "No! I am not that fortunate, it will be the caravan. Do not trouble the men. I don't want them spreading rumors that we have lost our nerve just because two horsemen were on the road. If it is Mongols, we will have time to assemble a sortie to repel an attack."

"As you command," Mundhir replied.

†

Byron picked up a gallop and rode as swiftly as he could towards the caravan. James lifted his hand, signaling the column to halt and then rode forward to meet Byron as Ishaq followed him.

"What news do you have, my friend?" James asked.

"It is not an abandoned outpost, but a great Saracen castle that guards the road?"

"What is its strength?"

"It is a large fortress of brick and stone with several towers and a strong keep."

"Merde!" James grumbled. "Is there a way around it?"

"No," Byron replied. "It is built upon a hill and commands the view from all directions."

"What do you want to do?"

"Ride to it and water the animals."

"Aren't you concerned about another entanglement with Saracens?"

"Yes, but to go around would raise suspicions. Besides, there is no need to enter the fortress. There are no great lords to pay homage to. Agreed?"

James turned to Ishaq. "What do you say, Don Fuego?"

"I agree, Sir James," Ishaq replied. "You must go past the castle on the road."

"What is your decision?" James asked Byron. "The priest left you in charge."

Byron looked up at the sky. "The day is getting on. It would be better to ride to the castle now. I cannot foresee anything that will make our circumstances more favorable." Byron looked at James and Don Fuego. "If it turns out ill for us, I would rather get this over with."

†

Mohammad and Mundhir watched from the ramparts as a large dust cloud appeared. Out of the dust, emerged a caravan of camels. "Do you believe they are the infidels?" Mohammad asked.

"That was the message of Prince Malik az-Zahir."

Mohammad frowned. "I cannot believe the Prince Malik az-Zahir would allow infidels to pass unmolested." Mohammad paused, deep in thought. "This is ridiculous! It is an insult to the land. I am not going to sit by and let infidels pass, desecrating our homeland."

"Our orders were explicit, my lord. You place the whole garrison at the risk of Salah al-Din's wrath if you disobey them."

"Salah al-Din can rot in hell. Allah would never punish a man for killing an infidel. The messenger of the Grand Vizier was a traitor who got the message wrong. Assemble the men. Bring my horse. The blood of the infidels will stain the sands before the sun sets."

"My lord, the messenger was not a traitor." Mundhir shouted. "I urge you to reconsider."

"Mundhir, you are acting like an old woman. Do as I have ordered. Assemble the men and get my horse."

"Yes, my lord," Mundhir said as he started to turn away.

"Salah al-Din will see his error," Mohammad gloated. "Allah and his prophet will reward me. You shall see, Mundhir."

Mundhir spun around drawing his shamshir, he stabbed the weapon deep into Mohammad's chest. Blood sprayed from the wound, splattering Mundhir's clothes with little droplets of red. A look of surprise filled Mohammad's face as he collapsed to the stone floor of the battlement.

"How dare you insult Salah al-Din," Mundhir grunted as he shoved harder on the hilt of the shamshir. "I cannot let you risk the lives of the men for your own personal glory."

Mohammad gasped, struggling for air. Blood ran from the wound and across the stones as his eyes bulged and then slowly glazed over in death. Mundhir pulled the weapon free and wiped the blood from the blade on Mohammad's tunic.

A soldier ran up the steps. "My lord, there is a prince at the gate. He is demanding to see the commander." The soldier glanced down at the body of Mohammad.

"That will not be possible," Mundhir said calmly. "Tell the prince politely that I will be down in a moment. Give him some refreshment and beg his forgiveness for my delay."

"He is a most arrogant lord," the soldier said, not even wanting to know why their commander was dead.

"Do what you can," Mundhir replied, and he turned to the rest of the soldiers on the rampart. "Take our commander below and see that his body is returned to the earth. It is my wish that Allah and his prophet give him his reward, but for those of us still here on earth, I remind you that the Sultan Salah al-Din will give you yours, and I have no desire to face the wrath of Salah al-Din."

The men nodded as two of the soldiers carried Mohammad's body away. Mundhir wiped the blood off his hands on his tunic as he descended the staircase that led from the rampart wall. He slowly made his way to the main gate; painfully aware he was covered with blood. He reached the main entrance and saw a tall handsome man standing next to a shorter man. The taller man was dressed in a black silk tunic embroidered with silver thread about the edges. An arrogant sneer was on his face. The shorter man, dressed in the manner of a man who worked for a living, was standing behind the prince.

"My lord," Mundhir said as he bowed, "I apologize for making you wait."

"You should. I have been waiting in the hot sun, and the only refreshment your rude men have offered me is water! And it is not even cold!"

"My apologies, my lord. My men are rustic. I will make amends."

"Too late! All I desire now is to water my camels and be gone." James stepped closer to Mundhir and saw the blood spatter on his tunic. "I wish to speak to the commander of the garrison, not his servant."

"He is not available, prince."

"What do you mean he is not available?"

"He has had a very bad accident. I don't think it is possible to see him."

James paused. "I don't know what has happened here," James replied slowly. "I think it would be best if I watered my animals and left."

Mundhir smiled coldly. "I think that would be wise, my lord. I also think that you should drink the water that was offered you. It is the best we have." James looked at the glass that was in his hand and slowly drank the water. When he finished, he handed the empty glass back to the soldier.

"Is there anything else you desire, prince, before you leave?" Mundhir said politely.

"No," James said.

"Excellent. Thank you for your visit."

James turned and began to swagger away, with Byron following him. "Don't you think you over did it?" Byron grumbled, once they had passed through the castle gate.

"No," James whispered. "Did you see that man? He is covered with fresh blood. If I didn't know better, I would say he had just killed a man."

"I couldn't see him. He was shadowed by the doorway. I wondered why you changed your tone when you stepped closer to him."

"We need to make haste. I fear there is an internal power struggle, and I am certain not everyone is in allegiance with the castle's new master."

Byron and James rode back to the caravan at a trot, doing their best to hurry, while trying not to look suspicious. Ishaq and Bashshar were at the head of the column. James brought his horse to a stop and told them what had happened.

"Christian, I would delay watering the animals," Bashshar said. "If there is a revolt, we need to move on swiftly. The Euphrates is still near, we can water them there. If fighting breaks out between the soldiers, it would be best if we are not caught in the middle."

"Agreed," James replied, turning his horse south and starting off at a trot. The caravan passed swiftly in front of the castle, yet to Byron, it seemed agonizingly slow. He held his breath and strained his ears for the sound of fighting. He expected to see Saracens spill from the gate at any minute, yet nothing happened. The last camel passed by the gate, and the walls of the castle slowly disappeared from sight. When they were a safe distance away, Byron relaxed.

✝

Muhtadi thought he was catching up to the Christians. However, each time he thought they would come into sight, all that was revealed was an empty trail. Husam al-Din kept sending riders, asking for updates on the Christians' location, and each time, Muhtadi sent them back with a vague answer.

The trail was clear. The Christians were hurrying south, traveling fast as if the devil himself was chasing them. He had one consolation. The castle of Qala' at ar-Rahba guarded the road, and the garrison would be able to tell him how far ahead the

Christians were.

When the Grand Vizier had sent Muhtadi to track the Christians, the old man had told him that he was sending messengers ahead of him, warning his commanders not to interfere with the Christians. The Grand Vizier had given Muhtadi the same warning of the painful death awaiting anyone who failed to obey orders. Muhtadi shivered at the thought of what would happen if someone foolishly did not heed the warning. He wondered what would happen to him if he failed to find the Christians and had to admit that his men had lost them because they were derelict in their duties. Fear filled his heart. He did not wish to find out, and he urged his horse on, hoping that at any moment he would see the dust of a hundred camels rising in the distance.

"Ahmed, hurry up!" he cried impatiently as he galloped down the trail.

"Quit shouting! This was not my fault," Ahmed said as he looked over at Nadim who looked down. "I am not the one who lost them!"

"Shut up and keep up!" Ahmed and Nadim did not reply.

Muhtadi rode at a reckless pace, pushing his horse hard. He galloped down the road. In the distance, he saw the walls of Qala' at ar-Rahba rising above the plains. Muhtadi urged his horse on, not caring anymore if he spared the animal. He and his men would get fresh horses at the castle and would continue the pursuit once they remounted. Soldiers issued from the main gate to block the road.

"I am Muhtadi," he shouted. "A servant of Allah and his prophet. A chief scout of Prince Malik az-Zahir of Aleppo! Has a caravan passed by?"

"Yes," one of the soldiers shouted. The soldier was about to say more when an officer appeared and the man grew silent.

"Are you Husam al-Din?" the man asked.

"No. Muhtadi, Chief Scout of Prince Malik az-Zahir. Husam al-Din follows. I am tracking a caravan of infidels for him."

"I see. I am Mundhir, commander of the garrison of Qala' at ar-Rahba. The Grand Vizier sent messages to expect you."

"I thought Mohammad was the commander. What has

happened to him?"

The soldiers glanced at each other uncomfortably. "Our late commander, Mohammad, had a grave accident," Mundhir replied.

"An accident? How unfortunate."

"Yes, indeed. How may I assist you?"

"We need new mounts."

Mundhir turned to two of his soldiers. "Bring new horses and get these men some water."

"You are very gracious," Nadim replied.

Muhtadi asked, "How far ahead are the Christians?"

"You should catch them by nightfall if you ride hard."

"Fresh horses will help. Did the Christians tell you anything of their destination?"

"No, they did not stay long. They are well disguised. If I had not been forewarned that they were Christians, I would have believed they were Saracens."

Mundhir's men arrived with the new horses and skins filled with water. Muhtadi dismounted, traded horses, and saluted Mundhir. "Farewell, my lord. Tell Husam al-Din that I am still following the Christians. I will send a messenger at nightfall." Muhtadi bowed, turned his horse, and took off at a slow gallop, Ahmed following behind him.

†

James kept up a grueling pace all afternoon without halting. Qala at' ar-Rahba was behind him, but the farther he could get from the Saracen stronghold, the better. He left the group as the day wore on and rode back down the trail looking for signs of pursuit, but all he saw was an empty trail. The disguise was working. The Saracens had not even given them a second glance as they rode passed.

It was getting late. He turned his horse and galloped back up the road to catch up to the caravan. When he reached the last group of camels, he found Bashshar riding rear guard, waiting for him.

"We need to find a place to stop and water the animals, especially the horses."

James nodded. "I will send Fitzwalter and Narvez ahead to find a place where we can water at the river." James put his spurs to his horse and rode to the head of the caravan.

"Fitzwalter, take Narvez and ride ahead to see if you can find a place where we can water the animals."

Byron motioned for Narvez to follow him, and both men rode off at a gallop to look for a place large enough to bring the caravan to the river's edge. It took some time, but Narvez found a promising place. Byron rode back to the trail and sat on his horse, waiting impatiently on the deserted road for James to arrive. The emptiness gave Byron an eerie feeling. Just as he was about to ride further down the road, James appeared, leading the way for the rest of the caravan.

Byron spurred his horse forward to meet James. "Narvez found a wide place on the riverbank." Byron turned his horse and rode back up the road, turned off the trail, and began riding down to the river's edge.

The animals crowded at the riverbank. James shouted at the men, "We don't have much time. I want to get moving again as soon as we get the horses watered." This was greeted with grumbling from the men.

Ishaq looked at Byron. Perhaps he could use this opportunity to weaken the Christians. He rode over to Byron who was leaning back in his saddle as his horse drank from the river . "Sir Byron, if you are concerned about being followed, then leave a false trail. Make the enemy think we crossed the river."

"It is late. The men are tired. Our clothes will not dry out before night fall."

"Yes, but if the Saracens are trailing us, it will throw them off our track."

James rode up. "What are you waiting for?"

"Don Fuego has suggested that we ride in the river bed to hide our trail."

James looked at the Euphrates and then at Don Fuego. "There

are deep holes along the bank. We could lose a man or an animal."

Byron crossed his arms as he looked at Ishaq suspiciously. "I don't know if it is worth the risk. If we had aroused the Saracen's suspicions, then we would have met our end at Qala ar at Rahba."

"It is only a suggestion, Sir Byron and Sir James," Ishaq said. "You can do whatever you wish. It is an opportunity, that is all."

James glanced at Byron. "It is an opportunity to throw off any pursuit."

Byron sighed, closed his eyes, and shook his head. He was tired, and he questioned if this was worth the effort. He pulled up his horse's head and turned to ride along the riverbank, his horse splashing in the water. As he passed each group of men, he passed along the plan to ride in the riverbed next to the bank.

When he reached the head of the caravan, he turned in the saddle and shouted, "Follow me!"

VonDurenberg's horse balked at the sight of the river, refusing to enter the water. Byron paused as VonDurenberg spurred and cursed the horse, but the horse refused to move forward, rearing in protest. At last, Narvez and Bashshar got behind the horse and started whipping it, forcing it to step into the water. The horse leaped into the water without warning, taking its rider with him. Byron could not help but laugh at the surprised look on Von-Durenberg's face. As the horse struggled back onto the shallow bank, Byron could hear the German cursing and shouting at the rest of the men who were also laughing.

Byron rode along the bank in the shallows, avoiding the places where the river had created deep holes in the riverbed. It was time consuming, and the sun was starting to sink into the west. After a mile, Byron had enough, and he took the first opportunity he saw to lead the caravan back to the road. When he reached the road, he turned south and picked up a trot, doing his best to get in every mile before the sun set.

The sun was past the horizon when Byron came upon a group of ruins jutting out of the sand. He stopped. He would camp here for the night. Without asking anyone else's opinion, he dismounted. He was wet and cold. At least, the ruined walls would offer some protection from the restless winds. Without any command, the men stiffly dismounted and started stripping the saddles from their horses. It was getting dark and Byron was exhausted. Slowly, he pulled the saddle from Enam's back and rubbed down his horse as best he could. He hobbled his horse and turned the animal loose to pick through the meager forage that grew among the stones and bricks of the ruined city.

Giodonni came up to stand beside Byron. "I do not like this place. It fills me with disquiet. Evil has been done here, I feel it."

"I am tired and cold," Byron replied. "I don't care. I am going to find a place to sleep out of the wind." Picking up his blanket, he tucked it under his arm and trudged into the ruins. Here and there, in the fading light, the brick walls jutted out of the sand casting long shadows across the ground. He walked along a path between the broken walls. He stopped and glanced around as the realization struck him that he was standing in the ruins of a city.

If Father Villhardain were still alive, the priest would have told him this was once the city, Dura Europa. In the gathering gloom of twilight, he could see the darkened arch of the city gate shadowed against the sky. Most of the walls had been thrown down and lay scattered on the ground, but here and there, parts of the rampart still stood. Like jagged sentinels, the dark shapes kept watch on the ruined city. Giodonni was right, a feeling of ill-boding crept over him. Shrugging off the feeling, he started to walk again. A wall blocked his path. A painted border of laurel adorned the walls top. The ceiling was gone and he could see a faint star appearing in the darkening sky. In the center of the wall, a faded image could still be seen on the chipped and cracked plaster.

Nymphs were dancing on the edge of a forest. In the dim light, he could make out the musical instruments of the half-dressed goddess' as they played music under the summer stars. On a green field in the center of the image, revelers enjoyed a feast beneath the boughs of the trees. It was an idyllic scene, and Byron, dusty and tired, wished he could step into the portrait to join the festivities.

He turned away from the wall. What had happened to the people who had lived here? As his eyes swept the ruins, he saw the answer. He had seen this kind of evidence before, the unmistakable signs of war. Enemies had surrounded the walls of the city, and in a bitter fight, they had breached the fortifications in several places. Even now, he could still see the defenders failed attempt to use scaffolding to shore up the damage to a wall. It had been futile, and the enemies of Dura Europa had surged in, overpowering the defenders, laying waste to everything in their path.

He turned around, and he saw it. A white skull, the eyes filled with sand. He looked at the white bony face and decided he would rather sleep out in the open. He was weary, but he had no desire to sleep among the ghosts that still might linger within the dilapidated buildings of the dead city. He found a mound of crumbled bricks that blocked the wind. He threw out his blanket, lay down, and within a few moments was fast asleep.

†

Muhtadi had been following the Christian's trail when it disappeared. Muhtadi stopped his horse.

"What is it?" asked Ahmed.

"The trail is gone. I have missed something."

"I told you we should have killed them."

Muhtadi ignored him. He dismounted and looked carefully at the ground. "We need to go back."

"Muhtadi, it's late and it will be dark soon. Let's find a place to camp while we still can."

"We are going to keep looking, until we find them," Muhtadi hissed.

Nadim dismounted and began searching the ground. Muhtadi walked back up the trail. He had spent his whole life tracking, and he was using every skill he possessed to find the Christians' trail. He cursed to himself for being careless as he walked back and forth on the trail. He found it. The camels had left the road here. His heart began to race. He cursed himself for not paying attention. Even the least skilled tracker would have noticed the trampled grass and bent reeds. He walked closer to the edge of the water and saw the distinctive round shapes with two toes. Camels had sunk into the mud of the riverbank.

"Allah, be praised!" Muhtadi exclaimed, but why would they cross the river? There was no road on the other side? There was nothing except rough empty countryside. He stood looking around, considering the evidence. He needed to make a good decision, if he didn't, it could take days to find them again.

Muhtadi looked at the far bank. "Nadim, do you think the Christians crossed the river?"

Nadim nodded. "Yes, Muhtadi, the sign is clear."

"What are you waiting for?" Ahmed demanded impatiently. "They crossed here."

Muhtadi smiled at Nadim. "No, they didn't. They just want us to think they did." He turned his horse south and began riding along the riverbank. "You have a lot to learn boy. Even if the sign is clear, look around before you blindly follow your prey. Sometimes things are not as they seem."

The sun was sinking, and Muhtadi did not have much time left to find where the Christians had returned to the road. He rode along the riverbank in the shallow water, his horse splashing with each step as it pushed though the reeds. At last, he saw it. A large herd of animals had emerged out of the river, chewing up a large swath of the riverbank, grinding the turf into mud. He was right. His enemy was cunning. He would be more careful from now on. The trail was clear, and he picked up the pace. The Christians would have to go into camp. Their animals were probably at the limit of their endurance.

It was twilight as he reached the top of a small hill. He strained his eyes in the failing light, and in the dim shadows, he could faintly make out the dark shapes of men moving back and forth caring for their animals.

He slowly turned and rode out of sight of the Christians. He and Ahmed would take turns watching at night. Nadim would watch during the day. No mistakes this time. The Christians were not fools, and with this knowledge, he would be on his toes.

CHAPTER 45
NODDABA

The morning sun streamed through the gaps of the brick wall and into Byron's face. He turned on to his side as he tried to go back to sleep. Small chips of broken masonry dug into his side, and he tossed and turned trying to get comfortable. At last, he gave up. He sat up; every muscle in his body ached. Slowly, he stretched to work out the stiffness in his limbs and stood up. James was up making his rounds, waking the men. After a quick breakfast, the animals were packed, and Byron set off following the river.

Each day was like the next, uneventful and indistinguishable until they became a blur. The men began to grumble. The Arab drivers were openly threatening to quit, and Bashshar had to threaten several of his men to force them to stay. The Christians were complaining among themselves. Giodonni had warned Byron that VonDurenberg was stirring up ill feelings against him among the men.

They had ridden hard all day. The wind had started to blow from the west. Byron's head was aching by late in the afternoon; his eyes watering with the pain. Bashshar rode up beside Byron. "We are drawing near Nehardea," he whispered. "Do you want to call a halt?"

Byron squinted up at the sky and turned in his saddle to look at the tired dusty men following him. "Yes, it is time."

Byron raised his hand, and the men halted and dismounted. Byron loosened the cinch on his saddle. He saw De Montgris, De Vale, and VonDurenberg gathered, talking in low voices. Speer who was standing next to his uncle looked up at Byron. The lids of the squire's eyes narrowed as the corners of his mouth turned up into a leer. Byron held the squire in his gaze for a moment and then looked away as he tied his horse to a palm tree. He sat down in the tree's shade and closed his eyes, hoping the pain would go away. Bashshar and Don Fuego came and sat beside him.

"Sir Byron, are you ill?" Ishaq asked.

"No, my head hurts, it is an old wound, it will pass. How close are we to Nehardea?" Byron asked.

"Christian, I do not know," Bashshar replied. "Why do you ask?"

Byron sighed. "I do not want to blunder into Nehardea unprepared. Can you take a horse and find out how close we are?"

"Have James do it," Bashshar replied. "I am tired."

"Damn it! Princes do not scout the trail!" Byron snapped. "For the sake of the risen Christ! Do what I ask!"

A look of anger filled Bashshar's face, and he glanced at Ishaq, who nodded. Mumbling, Bashshar got up and went to retrieve his horse. Tightening the cinch, Bashshar then swung into the saddle and rode off.

The sun was nearing the horizon when Bashshar returned. Byron looked up through watery eyes. A strange man was standing next to Bashshar. Dismounting, Bashshar stalked over to where Byron and Ishaq were still sitting.

"We are near the city," Bashshar said. "If we wish to remain unseen, we should cross the river soon."

The man standing next to Bashshar wore a coarse, black cloak frayed along the edges. A dark hood hid his face. Beneath this cloak, he wore a long tunic, grey from years of wear; no doubt, Bashshar had found a vagabond looking for a handout. The man turned and walked to Byron. He pulled back his hood to reveal a handsome face. He appeared neither young nor old. He wore no covering on his head. His black hair fell to his shoulders. Hazel eyes beneath dark eyebrows regarded the world with an air of superiority. His thin lips were pressed together giving the impression of disdain. The only blemish to his striking face was a dark mark near his temple. The man's hazel eyes fixed on Byron, and he smiled revealing white teeth.

"Bashshar has informed me that you need a guide to Babylon," he said in a pleasant voice.

"Do you know the way?" Byron asked.

The man scoffed, "Yes, I know Babylon. It is a great city."

Byron crossed his arms as he regarded the man. His initial misgivings of a beggar came back. "I thought Babylon was in ruins?"

"Who told you such a thing?"

"Our last guide."

The man laughed. "Your guide was misinformed. Babylon is not in ruin. No! It is still a great city. It is a haven for the weary. Food and strong drink in abundance." The man lowered his head as he looked up at James who was talking to Don Fuego. "And the women! Babylon has the most desirous women on earth. Their beauty is beyond compare." The man sighed. "I can set you on the path. The trail is not difficult, for it is well traveled. You are fortunate, you are near it now. It lies across the river."

Byron glanced at the man. "Why cross the river? I thought Babylon sat astride the Euphrates."

The man laughed. "It did long ago, but the land has changed. One must cross the river to reach the city."

Byron took out Father Villhardain's map from under his cloak and unfolded it. The man bent close and pointed to a spot between the two rivers. "See, it is right there."

Byron stared at the map. He had never noticed the mark before. Beneath the mark in small faint letters was the name Babylon, written in the priest's handwriting.

James walked over and looked over Byron's shoulder at the map. "Did you find something, Fitzwalter?"

Byron nodded. "Yes. I have not noticed it until now. Father Villhardain has marked his map with the place where the city of Babylon lies."

The man smiled as James stepped beside Byron and took the

map. James furled his brow as he stared at the map. At last, he looked up. "Strange, I have looked at this map several times and never noticed this."

Byron nodded. "Tis strange, verily... I have never noticed the mark either, but there it is."

"Indeed so, Fitzwalter. Your finding is timely. It looks like we are near the trail that leads us there."

Byron sighed. The pain in his head was growing. "The day is getting on. We should leave soon. Have the men mount up." James nodded as he walked away.

Byron turned to the man. "What is your name?"

The man smiled. "My name? I have had many names, for I have traveled in many lands, but you may call me Noddaba."

"That is an uncommon name."

Noddaba nodded. "Indeed. It is an old name, not used much anymore. I have lived here a long time. I know this land well, and I will not guide you wrong. I promise that I will deliver you to the Ishtar gate of Babylon."

Byron frowned as he looked over to see Bashshar and James talking. "What will it cost me?"

Noddaba smiled, but his hazel eyes remained unchanged as they held Byron in a steady gaze. "Nothing that you cannot afford. When we have reached Babylon, and if I have guided you well, there you can each give me a small reward."

"What kind of reward."

"That, you will have to decide, but do not worry, I will not ask for anything more than you can afford. Get your men across the river, and I will meet you on the other side."

Byron glanced at the sky and then said, "And how will I find you?"

"I agreed to guide you, did I not!" Noddaba paused and looked down, when he looked up again, he smiled. "My Lord Fitzwalter, you worry about crossing the river. Once you have done that, I will find you. Fear not." Noddaba pulled his hood over his head, shadowing his face. "Fear not," he repeated, "I will make sure you find Babylon." Turning, Noddaba strode swiftly down the trail disappearing from sight.

Byron watched him walk away. His head throbbed, and as he rubbed it to relieve the pain, he wondered to himself how Noddaba knew his name. He must have told him. He turned and wandered back to where Enam was grazing. Stepping into the stirrup, he mounted. Bashshar led the way, following the trail to a place where it led to a river ford.

"If you wish to cross the river Christian, this is the place to do it."

Byron looked across the slow flowing river choked with reeds to the green bank on the other side. It was getting late, and the thought of getting wet and cold filled Byron with loathing. Shaking his head at the thought and touching Enam with his spurs, he rode his horse into the river. The water surged up to his knees. Byron's tunic was getting wet from the splashing water. The wind had picked up, and the breeze made him shiver. Enam's hooves dug into the turf as he lunged up the bank, pushing his way through the reeds. When Byron reached the top, he drew his shamshir. He rose in his stirrups and looked around. The land was empty, Noddaba was nowhere to be seen.

"Christ! I knew it," Byron muttered as he put the spurs to Enam who started forward down the trail. Muttering dark curses, Byron rode on, in the hopes of finding his guide before nightfall. He dropped over a small rise and pulled Enam to a stop. In front of the roaring fire stood Noddaba.

"Come! Come! Rest!" Noddaba cried. "Warm yourselves by the fire."

Byron felt like a fool for doubting Noddaba. The sight of the fire brought a faint smile to his face. He turned and looked at the cold tired men following him. "We camp here." Byron swung his leg stiffly over the cantle of his saddle, dismounted, and stretched.

Noddaba motioned to Byron. "Come and enjoy the warmth." Byron stripped the saddle from his horse and carried it to the fire. Setting the saddle down on the sand, Byron leaned against it as he sat next to the fire. The men gathered near him for their meager meal. When the meal was finished, Byron stretched out to read.

James came and sat near him. "Fitzwalter, are you still feeling ill?"

Byron sighed. "No, the ache has lessened." Byron reached

into his saddlebag and pulled out the pages of the Odyssey. "I hope by tomorrow it will be gone." Byron untied the string that bound the pages.

James frowned, a look of worry on his tired face. He stood up. "I hope so." James looked down at his friend. "I will check on you again." Byron shook his head. He was fine. His head ached, but that was nothing new. Sitting in the firelight's glow, Byron immersed himself into the Odyssey.

Noddaba glanced at the pages of the book. "Ah, the Odyssey. The Trojan war is one of my favorites. Odysseus was a very clever Greek."

Byron looked up from the pages at Noddaba. "You know the story?"

"Ah yes." Noddaba stared into the fire. "It must be a good feeling to know that you are close to Babylon?"

"Yes. I hope to be there soon. In the morning we will ride. Do you have a horse?"

Noddaba shook his head. "I don't have a horse, nor do I need one. I'm surprisingly swift, as swift as the wind some say. Do not worry, My Lord Fitzwalter, I will not hinder your journey. If I need a horse, I will take one." Noddaba smiled. "I am just glad that I am able to aid you in your quest."

"I will be indebted to you," Byron said as he started to roll up the pages.

"Yes, you will," Noddaba smiled as he patted Byron on the knee. "If I may, I have some vision of the future." Byron stopped rolling up the pages of the book and looked at Noddaba. The flames of the fire cast a reddish hue to the guide's handsome face. "Fitzwalter, you will have success in Babylon. You will save Jerusalem, and for this great deed you will be rewarded."

Byron started to ask how he would be rewarded when Noddaba stood up. "I know your question. Visions do not come with explanations. They just are. I promise, the day after tomorrow you will see the Ishtar gate, and soon after that you will know the truth."

The morning dawned with a strong wind blowing. Dust whipped along the ground as the wind hissed through the gaps of the nearby rocks. The horses were saddled and the camels packed. Noddaba led the way. At last, they reached the trail, a well-traveled trench beaten into the earth by the many feet that had passed this way before. The wind was blowing harder. With his head bowed, Byron rode on, following Noddaba who ignored the wind. The miles passed, and they stopped at midday to rest. After a quick meal, they started again. The light of the sun was failing, and Byron turned in the saddle to see a brown shapeless wall of dust rushing towards them. Lightening flashed among the darkened clouds. "A storm approaches," Byron cried.

Noddaba looked back as the landmarks disappeared into the murky gloom. Sand pelted them. "Do not fear the storm. Stay on the trail and follow me."

"We should find shelter and wait out the storm," James shouted.

"I agree," Bashshar cried over the shriek of the wind. "It is a simoom. We must find a place to stop."

"Babylon is near," Noddaba cried. "Keep going. The walls of the city will shelter us from the storm."

"How long will this last?" Byron demanded.

"A few hours if we are fortunate, or a few days if we are not," Bashshar shouted back.

Noddaba looked back, his hazel eyes had a yellow tint in the gloom. "It will not last. Rest, warmth and good food await! We are close. Follow me!" Before Byron could answer, Noddaba strode forward.

James trotted up to Byron. "Fitzwalter, we need to stop. The animals will not survive this."

"We are close!" Byron shouted. "We must keep going!" Byron spurred Enam forward, ending the conversation. They trudged along the trail. The sand pelting them. Hours passed, at last Noddaba stopped.

Byron rode up to the guide. "The men can go no further!" he shouted over the wind.

"Do you not wish to reach Babylon?"

"Yes, but we must stop and rest."

Noddaba shrugged. "As you wish."

They found a small depression and gathered the animals into a circle as the wall of dust and sand engulfed them.

Byron huddled under the shelter of his blanket. He was holding his aching head when Noddaba appeared out of the blowing dust and bent near. "Keep hope, Fitzwalter. You will be there soon." Noddaba smiled and then disappeared into the dust.

Byron stood up, but Noddaba was gone. He could barely see the men around him through the blowing sand. It was hard to breathe, so he tied a rag over his mouth. The men huddled under their blankets as they waited for the storm to pass. The night went on, and the storm showed no sign of abating.

The sky lightened to a reddish-orange as the dawn came, and still the sandstorm raged. Noddaba was standing facing the wind, his black cloak whipping behind him. VonDurenberg and De Courcy were standing next to the guide. James, his head down, struggling against the wind staggered over to Byron. "You are not considering going on?"

Almost as if he had heard them, Noddaba came over. "Babylon is close. We would have reached the safety of her walls had you had more faith and continued on."

"We have no choice," Byron snarled. "If we stay here, we will surely perish. If we go on, I hope to find Babylon and safety."

"Yes," VonDurenberg shouted. "We could be enjoying Babylon's comforts, but here we are in this Godforsaken place in the middle of this wretched storm." Noddaba nodded and smiled at the graf.

In the dust, Byron could make out Bashshar. He motioned the Arab to join them. "We are going to continue on to Babylon," Byron shouted.

"I agree," Bashshar shouted back. "This is no place to stay. Allah willing, we will find shelter."

"This is madness!" James shouted as he turned and stalked away.

The men struggled to repack the camels. Parker's horse, spooked by the wind, reared up as it was being saddled and fell over backwards. Cursing, Parker picked up his saddle and restarted saddling the horse. Noddaba watched Parker pick up his saddle, and with a look of disdain, he turned and grabbed Father Villhardain's riderless horse. Swinging on to the horse's back, Noddaba took off at a run.

"Father Villhardain's horse has bolted!" James shouted over the wind.

Byron ignored James as he mounted Enam. It was obvious that in the blowing sand, James could not see that Noddaba was riding the priest's horse. Without waiting, Byron rode off following Noddaba. In the gloom, he could just make out Father Villhardain's horse. Noddaba was waiting for them. As Byron neared, Noddaba turned and rode off ahead of him. At times, they were forced to stop as gusts of wind obliterated the trail. Byron could barely see Noddaba a few feet in front of him. He put his head down, sheltering his face, as Enam plodded on. They had traveled for several hours when Byron looked up to see the ghostly image of Noddaba disappearing into the dust. Byron blinked and wiped the sand from his face. He called out to Noddaba, but Noddaba did not stop. The wind shrieked in his ears. Byron struggled forward, but there was no sign of Noddaba.

The trail went on. The horses were exhausted, and the men were tired. It was growing dark and still the wind blew. In the swirling dust, Byron could see something in the trail. A large rock. Byron drew close, and as he leaned over Enam's neck, he saw the head of a horse. Its eyes fixed wide open. He dismounted and knelt down. It was Father Villhardain's horse. He brushed the sand from the horse's head, but it did not move.

He stood up and looked around for Noddaba in the swirling sand when VonDurenberg came up. Giodonni and De Montgris were with him. "Where in the hell are we?" Byron did not answer. "My lord, I asked you a question," VonDurenberg shouted over the wind, his face white with exhaustion. "Where is Babylon?"

Byron stepped close to VonDurenberg. "I do not know. Father Villhardain's horse lies dead in the middle of the trail."

Giodonni stepped forward. "My lords, it is an ill omen. We should stop and let the storm abate. In the morning light, we will have a clearer view."

"Or the storm will bury us," De Montgris grumbled as he turned away.

"You had better hope Babylon is near," the German said.

"We should at least go on a little further. Perhaps there is a better place up ahead to take shelter from the storm." Byron tugged on the reins, but Enam refused to move. Byron tugged harder. Enam snorted and pulled back. Swinging around. the knight tried to whip the horse, but Enam deftly side passed away. "Damn it, horse," Byron cried, but Enam continued to pull back.

James trudged up. "The horse has more sense than you. We have gone far enough today."

Byron was too tired to argue, and giving up, he looked around. Noddaba was gone and trying to find him in the storm would be foolish. It was time to rest, they were next to a small bank and it would have to do. The men made camp and huddled beneath their blankets, making a vain effort to ward off the blowing sand. As the night wore on, the wind began to slacken, stars began to appear.

Byron rose and shook the sand from his blanket. The pain in his head was gone. In the growing light, he looked around. There was nothing to see but dust and rocks. Here and there a tangled shrub, struggling to survive in the desolate land. The horses and camels were huddled together. He took off his cloak and tunic and shook them, dusting the sand from his skin. He redressed and then walked down the trail to the dead horse. The head of Father Villhardain's horse was almost buried. He looked into the dull brown eye covered with flecks of sand. He paused, and then sighed as he walked around the horse's stiffened legs.

He had taken just a few steps when he stopped. He was standing on the edge of a thirty-foot drop to earth below. Jagged rocks jutted up from the ground. Byron gazed down at the rocks. If he had continued on his bull-headed way, he would have led his men over the cliff. Enam had saved him. Noddaba must have dismounted and fallen over the edge in the storm. He walked along the cliff's edge, but found no evidence of his missing guide. He sat down on a rock and stared down into the pit below.

The sun shone down on him, and in the morning light, he could see everything clearly. The jagged edges of the rocks below seemed closer than they were. He thought about the last several days. He was tired. He had almost led them to disaster. The dust was blinding. He gave a long sigh, Father Villhardain was gone, and now his new guide was nowhere to be found.

Byron pondered the fate of his missing guide. They should at least look for him. A cold shiver came over him. He was the only one who had spoken to Noddaba. No, he told himself, James had talked to Noddaba. Bashshar had obviously spoken to the man. The more he thought about Noddaba the more he began to question if Noddaba had been real. He put his hands to his face and rubbed his eyes.

The strain was starting to overcome him. Tears streamed down his face. He was lost. He had almost led his men to their deaths, and he was seeing people who were not there. The banshee, the fisherman, Noddaba. Was he going mad?

He shook his head as he wiped away the tears. "Lord, help me," he sighed. "Please help me."

He heard someone approaching. He stood up and wiped his eyes. Bashshar stopped next to him and looked over the edge. "Allah has favored us." Byron nodded. "Come," Bashshar muttered, "the others are gathering."

Byron followed Bashshar back to the place where Father Villhardain's horse lay dead. James was standing near the horse's head, the rest of the Christians were standing in a semi-circle around him. VonDurenberg stood across from James, his arms folded.

"We have been saved from disaster," James said as he looked at Byron. "The trail has been destroyed. Father Villhardain's horse lies dead on the edge of a sheer drop."

"So, now what?" VonDurenberg growled. "You seem unable to find Babylon."

"It is obvious," De Courcy cried, "we go home! The Saracens are following us. I have seen them through the swirling dust. Every moment we delay, increases the chance that they will attack."

James scoffed, "God's bones, De Courcy! The Saracens are not following us. No one could follow us in that storm."

The men looked at Byron. "We are not going back," Byron said. "There must be another trail. The city is here somewhere."

"I agree," Bashshar said. "We are in the wastelands between the Euphrates and the Tigris. If we head east, we should find the Tigris. We can rest there while we look for a new trail. Babylon is near. We will find it."

"Yes," Ishaq interjected, "the Tigris will give us a bearing. We need to let the animals rest. Then we can make another attempt to find the city."

Byron looked around at the tired faces of his men. No one spoke. "Go pack the camels and saddle the horses. We go to the Tigris and then we will try again."

Simon De Courcy stayed and looked back down the trail. "The Saracens are following," he muttered. He drew his dagger and looked at it. Shaking his head, he said, "I won't go back to Aleppo." He stared at his reflection in the blade. "You will help me, won't you?" He watched his reflection nod, and he shoved the dagger back into its sheath.

They set off heading east. Going cross-country, they trudged along until they reached a new trail that headed in the right direction. The sun beat down as the dust from the hooves swirled in the air choking the men. It was near evening when a dark line appeared on the horizon.

Byron stopped. Bashshar rode up beside him. "That line marks the river. We should reach it before night fall."

It was near dark when the Christians reached the bank of the river. Beneath the fronds of the palm trees, Byron stripped his saddle from Enam. As an apology, he spent more time than usual rubbing down Enam's back as the horse grazed on the green grass. The horse had saved him from the going over the cliff's edge, and he was grateful.

CHAPTER 46
QUEST PAR EXCELLENCE

The Christians camped by the river taking the entire day to rest by the cool water. Giodonni shot a gazelle, and for the first time in weeks, they enjoyed a good meal. The next morning, Byron sent Narvez and De Vale to ride in different directions in the hope that they would find a trail that might lead them to the city. Byron rode to the south but found nothing other than an empty, trackless wasteland. Discouraged, he returned to camp and loosened his saddle's cinch so his horse could rest. Pulling out the priest's map, he looked at the river and then the map as he tried to orient the map to where they were.

He was staring at the place on the map marked Babylon when Parker came running towards him, laughing. "Come see," he cried excitedly. "They're about to stone some Saracen wench on the other side of the hill."

Byron glanced up. "What?"

"Three Saracens have some woman on her knees," Parker sniggered. "They are gathering rocks." Parker turned and tore off back to the crest of the hill to watch. Byron stuffed the notes beneath his tunic and ran after Parker. VonDurenberg and several knights also hurried to the edge of the hill and looked out at the riverbank below.

De Courcy looked up at Byron. "I told you the Saracen's were following us. See, there they are! And they have a Saracen witch with them."

"M'Lord De Courcy, they're not here for you," Parker said. "Can't you see, they are about to stone her. I wonder what she did?"

"She is a witch, I tell you!" De Courcy snapped.

In the flat depression of grass stood three Saracen knights. Kneeling in front of them was a woman. The Saracens, in burgundy kaftans gathered stones. Shamshirs hung at their sides, shields slung on their backs. The sun glinted on their steel helmets wrapped with white turbans. The woman, in a green dress, had her head bowed in prayer. Four black horses stood tethered nearby.

"Witch or not she probably deserves what is coming," VonDurenberg said with a chuckle.

Byron could feel the anger rising inside of him. He was disgusted to even know these men, let alone watch the cruel act about to happen. One of the Saracens picked up a rock and tossed it at the woman. The second Saracen walked up to her and stopped, facing her. Reaching out his hand, he tore the hijab from her head, releasing her long dark tresses. He then grabbed her by the chin and looked into her eyes. With his other hand, he jerked something from around her neck, tossing it away.

As Byron watched, pain shot through him, and he heard a voice whisper, "Do not fail again."

He whipped around, but the banshee was not there. His face went rigid, his breathing became ragged as his mind filled with the faces of the dead Saracen women clutching their children, begging him to save their lives. He could stop this! He turned to go.

"Where are you going?" Parker cried. "Don't you want to see this?"

"My Lord Fitzwalter can't stomach blood," taunted VonDurenberg.

Byron did not answer. He ran down the hill past James, who was walking up to see what everyone was watching. His horse was still saddled. He jerked the cinch tight. Hurriedly he shoved the bit in Enam's mouth. He swung onto the horses back. "*Laissez aller!*" he cried as he put the spurs to Enam. His faithful horse leapt forward into a run. The long miles had formed a bond between horse and rider. The horse trusted the rider, and Byron had confidence in the horse. The union had forged the ultimate weapon, the knight with his fearsome steel weapons, carried by the speed and strength of the horse. Enam swiftly reached the crest of the hill.

"Come back, you idiot!" hissed VonDurenberg as Enam cleared the top of the hill with a mighty leap and slid down the other side on its hocks to the riverbank below. "This is not our business!"

Byron ignored the German as Enam thundered past, the horse's hooves pounding on the hard earth. Byron, no longer a mortal man, had become a god of war bent on wreaking vengeance on the unsuspecting Saracens below. The wind hissed in his ears. A Saracen was laughing as he picked up a stone to throw at the woman. Enam swiftly closed the distance, and with a ring of steel, Byron drew his shamshir. Before the Saracen's confederates could shout in alarm, Byron drew back his arm, and with the sweeping blow, the man fell dead, his head severed from his body.

The second Saracen turned to run. Bryon ran him down, Enam hitting him with his chest, knocking the man to the ground. Byron rose up in his stirrups as the man fell face forward, and with a mighty swing, the sword split the man's back, breaking his ribs and piercing his lungs. A fine mist of bloody foam sprayed Byron, staining his hands and his clothes.

Byron's horse slid to a stop. He spun Enam around to face his last opponent. He could hear the gurgling sucking sound as the man he just flayed gasped for air, suffocating to death.

"Fair Fight!" shouted the last Saracen as he drew his sword. His dark eyes locked on Byron. "Fair fight, or I name you a coward before Allah."

Byron paused and then raised his sword in salute. "Fair fight," he shouted. Byron nudged Enam forward and trotted over to one of the dead Saracens. Dismounting, he ripped the shield from the dead man's back. Keeping his gaze on the Saracen, he moved towards the man.

"I don't know who you are," the Saracen cried as he moved to circle Byron, "but this is not your concern!"

Byron did not answer, but launched his assault by ramming the boss of the shield into the Saracen and knocking him backwards. The Saracen turned sideways swinging his shamshir in an arc toward Byron, who skillfully blocked the blow with his sword. The two men circled, each seeking an opening to strike the other. The Saracen attacked, bringing his sword down on Byron's shield. Byron yielded to the blow by stepping back. The Saracen came at him again, attempting to cut Byron at the knees with a sweeping blow to the legs. Byron jumped back as the blade went by, cutting the empty air where his legs had just been. Off balance from the near miss, all Byron could do was block the Saracen's next blow, aimed at his torso.

Byron's face was unguarded. The Saracen, seeing an opportunity, swung his shield at Byron's unprotected face. Byron's head snapped sideways as the shield's edge struck him on the cheek. He staggered backwards. Blood trickled from the gash, and he raised his own shield to avoid another attack.

"You're not so good without your horse," taunted the Saracen as he stepped back to circle Byron again.

Byron ignored the insult as he concentrated on his opponent, looking for an opening. The Saracen attacked, but Byron was ready. With sword and shield they fought, striking and blocking as they tried to break through the other's defense. Out of breath, both men stepped back to circle once more. The Saracen was a skilled swordsman and tough, but Byron was patient, watching, waiting for the Saracen to make a mistake.

The Saracen attacked again, delivering another sweeping blow to Byron's knees. This time, Byron anticipated the move and with a downward stroke, severed the Saracen's arm at the elbow. The man gasped and jerked his severed arm towards his body, blood spurting from his severed arteries.

Byron continued his attack as the injured Saracen blocked each blow with his shield, the bleeding stump of his arm tucked against his kaftan. The Saracen did his best to defend himself. Byron admired the man's courage to keep fighting even though the end was no longer in question. The Saracen collapsed to the ground.

Byron lowered his sword. "My lord, you fought well. Such

courage should not perish. Do you yield?"

"Never," the Saracen cried through the pain. "I will not yield to a bedraggled Bedouin. You are a thief and a murderer. I will not debase myself just so I can live." Byron looked down at the man's arm as his blood spilled out over the sand. "I curse you," the Saracen gasped. "The woman was condemned under Sharia law. She is an adulteress! You have defied the will of Allah."

Byron leaned over the dying Saracen. "I shall not fear God, nor will I repent an act of mercy."

"Mercy?" the Saracen wheezed. "I shall be in paradise...," he whispered as the color drained from his face. Whatever else the man was about to say died with him, and with a slow rattling breath, he stopped breathing. The sweet, sickly odor of death began to fill the air. Byron had smelled it many times before. It was an odd, sickening smell that permeated everything around it, and he hated it. Byron turned away from the corpse.

CHAPTER 47
ZAHIRAH

Byron watched as the birds seeing death began to circle. The woman on her knees was holding her face in her hands, sobbing. Byron walked towards her, his sword in his hand. She glanced up, her eyes widened in terror. Scrambling to her feet, the woman backed away.

Byron sheathed his sword and held out his hand. "Stay, lady, your attackers are dead. I will not harm you."

The woman looked at him, tears in her eyes. "You fool," she screamed. "Do you know what you have done?"

"No?" Byron stopped and stood still.

The woman bowed her head and began to sob. She looked up after several moments. "You're still here? Leave! Haven't you done enough harm already?"

"What harm?" Byron demanded in astonishment. "I just rescued you from death, don't you want to live?"

"I was prepared to die." Her eyes darted to the three corpses surrounding her. "When my husband finds out his servants are dead, he will think my father has rescued me from my executioners. Your meddling will be the death of my father!" She paused as her own words sank in, and the extent of her situation came clearly into focus, and she started to sob again.

"My lady, stop crying. What's done is done. You are alive. Come, I will take you to safety."

"I don't want to go with you!" screamed the woman in protest.

"Lady, I cannot leave you here."

"Yes, you can!" she snapped.

Byron walked forward. "Lady, I cannot and I will not. Either you come with me, or I will take you against your will."

The woman stopped crying and stared at him. She wiped the tears from her eyes. She dusted the sand from her silk dress adorned with pearls. Byron walked over to one of the horses of the dead Saracens and led it to the woman. James galloped up as the woman was mounting.

"Fitzwalter, are you unharmed?" James exclaimed, pulling out a rag and tossing it to Byron to staunch the wound on his cheek.

"I am fine," Byron said as he mounted Enam.

"Fitzwalter, that was an outstanding fight, worthy of a song. You're almost approaching my standards."

Byron nodded blankly as he nudged Enam forward at a walk. Any other time he would have appreciated James' praise, but right now, he just wanted to forget the whole affair. He saved the woman from death, but his exploit was now shorn of its glory. He already had enough problems. He could not find Babylon, and if that was not enough, he went out of his way to create more trouble by saving this woman.

James stopped talking as he caught a glimpse of the Saracen woman riding beside them. She was tall. Her long, black hair cascaded around her face down to her thin waste. She was using a handkerchief to wipe away the tears from her dark eyes. Byron, absorbed in his own thoughts over the recent battle, ignored the woman. James, a connoisseur of women, knew beauty when he saw it.

"Who is this?" James said as a smile spread across his face as he admired the woman's figure.

"I don't know?" Byron replied. "I didn't ask."

James slowed his horse, crossed behind Byron, and rode up beside the woman who was now sandwiched uncomfortably between them.

"Hello," James said in his best sultry Arabic. "May I ask the lady her name? I am sure it is as beautiful as you are." The woman, in no mood for James' advances, looked daggers at him. James laughed. "Oh, come now," he said in his most charming voice. "It would at least be courteous of you to tell me your name if we are going to travel together."

"You're Franks, aren't you?" The woman demanded.

Byron's head whipped sideways to look at the woman. James raised his eyebrows as he realized that in his excitement, he had been congratulating Byron in French.

"You were just speaking French," the woman snapped.

James glanced at Byron who shrugged. "Yes, we are Franks."

"Norman French," Byron corrected with a frown.

The woman's eyes narrowed as her lips curled into a frown. "That explains your recklessness."

"Recklessness?" James repeated. "It is not reckless to save a beautiful woman from an undeserved fate." The woman looked at James darkly but said nothing. "So, Mon Cheri," James said, smiling at the Saracen woman, "how is it that you understand French." Before the woman could answer, James continued, "What shall I call you? What do you think, Fitzwalter?"

"You will not call me anything," the woman said angrily. "My blessed father who is learned and wise, a servant of Allah and his prophet, insisted his children receive the best instruction money could buy. He felt, unlike you ignorant barbarians who have disgraced our lands, that ignorance was a curse!"

"Barbarians?" James chuckled.

"Yes, barbarians! You butchers murdered, without conscience, the faithful of Jerusalem. You have robbed and plundered our caravans. You are ignorant and superstitious. You are dirty and don't wash!" She paused as she ran out of insults to hurl.

"Yes, that is true," James said with a smile, ignoring the woman's contemptuous looks. "But I must ask, why were you about to be stoned to death?"

"I suppose," the woman sighed in exasperation, "you will give me no peace until you learn my name. My name is Zahirah."

"Zahirah. What a beautiful name," James replied. "Wouldn't

you agree, Fitzwalter?"

Byron had stopped paying attention to them. He shook his mind free from his thoughts and answered. "Umm, yes, I guess, I suppose it is," he said, not knowing what he just agreed to.

"Fitzwalter does not have any real appreciation of women," James said.

"My husband is much like you. Once he tired of me, I was sent here to die."

"I have many faults," James said seriously, "but I have never sent a woman to die because I tired of her."

Zahirah's dark eyes flashed as she looked at James with contempt. At last, she looked away. "You could at least look for my necklace," she said. "It was taken from me by one of the men you just slew. It was a gift from my father, and I would like it back."

"We don't have time to look, and you don't need it," Byron said unsympathetically.

"Absolutely not," James agreed. "Your beauty should not be marred by a man-made trinket."

Zahirah sighed, giving up any hope that her rescuers would spend time looking for the necklace. She had no doubt that she would never get it back if she told the barbarians what it was worth.

As they crested the hill, the Christians gathered around Byron. Byron noticed they were all wearing swords. VonDurenberg stood in the center of the semi-circle of knights, his arms folded. Speer sat on the ground next to his uncle. On his knees, in front of the graf, was a Saracen with a dark moustache. He was dressed in black, his dark hair matted with blood. The Saracen looked up and watched as Byron helped Zahirah off her horse. Behind the knights, the Saracen drivers gathered.

"I see you armed the men," Byron said.

VonDurenberg scoffed. "I had to after you foolishly attacked the Saracens in the valley. Did you arrogantly think I would leave them unarmed? Besides, while you were interfering in the affairs of others, Narvez and DeVale on their return to camp captured a spy." The graf turned to the other knights. "My lords, this matter must be judged. What shall we do with our prisoners?"

"The woman is spoil of war!" Narvez cried. "She should be

shared. The spy...kill him."

"My lord, what do you mean shared?" Giodonni asked Narvez.

"You know what he means," Parker interjected with a grin as he stared at Zahirah. "She should serve our pleasure."

"No, I don't know what you mean," Giodonni snapped as he walked closer to look at Zahirah. The Italian knight reached down to caress a lock of her hair. "She is a lost soul who should be shown the path of salvation."

The Saracen knight started struggling to get up. DeVale struck him with the flat of his sword. "Do not move, devil worshiper. Your fate has yet to be decided." The Saracen looked at Zahirah, their eyes met. The Saracen began to pray.

"Foolishness!" Bashshar cried and then spat on the ground. "The woman is clearly a condemned adulteress. We should kill her. Spare the man, he can serve us as a slave." The Saracen drivers shouted their approval. Speer started to laugh.

VonDurenberg raised his hands. "I have no doubt the woman is a wicked Saracen witch, but she may prove useful. She is familiar with these lands. The spy, I do not trust." VonDurenberg turned to Bashshar. "We will keep the woman until she is of no further use. When we are finished... you can carry out your law."

Byron drew his sword and James followed suit. "She is my prisoner and under my protection," Byron cried. "Nothing will happen to her, and no one will touch her."

Narvez swept out his sword. "That is not for you to decide. We shall fight for her and let God judge the matter."

"God should judge the matter," Giodonni agreed.

"Yes," De Courcy cried, "and his judgement is that the Saracen devil worshiper should die." With a guttural cry, the grey haired knight drew his sword. His red, watery eyes gleamed with rage as he brought his sword above his head and swept off the Saracen's head. The head rolled to the ground as the body sagged and fell over.

"De Courcy, you fool!" James shouted. "It would have been wise to question the Saracen to see if he was alone or had companions!" James looked at the headless corpse. "But that will not happen now."

De Courcy fixed his gaze upon Zahirah as he bent forward to charge. James and Byron stepped in front of her, their swords at the ready. "Get out of my way!" De Courcy cried. "How dare you defend that Saracen witch?" Byron took a step forward as he prepared to defend Zahirah.

Ishaq leaped between both parties. "My lords, have you lost your senses? Stay this madness. We have business to do, and fighting over a woman will not aid our cause."

Ishaq had watched in horror as Byron had attacked the three Saracens who were obviously carrying out a lawful punishment. Now, these hotheaded imbeciles were about to fight over her, wasting precious time. They needed to get away from this place.

"My lords, put aside your differences," the assassin continued. "We need to leave this place least someone rides up and sees us so near the bodies of the men you rashly killed!"

VonDurenberg glanced at Don Fuego and then to Byron. "Keep the bitch. Fitzwalter, I will give you a few more days," VonDurenberg glanced at Zahirah, "and then I am turning for home. I will not waste any more time on this fool's errand." VonDurenberg walked off and Narvez followed. The rest of the men turned away.

Ishaq turned and pointed a finger at Byron. "You fool! This is not some lark or romantic quest to find courtly love! We are deep in the land of the enemy!" he shouted, losing his composure. "Those servants belonged to a great lord! Did you not bother to look at the fineness of their dress? What do you think will happen when this lord finds out the woman he sent here to die, lives, and his men who were sent to kill her, are dead?"

"Would you rather I stood idly by and let her be murdered," Byron grumbled indignantly.

"Yes!" Ishaq snapped, trying to regain his composure. "I mean, yes, Sir Byron." Ishaq shook his head. "Let us pray that whoever this lord is, he does not soon learn of his servants' deaths."

"What do you suggest, Don Fuego?" James asked.

"We move north and then double back. I will send Bashshar to pick up the bodies and load them onto a camel. We will dispose of them along the way, but we need to get moving now!"

"I agree," James replied.

"Now that you have made this mess, Sir Byron," Ishaq said, "you need to figure out what to do with that woman! She is your responsibility. If she endangers my men or my animals, I will hold you responsible!"

Ishaq walked away and began shouting orders to his men. Byron could see Bashshar glaring at him as he and a couple of the Arab drivers headed down to load the corpses onto two of the camels.

"What do you intend to do with her?" James asked.

"I don't have any idea," Byron shook his head. "I should have minded my own affair. Everything has turned ill today!"

"As your friend," James said with a twinkle in his eye, "I think you did a good thing. Don't worry about them. You don't know the future and neither do they." Byron startled at this as he thought about what Noddaba had told him.

"As far as your new love," James said mischievously as he saw Byron's expression sour at the suggestion, "we can't turn her loose. Don Fuego is right. Once these servants don't return, the Saracen's will look for them. The last thing we need is for her to be found and tell them about us."

Byron nodded his head and walked back to Zahirah who was sitting on the ground hugging her knees. She had heard all her life that the Christians were barbarians of the worst sort: raping, murdering, and pillaging the countryside. She wondered if Allah was punishing her with a fate worse than death now that she had become a captive of these monsters.

"Do you treat all of your prisoners this way?" she said as she pointed to the headless corpse in front of her.

Byron looked at the dead Saracen. De Courcy's cold-blooded murder had surprised him and it filled him with loathing. "Lady," Byron said, "there was no honor in the killing of that man. It was unchivalrous, and De Courcy will someday answer for it. As for you, you are under my protection, though I am at a loss as to what to do with you. I had hoped to at least have your gratitude for saving your life, but I know it is not so. I now have the quandary of not wanting to spend any more time with you, yet I cannot let you go either."

"So I can expect the same," Zahirah said as she pointed to the dead man, "when I become a burden."

"Do not insult me. I will not kill you," Byron snapped. "This is what I propose. You come with me willingly. When we are done with our business, and once we have reached our own lands, you are free to go wherever you will."

"You need not fear, I have nowhere to go," Zahirah said sadly. "My family is likely to die because of you and your recklessness." She broke down and began to weep.

James walked over and knelt beside her. "Don't cry, Mon Cherie," he said softly as he handed her a cloth to dry her eyes, "and don't assume the worst. Believe in God's deliverance. Your family may yet be safe, and in the absence of evidence to suggest otherwise, keep hope in your heart."

Zahirah took the rag and wiped the tears from her eyes, and for the first time, she smiled weakly. "You are right." She turned to Byron and said, "If you keep your promise, I will keep mine. Perhaps by the time we part, my husband will have chosen a new consort, and I can return to my family unnoticed."

Byron smiled at her. "I think it's time we go," he said, reaching out his hand to help her from the ground.

Bashshar returned with the dead Saracens draped over the back of two camels. Their hands tied to their feet in order to keep their bodies in place. A blanket that the Arab drivers used to cover the loads was thrown over the bodies and roped down. The sun was already past noon as the caravan set out on the road.

"Are you sure you want to go this way?" Zahirah asked as they turned north.

"Yes, adulteress!" Bashshar said, still angry at having to clean up Byron's mess. "Now be quiet and assume your place!"

There was no talking among the men as the grim realization of the danger they were in put a damper on their spirits. Byron could feel the angry glances of Narvez for selfishly keeping the woman for himself.

CHAPTER 48
THE STAFF OF AL-TUSI

Byron took the lead riding as fast as they could from the scene of his battle. He looked back nervously hoping the dead men were well hidden. He could see the arms and feet of the dead men dangling beneath the tarps. They were noticeable. Now, would not be a good time to be caught with the Saracen woman in their midst. Byron was already working on what to say should they be unlucky enough to run into anyone on the roadway. He knew he could talk his way out of a tight spot, but even he was a little worried that it would be hard to give a plausible explanation.

The hours passed and each mile took its toll on the men. The corpses were starting to smell, and the stench of decaying flesh hung in the air.

Zahirah rode shifting in the saddle, looking around, fidgeting with her reins. "You should turn around," she said.

"Be quiet, adulteress!" Bashshar shouted.

"I will not be silent," Zahirah cried as she turned to Byron. "You are leading your men into danger! Turn around while you still can."

"Fitzwalter," VonDurenberg shouted, "tell your woman to shut up!"

Byron turned to Zahirah. "Lady, please be quiet," Byron said as he scanned the land around him. "I have troubles enough already." He was hoping that soon the ruins of Babylon would come into view. But each time he thought he saw something man made, it turned out to be a rock or hill or some other natural feature.

It was nearing twilight, and there was still no sign that they were nearing the ruins of the city. James and Bashshar had ridden ahead to scout the area for a place to leave the road and get rid of the bodies. No one wanted to spend another minute with the smell of death. They had been gone for some time when Byron looked up to see them flying down the road, riding their horses at great speed. The look of concern on James' face told him something was wrong. Byron stopped his horse to await the bad news.

"We are on the edge of a large city," James exclaimed as he pulled his horse up abruptly beside Byron.

"I think it is Baghdad," Bashshar interrupted, coming to a stop beside James.

"It can't be. Damn it! Damn it! We will never find Babylon!"

"Babylon?" Zahirah asked. "Is that what you are looking for?" Byron went silent. Zahirah began to laugh humorlessly. "You're lost." Byron felt uncomfortable, not knowing whether to admit the obvious. "You are lost, admit it!" she said again. "I can see it in your face."

"My lady," James said, "we are not lost. No, we are just not sure of where we are."

"That is lost!" Zahirah said contemptuously.

"Then where are we?" Byron snapped.

"He is right," Zahirah said, pointing at Bashshar. "You are on the outskirts of Baghdad. The city where my husband is lord!"

Byron put his hand to his head. The magnitude of his recent foolish conduct slammed home. "Oh my God!" he said in shock. "You're the Sultana of Baghdad?"

"I was," Zahirah said, smiling grimly. "Now my husband is starting to wonder why his servants have not returned home with evidence of my death. In a few hours, his anger will be very great, and he will summon his officers to go and search for his most trusted servants. No effort will be spared to learn their fate, as well as mine."

"We need to get off this road!" James said urgently. "We need to get rid of those bodies, now!"

Ishaq, who had ridden up unnoticed, spoke up, "Night is coming! It will become much harder to find us in the wastelands."

"And once you are in the wastelands, where do you intend to go?" Zahirah asked. "Do you even know where Babylon is?"

"No! If I did, do you think we would be here," Byron replied.

Zahirah laughed, and the sound sent shivers down Byron's spine. "Why do you seek the city of the damned? It is cursed, and all who defy the will of Allah by entering the city are severely punished."

"We have our reasons," James snapped.

Zahirah scoffed, "Actually, you were near the city when you found me. As a final insult to my soul, my husband had ordered his servants to take me there and murder me, but they feared to enter the cursed Ishtar gate. Since no one would ever know where I died, they decided to make things easy for themselves and kill me by the river."

"Can you take us to the city?" Byron asked.

"I can," Zahirah said.

Byron leaned forward in his saddle as he examined Zahirah's face. "Our first guide died. Another guide led us into the wastelands and almost over a cliff. Can I trust you?"

Zahirah's full lips turned up into a smile, melting Byron's heart. "You must trust my word as much as I must trust yours. Is your promise good?"

Byron nodded. "Yes, lady."

"Then so is mine. Follow me," Zahirah said, turning her horse off the road and leading them into the desert.

After an hour of picking their way through the rocks of the barren landscape, she halted near some scrub brush covering a natural depression. Ishaq rode up beside her. "Leave the bodies here," she said. "No one comes this way. The brush will conceal them."

Ishaq nodded in agreement. "Bring a shovel. We don't need the vultures giving away their resting place."

Bashshar walked back to one of the camels and returned with a shovel. "You made this mess," he snarled, throwing the shovel down at the hooves of Byron's horse.

Byron was about to protest when James said, "I will help." Byron and James dug a shallow grave while the rest of the men ate a cold meal. The shallow graves were finished, and without ceremony, James and Byron heaved the four corpses into the trench. Byron wiped off the sweat from his forehead and walked over to Zahirah. He could see she had a wooden stick next to her. She had tied a series of strings to it at even distances and was in the process of tying small rocks to the strings. He stood and watched her work.

"What are you working on, my lady?" the knight said kindly.

"I am making the staff of Al-Tusi," she replied without looking up at him.

"The what?" Byron replied in astonishment, thinking she was bored and building some useless trinket for her amusement.

"An astrolabe," Zahirah said, continuing her work.

"Be clear, lady," the knight pressed.

She stopped tying a rock to one of the stings. She looked up at him, her lips pressed together into a frown. "An astrolabe is used to find our position on earth. The great Islamic mathematician, Sharaf-al-Din al Tusi, designed this staff to determine a position on earth based on its relationship to the stars. I intend on using this staff to determine our position so I can guide us in a straight line south so we don't get lost or waste time traveling in circles in the dark."

"You mean you can determine where we are by using the stars, a stick, and some rocks?"

"Allah placed the stars in the sky with a purpose. Wise men have looked to the stars to guide them. Now if you will let me finish, we can move on."

She looked back down at the rock and tied it to the string, tugging on the knot to make sure it was tight. Byron was stunned. He knew his knowledge was sadly lacking, but Father Villhardain had never talked down to him, nor made him feel stupid. At least he could carry on a conversation with the priest. The Saracen woman made him feel small, and for some odd reason, awkward. He turned and walked off in the dark to get his horse ready for the next ride.

James came over as Byron tightened the cinch on his saddle. "What is she doing?" James asked casually as he looked over at Zahirah in curiosity.

"I can't explain it. Something about finding our way in the dark by using the stars and a stick."

"Fitzwalter, surely you misunderstood."

"No, but if you wish to know, go ask her."

Byron watched as James swaggered over to Zahirah who was putting the finishing touches on her creation. He could see James talk to her, and then turn around and walk back to Byron.

"You're right. She told me what she was doing, and I still have no idea how her little stick works."

Zahirah took several measurements from the stars to determine their position on earth in relation to the sky. After she was satisfied with her results, she walked over to James and Bashshar who were mounted on their horses waiting for her.

"I have a rough idea of our position in relation to the star I have chosen to follow," she said as Byron walked over and handed her the reins of her horse. She swung into the saddle with the grace of someone accustomed to hours of riding. "By using the star as a guide, I should be able to keep us in a straight path in the dark. I should be able to bring us close to the accursed city."

Bashshar motioned for the caravan to rise and follow. Guided by the stars and a Saracen woman, the caravan moved across the desert.

CHAPTER 49
THE TALE OF THE EMERALD NECKLACE

Muhtadi was tired. He had tracked the Christians through the storm, following them as close as he dared. Hidden in the dust, he had followed the Christians, like a phantom, riding at the end of their column. Wise men would have stopped to seek shelter, but the Christians had kept on the move. Even more inexplicable, they had crossed the waste to the Tigris river. The Christians' course had been towards Baghdad, but then they turned south following the river.

Muhtadi doggedly stalked them, and after a long day riding, the Christians had stopped by the river and were starting to unpack their animals. Muhtadi found a small hill and dismounted. Leaving his horse, he crawled to the top of the rise to watch. "Damn them," Muhtadi cursed as he watched. He was tired and he had come to hate the sight of them.

Ahmed crawled up beside him. "Muhtadi, leave these mad men to make their camp."

Muhtadi did not answer, but watched the Christians through his glass. He lowered the glass from his eye and glanced at Ahmed. Muhtadi sighed, "I need to talk with Husam al-Din. I wonder how much longer we are going to track these fools." Muhtadi turned and slid down the small hill. Dusting the dirt from his tunic, he walked over to where Nadim was holding the horses. Taking his horse, he mounted and turned from the river. Husam al-Din would want his best guess regarding the next destination. Muhtadi did not have an answer.

Muhtadi rode across the desert. The green tree line of palms that marked the Tigris was at his back. In front of him was the dull brown landscape, empty and barren. Rocks jutted from dirt and sand. His horse picked its way down a path between tufts of scrub brush that clung to the land.

It was late in the afternoon when a line of horsemen came into view. Muhtadi kicked his horse into a gallop. Husam al-Din, riding his black horse at the head of the column, raised his hand, and the cavalry troop came to a halt.

"They have stopped," Muhtadi said. "They will make camp."

Husam al-Din nodded. "You have done well, Muhtadi. Allah has blessed you. It was no small feat to track the Christians through the dust storm."

Muhtadi bowed. "My lord, you are very gracious."

"Are you certain they will make camp?"

"Yes. They were unpacking their animals when we left."

"Good. Then lead us to a suitable place to rest. You will stay as my guest. I will send one of my men to watch in your place. Amjed!" A thin man with a dark moustache rode forward. "Go to the river and there you will find the Christians."

Amjed tilted his head as he held Muhtadi in his gaze. His lips curled downward into a sneer. "And where shall I find the Christians?"

"I will send Nadim to guide you," Muhtadi replied.

Amjed looked at the boy with contempt. "I think I can find it on my own."

Muhtadi turned his horse and pointed into the distance. "Then keep the sun at your back. As you approach the Tigris, you will see a clump of palm trees near a shallow bend in the rivers course. In that bend, you will see the Christians."

Amjed bowed. "I shall leave at once." Muhtadi watched Amjed ride away.

"Come, Muhtadi," Husam al-Din said. "Do not worry. Enjoy a

night of well-earned rest. Amjed will keep watch. We will pick up tomorrow."

Muhtadi wavered, but then accepted the offer, which was heartily welcomed by Ahmed and Nadim. Beneath the stars, Muhtadi and his men feasted, and as the fire died, they rolled out their blankets for the simple pleasure of a night of uninterrupted sleep.

The morning brought a surprise. Isma'il felt a hand shake him awake. He opened his eyes to find the night guard hovering over him. Isma'il rolled over and leapt to his feet.

"My lord, I am sorry to wake you, but I have something you must see." Following the guard, he made his way around the slumbering men. In the distance, the grey light of the dawn grew in the horizon. A Saracen was holding a horse. "Amjed's horse has returned to us without his rider."

Isma'il walked to the horse and looked it over carefully. Running his hand along its back, he looked at the saddle. Everything was in place. The horse was uninjured. Isma'il hurried to the place where Muhtadi slept. The tracker was awake. His cloak pulled about him as he watched the morning grey give way to the golden light that spread across the sky.

Muhtadi looked over at Ismail's approach.

"Grim tidings," Isma'il said, "Amjed's horse returned without its rider." Muhtadi stood up. "The horse shows no evidence of violence," Isma'il continued. "Perhaps it spooked and escaped from its master."

"Humph, or the Christians have him. I will awake my men." Muhtadi turned and went to the place where Nadim and Ahmed slept. Muhtadi looked down at Nadim wrapped in the blanket that his mother had woven for him. Nadim's mother had begged Muhtadi to take her son and train him as a scout. At the time, he had wanted to refuse, not wishing to be burdened with the task of training the boy. But she was so sorrowful and desperate that he had relented. Muhtadi stared at the boy, and then bent down and gently grasped his shoulder. "Come, we have work to do."

Nadim sat up. "What?"

"The morning has brought ill tidings. We must ride."

The boy stretched and stood up. "Yes, Muhtadi." He picked up his blanket, shook it, and rolled it up.

Muhtadi turned, and with the toe of his boot, he nudged Ahmed. "Get up. We must get moving."

Ahmed rolled over. "Have Nadim do it," he mumbled. Muhtadi frowned, and with more force, kicked Ahmed with his boot. "Get up now."

Muhtadi, Nadim, and Ahmed set off at once towards the Christians' camp. The desert was quiet. Only the dull sound of the horse's hooves striking the earth broke the silence. The track led to a small hill and stopped. The sparse grass was torn and uneven where a horse had grazed.

"Wait here." Muhtadi dismounted and walked slowly up the hill. He was half way up the rise when he stopped. Beneath a withered bush, long dead from thirst, lay a steel helmet wrapped by a turban. The dirt and sand near the bush was disturbed and scuffed as if someone had struggled upon the ground. Muhtadi frowned. With a sigh, he continued to the top of the hill and looked out over the edge. The Christians' camp was empty. He jogged down the hill and mounted his horse. "The Christians are gone," he said to Ahmed and Nadim. They rode swiftly to the abandoned camp. Muhtadi hoped that by examining the remains of the camp he might learn something useful.

He dismounted and slung his bow and arrows on his back. The Christians had left in great haste. He wandered about until he found a place where a large amount of blood had been spilled. He paused and bent closer to examine the ground. A body had been dragged to a camel. He found more signs where blood had dripped and pooled. He dipped his finger into the blood-soaked earth. He brought the damp dirt close to his face, rubbing it between his thumb and finger, confirming his suspicions. The blood was starting to thicken.

He stood up and scanned the area. He spied two more places where camels had stood and blood had pooled. Carefully, he followed the trail of blood down to the river. He stopped walking. The earth was torn and the grass crushed. A piece of wood that jutted from the ground caught his eye. Muhtadi knelt down and looked at it until he realized he was looking at the hilt of a knife.

The knife must have been pulled free from the dead man's body. Muhtadi picked up the knife and drew it from its sheath. The Damascus blade was inlaid with a golden crescent moon. Muhtadi sheathed the knife and stuck it in his belt. Muhtadi began to walk in an ever-widening circle until he found a place where a smaller person had knelt down.

A larger set of boot prints were nearby. He studied the new riddle. Muhtadi walked back and looked down at the smaller footprints, mere dents in the sand. He knelt down to examine them closely and saw a tiny pearl next to the imprint. A woman. They fought over a woman. He stood up and followed her tracks to where four horses had stood milling around as if waiting. He looked for the hoof tracks. The riders had come from Baghdad. He stood for a moment looking in the direction of the city. Three men and a woman had ridden here. The men were dead, but the woman still lived. Taken against her will by a Christian.

There was nothing more to see. He stood up and started to walk back to where Ahmed and Nadim waited. He had only taken a few steps when he saw something glittering in the sunlight. He walked over, and to his surprise, he saw an emerald necklace laced with gold and silver. He picked it up. The sun shone through the green stones. Muhtadi lowered it and examined it carefully. Each emerald was set in the center of golden leaves, strung together on a silver chain. No one would cast aside such a treasure. Perhaps she had tossed her necklace away as a token that she still lived. Whoever she was, she had merited escorts. A woman of importance, royalty or a favored wife.

"Muhtadi," Nadim asked, "what did you find?"

"Amjed is dead. Three others were slain here as well."

"Did the Christians fight amongst themselves?" Ahmed asked.

"No, murder has happened here. Why, I am not sure. What I do know, is the Christians are getting further away every moment we spend here. Ahmed! Return to Husam al-Din. Tell him that his man is dead. Tell him to make haste. The Christians are on the move towards Baghdad. I will leave signs for you to follow." Ahmed opened his mouth, and Muhtadi cut him off. "I do not have time to quarrel. Now go!" Ahmed glared at Muhtadi, then turned and rode off.

"Come, Nadim," Muhtadi said as he watched Ahmed ride away. "The trail is growing old. See how the animal dung has already dried. We must ride swiftly if we are to catch our prey." Muhtadi put the spurs to his horse and galloped down the trail, Nadim following behind him.

CHAPTER 50
ALI IBN UBAYDULLAH AL-AZIZ

Ahmed rode at a gallop. He was furious at having to retrace this morning's ride. He was a skilled tracker. Nadim was the errand boy. He had been riding for several hours, muttering curses to himself, when he saw dust rising in the distance. He halted. Husam al-Din could come to him. He dismounted and fished several dried dates from his saddlebags. He sat down in the shade of his horse and watched as a lizard scampered over a rock to hurry away.

At last, Husam al-Din appeared at the head of his men. Ahmed stood up and dusted his pants. Husam al-Din raised his hand and his men halted some distance away. Spurring his horse, Husam al-Din rode forward. He was followed by Isma'il and another man with a thin face. Husam al-Din stopped his horse beside Ahmed. The black horse snorted and pawed the ground, and Husam al-Din gave a sharp jerk on the reins to make the horse stand still.

Husam al-Din turned in his saddle and stared down at Ahmed. "What news do you have of Amjed's fate?"

Ahmed looked into the dark eyes of Husam al-Din. "He is dead."

"I knew it," cried a voice from behind Husam al-Din. "You sent him alone to his doom." Husam al-Din turned to see Kasim riding up uninvited. "His blood demands vengeance. You sent Kamal and Fadil to their deaths on the Tyre road, now Amjed?" Kasim turned on Isma'il. "His blood is on your hands as well! You had your chance to end this fool's quest. Now look, another man is dead, and what do we have to show for it?" Kasim's arms swept over the desert land. "Nothing!"

A ring of steel filled the air as Isma'il swept out his sword and leveled it at the man's thin face. "Kasim," Isma'il spat, "the Christians killed these men. If you whisper a word of this to the rest of the men, it will be your death."

Kasim smiled, his yellow teeth showing. "I don't need to say a word. Most of the men are with me already."

Husam al-Din turned his horse and trotted next to Kasim. Grabbing his long beard, he gave it a jerk. "The sultan has given me this task, and I will not fail. Hinder me, and you will feel the wrath of Salah al-Din."

"You hinder yourself, Husam al-Din. The men will not follow you much longer. Your time is almost at an end."

"And so is your disloyalty," Husam al-Din growled as he pulled harder on Kasim's beard.

"I am just the messenger. Kill me and you will seal your death."

Husam al-Din glanced back at the men waiting in the distance and let go of Kasim's beard. "You have been warned. Get back in line."

"And so have you," Kasim said as he turned his horse to ride back to the men.

Isma'il sheathed his shamshir. "Husam al-Din, you must say something to the men. I know the sultan has given you a task to carry out, but the men need to know why they suffer. Kasim is right. You do not have much time left before you have mutiny."

Husam al-Din nodded. "I know, and I will say something when the time is right." Husam al-Din looked down at Ahmed. "Speak a word of what you have seen, and you will suffer my punishment. Now take me to Muhtadi!" Husam al-Din turned his horse and raised his hand, signaling his men to follow.

Ahmed mounted his horse and took the lead, retracing his trail. The sun beat down and the dust rose, choking the men who rode in the rear of the column. As they drew close to the Tigris river, Husam al-Din rode up next to Ahmed. "What evidence did

Muhtadi find that Amjed is dead?"

Ahmed's brow furled as he looked down and spoke in a low voice. "Amjed was dragged to the Christian camp. Blood stains the ground everywhere. We did not find his body, but even more puzzling is that Amjed was not the only victim."

"What dark crime does Muhtadi think the Christians have done?"

"Muhtadi does not know, but he is following the Christians. I hope by the time we meet him, he will have an answer."

†

It was a long day of riding. Muhtadi began to worry; he was approaching the outskirts of Baghdad. The trail stopped, disappearing off into the desert.

"Nadim, Ahmed is following with Husam al-Din. Bring Husam al-Din here, I wish to speak to him." Nadim bowed and then galloped off. Muhtadi sat on his horse contemplating this change in direction. He dismounted and sat down on a nearby rock. The emerald necklace troubled him. Who could have owned such jewelry? It certainly was not one of the Christians. He picked up a stick and began to doodle in the sand. He was thinking about the mystery of the necklace when Husam al-Din rode up.

"What have the Christians done?" Husam al-Din asked in irritation. "I hear that Amjed is dead. Worse, I have been told that he may not have died alone."

"Yes, that is true. Amjed is dead and three others died with him."

"Ahmed said there were no bodies."

"Yes, they have taken them with them. They have ridden off into the desert again." Muhtadi looked up at the sky. "I assume they have left the trail to hide the evidence of their crimes." Muhtadi shrugged. "But why here?"

"My friend," Husam al-Din said wearily, "the Christians have not done one thing that I would consider wise, but if you had to guess their intent, what would you say?"

"My guess? I would say they are lost."

"Lost?" Husam al Din cried incredulously.

Dust was rising from the road. It hung like a cloud in the blue sky. Muhtadi turned his head to look at it. "Yes, my lord," he answered distractedly. "I think they are lost. My guess is, once they realized they were approaching the city from the south, they rode into the desert to get rid of the bodies."

The dust grew. Black figures riding towards them appeared.

"We have company," Muhtadi muttered.

"Christians?"

"No...Too many men and no camels."

Sixty men mounted on black horses were riding in two columns at a trot, their spears raised into the air. Their leader at the head of the columns stood up in his stirrups and shaded his eyes with his hand. Before either Muhtadi or Husam al-Din could move, a shout rose from the approaching Saracen cavalrymen, and to the surprise of Husam al-Din and Muhtadi, they began to charge.

"We are friends! Servants of Allah and his prophet!" Husam al-Din shouted as the cavalry troop galloped up. Without command, the columns split, moving swiftly around Muhtadi and Husam al-Din. The circle formed. They wheeled towards the two Saracens lowering their spears.

Husam al-Din sat quietly on his horse. Muhtadi stood up and faced the grim looking soldiers in front of him. Each soldier wore a hauberk, burnished bright, over a tunic of dark green. Beneath the long skirts of their hauberk, each man wore tall boots, polished to a shiny black. Mail hoods, topped with steel helmets with long nose guards, covered their heads. At their sides, each man wore a shamshir with an ornately engraved hilt. Husam al-Din eyed them, sizing them up; their accoutrements, their horsemanship. He decided it was best not to move.

The Saracen lord rode between two of his men. He sat tall in his saddle. A black cloak wrapped around his armor. His steel helmet, adorned with a gold emblem of two crossed shamshirs, rested on his head. He was pale, as if ill, or as some deep grief clung to him.

The frown upon his lips was accented by a thick black moustache. He looked at Muhtadi and Husam al-Din, and his dark eyes narrowed. "Peace be to you."

"And to you," Husam al-Din replied, not lost on the irony that he was outnumbered and surrounded by armed men.

"Who are you and who do you serve?" the Saracen lord demanded as he pointed at Husam al-Din.

"I am Husam al-Din ibn Abdul al-Subayil and I serve the Sultan Salah al-Din."

"I see," the Saracen lord said, unimpressed. "What brings you so far south? Salah al-Din is preparing to crush the infidels in Jerusalem, and yet he has sent his servants here?"

Husam al-Din nodded. "That is true. Prince Malik az-Zahir requested that I ride the south road to make sure Christian infiltrators are not attempting to interfere with supplies or reinforcements."

The Saracen lord tilted his head to the side. "I don't understand the prince's concern. His father, the sultan, has all the Christians surrounded in Jerusalem."

"I was not in a position to ask why," Husam al-Din replied. "I am only following my instructions. How can I be of service to you?" Husam al-Din asked, wanting to get down to business.

"I have been sent by my master, the Sultan of Baghdad, to find three servants who failed to return to the palace as expected. My master is deeply worried and ordered me to search for them."

"Hmm, I take it you have not had success in finding them."

"No. They were sent to punish a woman for her infidelities. My master is troubled that his servants might have been prevented from carrying out his will. I am hopeful that you might have information which might aid me in finding the missing servants or learn their fate?"

"Unfortunately, I cannot help you," Husam al-Din answered, shaking his head. "All I can do is save you the journey north. My men are a mile behind me. I assure you that on our southward journey, we have met no one."

"My master will not take this news well," the man said. "Not well at all."

"I can assure you," Husam al-Din replied. "We have not interfered with your master's justice. Nor would we prevent an adulteress from receiving her just punishment."

The Saracen lord frowned. "Then I ask a favor."

"You may, and I will do all within my power to help a brother in his time of trial, so long as it does not interfere with my own master's wishes."

"Excellent. I will continue to search. It would ease my burden if you would look for the three men and the woman on your return journey to Aleppo. Would you send a messenger to me if you find them, no matter their condition?"

"Your request is reasonable. If we find your missing servants, I will send a man."

"That is well. I will be searching near the accursed city of Babylon, for it was determined her soul should leave this life in that vile place. Send news to me there if you learn her fate and that of my master's servants."

"Before you take your leave," Husam al-Din said, "I thought the Caliph al-Nasar ruled Baghdad, who is this sultan you serve?"

"A complicated tale," the Saracen lord replied, shaking his head, "which I have no time to tell. Caliph al-Nasir still rules, but he has allowed Mahmud, the grandson of Mahmud Second of the great Seljuq Empire, to take the title of sultan."

"A pretender to the throne?"

"Time presses me. What happens in Baghdad is no concern of the servants of Salah al-Din."

"If I send a man to find you, whom should he ask for?"

"Tell your man to ask for Ali ibn Ubaydullah al-Aziz, captain of the sultan's guard."

"All shall be done as promised."

"Good," Ali replied. "May Allah bless the road you travel." He turned and shouted to his men. In an impressive feat of horsemanship, the mounted soldiers at the circle's center did a ninety-degree haunch turn. Each man followed suit until all of them were facing head to tail. Ali bowed to Husam al-Din and spun his horse to face in the opposite direction. On Ali's command, the Saracen cavalry moved forward at a trot, reforming into columns of twos. Muhtadi mounted his horse as Husam al-Din watched Ali's men disappear to the northeast.

"I did not know Baghdad had a sultan?" Muhtadi said.

"Neither did I," Husam al-Din replied. "It sounds as if a power struggle is occurring. I suspect this adulterous woman is somehow a pawn caught between two ruthless men. Who knows, and for that matter, it is not my concern."

Muhtadi looked down. "I have not had the opportunity to speak, but I think I know the fate of the missing servants of Baghdad."

"Speak to me," Husam al-Din exclaimed, concerned with the implications of withholding information from the angry sultan of a foreign land. "Tell me what you know."

"My lord, I did not speak of this earlier because I did not understand the meaning of the evidence I found. Now that I have heard the tale of the captain of Baghdad, the pieces have fallen into place."

"And what are your suspicions Muhtadi? Do you believe the Christians had something to do with this?"

"I do. I found evidence of bloodshed and murder in the camp of the Christians. I traced the path to the river where I found the place where three souls shed their life's blood on the earth. I followed the path their bodies made as they were dragged to two camels. The camels are part of the caravan we have been following."

Husam-al-Din put both of his hands on the top of his head and sighed in annoyance. "Christians! Only a Christian knight would be so impulsive and so stupid as to attack the servants of the most powerful sultan who ruled the region. What were these fools thinking? Deep in enemy territory, outnumbered ten-thousand to one, and yet they would act in such a reckless manner to bring attention to themselves."

Muhtadi scoffed, "Based on the evidence that I found it was the woman that caused this reckless act. She has been taken captive. At least that is my guess."

A look of surprise crossed Husam al-Din's face. "They fought over her?" Muhtadi nodded. Husam al-Din started to laugh mirthlessly. Muhtadi looked at Husam al-Din as if he had lost his mind.

"I can't believe the absurdity of this," Husam al-Din said.

"Absurdity of what?"

"Muhtadi, if you knew the Christian's purpose in the Levant, to risk capturing the woman would seem insane." Husam al-Din sighed, "She must have great beauty." He paused and shook his head. "No this is just plain stupidity."

"Do you really think they are lost, or is this a clever ruse to shake off pursuers?"

Muhtadi shifted uncomfortably on his horse. "I told you my guess, but besides being lost, I now think they left the road to dispose of the bodies of the Sultan's servants."

Husam al-Din sat on Anton looking down at the long black mane of the horse's neck. He was tired of following these fools, wearing out men and horses. Perhaps the Christians were circling back to the river. But which river? He could ride the shorter road if he turned and went straight back.

Isma'il was right. He needed to tell his men why they were here. He looked up. "It is time I told all of you what the sultan has commanded me to do. It is time we return to the men. We need to send the Baghdad cavalry home, or this will become very difficult!"

The two men turned and began to gallop back towards the place where the men should be waiting. Muhtadi's curiosity was overflowing by the time they reached the men. Husam al-Din called his men to gather around. There was complete silence when he finished telling his men that the Christians they were tracking were trying to find the lost Roman treasure.

"We must succeed!" Husam al-Din cried. "If we fail, the enemy will be strengthened. The infidels will bring new and larger armies into the fight. We must deny them the opportunity to win this war. We must send these invaders home, or deliver them back to the earth from which they came. My brothers, the enemy is unwittingly drawing us with him to the place where the treasure lies hidden. Once found, we will take it from them and deliver those we have not slain to the Gates of Aleppo! We will not fail! As sure as the sun will rise in the east, so is my faith that each of you will do all that is expected. The sultan has promised great reward, and I look forward to having the honor of being present when he bestows it upon you!"

The eruption of emotion was spontaneous as the men jumped to their feet and shouted, "Allahu Akbar!" Husam al-Din could see it in their faces. The waiting and work had not been a waste after all. In one moment, the morale of his men lifted immeasurably. Several of the men gave Kasim dark glances.

"My friends," Husam-al-Din said, raising his hands to quiet his men, "now that you know, you must keep this knowledge to yourself. We must be cautious not to warn our enemy of his peril! We must continue to lull him to sleep, into believing he is safe. We will let them do the work, and we will reap the rewards for our cunning. Muhtadi and his men will continue to watch, reporting their movements. We will swoop down upon them with vengeance and punish them for their incursion into our lands when the time is right. Now, go and rest. Muhtadi and I will finish working out our plan."

Husam al-Din, with Isma'il beside him, walked away from his men. Muhtadi, dazed from the enormity of what he had just learned, joined them.

"What do you think, my friends?" Husam al Din asked. "Are you surprised?"

"Yes," Muhtadi answered. "So, what is your plan?"

"First, I need you to send a messenger to find Ali at Babylon. I am thinking that Isma'il and Nadim should bring tidings of the death of the sultan's servants. Tell him it appears they encountered bandits, and make sure you tell them that the woman is dead."

"And if he wants to see the bodies?" Isma'il asked.

"Tell him we have buried them," Husam al-Din said. "That they were rotting in the sun. That should discourage Ali from attempting to verify the truth."

"As you wish, my lord," Muhtadi replied. "I will send Ahmed to follow and mark the Christians' trail."

Husam al-Din nodded. "Is there anything else we should do?"

Both men shook their heads. "Excellent!" Husam al-Din exclaimed.

"You should take this as a token of the woman's death," Muhtadi said, handing Isma'il the green emerald necklace. "I have no doubt it belonged to the woman."

Isma'il held up the necklace as it flashed and sparkled in the sunlight. "This has great worth," he gasped as he passed the necklace to Husam al-Din.

"True," Muhtadi said, "the woman was someone important. There is a good reason why the sultan wanted her dead. It is important the captain of Baghdad believes you."

"I agree," Husam al-Din muttered, not looking up from his admiration of the workmanship of the necklace. "She is important, whoever she is, and wealthy." Muhtadi handed Isma'il the dagger. "Take this as well." Isma'il took the knife and shoved it into his belt. "Take Nadim with you, the boy can help."

Isma'il nodded. "I will do what I can," he said, as he left to get Nadim.

"I expect nothing less," Husam al-Din replied. He turned to Muhtadi. "I want you to join me on the ride south." Husam al-Din was gambling. He was hoping this bold stroke would pay handsomely, and he would come out ahead of the Christians.

CHAPTER 51
THE SECRET OF ALI AND ZAHIRAH

The morning star was visible against the dark purple sky. Zahirah halted on the edge of a dry watercourse that cut across the land. Byron stopped his horse beside her. "We are near," she whispered. "The Euphrates changed course. It no longer passes through the city. Babylon is now the haunt of jackals and ghosts, its splendor faded and gone. Wiser men would have turned back."

"It is good then that we are not wiser men," Byron grumbled.

They followed the dry riverbed through the empty wasteland. In the ever-shifting bands of the mirage emerged a distorted vision of a wall of weathered mud bricks, half consumed by the sands. As they drew closer, the remains of a bridge which once spanned the Euphrates lay in ruins among the sand and stones of the long dry river bottom. The indistinct walls of Babylon became clear. The broad walls had been thrown down, and great gaping holes appeared where the ramparts had been breached. Through the invader's portals to the city, the indistinct crumbling buildings could be seen. No color, no gold, and no evidence of any wealth or power remained, just a nondescript collection of jagged walls without roofs. A blandness had descended upon Nebuchadnezzar's great city as the edifices of Babylon blended into the earth from which they were made.

Byron felt a shiver run down his spine as he sat on his horse looking over the ruins. He had seen this before. He had stood on Palatine Hill next to Father Villhardain as he looked out over the center of the ruins of Rome where the emperors had lived in splendor. Now, he was looking at mighty Babylon, the first of all great cities, a collection of crumbling mud bricks, sinking beneath the desert sand.

"This is it? This is Babylon?" Byron asked..

"Yes," Zahirah said. "I have read that the Emperor Trajan said much the same thing when he conquered this region for Rome."

Byron started at the name. "How do you know about Rome?"

"I can read," Zahirah replied. "A treasured gift that most barbarians do not know, nor appreciate." Zahirah tilted forward in her saddle, her dark eyes looked intently at him. "What do you seek here?"

Byron looked away from her as he surveyed the ruins. "I am not sure." He turned his horse and then glanced back at her. "At least not yet." He rode to where James had dismounted next to the city's wall. "The caravan should continue on to the river and make camp while we search the city. It will make us less noticeable."

James nodded. "I agree. There is nothing here for them to do except wait."

Byron walked off. After waiting for the drivers to gather around him, he told them his decision. There was no argument from the men. Let the Christian fools dig in the ruins. Bashshar grudgingly agreed to return with supplies, while Ishaq decided to stay and keep an eye on what the Christians were doing.

It took less time than usual for the drivers to get the camels lined up and moving off at a trot. Bashshar was in the lead. The banks of the Euphrates would be much more pleasant than the hot dry land of Babylon.

Byron leaned over to James and whispered, "Babylon will still be here tomorrow. We should look to our own camp. I am certain things will go better for us if we get a fresh start in the morning."

"Indeed," James replied, scanning the surrounding desert. "I could rest." Suddenly, he grabbed Byron by the arm. "Look!" he hissed. Byron looked towards the place where James was pointing. A cloud of dust was rising into the air. Byron could faintly see the dark shapes of horsemen riding in formation.

"Behind the walls!" James yelled as he turned to retreat, pulling his horse with him. The others followed, moving into the deserted city.

"Take the horses deeper in," Byron cried. "I will stay and see who our unwanted visitors are."

"I would like to stay," Zahirah said. "Maybe I can help."

Byron hesitated for a moment, debating the wisdom of trusting the Saracen woman. "You can stay," Byron replied at last.

James reached out for Byron's horse while Giodonni took Zahirah's horse. Zahirah bent down, crawled close to one of the holes in the wall and lay down in its shadow to watch. Byron crept beside her. As he lay next to her, he noticed her beauty, and a strange sensation swept over him.

"They will not dare enter the city," she whispered as she saw the horsemen draw near. Byron nodded. The sweet smell of her perfume was distracting as he tried to focus on the approaching men in front of him.

Two of the warriors dismounted and slowly began walking to the walls. One was tall and muscular, a steel helmet covered his mail hood. A black moustache on his tanned face gave him a fierce look. His hand rested on the hilt of his shamshir as he walked with a purposeful stride, his head up, looking at the ruins.

"There have been horses here recently," Byron heard the shorter man say.

"It could be anyone," the tall warrior muttered. "People ride here from time to time to look at the ancient ruins. I see nothing to suggest that the prints are from the servants sent to kill Zahirah."

Byron heard Zahirah gasp as she took a quick breath. "Ali!" she whispered, her face twisted with a strange emotion.

"Who is he?" Byron whispered.

"The captain of my husband's guard," Zahirah replied, her voice shaking. "He was my protector," her head dropping as she looked down.

Byron gave Zahirah a long look and then turned his head to

watch. From the shadows, he could see Ali and the soldier approach the wall, following the horses' tracks.

"See," the soldier said, "the camel tracks head to the river. It looks like Bedouins."

"Perhaps, Huran, but we should still overtake them and see what they know," Ali replied.

Huran looked at Ali with displeasure. "We have ridden all around the city. I doubt if they were ever here."

"I am aware of that, Huran. But I must be sure, unless you want to be the one to tell the sultan that we did not do all that was possible."

Huran became quiet. "I didn't think so." Byron's heart was racing as Ali began to walk towards their hiding place. He was almost to the wall when two horsemen galloped into view. Ali turned to face the riders.

"Peace to you!" said one of the newcomers. "Husam al-Din sends his greetings and asked me to bring you tidings. I am Isma'il, his second in command."

"And I am Ali ibn Ubaydullah al-Aziz, captain of the sultan's guard. What news do you bring?"

"I bring news of woe," Isma'il said gently. "You asked my captain for a favor, and he sent our men to search the land. One of our men found the bodies of three men and a woman, black and bloating in the sun. We surmised that they must have fallen victims to bandits who robbed and then murdered them, leaving their bodies where they fell. I have brought a few items that could be retrieved from the putrid smell of decaying flesh."

"Your news is full of woe!" Ali cried. "What has become of their bodies?"

"We have buried them, my lord, giving them a funeral as befitted men of their rank."

"And the woman?" Ali asked, his voice strained with a strange emotion.

"We dumped the woman into a hole with curses for her crimes."

"That does not ease my heart," Ali said, looking down at the ground. "Zahirah was a beautiful woman, and I was saddened to hear that she had been accused of adultery. I knew her, and I still find it hard to believe she would ever do such a thing."

"I do not know, my lord," Isma'il said, thinking that perhaps he should have been a little more tactful when he spoke of the woman. "We only acted based on what we were told, perhaps Allah knows different."

"Well he does. Tell me, what did they look like? Describe the manner of their dress."

Isma'il hesitated, he had not expected such a question and it took a moment before he came up with an answer. "I cannot tell you, my lord. The heat disfigured the bodies. The flies were thick, and already the vultures had been feasting on their flesh. I must confess, the smell was overpowering, and I did not spend any more time than necessary."

"No," Ali said sadly. "One does not linger under such circumstances. What do you have for me?"

Isma'il motioned to the boy that accompanied him. "Nadim, show this Saracen lord what we have found."

The boy turned and fumbled with his saddlebag. After a moment of tugging at the bag's laces, the boy held up a dagger and a green emerald necklace laced in silver and gold. Isma'il took the necklace and held it up in front of Ali. "Did this belong to the woman you seek?"

Ali's face went ashen. For a slight moment, his lips quivered, and then he stopped as if he had just mastered some deep grief. Ali took the necklace and examined it. The light of the sun shone through the gems, casting specks of green upon the ground. Ali sighed as he looked up at Isma'il, his brow furled. "You tell me that the servants of my master were robbed and murdered and yet you hand me this necklace. Do you have any idea of its worth?"

Isma'il's mind was racing. How stupid could he be! Of course, bandits would have taken the necklace. He felt his mind start to panic and then swiftly the answer came to him. "I don't know it's worth, my lord," he said as he shrugged. "I can only say it appears to be of great value. It was found in the grass near the bodies. My only explanation is that it came off when the bandits assaulted and killed the woman, and they were unable to find it again. Otherwise I have no idea why they left it."

Ali nodded. "Leave us," he commanded Huran. After waiting a moment for his men to withdraw, he said to Isma'il, "Walk with me."

The two men walked to the wall. They were so close now that Byron could reach out and touch Ali's boots. He held his breath and lay still. To Byron's amazement, Ali staggered, as if his ability to keep his emotion in check was now beyond his control. Ali bowed his head and began to weep. He leaned against the wall for support. Ali, completely unmanned, struggled to regain control.

Isma'il stood awkwardly next to Ali with a look of embarrassment, not knowing what to do. He looked around, trying his best to ignore the grief-stricken man beside him. Isma'il glanced down at the wall, and a quizzical expression crossed his face. The Saracen captain spoke, and Isma'il quickly looked back to Ali.

"I loved her," he rasped as he mastered his grief. Byron glanced at Zahirah. He could see the anguish on her face as she looked up at the Saracen captain. A thrill of fear swept over Byron. The thought that she might call out to Ali and betray him filled his mind. Just as he was trying to decide what to do, she buried her face in her robes.

"I loved her," Ali repeated. "She did not deserve this, I failed her."

"You are the cause of her death?" Isma'il demanded, aghast at the revelation.

"I never caused this," Ali sobbed. "My master is a cruel man." Ali bowed his head. "It was my duty to protect the sultana."

"You seduced her and now she is dead," Isma'il said unsympathetically.

"No," Ali replied. "I loved her. Now she is dead."

"My lord," Isma'il said in a softer tone, "I see you are grieved, but you must pull yourself together! Your men are watching. For your sake, take the evidence I have given you and return to Baghdad with the news of her death. If you loved this woman, then heed my advice. Look for her no more. Events may not be as evil as you think." Isma'il looked directly into the captain's eyes as he said this. Isma'il could see comprehension flicker in his face.

Ali paused for a moment and wiped the tears from his eyes. "Isma'il, I will heed your advice. Say no more about her, but I must know, are all three servants dead? It could prove awkward and place me in grave danger if one still lives and returns to Baghdad."

"All are dead," Isma'il replied with certainty.

"Hmm," Ali said as he took a deep breath to compose himself. "That is enough, I will return to Baghdad. My master will not be pleased, but evidence of his wife's death will compensate him for the loss of his servants. He is a cruel man."

"Most are," Isma'il muttered.

"Indeed," Ali replied, the confidence returning to his voice. "Isma'il, may Allah bless you and give you a safe journey home to Aleppo. I will not forget your kindness today."

"You are very gracious, my lord," Isma'il said, saluting. "I think it is time to leave this place. Husam al-Din will become impatient, and I am sure it would be better for you to deliver the news sooner than later."

Byron watched the two Saracens walk away and mount their horses. He was relieved as he watched the Saracen cavalry ride away from the ruined city. He was already cramped and uncomfortable from hiding, and it felt good to stand and stretch. Zahirah stood up, the tracks of her tears still evident in her face.

"Was that your lover," Byron asked gently.

Zahirah shook her head. She looked down and hid her face as she began to weep. Byron was at a loss as to what he should do, and without any real thought, he put his hand on her back and pulled her close. They stood together in the empty space between the wall and the city not saying a word as he comforted her in her grief. At last, she stopped crying.

"We should go," Byron said softly. They started to walk through the sand filled streets as they looked for James and the rest of the men.

"I suppose you are going to mock me to your men," Zahirah said, breaking the silence.

"That would not be chivalrous. We build our own crosses. How we carry them defines us, at least that is what I think."

Slowly, they searched the empty streets. The walls of the buildings cast shadows on the sand. They walked past the darkened doorways and empty windows without pausing to look, clambering over piles of bricks strewn about their path. At last, Byron spied the hoof prints in the sand and started to follow the trail, looking for the rest of the group.

Zahirah spoke again as they turned down another empty street. "I don't think you are a barbarian," she said. "I am grateful for your rescue."

Byron nodded. "Lady, you are welcome."

Zahirah smiled, leaned over, and kissed him on the cheek, causing Byron to blush. He turned the corner of what had once been a large roofless building and saw James and Narvez holding the horses. The rest of the men had spread out across the street with weapons at the ready.

Byron stopped in the shade of the wall to wipe the sweat from his face. "The enemy is gone. They have ridden off. I don't expect them to return."

The men relaxed and began to talk among themselves. Byron left the shade of the building and retrieved his horse from James. "We should leave this place. Once we make camp, we need to talk."

CHAPTER 52
THE CENTURION'S MEN

Byron led the men to a grove of palm trees within sight of the jagged walls of Babylon. As the men dismounted, Speer crept away and crawled up a small hill. Among the rocks, the squire sat staring at the ruins of the city. Speer started to weave back and forth, singing a nonsensical song of screeches and guttural sounds. Byron looked up and frowned at the noise. He was about to tell the squire to stop when Speer abruptly quit singing. Throwing dust in the air, Speer stood up and walked away.

Byron watched the squire disappear and turned back to the task of laying out his blanket. When he finished, he sat down on a nearby rock and drew his shamshir. He examined the patterns of the Damascus blade. It was still marred with dried blood. He had not had time to clean his blade since rescuing Zahirah. Taking his water skin, he poured water on the steel which ran in small rivulets down the blade. Using the hem of his cloak, he polished the shamshir. Slowly, the blood washed away until no trace of it remained. Holding the sword before him, he examined it. The shamshir glistened in the light of the setting sun. Satisfied, he put the weapon back in its sheath and took out Father Villhardain's notes.

He wished the priest was still here to guide him. His first sight of the ruins of the city told him finding the palace was going to be difficult. Every building looked the same. He sighed at these thoughts and unfolded the map. He held it to the light. He glanced at the city in the distance and then to the map. The map showed the city as it was, not as it now existed. He looked back to the ruins and shook his head. He carefully folded the map and put it away as he saw Zahirah approaching. He wanted to ignore her, but found himself stealing a glance at the woman as she sat down across from him.

"I have made a place for you to sleep," Byron said indifferently. "It's not much, but it's all I have to offer." Her dark eyes rested on him. An uncomfortable warm feeling filled Byron, and he looked away.

"What do you mean?" she said.

"Lady, unless I am mistaken, you do not have anything to sleep on."

"I can't take your blanket."

"Lady, I have my cloak, and I will not need the blanket anyway. It is my night to stand watch, so I will not miss it." Zahirah was about to argue, but decided to do so would be insulting, and it would be best to accept his simple gift of charity.

Byron stood up and gathered some sticks and grass to build a small fire. He missed his dagger he had left on the body of the priest and made do with a small knife. He shaved several of the sticks, careful to keep the small feathered shavings attached. After he had made several of these wood-feathered sticks, he formed a ball of dried grass and placed it on the ground arranging his rustic woodcarvings around it. Picking up a flint and steel, he began to strike them together at an angle, working to produce a spark. After several attempts, a spark landed in the grass and started to smoke. He carefully lifted the ball of grass to his lips and began to blow gently, bringing the flame to life. The grass burned brightly, and he hurried to add the feathered sticks to his little blaze. As the little feathered sticks ignited, they burned brightly and were quickly consumed, turning to ash as they collapsed into red glowing embers. He added sticks of more substance and strength as his small fire grew larger. With a snap and crackle, the fire demanded more wood as the heat grew, and Byron placed several larger pieces onto his creation. Satisfied with his work, he sat down, stretching out his legs to enjoy the flames. Zahirah came over and sat down beside him.

"Lady, why did you not call out to Ali? He was so near. You could be far away from here."

A faint smile crossed her lips, as if a pleasant memory stirred and then faded away. "To what end? Hunted by my husband? Everyone I care for...slain on the suspicion of helping my escape? No, I am dead and Ali will take that message back to Baghdad."

"Lady, I am sorry."

They sat quietly together staring into the yellow flames. The coals glowed in the gathering darkness. The solitude was broken as James joined them. His princely robes glittering in the firelight.

"Getting along nicely I see," James said as he sat down as close as he could to Zahirah, who abruptly moved, creating more space between them. James smiled. "You wanted to tell me some strange tale?"

Byron nodded, though he felt a strange annoyance at his friend's intrusion. "Yes, the oddest thing happened at the wall." Byron began to tell James of the conversation of Ali and Isma'il. When he had finished, Byron asked, "What do you make of it?"

"Our danger has increased. We need to hurry and be gone from this wretched place."

"Hurry. What compels you to travel here?" Zahirah asked.

James and Byron looked at each other. "Do you wish to tell her?" James asked.

Byron gazed at Zahirah. Her face, lit by the firelight, glowed, and as he looked at this woman, he felt himself falling under the spell of her beauty. He sighed. "We have come a long way. If Father Villhardain was here, I would not tell you our purpose, but he is dead; therefore, I will put my faith in God and tell you, with the hope you will not betray us." Byron looked down and began to recount the story of Achatius Licinius Geta's journey to Babylon. It was dark when Byron finished his tale. The only light came from the red and yellow flames of the fire.

"Treasure?" Zahirah said quietly and then paused. The wind sighed as the branches of the palm tree waved above them. "That is why you are here. You need the treasure to defeat Salah al-Din." She turned to Byron. "Go home. Babylon is cursed by God. Death comes to all who dare to venture within the walls of the city."

James chuckled. "I don't believe a word of that."

"Have you never heard of Alexander the Great?" Zahirah snapped.

"The Greek?" James asked.

"Yes," Zahirah replied. "Alexander decided to rebuild Babylon as his capital. Yet, as he dwelt in the palace of Nebuchadnezzar, he was struck down... and died."

It became quiet as the fire crackled, throwing sparks into the air. A nagging doubt started to fill Byron's mind. The Holy Father had blessed this journey. They were under the protection of the Church, yet Father Villhardain was dead. Had that been a sign?

Zahirah spoke at last, "Do you want to know what happened to the Roman soldiers?"

Byron frowned. "Killed by bandits."

Zahirah looked into the red embers of the fire. "The Romans never left the city." She looked up. "Very few remember the story of the Roman soldiers who came to Babylon." She picked up a stick and thrust into the fire. "Just before the fall of the western empire, Roman soldiers marched into Babylon and camped within the walls of the city. No one knew why the Romans came to Babylon, but they stayed, defying God, mysteriously laboring within the city.

"When they had finished their work, they brought wine and harlots within the walls. Drinking and whoring as the moon rose, the soldiers engaged in sin as black and evil as the night. As the revelers became wilder in their sins, God sent the angel of death into the city to punish them for their wickedness. In the pale moonlight, God slew each and every one of them, so that not one soldier remained when the sun rose to drive away the darkness. Consumed by their own evil, their bodies withered away, returning to dust so no evidence of their existence remained."

A wild laugh split the night. Byron jumped to his feet. Speer had crept up behind them and had been listening to Zahirah's tale. He laughed again in the darkness, just beyond the light of the fire.

James jumped to his feet, but Speer bolted off into the darkness. James hesitated, weighing the effort to chase the squire. At last, he sat down again. It would be fruitless to pursue Speer through the darkness.

"I have had quite enough of him and his master," James muttered as he turned to face Zahirah. "Lady, I enjoy a good ghost story, but I don't believe a word of your tale."

"What do you believe then?" Zahirah asked.

"I believe the centurion held a feast for his men and then poisoned them."

"Humph! You discount the power of Allah?" Zahirah cried.

"No," James snapped. "But I believe men make up tales like this as means to influence the weak minded."

Zahirah's face turned red as she jabbed a finger at James. "Weak minded? That is bold talk for an illiterate barbarian!"

"Enough!" Byron cried. "We are going to Babylon in the morning, and we have to find the Ishtar gate. I have no idea what that is."

Zahirah turned on him. "What makes you think I will help you recover the treasure for your new war of conquest?"

"Lady," Byron replied, "we will find this treasure with or without you. It will be sooner if you help, but if choose not to, it will be later. The longer we are here, the more likely it will be that we are found, and your husband learns that you are not dead." Zahirah looked down at the mention of her husband. "And what do you think will happen to Ali?" Byron paused to let the thought sink in. "They will take you back to Baghdad as a prize. His death and yours will be cruel."

"You make your point," Zahirah muttered as she eyed him darkly.

Byron nodded as he pulled out his map and Father Villhardain's notes from beneath his tunic. "The priest was teaching me to read, but alas, he died too soon. I have his notes and this map, but after seeing Babylon, I am not sure where to start." Byron smiled. "So, m'lady, what is the Ishtar gate?"

Zahirah looked at the leather folder of parchment in his hand. She snatched it away and opened the folder. She sighed, mumbling to herself as she sorted through the papers. She unfolded the map and held it up for a moment and then folded it back up. "The Ishtar gate is at the north end of the city. Nebuchadnezzar built it as the entrance to the city. It is known as the processional way, or as the Babylonians called it the road that the enemy shall not pass."

"So, what is Ishtar?" James asked.

"Ishtar," Zahirah replied as her eyebrows lowered to give James and icy stare, "is the name of the Babylon goddess of love and war. I thought you would have known that!"

"Once we pass through the gate," Byron said, ignoring the jab, "we need to find the palace of Nebuchadnezzar, where Belshaz-zar saw the writing on the wall."

"That would be the north palace, next to the Ishtar gate," she said. "None of this will be hard to find in the morning." She stood up. "I am tired, it has been a long day." She turned and walked into the darkness.

James stood up and threw a few more sticks on their small fire. "Perhaps tomorrow, fortune will favor us, and then we will be on our way back home."

"Not likely," Byron said, pulling his cloak about him and laying down to get some sleep before his turn came to watch the camp.

†

Speer stopped running when he saw James sit back down. He circled back and headed to join his uncle. VonDurenberg was sitting by his own fire. Narvez was sitting next to him. Across the flames of the fire, sat De Courcy and Parker. De Montgris and De Vale stood near the graf on the edge of the firelight. Narvez was ranting to VonDurenberg at Byron's selfishness in keeping the woman when Speer sat down next to his uncle and whispered something into his ear.

"They have a map!" VonDurenberg exclaimed. Speer bobbed his head up and down. "See!" VonDurenberg cried to Narvez. "I told you they were keeping things from us. I wonder what else they are not sharing."

"The woman for one," Narvez replied.

"Agreed," VonDurenberg retorted. "If they're not willing to share the woman, then what else are they planning not to share?" VonDurenberg looked around at the men seated around him. "No doubt, planning to keep the treasure for their own. They will either claim all the glory and rewards for returning it to Rome, or keep it for themselves when they betray the Holy Father." VonDurenberg paused as he leaned forward and said in a low growl, "Either way, there will be no rewards for our own sacrifices."

"Then what do you propose to do?" Parker demanded.

"Kill them now," De Montgris said. "Take the map and find the gold ourselves."

"Be patient," VonDurenberg replied. "I am the military leader of this expedition; the Church gave me that title. These imbeciles have usurped my authority, but soon I will have my revenge!"

"And what is your plan," De Montgris growled.

"We wait. Once the treasure is in our hands, we kill both of them and take the woman. Do you not think that I have suffered all of their slights for not? All I ask is that you continue to befriend them until the treasure is in our possession."

"Are you sure we should kill them?" De Vale asked. "I don't really think they deserve that!"

"Yes, they do," VonDurenberg replied sarcastically. "If you doubt they deserve death, wait until they have the treasure. Then they will reveal who they truly are. They have kept the woman. What do you think will happen when they have the gold?" De Vale frowned. "When the time is right," VonDurenberg said, "I will strike! When I am finished, I will make sure everyone receives his rewards once we have returned to Rome!"

Speer was working his hands together furiously as he sat listening to his uncle plan the murder of James and Byron.

"Then it's agreed," Narvez said. The men nodded.

"What do you intend to do with the woman once Martel and Fitzwalter are gone?" De Vale asked.

"She is mine," VonDurenberg said.

"When you tire of her, my lord," De Vale said, "I would like to have her."

VonDurenberg eyed De Vale suspiciously. "When I tire of her?"

Parker stood up and took several steps back from the fire to stand near De Montgris. "Are you certain that we should kill them? None of this bodes well. Babylon is a place of evil, black spirits live within the walls." Speer slowly crept up in front of Parker and stared unblinking at the knight.

"Parker, you are a fool!" De Courcy growled as he turned to look back at Parker. "I spilled the blood of that Saracen spy, and I will spill the witch's blood too. Kill Fitzwalter. Kill Martel. Kill the Saracens. Kill them all. Kill every last one! Send them all to hell."

"Ha! Ha! Ha!" laughed VonDurenberg. "Well said, my lord. Evil spirits! Ghosts! Parker you are craven! Grow some courage." Speer laughed insanely, the sound echoed in the night, causing the men who heard it to shiver. "I have heard enough! Ghosts!" VonDurenberg stood up and looked down at Parker in disgust. "It is time to rest. You stand first watch, Parker, unless you are too afraid?"

Parker leapt to his feet. "I fear none."

Simon De Courcy chuckled as he rose to his feet. "Boy, you have killed none. When you have slain your first man, then you can brag about your courage." He gave Parker a shove. "Until then, do your best to stay awake."

Ishaq, standing in the shadows, quietly withdrew. He had been keeping an eye on the graf, for he knew a conspiracy when he saw one. They were plotting to kill Fitzwalter and Martel. He walked back to the place where he had laid out his bed, pondering what to do with the information he now had. He lay down and looked up at the stars glittering against the sable backdrop. At last, he closed his eyes and fell asleep.

CHAPTER 53
THE ISHTAR GATE

Byron woke to someone shaking him. He grabbed for his dagger, but it was not there. "Do not fear Christian, it is just me." Bashshar said. Byron relaxed and with a groan, sat up. "And you are fortunate it is just me. Too slothful to set a watch?"

Byron rubbed his eyes and sighed. "I set a watch."

"So, you thought. Christian, you're fortunate to be alive," the Arab replied. "Saracen cavalry passed our camp by the river last night. Had they come this way, you would all be dead."

"Parker," Byron mumbled as he rose to his feet.

Bashshar's face twisted into a smirk. "I woke him this morning. He had fallen asleep. At least he had his sword drawn."

Byron rubbed his face. "I will take care of this."

"Indeed Christian. If your men don't stay awake, you will not live to see another sun rise." Bashshar stood up.

"I expected your return last night," Byron said.

"That was my intention, but when I saw the Saracen cavalry on the road, I changed my plans."

"How many were there?"

"I did not count them, Christian." Bashshar turned to walk away. "All I can say is that their numbers are greater than yours."

Byron watched the Arab walk away. The thought of Saracens

patrolling the road troubled him. They were fortunate this time. He dusted the sand from his clothes. He needed to deal with Parker's carelessness and set off in the direction of VonDurenberg's camp. The graf was sitting on a rock, his blanket draped over his shoulders. Narvez was sitting next to him. Parker, standing in front of the graf, saw Byron approach and turned to leave.

"What happened to last night's watch?" Byron demanded.

"Why do you ask, lord?" VonDurenberg replied.

"Because I was awakened by Bashshar who said he found Parker asleep."

Parker opened his mouth, but VonDurenberg cut him off with a sharp wave of his hand. "My Lord Fitzwalter," VonDurenberg said as his lip curled in a sneer, "you are not a graf or a baron. You are just a lowly landless knight. I remind you, Lord Fitzwalter, the Church gave me authority over military matters, did it not? I will decide what punishment to mete out, not you."

Byron's face flushed as his jaw muscles tightened. He stared the graf down. "Indeed, it did. If that is the responsibility you still claim, then I expect you to take care of the problem." Byron turned to glare at Parker. "Saracen Cavalry were on the road last night."

VonDurenberg laughed as if to dismiss Byron's concern. "The country is crawling with Saracens."

Byron jabbed a finger at Parker. "I want him dealt with! If you cannot, then I will."

Narvez stood up menacingly. "The graf said he will take care of the problem. If you have nothing else, then go back to your woman."

Byron could feel the hatred of the Spanish knight and decided there was nothing more to gain from arguing with VonDurenberg. "We ride within the hour," he said curtly as he turned and walked away.

It was still early morning by the time the men were saddled and ready. Byron could see the dark glances of the men as he took his place next to Zahirah at the head of the column. Zahirah led the way eastward towards the shadowed walls of the city. The horses trudged through the soft sand. The city of Babylon slowly grew closer. Scorpions scuttled across the hot sand. The heat was suffocating and it was a relief when they finally reached the shade beneath the walls that had once kept the enemies of Babylon at bay. The walls towered above them, rising thirty feet into the air. Built from mud brick, the tops of the walls had eroded into dust. Byron could see the foundations of watchtowers at even intervals along the wall. Built of the same mud bricks, the towers had collapsed leaving only their broken and jagged outlines against the blue sky.

Zahirah turned north, following a narrow trail that led towards the Ishtar gate. Byron had the feeling unfriendly eyes were watching him. Each time he glanced at the ruined walls trying to catch a glimpse of the cause of his unease, he saw nothing. Only dust danced in the wind as it lifted skyward from the decaying mud bricks, soaring its way into the heavens. Byron shrugged off the feeling as nothing more than his imagination, blaming his unease on Zahirah.

Ghosts, he scoffed to himself. The Pope had prayed for him, the Church protected him; yet the thought of God killing the centurion's men weighed on him. He shrugged the feeling off. James was right; the centurion had murdered his men.

They reached the edge of the north road. Sand had piled deep in places along the stones of the roadbed. In the distance, two tall boulders marked the place where the bridge to the Ishtar gate had once stood. As they grew closer to the boulders, they became recognizable as headless statues of men with long robes with wide sleeves. Each figure held a long spear pointed to the sky. In front of the stone images, an oval shield rested in front of the headless warrior's knees. Beyond the statues, the chasm of the empty watercourse cut through the earth where once the Euphrates had flowed.

The bridge to the Ishtar gate was thrown down. Only the foundations remained to mark where it had once spanned the river. Sand filled the riverbed, effacing the height of the bank. Zahirah led the way down into the depression that once had been the course of the mighty Euphrates River. Reaching the other side, her horse lunged up the embankment and onto the broad roadway paved with great flags of stone, worn smooth over the centuries by an untold number of feet.

Enam, in a series of lunges, climbed up the bank and onto the road. Byron lifted his hand tightening the reins, bringing the horse to a halt. As Byron waited for the rest of the men to cross the dead river, he looked at Babylon. A great ramp rose from the desert floor to the distant blue tiled Ishtar gate.

Zahirah looked at the man next to her. His blue and white ghutra stained with sweat. His tunic, covered with dust, hung loose on his shoulders. He was looking at the towering blue gate rising in the distance, and she wondered if he knew its significance.

Babylon the great. The city of Nebuchadnezzar. Men had been drawn by its wealth. The Persian Cyrus, Xerxes, Alexander the Great, the Roman Emperor Trajan. All had conquered Babylon, but not one had held the city for long. Like an old hag whose youth and beauty had fled, the city remained, but she was no longer the object of men's desire. Forgotten, and withered, the once magnificent place was crumbling into dust as the individual bricks of her mighty walls surrendered to the earth from which they had been made.

Byron looked behind him as the last man crossed the riverbed. Nudging Enam forward, he rode towards the gate. Rising steadily, he reached two tall ramparts on both sides of the road. The squeak of saddle leather and the sound of horse's hooves echoed eerily off the walls.

Sand had drifted in small dunes here and there next to the blue tile walls, forcing Byron and the rest of the men to ride around them. The Ishtar gate was growing closer. Byron glanced at the wall. A golden lion walked next to him, its mouth open in a roar. The golden gilt of the beast's mane was peeling away, but it still held him with its baleful gaze as if warning him to stay away. Ahead of him, more lions with manes of alternating colors of red and gold lined the wall. Following in a line, the lions led the way to the gate. In the distance, the blue battlements of the gate rose before him. The second battlement, taller than the first, blocked the road, denying entrance to enemies of Babylon. On each side of the gate, two large towers stood against the sky. These imposing bastions had once guarded the gate should anyone be foolish enough to make a direct assault against the city. Now they were empty, except for a black raven who turned its head to the side to watch the Christians approach.

Byron stopped in the shadow of the great gate of Babylon, the blue enameled walls rising fifty feet above him. Embossed on the walls of the gate, a line of golden bulls strode across the blue tiles. Above the bulls, walked a line of golden dragons with long necks, their tails stretched out behind them. The tiles, despite their age, had fared well in the desert sun, but here and there, the glaze had cracked, chipping away, exposing the earthen bricks beneath the blue glass. Several of the dragons had succumbed to the elements. Now, only an earthen outline remained as they faded away into nothingness. A cool wind funneled through the empty gateway. Byron, in his sweat soaked tunic, enjoyed the feeling. It was all the power that remained to the gods of Babylon to deny him entry.

James stopped beside Byron and sat on his horse looking at the gate. "This is mighty Babylon?"

"Yes," Zahirah replied. "This is the Ishtar gate."

A jackal, resting in the shade of the arch, was disturbed from its slumber. The wild dog jumped up from its makeshift den and ran off down the processional way. The sight of the jackal startled Enam, and the horse snorted in fear, its ears forward, alert, tense. Byron reached down and stroked Enam's neck.

Bashshar, leading the two camels loaded with supplies, rode up. "Are we going to stand here all day in the heat, or are we going to enter the city?"

Byron nodded begrudgingly, not wanting to leave the cool air. James, nudging his horse forward, rode into the shadow of the archway and onto the road that the Babylonians once called the enemy shall never pass.

Zahirah started to follow when wild laughter came from the top of the gate. Startled, she looked up. Peter Speer, outlined against the sky, was standing on top of the gate, his hands on his hips. Speer glared down at the knights and began pointing at them, like Zeus hurling a thunderbolt, shouting, "Ha!" with each motion of his hand.

"Get down from there!" VonDurenberg shouted. "Get down. Now!" Speer paused for a moment and ignoring his uncle, sat down.

"What is wrong with him?" Zahirah asked.

"I don't know," Byron replied. Having seen enough, Byron nudged Enam forward and passed through the gate and into the city of Babylon, leaving VonDurenberg to deal with his insolent squire.

CHAPTER 54
THE PALACE OF NEBUCHADNEZZAR

The Aibur-Sabu, 'the enemy shall never pass'. James rode a short distance down the broad road and stopped at an archway guarded by two large mounds. Once the figures of lions, the mounds sat at each side of the archway, facing the street. Long years had erased the lions' majestic manes leaving only blurred lines carved into the stone. Stumps of broken teeth showed in their open mouths. James rode past the weathered sentinels and halted in the gateway to the palace courtyard.

Beyond the courtyard, stood a roofless shamble of a large building built of mud bricks, it had collapsed, crumbling in the hot desert sun. Darkened holes, once windows, stared out from the dilapidated wall like empty eye sockets in a weathered skull. A sensation of uneasiness crept over James as he beheld the empty places, as if someone, or something, was looking back at him. James scanned the ruined walls of the building, but he saw nothing other than the dust swirling in the wind. James, transfixed, did not stir as Byron and Zahirah rode up beside him.

"The palace?" Byron asked as he pointed to the ruined buildings.

Zahirah nodded.

"Let's see if the knave is home," James said, and he rode into the courtyard.

Byron followed James into the expansive courtyard as the rest of the men filed through the archway behind them. Nothing grew here; only the broken, twisted trunks of old trees and shrubs remained where they had died from the lack of water. The only sound in the stillness of the courtyard was the sound of lizards as they tottered along the brick walls of the palace, unconcerned by the new visitors on horseback.

The remains of another arch stood at the far end of the courtyard; this one roofless, its graceful curve crumbled into a pile of bricks was now blocking the entrance to the next courtyard. All around the walls of the palace, the collapsing masonry still showed the layout of the huge palace complex; a distant memory of the comfort the royalty of Babylon had once enjoyed.

"Do you know where to go next?" James asked Zahirah, as he surveyed the ruined palace, imagining the enormous number of rooms they would have to search.

Byron frowned. "We need to find the place where a ghostly hand wrote a message on a wall. It has to be a large room."

"What do you mean by ghostly hand?" Zahirah asked.

"He is referring to Daniel," James interrupted. "We are seeking the place where a ghostly hand delivered a message to the king."

"So, you are seeking the place where Belshaz-zar learned his doom," Zahirah said.

"Yes," James replied. "Do you know where it is?"

"No, I have never been here."

Byron was disappointed and it showed on his face. He had hoped Zahirah would know how to find the throne room, but it appeared she knew as little as he did, and the thought of the enormity of the search started to overwhelm him. "Any thoughts of where to start our search?" Byron asked hopefully.

Zahirah shook her head.

James frowned and then dismounted. "Well, staying here accomplishes nothing." James turned to the men. "Spread out! Perhaps luck will favor us and we will find this throne room without too much trouble." The men dismounted and began poking through the rubble searching for a large room.

Byron led his horse to the collapsed archway and stopped, examining the mound of bricks blocking the path. Bashshar came up beside him. "Christian, I will hold your horse. You can search," Bashshar's eyes swept the palace, "I will wait here in the shade."

"I think, Sir Byron," Ishaq added, "I will also stay with Bashshar. Help guard the horses until you return."

Byron nodded as he motioned for James to join him. De Montgris and De Vale started to search the first courtyard. Von-Durenberg sat down in the shade of the wall to watch, waiting for his unruly squire to return from his antics at the gate. Byron, surveying the mound of bricks blocking the entrance to the next courtyard, glanced over his shoulder and saw Speer slink through the gate. The squire ambled over to his uncle and sat down. Von-Durenberg jumped to his feet and slapped his squire across the face. Grabbing Speer by his tunic, the graf bent down and shouted. "You will do what you are told."

Byron saw the graf strike his squire and then turned away. Motioning for the rest of the men to follow, he clambered over the crumbling mound of bricks, which slid and clattered with each step. Once Byron reached the top of the mound, he slid down the unstable pile of rubble to the other side. James followed, reaching out his hand to help Zahirah from the top of the mound.

Byron surveyed the new courtyard. It was smaller than the first. In this courtyard, stood two buildings of great size that faced each other. The building on the right was intact, its bronze door ajar revealing only darkness. Faded bands of red paint remained on the wall. A stone statue of a bull with a man's upper body stood next to the door. The statue's muscled arms bent at the elbow as if holding out its hands to receive something. Its broad shoulders culminated to a stump, for the decapitated head was now lying face down in the sand. Only the jagged front wall of the building on the left remained. The roof had collapsed, pulling the walls down with it, leaving only a heap of bricks and a few beams that rose skyward from the mound of rubble.

Byron put his hand on Giodonni's shoulder and pointed to the intact building. "My lord, take the men and search that building. Martel and I will move on to the next courtyard."

"And if I find anything?"

Byron wiped the sweat from his brow. "If you find anything,

Martel and I will be in the next courtyard." Giodonni nodded, motioning for the men to follow him into the building.

Byron led James and Zahirah between the two buildings to the next courtyard. At the far end of the courtyard stood another archway covered with blue glazed bricks. At the base of the arch, a line of golden lions walked above a golden border. Above the lions was a row of columns topped with three round orbs painted on the wall. Byron paused; the orbed columns reminded him of trees. He almost asked Zahirah their significance, but then remembered her response to his question about the staff of Al-Tusi and decided against it.

"We are not here to sightsee, My Lord Fitzwalter," James called out as he and Zahirah entered the archway.

Byron looked away from the wall and walked to the entrance of the arch. Two bearded men looked down at him from the opposing walls. The figures wore feathered crowns. Long robes, adorned with wheeled symbols, hung down to their feet. In their left hands, they held a symbol shaped like the hilt guard of a sword, and at their feet, like a protective dog, lay a golden dragon.

James stepped closer to the image on the wall. "Who is this?" James whispered to Zahirah.

Zahirah moved next to James and reached out her hand to touch the image. "This is Marduk, the God of Babylon. We must be nearing the courtyard of the kings."

"The palace must be near," James muttered.

Zahirah withdrew her hand from the wall. "Yes... the place where the hand of God's messenger pronounced this city's doom."

The temperature was rising as the sun punished the land, yet Byron felt a shiver run down his spine. "Let's press on," he said. "Evil abodes here, I can feel it."

They passed through the arch and into the largest courtyard they had seen so far. In front of them, a blue walled building extended across the courtyard. The roof was crowned with thorns of crenellation, fashioned into a line of angular points. Beneath the crenellation, tall narrow windows frowned down upon the mortals who dared to enter the courtyard of Nebuchadnezzar.

"That must be the throne room," James said confidently.

Zahirah nodded as she looked around at the rest of the crumbling structures. "Blue is the color of the kings."

Byron said nothing as he gazed at the throne room of Nebuchadnezzar. In the center of the palace's smooth façade, stood a large archway with broad steps littered with the rubble. Two bronze doors, decorated with dragons with wings spread like fans, lay thrown down in front of the darkened doorway.

In the bright sunlight, the palace looked forsaken. The blue tiles, chipped and damaged by the sun, were flaking away. Sand had drifted into small dunes against the walls, yet at one time, this single building had been the center of the civilized world. A place of enlightenment; where wise men gave advice to the king, where courtiers waited shamelessly for a mere nod from their monarch. This single throne, the first of its kind, feared no rivalry from the lesser empires that surrounded her. Even the Hebrew slaves held captive here could not dispute Babylon's greatness.

Only the Hebrew God was unimpressed, and at the height of Babylon's glory, his prophets proclaimed the city's doom. Unheeded, the warnings were ignored as nothing more than the ravings of an accursed race, jealous of the power and wealth of Babylon. Yet standing in the courtyard of the king's, Byron could see that it had all come true.

Byron hesitated as he looked in at the dark opening that once led to the exclusive haunts of the privileged few of Babylon. A fear that he could not explain made the hair on the back of his neck stand up, and though it was broad daylight, a coldness surrounded him. James felt it too, and he looked at Byron who was doing his best to shake it off.

"Do you feel it?" Byron whispered.

"Feel what," James snapped, striding off towards the doorway.

"You feel the curse of God," Zahirah whispered. "I warned you not to enter."

Byron stared at the dark doorway of the throne room. "We are here to do God's work. God will protect us."

"I have warned you," Zahirah replied.

Byron looked at her. "Great deeds are never done by the faithless or by those who lack courage." He turned to follow James into the throne room. Zahirah followed him as he crossed the courtyard and went up the broken bricks that had once formed the steps to the hall of the kings.

The overpowering smell of urine and feces greeted them. Jackals had moved into the palace and had turned it into their den. "My god!" Byron gasped as the overpowering stench slammed his senses. He quickly pulled a rag over his nose and mouth, as did Zahirah as she entered behind him.

Byron paused, his hand resting on his shamshir as he scanned the empty room. Shards of broken pottery lay scattered across the floor. Here and there, sand had accumulated against the walls. In places, the roof of cedar beams had given way and had crashed down onto the floor. Shafts of sunlight streamed through the ruined ceiling, as if pillars of light supported the roof. At the far end of the hall, Byron could make out the shadowy figure of James who had stepped just beyond the light into the darkened end of the hall.

Warily Byron and Zahirah crossed the room. The smell became less as they moved deeper into the throne room, and Byron removed the rag from his face. At the far end of the immense hall, Byron could see a blue tiled wall with tarnished gold lions at the base. A row of tiles shaped like pillars rose above the lions, while paintings of images, no longer discernible, adorned the surrounding walls. The faded art reminded Byron of images he had seen in Rome, and he wondered if Alexander the Great, in his brief lordship over the city, had ordered the work.

An immense throne, the sides shaped like two standing winged lions, sat in the center of the blue tiled wall. The wings of the lions had once wrapped around to form the back of the throne, but were now broken and lay cast aside on the floor. James was looking down at a curious bundle on the floor in front of the throne. As Byron moved closer, he realized he was looking at the headless body of a man in armor. A javelin driven into the corpse's back secured the cadaver to the floor. Jackals had feasted on the body. The bones of the arms and legs lay scattered around the room while the armor had protected the torso from the ravages of the wild dogs. A curious helmet plumed with horsehair lay near the corpse. The head was gone, the jackals having carried it off; but the wild dogs, having no interest in the bronze helmet, had left it lying on the floor. James bent over the body.

"Nothing interesting, about it," VonDurenberg said. The graf had entered the throne room unnoticed. He walked over and gave the corpse a dig with the toe of his boot. "Why are we in this stinking hovel anyway?"

"To search," Byron replied as he looked over his shoulder at VonDurenberg. "My lord graf, did you tire of beating your squire?"

VonDurenberg scoffed. "The boy is incorrigible, but he will think twice before he disobeys me again!"

Byron looked away. "Indeed. Well, my lord, this has to be the palace where the ghostly hand wrote upon the wall."

"Well, the search of the other courtyards has proved fruitless." VonDurenberg scowled as he looked around. "I don't see anything here either."

"I do," James said, pointing to a place in the wall near the broken throne. Chiseled into the blue tiles of the wall, the word babel was scrawled.

"Babel?" Byron asked, his face twisted into a quizzical expression. "Do you have any idea what that means?"

"No, other than to babble like a fool," James said, looking at VonDurenberg.

Byron moved closer to get a better look. He knelt down on one knee to examine the corpse of the dead Roman and then glanced up at the word babel. The graf walked up to stand behind Byron. "There's nothing helpful here. Babel!" VonDurenberg scoffed. Byron turned to reply, but VonDurenberg cut him off with a wave of his hand. "Don't weary my ears, Fitzwalter. You don't know what it means. Stay and smell the dog shit. I am going outside!"

"The writing on the wall," Byron muttered.

"Did your priest say anything in his notes about the throne room?" Zahirah asked in a voice muffled by the handkerchief she held against her face.

Byron pulled out Father Villhardain's notes and shuffled through them. "No, whatever his plans were, they died with him."

James smiled. "Fitzwalter, give the Saracen lady the notes and see if she can find an answer." Byron handed Zahirah the parchment. She rearranged the pages. Once satisfied that the pages were in the right sequence, she began to read.

Zahirah looked up from reading Father Villhardain's notes. "Your priest apparently translated his notes from the centurion's original text. Several times, he has underlined a passage he obviously felt was important. It says here, Mene, Mene, Tekel, and Parsin."

"Then from his presence the hand was sent, and the writing was inscribed. And this is the writing that was inscribed: Mene, Mene, Tekel and Parsin. This is the interpretation of the matter:

Mene, God has numbered the days of your Kingdom and brought it to an end;

Tekel, you have been weighed in the balances and found wanting;

Peres, your Kingdom is divided and given to the Medes and Persians."

A feeling of unease passed over them. Here in this very place, God had sent his messenger to pronounce the city's fate. In this room, the prophet Daniel had read these words, announcing God had rendered judgment and that frightful end was near. Byron looked at the broken throne.

†

The party was probably at its height. Belshaz-zar sat there on his winged throne, enjoying the entertainment. Perhaps he had been leaning on the armrest of his great throne as he drank from a golden vessel taken from the Jewish Temple. Surrounded by his sycophants, Belshaz-zar had not one care. He was king of the mighty empire. All feared the power of Babylon. He lifted the cup to his lips to drink, when over the rim of the cup, he saw it. A disembodied hand that glowed with pale light. It drifted across the room until it reached the wall. With its index finger, it began to write. The letters flamed with red light as the finger traced upon the wall until all could see the words Mene, Mene, Tekel and Parsin. As the last letter was laid down, the hand began to glow brighter and brighter until the light became unbearable. Belshazzar shielded his eyes and then it was gone.

The king jumped to his feet, the color gone from his face. Motioning to a servant to come near, the king bent down and whispered in the servant's ear, "Find Daniel and hurry. Speak to no one. I do not want fear to spread until we know what this means."

The revelers must have stood in dread as Daniel entered the silent room. The prophet approached the wall, Belshaz-zar following close behind in apprehension, asking the prophet what the words foretold. Daniel read the words to himself. Belshaz-zar pressed the prophet for an answer, impatient to know. At last, Daniel stood back, and in a loud voice so all could hear, he told them the meaning. No doubt, great fear descended as the faces of the privileged of Babylon turned ashen. It could not be true. They were made of finer clay. No, this could not be true. The moment was broken as a soldier with blood running down his face ran into the throne room. "Great King!" he cried. "The Persians are upon us! They have broken through the Ishtar gate. Darius is here, and he has come with a great host! Chaos erupted as the crowd scattered, running from the palace, screaming as the Persians of Darius set upon killing them all.

†

Here, the passage was no longer a vague story to be read half-heartedly and dismissed. Zahirah's voice echoed off the walls of the palace and it gave power to the passage that had been unnoticed when Father Villhardain had read the same words in the Lateran. A strange silence descended as they looked at each other, the implications of the words sank in.

"There is more," Zahirah whispered.

"In Babylon, beneath the place where the languages of men were born. At the door of Marduk, you will find a mark. The sign of Constantine's victory over Maxentius. Loyalty to the emperor will unlock the door. SPQR."

"That is not helpful," James said quietly as he looked around at the walls of the throne room.

"Did I overhear you say the priest told you the Christian Bible was used as a guide to the treasure?"

"Yes," Byron replied.

Zahirah paused and looked down at the parchment in her hand. "Then I have the answer."

"And?" James demanded impatiently.

"The treasure is hidden in Ziggurat Etemenanki."

"The what?" James said. "I have never heard of it."

"The tower of Babel," Zahirah said. "Have you not heard of the great tower?"

Byron frowned. "No."

Zahirah sighed as she rolled her eyes to look up at the beams of the ceiling and then back to the two knights standing in front of her. "In Genesis, man ignored the will of God by building a tower to reach heaven."

"Yes, I know that," James interrupted. "But what does that have to do with Babylon and the ziggurat of...Eeky Weeky?"

Byron burst out laughing. The sound of his laughter filled the hall, bouncing off the walls, echoing and re-echoing eerily until it faded away. They looked at each other as the last echo died away, at last Zahirah spoke, "E-temen-an-ki," she said softly. "People believe the Ziggurat of Etemenanki was the foundation for the tower of Babel. The centurion has left the treasure there."

"And what is a ziggurat?" Byron whispered.

"A ziggurat is a stair-stepped pyramid," Zahirah replied. "E-te-men-an-ki means the house of the foundation of heaven on earth. It was dedicated to the God Marduk and his wife. It had seven terraces, each smaller than the first. The last terrace was reserved for the gods and the Chaldeans, who looked to the stars for answers to their earthly questions."

"Where is this tower of Eeky Weeky?" James asked.

Zahirah's eyebrows lowered as she gave James a look of disdain. "Etemenanki stood near the palace."

"We are that close?" Byron said.

Zahirah looked up at him. "Yes, you are very close."

Byron felt his excitement rising. They were close, soon this would all be over, and they would be on their way home. "There is nothing more to see. Let's leave this wretched place."

"No, stay a moment," James said, looking at the wall. "We have the writing on the wall. What about the hand that wrote it?"

"What about it?" Byron said as he turned to walk to the entrance.

"James is right. The centurion specifically quotes the moment that the hand appeared and wrote its message on the wall. We have the message, perhaps there is more?" Zahirah moved closer to the corpse and examined it. The arms were gone. She walked around it, looking at the floor. "The body was placed here with a purpose. Perhaps this soldier committed some crime. The penalties for failure in the Roman army could result in death." She looked at James. "Pull the spear."

James took hold of the pilum and gave a steady pull, but the javelin did not budge. Putting both hands on the shaft, he pulled harder. The javelin moved. Improving his grip, James pulled with all his strength and the pilum slowly gave way. Byron reached down, grabbing the corpse by the armor and drug it out of the way. James scuffed the floor with his boot, revealing several brown tiles outlined in gold. Byron and Zahirah got to their knees and started brushing the dust away with their hands. Slowly, an image appeared. Tile by tile a great lion with folded wings appeared on the floor. Byron stood up and looked down at the image as the memory of the dream of a winged lion came back.

"The symbol of Babylon," Zahirah whispered.

Byron walked around the image. Reddish brown tiles formed the mane of the great beast, but as Byron looked closer, he saw that several of the tiles near the lion's heart were brown, discolored, as if a crude patch had been added. He knelt down and reached for the javelin in James' hand. Using the tip of the javelin, Byron forced the tiles up and slid them out of the way, revealing a dust covered black square. Byron ran his hand over the top. It was a piece of wood, painted black. Shoving his fingers in the gap between the black board and tiles, Byron lifted the wood from the floor. Slowly, the board emerged from the floor's tight embrace, revealing that it was not a board at all, but a black box. He pulled the box free and set it on the floor.

James and Zahirah were hovering over his shoulder, watching. "Open it," Zahirah said.

Byron looked at the box and then to James who nodded. "Open it, Fitzwalter."

The bronze hasp of the latch was unadorned. Beneath the hasp, carved into the wood were the letters SPQR. Byron glanced up at Zahirah. "SPQR, it's Roman," Zahirah said excitedly. "The Senate and People of Rome."

Byron lifted the hasp, slowly opened the lid, and then inhaled sharply.

"What?" Zahirah cried as she and James pressed closer to see. Byron tilted the box. Inside was a black hand. Its palm open, its fingers spread apart.

Zahirah leaned her head closer. Her long, dark hair brushed against Byron's arm. "A signum manus."

"And by Gods bones, what is a signum manus?" James demanded.

Zahirah ignored James as she lifted the blackened hand from the box. "This hand once topped the standard of a Roman century. It represented loyalty to the emperor." She rubbed the palm of the hand with the hem of her dress. Slowly, a small spot of silver began to show. "The ages have turned this dark. Once, it was held at the head of the Century, guiding it into battle. Only the best and bravest soldiers carried the signum standard." Zahirah looked at Byron with her dark eyes. "We need this." She gave the hand back to Byron who placed it back into its box. Byron closed the lid and stood up. He tucked the box under his arm. Grasping the pilum, he held it out in front of him.

"What do you want with that?" James asked, pointing at the javelin. "It is just extra weight."

"It interests me," Byron said, looking at the Roman javelin. "A souvenir. Might be the only tangible thing I get for all my trouble." Shouldering the pilum, Byron turned to leave. As they neared the entrance, Byron looked back at the vacant throne. In the gloom, it seemed as if a dark shadow was sitting upon the throne of Nebuchadnezzar. Byron flinched and quickly looked away as he picked up his pace to the doorway.

In the bright sunlight, Byron took a deep breath of fresh air and looked around at the walls of the palace. The thought of the shadow on the throne made him shiver. He must have imagined it he told himself, and dismissed the thought as he scanned the cityscape looking for the famed seven-tiered ziggurat of Babel. "I don't see the ziggurat!"

"I don't see it either," James said, looking around for a structure that by Zahirah's description should dominate the landscape.

"You don't see it," Zahirah said, "because it's not there."

"What do you mean it's not there?" James growled. "You just gave us the whole history of Eeky Weeky, and now you tell us it is not there." James turned to face her. "If you knew it was not there, why did you not say so?"

"The foundation is still there," Zahirah said, "but the tower itself is gone."

"What happened?" asked Byron. "Did it crumble away?"

"Yes," Zahirah answered. "Come, I will show you."

VonDurenberg and the men were resting in the shade of a wall as Byron, James, and Zahirah returned to the first courtyard. "Do you see the box Fitzwalter's concealing beneath his arm?" Ishaq whispered to Bashshar who was leaning back against the wall with his eyes closed.

Bashshar half opened his eyes to squint at Byron. "Hmm...looks like they found something."

"Wonder what it is?" Ishaq said as he got up and untied Enam. As Ishaq led the horse to the knight, he intently studied the box under Byron's arm.

Byron took his horse and started to lead him towards the

processional way.

"What now," VonDurenberg demanded. "We have found nothing. There is nothing here."

Byron stopped. "Our search was not fruitless."

"And what did you find," sneered VonDurenberg. A rusty spear and a box of dog shit?" The men started to laugh.

Ishaq's curiosity was overflowing. "What is in the box, Sir Byron?"

"A hand."

"A hand? Surely it is not real?" The men crowded around as Byron opened the box to reveal the blackened hand.

"And what use is that?" the graf demanded.

"I am not sure yet," Byron said as he snapped the box closed. He handed it and the pilum to James. Once Byron was mounted, he looked down at VonDurenberg. "If you wish to know its use, then follow me."

Giodonni stepped next to VonDurenberg and looked up at Byron. "My lord, are you sure we should disturb anything here? There is evil here. Perhaps we should turn back."

"Turn back?" James cried. "Surely you jest! We are not turning back. You wanted to turn back when the priest died. You wanted to turn back in the sand storm. Do you fear death? I tell you, Lord Giodonni, everyone here is a dead man, sooner or later."

Giodonni's eyes smoldered in rage as he locked his gaze upon James. "Just because I have the good sense not to meddle in the affairs of God does not make me a coward! This city is cursed, down to the last grain of sand. Being here is an offense to God. I feel it!"

"Yes, well God hates a coward," James snarled as he handed the box and pilum to Byron. "I will not hold you here, my lord, if the spooks and demons trouble you. Go if you wish." James mounted his horse and turned to face Giodonni. "The choice is yours." Muttering, Giodonni left to get his horse.

Byron rode to the processional way and stopped near the lions. James came up beside him. "I grow tired of the whining." Byron nodded. "The sultana likes you."

Byron scoffed, "You think so?" Byron said as he scanned the walls.

James moved closer. "Yes."

Byron looked away. "Well, my friend, I have lots of concerns; romance is not one them." Zahirah passed through the arch, abruptly ending their conversation.

"Where do we find this invisible Eeky Weeky Ziggurat?" James asked, changing the subject.

"Go south and follow the processional way," she said, pointing down the road. "There, you will see the foundations of the ziggurat."

James' eyes were alight with mischief as he smiled. "Why don't you lead?"

Zahirah scowled at him and turned to mount her horse. "I might as well, it will be faster, and then I shall soon be rid of all of you."

They rode in the shade of the wall that lined the processional way. The sun was past midday. Zahirah stopped where the wall parted into a long street, lined with battlements. Dead grass protruded between the flagstones that paved the street. At the far end, the ruins of what was a tall fortress gate. Like the Ishtar gate, Marduk's bulls and dragons decorated the walls in alternating bands. Crenelated battlements topped the wall that was once graced by an arch of blue tile, but only the stump of the arch remained. The southern half of the gate had been destroyed. Beyond the ruined gate, was a great forbidding mound, the remains of the Ziggurat of Etemenanki.

CHAPTER 55
THE ADVENTURES OF ISMA'IL AND MUHTADI

Husam al-Din sat in the shade of a palm tree waiting for Isma'il and Nadim to return. He wondered if the lie of the sultana's death would convince Ali to return to Baghdad. It had been some time since Isma'il had departed, and Husam al-Din was beginning to worry. He started to fidget, glancing about the sky to see if there were any telltale signs that his lieutenant was returning. At last, he saw a faint stream of dust rising into the air. Far off, he could make out the faint shape of two men on horseback. It was Isma'il, followed by Nadim. He stood up to greet them.

"Did all go well? Was the captain of Baghdad convinced?"

"All is well," Isma'il replied, dismounting and slapping the dust from the sleeves of his tunic. "The captain of Baghdad believed our story and has left, but that is not near as important as what else I have learned."

"And what is that?"

"I saw the Christians! They are in Babylon."

Husam al-Din's mouth opened, and for a moment, he was at a loss for words. "In Babylon? Why?"

Ismail shrugged. "I have no idea."

"Tell me what you know."

Isma'il related to Husam al-Din the events at the walls of Babylon: the startling confession of Ali, and the tact he used to convince Ali to drop his search and return to Baghdad.

"And then," Isma'il said, relishing the suspense, "I saw him! One of the Christians. He was lying in the shadows of a hole in the wall, and I would swear he was listening to our conversation. Even more surprising, I saw her!"

"Who?" Husam al Din demanded impatiently.

"The sultana. She was with the Christian."

"A prisoner?" Husam al-Din cried.

Isma'il shrugged. "I do not know. She did not appear to be restrained. What do you want to do?"

Husam al-Din motioned to Muhtadi. When the scout had joined them, Husam al-Din spoke, "The Christians are in the dead city. The sultana is with them. What do you suggest?"

Muhtadi frowned. "Well that answers a good many questions. I suggest Nadim and I enter the city to see what they are doing." Muhtadi could not see Nadim blanch at the suggestion.

"Good," Husam al Din answered. "Do you think the treasure is in the city?"

Muhtadi nodded. "I do. We are close now. The Christians could not find Babylon! I would guess the sultana is now helping them since her capture."

"So, it would appear," Husam al-Din said. "I cannot make up my mind if her helping them is good or bad."

"Well, if you want to stop wandering the desert aimlessly, it is a good thing," Isma'il said.

Husam al-Din nodded. "When can you leave?"

"Now," Muhtadi said as he glanced at Nadim.

"Good. Send a rider when you learn their purpose for being in Babylon."

Muhtadi nodded as he turned to leave. "Come, Nadim, we have work to do."

Nadim hesitated, his face pale. "But, Muhtadi, Babylon is cursed by Allah. Are you sure we should enter?"

Muhtadi glanced over his shoulder at Nadim. "The Christians are there, and therefore we go there as well. To watch." Muhtadi turned his back and walked away. Nadim did not move, hoping Muhtadi would stop and change his mind, but Muhtadi kept walking. Nadim sighed and started to follow, his head bowed as if some great weight had fallen upon him.

Husam al-Din sat down on the sand. Isma'il sat facing him. "It appears Allah favors us."

"Yes, the time for avenging Kamal and Fadil draws near. Allah has blessed you with a stroke of luck."

"Indeed," Husam al-Din said. "Soon this will be over. I am ready to go home." Husam al-Din tilted his head in the direction of Muhtadi. "I want you to go to Babylon. That boy is frightened. It would be better if a stout heart went into the city with Muhtadi. I don't want to be given away by the boy's foolish fears."

Isma'il nodded as he stood up. "The fear of Allah's wrath is not foolish, but I will go."

Muhtadi walked to his horse. As he saddled, his mind whirled with how he was going to get within sight of the Christians without being seen. He was pulling his saddle's cinch tight when Nadim came up to him, leading his horse. Muhtadi mounted and turned in the direction of Babylon. He was about to ride out of camp when Isma'il rode up to join them.

"Husam al-Din asked me to ride with you."

"And you are welcome to join us," Muhtadi replied.

Isma'il smiled and bowed. They reached the edge of the camp, and Muhtadi was about to kick his horse into a trot when he turned his head and frowned. He lifted his hand to shade his eyes as he looked into the distance. Far away, a rider on horseback appeared, riding in great haste.

"Someone is coming," he muttered.

Isma'il turned to look. Slowly, the horseman drew near. Muhtadi dropped his hand. "It is Ahmed."

Ahmed rode up and stopped in front of Muhtadi, his horse covered with flecks of white foam. "The Christian's are in Babylon," Ahmed croaked as he dismounted. "I tracked them across the wasted lands into the city." Ahmed pulled his water skin from his saddle and took a drink. "I also found where they left four bodies in the desert."

Muhtadi looked at Ahmed's face streaked with dust and sweat. "Well done, Ahmed. The Christians are in Babylon, eh. Very good." Muhtadi paused. "You have earned a rest after a hard ride."

Ahmed's dark eyes narrowed as his face tightened. "You know… don't you," he snapped.

Muhtadi nodded as he sighed. "Yes. Allah has blessed us. Isma'il spied one of the Christians hiding in the shadow of the walls."

"I saw the Baghdad Cavalry," Ahmed sighed. "All my efforts were for not."

"That is not true," Muhtadi replied. "Isma'il saw one. Now I know that all of the Christians are in the city."

"Not all of them. The Christian's sent their camels away before the Baghdad Cavalry overtook them."

"And that is news I did not know," Muhtadi said as he patted Ahmed on the shoulder. "Go rest. You have earned it. Isma'il and I are going to Babylon to see what the Christians are doing there. In the morning, I want you to pick up the camel's trail and find out where they were sent to wait."

Ahmed sighed. "I have ridden hard for the last several days. Couldn't you send Nadim?"

Muhtadi put his hand on Ahmed's shoulder. "You have done all that I have asked of you. We are close now and this is important. The Christians will need the camels to move the treasure. If the camels leave the river, it will be because they have found the treasure. If that happens, return here and report to Husam al-Din."

"As you wish," Ahmed said tiredly. He turned and led his horse away.

Muhtadi watched Ahmed go and turned to Isma'il. "I hope the elusive Christians are still there and have not disappeared again," he grumbled as he kicked his horse into a trot.

They rode slowly in a wide arc to the city, careful not to raise any dust that would give away their approach. They halted in a small depression in sight of the walls of Babylon.

"Are you sure it is wise to camp in the city tonight?" Isma'il asked, looking at the walls of Babylon. "I have heard tales that would make your blood run cold. It is said that when the sun goes down, the dead rise to walk among the ruined walls of the city, waiting for the last day when judgment is rendered for their sins."

Nadim looked at Isma'il with alarm and then stared intently at the city walls as if he were looking for ghosts among the shadows. The corner of Isma'il's mouth turned up slightly as he winked at Muhtadi.

"I have heard the same," Muhtadi replied solemnly as he watched Nadim turn pale. "The dead prowling the streets, waiting to drink the blood of the unwise who stray into the city after dark...but I do not believe any of it," he added, deciding that perhaps he should not scare the boy too much.

"I do not fear ghosts!" Nadim snapped as he looked away from Babylon.

Muhtadi smiled. "Good! Then we shall camp near the south wall and enter the city by first light." Muhtadi got off his horse and lay on top of the small rise to look at the city through his glass – nothing moved.

Isma'il came up beside him. "Anything?" he asked.

"No, all is still," Muhtadi whispered. Scorpions scampered about them, their tails raised in an arc as they moved along the sand. The sun beat down as they waited and watched. Isma'il looked behind him to see Nadim sitting in the shade of the horses as he held their reins.

"They are coming out of the city," Muhtadi hissed.

Ismail turned back to look. In the distance, he could see vague figures moving. "What do you see?" he whispered.

"I see men on horses. Ahmed is right, there are no camels with them. I wonder what they have done with the camels?" Muhtadi asked aloud.

"Perhaps they sent them to the river," Isma'il answered. "Ali's scout said their trail led towards the Euphrates."

He got up and walked down the rise to Nadim. "Nadim, ride to Husam al-Din, tell him the Christians have left the city for the day."

"Yes, Muhtadi. Do you wish me to tell him anything else?"

"Tell him that I believe the treasure is in the city. Hopefully, the Christians will lead us to its resting place. We will wait for you at the south wall. Oh! And bring some more water skins back with you!"

Nadim bowed. "Yes, Muhtadi."

Muhtadi climbed back up the rise and joined Isma'il.

"Do you think they will come back to the city?" Isma'il asked.

"Not tonight. In the morning, they will return. The treasure must be in the city."

When Muhtadi deemed it safe, he and Isma'il shadowed the Christians to a small group of palms near the walls and watched them make camp. When Muhtadi was certain they were going no further, he stealthily crawled to a small vantage point where he could lay down and watch the enemy. The sun beat down, turning the sand into a furnace. Hours passed. When Muhtadi was certain the Christians were in camp, he stood up and slowly returned to where Isma'il held the horses.

"They're done for the day and so am I," Muhtadi said, wiping the sweat from his face. "Let's attend to our own needs and find a place to spend the night."

They stopped under the lip of a small dune near the south wall. The hill gave them some shade from the relentless sun as they sat drinking water, waiting for Nadim to return. Nadim rode up as the sun was starting to sink beyond the horizon.

"Husam al-Din sends his greetings and thanks for the report," the young man said with a smile. "He said to tell you that he has men patrolling the road to make sure no one comes and disturbs our Christian guests. He wants to make sure their work remains uninterrupted," Nadim said, smiling.

"Excellent," Muhtadi replied.

The sun sank into the west, and as the grey shadows stretched across the sand, it began to grow cold. Muhtadi wrapped his blanket around his shoulders. The night was long and sleepless. When the sun rose, Muhtadi was awake to greet it. After a cheerless breakfast, Muhtadi and Isma'il made plans to enter the city to wait for the Christians return. Nadim did not complain when Muhtadi suggested he stay and tend to the horses.

After prayers, Muhtadi and Isma'il quickly crossed the sand and slipped through a hole in the wall. Muhtadi carefully climbed to the top of the decaying battlement. Once he found a good place to conceal himself, Muhtadi turned to see Isma'il lay down behind a crumbling pile of bricks. They waited. The wind stirred, bringing some relief from the heat as Muhtadi watched the lizards scampering in short spurts here and there along the bricks, ignoring him as they went about their business.

It seemed like an eternity as Muhtadi sat on the hot bricks baking in the sun. He was miserable with nothing else to think about except the heat and the sweat running down his back. It was a relief when he saw the telltale sign of dust that signaled the Christians were returning. His misery forgotten as he watched them ride along the edge of the wall. The Christians passed from sight. Muhtadi had to move. Using great care on the unstable bricks, he darted between the open spaces that were used by the ancient archers as he kept the Christians in view.

The tall handsome Christian with dark hair was leading the group. A smaller man mounted on a bay horse, rode beside him. A beautiful woman of Saracen descent was next to the man on the bay horse. Several Christians passed. In their midst, Muhtadi saw a blonde haired arrogant looking man. As the last of the Christians rode by, Muhtadi noticed a man with a beard bringing up the rear of the column. The man looked out of place, almost like an Arab. Muhtadi wondered about the distinguished looking Arab, surely this man had supplied the camels. He wondered how much the Christians were paying him.

As Muhtadi carefully scurried along the walls keeping up with the riders, the Christian on the bay horse seemed to sense him. The man kept looking around scanning the walls, watchful and alert. Muhtadi's heart stopped when the Christian looked right at him, as if he saw him. Muhtadi, darting back to hide, lost his balance. To his dismay, several bricks came loose and clattered down the inside of the wall making a terrible racket.

Muhtadi froze, his heart beating wildly. He glanced down at the Christians fearful that he had given himself away. To his relief, they appeared to have not heard the noise. They were continuing on their way, unaware of his presence. He looked over at Isma'il who was shaking his head and frowning.

It took some time for Muhtadi to get his nerves under control. At last, Muhtadi was calm enough to begin stalking the Christians again as they worked their way to the Ishtar gate. The Ishtar gate proved to be a challenge. The rampart had been reduced to a crumbled point, sloping away on both sides of the wall. Muhtadi had to content himself with spying from a distance as the Christians paused at the gate.

A cry of rage pierced the silence. Muhtadi froze in place. He looked to the place where the sound had come. To his amazement, he saw one of the Christians standing on top of the Ishtar gate. Muhtadi watched as this strange Christian danced from one foot to the other screaming and pointing at the others. He looked at Isma'il to see if he had an explanation, but Isma'il only shook his head and shrugged.

Muhtadi glanced down at the rest of the Christians to see what they would do, but they sat on their horses looking up as if they did not know what to do with him either. The man must be insane. One of the Christians began yelling at the young man in Frankish, but the young man defiantly stood up on the gate refusing to obey his master. To Muhtadi's disbelief, the Christian's master threw his hands up and rode off, leaving the fool sitting on the top of the Ishtar gate.

"Do you think we should try to capture him?" Isma'il whispered.

"To what end?" Muhtadi replied. "What could we learn from him? Clearly, he is possessed! The most that could come from such an attempt is he escapes from us, or someone comes to look for him. Either way, he does us no good." Isma'il nodded. "We need to move," Muhtadi whispered. "They're almost out of sight."

The young man was now tossing pebbles from the top of the Ishtar gate onto the roadway. Muhtadi took one last glance at the young man to make sure he was not looking their way before he moved to follow the Christians. To his shock, the young man was looking right at him, an unpleasant grin on his face. Muhtadi stood still. He waited, watching to see what he would do. To Muhtadi's surprise, the young man smiled broadly and put his finger in front of his lips in a gesture to be quiet. The young man stood up, dusted off his clothes, and then walked off, disappearing out of sight.

"Did you see that!" Isma'il hissed in fear. "He saw us! He is going to warn them."

"Let's see what happens, I am not so sure. Would you believe him?"

"No," Isma'il said after a thoughtful pause. "No, I would not."

"That's right. Men are reluctant to believe the truth under the best circumstances. Imagine the weight they would give to a messenger who is crazy."

Muhtadi was right, nothing happened. It was a long afternoon of sitting and watching. He had inadvertently dozed when Isma'il nudged him. The Christians had emerged back on to the processional way. The Christian with the bay horse had a black box tucked under his arm. Muhtadi stared at the box trying to guess its contents. More curious, the Christian was carrying a javelin. Muhtadi stroked his beard as he pondered what the Christians had found, or how these tokens would help them find the treasure. The box was intriguing. It was not a large box. The Christian held it close as if it was important. The Christians mounted again and began moving down the processional way.

There was no way to slip down the wall without being seen. By late afternoon, the Christians had disappeared from sight. Whatever they were doing, he would have to wait to find out. The sun began to set when the Christians reentered the roadway. He did not pay very close attention to them at first, but then realized the Christian on the bay horse was injured. The man's head was covered with a green bandage soaked with blood. He appeared to lean on the woman and the handsome Christian Knight. As Muhtadi watched the Christians, he wondered what could have happened. When the Christian's were gone, he stood up and stretched.

Isma'il walked stiffly towards him. "What are your plans? Shall we go see where they have been?"

"No," Muhtadi said. "I am tired and thirsty, and I have not eaten all day. We will come back tonight to look around. I want to be sure that the Christians have left for good. I don't want to start poking around only to be discovered because they have returned for something they forgot."

CHAPTER 56
ETEMENANKI
"Eeky Weeky"

Byron rode through the pillars of the gateway to Etemenanki and stopped. Thrusting the pilum into the sand, he dismounted. Setting the box down in front of him, Byron leaned against the javelin and looked at the mound of crumbling bricks in the distance. He took a sip of water as James came up to stand next to him. Byron nodded towards the remains of the tower of Babel. "It looks like a mound of dirt."

James shaded his eyes against the sun's glare. "Not what I was expecting."

The rest of the men slowly entered the courtyard and sat down in the shade of the broken wall. The entire southern wall destroyed, leaving the foundation and a few scattered bricks to mark where it had been. The courtyard was filled with dead trees whitened by the desert sand, a reminder of when they had been planted for the pleasure of the God's of Babylon. Sand filled the grounds as it sifted in, consuming the land, making it difficult to see the road that lead to Etemenanki. Clumps of grass and weeds waved in the wind. The mound of the once towering ziggurat waited for them in the distance.

Byron capped his water skin and picked up the box. Taking the javelin, he leaned it against the wall near the ruined arch.

"The day is getting on," James said as he looked up at the sky.

"What about the rest of the men?" Byron asked.

James shook his head. "If we need them, we can come back."

Byron motioned to Zahirah to join them. He found himself watching her as she walked towards them, her green dress swaying with each step. Once again, a strange sensation of excitement stirred as she drew close. Not wanting to give away his feelings, he said stiffly, "My lady, we are going to look for Marduk's door...if you wish to join us?"

Zahirah shot a glance back at VonDurenberg and the dust-covered men leaning against the wall. She smiled at Byron and nodded. Zahirah, her shoulders back and her head up, walked beside Byron, who kept the black box tucked beneath his arm. James walked behind them, his hand resting on his shamshir.

Only the ziggurat's foundation remained. Forty feet high, the foundation wall was spaced with recesses that gave an aesthetic appearance to the otherwise bland structure of tan bricks. A band of blue enamel bordered the top of the foundation. Above the blue enamel was a mound of dirt and broken bricks.

James stopped and stared at the ziggurat. "Weighed," he said quietly to himself.

"What?" Byron asked.

"Weighed and found wanting. What does the centurion mean?"

Zahirah stopped and turned to face James. "Belshaz-zar was found unworthy by God. That is what weighed and found wanting means."

James crossed his arms across his chest. "I was looking for a more pragmatic answer. Does the centurion mean that we have to weigh ourselves to prove our worth?"

"No," Zahirah snapped. "Weight has nothing to do with it. It is who you are! What you are. God sees all. The thoughts. The deeds. The evil you hide from others, versus the face you show to the world. All is laid bare. God knows who you truly are." Zahirah glanced in the direction of the ziggurat. "Whatever he has devised, we first must find the door of Marduk. Then perhaps we shall have a better understanding of what the centurion means."

Byron sighed and started towards the mound of dirt and bricks.

The huge mound at the top of the foundation was all that remained of the seven terraces that rose to the blue enameled temple high above the desert floor. As the sun rose and set, the mud bricks had weakened as the succeeding generations of Babylonians had neglected its care of what their grandfathers had built. By the time Alexander the Great had conquered Babylon, the temple was beyond repair. As the jewel of his empire, Alexander decreed that Babylon should be rebuilt more glorious than before. On his orders, his soldiers started to remove the decrepit monument, clearing the land for a new, more elaborate temple, but Alexander died and with him died the rebuilding of Etemenanki.

Byron reached the foundation and looked up at the ruined top. Dust was rising from the mound as it drifted away with the wind. Zahirah and James joined him.

"I wonder if the centurion's mark even remains," Byron said.

"I don't know," James replied.

"I wonder where we should start," Byron said as he looked at the lines of dirt that snaked down around the bricks, like fingers reaching for the earth. "We could search forever."

"Your priest writes, *'in the shadow of the place where the languages of men were born',*" Zahirah said. "It is going to be under the ziggurat."

"And what do we look for?" Byron asked.

"A dragon," Zahirah replied. "Marduk's dragon will mark the door."

Byron nodded as he turned to go. "We should split up and take a side. The search will go faster. I will search the back wall."

Byron walked beside the ziggurat looking for anything that might help find the door. He turned the corner. In the wall's shadow, he stopped to look at the graven images of a line of bearded warriors armed with bows. Each archer wore overlapping scales of plate armor that hung down to their knees. At one time, the image would have impressed those who saw it. Common men dressed in armor, armed with the latest weapons that only a great power could provide. The soldiers glared down at him with their baleful elongated eye, but Byron heeded them not. The only power that remained to Babylon's military might was curiosity, and once Byron was satisfied, he moved on. He walked beside Nebuchadnezzar's archers. An army of scorpions scampered in front of him. He reached the middle of the wall to find a long stairway blocking his way.

The stairway buttressed the wall like a great wedge that rose from the desert floor to the top of the terrace. An insurmountable barrier. Byron turned to trudge beside this inconvenient obstacle. At last, he reached a place where he could jump up and pull himself onto the stairway. Arms straining, he lifted himself up as the bricks crumbled under his weight. Standing up carefully, he crossed the stairs to the other side and jumped down into the soft sand. The sun shone on him as it moved towards the western hills. Byron walked along the edge of the great stair as it gradually rose above him. He reached the main wall of the ziggurat and stopped.

Beside the embrasure, next to the stairway, two kings carved from the bricks faced him. Robes embossed with round symbols of rays and stars cascaded from their shoulders down to their ankles. On their stony brows, sat tall crowns that widened from the king's head to a broad flattop. Byron looked up at them as they stood guard armed with staves. He backed up and looked at the space between them. The width of a door. He moved forward and touched the wall, his hand feeling along the bricks. Finding nothing of interest, he knelt down, setting the box down beside him, he started to dig. As the hole grew, a thin line of gold emerged. He paused to look at the golden line and then started digging faster.

The line became a horn that curled forward to a point. An eye appeared. Slowly, a snakelike head covered in brown scales emerged from the sand. The serpent's tongue flicked from its mouth, curling like a lash. Byron stood up and admired his work as the serpent's dark eye glittered in the light as if it was watching him. Byron leaned back to stretch his back and then knelt down to continue digging. Slowly, under the dragon's watchful stare, a bronze door dark with tarnish stood before him.

The snake dragon was standing on its back legs, its head turned to the side, its claw raised as if to strike. Byron's heart was racing, his gaze transfixed on the image. Carved into the serpent's scales was an X with the letter P crossing the center. The

Chi Rho, the sign of Constantine's victory. He almost jumped in triumph. The memory of Father Villhardain's words at the arch of Constantine, "In Hoe Signo Vinces", came back to him. He stood there savoring the moment. Father Villhardain had been right. He looked up and wished the old priest could be with him to share the excitement.

He cleared the last of the sand from the doorway and leaned back against the wall, savoring the moment. Father Villhardain would have been pleased. All of his work was coming to completion. Byron stood up and looked at the sun dipping towards the horizon. He dusted off his handiwork and looked closely at the cross on the door. In the center of the cross, he saw four round holes within a circle. Byron stared at the circle for a moment, and then decided he should gather the others. He picked up the box and walked back like a conquering hero, ignoring the reproachful stares of the stone archers. He spied Zahirah at the far end of the ziggurat and picked up a jog to tell her of his find. They found James, and the three of them returned to Marduk's door. The sun was nearing the horizon, and the dark shadows were creeping across the sand as they stood in front of Marduk's dragon.

"Interesting," James said as he ran his hand down the serpent's scales. "Do you think we can get the door open?"

"I don't know... I did not try," Byron replied.

"We could force it," James said as he stepped back to look at the bricks that framed the doorway.

Zahirah lowered her chin to give James an impertinent glare. "Yes, and you will collapse the entire entry." She stepped forward and ran her hands down the doorway. "Some subtly is required here." She searched the door for some slight changes in the bronze. When she reached the circle in the center of the cross, her hand stopped and she frowned. "Loyalty to the emperor will open the door." She glanced at the box tucked under Byron's arm. "Give me the signum manus."

Byron opened the box and took out the black and tarnished hand. Zahirah held it up and looked at it. Each finger was a different length. She looked at the four holes that were in a straight line with the door.

"Try it," James said.

"Wait! Does it turn up or down?" Byron asked.

"I don't know," Zahirah replied. She bit her lower lip as she sat staring at the hand and then the circle. Without a word, she thrust the fingers of the hand into the holes, and grasping the thumb, she started to twist. The circle moved slowly, grinding as the sand in the mechanism was crushed. The circle stopped moving. James reached out to help push. Groaning, the circle started to turn again, and with a crunch and a snap, the thumb stopped, pointing to the side. James gave a shove. Nothing happened. Byron put his shoulder against the door as both he and James pushed. With a scrapping sound, the door moved. Both men pushed harder. Inch by inch, the door moved until suddenly it let go. With a screech, the door swung open.

Byron brushed the dust from his tunic. "How did you know which way it would turn?"

"In the colosseum, the Emperor would signal the death of a gladiator by turning his thumb to the side. The centurion is warning us not to enter." Zahirah shrugged her shoulders. They stood looking into the darkness. Loose dirt from the mud bricks fell in small sifting streams of dust that drifted down in front of the open doorway.

"Do we go in?" Byron asked.

"Of course," James replied. "I will get the torches."

James jogged towards the entrance of the courtyard. Until this moment, he had doubted they would find anything. He had half-heartedly believed the story in the beginning. The only reason he had continued this journey was to receive absolution for his sins. Here in Babylon, the proof had become irrefutable: the word babel, the body of the Roman officer, the hand. No one would go to such efforts if the story were not true. Still, a doubt lingered that the treasure was still there. It was likely robbers had looted the treasure long ago. He pushed aside this doubt. They were so close, and he was starting to believe that maybe, just maybe, the treasure might be there after all.

At the wall in the courtyard, VonDurenberg sat next to Narvez, waiting.

"What are they doing?" whispered the Spanish knight.

"Looking for a way to enter the ziggurat," VonDurenberg said in a low voice.

"Do you think we should help?"

VonDurenberg gave Narvez a sideways glance. "It's hot out there! Let them take the risks. They will come get us when they have found what they are looking for."

"And if they don't find anything?"

"If they don't find anything, then we go home. I will make sure the world knows of their failure."

"And the woman?"

"I will have to think about that."

De Vale was waiting further down the wall beside De Montgris. Parker was not with them. They had sent him to get water and were now taking this opportunity to avoid him. De Montgris was tired of this journey. Had he known what he was getting himself into, he would never have volunteered.

"I am tired of waiting," De Montgris whispered to De Vale, kicking at the sand with his boot. "If these fools find the treasure..." De Montgris raised his eyebrows. "All I want is what's rightfully ours."

"Agreed," De Vale whispered back. "You and I both know that no matter what happens we will get nothing for our troubles."

"Indeed. VonDurenberg is right about that, but he is also in it for himself!"

De Vale glanced in the direction of approaching footsteps. "Here comes that stupid Spanish Don."

Ishaq had wanted to explore the ziggurat with James and Byron, but he decided that he needed to keep an eye on VonDurenberg. As he approached De Vale and De Montgris sitting in the shade, he saw the dark glances they gave him. Ishaq went further down the wall and sat down. Only a few more hours of daylight remained. Just as Ishaq was about to give up on finding the treasure today, James appeared. "Come!" he cried excitedly. "We have found the door."

The knights gathered around James. A feeling of excitement was in the air. They were close now. Everyone could feel it.

"Bring the shovels and torches," James said eagerly. The men scrambled to gather the equipment and followed James to the back of Etemenanki. They gathered around the door and stared at the steps leading into the black hole that descended down into the depths of the earth.

"You found it, you search it!" VonDurenberg declared.

Byron seized a torch from Narvez and lit it. "I expected as much!"

"I will go with you," James said.

"I would like to go," Zahirah said. "I want to see the inside of Etemenanki."

James looked at Zahirah with an impish grin. "Eeky Weeky is full of spiders and snakes." Zahirah gave James a dark look of disgust.

Byron was dreading entering the dark tunnel, and James was not helping. As a boy he and his brothers had been playing war. His older brother had taken him prisoner and locked him in a crate in the armory of Kilkenny castle. If he let his mind dwell on it, he could still feel the sides of the wood box, pressing against him as he struggled to get free. Now, the familiar fear was back, and the thought of going into the confined space made his skin crawl.

He was staring at the entrance when James brushed past him and headed down the steps into the darkness. Zahirah followed. Byron watched her disappear. At last, his will took over, and he forced himself to walk into the entrance. He hesitated for a moment. Then with all the willpower he could muster, he continued on.

James led the way. The torchlight flickered on the ceiling as he descended the seven steps into the darkness below. Zahirah followed. Byron walked behind, his hand touching the wall. The low ceiling of the square hallway forced him to stoop, and he felt like the tunnel was growing tighter with each step. A damp musty smell filled the air.

The walls gave way to another stairway that led down into the darkness. Black bulls with golden horns had been painted on one side of the wall. On the other side, a line of dragons marched into the darkness.

"Come look at this," Zahirah said as she moved to examine a clay tablet beneath the bull. James moved next to her and held his torch aloft so that it shone on the tablet marked with lines and symbols.

Byron brushed past them. He started down the stairway, forcing his feet to move. The darkness closed about him, but Byron dared not stop, least his fear overwhelm him. He had descended ten steps when he came to a short hallway. At the end of the hallway stood two pillars shaped like the trunks of palm trees, their fronds spread across the roof. Between the trunks, a black opening.

Byron was breathing hard. Damn it, he thought as he cast a glance at James and Zahirah, what is taking so long. He looked up in irritation at the ceiling and caught glimpse of something above him. He grabbed for his dagger, but it was not there. His hand swept to his shamshir as he prepared to face the unknown menace. As he drew his sword, he looked up to face his enemy and found he was looking at himself.

A copper mirror hung between the pillars. The long ages had tarnished the mirror, turning it black. Byron moved closer to stand beneath his image. Only the center of the mirror remained clear enough to see a reflection. His lean face, darkened by a beard, was etched with lines of fatigue. Streaks of green corrosion stretched across the mirror, marring his face. He almost did not recognize himself. He took a step forward to see if a different angle would reveal the mirrors purpose. Something caught his foot and he fell forward. A sharp blow struck him on the shoulder. He felt pain as something hit him on the head. Bricks were falling. Before he could move, a great weight slammed him to the floor. Dust filled the air. He could not breathe; his face was shoved against the sand on the floor and then all went black.

†

Byron opened his eyes. He was face down on wet sand, water was washing over his legs. He pushed himself up and found he was standing on a white beach. Beyond the beach, green hills rose in the distance. He walked from the surf, his wet clothes heavy, dripping with water. In the distance, he saw a man in a white tunic sitting on the sand facing the surf. He seemed unaware of Byron's presence. Byron walked towards the man, his boots sinking in the sand. As he drew closer, he recognized the man. It was the fisherman. The fisherman's long black hair was combed, the sweat was gone from his brow. He glanced at Byron's approach.

"You have returned," Byron said.

The fisherman tilted his head to look at Byron. "I never left."

Byron frowned. "But I saw you walk away."

The fisherman smiled. "Did I, or did you leave with your friend James Martel."

"I don't know," Byron said as he sat down by the fisherman and looked out at the sea.

"How are you, Sir Byron Fitzwalter?"

"I am tired."

The fisherman looked at Byron, his dark eyes examining his face. "Yes, you look tired. I suppose it was hard on you when Father Villhardain left you."

"It was a hardship. I have managed."

The fisherman chuckled. "Yes, but it is Zahirah I think that has helped you most in the priest's absence."

"You know about Zahirah?"

The fisherman smiled. "I know a great many things."

"Yes, saving Zahirah has proved to be a great boon to me." Byron looked out at the sea and sighed. "It seems pleasant here."

"It is. The sun rises and I fish. When it sets, I sleep beneath the moon and the stars."

The two men sat in silence, listening to the waves washing on the beach. "It seems lonely," Byron said at last.

"There are others," the fisherman replied as he looked away down the empty beach. "Eithne! Come here child."

A small figure, silhouetted against the sun, appeared. A feeling of apprehension filled Byron as he watched the distant figure walking towards them. The light shimmered around the dark shape as it grew larger. Byron felt his heart beat faster, as if in anticipation of some mysterious threat. The figure drew closer, and to Byron's relief he saw that is was a small girl with golden hair. The girl came and sat next to the fisherman. She leaned forward and looked at Byron with her blue eyes. She seemed familiar, but Byron could not remember where he had seen her. Eithne smiled, but her unblinking gaze made him uncomfortable. At last, he asked. "Do I know you child?"

The girl nodded. "Do you not remember?"

Byron searched his memory. Her dimpled face was clean, her blond hair shown in the sun. Her dress, white as the snow, hung from her shoulders. Byron shook his head. "No, child, I have never met you."

Eithne rose to her feet and stood in front of Byron. Her face grew hard. "Change your road," she hissed.

Byron scrambled backwards and jumped to his feet. "You!" he cried as he pointed his finger at her. "You're the banshee!"

"Yes," she replied and suddenly threw her arms around him and hugged him, "and I have been waiting for a long time to tell you that I forgive you."

"Do you remember now?" the fisherman asked.

"I thought she was a banshee sent to foretell my death."

The fisherman scoffed, "That you thought she was a banshee was your own foolishness. She was sent to get your attention. To get you to do what was required."

Byron nodded as he wiped the sudden tears from his eyes as he looked at Eithne. "You are the Celtic girl."

"There are no tears here," the fisherman chided.

Byron nodded, but he could not stop weeping. "I know... but I don't deserve... to be forgiven. I don't deserve to stay."

The fisherman frowned, his eyebrows furling over his dark eyes. "Of course, you don't. No, you do not deserve any of this... but fear not... our Lord paid your ransom long ago. So, dry your tears and be comforted."

Byron sighed deeply as he wiped the tears from his eyes. A feeling like he had never felt came over him. He could not put his finger on it: joy, love, tranquility, he was not certain, but with a sigh of contentment he said, "Then I would like to stay. Are there good horses in this country? I would like to ride those hills." Byron pointed to the green fields on the distant hills.

"There are many good horses in the master's land." As the fisherman said this, Byron saw several horses running across a distant meadow. He looked back at the fisherman who was watching him. "But if you stay, your story will end," the fisherman raised his eyebrows. "Are you finished?"

Byron frowned as the feeling of contentment left him and he looked back at the dark blue water. "No, I have more to do."

"I agree. I think you have more work yet to do too."

Byron nodded. "What is your name?"

"I am called Simon," the fisherman said as he stood up and took Eithne by the hand. "We will wait for you, but before you go, Father Villhardain asked me to tell you something." A slight smile appeared on Simon's face. "He said that you should pay more attention to the warnings that he left for you." Simon chuckled. "He also said that when all grows dark, follow the lion with wings."

A large wave curled up and rolled towards the beach. The wave flecked with white foam swept over Byron. With the roar of the water in his ears, he was pulled back into the sea.

Byron woke to the concerned faces of James and Zahirah looking down at him.

"He is coming back," James said excitedly. "Thank god!"

"Water," Byron mumbled. He began to cough. Byron sat up, his head throbbing. He reached out and grabbed Zahirah's hand to steady himself.

"He is bleeding," Zahirah said as she tore a strip of cloth from the bottom of her skirt. James knelt beside his friend, holding the torch so he could see the gash on the top of Byron's head. Years of fighting with edged weapons had given him more than a casual acquaintance with bandaging wounds.

"Fitzwalter," James said as he started wrapping a bandage around Byron's head, "I have never seen someone take a blow like that and live." James nodded towards the pile of bricks that had fallen from the roof.

"Where am I?" Byron asked as he looked around. "Where is the fisherman?"

"You're in the ziggurat," Zahirah replied as she knelt down and put her hand on his cheek. "There is no fisherman here. There is no water."

Byron looked around and sighed, "I should have stayed."

"Stayed where?" James replied. Byron frowned, but said nothing. "Fitzwalter, you are needed here," James said. "God has favored you again. The rope broke, otherwise you would have been crushed when the entire ceiling caved in...or trapped in darkness on the other side."

Zahirah held up her torch. In the light, Byron could see that the Romans had undermined the entire ceiling. They had placed two wooden beams between the pillars to hold the bricks in place until the moment some unsuspecting person tripped the rope, bringing the whole roof crashing down.

"Help him up," Zahirah said, bending over Byron, putting her arm around him as she helped him struggle to his feet. Byron gasped. His whole body ached. Every breath hurt, yet a strange feeling swept over him once again as he felt Zahirah's closeness. A tingling sensation of excitement filled him with desire. He took a breath and the pain drove the feeling away. Good, he thought. The last time he had felt like this was when he had been near Isabella de Clare, and that had ended in heartbreak.

"How bad is it?" Byron gasped.

"Your head is not as bad as it looks," James said. "Of course, when the wound heals, you will not be as handsome as you were; but then again, you never were that handsome in the first place."

James and Zahirah slowly helped him back up the steps. Byron's head was throbbing, he felt nauseous and fell to his knees. James helped him to stand. Stumbling, he made his way back through the doorway into the fresh air.

"What happened in there?" Ishaq cried as Byron emerged, blood seeping through the green bandage around his head.

"The roof almost caved in," James said, after he took a deep breath of clean air. "Our Roman friends didn't want anyone going in."

"Are you going back down there?" De Vale cried as he looked at the dark opening.

"No," James said. "It's getting late and the sun is setting. The ziggurat isn't going anywhere," he said looking around. "We will take Fitzwalter back to camp, clean up his wounds, and try again tomorrow."

"So, what kind of device did the Romans set," De Montgris asked as he walked to the entrance and looked in.

"They set a rope between two pillars at the base of the stairs," James replied suspiciously. "Fortunately, the rope broke."

"God favored you," Giodonni said as he crossed himself, looking at Byron and then back to the entrance.

The men gathered up their tools and returned to the processional way where the horses were tied. The sun was setting in the west and the sky was lit a crimson red as if it were on fire. Byron looked back at Etemenanki, whether it was a trick of the light, or his sight was still blurred from the concussion he just received, he saw a vision of the ziggurat. A great dark pyramid against the fiery background. The memory of the dream of the lion came back to him. His mouth sagged open.

"Are you well, Byron," Zahirah asked, her dark eyes filled with worry.

"It is nothing," answered the knight distantly. "It is nothing at all."

It was dusk by the time they returned to camp. Byron stiffly dismounted. His head ached. He sat down and Zahirah rebandaged his head. After a quick meal, Byron lay down. The pain was excruciating and he quickly got up. He saw a small hill of sand and dirt. He sat down and leaned back against the mound. It was uncomfortable but he was too tired to care. He watched as the rest of the men settled in for the night. As the stars grew brighter in the night's sky, he thought about the ziggurat and wondered about the fisherman. Had it been a dream? As he thought about the memory, he could hear the waves rushing over him dragging him back. Perhaps he should have stayed sitting on the beach next to Simon listening to waves as they swept ashore. As he thought about that tranquil place, he closed his eyes and fell asleep.

CHAPTER 57
SILKEN BOWSTRINGS

Nadim passed the time waiting for Isma'il and Muhtadi by throwing stones at the scorpions that scampered around him. His intended victim had scampered behind a rock. Nadim's arm was back, a smooth pebble in his hand as he waited for his prey. The scorpion darted forward. Nadim took a step forward and threw. The pebble, landing just under the scorpion, flipped it over in an explosion of sand.

"Missed," he muttered. He kept his eye on the scorpion as he stooped down to scoop up another projectile. He was about to throw when he saw Muhtadi and Isma'il walking towards him from the city. The scorpion forgotten, he dropped the pebble and hurried towards Muhtadi.

Muhtadi stopped near a large boulder and unbuckled his shamshir. Unslinging his bow, the scout carefully set it against the rock. He sat down and took a long drink from his water skin. He leaned back against the rock and closed his eyes. He was about to take a nap when Nadim jogged up and stood in front of him.

"Muhtadi, did you find the Christians? Were they in the city? What were they doing?"

Muhtadi opened one eye and looked down his hooked nose at Nadim. "Go away, boy. I will tell you later."

"Muhtadi, what did you see? What does Babylon look like?"

Muhtadi closed his eyes again as he moved his shoulders to get comfortable. "Babylon is a ruin of dirt and bricks, sand and dust. There is nothing more to tell."

"Muhtadi, surely you saw more?"

With a sigh of exasperation, knowing the boy would not go away, Muhtadi opened his eyes and sat up. After every bit of information had been shared and discussed, Nadim left satisfied, and Muhtadi lay back again to enjoy a short nap.

Muhtadi awoke feeling refreshed. The sun was setting, and he decided that a small fire would go unnoticed. Craving qahwa, he put a small copper kettle on the fire. He unrolled his carpet and looking towards Mecca offered his evening prayer. When he finished his prayer, he poured a cup of qahwa and leaned back against the rock to watch the sun disappear beyond the horizon.

The moon was rising, and Muhtadi knew the time had come to go back to the city. Isma'il was not happy with the decision, yet he knew what was at stake. Walking among the shadows, Muhtadi and Isma'il crept into the city. Muhtadi's curiosity was overflowing. What were the Christians doing at the ziggurat? He and Isma'il carefully skulked down the processional way. The street was dark, and the new moon did little to drive away the shadows. Muhtadi cursed as he bent close to the ground to follow the Christians' trail. He reached the ruined gate that led to the courtyard of Etemenanki and paused. The stump of the ruined arch cast a shadow over half of the entrance. The Christians had entered through the arch. The scout carefully picked his way through the fallen bricks. He stopped and smiled to himself, despite the windblown sand he could still see their trail, and it led to the ziggurat.

Isma'il, who had been waiting patiently for Muhtadi to find the right set of tracks, followed him into the courtyard, keeping his distance just in case Muhtadi fell into a pit set for the unwary.

Muhtadi reached the base of the ziggurat and stopped. Isma'il looked at the old ruins silhouetted in the dark. The sight gave him the shivers. "I need a rest," Muhtadi sighed as he sat down and leaned against the wall. Isma'il sat down beside him and looked out at the courtyard.

"Dark tonight," Muhtadi said as he took a drink of water. "We are close now."

Isma'il raised his hand. "Shhh," he whispered, "someone's coming!" Muhtadi stood up, and both men slipped back into the shadows to watch. Torchlight lit the walls of the gate, the glow grew brighter, and two men leading horses appeared. They paused to tie the horses at the wall and walked towards the ziggurat.

✝

As Muhtadi and Isma'il prepared to return to Babylon, De Montgris sat up and watched the new moon rise into the sky. When he was sure that everyone in the camp was asleep, he walked over to De Vale and shook him.

"It's time, if you still wish to go," the Norman said gruffly.

"Yes," De Vale whispered as he got up and quietly got ready.

They stealthily saddled their horses and rode off towards the city. The night was still and the darkness pressed close. They rode across the dark and shapeless land, only the faint outlines of the walls of Babylon were visible in the distance. Dark, jagged walls silhouetted against the night sky.

The walls of the city rose before them as they reached the headless sentinels that guarded the dry riverbed. They crossed the riverbed and onto the road. The walls pressed close as it funneled them up to the black outline of the battlements of the Ishtar gate. An oppressive gloom settled on De Vale as he rode to the gate. In the darkness, dragons and bulls stared down at them, their unblinking eyes glittering in the starlight.

The two knights paused before the archway. The horses, sensing their rider's fear, stamped with impatience as the men lit two torches. Dark smoke curled from the flames as it rose up into the night's sky to be lost from sight in the darkness. De Montgris rode into the blackness of the entrance. De Vale hesitated and with a sigh, bowed his head and followed. Once beyond the gate, the mud bricks of the city walls shown red in the torchlight. De Montgris stopped his horse. The processional road continued beyond the flickering light, disappearing into the inky blackness.

"We don't have much time," De Montgris muttered. "We must be swift."

Through the darkened ruins, the two men passed unaware that more than one danger lurked in the shadows. De Montgris paused next to the ruined lions in front of the palace courtyard. He glanced about and then started past the archway. As he passed the archway's center, he glanced into the darkness towards Nebuchadnezzar's palace A pair of yellow eyes looked back at him and then vanished. De Montgris' horse snorted in fright as it shied sideways.

"Did you see that!" De Vale hissed.

De Montgris scoffed as he gave the horse a sharp jerk with the reins and thumped it in the ribs with his outside leg to get it moving forward. "Jackals," De Montgris growled. "By the sounds of it, several of them."

The knights finally reached the gate to the ziggurat. "What now?" De Vale asked as he tied his horse at the wall.

"Simple, we go to the door that leads into the ziggurat and take what we are owed."

†

From the shadows, Isma'il and Muhtadi watched the two figures approach.

"What do you want to do?" Isma'il hissed.

"Follow them."

"And then what?" Without reply, Muhtadi handed Isma'il a silk bowstring.

De Montgris and De Vale approached the ziggurat, the light from their torches reflected upon the walls. Black figures danced in the shadows of the torches following the two knights as they groped their way to the door that led to the depths of the temple. They turned the corner to the south wall. The light cast long shadows upon the faces of the stone archers. De Vale stopped beneath the temple guardians as he scanned the empty courtyard.

The new moon shown down, its light reflecting off the sand, stretching to those places where the darkness held sway. All was quiet. They moved across the empty square to a place where they could cross the stairway. De Vale started first. As he put his boot down, a brick cracked and then crumbled away. Small pieces of masonry clattered down the steps, echoing in the still night.

"Do you wish to wake the dead?" De Montgris snapped. "God's bones! Use more care!"

De Vale's face twisted in anger. "I am using care," he hissed. Turning his back, he crept across the stairs and jumped down to the other side.

De Montgris followed. "Fool," he muttered to himself, "even that stupid Spanish Don would be quieter."

De Vale stopped as De Montgris came up behind him. In the distance, the two stone kings stared down at them. The opening of the door was in front of them, a large black hole surrounded by jagged bricks.

"I will follow you," De Vale whispered to De Montgris.

"Not stout enough to go first?"

"I am. I thought you would want to see the gold first."

De Montgris' mouth twisted into a sneer. "I see," he scoffed. "Follow me then...If you dare."

De Montgris took a step forward, Muhtadi slipped behind him. With a swift motion, he brought his hands down on either side of the knight's neck. Wrapping the bowstring around De Montgris neck, he pulled it tight. Leaning back, Muhtadi put all of his weight into the noose. De Montgris grunted and began to struggle. Gagging, De Montgris fell to his knees as he threw his weight forward trying to throw Muhtadi off his back.

"Infidel pig!" Muhtadi cursed as he pulled the noose tighter.

De Vale cried out and grabbed for his sword. Isma'il whipped his bowstring swiftly over the French knight's head and wrapped it around his neck. Jerking it tight, Ismail held on as the French knight squealed, clawing at his throat. De Vale tried vainly to save himself, but with each passing moment, his flailing became feebler. He collapsed to his knees and fell face down into the sand, taking Isma'il down with him. Isma'il stood up. "Infidel bastard," he spat as he kicked De Vale. He wiped the sweat from his brow as he sat down to rest. He looked at the door. "Do you want to go in?"

"No!" Muhtadi replied sharply. "Let the infidels take the risk! They will return tomorrow."

"And what do you want to do with them." Isma'il asked, looking at the corpses of De Vale and De Montgris.

"Leave them. It will give the infidels something to worry about."

"Or spook them into leaving."

"Their greed will overcome their fear. Do not worry." Muhtadi turned away from the bodies. He had never enjoyed killing, but it had been necessary from time to time. It would bother him later. The killing done, he wanted nothing more to do with the bodies. Let them lay. Either the Christians would bury their dead, or the creatures who made Babylon their home would dispose of them, either way it was not his problem.

Isma'il stood up and dusted himself off. "It has been a long day."

Muhtadi nodded. He was tired of this unpleasant place. He turned and retraced his steps to the gate. Muhtadi and Isma'il stopped to look at the two now ownerless horses tied next to the archway.

"Should we leave them?" Isma'il asked.

"No, turn them loose. Let them bear the message to the Christians that their men are missing."

Isma'il pulled the bridle off the first horse and then the second, slapping it on the rump. The horse tucked its tail down, but did not move. He gave the horse a second slap and it took off running down the processional way. The first horse, seeing its comrade leave, took off at a run.

"Come my friend," Muhtadi said. "Tomorrow will be a long day."

Ismail nodded. "Yes. Besides Nadim is probably scared shitless by now."

Muhtadi scoffed, "I am sure by now the ghosts have him surrounded." The two men turned and left the courtyard.

Speer watched Muhtadi and Isma'il leave. After he was sure they were gone, he crept out of the shadows and over to the corpses of De Vale and De Montgris. He had followed the two knights to the ziggurat, where to his amusement he watched as Muhtadi and Ismail strangled the two men. He rolled De Vale over to stare into his sightless eyes. Speer lifted De Vale's head, twisting it from side to side, playing with his face, moving his mouth, opening his eyelids wide. He dropped De Vale's head back into the sand. Speer sat with his head bowed, and then he looked up as a smile spread across his face. He had work to do.

CHAPTER 58
THE ARMY OF THE TOWER OF BABEL

Byron woke to a golden light that stretched across the eastern horizon. He lifted his head and found himself face to face with a scorpion sitting on his chest. The scorpion's black armor glistened in the growing light. Byron held his breath as the scorpion raised its tail to strike. The scorpion regarded him, its stinger quivered and then after a moment, it scampered off his chest and scurried away. Byron exhaled, his head ached, and he debated whether it was worth getting up. He slowly sat up from the small hill and looked over to where James slept, but he was not there. James was awake, sitting quietly near him with his blanket over his shoulders, a strange look on his face.

"You look unusually thoughtful," Byron said sleepily.

"I had a dream," James muttered.

"Which was?" Byron replied.

"I saw Jesus Christ," James whispered.

Byron paused as he examined his friend's face to see if he was making a jest, but James did not smile. If anything, his face became more troubled. "You saw Christ? Did he say anything?"

James shook his head. "I don't remember."

"You don't remember?"

"No ...I don't remember."

Byron nodded, not knowing what else to say. He had not

wanted to discuss his own visions which had plagued him since his head injury at Hattin. They sat in silence. James stood up. "I need to eat. By the end of this day I want to be on our way home."

Byron pulled his cloak around his shoulders and thought about James' vision. A vision of Christ. Byron wondered if the vision was a good omen. It had to be. The Church had blessed this after all. Byron gazed at the new morning, the golden rays of the sun shot across the reddening sky. It was a good omen. Jerusalem would be saved. He saw Zahirah wake, and watched as she came over to sit beside him.

"I want to check your wounds." She took the bandage off his head and carefully began cleaning the dried blood from his hair.

"How does it look?"

"Not too bad," she said as she started wrapping a new bandage around his head.

"Thank you for your kindness, my lady." To his absolute shock, Zahirah bent over and kissed him on the cheek. She stood up, and as she was turning to leave, Byron reached out and took her hand.

"Lady, stay for a moment. I have been thinking about what happened in the ziggurat."

Zahirah stopped and sat back down. "What is your question?"

"Weighed and found wanting. Do you think that was the trap that almost killed me?"

"Perhaps. We shall know soon if that was what the centurion meant."

"But the mirror on the ceiling, the image was dark and corrupted. I was looking up." Byron sighed. "I should have used more care."

"Yes, well you are fortunate you are not dead, or worse, trapped in darkness on the other side."

Byron nodded. Zahirah rose and touched him on the cheek. "And that would have made me sad. I have grown fond of my rescuer." She turned and left to join James who was sitting and eating his morning meal.

Byron was still enjoying the afterglow of what Zahirah had just told him when Narvez walked up. "No one was on watch last night!" the Spaniard shouted.

James stood up. "What do you mean! De Montgris was

supposed to watch the camp, where is he?"

"I don't know!" Narvez cried.

James walked over to where De Montgris slept, but the dour knight was not there. "Where is Montgris?" James cried. All of the men looked up from eating.

"I have not seen him," Giodonni replied. "For that matter I haven't seen De Vale either."

VonDurenberg walked over. "What do you want, Martel!"

"We are missing two men!" James snapped. "Or didn't you notice."

"Do you think it is my responsibility to keep an eye on everyone?" VonDurenberg shouted. "Do you ever suppose they have left to take a shit!"

James raised his eyebrows. "Together?"

"Lord Martel!" Parker yelled from where the horses were tied. "Over here."

James hurried over to stand beside Parker. As he reached the end of the line of horses, he found De Montgris' and De Vale's horses standing, saddled with no bridles.

"Do any of you have an explanation?" James demanded as he looked around at the faces of the men.

"We have been betrayed," Byron grumbled.

"De Montgris and De Vale would not do anything of the sort!" Parker yelled angrily.

"Well they are gone," Byron replied. "Faithless to the end."

"It is Babylon," Giodonni cried. "Evil lives in the city after the sun has left the sky. Dark spirits that lurk in the shadows of the city seized them."

"Horseshit!" VonDurenberg shouted. "Nothing has happened to them, they will turn up and everything will be explained."

Ishaq standing in the back smiled. The superstitious Christians were afraid. He scanned the worried faces. Perhaps he could use this to his advantage. "I have not spoken about this until now," Ishaq said in a somber voice. "The treasure is cursed by the ghosts of the Romans who left it. Their undead spirits still haunt it, protecting it from anyone who tries to take it."

Peter Speer quietly slipped up to stand beside his uncle. As the squire listened to the debate of the fate of the missing men, the corner of his lip twitched into a slight smile.

"Do you think...," Parker stuttered. "Do you think that De Vale and De Montgris were killed by ghosts?"

Zahirah spoke up. "Don Fuego is right," she said, breaking the silence. "The Romans were slain for defying the will of Allah. You are in grave peril, nothing good will come from you disturbing the resting place of the treasure buried in Etemenanki."

"Woman be quiet!" VonDurenberg shouted. "If I wanted counsel from a Saracen witch, I would have asked."

Byron stood up and raised his hands. "The Church has blessed this. The Holy Father has commanded this. Gird yourself! You are knights of the Holy Sepulcher, for God's sake. Be of stout heart."

"Yes, be men," James snapped. James motioned to the horses. "Mount up!"

The men left the highline to prepare to return to the ziggurat. When James finished saddling, he led his horse to where Bashshar was waiting. "Bring the camels to the city today," he said in a low voice. "This will be the last day we are here."

"I can," Bashshar said with a look of disgust, "but you had better have the treasure above ground."

"It will be done," James replied and led his horse away.

†

On the other side of the city, Muhtadi rose. Turning towards Mecca, he spread his prayer rug on the ground. He sat for a moment and watched as the sun spread its golden light across the land. Bowing his head, he prayed to Allah. When he was finished, he rose to join Isma'il.

"Isma'il, I want you to ride to Husam al-Din," Muhtadi said between mouthfuls of food. "Tell him to bring his men within sight of the walls near the Ishtar gate and wait. Today will be the day the Christians bring the treasure out of the ziggurat. He needs to be ready to intercept them."

"Why now?" Nadim interrupted. "Why not wait until they are on the road?"

Muhtadi smiled. "They can't see us once they are behind the ziggurat's south stairway. They will not see us coming until it is too late. When we attack, they will be trapped in the enclosed courtyard. We will slaughter them like sheep in a pen."

"And a glorious slaughter it will be," Isma'il replied.

"Look for three flashes," Muhtadi said as he held up a small glass. "I will repeat the sign several times. Look to the Ishtar gate and you will see the signal."

Isma'il bowed. "We will be ready." Isma'il finished eating, then rose and saddled his horse. He rode back to Muhtadi, who had slung his bow and was preparing to enter Babylon. Nadim, his fears of demons and other dark spirits forgotten, was going with Muhtadi.

Isma'il pulled his horse to a stop and looked down at Muhtadi and Nadim. "The gold will be ours by the end of the day, and the Christians will either be dead or prisoners. Allahu Akbar!"

"Allahu Akbar!" Muhtadi replied.

Isma'il turned and with a wave of his hand rode swiftly away.

†

Byron led the men to the city. He crossed the dry riverbed and took off at a gallop leaving his men behind. His horse clattered up the stones past the line of lions. By the time he reached the shadow of the Ishtar gate, his mouth was watering. He leaned to one side of his horse and wretched. He glanced behind him, the rest of the men were still crossing. Satisfied that no one had seen him, he sat up in the saddle. He sat in the shade resting, his head ached and he felt dizzy. They were going to find the treasure today, and he needed to keep the perception that he was well enough to lead. If he showed any weakness, VonDurenberg would exploit it.

He swallowed hard.

Zahirah rode up beside him, leaned over, and looked at him. Her dark eyes filled with concern. "Where did you go? I was worried."

A faint smile crossed his pale face. "I wanted to check the road, my lady." He glanced behind him as the rest of the men rode up. "The disappearance of De Vale and De Montgris troubles me," he said a little louder than necessary. Byron stood up in the stirrups and turned to face the men.

"I see no signs of De Vale or De Montgris," he cried, "but we shall continue to look." Byron nudged Enam forward and the horse picked up a jog.

"I did not know that he cared?" Narvez whispered to VonDurenberg.

"He doesn't," VonDurenberg snapped.

Byron ordered a dismount once they reached the ruined arch of the gate. He tied his horse next to the pilum that he had left leaning against the wall. James came over to him.

"Do you think Saracens have captured De Vale and De Montgris?" James whispered.

"No," Byron replied. "They would have attacked by now. Something else has happened. I know it."

Byron stripped his saddlebags from his saddle and slung them over his shoulder. The men gathered up several torches and followed Byron as he led the way around the south stair of the ziggurat to the door. Two dark objects were hanging beneath the feet of the kings. At first, Byron could not make them out, but with each step, the objects became clearer. He stopped dead in his tracks. De Vale and De Montgris were hanging from the wall, a wooden stake driven through each of their mouths, pinning them to the wall. The dead men's eyes had been gouged out leaving the red flesh of the empty eye sockets to look out over the courtyard. VonDurenberg blanched at the sight. The men slowly gathered around. Several of the younger men were visibly shaking.

"This place is cursed," Giodonni muttered as he crossed himself. "This is the work of the devil!"

Byron reached up and pulled the wooden stake holding De

Vale's body from the wall. De Vale's corpse slid to the ground and then toppled onto its side. Byron walked over to De Montgris and pulled his body free. Everyone moved clear as the body fell to the ground. Parker, standing near the wall, was weeping quietly at the death of his friends. James and Byron drug the bodies away from the temple entrance.

"Who did this?" James whispered.

Byron slowly examined the corpses of the two men and shook his head. "I don't know, but we are not alone."

Ishaq pushed several of the Christians aside and stood next to James. "Don Fuego, do you have any idea what killed them?" James asked.

Ishaq looked closely at the corpses. His experienced eye spied the swelling around the base of the jaw and the slight red marks around their necks. Having used bowstrings himself, Ishaq knew the telltale signs. "Some dark force is at work here," Ishaq said. "It led them here and then it killed them."

James tilted his head to one side as he gave the Spanish Don a skeptical glance. "Or someone."

Byron turned to James. "We must hurry before that someone returns and with greater numbers."

James nodded as he picked up a torch. "Are you going in?"

Byron looked at the open door and sighed. In answer, he grabbed up a torch. Taking his saddlebags from his shoulder, he tossed them on the ground and unbuckled his shamshir. The sword would be in the way and useless in the tight corridor. James took off his sword and set it next to Byron's. The torches were lit, the black smoke rising into the blue sky. Byron hesitated in the doorway and plunged in.

James stopped and turned to Zahirah. "Are you coming with us." Zahirah nodded and followed James into the darkness.

Ishaq watched as Byron, James, and Zahirah passed into the shadows of the doorway and out of sight. He was inwardly disappointed his attempt to scare the Christians away had failed. He stood for a moment and then with a shrug, picked up a torch and followed them in. It would be good to see how much gold he was going to have to steal.

Byron felt the walls closing in once again as he passed the threshold. He was having trouble breathing as the fear of being buried alive gripped him. Pushing himself forward, he hurried down the steps. Had he been outside in the sunlight he might have taken the time to admire the image of the bulls with their golden horns, but here in the suffocating darkness, he heeded them not. The pillars of the palm trees were ahead of him, he could see the bricks littering the floor. Byron glanced at the mirror. The green bandage on his head shone in the torchlight. He stared at himself, a haggard face with its mouth open, gasping for air. The feeling of being buried alive came over him. He could feel the weight of the bricks falling on him. Byron felt his stomach twist, he was about to be sick again when he felt a hand on his shoulder.

"Slow down," said the soft female voice. He glanced over his shoulder to see Zahirah behind him. He looked into her eyes, and a feeling of confidence came over him. The torch flickered in the still air as he looked at the concern in Zahirah's face.

"I didn't think you should have come down here again," she whispered.

"I have to. It is my duty." he replied.

Zahirah touched his arm. "Before we go further, we should look to see if the centurion gave us any warning as to what else lies in wait." James, standing next to her, held his torch aloft, the light reflecting off the ceiling.

"Mene, Mene, Tekel, and Parsin," Zahirah muttered. "Mene, God has numbered the days of your Kingdom and brought it to an end; Tekel, you have been weighed in the balances and found wanting; Peres, your Kingdom is divided and given to the Medes and Persians."

"It is not in order," James said. "If Byron was weighed and found wanting." James grinned at Byron who scowled back at him. "Numbered and ended that should have come first."

"Perhaps you missed the first of the warnings," Ishaq replied.

James turned to find Ishaq standing behind him. "Don Fuego! Excellent! I am glad to see that you have joined our expedition."

Ishaq gave a small bow.

"Don Fuego is right," Zahirah said, "perhaps the centurion left his mark somewhere near the entrance. We should check." Zahirah turned and went back up the steps. Holding her torch close, she stopped to peer at the image of each bull.

"Fitzwalter, stay here," James muttered, "and don't move."

Byron watched as James went up the stairs, the torch reflecting on the dragons on the opposite wall.

"Don't move," Byron grumbled to himself, watching Zahirah and James talking to each other in whispered tones as they looked at the bull closest to the door.

"I admire your courage, Sir Byron," Don Fuego said, making Byron jump. "It is not an easy thing to return to the place that almost caused your death."

Byron nodded, not wanting to discuss his fears with the Spanish Don. "What do you think the centurion means by numbered?" he said, changing the subject.

The Spanish Don sucked in air and sighed. "Depends, if he was a pagan it could mean the moment the fates cut the string of a man's life. Although, I think he probably means linear. Such as a journey, the number of footsteps in a destination, or the sign of death."

Byron started to laugh. The echoes filled the chamber. James and Zahirah turned to look at him.

"It was the lock," Byron cried. "It was the lock. My lady, you are the one who told me." Byron looked at the blank stares of James and Zahirah. "The hand. The centurion was telling us which way to turn the hand. Turn the hand so the thumb comes to rest on its side. The sign of death? Your days are ended."

"Yes," Zahirah said, "that could be an interpretation of the matter."

"That's it then," James cried. "All that is left is divided. Half and half."

James turned and headed down the stairs, Zahirah followed him. When they reached the bottom, James stopped in front of the pillars and looked up at the mirror above him. Zahirah crowded next to him. "Do you think this has some other significance?"

Zahirah held her torch up as she looked at their image. "I don't see anything."

As Byron watched them, a little pang of jealousy filled his heart and he stepped closer. He was leaning against the pillar of the stone tree when he noticed the letter "c" scrawled at the base. Byron knelt down and dusted the sand away from the base with his hand. In the glare of the torch light, he could make out the shadowed letters of the word centuria. He stood up.

"Did you find something, Sir Byron?" Ishaq asked.

Byron furled his brow as he stared at the word. "I don't know."

"Let me see," Zahirah interjected as she stepped over to stand next to Byron. "Centuria," she said as she peered at the word in the dim light. "There is more." Zahirah dusted more sand away from the base, a Roman numeral II appeared.

James scoffed, "Probably a soldier's vandalism."

"I am not so certain," Byron muttered. "Perhaps it is another warning. We have missed the others so far. Almost to our doom."

James smiled. His eyes alight with mischief. "Yes, Fitzwalter, and you have done well at ferreting out the centurion's devices. I was thinking of sending you on ahead."

Zahirah spun on James. "That is terrible! How could you say something so mean spirited?"

"Fitzwalter knows I would not sacrifice him," James chuckled. "Not willingly."

Byron sighed. "What does the does II Centuria signify?"

Zahirah bit her lip. "I think it means the Second Century. Of what legion they were attached to, it does not say." She dusted further and then shook her head. "No, nothing."

James looked down the darkened stairway between the pillars. "We can stand here all day, but it will not get us any further." James stepped down on to the first step and headed cautiously down the stairs, counting each step.

Byron hesitated, looking for the first time at the walls in the torchlight. The line of golden dragons with long outstretched necks marched in a procession, leading the way to the depths below. Time and decay had filled the floor at the entrance with sand, but the floor changed as they went down into the depths. Bricks carefully laid with skill so the seams were even and level, now lined the floor. James' muffled voice from counting his strides echoed from below. The quiet stillness was filled with the muffled sounds of their boots as they slapped against the smooth hard floor. The sound echoed off the walls in the enclosed space. Each step magnified against the last, until the echoes sounded like hundreds of feet were following them.

A feeling of being watched by some malignant force crept over him, and Byron found himself glancing behind him, expecting to see the shadows of dead Roman soldiers following him with their swords drawn. Each time he looked back, all he could see was the blackness. He told himself to ignore the fear, but the primeval part of his mind kept screaming, run - get out of here. Each step was becoming harder and harder to take. His senses were tingling, and every fiber in his body was on alert, ready to turn and fight against a sudden attack.

James reached "seventy". The air was now thick with the smell of water, and the walls of the hallway were damp with moisture.

"The water table must be rising," whispered Zahirah.

In the dark, Byron nodded but said nothing. Holding their torches up, they looked at the walls. Nothing. The walls were damp and smooth. The image of the dragons marched off into the distance disappearing into the darkness.

James started counting again. They were now really starting to descend. James counted his strides, his voice evenly intoning each step. "Seventy-seven, seventy-eight, seventy-nine."

Byron saw James' torch disappear. A cracking sound echoed in the darkness. Everything became confused. Without thinking, Byron shoved his way forward, pushing Ishaq and Zahirah roughly out of the way. His torch cast its light where James had been, and he looked down as James started to push himself off the floor.

"That was close," said James as he stood up.

"What happened?" asked Byron, breathing hard as he tried to keep his voice from squeaking.

"I am not sure. I heard it release, and as I jumped backwards, I tripped and fell," James said as he picked up his torch from the floor. He relit his torch. He thrust it forward to see what had happened. Byron could see a wooden pole with a rust covered blade lashed to its shaft. Above and below the blade, long wooden spikes were sharpened to a point. Sharp as spears, the spikes were long enough to drive through a man's body and out the other side.

James gasped. "That was fortunate; the pole must have lost its spring in the damp air."

Byron ran his hand along the pole as he examined it. James was right. The pole was warped from having been left in a bent position too long. James was lucky indeed, if the pole hadn't lost its spring, he would be dead.

"Divided?" Byron asked as he looked at Zahirah.

Zahirah shrugged. "It is not what I had envisioned."

"Very cunning! Very cunning indeed," Ishaq said as he admired the device.

"I am certain this is not the only one," Byron said grimly. "There will be more."

"Do you think the distance will be the same?" James asked Zahirah.

"Yes. Now I know why *second centuria* was carved on the pillars. He has numbered the stairs for each one of his men."

James rubbed his face with his hands and then turned to face Zahirah. "I thought century meant one hundred."

"It does. but in the late empire, a centuria was reduced to eighty men."

James threw up his hands as he turned away. "That would have been useful to know!"

"How am I supposed to know what you know and don't know!" Zahirah cried. James shook his head, but said nothing.

They slowly continued down the hallway. The paint was now peeling in the damp air, and the lines of marching dragons were deformed. At eighty steps, James found the next device pulled back and waiting. It was hard to see in the dark. It took James some time to trip the trigger to make it safe. It was tedious work as they moved forward apprehensively. James found the third weapon so deformed that it hardly snapped forward.

"We are deep under the ziggurat. Do you think we have much further to go?" Byron muttered as he looked around.

Zahirah swept the walls with her torch, double-checking to make sure no clues had been missed. "No, but we still must use care."

It seemed they had been in the ziggurat for hours. Byron was starting to think the nightmare would never end when the walls gave way, opening into a large chamber. Byron could hear his boots splashing in the water.

"Someday this will all be underwater," Zahirah whispered.

Byron tripped and almost fell. He looked down and jumped back. A long white bone glimmered beneath the water. He held his torch closer. There were more bones. Ribs, vertebra, arm bones, and leg bones all scattered across the floor. In the center of the darkened chamber, something reflected in the red torchlight. Byron stared into the dim light; he saw them - a Century of Roman soldiers standing at attention, lining the walls of the chambers. The white bones of their faces stared back at him. Zahirah gasped, the sound echoing in the chamber. Nothing stirred. Only the sound of water broke the silence as it seeped through the walls from the world below, gathering in this place that knew neither sunlight nor life, nor the wind in the grass, waiting with the dead never to return to the sky.

Byron slowly walked forward to get a closer look at the men who never left Babylon. Their skulls had been impaled on their spears. Their furcas had been lashed to each spear as a cross member for shoulders. Still dressed for battle, the Lorica hamata had been draped on the wooden cross that now formed the soldier's bodies. Helmets with long cheek guards had been placed on the skulls, while the razor-sharp spatha swords rested at their armless sides. As Byron gazed into the empty sockets of their eyes, a twinge of sympathy passed through him. These men all had dreams, but it had ended here, and here they stood still doing their duty, guarding the gold for an empire that, except for the pretender in the east, no longer existed.

Ishaq walked to the center of the chamber. Hundreds of crates were stacked in the middle. He saw the image of an eagle with outspread wings surrounded by a circle of laurel. He held his torch over the crates. The letters SPQR were still visible.

"SPQR?" James said, looking over Ishaq's shoulder.

James walked over to one of the skeletons and from the belt of the dead soldier, drew a spatha from its sheath and walked to one of the crates. He shoved the sword under the lid and began to pry. With a shriek, the lid slowly opened. The sound echoed repeatedly in the chamber. James shoved the sword in deeper to get more leverage. The lid popped open and fell with a splash onto the floor. Rows of golden coins filled the box. Stacks and stacks of them all neatly arranged, glittering in the torchlight. The entire group stood quietly, gazing at the imperial gold brought from Ravenna by Achatius.

"I never thought we would find this," James said in disbelief.

"So, when do we start moving the treasure?" Ishaq demanded, his eyes shining with excitement.

Byron looked at the walls of the chamber and back up the tunnel that led to the world above. He hated being here, but he had a job to do. Time was slipping away, and they needed to get moving. The memory of De Vale and De Montgris came back to remind him of why they were hurrying.

"James, what is your plan?" Byron asked.

"You and Zahirah stay here and start pulling the lids off the crates. I will go back up to the top and start sending the men down with baskets. Don Fuego. Don Fuego!" James repeated.

"Err, what?" Ishaq answered. He was so absorbed with the sight of the gold he had stopped paying attention to anything around him. "Yes, what do you want?" he answered, irritated at having his pleasant daydream of being rich interrupted.

"Come with me," James demanded. "I need you to supervise the loading of the treasure on the camels."

"Of course," Ishaq replied, delighted with the request.

†

The men were standing around the remains of De Montgris and De Vale, grief stricken. Even VonDurenberg seemed upset by the sight. As the men waited, Bashshar arrived with the caravan.

The camels filled up the courtyard as they milled around. The men gathered around as James emerged from the depths of Etemenanki.

"Did you find anything?" Giodonni asked gloomily, expecting James to say it was gone.

"We found it!" James replied. "Crates of gold! Hundreds of them!"

"God be praised!" Parker shouted excitedly, all sadness for his friends forgotten.

The men jumped to their feet. All concern about entering the ziggurat was gone as they started for the doorway. In a wild rush, they pushed and shoved as each man jockeyed to be the first to see the treasure.

James blocked the way. "Two at a time! Leave your swords! It's crowded and they get in the way. Take a basket with you when you go! When you return, I will send the next two down."

VonDurenberg moved to stand beside James. "Do as he says." The men needed no further encouragement and hurried off to get baskets. Narvez and Parker were the first to return.

"Parker, I need you to watch the gate," James said. "I will send someone else down in your place."

"Why me! I want to see the treasure!" the young man whined, not wanting to miss the adventure.

James felt a flash of anger and then relented. What would it hurt if he let him go down once? His curiosity would be satisfied and perhaps he would do a better job watching. "Fine," James said. "You can make the first trip, but then I want you at the gate. I don't want anyone sneaking up on us."

"I give you my word," the young man replied as he hurried to catch up with Narvez, who was just about to enter the ziggurat.

The men made continuous trips to the chamber all afternoon, loading their baskets and returning. Before long, a large number of baskets were stacked around the entrance waiting to be loaded on the camels.

"There are only a few crates left," Giodonni told James as he sat down to wipe the sweat from his brow and take a drink of water.

Bashshar was irritated with the lack of planning in loading the camels. He had enough and angrily walked over to Ishaq, who was giving instructions to one of the Arab drivers. "A word!" the burly Arab snarled. "I want to move the camels that have been packed into the processional way."

Ishaq leaned close to Bashshar and whispered, "This is all part of my plan. The confusion will make it easier to kill them one by one."

A smile crossed Bashshar's face showing his yellowed teeth. "Indeed, it is about time."

"Very soon, my friend," Ishaq said. "Let's take the few camels we have loaded into the street."

Bashshar grabbed the lead ropes to three of the camels and led them through the courtyard into the street. Ishaq followed Bashshar, leading three more camels.

Ishaq stopped just before the ruined gate to look around. "Where is Parker?" he asked.

Bashshar shrugged. "Probably couldn't stand the suspense any longer and went to take another look at the treasure. You know how undependable he is."

"James should have picked someone more disciplined for such an important assignment."

Ishaq walked through the gate, avoiding the overhanging half of the arch and turned south. He walked for some distance, making room for the rest of the camels so they would not have to move the camels each time they brought a new group into the street. He turned to Bashshar when he was satisfied that he had left enough room.

"Stay here and wait," he said, "I am going back to the ziggurat. I will send someone to take your place."

"Take your time boss," Bashshar said as he sat down in the shade of a palm tree. "There is shade here, and I am tired of dealing with childish fools."

Ishaq smiled. "I am thinking we won't have to suffer their company much longer." He turned and walked quickly back to the ziggurat.

†

Muhtadi was setting his own plan into motion as Ishaq and Bashshar were moving the camels into the street. He and Nadim had stealthily crept onto the south wall of the courtyard and watched. Muhtadi had been surprised to see the bodies of De Montgris and De Vale hanging at the feet of the Babylonian kings. He and Isma'il had left their bodies lying on the sand. The Christians had another enemy lurking nearby. He did not have time to contemplate who that might be. He watched the injured Christian with a green bandage around his head disappear into the depths of Etemenanki.

When the injured Christian was out of sight, he saw the rest of them gather around the blond Christian with a pockmarked face. As the blonde Christian spoke to his men, the caravan of camels arrived in the courtyard. Muhtadi leaned back against the battlement as he watched the camels mill about. He was getting bored when the handsome Christian burst out of the ziggurat. Muhtadi sat up. By the reaction of the men, he knew they had found it. The treasure was now within reach. Muhtadi was just as excited. The Christians split up and gathered the large wicker baskets from the camels. Muhtadi watched intently as they brought up the baskets of gold from the depths of the ziggurat. One of the knights left the group to guard the gate. Muhtadi shifted his position to watch this man. This knight was obviously bored and not doing a very good job of protecting his comrades. He wandered around aimlessly looking at stones, throwing rocks at the half arch that hung precariously over the sand. Muhtadi was devising a plan to kill him when the young knight, apparently not able to take the boredom anymore, walked away to rejoin the rest of his comrades bringing up the gold.

"Nadim!" Muhtadi whispered harshly. "Come with me."

Muhtadi carefully crept along the wall to the processional way. He paused to look at the street. It was empty. He jumped down from the wall, pausing again, taking a second glance to make sure he had not overlooked any threats.

"Nadim, stay here and keep watch. I am going to the Ishtar gate to give the signal." Muhtadi hurried to the Ishtar gate. He quickly scaled the wall beside the gate and took out the small glass. Angling the glass to catch the light, he rocked it back and forth three times, pausing and repeating the process.

†

Husam al-Din was walking through the camp talking to his men as they sharpened their swords or polished their armor, preparing for the confrontation they all sensed was coming. All the men stood up as they saw Isma'il ride into camp.

"The Christians have found the treasure," Isma'il said breathlessly. "Muhtadi thinks they will try to move the treasure out of the city today. He has sent me to bring you within striking distance of the city. He will signal us when the time is right."

Husam al-Din smiled. "I know. Ahmed returned at first light and told me that the camels and their drivers left the river. The Christians must think they have the treasure." Husam al-Din laughed. "But not for long. Get a drink and rest. Once we are ready, ride with me. Today we will avenge Kamal and Fadil."

When every man was mounted, Husam al-Din rode between the two columns inspecting his men. He stopped when he reached Ahmed. "I see you found a spear. Does this mean you are riding with us into battle?"

Ahmed nodded. "I have waited a long time to exact justice upon these Christians."

Husam al-Din smiled. "Allah will soon grant your wish. You are fortunate, Ahmed. You are riding with the best. You will soon see why the Christians fear us."

Husam al-Din led his men in a slow gallop. No longer would Husam al-Din wait upon the enemy. It was his turn now, and when the sun set on this day, the Christians would be his prisoners and the treasure in his custody. He wished he could see the face of the Christian Pope when he learned that his attempt to finance a new crusade had been crushed.

Husam al-Din led the Saracen Cavalry a safe distance from the walls of the city and halted. Isma'il and Husam al-Din sat on their horses watching the Ishtar gate. The afternoon slipped by. Just as Isma'il was starting to think it would be more comfortable to dismount, it happened! A flash of light. The flash repeated itself three times and then stopped.

Husam al-Din turned to address his men. "The time has come! If the Christians fight, kill them! If they surrender, take them prisoner! We will move up quietly, and once I give the signal, we charge. There is no god, but God! Allahu Akbar!" With a wave of his hand, he motioned his men forward.

They galloped forward in military order, jumping the remains of the Euphrates and galloping up to the gate. They paid no attention to the artwork on the walls, the city's place in history, or the curse upon the land. Each man focused on the coming fight, rehearsing in his mind what he would do based on the countless times he had engaged the enemy before. This was not the first time these men had fought the Christians. They knew what to expect, even with the element of surprise and overwhelming numbers, the enemy would fight. How hard they would fight was the unknown. The fanatical Templars would fight to the death. Husam al-Din hoped these men would give up once they realized the overwhelming odds, although, there was no doubt that the gold would strengthen their resolve.

Muhtadi stood in the archway of the Ishtar gate waiting as Husam al-Din and Isma'il rode up. "All of the Christians are at the south side of the temple. The south stairway will hide our approach," he said. "Fortunately, they are so obsessed with finding the treasure that they have become careless. No one watches the entrance to the courtyard."

"Good," Husam al-Din said as he smiled. "Let us teach the infidels a lesson as to why you always leave a rear guard!"

"Ride with me, my friend," Isma'il said, taking his foot from his stirrup and reaching down with his hand. Muhtadi took Isma'ils hand, stepped into the stirrup and swung up onto the back of the horse. Isma'il led the way.

When Husam al-Din reached the ruined arch of the gate, Nadim slipped out of the courtyard and into the processional way to greet him. "The Christians are still at the back, unaware of your approach."

Husam al-Din smiled cruelly, and without a word, he rode beneath the stump of the gate arch. The Saracen Cavalry followed, flooding the courtyard. He turned to Kasim, who was just behind him. "Kasim, return to the road and guard the entrance to the courtyard. I don't want to be caught like we are about to catch the Christians." Kasim nodded.

"Nadim! Come here, boy. And be quick," Husam al-Din cried. The boy jogged to the front of the column. "I have a special task for you and it requires diligence."

"Yes, my lord." The boy bowed. He was breathing hard, his eyes wide with excitement.

"I want you to guard the courtyard of the ziggurat." Husam al-Din pointed to Etemenanki. "If there are Christians still inside, I don't want them coming out of an unseen exit and attacking us from behind." The boys head bobbed up and down. "Every man here is depending on you. Now go and take your post."

Husam al-Din watched Nadim run to the ziggurat's wall. It was the best he could do to keep the boy out of harm's way. He stood up in his stirrups and looked at his men. "The bowstring has been drawn. It is time to release the arrow. Allahu Akbar!"

"Allahu Akbar!" his men repeated the cry as they drew their swords. With a wave of Husam al-Din's hand, the men charged, sweeping around both sides of Etemenanki towards the unsuspecting Christians on the south wall of the temple.

†

At the very moment Husam al-Din was riding to the Ishtar gate, VonDurenberg watched as the last of the treasure was brought from the chamber. The time had come to put his plan in motion. Watching each basket of gold pass by, VonDurenberg brooded on the wrongs James had done to him: the beating at Aleppo, questioning his authority, exposing him as a fool. He hated him, and as the minutes ticked by, his anger grew into a rage he could barely control.

He walked over to Narvez. "Are you ready to strike a blow?"

"No," Narvez whispered. "If you kill Fitzwalter and Martel, do it on your own. I want nothing to do with it."

"Coward!" VonDurenberg snapped. " I will remember this."

"So will I." Narvez pointed to the stiffened corpses of De Montgris and De Vale. "God is against this! Do you not see the signs?"

"I see nothing!" VonDurenberg said as he turned and walked off.

VonDurenberg's countenance changed to a smile as he approached James who was directing the loading of the camels. "Are we almost done?" the German asked in the friendliest manner he could manage.

"This is the last," James replied.

VonDurenberg smiled. "I would like to see the chamber before we leave. Would you show me the way? Perhaps we can go and tell Fitzwalter and the Saracen woman that we are almost ready to go."

"I can do that, " James said pleasantly. "I am sure Fitzwalter is ready to come up and breathe some fresh air."

They entered the doorway of Etemenanki and went down the steps between the images of the bulls and dragons. The shouting of the men loading the camels grew faint as they walked deeper into the ziggurat. James paused near the pillars where the ceiling had been undermined.

"This is what almost killed Fitzwalter," James said as he held his torch up to look at the mirror. "A clever deception." James motioned up to his image. "Fortunately, the rope broke, but all it would take is for someone to pull on it and the whole thing would come down."

VonDurenberg paused to look at the lintel and posts holding the bricks of the ceiling in place. "Devilishly clever," VonDurenberg muttered.

"It almost worked," said James as he started down into Etemenanki. "I can't decide what would be worse. To be crushed to death, or trapped here forever entombed in darkness."

†

The last crate had been emptied. No more gold remained. Byron and Zahirah looked around at the soldiers of Rome. Their purpose was now gone, nothing remained for them to guard; yet, no release from service would ever come. Here they would remain forgotten by family. Forgotten like the empire they had served. Perhaps God had not forgotten them, but Byron would never know.

He took Zahirah's hand and they walked to the tunnel that led to the land of the living. Byron was tired of this place. His mind had already leapt to the future, Rome was waiting, and the treasure would bring new energy to the fight. If Jerusalem fell, perhaps its loss would only be temporary. He glanced back at the Century of Roman soldiers. He hoped his sacrifice would not end up like theirs, an empty death.

"It is time to leave this place," he said. They started climbing the steps towards the entrance. Byron saw torchlight approaching. As it grew closer, he could see James. Someone was following him, but the light cast a shadow over the man's face.

†

VonDurenberg saw Fitzwalter. He was holding the Saracen witch's hand. He had not expected this. With each step, he had nursed his hatred which was now boiling over as every grievance came to bear. The opportunity was now within his reach, and he acted swiftly. With rage he struck, just as Cain attacked Abel long ago, driving a knife deep into James' back. The suddenness of the blow caught James by surprise. It felt like a heavy punch, the seriousness of the injury not immediately apparent. James spun to face VonDurenberg as the next blow fell, the knife plunging into his upper chest. James grabbed VonDurenberg's wrist, forcing his arm straight up. Blood running down James' clothes. The pain intense, he ignored it as he focused on defeating VonDurenberg. He stepped in, struggling with the man who could only attack him from behind. With all his remaining strength, he twisted the knife out of VonDurenberg's grasp and it clattered to the ground. James seized the weapon and turned to slash at VonDurenberg, who began retreating up the stone corridor of the ziggurat.

"VonDurenberg!" came a cry from above that echoed off the stone walls. "We are under attack!" VonDurenberg, hearing the cry, started to run.

"Come back!" James gasped as he collapsed to his knees. "Come back so I can finish what you started!" A pool of blood was forming on the floor. James stared at it in disbelief.

Byron could not believe his eyes as he watched VonDurenberg stab James in the back. Byron ran up the stairs, ignoring the pain in his head. He was almost there when he saw VonDurenberg turn to flee. James was on his knees. VonDurenberg was running up the stairs. Byron was closing the gap. He could just make out VonDurenberg's shadow ahead of him.

"Let him go!" Zahirah shouted. "James is dying!"

Byron stopped and turned to see James lying on the floor. He ran back down the stairs and knelt beside his friend.

Dropping the knife, James fell forward onto the floor. "Do you remember this morning?" James whispered. "I saw Christ?" He paused, choking on blood. "I remember what he said... he told me....he told me... he would see me soon." James closed his eyes and with a ragged breath, lay still. Byron bowed his head as tears streamed down his face.

†

VonDurenberg ran up the hallway. He tried to shake off the feeling that like Cain, he was now a marked man. He stopped beneath the mirror and looked up at his image streaked with green and black. The sound of swords ringing echoed down the empty hall. On impulse, he picked up the frayed ends of the rope. Turning to face the pillars of the stone trees, he backed away until the rope went tight.

"Fitzwalter! You and the Saracen witch enjoy the darkness!" VonDurenberg leaned back and gave a sharp tug. The beams fell. The center of the ceiling gave way. A cloud of dust rose up obscuring VonDurenberg's view. It would take Fitzwalter weeks to dig his way out. He turned and ran to the entrance, grabbed his sword at the doorway and rushed out to join the fight.

The sound of the collapsing ceiling echoed down the hallway. Byron's head began to throb. A strange feeling overtook him, as if a lightning storm had seized him in its grip. He fell to the floor in convulsions. Zahirah watched in horror as Byron lay in throes of violent spasms. Dropping to her knees, she cradled his head as he shook and thrashed about.

The lightning storm in Byron's head raged, reaching a crescendo and then it was gone. He heard laughter. Byron opened his eyes and found he was lying face down on a stone floor. He raised his head. A red light flickered in the distance, casting a dim light on the black rock walls of a tunnel. He rolled over and saw Noddaba standing over him. Noddaba's hood thrown back, his handsome face outlined in the darkness.

"I thought you were dead?"

He shook his head. "I am not dead." He bent closer. In the tunnels light, his face had a pallid hue. His lips curled in a smile, but his dark eyes were fixed and cold. "I see that you have found Babylon. Have you found the gold?"

"Yes! No thanks to you," Byron snapped as he sat up shivering. "You led us to a pit in a storm and then left. Had it not been for the priest's horse, we would have gone over a cliff. You are a faithless guide Noddaba."

"Faithless? I think you are in a poor position to judge of faith." He stood up. His dark outline seemed to grow. "Did you not find Babylon? No one ever promised it would turn out well for you. Did they?"

"You did. Noddaba, did you not tell me that I would save Jerusalem!"

The corner of his mouth twitched into a slight smile and then faded from his face. "Noddaba," he repeated to himself, "Noddaba did tell you that...didn't he?" He looked down at Byron, his eyes red in the tunnels light. "But alas, I am not Noddaba. I am Abaddon. But a monkey like you could not figure that out." Abaddon scoffed. "I will never understand what he sees in any of you. Not that it matters, I have you and I will soon have all the rest." Abaddon bent closer, his teeth bared like fangs. Abaddon reached out his pallid hand that glistened in the red glare.

"He is not yours," said a small voice. Byron turned his head to see Eithne standing beside him. Her white robes shown with incandescent light.

Abaddon withdrew his hand and turned. Putting his hands on his hips, Abaddon towered over the Celtic girl. "And you are going to stop me?" Abaddon frowned as he looked over at Byron. "Shows how much he cares for you. Did he send any of his mighty angels? Did he send the Archangel Michael? Did he send his messenger Gabriel? No! He sent a small girl!" Abaddon chuckled and then leaned forward to seize him.

"He is not yours." Eithne's lips moved, but it was not her voice. Instead, it was a deep voice. The voice was not angry. Its tone was as if stating a fact; nevertheless, the voice shook the tunnel's walls. Every fiber in Byron's being tingled. A feeling of great joy overcame him, like the sunshine of a warm spring day. He leapt to his feet. Eithne raised her hand. A white light shot across the room, filling the tunnel with blinding light. Abaddon snarled as a white mist blocked Byron's sight.

Byron opened his eyes. His headache gone. Zahirah cradling his head was calling to him. "Come back. Come back," she whispered. "Do you hear me?"

Byron groaned. He slowly sat up and wiped the tears from his eyes. He felt as if a great storm had passed. He felt weak. He sighed and struggled to regain his senses. He looked over at the body of James. The memory of his friend's death came back to him. He sat up and after a moment, rose to his feet and stood over James.

James' vacant eyes were fixed on the ceiling above, their luster was gone. A pale, waxy hue had fallen on his face. Byron knelt down and arranged the body so it looked like James lay in peaceful sleep. Placing his hand on James' face, he closed his eyes. "Someday we will meet again, but until then... lie here." Byron glanced up at the walls. "In a monument fitting for the scion of Charles the Hammer and Charlemagne." Byron stood up and looked down at his friend, hoping that perhaps he had made a mistake and James would wake and sit up. At last, Byron looked away. Tears streamed down his face. He took Zahirah's hand and started back down to the chamber.

They walked in silence until at last, Byron asked, "How are we going to escape this doom?"

"Ziggurats have more than one entrance. I hope Eeky Weeky is the same." Zahirah bit her lip as Byron looked down and sighed.

Entering the chamber, Byron and Zahirah spread out and started looking for anything that might resemble a door. The torches were starting to sputter; they did not have much time. The dead Romans were in the way, and Byron did not hesitate to shove them aside in his search for an escape. Bones and armor fell with a splash. Zahirah worked her way carefully through the corpses. She had not gone very far when her torch sputtered and then slowly went out. Dropping the torch, she hurried across the chamber to stand next to Byron as he shoved his way through the skeleton army.

He neared a recess in the far wall. In the dim light, he saw it. A glimmering gold outline of the winged lion of Ishtar. Father Villhardain had not forgotten him. This was it! The entrance for the priestess of the Babylonian goddess. He leaned forward and shoved, the door moved. He jumped back and threw his weight against the door. It opened a few inches more.

"God help me!" Jumping back again, he threw his weight against the door. The door opened.

He saw a broad hallway lined with golden lions leading up from the chamber, walking head to tail, leading the way out. He saw light shining in the cracks of the doorway at the other end. Even once they reached the courtyard, he would still be in danger.

Something was wrong. He could hear the cries and the clash of swords. He turned to the remains of two of Rome's best soldiers and unbuckled their sword belts, the leather cracked from age as he worked it through the buckle. Quickly, he pulled the two spathas from their sheaths and checked to see if they were still capable of inflicting death. The swords were rusted near the hilt, but the blades glinted in the torchlight.

They were not his first choice of weapon, but they were better than nothing. The legions of Rome had conquered the world using the gladius hispaniensis, the Spanish sword, but by the later empire it had been replaced by a longer sword, the spatha.

He slung the weapons over his head and grabbed Zahirah's hand. They made their escape, running up the hallway towards the light, excitement building with each step as they neared freedom, escaping the clutches of the grave.

CHAPTER 59
SHORT SWORDS, LONG SWORDS, AND SHAMSHIRS

Bashshar sat in the shade of the palm tree waiting for someone to come and take his place, but no one came. He leaned back against the wall. He was tired, and the cool shade made him drowsy. He had just closed his eyes when he heard the scuffle of approaching feet. He opened his eyes to see Ishaq running towards him. Ishaq, breathing hard, stopped and leaned against the camel in front of his lieutenant.

"You're a little out of shape," Bashshar said as he watched his boss gasp for air.

"Shut, up!" Ishaq snapped. "It's about to happen. VonDurenberg is going to kill Martel and Fitzwalter."

"Ha! Unlikely. He will fail."

"Yes, but even then, the Christians will be in turmoil. Come, I need you at the ziggurat."

"I would be there now if you had sent someone to take my place," Bashshar grumbled as he rose to his feet.

Ishaq threw up his arms in irritation. "Yes, fine, I forgot. I will send that crazy Christian De Courcy out here. When he gets here, hurry back. I am going to need you." Ishaq whirled back to the ziggurat's gate, took a step and then stopped. "Oh shit!" he whispered.

Bashshar stood up and saw the source of Ishaq's concern. A host of Saracen Cavalry was entering the gate to the courtyard. Both men dared not move as soldier after soldier, with shamshirs drawn, passed into the courtyard. When the last soldier had passed through the gate, Ishaq turned to Bashshar. "Come, my friend, Allah has spared us."

"Shouldn't we warn our men?" Bashshar said as he followed his boss to the kneeling camels.

Ishaq climbed on to the back of the nearest camel. "There is nothing we can do for them. Except die with them. Do you want to fight?"

Bashshar looked in the direction of the gate and shook his head. "The odds are not in our favor." Bashshar mounted the camel next to him. He reached out for the lead ropes of the of the other camels when he heard men shouting Allahu Akbar. The four camels, spooked by the noise, rose to their feet and bolted.

"They're getting away?" Bashshar cried. He kicked his camel to give chase.

"Let them go!" Ishaq yelled. "Let them go. We will find them later."

The shouting stopped. Ishaq could hear the sounds of fighting. It started gradually, but the clash of steel was unmistakable as it grew, reaching its crescendo. "Come on, my friend, it is Allah's will!" Ishaq cried. Banging his heels on the sides of the animal, Ishaq rode off through the ruins of the city.

✝

Husam al-Din swept around the south stairway of the ziggurat, his surprise was complete. The Christians stopped moving, looking at him in complete shock. Husam al-Din bore down. The Christians scattered, running to retrieve their swords stacked against the wall of the ziggurat.

"The devils are upon us!" De Courcy cried as he swept up his sword and turned to face the Saracen onslaught. A Saracen horseman seeing De Courcy waving his sword lowered his spear.

"Come on! Saracen dog!" De Courcy yelled as the Saracen bore down on him. De Courcy, his eyes on the Saracen, took a step back. Catching his foot on Byron's saddlebags, he stumbled and started to fall. Ahmed spurred his horse to run harder, and adjusting his aim, he drove his spear through De Courcy's chest. Shoved backwards by the force of the lance, De Courcy fell across Byron's saddlebag. The pages of the Odyssey burst into the air as Ahmed's spear tore the saddlebags open. Caught by the wind, the pages drifted in the breeze as they came fluttering down across the courtyard. Ahmed pulled his lance free. He glanced down at De Courcy's face, his lips turned up in an odd smile. Ahmed shook his head. He turned his horse in search of another victim.

The battle was reaching its height. The Christians, fighting individual battles, were being slain one by one. The Saracen drivers, seeing their countrymen attack, threw themselves on the ground, begging for forgiveness.

"Rally, you bastards!" Narvez shouted, raising his sword. "Rally, damn you, or we will all be killed!"

Narvez looked over his shoulder and saw VonDurenberg standing in the doorway of the ziggurat. "VonDurenberg, for God's sake, rally the men!"

VonDurenberg hesitated, his face white with fear. He saw his men being cut down one by one. He glanced at the opening in the south wall. His choice made, he ran. Ducking the shamshir of a Saracen horseman, he ran faster. The wall was growing nearer. Without one look back, he leaped through the opening. Tripping, he fell, cutting his hand on the bricks that lay scattered on the ground. On his knees, he heard a sickening smack. VonDurenberg looked back through the opening and watched as a Saracen drove his lance through the back of a fleeing Christian. Fear overpowered him. Without the slightest idea of where he was going, the graf leapt to his feet and ran.

Narvez watched in disgust as VonDurenberg ran, disappearing through the opening in the wall. Narvez was alone, yet he would not surrender. He raised his sword in defiance and called out one last time, pleading for the few men left to rally to him.

Husam al-Din saw a dark faced Christian raise his sword and cry out to his confused and dazed men. Husam al-Din needed to kill him. If their leader died, the rest would give up. Husam al-Din turned his horse and galloped head long at Narvez. Isma'il, seeing his commander change course, swerved to join him. Narvez lifted his sword defensively to deflect the coming blow. Husam al-Din delivered his strike. Narvez swung upward to meet the Saracen's sword, deftly redirecting the blow, but Narvez could only fight one foe at a time. As he deflected Husam al-Din's sword, Isma'il struck. The force of the curved shamshir severed Narvez's head from his body. As Isma'il rode past, Narvez's body slowly toppled sideways, the blood pooling on the sand.

Parker and Giodonni, rushing to Narvez's aid, stopped and watched his head fall to the ground. The delay was fatal. Two of Husam al-Din's archers drew back their bows and sent their arrows into both men. Parker fell to his knees, screaming. Giodonni, hit in the shoulder, broke the arrow off and began to run to attack his assailants. He closed the gap as two more arrows struck him. Collapsing, with an arrow through his heart, Giodonni fell onto his back and died, staring up at the bright blue sky.

†

Byron threw open the door. He could hear shouting and he paused to listen. Through the din, he could hear the cry 'Allahu Akbar'.

"The enemy is here," he whispered.

He stepped through the doorway. To his surprise, he saw a Saracen boy looking at him. The boy's dark eyes were wide with fright as he fumbled to draw a dagger from his belt. The boy, running backward, tripped and fell. Byron sprang upon him, and holding a spatha to the boy's throat whispered, "Let go of the knife boy." The boy swallowed hard and then let the dagger slip from his hand onto the sand. Byron glanced at the dagger. Still holding the spatha to the boy's throat, he pulled him up. Reaching down, Byron drew the boy's shamshir and tossed it away. "You can come back for it when we are gone." The boy looked at Byron unsure what to do. "Run to your master. I will not have your death on my conscience today."

The boy nodded and scampered away.

Screams and shouts echoed in the courtyard. Byron looked towards the sound of battle as he absent-mindedly leaned over and picked up Nadim's dagger. Handing the dagger to Zahirah, he said, "Wait here."

"No!" She cried. "You owe them nothing!"

"Lady, I am a knight of Saint John! It is my duty!"

Zahirah grabbed his hand. "Do not go. They abandoned you. Did they not kill James?"

Byron hesitated. She looked down and caressed his hand. "Do you believe that VonDurenberg acted alone?"

Byron stopped. Did the men know? Of course, they knew. VonDurenberg would not have acted without their consent.

Speer, listening to the fighting, skulked along the edge of the ziggurat. He turned the corner and spied Byron and Zahirah. He smiled to himself and knelt down to watch. The knight was looking at the woman. Speer saw something shiny lying in the sand. He crept closer and saw that it was a shamshir. Crawling on his knees, he crept to the sword and lifted it from the ground. Fitzwalter had his back to him. The woman was looking down, holding the knight's hand.

With a scream, Speer charged. Bryon turned as Speer slashed at him with the shamshir. Byron ducked, the sword swished over his head. Stepping back, Byron brought the spatha to a guard position above his head. Speer attacked again. Byron blocked the next blow with the spatha and kicked the squire in the stomach. Speer stepped back with a gasp and then looked at Byron as a malicious grin spread across his face. Byron drew the other spatha. The two men circled each other. Speer laughed and then attacked in a swinging arc, chanting in some nonsense tongue. Byron felt the blow run down the spatha through his arm. The strength of the blow surprised him. He countered with his other sword, missing Speer's head by inches. Speer gave another guttural laugh as he attacked again with repeated blows. Byron fended off the attack, using one sword after the other. Speer circled, watching for an opportunity to strike.

Byron needed to end this. The sounds of fighting were dying down. He lunged at Speer as he attempted to stab the squire in the chest, but Speer turned sideways as the spatha went by. Byron had overextended himself, and Speer, seeing an opportunity, brought the butt of the shamshir down on Byron's bandaged head. Byron gasped and fell to the ground. The pain was searing. As Byron pushed up to regain his feet, Speer leaped on his back, pinning him to the ground. With a guttural cry, Speer raised the shamshir in triumph as he turned the sword blade down. As the squire was about to stab Byron in the back, he felt a hand take hold of his hair near the scalp. A dagger flashed beneath the squire's eyes as it slashed his throat from ear to ear.

Zahirah let go of Speer's hair and stepped back. In her hand, Nadim's dagger was red with blood. Speer let go of the shamshir and reached for his neck. The dark, red blood streamed between his fingers. The squire turned pale as he tried in vain to staunch the wound. Byron, not realizing what had happened, pushed up, throwing Speer to the ground. Turning, he saw Zahirah standing near him with the dagger in hand. He looked down. The squire was lying on his back twitching. Speer's mouth sagged open as he struggled to breathe.

Byron did not pause to watch Speer die. He grabbed Zahirah's hand and took off at a sprint. Horses and camels were running wildly in the courtyard. He ran to the ruined gate and turned towards the horses. A shout went up and he spun to see a mounted Saracen bearing down on him with his shamshir drawn. Byron seized the pilum leaning against the wall. His souvenir had a use after all. The Arab horse was almost on him. Byron jammed the butt of the pilum into the sand and aimed the metal shaft at the horse's chest.

To his horror, Kasim saw Byron level a javelin at his horse, but it was too late to change what was about to happen. The horse drove onto the javelin with the power beyond the strength of a man. It went deep into the horse's chest, piercing its heart and lungs. With a scream, the horse reared straight up and then toppled over onto its back, crushing Kasim beneath him. Byron could hear the snapping of bone and the exhale of burst lungs as a thousand pounds of horseflesh fell on top of its rider. The horse, in its death throes, rolled and tossed on top of the corpse of his late master, taking him with him as he died.

Byron did not linger to watch. He was already turning to run the moment the horse reared. He untied Enam. Zahirah was already on her horse. Byron swung into the saddle. "Laissez-Aller," he yelled, furiously spurring Enam into a dead run. He looked over his shoulder, satisfied to see that Zahirah was following.

†

The attack was over. Half of the Christians were dead. Seeing the death of Narvez, the rest of the Christians threw down their weapons. Husam al-Din's men pounced on them as soon as the last Christian dropped his sword, forcing them to their knees. A spontaneous yell of triumph filled the air once the Christians were shackled in chains.

It was over! Husam al-Din had crushed the Christian's dream to finance their war. He was about to shout in triumph when Nadim came running up.

"They are getting away!" the boy cried.

Husam al-Din turned. "Who is getting away?"

"The traitor princess and a Christian!"

Husam al-Din wheeled to Isma'il. "Take several men and go after them."

Isma'il leapt on his horse and took off at a run calling to several of the men to follow him. As Isma'il disappeared behind the ziggurat, Muhtadi rode to Husam al-Din. "My lord, you have triumphed over the enemy! What do you wish to do with the

Muslim traitors who aided our enemies?"

Husam al-Din looked around at the twenty-men face down on the ground, begging for forgiveness. The remaining Christians sat apart in chains, looking dejected. "Have the men punish them for their stupidity, and then put them to work loading the gold. They can labor for us, and if they work hard, live. Anyone shirking his duty will forfeit his life. Make sure they know this."

"You are wise and just, my lord. All will be done as you command."

"Good, Muhtadi, I leave it to you to see that it is done." Muhtadi bowed and rode away to give orders to the men.

Husam al-Din walked back to his horse and retrieved his prayer rug. He walked to a quiet corner of the courtyard where he rolled out his carpet. Allah had rewarded him and he needed to express his gratitude.

†

Enam was running hard, Byron glanced back to see that Zahirah was just behind him. He looked further back as a Saracen archer ran through the ruined arch and dropped to his knee. The Saracen drew his bow. Byron ignored him. An arrow flew over him and he glanced back. The Saracen was nocking another arrow. He looked forward again, and to his horror, saw a wall of discarded broken bricks and dirt looming in front of him. Alexander's soldiers, in their removal of the old bricks from the ziggurat, had thrown the refuse into the street. The road was blocked.

Only now, did he understand why the centurion had brought them through the Ishtar gate. It was too late to change course. He put his spurs to the horse, and in a leap of faith, prayed there would be a place to land on the other side. Time and the elements aided him. The desert winds had filled the mound with sand as the bricks had crumbled into dust in the heat of the sun. He felt Enam lift up as the horse jumped onto the man-made plateau.

Scrambling to keep his feet, the surefooted horse stumbled among the jumbled bricks and sand.

Byron looked back just as Zahirah's horse landed behind him. Her horse stumbled and went down to its knees, throwing Zahirah from the saddle. She rolled across the bricks and sand as her horse struggled to stand up. Byron pulled his horse to a stop. Zahirah rose to her hands and knees. Turning, Byron put his spurs to his horse. Clattering along the uneven surface, he ducked an arrow that pierced his cloak, tangling in the cloth.

Zahirah was on her feet as Byron rode past. Placing his horse between the Saracen archer and Zahirah, Byron kicked his feet out of his stirrups and reached down. Grabbing her cut hand, slick with blood, he held tight. With all his might, he pulled her up. Stepping into the stirrup, she swung onto the horses' back.

Byron turned Enam towards freedom as he glanced back to see another Saracen ride through the gate. Squeezing Enam up between his legs, he pushed the horse forward. Turning and twisting, he guided Enam between the holes in the rubble and sand. Another arrow flew past him, just missing his head. The Saracen's were closing in. Byron urged Enam to go faster. At any moment, the Saracen archer would be on the mound. Enam stumbled along. The edge was drawing closer. Out of the corner of his eye, he saw Zahirah's horse following. He reached the edge. Below him stretched the desert floor and his escape. With a mighty leap, Enam jumped from the plateau. He pulled his horse to a halt and watched as Zahirah's horse followed.

"Come on then," Byron shouted as Zahirah's horse raced up to stop beside him. They made it, but the danger had not passed, he needed to put more distance between them and the Saracen's in Babylon.

"Get off!" he said in a harsher tone than he meant to use. "Enam can't carry both of us!" He reached out to grab the bridle of Zahirah's horse. Zahirah slid off and remounted. As soon as she was back in her saddle, Byron started off at a run, Zahirah riding beside him. Byron glanced back at the mound. Silhouetted against the sky, two Saracens stood on the mound of bricks. Several more joined them. Byron watched them over his shoulder, but they did not move. Byron looked forward and urged his horse to greater speed. He had barely escaped. He slackened the pace after an hour of hard riding and stopped. Breathing hard, he looked behind him for any sign of pursuit. The road was empty.

†

Isma'il stood on the mound of bricks watching Byron and Zahirah ride away.

"Should we go after them?" Ahmed asked.

"What for?" Isma'il asked. He glanced behind him to see the rest of his men scrambling over the bricks. "I will not risk one horse clambering over this. Nor will I risk the life of one man to kill the Christian. We have what we came for and that is enough." Isma'il scuffed the ruined bricks of Etemenanki with the toe of his boots. "Besides, we need a messenger. I want the infidel Pope to know his failure. I want him to know that we took the treasure from him." Isma'il turned and started to walk back across the mound to his horse. "After all, I promised Ali that his mistress would live." Isma'il scoffed, "She showed her allegiance to the Christians. Let Allah deal with her."

Byron rode to a grove of palm trees and stiffly dismounted. He held the horse's reins in one hand and reached up to help Zahirah dismount. "Let me see your hands."

"They're fine," she replied curtly.

"No, they are not," he said, grabbing her wrist, looking at the cuts and scratches on her arms and hands. He took his water skin and poured water on the cuts. He pulled a rag from around his neck. "Let me see your dagger." Zahirah fumbled with the belt around her dress and handed Byron the dagger. Byron held it up to cut the rag in half and then stopped and stared at it as if he had been suddenly stricken. "Where did you get this?"

"You took it from the boy."

Byron held the knife in front of his face. "This is mine. I left it on the body of Father Villhardain." Byron trembled as he lowered the knife and stared at it in disbelief. After a moment, he sighed and cut the rag in half. Shoving the dagger in his belt, he started bandaging her hands. When he finished, he walked over and sat down beneath a palm tree. As he leaned against the tree, he took out the dagger and stared at the engraving. Numbers 6:24-26, may the lord bless you and keep you. Everything he had done had been a waste of time and effort. All that was left for him to do was to turn for home and return empty handed.

Zahirah came over and sat down beside him. He stared at the toes of his boots. "Where do you want to go?" she asked. Byron did not answer. "Where do you want to go?"

Byron sighed. "I guess I will ride to the river and turn south. If the Saracens followed us from Aleppo, they will not go that way."

Zahirah smiled and rubbed her hand on his cheek. "No, they won't expect that."

"There is no reason for you to stay, my task is over," he said sadly. "I release you."

"And where would I go?"

Byron looked over at her. Zahirah smiled. "Besides, you need me. For I am certain you will get lost should I leave you."

"Doubtless," he said, shaking his head. "Everything else has failed."

She stood up and dusted off her dress. She reached out her hand and held it out to him. "You didn't fail!" she said sternly. "You did everything you could! This is not the end. You cannot see what is next. Can you?"

He took a deep breath. He looked at the empty land around him and then took her hand. This journey had cost him deeply, and yet he had been spared. It was done. Brooding would not change a thing. He took another deep breath. His face brightened and he smiled at her.

"Lady," he said tiredly, "I would welcome your company, wherever this journey may take us."

Zahirah smiled and kissed him on the cheek. "That's better!"

He smiled back and as they looked into each other's eyes, they drew closer. An irresistible force pulled them together. Her lips parted and he cupped the back of her head gently with his hand, his fingers running through her soft, dark hair. He looked into her eyes and gently kissed her on the lips. They parted for a moment and then kissed again.

She broke away and smiled. "We should be going."

"Yes," he replied reluctantly. "We should be going. It would be wise to cross the river before nightfall."

They remounted and rode to the banks of the Euphrates where they stopped to water the horses. Byron sat on Enam scanning the countryside. Three camels tied together were standing near them, the baskets of gold still on their backs. He looked at them in disbelief. They must have bolted when the Saracens attacked. He slowly rode to the camels and cautiously reached out, grabbing their lead ropes. He looked over at Zahirah, who shrugged. Perplexed at his good fortune, he did not know what to say.

"I told you this was not the end, and look, you have been given a gift."

"Well, I didn't expect this," he answered.

"God is mysterious." She shrugged.

They crossed the river and started riding into the sun as it was descending towards the horizon. Zahirah smiled. "I will follow your lead."

†

Far away on a small hillside, Ishaq sat mounted on his camel looking at the city below. Bashshar was beside him. Ishaq watched as Byron and Zahirah made their escape. He had seen enough. He took one last look at the ziggurat and felt a pang of regret for leaving his men behind, but there was nothing he could do for them except join them as a prisoner. He would make sure that he compensated their families.

Maybe Saladin's soldiers would be generous, one could always hope. Ishaq had always heard the Great Sultan was a generous man. Perhaps that trait would also influence the men beneath him. As he turned to go, he looked down and saw VonDurenberg clawing his way up the slope of the rocky hill. The graf collapsed on his knees in exhaustion, gasping for air.

"Don Fuego, for God's sake, take me with you!"

Ishaq stared down at VonDurenberg for a moment. Ishaq laughed. "Fool! I would never take you with me."

VonDurenberg started to shake with fear. Salvation was slipping away. The affable, inept Spanish Don existed no longer, instead a new person looked down from the camel, and this person filled him with dread.

"I am Ishaq of Tyre, and I would never take a man who has betrayed his comrades, his religion. How could I ever trust you?" Ishaq turned his camel sideways as he glared at the pathetic German on his knees.

"For the sake of God," VonDurenberg pleaded, "don't leave me. Take me with you!"

Ishaq paused for a moment and looked up at the sky. "So, what will become of you, VonDurenberg, now that you have betrayed all of those around you? Thinking you needed them no more. Would not Fitzwalter or Martel have helped you? They would not have left you here to die."

VonDurenberg stared at Ishaq, his mouth open in the realization that no amount of begging would change Ishaq's mind.

"Odd isn't it," Ishaq continued, "that when you were betraying your fellow Christians, you were in fact killing yourself, Wilhelm Helmuth Graf VonDurenberg." Ishaq said thoughtfully, "I will not help you, nor will I kill you." Ishaq looked up again to the sky. "I will let Allah determine your fate; perhaps he will be merciful and rescue you from this fiery furnace." Ishaq made a sweeping gesture with his arm. "But I think not. You could always run back to Salah al-Din's men. The choice is yours," Ishaq laughed. He turned to Bashshar. "Let's go, my friend, and leave this wretch to ponder my words."

Ishaq and Bashshar turned their camels north towards Baghdad and rode swiftly away. VonDurenberg watched them disappear from sight. There was no escape. He pulled out his dagger and looked at it. He could speed up the inevitable and make his death swift. He looked back at the city. Even now, he could make out the survivors being led away into captivity. He stared at the knife, his face distorted and twisted by the blade's reflection. He staggered to his feet and began to run like a wild man after Ishaq, cursing the assassin.

He had only gone a short way when his strength gave out, and he collapsed in a heap. He looked across the burning sand and saw a man distorted in the rising heat of the mirage. The man turned and walked away.

"Help me," VonDurenberg cried, but the man slowly sank from sight. "Help me!" He staggered back to his feet. The sun beat down upon him, and he cursed God with each painful step. Babylon had now disappeared from sight. He had gone a short way when in the distance, he saw the man again. The sun shone brilliantly behind his head, shadowing the man's face.

The phantom spoke, "Why are you here, Wilhelm. Why are you in Babylon?"

"Go away foul daemon!" VonDurenberg cried.

The man laughed. It sent shivers down VonDurenberg's spine. "Where is James? What have you done?"

"I have done nothing," VonDurenberg shouted.

"You lie," the man hissed. His image faded away into the mirage.

"I do not lie!" VonDurenberg cried, "I do not lie." He shook his fist at where the image had stood. He stopped. Hot wind blew in his face, and the sand swirled past him. The magnitude of his punishment sank in, so did the memory of Fitzwalter and Zahirah escaping from Babylon. Fitzwalter had escaped Babylon with the true treasure. He had been blind. VonDurenberg tilted his head back, and with a cry of rage, cursed the name Fitzwalter.

CPSIA information can be obtained
at www.ICGtesting.com
Printed in the USA
BVHW080806270521
608292BV00004B/714